FROM COMFORTABLE DISTANCES

JODI WEISS

This book is a work of fiction. All incidents, dialogue, names, and characters are the products of the author's imagination. Where real-life locations appear, the situations, incidents, and dialogues concerning those locations are entirely fictional and are not intended to change the entirely fictional nature of the work. In all other respects, any resemblance to persons or events is entirely coincidental.

For information about permission to reproduce a chapter or selection from this book, or to offer comments or questions, contact the author through her website.

www.JodiWeiss.net

DEDICATION

To my mother and father, who taught me to reach for the sun, the moon, and the stars.

Table of Contents

From Comfortable Distances

For this is action, this not being sure, this careless

Preparing, sowing the seeds crooked in the furrow,

Making ready to forget, and always coming back

To the mooring of starting out, that day so long ago.

John Ashbery, "Soonest Mended"

CHAPTER 1: INSANITY

I have often felt completely alone.

There is always in this life something to discover.

The days and years have gone by in some sort of blur.

On the whole, I am satisfied. – Alice Munro

The sun still a promise in the pre-dawn sky, Tess Rose glimpsed a figure in the middle of the street as she approached the stop sign at the Whitman Drive intersection. He seemed to be trying to walk on the double-yellow line that divided the road, like a drunk testing his sobriety.

Only no, up closer, Tess could see that he was staring up into the sky. Nothing happening up there except some pigeons flying by.

She slowed down when she was a few feet from the man, beeped her horn, and opened her window. The dank April-morning air from Jamaica Bay chilled her. Being situated on the water was the catalyst for a strong real estate market in Mill Basin, a remote corner of southeastern Brooklyn. Families liked boats and beach in an urban environment.

1

"Wake up, mister," she said. "Get out of the way or I'll run you over."

He grinned at her, nodded his head, and waved. Surely, he must be high on something. He grew faint and distant in the rearview mirror as she sped past him. That was it. She was going to have to meet with the neighborhood association. She was not going to let these crackpots wander the neighborhood if she could help it. She paid enough in taxes to have her say.

Goodness gracious! She screeched her brakes the moment before impact. She had been so caught up in the jerk behind her that she almost slammed into a fat, mangy, orange cat as he darted across the street, pausing directly in front of her car. Just what she needed – to start off her week killing Garfield. She beeped and the cat fled as quickly as it had appeared.

When she hit the red light at the four-way intersection of Avenue U and 66th street, her image on the billboard at the bus-stop shelter smiled back at her. Below her cheesy, smiling face, the caption: *Why buy from the rest when you can buy from Best Realty? If you are in need of Real Estate solutions, call Tess Rose at 1-800-TRY-BEST.* Did she really look that old? In the rearview mirror she lifted her eyebrows and rearranged her strawberry-blonde curls with her fingers, working the banana curls this way and that from the roots. The dew always managed to frizz her hair so that she looked like Shirley Temple. So much for living on the water. More wrinkles on her brow, more surrounding her eyes. Every day now, more wrinkles. She pulled out her blackberry and scrolled to her to do list: *call photo guy*, she typed with both fingers, her foot pressing the brake. *Fix up face and* tossed it back into her bag. After all, it was quicker and less painful to fix her face in a photo than it was to get plastic surgery. She tapped her steering wheel. The traffic light seemed to take forever but then she remembered that she was one of the advocates in getting the civic association to put in turn arrows after all those accidents. Houses didn't sell well on a block that had a history of car accidents. In her rearview mirror, the character in the middle of the road was making his way towards her. Freak. The way his bald head shone in the early-morning light reminded her of Mr. Clean.

Some days the 15-minute ride to her office was luxurious: precious minutes to shut off from the world and gather her thoughts. Other days, like today, the ride seemed to last forever. She had three real estate deals to close this morning, which meant that she had on her black power suit, the skirt falling just above her knees with a slit to show off what she thought to be her best feature: long, shapely, well-defined legs. The blazer was double breasted and hugged her narrow frame. As she drove past the stores on Avenue N, her black BMW convertible reflected off the storefronts. Michael, her ex-husband, had fought her on getting the black. He thought it was too much of a funeral procession car. She, on the other hand, had seen it as sharp and sophisticated, and after splitting from Michael, whom she had promised herself was to be her last husband, she wanted something hot and sexy in her life.

She waited for a clearing to make a left turn into the parking lot of Best Realty. One car sped by, then another. This was one of the many things she *loved* about Brooklyn: no one would stop to let her turn. The more she looked at the mustard-yellow and white Best Realty sign, with its fancy scrolled lettering, the more it reminded her of squiggly lines of mustard on hot dogs. Michael was opposed to changing it. He liked to remind her of what the big-wig marketing consultant who had convinced them that it was the right logo had told them: that the yellow and white coloring would remind buyers of a price tag, so when they came to Best, they would think *buy*. "Besides," as Michael said, "If it's not broken, why fix it?"

She pulled into her reserved-for-owner spot and immediately saw Michael's pale-blue Mercedes in his spot across from hers. Couldn't she get one morning of peace and quiet? Tess's third husband, David, had introduced her to Michael, and was instrumental in bringing Michael on-board as Best Realty's in-house lawyer. Tess had never imagined herself with Michael, although she found him handsome with his steely blue eyes and his salt and peppered hair. There was something too Ken-like about him, and yet the first time they kissed, Tess had fallen for him. It wasn't long after that she and David split and Michael and his wife split, and Michael moved into her house in Mill Basin. Why she married Michael, she didn't know. She wondered sometimes if they hadn't gotten married if they would still be in a relationship. But if they hadn't have gotten married and then divorced, she wouldn't have gotten to sell him her dream house in Mill Basin, and it would have killed her to have sold that house to just anyone.

"All I want is a few hours here alone to get some work done. Is that too much to ask?"

"Good morning to you, too, Tess. You asked me to meet you here early today, remember? We need to go through some contracts before your meetings."

"Have you put on the coffee?"

"Has anyone ever told you that you're a piece of work?" Michael asked.

"You did, dear, all two years we were married."

"Shhh. Listen. Hear that? Either the Gods are peeing in the kitchen, or maybe, it's coffee brewing."

"Do you ever get tired?" Tess asked.

"At around 12:00 a.m. each night."

Tess dropped her bag on her desk and plopped down on her chair.

"How is it that I can be exhausted already, and the day didn't even begin?" she said.

"You'll drink your coffee and feel fine."

Tess traced the lines on her forehead, creasing her brow and releasing it. The pockets under her eyes felt puffy.

"Michael."

"Tess?"

"Do you think I look old in the billboard ads?" Tess asked.

"My dear, if you look old, then I look old."

"And your point is?" Tess asked.

"We're both 55."

"Will you answer my question?"

"No, Tess, you don't look old. And if you think you do, go to a plastic surgeon," Michael said.

"Just what I want. Someone cutting my face up."

"How was your weekend?" Michael asked.

"There was a weekend?" Tess said.

"Tell me you weren't in here working all weekend."

"I wasn't in here working all weekend," Tess said.

"Now tell me the truth," Michael said.

"I was in here working all weekend."

"Did you relax at all?" Michael asked.

"I watched *The Sound of Music* on Saturday night."

Michael sat down on the edge of her desk, knocking over one of her hollowed metal tristate Realtor of the Year awards, which he quickly picked back up, smirking. She knew he thought her displaying the awards was tacky and she generally agreed with him, but she felt that they served as a reminder to her staff of her credibility.

"I love the fact that inside that workaholic exterior, you're a sap. How many times have you seen it now?" Michael said.

Tess shrugged. "I lost count."

"What is it with you and that movie?"

"I love that Maria does the unexpected. Maybe it makes me think that there's hope for me."

"Do you have plans tonight?" Michael said.

"It depends."

"Don't worry, I won't try to woo you. You've made it clear that it's a losing battle. Besides, I'm waiting for you to come to me and tell me that you're in love with someone else."

"Well, you'll be waiting a good, long time, because that's not going to happen," Tess said.

"Man-lover to man-hater."

"I am not a man-hater, Michael. I just don't want to be bothered with romance anymore. It gets me off my course."

"And your course is?"

"Work," Tess said.

"Go with me to a yoga class tonight. My treat," Michael said.

"A yoga class?" Tess asked. She pushed herself away from her desk and propped her legs up on it.

"Don't start, Tess."

"Don't start? I'm intrigued by your venture into spirituality, go on."

"It's not a venture into spirituality. One of my golf buddies told me that yoga has helped his game and that the teachers are pretty attractive, too."

"Oh, now I see. You want me there so that you don't look desperate when you hit on other women. If you're there with me, they'll think you can't be half so bad, right?" Tess said.

"There's an 8:00 p.m. class – we could shoot into the city after work and give it a whirl."

"Michael, my dear, I gave up yoga when I was a teenager, or have you forgotten that my mother was, is, the spiritual, Buddhist, healer of Woodstock? My yoga days ended when I left that god-forsaken upstate town."

"Was your mother a stressed-out workaholic?"

"Well, no, because she didn't work. Unless you consider being a guru work."

"Tess Rose, your mother is the freest, most joyful person that I've ever met."

"Let me remind you of your reaction when I first took you to Woodstock – you felt sorry for me for having grown up there, and when the folks started piling into my mother's house at 6:00 am to meditate, you were ready to check into a hotel."

"Look, just come with me. What do you have to lose?"

"I do not need yoga. I'm glad to leave my past in the past. But thanks for thinking of me."

"If you ask me, you've spent the last 30 or so years of your life trying to undo your past and it doesn't seem to have gotten you anywhere."

Tess dropped her legs to the floor and pulled herself closer to her desk.

"What's that supposed to mean?"

"It means that you fled from upstate New York to Brooklyn, got an MBA, married four husbands, own a thriving real estate business, and lead a stressed-out, neurotic life."

"For your information, I'm far from stressed out," Tess said. "Is that coffee ready yet? I don't hear it dripping anymore."

"I'll pick you up at your place at 6:30 tonight and don't tell me you need to work late. It's 7:00 am. Get to it. I can't wait to see you in your yoga clothes.

CHAPTER 2: STATE OF MIND

"It's an incredible property," Tess said. "And you couldn't ask for a better area. Brooklyn Heights boasts some of the hottest real estate around. Great shopping, cafes, restaurants. Some pretty good private schools, too, not to mention playgrounds nearby."

She guessed Kyle, the prospective buyer, couldn't be more than thirty. On his application form, he had noted that he was a broker for Morgan Stanley, earning close to $500,000 a year plus a substantial bonus. That had made her laugh. *Substantial.* Normally, his smugness would have turned her off, caused her to dismiss him as a pretentious young punk, but something about him, perhaps it was his hair – Tess connected with curly haired people – eased her up. He reminded her of her son, with his penetrating, black eyes. They had the same quicksand quality as Prakash's eyes. The girl he was with, Dale, his fiancé, twirled her long, wavy, chestnut hair over and over, so that Tess wanted to tie her hands down. The way she coasted around in her tall, lanky body made Tess pause. There was a floating quality to her that registered with Tess: this girl was not ready to settle down and move in.

Tess leaned against the kitchen counter. Charcoal gray and white granite. Nice touch. The three-floor, eleven-room brownstone had just the right mix of old and new with its high ceilings embellished with an intricate woven pattern at the corners and exposed silver pipes. Charming was how she'd describe it to a more mature couple. She was dying to take her shoes off, kick back and relax on the ivory leather sofa that she had positioned adjacent to the fireplace. She had learned that the best way to make a property that she was showing appealing, was to put some comfortable couches in the living room and a coffee table that was the perfect height to put papers on that needed signing. No reason to make the house-seeker bend down too much. Pain and selling a house didn't go together. Her colleagues believed in baking pies in the oven of a property to make it smell "homey" and inviting. Tess believed in sprinkling the plush ivory rugs she brought in with baby powder to make the house smell fresh, clean. She'd certainly prefer to move into a house that appealed to her sense of freedom rather than her stomach.

Kyle looked up at her and exhaled, as if he were a balloon losing air.

"When I saw this property, I thought of you right away," she said.

"It's a great place," Kyle said. It sounded more like a question to Tess. He passed his hand through his thick, black curly hair and shook his head as if he were waking himself up.

"But –" Tess said. There was always a "but."

"But, well." He glanced to his fiancé. When their eyes met, she shrugged her shoulders.

"I think we're interested in something smaller. Something more along the lines of a first house," he said.

"I see," Tess said. She had learned that the best approach when you were dealing with young people who had a lot of money to spend but were confused how to spend it, was to intimidate them.

"You're interested in a starter home?"

"Exactly," he said.

Tess cleared her throat and rolled her eyes, but not before she was sure that Kyle was watching her.

"Got it," she said.

"Is there something wrong with that?" Kyle said. He glanced toward his fiancé, but she was staring out the window.

"No. It's just that in my experience starter homes become the only home you ever live in. Most people think they'll move after a few years, but then a few years come around and well let's face it – no one wants to pack up all their stuff again and move after that first nightmare experience of an initial move. Not to mention if you have some kids by then – packing up and moving with kids is a mess."

He looked away from Tess and moved his hands through his hair again.

"It's not that I don't love this place – I do. It's incredible."

Tess opened her mouth to say, "With a deposit down, it could be yours," and then stopped. If there was a chance that they would split up before the paperwork for the house sale went through, then what was the point of going in for her killer close?

Dale sat at the window seat, an octagon shaped wedge built into the dining room wall. The way she pressed her head against the glass made her look just the right mix of lazy and elegant – *ennui* was the word that came to Tess. Normally the look would have annoyed Tess, but there was a lack of self-consciousness to Dale just then that intrigued her. Dale turned abruptly and glanced at Tess, their eyes locking for a long but not uncomfortable instant, before she pulled her hair up off her neck and twisted it into a bun with one sweep of her hands. Tess cleared her throat and turned back to Kyle, her tone softer.

"Look, I can show you starter homes in Brooklyn or Queens, but you're not going to be this close to the city, not to mention have an investment that's most likely going to double in less than two years' time. Sure, it's 2003 and 9/11 is still in the air, but a few years from now, I predict this real estate is going to go through the roof again. Besides, brownstones like this rarely become available. The only reason this one is on the market is because the woman who lived here had to relocate to London for business."

"I can't imagine not living in Manhattan," Dale said. "I don't know if I can do the Brooklyn thing."

"Honey, Dale, it's just a few minutes outside of Manhattan. We've been through this already. For what we'll pay to buy an apartment in the city, we can buy a home elsewhere."

Dale shook her head. "I just don't know if I want to live outside of the city, in a suburb. Suburbs depress me."

13

"Brooklyn Heights is just like Manhattan," he said.

"Says you," she said. "To me, Brooklyn Heights is like Brooklyn Heights. I feel far away from everything."

"You work in downtown Manhattan," Kyle said. "You're closer to your job living here than you are living on the Upper East Side."

"Yes, but I can't walk to work from here."

"You can walk across the bridge," Kyle said.

Dale laughed. "Oh, right. I'll stroll across the bridge each morning. Sounds great. I'll be sure to wear my painter overalls so that my clothes don't get full of traffic soot."

"Perhaps we should meet up again when you're ready to talk seriously about a house," Tess said.

"No! I mean, we are ready to talk seriously now," said Kyle.

"If you are, then I can't imagine having a better place than this to show you that's close to the city and this beautiful, not to mention in your price range."

"I wouldn't say this is exactly in our price range," Kyle said.

"Money," Tess said, "is a state of mind."

"I'll be sure to tell that to my bank when I try to withdraw money that I don't have," Kyle said.

"How long have you been living in Manhattan?" Tess said. She was facing Dale.

"Born and raised," Dale said. "All 27 years of my life."

Tess believed that decisions made before 30 weren't to be taken seriously and she would have shared that insight with Dale, only her son had drilled into her that free advice wasn't worth much.

"Aside from the location, all of this space scares me," Dale said.

Tess glanced at her watch. Clearly consensus wasn't one of this couple's strong points.

"I don't mean to rush you, but I need to be on my way," Tess said. "Why don't you two discuss what you're looking for and get back to me?"

"We're looking for a place just like this," Kyle said.

"You just said that you wanted a starter house, and the space and location scare your lovely fiancé," Tess said.

Keep them real. That was her way to avoid wasting time.

"I love this place," Kyle said.

Dale closed her eyes, exhaled loud, and shook her head so that her hair scattered all about her shoulders. "I need a cookie," she said.

"A cookie?" Tess said.

"She's got this cookie thing," Kyle said. "It's how she deals."

"Right," Tess said. She stifled a laugh and smiled. A girl who didn't want a gorgeous home and dealt with conflict by eating cookies. No, Tess didn't have time for these two.

"Chances are that I'll get some bids on this place before the week is up," Tess said.

"Dale, what do you say? We've looked at over a dozen places already, baby. This place is incredible."

This was the first place she had showed them, so obviously the other realtors had gotten fed up with them. Perhaps what was needed to help them focus their energy was to change the subject.

"Where are you two getting married?" Tess asked.

"To be decided," he said. "That's Dale's department. My job is to find a place to live. Right?" he said, his eyes on Dale.

"Sure," she said.

"Good luck," Tess said. And then, in answer to Dale's off-center gaze. "With your marriage." She had meant to say with the planning.

Dale's eyes were intent on Tess, as if she were seeing her for the first time. It was a sharp glance, and Tess recognized something in her eyes, but she couldn't pinpoint exactly what.

"Why don't you two take some time to think about where your dream house is located and what it looks like, and get back to me? I'll be glad to put you in touch with one of my agents to help you when you know what you're looking for."

"Why can't we work with you?" Kyle said and Dale was standing behind him now, her eyes on Tess as if they were both about to charge into her.

"Goodbye then," Tess said, seeing them out the front gate.

"I'll be in touch," Kyle said.

CHAPTER 3:THE AWAKENING

The scent of nag champa incense – sweet and spicy – filtered through Tess as she made her way up the two flights of stairs to the yoga studio. Michael had insisted that they beat the crowd in the lobby waiting for the elevator by taking the stairs. For a moment, just as she was reaching the top stair, she closed her eyes and thought of her childhood home. Michael caught her from behind: "steady there, Tess. No accidents before we make it into the studio." He pulled the heavy steel door open and suddenly the scent enveloped them full blast.

"Your shoes!" the girl behind the counter screeched. "Please! Take them off before you walk in."

"Oh," Tess said, turning to Michael and leaning on him for support. She pulled one black suede Gucci loafer off and then the other, putting them in her tote bag.

"What are you doing?" Michael said.

"What does it look like I'm doing?"

He stuffed his sneakers into the shoe-holder egg crates.

"Why don't you put your shoes next to the rest of them," he said.

"Are you kidding me?" Tess said. "These shoes cost $550."

Michael rolled his eyes. "Since when did you become so paranoid?"

"If I were wearing a pair of out-of-date sneakers like you, I'd gladly put them on the shoe rack or in whatever that is – the shoe cubby thing."

"Excuse me!" the girl behind the desk whispered loudly. She pointed to a circular white plaque that had the word *talking* on it in red caps with a line through it. "Please obey the rules; we don't speak while a class is in session."

The studio was a mix of light Danish wood benches and matching built-into-the-wall shelves filled with precisely folded yoga clothes and books. Across from where the elevator let out, there was an oversized semi-circle shaped wooden desk covered with sign-in clipboards. Tess squinted up at the high ceiling. Exposed silver beams and silver track lighting rods were interspersed with extra small light fixtures. From their glow, she imagined they had used either hot pink or dim-orange bulbs, which created a nice echo effect. Spacious is how Tess would have described it. Sophisticated, airy, and spacious.

The girl behind the counter smiled sugar sweet at Michael when they approached. That was all he needed to be hooked: a twenty-something year old flirting with him the minute he walked in. She looked like a cheerleader to Tess, with her tawny blonde stick straight hair, and her red bra top that did nothing for her concave chest, although her flat stomach was, Tess noted, appealingly accentuated by her low wasted skin-tight black leggings that flared out at the bottoms. Yoga clothes had come a long way from the oversized t-shirts and the flowing bohemian tops that all the men and women who used to come to do yoga with her mother wore.

"Have you been here before?" the girl said.

"No, we haven't," Michael said.

"You'll have to fill out a release," the girl said. She handed Michael a clipboard with a form on it and pushed one in front of Tess. "Let's put your name into the system so we can at least get you paid up," she said, her eyes on the computer screen she was tapping information into. "Will you be paying for your wife, too?" she said.

"I'm not his wife, but yes, he'll be paying for me, won't you, Michael?"

"I dragged her here, so I guess I have to pay," he said. The girl grimaced at him, as if they were sharing a secret, and Michael winked at her. Tess's bullshit detector was ringing at full volume.

"Will you need to rent mats?" the girl asked Michael.

"Yes, we both need to rent mats," he said, handing her his credit card.

The girl smiled a cheesy smile at Tess. "Splendid," she said. "If you could just move to the side to fill these out so that I can take care of the other people," the girl said, motioning to the line that had formed behind them. "I'll give you your card back when you return the forms."

The people on line were pulling yoga clothes out of their tote bags, unbuttoning their shirts, undoing their belts. Tess sat down next to Michael on the bench adjacent to the counter to fill out her forms. *Was she pregnant? Taking any medication? High blood pressure? How many days a week did she exercise? The regularity of her yoga practice. Was this her first yoga class? How'd she learn about the studio?*

Tess tried to concentrate, but everyone around her seemed to be scrambling; the activity was making her anxious. Some formed a line to use the bathroom, while others waited on line to get into the dressing rooms. No one talked, which magnified the sound of their movements.

"Can you believe how many people are here? You need a valium just to deal with this chaos," Tess said, a bit too loudly she supposed, because two of the women on the bathroom line turned and glared at her.

"Do you think I should be wearing shorts?" Michael said. The man standing in front of him wore a short, fitted tank top and blank cotton spandex shorts so that nothing about his tight, firm body was left to the imagination.

"I wouldn't be seen with you if you wore those shorts," Tess said.

"Are you saying that I don't have the body for them?"

"I'm saying that I think private parts are more appealing when you keep them private."

The girl behind the counter leaned over from her waist so that she was in full view of them. "I wasn't kidding about the talking," she said. "Please, respect our rules. Are you finished with the forms?"

Tess cleared her throat. "Bitch," she said loud enough for Michael to hear.

"Be nice," Michael said, holding out his hand for Tess to hand him her clipboard.

"Next time I let you drag me somewhere, remind me to get my head examined."

The girl grunted when Michael handed her back the clipboards and shook her head at Tess. Tess had an urge to stick out her tongue at her. The last thing she needed after a stressful day was to be reprimanded by the yoga studio counter girl.

"The mats are in the back of the room," the girl said. "When you're finished with class, fold them up just how you found them and put them back."

"Yes, ma'am," Tess said. Michael pulled her arm down before she was able to salute the girl.

"She's just doing her job," he said close to her ear.

"I suppose she gets paid extra for being a drill sergeant."

When the doors of the yoga room opened into the waiting area, herds of sweaty women and a few men streamed out; most of them had sopping wet hair.

"Great. Just what I was hoping for, a sauna. If I wanted to sweat,

I could have turned on my oven full blast and put on my flannel PJ's," Tess said.

"Will you stop complaining already?"

"Look who's talking."

The girl behind the counter chimed a bell, and the yogi's-in-waiting rushed into the yoga room.

"I guess that's our sign that it's safe to enter," Michael said, nudging her ahead of him. "After you."

"If I have to."

Michael pushed her into the room, jabbing her back with his fist. She picked up a mat at the back of the room; it smelled to her like feet, and a wave of nausea rushed through her.

"So sanitary," she said, handing Michael a mat. It was still streaked with sweat from the last person who had used it.

The walls and ceiling of the yoga room looked as if they'd been bleached. Optical white. That's what Tess would call it. If she focused on the whiteness, it overcame her, as if she were staring into a cloud. Tess chose a spot near the wall, in the third row. Michael set up behind her.

She lay down on her mat while people settled themselves in around her. The ceilings were high and decorated with ornate, swirly designs at the four corners of the room. Tess searched for a way into the swirls, but each bend seemed to begin and end without leading into the next. The night sky shone through the three large square windows on the ceiling. Free. Quiet. Safe. That's how the room made Tess feel, until the nag champa incense filtered through her, unsettling her. Growing up, the smell had permeated her house so that it was imbedded in her clothing, her skin. Whenever she had walked into her classroom at school, the whole class had started sniffing, reminding her that she was different. Some of the children teased her and passed her notes that said that she smelt funny, and yet the smell had always given her comfort, and often, in the middle of the school day, she had brought her shirtsleeve to her nose and inhaled.

In her mind's eye, she could see her mother's devotees in her home in Woodstock practicing yoga each morning before sunrise. The daily meditation sessions that her mother made her take part in each day before she went to school. She could see herself walking to the bus stop in the bright colored t-shirts and ponchos her mother dressed her in. At lunchtime and after school the other kids called her a Hare Krishna, chanting Hare Krishna and clapping whenever she was around. The incessant teasing by her schoolmates, who would whisper within her hearing that she and her mother were freaks, hadn't bothered her much. She, too, had thought of her mother as a freak for a while, wishing with all her heart and soul that she had some other mother, that she lived in some other home in which she was allowed to watch TV after school and eat cookies and junk food.

Her mind darted to her son, Prakash. Unlike her, Prakash had been captivated by her mother. He had bought into it all early on – yoga, meditation, Buddhism – so that by the time he went off to college, some dozen plus years back, his guiding principles were of a Buddhist nature, although he wasn't caught up with the need to look the part. Tess had admired that about him: his ability to be his authentic self without trying to impose his beliefs on anyone else. Prakash had always seemed to her as if he were her mother's child, with his Asian complexion and black eyes. Tess's red hair, blue eyes and fair complexion made her feel like an outsider.

A hint of lavender waffled through the room, and for a moment she smelled the pillow that she had slept with as a child, the pillow that her mother had scented each night with lavender oil before Tess got into bed. To Tess, it was the smell of sweet dreams. Her shoulders fell until she felt herself folding up into herself.

"Oh!" Tess jumped, sitting up.

Michael had jabbed her. "You fell asleep," he mouthed, to which she shook her head no.

The yoga teacher was talking, instructing the class to find a comfortable seat. Her voice was like a lily flower to Tess – delicate, distinct, and sweet. They were to begin class with meditation.

"Close your eyes and begin to go inward. Follow your inhales and your exhales. Begin to slow everything down. Forget where you were today, where you need to be later, what you'll be doing tomorrow. All that matters is this moment. Listen to your breath. It will let you see where you are inside. Focus on your inhales and your exhales."

By the time the teacher instructed them to come to the front of their mats, standing tall and at attention, the four corners of their feet firmly pressed into the earth, their shoulders down, their neck lose and free, their arms light and long by their sides, Tess felt herself letting go, easing up. She breathed in long and hard through her nose, and when she exhaled, it was as if everything that had been sitting on her chest – things that she hadn't known were there, making her feel heavy and suffocated – drifted away from her. With the first swoop of her hands upward and towards the sky, Tess felt as if she were flying.

As much as Tess tried to focus on her movements, to modify her poses per the teacher's directions – tuck her tailbone, engage her abdomen – her mind continued to dart about. The movements were so familiar to her, so that with each upward motion of her arms, she felt as if she were diving into her past, exhaling her face up to see her mother smiling at her; in downward facing dog she could feel her mother's gentle hands easing her shoulders down her back, away from her neck. She heard her mother's voice in the teacher's voice, everything blurring, so that each time she looked at the girl on the mat in front of her, she realized she was one step behind what the rest of the class was doing.

"If you feel like you need a rest," the teacher was saying, "then by all means take child's pose." After one more sun salute – arms coming around and up towards the sky, then exhaling and folding down towards the floor, inhaling, her face up, and then exhaling one foot back and then the other, lowering down towards the floor, her upper body lifted as though she were at the top of a push up, her knees and thighs lifted, and then exhaling into downward facing dog – Tess took child's pose. She needed to be quiet and small, to let go of everything that was going on around her, shut down her mind. In a few moments, the rest of the class moved onto standing poses, while the teacher bent down by Tess and whispered for her to take rest, shavasana, on her back. The teacher massaged Tess's neck, loosening her up; the smell of lavender, on the teacher's hands, soothing her, helping her to further let go. There was so much tenderness, so much warmth in the teacher's fingers that Tess felt as if she were in mother's care, safe in her mother's yoga room, her mother presiding over her. In this cocoon of the present meshed with memory, it amazed her how easy it was to stop thinking, to relax, to rest.

"Nap time is over," Michael said. He was leaning over her, on his elbows, so that Tess jumped up. He smelt like sour milk. Everyone around Tess was moving, folding up their mats, sipping from water bottles.

"I was asleep," Tess said. She popped up, not sure if she was back in her mother's house or if it was a dream.

"Really? No?" Michael said.

Tess closed her eyes and opened them. No, she wasn't back at her mother's. She felt as if she had slept for days.

"I feel amazing," she said, and it surprised her that she did. A feeling of joy, serenity, displaced the dread and fear she had felt coming to the studio, of returning to yoga.

"I'm glad one of us does. I feel dead," Michael said. "So much for me and yoga. While I was struggling through one downward dog after the other, you were snoozing."

"You smell bad," Tess said.

"Thanks," he said.

Tess folded up her mat, placed it on the stack at the back of the classroom, and was about to follow Michael out when the teacher stopped her.

"I hope you come back," she said.

Tess smiled at her. "I will be back," she said.

"You needed the rest."

"I didn't realize it, but yes, I guess that I did," she said. Tess felt as if she were floating.

"Namaste," the teacher said, and Tess repeated, "Namaste."

It was the way the girl walking out in front of her swooped up her long locks in one instant and then sorted through her bag, pulling off a chunk of something – from behind it looked to Tess like a piece of cake – that caught Tess's attention. When the girl turned toward her, Tess could make out that it was a piece of a cookie that the girl stuffed in her mouth. In a moment of mutual confusion and recognition, their eyes locked.

"The brownstone," Dale said, and Tess nodded. Dale wiped her hands on her black yoga pants and smiled. "You must think I'm awful," she said.

Her demeanor, her smile – it was as if she were a completely different person. She stood upright and tall and there was a softness to her, a humorous side that Tess would have never guessed existed in her.

"No, I don't think –"

"I'm sorry," the girl said catching Tess's forearm. "I don't usually carry on like that. It's just that Kyle seems to have convinced himself that we need to move and is on a mission to find us a place when there's no reason for us not to stay in my place."

"I'm sure you two will figure it out," Tess said, her voice low. Talking business seemed like another language to her right now. She felt as if she had overdosed on muscle relaxers.

Dale's head moved back as if she were trying to distance herself from Tess while she studied her. Her lips were a straight line.

"I mean that you don't have to explain to me," Tess said.

"Right. Thanks for your vote of confidence. I'm sure we will figure it out," Dale said.

Michael was standing beside her now. He and Dale nodded and smiled at one another, and then the girl pulled open the door to the stairs and was gone. Tess was lost as to what had just happened; she wished that she could transport herself from the yoga studio into her bed. That was where she needed to be in her present lost-in-space state of mind.

"Shall we go?" she said to Michael.

"Cute girl," Michael said.

"She's taken," Tess said.

"So were you," Michael said, and with that Tess made her way to the elevator, grabbed a schedule from the bulletin board, and pushed the down button.

CHAPTER 4: SEEK AND YOU SHALL FIND

Tess made a sharp turn from Avenue U onto 66th street and hit the gas. Homeward bound. It had been a long day, but a good one – she closed two houses and her two top-producing agents had each closed one. It was like this each spring: real estate deals closed with the steadiness of planes landing at the airport, coming in one after the other. Spring and summer, Tess knew, was wedding time, and the feeling of optimism in the air, the promise of new beginnings, the desire to please future mates was contagious to house shoppers. Sometimes while showing a home to a young, hopeful couple, Tess envisioned them down the road, weathered, kids rushing through the house, noise, dirt, bills to be paid scattering the counter, and she wanted to tell them it wasn't worth it – that in a dozen years, this home would become their jail cell.

Tess sighed and felt her shoulders fall from their perches by her ears. She looked forward to drinking a cup of chamomile tea and soaking in a bath. At the stop sign, she fiddled with the radio. There never seemed to be anything on except for deejays talking to people who were struggling with relationships. A woman was telling the deejay that she was divorced, middle-aged, and that she wanted to find her soul mate. For an instant, Tess wondered how many more days of her life she would zoom down 66th street at 8:00 pm on her way home to an empty house, and a wave of something – sadness, despair – washed through her. But her day had been too full and there was too much she had to accomplish tomorrow to feel anything other than anticipation for her cup of tea and a bath.

In the darkness, she spotted his white shirt and shiny head as she fiddled with the scan button on the radio, trying to stop it from skipping from station to station. It was *him*, the guy with a death wish, the middle-of-the-street walker. Only this time he was on a bicycle, on the opposite side of the road, riding in the middle of the street in the darkness. She beeped at him, and opened her window, ready to scream to him to get out of the street, but he smiled and waved at her and at that moment, church bells rang. A car behind her beeped at her and Tess pulled over to the curb. All those years of living in Mill Basin and Tess couldn't remember the last time she had heard the church bells from St. Bernard's Church over in Bergen Beach. The chiming soothed her, took her back to the other night, the yoga room, the bells chiming to invite them into class and then at the end of class, the teacher using them to stir the class from their rest. Tess had been sleeping, hadn't heard them consciously, but somehow their sound had seeped into her.

She made a U-turn so that she was behind him. He looked back at her and smiled, bobbing his head from side to side, as if he were trying to get water out of his ears. She wasn't going to let this kook job freak her out. She was going to find out his story and then be on her way. If there was someone insane in the affluent Mill Basin as she liked to call it when she was in her selling mode, she wanted to know about it, if only to be able to acknowledge him when she was out with potential buyers, explain his story and quell any anxiety that her customer's might feel.

She lost him at the light at Avenue U, but then she was behind him again after the light changed, and when he got to St. Bernard's Church, he parked his bike on the side of the building and went in. Tess sat in her car for a few moments, waiting, watching, and suddenly, she was pulling into a parking spot and getting out of her car. She wasn't in the habit of following strangers, and yet she couldn't seem to quiet her curiosity.

Tess eased open the heavy wooden door of the chapel and was hit with cool air and the smell of sharp incense – a mix of frankincense and licorice – seeped into her throat and then her chest, so that she felt heavier. She had never stepped foot in this church in the 30-plus years that she lived in Mill Basin. The only temples she had visited were the Buddhist ones her mother had dragged her into.

The chapel was sparsely lit with long stemmed candles and a dim drop-down light in the center of the room. In the back where she stood, there were rows intermixed with burning votive candles and ones that were yet to be lit. Beside the table was a worn wooden donation box with a chain and padlock around it. The stage was adorned with candles, as was each of the window ledges, the dancing flames illuminating the stained-glass panels of Christ and Mary and men who Tess guessed where the apostles. Their agonized faces glowed surreal so that from certain angles, they looked as if they were about to fall out of the panels and land before Tess, begging for help.

There were rows of wooden benches, all empty; a glistening hard wood floor, and a high ceiling that gave the room a hollow feeling. If she focused on the crisp, white wall opposite the windows, she noted the angels etched into it. They struck her as tacky, over the top – the angels were too far away and out of reach to help anyone.

The backdrop of the stage was an enormous cross with a worn and weary Mary holding a dying Jesus across her lap. The image stilled Tess. To be a mother. To lose a son. To hold him dying. Tears came to her eyes, and she laughed at herself; she didn't understand where this emotion came from. Prakash was safe and well in San Francisco – she had just talked to him that morning. On the stage was a pulpit with a microphone and a table dead center with candles and some prayer books stacked on it. Tess found a seat in a pew in the back of the room, took a daily prayer book on her lap, dusting it off, and closed her eyes. It felt nice to be sitting in this foreign place, the air cool and fragrant; she had grown accustomed to the smell of the incense by this time. They were not sweet like the nag champa incense, but harsher, more intense.

Tess didn't know how long she had zoned out when the door creaked shut. She felt refreshed, as if she had awakened from a long, deep sleep, and she thought of the other night, the yoga class. She didn't think of herself as the type of person to fall asleep in public places. She imagined that Michael would have a field day at her expense over this new phenomenon.

The crazy man made his way down the center aisle. He walked slowly and precisely, as if he were balancing a book atop his head. He stopped when he was a few feet from the stage and made the sign of the cross.

"Hail Mary, full of grace, the Lord is with you. Blessed are you among women and blessed is the fruit of your womb. Holy Mary, mother of God, pray for us sinners now and at the hour of death."

His voice was gentle, soothing. Not what Tess expected to come out of him. His clean-shaven scalp glistened in the flickering light. The way his chin jutted into his chest reminded her of a child – shy, insecure – and she felt foolish for having yelled at him, for following him this evening. She moved in the pew, sending the prayer book to the floor with a thump and he looked up, slowly, as if he had been caught.

"I'm sorry to disturb you. I thought I was alone," he said.

"You were," Tess said. She placed the prayer book back in its slot and stood up.

She followed his eyes and looked down at herself. The way he was looking at her made her feel as if a giant spider was crawling up her. "Is something wrong?"

"No," he said.

"Well, excuse me, then," she said, preparing to leave.

He nodded and smiled at her, taking all of her in, so that she wasn't sure what to say or do next.

"You know, you ought to be more careful where you walk or ride your bike. Someone will run you over if you dally in the middle of the street."

He smiled and nodded again; he looked as if he was amused.

Either that, or he was stupid.

"Well, I'm going," she said.

"Goodnight," he said.

She pursed her lips. There was something penetrating about him and kind and open at the same time. If she were out selling a house to someone with those eyes, she guessed that he wouldn't be an easy customer, that he would do his homework on the house, uncover whatever there was to uncover, and share his knowledge with her, a smile on his face, his voice low and sure as he demanded a better price. She would like to spar with him like that, settle once and for all who was made up of what.

"I'm Tess," she said, holding out her hand. "Of Best Realty."

The moment she said it she felt ridiculous. He stared at her hand and bowed his head again. Tess retreated her hand, her eyes on him. Perhaps he had a disease and didn't want to touch her. He was attractive: smooth ski-slope nose, hollowed-out cheekbones, soft, pool-blue eyes. He had the face of someone who never raised his voice.

"You haven't told me your name."

"Neal. Neal Clay."

"So now when I see you strutting in the middle of the street, I can yell at you by your name."

"You were on your way out?" he said.

"Yes," Tess said.

"After you," he said, following her. Neal opened a door of the chapel that led into the church's deserted hallway, so that for a moment Tess was disoriented. She had expected to be back out in the street.

"You're the woman on the bus stop ad," he said.

He watched her with an intensity that made her uncomfortable. She shifted her weight from one foot to another and jingled her car keys in her blazer pocket, wedging the sharp-edged key in between her knuckles.

The hall was narrow and long; Tess's stilettos made a clicking sound against the pale ivory linoleum.

"Do you like what you do?" he said.

"I've been in the real estate business for over thirty years now. It's all I've ever done," she said.

"Just because you do something for a long time, doesn't mean you like it."

"No. I suppose it doesn't," she said.

Neal stopped when they got to the end of the hallway. "But then again, you might like what you do. Blessed are those who love their work." He looked up at the ceiling, insinuating God. Tess couldn't tell if he was in earnest or poking fun.

"I guess I do love my work. Although I don't always love how much I work," she said.

He had a way of being quiet after she spoke that made her unsure of what to do or say next.

"Do you live in Mill Basin?" Tess said.

"I've come to visit for a while." Then, as if it would shed some light on his visit, in a lower voice, "I'm writing a book."

The end of the hall led to another hall with candelabra on the walls, illuminating the paintings in their elaborate gold frames. She paused by the painting of a young, small girl who held an abundance of roses in her hand. Draped in one of her elbows was a wooden cross with Christ on it. Across the center bottom of the painting's frame there was a gold plaque with an inscription that read:

I have never given to the good God anything but love. He will return that love. After my death I will let fall a ceaseless shower of roses upon earth.

– St. Theresa of Lisieux

"She was a very strong and beautiful soul," Neal said.

"What did she do?"

"She became small for the sake of God," Neal said.

Tess envisioned her shrinking, like the witch in the *Wizard of Oz*. "She became small?"

"Not physically. Her becoming small had to do with how she lived her life. She was faithful to the little things in her daily routine, doing everything for God's honor and glory. She lived a peaceful and hidden existence in the Carmelite Order. She became small so that she could lose herself and devote herself to Christ."

Neal inhaled the painting. Tess couldn't tell if he was deeply religious, or if he was truly nuts.

Neal pointed to the last line of the inscription: "Whenever you see a rose on the ground, think of St Theresa."

"My last name is Rose," Tess said.

"Well, then you're a sign from St. Theresa – a reminder to live small and be faithful to the important things in your life."

Tess studied him for a moment; she'd never come across anyone as over the top as this clown and yet there was an earnestness about him that touched her. She recognized something of her mother's intensity and naivety in Neal that made her feel that he was for real, that this wasn't an act for him.

"What's your book about?" she said.

"Religion," Neal said.

"That's a broad subject," Tess said.

"I wouldn't want to offend your religious beliefs," Neal said.

Tess laughed. The idea of someone offending her religious beliefs, whatever they were, tickled her.

"Try me," she said.

"My book unites all religions; it breaks down the barriers humans create in the name of religion. At least that's what I hope it does when I finish writing it."

"Sounds like you have your work cut out for you," Tess said. She paused in front a painting of Mary holding the baby Jesus with a halo around his head. It could have been any woman holding her son.

"I take it you're not a Catholic?" Neal said.

"No," Tess said. She turned to face him; his eyes were on the painting. There was something in the way he took it in, as if he were looking for a clue. "Apparently you are," Tess said.

"Yes," Neal said.

"I was raised Buddhist – Tibetan Buddhist. The Four Noble Truths and The Eightfold Path and all that. My mother was from Thailand."

"That's interesting."

"If you buy into it all, I suppose," Tess said.

One of the candles in the hall flickered and for a moment it looked as if it was going to die out until as if spurred on by a spirit, it burned brighter.

"And you don't?" Neal said.

He walked on and she followed him, until they stood at the end of the corridor where there was a sign that said: *NO ENTRY, Church Personnel Only.*

"When I was a child, it was hard for me. All that stuff about suffering and being on the path to end suffering. I wanted to have fun. Suffering seemed like a drag. I rebelled," Tess said.

"Were there any turning points?" Neal said.

Tess hugged her shoulders and looked around to see where the draft was coming from. Neal walked slowly beside her, and she debated if it were time to go, to say goodnight. She wasn't one to share details of her life with a stranger and she still wasn't sure if she were talking to a crazy man or a sane one.

"Sometimes as we grow older things we fought begin to make more sense," Neal said in a low voice that made her wonder if he were addressing her or himself.

"I don't think I'll ever be a practicing Buddhist, but yes, now I can appreciate some of the concepts a bit more," Tess said.

"I admire you," he said.

"Admire me? Why?" she asked, her voice cracking. She felt his eyes on her, but when she turned to him, he stared straight ahead.

"It's easy to get brainwashed as a child, to do as our parents say, but you seem to have had your own ideas as a child and maintained them. That's brave."

"I don't think it's brave. It was just how my mind worked – I questioned everything when I was a child. If things didn't make sense to me, I couldn't just believe them." She stopped. "What is that?" she asked pointing to the necklace he wore.

Neal rubbed the necklace's centerpiece, which consisted of two squares of woolen cloth connected with each other by two strings or bands; the front segment rested on his chest, and she imagined that the other part of it hung down his back.

"It's a scapula," Neal said. "It's supposed to help guide people. When you pray to it, you never say Amen because the prayer is continuous. It doesn't have an end."

"For someone writing a book that equates religions, you seem to be a pretty devout Catholic," Tess said.

"Religion has played a big role in my life. The book is helping me to make sense of what my truth is," Neal said.

He rubbed his scapula and glanced up at Tess and then down at the floor, as if he were checking to see if it was still there. There was an innocence to him that she couldn't place, a shyness around her, and she wondered if he were gay.

"Are you far along with your book?"

"I've had a lot of false starts, but I think that I'm on the right path now. I've written a few chapters in the past week."

She couldn't place his accent: Midwest?

"Well, that's good news. Hopefully you'll figure out your truth in no time at all."

They stood in front of a painting of a young, bare-chested Jesus holding Mary's hand, pulling her along a road. The sky in the painting was parting so that Jesus and Mary's faces radiated. Tess felt herself growing warm, and then they were moving on again.

"Are you from Brooklyn?" Tess asked.

Neal nodded. "I grew up in Mill Basin." They walked down another corridor. "It's nice to be back in Brooklyn," he said.

"That depends on where you've been."

Neal stopped rubbing and stared down at his hands, as if Tess had asked him to pull a frog from his throat. She envisioned a nasty divorce, his going bankrupt, an illicit affair. She had learned that it was better that people didn't know one another's secret lives.

"I've been up north, Canada."

"I've never made it to Canada. Sometime you'll have to tell me about your life there."

He looked as if he was about to hyperventilate, and she would have said something witty – that Canada could be his secret – but his hands on his chest made her lose her thought. Smooth and strong, with fingers that were long and lean with well-kept nail beds, glossy and pink white. They were the hands of someone that was precise, deliberate; they were the hands of someone who didn't do manual labor.

What was that glow on his head? Aside from dull lights overhead this end of the corridor, it was dim. There was no stained glass where they were standing. She saw the way the red and orange and yellow merged seamlessly from his forehead to the crown of his head. A rainbow! It was a rainbow. Were you supposed to wish for something when you saw rainbow? Just as she was about to tell him, the rainbow vanished.

"Are you okay? Is something wrong?" he asked.

"Oh. No. I'm fine," Tess said. A rainbow on a man's head? She smiled to herself.

"Did you grow up here?" Neal said.

Tess shook her head. "Woodstock. Upstate New York."

"I've never been," Neal said.

"It's an interesting little community. Eighteen years of my life there was enough for me. Living in a small town is a small life," Tess said.

"Your life is as big as you make it," Neal said.

The things he said and the way he said them, matter-of-factly, made her feel as if his words were riddles to be solved. Standing beside him, she felt as if she were a different Tess – nicer, quieter, more receptive. Tess couldn't remember the last time she had felt this way in the presence of another person.

"Why are you here, tonight?" Neal said.

She patted her wavy locks and brushed the dangling wisps off her face. She felt her jutting collarbones and smoothed her black sweater. Her belly protruded – slight and compact, like a mini sack meant to hold her lipstick or a pack of tissues. After being bone skinny all her life, this little bulge comforted her now. Her clasped hands rested on it.

"I'm not really sure," Tess said. "I'd never come in here before tonight."

Neal rubbed the scapula between his hands, as if a genie would come out of it.

"Sometimes the things we do are driven by a higher power."

Tess was not going to entertain his holy thoughts. No, she had limits.

"Why are you here tonight?" she asked.

"I used to go to this church," Neal said. "I went to elementary school and junior high school here." Neal looked around. "They've redone it quite a bit. It's beautiful now."

The narrow halls, the glistening tiling, the high ceilings with etchings on them. The light was just right – enough to seduce without overpowering the eyes.

"Yes. It's quite lovely," she said.

The chiming church bells startled Tess. They listened to the bells in silence as she followed him outside.

The night air was dry and crisp, the temperature had dropped. Spring. Tess shivered. Under the vast sky, she felt small.

"Do you like your life?" Neal asked when the church bells grew silent.

Tess laughed. "That's quite a question to ask a stranger."

Neal nodded and bowed his head. There it was, that unexpected shyness.

"I suppose I do," she said. "It's the only life I've ever lived."

He smiled at her, his eyes focused on hers, intent, full of what seemed to her curiosity, as if she were some strange creature.

"Would you change anything?" he asked.

"I wish there were more hours in the day to get to all the things I'd like to get to," she said. "But I guess that everyone feels that way."

"I've lived a long time by the rule that you need to find time in your day for solitude, companionship, food, reading, silence, noise, sleep."

"Sounds like a 36-hour day," Tess said.

In the moonlight, Neal's eyes were a deep navy-blue with glimpses of white that made her think of the ocean from a plane window.

"Look at all the stars," Tess said.

"Make a wish," Neal said.

She couldn't remember the last time that she had made a wish upon a star. She wished that she could keep the feeling she felt now – peace, serenity – with her.

She turned to smile at him and had an instinct to hug him, as if she hadn't seen him for a while. He smiled back at her, and she felt as if they were in something together.

"I bid you, adieu, my new friend. Goodnight and farewell. Don't worry, though, I won't sing you the song."

"The song?"

"The one the children sing in *The Sound of Music.*"

Neal shook his head.

"The movie – *The Sound of Music.*"

"I never saw it."

"You have to. It's a beautiful movie," Tess said.

"And you have to find time in your days to get to the things you wish to get to."

"Maybe in another lifetime." She made her way to her car.

"Good night, Tess," Neal called to her

"Good night," Tess said before she pulled her car door shut.

In her rearview mirror, she could see Neal mounting his bike and riding away, his jacket flapping in the cool April breeze, so that he looked as if he was about to take flight.

CHAPTER 5: MUCH ADO ABOUT NOTHING

Tess scrolled down the list on her blackberry:

- House on Mill Avenue – to list? Follow up with Frank Landow/owner

- Call back the Weinstein's re potential buyer – offer for $680K

- Review property taxes for Bergen Avenue corner property

- Follow up with Kyle on Brooklyn brownstone

- Go over contracts with Michael for 2 new closes

- Interview realtor from Podomeyer – what's he looking for in terms of compensation? Run background check on him if appropriate.

- Touch base with Best realtors to see where their deals are at – calculate how many possible closes there are for the month and update forecast

- Review March's numbers with the accountant; go over April's numbers to date

How was it that so many things to do accumulated each day? Hadn't she just cleared off her to do list last night before she left the office? It was only 7:00 am and already she felt behind. She pulled out a wad of post it's from her pocketbook. Powder blue was her shopping lists: soy milk, Tetley green tea bags, Stella Doro breakfast treats, Dove soap. Orange was urgent – people she had to call back, deals pending: call the Weinstein's. Yellow were annoying tasks she hadn't gotten to: call the gardener to discuss last month's bill (he had not planted the pansies that he had billed her for, and her evergreen trees looked like they were wilting); pick up her dry cleaning.

Her cell phone was ringing – an unknown number – and she hit ignore, sending it to voicemail. Wednesday, hump day. She didn't always understand why she had so many tasks to do; she was the CEO, didn't that count for anything? Wasn't she supposed to have her staff taking care of this and that for her? She was sure, though, that the reason she was taking care of it all was because she chose to. She couldn't remember ever asking for help from her staff and not getting it. She was looking for her favorite pen in her bag when she came upon the yoga schedule that she had stuffed into her bag the other night. Her instinct was to toss it away, and then she paused. Thinking about how light and free she had felt after class, she studied the schedule – she couldn't make the Wednesday or Thursday night classes as she had houses to show tonight and tomorrow night. On Friday there was an all-levels class at 4:30 pm and an all-levels wind-down class at 6:30 pm. She could make the later one for sure. She pulled up her calendar on her blackberry and booked herself from 5:00 pm on for Friday, inserting a reminder to go off at 6:00 am Friday morning to put yoga clothes in her car. Hmm. She'd try to get to the studio early to buy a yoga mat there – she was sure she saw some for sale over in the corner; she couldn't deal with smelling the rental mat sweaty-feet smell again.

Michael stood in her doorway. When their eyes met, he knocked, and she tossed the yoga schedule on the floor.

"You dropped something," he said.

She swiveled her chair closer to her desk to keep the schedule from his view. "It's nothing," she said. "Is that your new technique? Wait until I see you and then knock?"

"You seemed to be busy communicating with yourself and studying whatever it was that fell on the floor. I didn't want to disturb you."

"What's up, Michael?"

"*Waz up Michael.* Is that your home girl rap?"

"Don't you have work to do?"

"Just wanted to know when you wanted to go over the contracts."

"Is it complicated stuff?" Tess asked.

"Complicated? No, I mean, nothing too unusual."

"Can we do it later? I need to make some calls first."

"Did you call your gardener yet?" Michael asked.

Tess smiled. Michael had dealt with the gardener when they lived together; that was one of his tasks. "No, but I will."

"The offer still stands; I'm glad to call him on your behalf."

"I can handle it just fine, Michael, but thanks."

"Call me when you're ready to go through the contracts."

"Hey, do you think we need another realtor?" Tess asked.

"It depends if you're talking about a producer or a newbie."

"Not a newbie; he seems to have some years in the industry. He had a blow out with Podomeyer, so he's looking to make a switch."

"Worth talking to him, but you know how those Podomeyer folks are. To use your words, 'pushy scheisters.' I'd check on his licenses right away, too. Remember last time? Turned out the guy you spoke to about a job didn't even have a valid license."

Tess laughed. "Pushy scheisters. I came up with that? Not bad. I'll give him a call at the least and see what he's about."

"Anything else?" Michael said.

"A cup of coffee would be nice."

"Sure would; I'd like mine with milk and sugar," Michael said.

"You're always the accommodator."

"I took a look at the house on Mill Avenue," Michael said.

"What do you think?" she asked.

"It needs work. I guess it could sell as a starter home. Couldn't see you getting more than $150K for it."

"They want to sell it for $300K. They paid $95K for it about 10 years back," Tess said.

"Yeah, and since they let it go and didn't update it, it's not worth much more than that. Knowing you, you could push it for $200K, but I can't see it going for more than that," Michael said.

"I'm not sure if it's worth the time and energy of an exclusive sell if I don't know if I can push it. The thing is, though, we don't have many starter homes in Mill Basin and you know that wedding time is in full bloom," Tess said.

"You have a point, but the folks who get married and want to move into Mill Basin generally have bucks, and if they don't, they move to Bergen Beach – all those starter homes there on 69th street."

"Bottom line: if I move it for $250K say, I could cut a $50K commission. I'd give it to one of the junior agents."

"Sounds like a plan," Michael said.

Tess nodded. "Oh, don't let me forget that I need to go over the property taxes with you for the house on Bergen Avenue."

Michael nodded. "Right, I need to pull up that information."

"Get to it sir; you don't have time to dawdle in my doorway."

"You were talking to me."

"You're in my office."

Her phone was ringing.

"Saved by the bell," Michael said, and she nodded yes when he motioned to close her door.

"Contesta."

"Hello, Mother." Tess shifted in her seat and took in a deep breath. Tess's daily phone calls with her mother had begun two years back, when her mother had been diagnosed with Leukemia. Her mother's ayurvedic doctor had been the first to notice the drop in her mother's energy levels and when he hadn't been able to do anything about it, he had sent her to a Western doctor – he had been the one to diagnose and confirm that her mother had cancer. After a lifetime of dismissing Western medicine and relying on Eastern remedies, her mother had acquiesced to chemotherapy and cancer drugs; she had been in remission for six months.

"It's a glorious day, Tessy. Spring is in the air. The birds are alive with their songs. It's the type of day that you would love."

There was a quality to her mother's voice that stilled Tess, told her in the silences of their conversations that her mother understood Tess's choices, accepted them – that she always had. The prospect of losing her mother had filled Tess with a need to know her mother, to be close to her. "Our differences are what enable you to be you and me to be me. Our love is made up of differences and acceptance," her mother had told her one afternoon, and Tess had clung to those words, a lifeline between them.

"You sound well, Mom."

"We both woke up today. We're alive. What could be better?"

It was hard for Tess to take her hectic, rushed life seriously when she heard her mother's voice – so free, so alive. Her mother's tone had a way of slowing Tess down, of making Tess feel silly for struggling so much to get it all in. Everything would get done. It always did.

"What's new and exciting in the world of Woodstock?" Tess asked.

"I took a lovely walk this morning – so many people outside. It's always so nice when it thaws out," she said.

Tess breathed in deep and swiveled in her chair so that the world outside was her backdrop: storm clouds had formed above, tinting the world a hazed gray. The country seemed so far away to her with its lush spring palette of yellows and greens and its crisp, bright-blue skies.

"Tell me about you, Tess. How is your life on this Wednesday?"

Tess's reflection gazed back at her in the glass. She adjusted some stray curls behind her ear. As a child and adolescent, whenever anyone had said that Tess was beautiful in the company of her mom, her mother had said that she was beautiful on the inside, too.

"My life is the same as yesterday. Busy. I'm working hard, Mom." She had an urge to break down, to cry, to tell her mother about anything, everything – to be a child.

"You were always a hard worker."

"Yes. I suppose that's true."

"Try not to lose your life in the work," her mother said.

"Mom —"

"I know, you like to work, but don't lose all the other things in your life, Tess. That's all that I ask of you. Honor yourself."

The lights on Tess's phone were lighting up, signaling another call coming in, and then another. The world would wait. That's what her mom would say if she were to see the calls coming in.

"I should get back to work, Mom."

"Of course, Tessy. I'll be praying for you."

Tess smiled. "I love you, Mom."

"I love you, my daughter."

Tess didn't realize her mother had hung up until the line went dead and the silence resonated in her ear. It pained her to think that at times, like now, that she rushed her mother off the phone. How could she be too busy that she didn't have time to talk to her? And yet, she had work to do; if she didn't do it, there was no one else that would. She picked up the phone to call her mother back and then paused. No. What else was there to say? She could call her later, or tomorrow. As she started to go through her emails, what came to her was that there would be a time, not too far off, when she would call her mother and not be able to reach her – a time when silence would prevail on the other end of the line.

CHAPTER 6: CHANCE MEETING

She had woken up before sunrise Saturday morning and without giving much thought to all the things she had to catch up on after the work week – food shopping, house cleaning, laundry – Tess had put on a pair of black stretchy exercise pants, a t-shirt, and a zip-up hooded jacket over it, and gone outside to take a walk around the neighborhood. It was something she always wanted to get to, but there never seemed to be time to do in the routine of her life. The Friday evening candle-lit yoga class had left her feeling delicious and made her sleep sweeter than she had remembered in a long time. Later in the day, she would drive into the city and take a late afternoon yoga class. It amazed her how much she enjoyed the classes, how much she couldn't wait to get back to the stillness of the yoga room. Michael would point out her addictive personality if she'd let him know that she had been back a few times since she first went to the studio with him.

Tess smiled in the cool, early morning air and a slight chill – something like excitement, anticipation – filled her. The spring always made Tess feel unhinged, as if a part of her was about to melt away and she had to work hard and fast to secure the parts of herself that she didn't want to lose.

She walked through the gates of the Bergen Beach Yacht Club across from her house and followed the gravel path onto the wrap-around wooden dock. Most of the boats on the private docks were still covered with canvas. Tess imagined it was too cold out on the water for any of the boats to set sail just yet. Beyond the wraparound dock were backyards, each of which had stairs leading down to the sand where the wraparound deck could be accessed. The waters of Jamaica Bay glistened green with slimy algae. And yet it was nice to be by the water – sometimes it didn't seem possible to her that behind all the houses there was that body of sand and water. She had worried years back if the houses could float away in a storm, but it hadn't happened in the last 30 years. When Prakash was a toddler, they used to sit by the shore, Prakash tossing pebbles, mesmerized by the splash. Staring into the water now, Tess felt as if she were moving towards something. The tide drifted in, slowly, surely, and drifted away. Tess tossed a stone in the water and saw her selves in the rippled effect. So many different Tess's. The surface resounded as she tossed another stone, then another. She didn't know what she was sending away from her, but with each toss, she became lighter, freer. Circles opened where the stones had vanished, like little black holes.

"Are you trying to wake up the fish?"

Tess turned toward the voice.

"Neal." Tess smoothed her hair; in the cool early-morning dew, her curls were frizzy and tight.

"It's nice to see you out so early. I was beginning to think I was the only one in this neighborhood who was up early."

"I didn't think anyone came out here," Tess said.

"The sea gulls were circling above; I came to see what the commotion was about."

A flock of sea gulls, gawking and moving round and round, as if in a whirlpool, were overhead. Tess hadn't heard them until now. As quickly as she noticed them, they flew off.

"There they go," Neal said.

The early morning mist was rising from the water like a curtain between pulled up. In a few moments, the sun would rise.

"It's a beautiful morning to be out walking," Tess said.

"There's something to being out before the world

comes alive that's always appealed to me." Then, "I've never seen you out here," Neal said.

"I can't remember the last time I was out walking in the morning. Probably over 30 years ago. I'm usually busy," Tess said.

"What made today different?" Neal asked.

He wore a white thermal long sleeved top just tight enough so that she was able to make out the outline of his muscles in his chest and arms. He was in good shape.

"I'm not sure. I just felt like I needed to be outside," Tess said.

Neal bowed his head. "I'll leave you to enjoy your morning."

"No. I mean, your company isn't bothering me. I was on my way to walk."

Now that he was there with her, Tess realized that somehow, she had wanted to see him again. Neal started to walk, and she fell in line beside him, the two of them making their way from the dock and back onto 66th street.

"I drive around this neighborhood so much, but walking it is a whole different thing. There are so many things you don't notice while you're driving," Tess said.

They moved beside one another in silence. Every now and then Neal glanced behind him, as if he was worried they were being followed. Tess glanced behind her as well: no one in sight.

"Everything okay?" she asked.

"Fine," Neal said. "Everything is fine."

Spring had already begun to transform the neighborhood. Tulips were coming into bloom in the gardens in vibrant hot pinks and pale yellows and reds. The shrubs were rich and full in deep emerald green. It was magical the way everything came back to life with spring.

"How long do you plan to be visiting Mill Basin?" Tess asked.

"Why?"

"Just asking," Tess said. She pursed her lips. Nosy, that's what Michael had called her at times.

He led the way, veering them from 66th street, the main road, down Dakota Place to Basset Avenue. When Neal led her through Ohio Walk, she marveled over the fact that she hadn't been down that lane in at least 30 years – not since she had wheeled Prakash in a baby carriage. Neal bent down to pick up a damp yellow-green leaf on the ground, twirling it in his fingers by its stem.

They passed the houses she was selling on Mayfair Drive South, and she began to fuss with her hair, check her lips to feel if she had lipstick on. It was still strange for her to see Best Realty signs on the front lawns with her picture on them, as if she was a politician. She was a private person at heart. How did her face end up on people's lawns? Neal seemed to be in a trance of his own. She would need to tell her folks to clean up the evergreen trees on the lawn of one of her houses, which reminded her that she needed to check her work voice mail to see if one of her agents had closed the deal last night on the one-family house in Bergen Beach.

Neal stopped mid-block so that Tess almost stumbled into him.

"I have to go," he said.

"Oh," Tess said. She pulled down on her sweatshirt and felt the hint of perspiration in her armpits. "Sure."

He held out the leaf to her. "When summer comes, perhaps you'll look back at this leaf and think of this spring morning."

Tess nodded. "I will," she said, and with that Neal bowed his head and began to jog away from her and then all out run toward the end of the block, so that in moments he was gone from her view. She couldn't quite remember the last time a man had sprinted away from her. Strange. She put the leaf to her nose: it was a faded yellow – the color of in-between. She wondered where Neal had suddenly vanished. He must have a wife. Or maybe he was on the run? He didn't strike her as a criminal, but nowadays who knew? It was creepy, but she didn't feel afraid. They had been alone on the beach, and she hadn't felt threatened. And he had been at the church. Unlikely that a criminal was visiting with God. Unless he sought repentance? She kept moving towards the end of the block, which would intersect with 66th street, from where she would be able to turn around and make her way back to her house, her life.

Tess saw the curtains – were they velvet? Maroon velvet? – of the house she was approaching sway, as if someone were behind them, looking out. Shrubs and trees covered the lower level of the house, except for the front room windows. If Tess were to sell this house, she would get those shrubs cleared away immediately. Privacy was one thing, but this house looked as if it belonged in the middle of the wilderness. Right then Tess got a glimpse of a woman peeking out from behind the curtains – she was older, short hair, in a house dress. Or a robe. The house was situated differently than Tess's house, so that she wasn't sure if the room the woman looked out from was a den or a living room. She lingered, bending down to tie her sneaker, trying to get a better glance at the woman. Something was certainly strange. Was the woman watching her or scanning the street? 56 Barlow Drive. Tess must have driven past this house countless times without noticing it. When Tess stood back up, she saw the woman dart from the window, as if someone inside the house had called to her.

CHAPTER 7: THE SOUND OF MUSIC

Michael shuffled through the Best Realty papers in front of him. He put his feet up on Tess's glass octagon-shaped kitchen table and glanced over at Tess by the stove as she grilled French toast. She glared back at him.

"Excuse me," she said.

"What?"

"We don't put our feet up on the table where we are going to eat," she said.

Michael took his feet down and shook his head.

"Really, Michael. I can see that living alone has destroyed your social skills."

"Will you get off my case?"

"In my house, we still obey basic social skills."

"In your house."

"Yes, my house."

"Once upon a time this was *our* house."

"Once upon a time is not now," Tess said.

"I thought all the yoga was lightening you up."

"Perhaps if you didn't give up on it after one class, it would help you, too."

"I don't need help, Tess," Michael said.

"Oh, got it. You're just perfect, Michael."

"I'm glad you can admit it. What are you putting on the French Toast?"

"Blueberries," Tess said.

"Frozen blueberries on French Toast. Yum."

"When I'm done cooking them, they won't be frozen," Tess said.

"I'm sure it will be delicious."

"I have better things to do than cook you dinner," Tess said.

"Like what?" Michael said.

"Like live my life."

"We could have gone out for dinner," Michael said.

"You're the one who showed up here – be grateful I invited you to eat over."

"Sunday dinner just like momma used to make it," he said.

Tess turned the French toast over in the pan and pressed it down with a spatula so that the olive oil hissed. In her free hand, she dipped a fresh slice of 7-grain bread in the mix of egg whites, cinnamon and cardamom, letting it soak the mixture in.

"Are the papers you need there?" Tess said.

"All here," he said.

"It's a good deal, no?" Tess said.

Tess put a plate down in front of Michael, steam rising off it. She took the strawberry preserves and butter out of the refrigerator and placed them down in front of him.

"So gourmet, Tessie," he said looking into her eyes and winking.

"The deal – what do you think about it?" she said, back at the stove making herself two slices of French toast.

"There's a nice commission for you. It looks good. There shouldn't be a problem closing it." He leaned down to the plate and examined the bread.

"What are the black dots in the bread?"

"Flax seed."

"Now you're into bird bread? I leave you alone and you fall apart, Tess."

Tess put silverware down beside him and draped a napkin across his lap before she sat down with her own plate.

"Do you have any idea how many houses you closed last month?" Michael said.

Tess shook her head.

"About a dozen," he said.

"Not too shabby," Tess said.

She spread the preserves across her French toast.

"Do you realize how much money you're making?"

"Do you realize how much I have to pay out for my business?" she asked.

Michael cut the toast in half and put one half in his mouth. Tess shook her head at him.

"I'm a growing boy," he said. "Give me a break; it's a piece of toast."

"Anyway, I met the new neighborhood freak up close the other night. He's quite interesting."

Michael held his fork and knife frozen over his toast and watched her take a bite.

"Oh Michael, get over yourself. I'm talking about the guy I mentioned to you the other morning – the one that was walking in the middle of the street."

"You met him the other night?"

"And, then I ran into him yesterday morning while I was out walking."

"You were out walking? Since when do you go out walking?"

"Since I felt like going out for a walk yesterday," Tess said.

"Hmmm," he said.

"Anyway, we were walking along and then he had to go and darted off. Literally."

"Did he dart off with your wallet and keys?" Michael said.

"You think he's a criminal?" Tess said.

"How old is this guy?"

"In his forties, I guess," Tess said.

"Do we know if he even lives in Mill Basin? He could be sleeping on a bench in Lindower Park," Michael said.

"He seems clean," Tess said. "He did tell me that he grew up here and that he's writing a book now. He was in Canada for a long time. He seems harmless."

"So do most serial killers from what they say," Michael said. "Canada? A great place to run from the law. And writing a book? Prison pastime if there ever was one."

Tess jutted her chin up at the ceiling with her eyes closed – what

Michael had called her God-to- the-rescue expression before she glanced at Michael and hesitated, pursing her lips.

"Say it," Michael said. "Say what you're thinking."

"There was something odd. When I was making my way down Basset Drive, after he darted away, a woman seemed to be watching me from behind the curtains. Could have just been my imagination, but –"

"Either his wife or the woman he's kidnapped trying to get your attention to help her. You know how to pick 'em, Tess."

"Oh, Michael, he's just a nice guy; the woman probably had nothing to do with him – I don't even know why I mention these things to you."

"Or she could be his accomplice or his sex slave. Next time you see him be sure to check for tattoos."

Tess choked on her mouthful so that she had to clear her throat.

"Tattoos?"

"If he's a convict, he'll have tattoos. And nice pumped-up muscles – those convicts have plenty of time to hit the gym."

"I'll be sure to scan him for tattoos. *Excuse me, Neal, can you take off your shirt so that I can check your flesh?* Charming."

"If I didn't know any better, I'd say you like him."

Tess rolled her eyes and shook her head.

"Michael, how in the world do you deduce that I like this man?

He's weird. I'm telling you about him like I'd tell you about…about an unusual house."

"My dear Tessie, you forget how well I know you. You like mystery. If you ask me, I'd say that you saw him out walking yesterday morning, decided to go out for a walk yourself so that you could conveniently run into him, and then you had a little tête-à-tête with him while you walked."

"You know me, Michael. Out stalking men whenever I can."

"Oh, right, I forget – you've decided that you're done with relationships in your old age."

"I resent that," Tess said.

"Excuse me. In your middle age," he said.

"That's not what I was talking about."

"Should I start going out for walks in the morning now? Would that make you more interested in me?" Michael asked.

"Will you stop?" Tess said.

"Did you ask him for a date?"

"I didn't mention that I asked him to have sex? He didn't have condoms, so it was a no go," Tess said.

Michael laughed and focused on his French toast, piling blueberries up at the tip of his fork.

"You should see your face right now – all smug. You like this man," Michael said.

"Haven't we been through this? You know I'm done with all that. I'm focusing on my career, remember?"

"I don't know, Lady Tess," Michael said.

"You said it – you *don't* know."

"Don't get annoyed at me – with all your marriages, you're the one who created the drama around you."

Outside the kitchen window, the cherry orchids' petals swayed in the wind. It was beginning to drizzle. Raindrops swam down the window, and for a moment, Tess felt something in her sinking, too. She ate the blueberries on her plate one by one.

"What's on your agenda this Sunday night, Tess?"

"Oh, maybe I'll bake a cake."

"With your expert cooking skills, I'm sure it would be super."

"If you're going to insult my French toast, I won't hear it."

The rain came down harder now, so that it sounded as if someone were throwing gravel at the window.

"Look. Rain," Michael said. "It's your lucky night, Tess."

When Tess had first told Michael that she loved the rain, how being out in the rain when she had nowhere to go, letting it soak her, she felt recharged, Michael had laughed. "I just feel wet," he had said. That was years ago, when they were married to other people. They were always better friends than they were lovers.

Michael glanced at his watch and wiped his lips with his napkin.

"I need to get going," he said.

"Where do you need to get going to?"

"I have a conference call at 8:30."

"You're working tonight?" Tess asked.

"That's how it goes when you have a boss that's a workaholic."

"Don't blame your workaholic ways on me."

"You once told me to blame my workaholic ways on you, remember? That was when I was married and we were having an affair, I believe," Michael said.

"That's senility for you," Tess said.

"What was the address on Basset Drive where the stalker woman lives?"

"56," Tess said. "What are you going to do? Ring her bell?

"Just see who owns the house," Michael said.

"You're terrible," Tess said.

"You didn't have to tell me the address. Peace," he said.

"Goodbye Michael," she said, and then he was gathering up the papers he needed, kissed her forehead and she followed him down the stairs to let him out. He beeped twice and waved as he pulled away.

The rain had subsided to a slight drizzle again. Spring. Her old fogey neighbor who lived in the house to the left of her was out on her driveway in a poncho and was scrubbing the bricks with what looked like some sort of broom. Probably to save money on using water, Tess supposed. Cheapskate. Who scrubbed their driveway in the rain? Once, the "cleaning lady" as Tess had nicknamed her with Michael, had been married to a dentist and her grown son, also a dentist, had lived with her. Since her husband died and her son had moved out and gotten married, she had become an obsessive cleaner. She would walk out of her house each evening with bags of garbage wearing a do-rag and old ragged clothes and rubber gloves on her hands. She and Tess were on nodding terms.

Tess walked outside and stood behind the evergreen tree that shaded her porch. She sensed that the cleaning lady heard her walk out on porch, but she didn't look in her direction. Tess used to stand or sit in this spot when she craved being outdoors and didn't want anyone to see her. Everything inside of her was moving fast; there was something about Michael's presence that managed to make her feel uneasy, restless. She inhaled the damp tree's piney mint aroma. Sometimes she wished that she could live in her own planet, far away from everyone, if only to be able to hear herself, feel what she felt for a few minutes without anyone imposing their thoughts on her. Michael did know her in many respects, she couldn't deny that, and yet the way he summarized her frustrated her, or maybe it was that he reminded her about versions of herself that she wanted to let go of, bury.

And what if she did like Neal? Not that she did, but she didn't want to have to justify herself to anyone, let alone her ex-husband. Was it so bad, though, to be curious about someone, to want to know more about them? She wanted to know what Neal had been doing all those years when he wasn't in Brooklyn. She wanted to know if he was divorced, if he had children, if he was a long-standing bachelor. The rain started to fall again, softly and quietly, and Tess closed her eyes, looking up toward the sky, letting the drops stream her face. When she was a young girl, she used to sit up on her rooftop in Woodstock and let the drops swim her face until touching them midstream, they felt to her like her own teardrops. In a moment, the rain stopped, and Tess smiled up at the heavens. The unpredictable-ness of life was a constant. Her mother had promised her that much; she had instructed her to accept that the only certainty in life was uncertainty. She had fought her mother over that, insisting that there were certainties – one of which was that Tess was not going to live the life of a Buddhist tucked away in Woodstock.

There was something about Neal – Tess couldn't say what just what – that reminded her of her mother. A gentleness, an instinct that he had seen another side of life; a side reserved only for a special few. It was more a thought than a feeling, but she believed that if she could learn more about Neal, she would also learn more about her mother. Maybe that was her mind playing tricks on her, inventing justifications as to there being a value in her getting to know Neal, or maybe there was something to it. This much she was sure of: neither Neal nor her mother fit into any of the categories of people that Tess knew. There was a freshness to Neal, a vulnerability, a sense of peace and good humor. It was more than that, though. It was as if when he looked into her eyes, he saw something in her that she hadn't yet seen in herself, and she wanted to know what he saw.

It amazed her – this concept of intersecting with another person in this great big world. She believed that there was a reason that certain people crossed one another's path, although she didn't claim to know what that reason was. But she did believe that it was more than just by chance.

The evergreen tree shimmered in the breeze, its bush brushing against Tess's knee, as if it were pushing her away, back inside. There were moments, such as this one, that Tess wished she never had to go in doors. Being outside made her feel endless, as if the perimeters of her life didn't exist. Once indoors, her life, the one she had created, seemed to close in on her until exhausted and defeated, there was nothing for her to do but collapse on her bed and close her eyes until it was time for her to start again.

She imagined her mother liking Neal, being able to say something definitive about him, precise, that would make Tess nod her head and have clarity as to why she kept thinking about him when she had no reason to keep thinking about him. Maybe Michael was right: she was a basket case. Or maybe she wasn't. Maybe she was just living. Maybe this is what life was – a journey full of twists and turns, a chance to work hard and to love and sleep and think and feel and lose and find yourself. Tess liked getting to know people – liked how it felt to let someone into her life. She had forgotten that about herself. After so many years of trying to people keep out, she had forgotten the joy of letting someone into her life, and it made Tess wonder if she had ever really let anyone into her life. Even with her four husbands, there had always been so much of her that they never knew, so much of them that she would never know. The little barriers put up had become walls over time, insurmountable, so that looking back now, it was clear to her that the only person that she had ever allowed in had been herself, and she even fell short in that respect, because there were so many times in her life when she couldn't grasp what she sought.

Somewhere along the way, Tess had come to believe that the most that you could hope for in life was a parallel road to travel alongside a person. But deep inside, in the places that Tess never shared with anyone, she believed that there were some people in this world that she would intersect with in a more meaningful way – that their paths would collide so that they would stake out a new direction together. She believed that those were the people worth seeking in life.

Tess yawned. She didn't always know where the silliness she thought about came from. The sky had become a light show, the air a bit cooler, damper. Her cleaning lady neighbor must have gone inside at some point. Tess smiled. She couldn't quite say what she was happy about, but for the first time in a long time, she felt quieter inside, calmer. She closed her eyes and let the breeze pass through her one last time before she left the world behind and went inside.

CHAPTER 8: YOUR BOUNDARIES ARE YOUR QUEST

"Lokaha samasta sukhino, bhavantu." Tess repeated the chant in unison with the class. *May all beings everywhere be happy and free.* She closed her eyes and sang louder, losing the sound of her voice amidst the others, so that all she felt coming out of her was a vibration. In the moments of silence following the chant, she saw her mother bowing down to the shrine in their living room as she did each night, singing in Sanskrit as she counted her mala beads, her eyes closed, her head moving to melody coming out of her, as if she were in a trance.

The teacher was asking them to make their way onto their hands and knees to start warming up their spines. This was the part of class that Tess loved most: everything in her full of anticipation, and a good fear, as if she were about to climb up a steep ladder from which she'd dive through the air and float to a safe landing. It was the moment of all-potential, when anything was possible: she could fall or fly, depending on how light and free she was.

In the yoga room, she was able to lose herself. Each time a thought about work popped up, the teacher's voice, instructing them into the next pose, brought her back to the moment. There was no time to think in yoga: it was all execution. One pose blended into the next so that time and space didn't exist, just movement and feeling, like floating through water.

When they reached the end of the class, Tess willed herself up into a backbend, full wheel, her elbows shaking, her feet unsteady below her. She felt as if she may break in two. Her breath became short and shallow, so that when the teacher approached her, she was about to let go and plop back down onto the mat, until the teacher loosened up her shoulders, massaging them, and holding onto Tess's hips, instructed her to bring her feet closer together and to press her hips up to the ceiling, open her chest, let her heart breath. Tess was about to say, *stop, let go*, and collapse, until all at once, something in her opened, a small splitting feeling, and with her legs closer together, her hips rising, she felt as if her heart was being freed from a web that had been confining it. The teacher held her loosely round the waist as Tess eased down onto the mat. The teacher instructed her to bring her knees to her chest to release her back, and she pressed gently on Tess's shins, so that Tess was able to feel her lower spine ground. Tess sighed. For a moment, she worried that she would fart, and she froze, and then the moment passed, and she was letting go again. It felt nice to massage her spine against the hardwood floor. Then, after all her hard work and exertion, the teacher led them into the final pose, shavassana – literally, dead-corpse pose. Tess let the ground beneath her cradle her, and in a few moments, she was out cold. She didn't wake up until the class was sitting cross-legged, eyes closed, chanting "Om."

With the final Om, Tess rolled over on her right side, rest there a few minutes, and then sat up. She folded up her mat slowly, methodically. No thoughts went through her head, just an airy, peaceful feeling as if she was drifting through a cloud.

The lobby was chaotic and noisy as it always was after class. It reminded Tess of being behind the scenes at a Broadway play before the curtain was about to rise, with everyone scrambling to change their clothes before the next scene. Tess had learned to hang back from the activity for a few moments if she didn't want to be robbed of the effects of the class.

The teacher tapped Tess on the shoulder.

"Nice class," she said. "You've made a lot of progress in a short time," the teacher said. "How many classes has this been for you?"

"Oh, thank you. I think it's been five or six classes."

"You're definitely a natural."

"Thanks," Tess said. "I feel great. If I could, I would be here every day, but it's not possible."

"Well, in the end, it's you that counts, not work."

"I own my business," Tess said. "Me and my work are one and the same."

"That's what I used to say," the teacher said. "I was a corporate slave – I worked as a designer in the publishing industry. I loved my career, never thought I'd leave it, but then I found yoga."

"You left your career to become a yoga teacher?"

"Not all at once. But little by little, the more I got into yoga, the more I started to analyze what I wanted in my life – what mattered. I always felt as if I was rushing around, living on a time schedule – I'd show up late for every yoga class. Everything about my life was messy and frantic. Yoga helped me to get a grip on my life. Pretty soon, I was leaving work earlier to make sure I'd get to class on time. My priorities shifted."

Tess nodded. She felt like she was listening to an infomercial on why to become a yoga teacher. Frankly, she just wanted to be quiet. Seep in the rewards of her class. How didn't the teacher get that? The crowds were beginning to disperse. Tess spotted an empty changing room.

Tess smiled at the teacher. "I'm glad it worked out for you," she said.

"You should check out the teacher training program. There's a reason you found yoga at this point in your life. Once I took the teacher training program, it wasn't long before I left my career and began teaching full time."

"Sounds like you found your calling."

"I've learned firsthand that it's never too late to change your life," the teacher said. "Besides, the studio could use some teachers like you. I think it would be very inspirational for students to see that yoga is for all ages."

Tess had heard enough. Was the teacher insinuating that Tess was over-the-hill? Sure, she wasn't in her twenties or thirties, but she wasn't a senior citizen either. She was about to tell the teacher she was in her thirties, see how she'd handle that one, but then she caught herself. Who cared what the teacher said? And yet how dare the teacher bother her like this after class. Wasn't she allowed to be quiet and enjoy the peaceful feeling?

The teacher reached over to the stack of flyers behind the desk and gave one to Tess. Tess glanced at it, folded it in half, and smiled a cheesy smile. "I need to be going," she said.

"Trust me, when I took the training, I never thought I'd become a yoga teacher. Oh, and classes and all the training sessions are at night and on weekends – it's set up for people who work full time."

"Thanks," Tess said. She would make it a point to never take her class again.

She put her hand on Tess's shoulder and smiled into her eyes. What was going on – why wouldn't she back off Tess and let her be? There were plenty of other people that she could go bug to take the teacher training program. What did she want from Tess?

Tess slipped on her loafers and was at the elevator, pushing the down button without taking the time to change into her street clothes. She didn't want to risk having to listen to another minute of the teacher's lecturing.

Just as she got into the elevator someone screamed hold it, and in walked Dale. Tess was already plotting to find a new studio to go to. She imagined that there were dozens to choose from in the city. Between the teacher salesperson and now Dale, the girl who had issues with homes, Tess was beginning to feel more stressed out than she had when she first walked into the studio after work.

"Hello, Tess."

Tess smiled pleasant enough and nodded. No. N-O. She was not going to deal with anymore banter. This was her night. Her peace of mind.

"I was going to take the next class, but when I realized who was teaching it, I couldn't do it." Dale nodded at the paper in Tess's hand. "She's fierce, huh?"

"She hit on you for the teacher training program, too?" Tess said.

"I think that she tries to convince others to become a yoga teacher in order to help her deal with her insecurities that she traded in her career to become a yoga teacher."

"And I thought I was special," Tess said.

"The good news is that she only teaches one class on Tuesday nights. That's why I take the later class on Tuesday nights, the one after hers, but turns out she's subbing it tonight."

Tess laughed. "Thanks for the tip," she said. "Now I'll know better."

"Let's face it, we come here to detox," Dale said. "Not to get stressed out even more by a yoga teacher. And she is a great teacher, it's just the after-class lecture that's too much for me."

"I guess that if you take her class, you need to come prepared to dart right after it."

"Oh, she'll track you down after class if she wants to. One night after class, I swear she followed me to The Bakery to badger me about becoming a yoga teacher. The funny thing is that I heard yoga teacher training is sold out," Dale said. "At least that's what the Grinch behind the desk was saying to someone last night, so I'm not sure what she's doing."

Tess smiled – the Grinch. The elevator hit the ground floor with a thud so that they both stumbled.

"That's why I prefer to take the stairs," Dale said as they waited for the elevator door to open. "Not a chance about me becoming a yoga teacher. I may not know where I want to live, but I know that I don't want to be a yoga teacher. My mother is already on my case about being a social worker and working with runaway teens. She thinks I'm throwing my life away. Imagine if I told her that I was leaving that career to become a yoga teacher? She'd have me exported to Brooklyn at the least." She laughed. "That was a joke," she said.

"And should you ever get exported there, you could live in a very beautiful brownstone," Tess said.

The air was cool, crisp, fresh. Tess wished for a moment that she didn't have the 40- minute drive home, that she could just get under the covers now and let sleep take over. In her lazy state of mind, she would easily join Dale's Brooklyn boycott.

"How often do you come here?" Tess said.

"Most nights," Dale said. "And weekends." She laughed. "I guess I've gotten a little addicted," she said.

"I hope to see you here soon," Tess said. She meant it. "Just not Tuesday night at 6 pm."

CHAPTER 9: IN SEARCH OF

So, you think that surprising her with a house is the best plan of action?" Tess said. She was stopped at a red light. Kyle, beside her, was scanning his blackberry. He shook his head at whatever he was reading before he surfaced again.

"Absolutely. She's the one who wanted to move out of the city in the first place. After 9/11, she said she was done with the city. That's what led me to look at places outside of the city."

"Kyle, 9/11 was two years ago at this point and she is still living in the city."

"And your point is?"

"I think it's wonderful how much you want this to all work – I mean finding a dream house for the two of you, but I don't think that surprising her with the brownstone is the best plan of action for you right now."

Kyle put down his blackberry and watched Tess. She was driving up and down Montague and Hicks Street in Brooklyn Heights, looking for a parking spot.

"Aren't you supposed to be coaxing me to buy the property?" he

said.

"I only coax people if I think they're doing the right thing."

"Look, you called, told me that you had another offer, and I dropped everything to meet you to see the brownstone again. Right? Isn't that what happened? But now you're telling me that you don't think I should buy it?"

"I called you because I gave you my word that I'd call you when I had another offer, which I do. And it's a good offer, but I wanted to play fair and let you know. You're the one who wanted to come here to see it again – that was your request."

"I saw how you were when Dale was around the other night," he said.

She imagined that Dale hadn't mentioned their meeting up at the yoga studio. A car was beeping her; she started to move again.

"I know you may think she's a bitch, but she's not," he said.

"Trust me, I wouldn't be marrying her if she was, and between us, Dale doesn't always know what she wants. Last year she didn't even want to get married. We had a matter of fact talk one night at dinner and she told me that she didn't really see the point of getting married. That if you loved someone, that was enough – marriage, the whole concept of it, seemed ridiculous. But then I asked her to get married a few months later and she accepted."

Tess stopped again and faced him. "Did you not believe what she told you about marriage?"

"Dale's a walking contradiction. She'll be the first to tell you that."

"So, you're saying that you think she really wants the brownstone and expects you to buy it?"

"I don't know what I'm saying," Kyle said, and Tess laughed. He was endearing – that was the single most quality to him that reminded her of her son. No matter how much Prakash thought he had it figured out, he was always the first to admit that he didn't have all the answers.

Her phone was ringing. She glanced over and saw that it was her mother.

"Don't not answer on account of me. It may be my competition for the brownstone," Kyle said.

"It's my mother, Kyle, not your competition; it will be too long a conversation for right now."

'There," Kyle said. "A spot. That guy is pulling out right in front of the brownstone."

The brownstone was painted a deep terra cotta with eight steps leading up to the front door, a wrought iron scrolled railing and matching screen door. Beside the screen door there were two flower boxes on each side filled with cacti. It looked out of place on the block – like it belonged in New Mexico with its Aztec design. She imagined all the comings and goings up and down those steps, opening the front door each day, pulling it closed. There was something to the threshold of a house that held her interest: walking into one's separate universe, walking out into the world.

Sitting alongside Kyle in her car, she nodded at the brownstone. "It's lovely," she said.

"You think we should stay in New York."

"I didn't say that. I happen to think change is good – and making a change together is even better. But I think you should act as a couple," Tess said.

"What if only one person in the relationship is good at making decisions?"

"You try to find out why the other person is having a hard time making a decision. Listen to what she has to say, and if that doesn't work, a pros and cons list does the trick sometimes."

"Isn't there usually one decision maker in every relationship?"

"If it's a dictatorship, sure," Tess said.

"Were you ever married?"

"More times than I care to admit, Kyle."

"So that's what this is about," he said.

"What does that mean?" Tess asked.

"It means that you're cynical about the marriage stuff and think that if there's a chance we may end up divorced, why bother making such a big investment," Kyle said.

"Thanks for the psychoanalysis, Kyle, but I'm sorry to say that's far from the truth."

"Then what's the truth?"

"The truth is that most of the time I was married, I acted as if I wasn't. I did what I wanted, when I wanted, and didn't have much regard for my husbands. I was more outside of my relationships than I was in them, and it was my own doing, because I never let my husbands into my life. It starts with your making one decision on your own and then it somehow becomes routine, until one day you'll start wondering why you even need this other person in your life, because the truth is, you're just fine being married to yourself. And don't ask me why I'm telling you this because I don't tell my stuff to clients."

She took the car keys out of the ignition. "Shall we go inside?"

"You're right. We can stay in the city for the next year at least. Take it from there. I can find us a bigger place to rent on the Upper East Side and then after a year, we can figure it out together," Kyle said.

"So, you want to leave? Are you sure?"

Kyle nodded. "I'm sorry, Tess –"

She put her car keys back in the ignition and smiled at him.

"No problem," Tess said.

"I didn't mean to waste your time," he said.

"It's fine," Tess said, her voice devoid of expression.

This was why she didn't let herself get personally involved with clients' decisions. It led to drama, and in the scope of her life, in which she viewed time as a precious commodity, drama ate up minutes and hours, which once gone, she couldn't get back.

"Can I ask you a question?" Kyle said once they were moving back towards New York City. "What led you to divorce?"

"That's like asking me *what's the meaning of life*, Kyle."

"Right, but I'm asking you to tell me, based on your experiences, what were the shortcomings of marriage?"

"Every relationship has its own ingredients, Kyle. What made my relationships fail isn't universal. Tons of relationships do work, and to be honest, if you ask my ex's, they may tell you that our relationship did work until I lost it and decided I wanted a divorce."

"You just woke up one day and decided you wanted a divorce?" he asked.

Tess coasted into the center lane. 4:00 pm. So far, so good – she hadn't hit traffic.

"I hate to intrude reality on the counseling session, but where would you like me to drop you off?"

"Back at my office is fine," he said.

"Look, Kyle. You're a good kid. Probably a better kid than I gave you credit for being when I first met you."

"That's comforting."

"Your office is off of Duane Street, right?" Tess asked.

Kyle nodded. "Yes."

"I wish I could sit and talk to you about marriage and divorce, Kyle, but the truth is, my stuff is reflective of my life. And to answer your question, no, I didn't wake up one day and decide I wanted to get a divorce. It was an accumulation of everything. More like, I woke up every day for some time knowing that it was time for me to move on alone, and then one day I woke up and asked myself what the day was going to feel like when I finally shared what was going on inside of me with my husband."

"I don't want to get divorced," Kyle said.

Tess inched to a stop at the corner, before the traffic moved forward again. She felt Kyle's eyes on her.

"I don't think anyone ever wants to get divorced, Kyle. People change, though. And that's okay, too. It's part of life. As quickly as you grow with someone, you can grow apart from them. It happens sometimes. I will say this – divorce isn't always a bad thing. Each time I walked out of a relationship, I grew a little bit more. Not that I'm advocating divorce; all I'm saying is that it's okay if you grow apart from a person. It's real. It happens."

"Right here," Kyle said. "My office." Tess pulled to the curb in front of the building to her right.

"Talk to Dale. Communicate. Don't let things like buying a brownstone create a barrier between you two."

"For a long time, I felt like a team with her, but lately, I don't know."

"Ask her what's going on," Tess said. "It's amazing what people will tell you if you ask them."

"You're real, Tess. When you step out of your salesperson mode, you're real."

"Thanks. I think," Tess said.

"So, I guess this is goodbye for now. Of course, once I tell Dale that let the brownstone go, one never knows if she'll decide she wants to live there."

"I'll wait to get your confirmation tomorrow morning that you're officially out of the running for the brownstone."

"You're great," Kyle said.

"Goodbye, Kyle," Tess said.

He slammed the car door shut and, in a moment, his charcoal gray suit was lost in the crowd. She had a fleeting urge to run after him and tell him something; only she wasn't sure what it was she would tell him. To marry Dale? To let her go?

Tess hit play on her voicemail and then she was driving again, making her way back to Brooklyn, back to her life. "Contesta, it's your Mother. I was thinking of you my dear. Please do call me when you have a moment."

Her mother picked up on the third ring.

"My darling," she said.

"Mom."

"You don't sound like yourself, dear. What's wrong?"

"Did you ever make bad decisions, Mom?" Tess asked.

Her mother chuckled. "Of course. We all make bad decisions sometimes, but the good thing about life is that we often have a chance to redeem ourselves by making better decisions."

"Sometimes I feel like my life doesn't make sense," she said.

"No one's life makes sense, Tess. We just have to live and accept what happens and try to have a good time and be good to others and find our way and let others find their way."

"You make it sound so easy."

"My dear, it's not easy. What happened? What brought you down?"

"Oh, it will pass. A client. He's young, in love, trying to make a relationship work. Makes me wonder what the point of it all is – relationships, buying houses, moving in, divorces. It seems like more of a mess than it's worth."

"Just because marriage may not have always worked out how you wanted it to, it doesn't mean it will be that way for this client. It doesn't mean it will always be that way for you, Tess."

"I know. I met his fiancé last week with him and there was something in her expression, or her tone; something, that I recognized."

"It's not your job to save anyone, Tess."

"Yes. Tell me how you are. What you're doing today?"

"I'm out planting. What a glorious month April is. The garden is coming to life."

Tess smiled, the slant of sun penetrating her window warming her. In this safety, this warmth, she wished that her mother would be here forever, that she would always have her to call, but there were moments, such as now, when the sun hid behind the clouds, that she knew that there would come a time when her mother would be no more, and an unsettling feeling overcame her. There was so much she had yet to cover with her mom, and yet something held her back. Shyness, fear. She didn't know which, or if it were both, or where it came from, and it confused her.

"I've taken a few yoga classes," she said. She had wanted to tell her mother after her first class but had waited. She didn't want her mother to think back to those teenage years, when Tess had fought her about yoga, refusing after a while, to practice.

By the way her mother's breath stilled, she could tell that her mother had put down whatever garden tool she had been using. Tess imagined that she was kneeling now on her shins, fully listening.

"That's wonderful, Tess. Did you enjoy them? Tell me, what was it like?"

Tess smiled. Her mother was trying not to be overly eager, but it was clear in her voice that she was, as if Tess told her that she was going to be moving back to Woodstock.

"I did enjoy them, Mom. You see, everyone comes around,

right? Maybe there's hope for me yet."

"You were a wonderful yogi as a child, Tess. So peaceful and so supple; I used to look at you and wonder where you were inside when you practiced."

They both paused.

"I'm not worried about you coming around, Tess. I just want you to be happy in your life. Yoga is a wonderful tool. If it helps now, I'm thrilled for you."

"Yes," Tess said. She felt the beginnings of a headache from the sun beating down on her and moved her sunglasses further up on her nose. "I should let you get back to planting."

"It's always nice to hear your voice. I love you, Tess," she said.

"I love you, Mom."

Tess rolled down her window, the breeze lapping her face, and she wished, then and there, that she could close her eyes, lose the world if only for a few moments. She felt depleted and lost and suddenly cold. She put the window up and she thought of calling someone else – her son, Michael – only it seemed too far to go to reach out to anyone and besides, she knew better than to try to fill the voids that traveled through her; the fillers only made her feel lonelier in the end.

Cars passed her on the BQE, and she slowed down, moving into the right lane. She was tired of moving fast, of trying to get there before everyone else. Where, after all, was she going in such a hurry?

Tess got off at the first exit without looking where she was. She needed to stop. To slow the pounding in her heart. She eased into a parking spot under the train tracks and gripped the steering wheel, focusing on her breath. A bunch of kids wearing jeans falling too low on their waists whistled and waved at her Mercedes, screaming "Yo mama," so that in a moment her foot was on the gas again. That was life: even when you needed to stop there were things that made you keep going, leaving you no choice but to act without always having a minute to think. Where the heck was she? Maybe Michael was right – maybe she was a total disaster. Maybe her mother's way of life was the better path. Maybe she should be at home working in her own garden, but thinking of her mom, in her home, alone, a desperate energy flowed through Tess, a loneliness that was familiar and dreaded. A thought washed through her, a truth being formed, that for as much as she craved her independence, sought it and carved it out in her life, she was afraid of spending the rest of her days alone. What had been hardest for Tess growing up was the feeling of being utterly alone in the world. Her mother had preached about non-attachment as early on as Tess could remember and once she was old enough to grasp the concepts of attachment and non-attachment in her early teens, she had vowed to attach herself to anything and everything that she could. She didn't want to live her life feeling as if she was floating and that everything around her was out of her grasp. She wanted to feel the ground beneath her feet. She wanted the security of knowing that when she went to sleep at night, she would awake to a day in which everyone and everything in her life was intact. It didn't matter to her back then if what she sought was impossible – that life didn't come with guarantees, that one day she would find herself unhinged and alone. She had wanted what she wanted just the same.

One deep breath followed by another. That's what she focused on. She eased back onto the highway, her foot on the gas, moving steadily and carefully alongside the cars. She waited for an opening and then inched into the middle lane. That was how life worked: you waited for an opening and then squeezed your way in. How many emotions she was capable of in a five-minute span. She laughed at herself and glanced in the rearview mirror to gauge her options. What she felt for her mother now was love. A solid, impenetrable love. And the residue of guilt, she supposed, for having fled. She couldn't even say what she'd been running away from. The thing about running away was that once she got started, it was addictive. She got scared, felt out of her safety zone, she ran. How small a life could become, how predictable. The running hadn't gotten her any closer to knowing who she was or what she was all about. She had struggled to find herself, as if she were navigating a territory, failing to realize that all along she was the one creating the map. All the struggling and wishing and wanting and trying so desperately to differentiate herself from her mother, as if anyone cared. And after all of it – her fear, her running – what did any of it matter? *What did any of it matter?* She saw now, as if a banner hung before her, stating it, that her only job in life was to be Tess, and all these years, she had avoided it by one means or another.

CHAPTER 10: STRANGE COINCIDENCES

His back was to Tess as she approached him by the water's edge. Jamaica Bay. She remembered telling a family once that the house she was taking them to see was on Jamaica Bay and the young son had said that he didn't want to move to Jamaica.

It wasn't until she was up close that she was sure it was Neal.

"I don't think this neighborhood is big enough for the two of us," Tess said.

Neal jumped, turning around, so that the mass of pigeons he was feeding scattered in a multitude of directions all at once.

"Oh, my. I'm so sorry." She started to laugh. "I didn't see what you were doing," she said. "I didn't mean to startle you."

"It's fine," Neal said. He smiled shyly and opened his palm full of birdseed once again until one of the birds landed on his fingers and pecked at the food in his palm. Another one landed while a troop of pigeons looked on, as if they were eager for their chance to get closer to Neal.

Tess backed away – she didn't want any of those birds on her with their germs and diseases, and yet witnessing their careful movements as they dipped their beaks into his palm and then watched him as they swallowed, was one of the sweetest things she had ever seen.

"I was expecting you," Neal said.

"You were?"

Neal flicked the rest of the birdseed away, sending the birds back into flight and unzipped the front pouch of his navy and yellow anorak, producing a Ziploc bag packed with cookies.

"Oatmeal raisin and gingersnap. I hope you like them."

Tess took the bag from him, pressing it to her nose. The cinnamon-sugar smell was intoxicating. She couldn't remember the last time, if ever, someone had baked her cookies. Her mother had avoided sugar as if it was poison. A man who baked her cookies! She imagined him mixing the ingredients, thinking of her as he did, hoping that they would turn out just right, that he'd see her to give them to her. The more she thought about it, the more nauseous the kindness of it made her. She didn't even know if she liked him. She hoped she wasn't leading him on. It wasn't like she was home baking cookies especially for him.

"That was very sweet of you, Neal."

She pulled a piece from one of the cookies and inhaled it before taking a nibble.

"Mmm. Delicious," she said before she ate the rest of the cookie. "Incredible. Thank you. Unfortunately, I'll probably eat them all."

"There'll always be more," Neal said.

octocrab::rate_limit

Tess tilted her head and smiled at him with her best you-poor-fool face.

"You don't have to bake me cookies, Neal."

Neal looked confused for a moment, as if she had just asked him to count backwards from 100.

"I bake every morning."

He was just being nice. Neighborly. He had probably been planning to feed the batch he gave her to the birds.

"Is that what you do for a living?"

She could handle that – a baker. That could explain why he was in Canada –French baking or something of that nature.

Neal took her in for a few minutes as if he were debating an answer. She wished that his lips and his jawbone weren't so commanding, so masculine. She wondered if he could see desire in her eyes; she tried to straighten her lips, glanced down at the floor to compose herself. How in the world could she be attracted to a man sitting on the sand feeding pigeons from his palm, wearing cheap tan chinos and a zippered up yellow and navy anorak?

"No. I'm not a baker."

"Do you have a career?" Tess asked.

"I'm on a leave of absence," he said.

Tess looked around; they were all alone, not a soul in sight. She felt a thickness in her throat, something like fear beginning to well up in her. The way he chose his words. *A leave of absence.* Michael could be right – parole? She should probably run, get away quickly, before he knew where she lived, although he already knew she was with Best Realty and could find her. No, it was probably best for her to treat this gently. To ease away from this conversation, from him.

"Like I mentioned, I'm writing a book and I bake for a nursing home on Shore Road. Baking is just something I like to do," Neal said. "I've become famous for my cookies," Neal said.

A pigeon that he was feeding was moving close to him until it was right there, and Neal began to pet its head. It made Tess smile. Bad people didn't pet pigeons, did they? She cleared her throat. She wanted to say, okay, look, what's your story? Tell me who you are and what you are doing here.

He looked up towards her with a still face and those blue eyes – they were eyes that she knew could get her in trouble, eyes that she wanted to look into, to be up close with. No, now wasn't the moment to ask him for his life story. What had she shared with him of herself? Tess fingered the cookies and put them in her jacket pocket.

"You feed the birds once, and they'll always be expecting you to feed them," Tess said.

"As long as I can, I will."

The sun was about to make its way over the horizon. Tess always thought of Humpty Dumpty when the sun rose. If he could just get up over that wall. The glare was already cutting the water in two.

Tess sighed and stifled it as a yawn. As spring became more of a presence each day, her winter – full of long hours at the office and nights cuddled up alone under her blanket, updating her to do list on her blackberry for the next day – faded like a dream.

Neal began to walk, and she moved alongside him, her shoulders falling, her breath easing. Neal's soap, a clean, peppermint aroma, filtered through her. There was an antiseptic quality to it, yet amidst the sour smell of the bay, it was comforting. If he were a mass murderer, his moment to make a move had come and gone.

"I never get tired of looking into the water," he said. "Every time I look, I see something different."

In the water's rippled mirror, her image was disjointed: a snake like Tess, wiggling from top to bottom, which made her feel momentarily unbalanced so that she looked away.

"What do you see today?" Tess said.

"I see that what comes to shore, leaves the shore."

There was something about him that made her smile despite herself. Simplicity; no static.

"How's your book coming along?" Tess said.

"Writing is a slow process. There's never a shortage of distractions. And yet each day, whether it's for 10 minutes or an hour, I become totally engaged in it and lose the distractions," Neal said.

"Then I guess I'm always engaged in my business, because I

don't seem to notice that days come and go while I'm working. What do you like most about writing?" Tess asked.

A pigeon crept up beside them and then another one landed. The way they made their way closer to Tess and Neal, carefully, looking around them before they made their next move; they looked like they were eavesdropping and Tess shooed them away with her feet.

"There's a truth that comes through the writing each day – I may not always like what I discover, but somehow once I face it on a page, I feel freer. Committing to the writing is the hardest part – the rest just happens," Neal said.

"And what if you don't write one day?" Tess asked.

"As far as you would be able to tell, nothing. But on the inside, I feel as if I'm at a distance from myself, like my mind is sleeping and my legs are running. I start to malfunction a bit, I suppose."

He smiled at Tess, and she smiled back.

"I've learned that if I don't write, I'll never get to know what I'm thinking or feeling. My mentor used to tell me that if you disappear a bit, explore what's going on inside, the world will wait. Nothing will be lost or missed. It took me a while to be comfortable with tucking myself away from all that's going on," he said.

"I don't know if I believe that the world will wait," Tess said. "Life is happening all the time. While I'm out here taking some time for me, all the stuff I have to do piles up."

"No one is ever going to give you permission to slow down and take time for you, Tess – you need to give yourself permission. Trust me, though, the world *will* wait – it's only going as fast as you want it to go. You are your speedometer."

"If I'm my speedometer than I've probably accumulated a lot of speeding tickets." Tess laughed. "Do you know that when I was younger, I used to daydream about walking out of my office one day and not going back," Tess said.

"Where would you go?"

"I don't know. I guess that's why I never left," she said.

"What made you want to walk out?" Neal said.

"Too much to do. I'm always rushing to get stuff done, and then there's always more to do. I'm tired of rushing," Tess said.

"You're not rushing now."

"No, I suppose not." Tess focused on the water, the way it drifted from the shore, slowly, steadily, as if it was in a trance.

"I think that if you don't know what you seek in life, you can spend a lot of time moving in place, or worse yet, moving in the wrong direction," he said.

"Is that what happened to you?" Tess said.

The tide flowed onto the shore, not crashing so much as arriving. The rhythm mesmerized Tess. She thought of something her mother used to say about grace, how it had to do with flowing versus force.

"Isn't that what happens to us all at some point?" Neal asked. He stared straight ahead, his expression calm, serene. He could have been saying anything with that face.

"Right now, if I granted you the freedom to do anything that you wanted to do, what would you do?" he asked.

Tess looked into his eyes. This man didn't even know her. Why did he care what she wanted to do? His eyes were so intensely focused on her that she wondered if he were trying to win her over – or if he just sought conversation.

"I'd be here, where I am."

Neal smiled.

"Ah," Tess said. "Right answer?"

"Only if it was the truth."

"Oh, Neal. Truth smuth. We barely know one another, and I'm not known for spilling out my dreams to strangers. Besides, I'm weary of people who presume that they've got it all figured out," Tess said.

He smiled and cleared his throat; she had amused him.

"I don't presume any such thing," Neal said.

"What's your story then? You realize that you're beginning to sound like a philosopher."

"I'm a simple man trying to live a simple life," he said.

"I don't know what you've encountered in your life, but in my view, life isn't simple, Neal."

"People complicate their lives. I see it as a choice," he said.

"People have jobs and families and bills to pay and responsibilities – sick relatives, home repairs – life is messy. I think that if you asked most people they would rather not work or worry and prefer to rest on a hammock all day and live uncomplicated lives. I don't believe people try to complicate their lives," Tess said.

Neal was silent and Tess wondered if she had gone too far. He was a new acquaintance. He didn't know how outspoken she could be. And yet in the silence, she couldn't help wonder if she had chosen to complicate her life – between her leaving Woodstock, her relationships, her career. She wasn't sure what her life was now, if it could be measured in terms of simple or complicated. It was more of a routine: she went to work, kept busy, came home and worked some more and went to sleep.

"We all have responsibilities. It's up to us to do them with a clear mind or to cloud our minds and create drama around responsibilities. Look at the birds of the air, Tess. You don't see them worrying about where to live or their bank accounts. They just coast about," he said.

"How do we know they don't worry? Tess said. "We can't read their minds. For all we know, they're just as neurotic and screwed up as the rest of us."

Neal laughed and smiled at her and led the way from the docks out through the front entrance of the yacht club and onto 66th street. She wasn't sure if she were supposed to head back home, say goodbye, or follow.

"You're an interesting woman, Tess," Neal said.

The alleys of Ohio walk were filled with old oak and faint yellow leaves. She followed in silence, everything inside of her easing; he could be playful. She liked that. Her shoulders, which she hadn't known had inched up to her neck in attack mode, loosened. Up close, she could see that stubble was growing in on his head; it reminded her of a Chia pet. She wondered if perhaps he had been in the hospital, undergoing surgery – that would explain his leave of absence, why his head was shaved and now growing in. Only he looked too healthy to be recovering, unless months had passed.

The church bells rang in the distance.

"In Buddhism, the sound of the bell is a reminder to come back to your heart. My son, Prakash, loved that concept growing up. He rang the little bell my mother gave him all the time. I'd hear him ringing it up in his room. It used to make me feel sad."

"Why?" Neal asked.

Tess shrugged.

"Maybe it made me wonder why I didn't fancy Buddhism the way he did. I don't know."

"What do you know, Tess?"

"I know that I'm walking right now while I should probably be at my office."

"Forgive me if this puts me in the philosopher realm, but I'd say you're exactly where you need to be by essence of the fact that you're here," Neal said. "There are no coincidences in life."

"Well then that's something we agree on: I don't believe in coincidences either," Tess said.

"What do you believe in?" Neal said.

"Action, doing, putting your money where your mouth is," Tess said.

Neal cradled the v of his chin in the web of his thumb and pointer finger, moving his fingers back and forth as if he were checking if he needed a shave. They were by the Key Food down at the Avenue U intersection where traffic turned into Mill Basin. Tess always felt ungrounded at this corner – cars turning, cars speeding past, the B100 bus stop with her face plastered on the bus stop shelter, people boarding the bus, people getting off, the bank there on the corner, the supermarket. Everything at once.

"Does your son live locally?" Neal asked.

"No. He went to college on the west coast and made that his home. He's out in San Francisco. An architect."

"Do you miss him?" Neal said.

He certainly asked a lot of questions, but Tess didn't feel as if he was intruding on her life. For all she knew, he was going to add in information on her and her Buddhist upbringing to his book.

"I feel closer to him while he's away," she said. "If that makes any sense. He's off doing his thing and I'm here doing my thing and I know that whenever I want, I can pick up the phone and call him," she said.

They crossed the avenue U intersection and kept walking down 66th street, towards Avenue T. The houses were smaller here, closer together. It was considered Old Mill Basin. The row of trees that lined the block right before the curb somehow made the houses seem protected from the street. Tess had sold two houses on this block in the past year. Not much money to be made, but they were seamless transactions – the banks never hesitated to give loans to young families. Children were waiting on the corner with parents for the school bus. Tess had never been one of those parents that saw Prakash off to school. The school bus picked him up right on the corner of her block. She couldn't remember now if Prakash had told her that he could go alone, or if she told him it was fine for him to walk and wait alone.

The light turned green at the corner of Avenue T, and they crossed the street.

"Do you have any children?" Tess said.

"No," Neal said.

"Why not?" she said, so that Neal took her in with that expression of his that she was growing familiar with. It seemed to say, it's not that I don't want to tell you my whole life story, it's just that it's too involved. It was an endearing expression, one that made the mystery of Neal inviting to her when she was near him versus fearful.

"It just never fit into my lifestyle, I suppose," Neal said so that Tess smiled smugly. He's gay. Definitely gay. With that body, it all made sense. She would let him keep his secret until he was ready to share, although she had an urge to tell him, it was okay by her, that she wasn't one to judge.

"Children change everything. Your life becomes this other life once you have kids. I never envisioned myself having kids. All through growing up and even when I first got married, I didn't imagine having kids," Tess said.

"What changed your mind?" Neal said.

"Getting pregnant," Tess said.

They were in front of St. Bernard's Church; it was hectic with children being dropped off for school. Parents were beginning to congregate and chat as the children pulled open the heavy church doors and disappeared inside. The church looked different to Tess in the daytime than it did in the night. Tess shivered at the thought of spending one's days inside the church. It reminded her of an institution, until she studied the stained-glass windows, whose colors dazzled and sparkled under the glare of the sunlight. Squinting, the colors melded into a rainbow. How odd – it was the second time in one week that she'd seen a rainbow and it hadn't even rained.

"Do you see it?" she asked. She was afraid to look away and lose it. "There," she said, pointing ahead. "The rainbow."

"My mother used to tell me that the other half of the rainbow was beneath the surface. She said that there was always two arcs to it – one I saw and one I didn't, and that there was no pot of gold," Neal said.

Tess had never heard that; it took her a moment to process. She couldn't tell if it was a hopeful comment or a sullen one.

"Is your mother still alive?" Tess asked.

"Yes." He was silent for a few moments. "Shall we head back?"

"Sure," Tess said and once they made the turnaround, "Is your father alive?"

"No," Neal said. "My father passed a few years back – he was sick."

"I'm sorry," Tess said.

"Death is a part of life," Neal said.

Tess couldn't figure this guy out; at moments he was tender and others he sounded robotic, like he was giving her stock answers from some script in his brain.

"What about you?" Neal asked.

"I don't know where my father is," Tess said. "I haven't had any contact with him in decades."

She felt him looking at her, but her eyes were transfixed on the waving tree limbs in the distance.

"My father was an American businessman who met my mother

while he was in Thailand on business. He brought her over to the US. I'm sure that they were in love, but the Buddhist way was more important to my mother than bonds. She was an advocate of nonattachment."

"That mustn't have been easy for you as a child."

"I didn't understand it," Tess said. "My father packed up and went back to the Midwest when I was two, and my mother stayed on in Woodstock. I think that was the beginning of my not buying into Buddhism. My mother and her groupies were all about freedom and liberation. They claimed that the road to bliss was all about nonattachment, and yet they were the ones who clung to their beliefs more than anyone I had ever met."

"Sometimes we get so caught up in what we practice that it becomes hard to see the contradictions."

"I resented my father for leaving me with her. For not fighting for me. I blamed him."

"Maybe he thought that way of life would be best for you."

"Maybe."

Above, clouds were moving in; a cool breeze had crept into the air. The trees' limbs shimmied as if they were swaying to a melody.

"I spent most of my childhood hoping that one day when I woke up or when I came home from school, my father was going to be there waiting for me. I don't think that I ever stopped hoping for that, but then suddenly I was older, and I was going away to college, and I wasn't waiting for him any longer."

"You've never reconnected with him?" Neal asked.

"No," Tess said. "I guess my sense of loss had something to do with my having four husbands."

"Four?"

Tess smiled and nodded. "No regrets. They all had their place in my life. Or at least that's what I like to tell myself."

"What about your son's father?"

"Marc. My first husband. He had an affair and left me to be with her. He was my college sweetheart. I bought the house I live in now while I was married to him."

The sky looked as if it were about to burst. They were still a ways from her house, but she didn't move any faster.

"Marc had lots of issues," Tess said, her eyes still on the sky before she turned sideways to Neal. He stared straight ahead; his eyelashes were long and thick; luscious was the word that came to her.

"I think that the fact that I was more successful than Marc killed him. Back then men were still supposed to be the breadwinners. And of course, he didn't appreciate the fact that I bought our house without consulting with him. But what was I supposed to do? I loved that house – the first time I was out showing it to a couple, I had a vision: I saw myself living there, and it wasn't necessarily that I saw myself living there with him, but I saw very clearly that I was meant to live there. Does that make me crazy?"

"No," Neal said. "Especially since your vision came true. You're still living in the house."

"My son thinks I'm clinging to the past in that house. If it were up to him, I'd be living on the west coast. He can't imagine why anyone would want to stay in Brooklyn when there's a whole world out there."

"Brooklyn isn't so bad," Neal said. He smiled at Tess. "We've got Jamaica Bay, trees, flowers."

"We've got bagels," she said, and Neal laughed.

"Were you really married four times?" he asked.

"It's hard for me to believe myself. But every relationship was like a whole lifetime unto itself. Each time one ended, I was so sure it was my last."

"Do you have a favorite relationship?"

"Brad. My second husband." Tess smiled. There was a joy in remembering phases of your life that you would never have to repeat. "Brad adopted Prakash. That's who Prakash considers his father. The two of them were close. I used to wonder if I married Brad for Prakash's sake. Not that that's an awful thing. Brad and I were the best of friends and Prakash was nine at the time. It was important for him to have a father."

"What happened?"

"Brad made me nervous. I was always anticipating his falling out of love with me. It made me feel unhinged. I'd never felt that way with anyone else. I guess that I was tainted from Marc's leaving me. Brad and I got married at the Bronx Zoo."

"Were the animals invited?" Neal asked.

"We said our vows by the chimpanzees. It was Brad's first marriage. Once I got to know Brad better, though, I realized that he wanted to get married at the zoo because it would be another story to tell. Brad was all about stories – he was a nonstop show. I guess you could say I got tired of watching Brad perform after a while."

They were almost at her house. She inhaled the hydrangeas that seeped out through the figure eight cut outs in the cement fence on the house on her corner.

"What about your son?" Neal asked.

"I think Prakash began to hate me. Brad was a toy designer. At night, when they played, he would make all these weapon contraptions with Brad and try them out on me. After eight years of marriage, I felt tired. So tired. I couldn't believe that you could feel that tired at 41-years old. I didn't want to lead the lifestyle that I was living with Brad – it was as if he was always on stage. Something inside of me told me to walk away, be alone. Prakash didn't speak to me for a while after Brad and I split. I thought that Prakash was going to choose to go live with him, but then he came to me one night. I was in my bedroom, reading, and he told me that he wouldn't leave me. Brad lives in Los Angeles now. He and Prakash still see each other once a month or so."

"Did you ever ask your son what made him decide to stay with you?"

Tess shook her head. "I didn't. It didn't seem to matter to me. I just felt relieved that he was going to stay with me, even though he was to leave for college within a year. I needed him with me. I believed that if we didn't reconnect then, we might not ever."

Tess thought of her mother, how once she had left for college, there was no going back, how if she had been disconnected from her prior to leaving, being away from her mother had only made her more disconnected. There was a loneliness she still associated with leaving her or perhaps it was regret.

"Prakash and I managed to bridge the gap between us. I'm not sure how we did it, but we did. We made peace."

"Peace is good," Neal said.

Tess nodded. They had reached her house. The cherry orchid's petals scattered the side lawn, so that it looked like snow, and for a moment, Tess had an image of December, her birthday, and she shivered.

"You're cold?" Neal asked.

"No," Tess said.

Neal looked behind her, as if an answer to why they stopped was there, waiting.

"This is home for me," Tess said.

The cleaning lady neighbor was outside watering her lawn in tall black rubber boots, old sweatpants, a matching top, and rubber gloves. In the sunlight, her bright red Afro shone. Tess nodded to her, and she nodded back, stopping her hosing for a moment. Tess assumed she was wondering if yet another man would be moving into Tess's home. She had once asked Tess how many different men had lived in her house; that was when her husband had still been alive, and she hadn't been a cleaning freak.

"Right across from the Yacht Club," Neal said.

"Yes," Tess said. She moved past her neighbor so that they were closer to her other neighbor's house, the sloppy woman who had married an Israeli man. "I'm sorry for talking so much today. I don't usually tell people that I've just met my life story. I hope that I didn't intrude on your morning walk."

"I enjoyed listening to you and walking with you. I still have two more husbands to hear about."

"I promise to spare you," Tess said.

Neal stood with his hands clasped behind his back, as if he were ice-skating.

"Would you like to come in for tea?" she asked.

"Oh, no. Thank you. I need to be going."

"Sure," Tess said.

He turned to leave and then stopped.

"If you didn't leave things behind, there wouldn't be room for the new," Neal said.

117

"I suppose so," Tess said.

Neal smiled, bowed his head, and then he crossed the street. She liked the way his lean body moved, his arms swinging slightly at his side. There was an economy to his movement, a steadiness.

The cleaning lady was watching her as she made her way to her porch and Tess had an urge to skip or wave to her, only she didn't. Better to let the cleaning lady think of her as a flirt than crazy. As she opened her screen door, a gust of wind flicked cherry blossom petals onto her porch and with them came a beat-up, orange-striped cat, pouncing the falling petals in attack mode until it locked eyes with Tess. Her initial reaction was to scat it away and yet the cat's glare mesmerized her. Could this be the same creature she had almost hit in middle of the road that first day she had seen Neal walking in the street? No. She imagined there were hundreds of stray orange cats roaming the neighborhood. She had a sense of loathing and intrigue towards this creature. Another gust of petals came flying toward her porch, spooking the cat, which darted off her porch as quickly as he had appeared.

CHAPTER 11: SMELLING THE ROSES

Tess turned the page of the photo album in her lap. She leaned
back against the bed board. There was Prakash, standing in the driveway,
waving back at her. He couldn't have been more than five-years old. It
was before any of the divorces. He had been such a happy little boy.

"Remember when you had the big white parka jacket?" Tess
spoke into the air, the speakerphone microphone a few feet away. She
laughed. "You looked like a polar bear."

"You scare me when you talk to me and look through old photo
albums, Mother."

"You scare me when you call me Mother."

"Are you in my room?" Prakash asked.

Tess had left Prakash's room as it was when he left for college
on the west coast. White walls with a navy trim on the baseboard and
around the window. The comforter was navy, and all the accents were
deep tan – pillows, frames, knick-knacks. A mixture of Ralph Lauren
nautical and minimalism. Something in her gut had told her that he
wouldn't come back east, but she had decided against changing his room.
She liked feeling as if a teenager was still present. She lingered on his

framed black and white aerial view photos of the Brooklyn and Golden Gate Bridges. Three Frank Lloyd Wright books still sat on his desk along with a picture of him and his college buddies at Berkeley. He had always wanted to be an architect – even when he was a young boy.

"I can tell you're in my bedroom," Prakash said.

"How can you tell?"

"For one thing you've got me on speaker phone, and you always get this weird tone when you sit in my room. Nostalgia overcomes you."

"I'm an old lady, Kash. Let your mom get her kicks thinking of you as a little boy. Wow. You should see some of these pictures. Remember when you had the guinea pig? There are pictures of you kissing it. I never realized how ugly guinea pigs were."

"His name was Seymour."

"Right. Seymour," Tess said.

"How's the yoga going?"

Tess turned the page in the photo album. "Okay. I took a few more classes."

"Next time you come to visit we can go to yoga classes together."

Prakash had started practicing yoga when he was a freshman in college. When he told Tess back then that he was debating becoming a yoga teacher on the side – something to do in the summer while he was doing an internship – her first instinct had been that he was gay. That was before his manic girl dating phase began: one affair after another.

"I'd like that."

"You should come out here for good, you know," he said.

"We've been through this, Kash. I am not moving to San Francisco. The west coast makes me antsy. Besides, what would I do out there?"

"Live."

"My life is here, Kash."

"Broaden your horizons, Mom. Enough with your real estate junk. If you come out here, I'll build you your dream house."

"Don't talk to me about broadening my horizons. I've lived a lot longer than you. What's going on with the girls? Find anyone you're ready to settle down with and marry?"

"Like I've told you before – you've had enough marriages and divorces for both of us."

"You have such a way with words sometimes."

"Mom, I don't want to deal with a long-term relationship. I'm fine – I'm having fun. Besides, I'm married to my job now, like you."

"For your information, I'm not married to my job, Kash."

"Admitting an addiction is the first step to getting over it."

"Thanks. I'll consider that. When you find someone you love, it's a beautiful thing to make them your partner. Life is too short to waste even a moment, Kash. "

"People who try to scare you into believing that life is a flash are people who need to learn to mellow out. I refuse to live my life as if I'm on speed," he said.

"I just don't want you to wake up one day and realize that you've watched your life pass by you without experiencing everything."

"Mom, really, do we have to go through this again? This all applies to you, too, you know. Are you really experiencing your life working away all day, all weekend?"

"My life is on the down slope, Kash. I've already lived plenty."

"In Brooklyn, sure. There's a whole world out there – so many options."

"Point taken. We won't go through this again."

"Thank you," Kash said.

"But it's lonely not having a partner in life," Tess said.

"It's hard for me to take that advice from you when you have left one partner after another."

"I guess I am not the best role model," she said.

Tess took the photo that caught her eye out of the album. Prakash was sitting on the floor, cross-legged, staring up at the person taking the photo. He wasn't smiling or frowning. He was pensive, and the look on his face – as if he was in the midst of a higher communication – frightened her. She remembered a phase he went through in which he had decided that he was going to become a Buddhist. He couldn't have been older than 12 or 13. Tess had reprimanded her mother – warned her that if she kept infecting Prakash with her religion stuff that she was going to forbid him from visiting her up in Woodstock.

"What did you do when you used to go up to your grandmother's?"

Prakash laughed. "I'm glad to see we're off the relationship tract," he said.

"Did she teach you about Buddhism?" Tess asked.

"I don't think she taught me about it so much as she just practiced it."

"Did you think it was silly – all her meditating and praying to idols?"

"Silly? No. Just the opposite. I was interested in it. I don't know. I guess it was a little confusing with her being so into it and you being against it."

"I was never against it."

"I thought you were," he said.

"I wanted you to follow your own path, Kash. I didn't want my mom to persuade you."

"My grandmother was not one to persuade, Mom."

Tess closed the photo album and studied the picture of Prakash up close one last time before she placed the picture in a crack in the edge of the mirror in his bedroom.

"Did she persuade you?" Prakash asked.

"I think that she taught me what she knew, what she practiced. So, it wasn't so much persuading as it was being her daughter, living with her. I suppose that's what all mothers do. They expose their children to what they believe in and as a child, you either buy in or you don't."

Tess leaned back on his bed, positioning one of the throw pillows under her head, and closed her eyes. What had she exposed Kash to? What had she believed in back then aside from work and not being a Buddhist?

"You're quiet," Kash said.

"I wanted you to follow your own path, Kash. You know that, right? I didn't want to force you into anything," Tess said, her voice gentle.

"I was a kid, Mom. I don't know if kids have their own path to follow, or maybe they do, just at a certain age. When I went to visit my grandmother, she believed so strongly in so many things."

"Yes. She did," Tess said. She had been a blank slate to Kash. She wondered if she had seemed boring to him in comparison to her mother.

"You still there?" Kash said.

"I'm here."

"Mom, it all turned out okay," Kash said.

She laughed. "If you say so," she said. Then, "Did you just hear that?"

"Hear what?"

"That – a knocking – is that on the phone?"

"I don't hear anything."

Tess picked up the portable phone, switching off the speakerphone. She moved from Prakash's room to her own bedroom and stood adjacent to the window that overlooked the backyard. She couldn't see anyone out there. She moved into the hallway and looked out the side window.

"Mom? What's going on? Is someone there? Are you okay?"

Outside, she saw a person – it was a man – toss something up towards the window. Was it Neal? She pressed her face to the glass and saw his bald head in the twilight. It was Neal!

What was he doing tossing rocks – were they rocks? – at her window.

"Are you okay?"

"I'm fine," she said. "I have to go, Kash."

"What the heck is going on?"

"Someone is here for me. I think it's Michael."

"Okay. Send my regards."

"Sure thing. Can we continue this conversation another time?"

"Yes, Mom."

"Love you," she said.

She pulled open the window.

"Neal?" she called.

He froze, but he didn't seem afraid to have been caught.

"Hello, Tess."

"What are you doing? Why didn't you ring the doorbell?"

"I didn't know if you were busy."

"Go to the front door," Tess said.

The moment she opened the front door, there he was. His hands were behind his back now, as if he was about to pull a rabbit from them, and for a moment Tess felt afraid. There were so many crazy people around – what was she doing opening her door for this man?

"What's going on, Neal?"

He pulled a bouquet of roses, red-black under the setting sun and offered them to Tess.

"For you. I picked them from my own garden. In honor of your patron, St. Theresa."

They were beautiful – fully bloomed. He held them out to her and looked down at the floor when she took them from him.

"They're gorgeous," she said. "Thank you. I don't remember the last time someone brought me flowers."

She had always told the men in her life that she didn't like flowers – that giving someone something that died in a week was a bad omen. Now, though, holding this bouquet, she felt intoxicated. She had never realized how powerful an effect flowers could have.

"Come in," she said holding the screen door open for him.

The neighbor who had married an Israeli man was outside in her driveway with her six-year-old son who went to Yeshiva and always seemed to be in trouble from his mother. She was trying to coax him to go into the house with her, but he seemed to want to run up and down the driveway to avoid her. Once he saw Tess outside, he ran ahead of his mother up the porch and into their house.

Neal pointed up at the sky. The stars were beginning to appear.

"It's such a gorgeous night," he said.

Tess came out onto her porch in her bare feet and sat down on the top step. Neal sat down beside her. The breeze came in waves. There was a softness to the air, a hint of summer tinged with the coolness of the evening bay breeze. Holding the bouquet between her knees, she wrapped her cardigan around her tighter.

"Are you cold?"

"Feels good," she said. Then, "I haven't seen you around in a few days."

"I've been writing through the mornings," Neal said.

"Your book?"

He nodded. "I usually get to work by 3:00 a.m. and stop by 6:00 a.m. or so to take a walk, but when I am coasting along, it's hard to stop. This week I've been losing track of time, so I've been letting myself go with it."

"You get up at 3:00 a.m.?" Tess asked. She held the flowers clasped in her hands now. In the breeze, the petals danced.

"I guess some habits don't die," Neal said.

"You've been getting up at 3:00 for a long time?"

"For at least 20 years," Neal said.

"Does everyone in Canada get up that early?"

He looked at her for a moment without saying anything.

"Look at the moon," Neal said. "Just a slither and yet so bright. Just a few more days until the new moon."

The night sky was a deep navy blue, the stars suspended like snowflakes. Tess hugged herself; the sea breeze became cooler. She felt the spring in every ounce of her.

"Want to go for a walk?" she asked. She felt the residue from her talk with Kash. A walk would be good for her, get her out of her head a little.

"Now?" he said.

"Now," she said.

"I could go for a bit, I suppose," Neal said.

Tess was about to ask him what he needed to do at home, but instead she picked up her bouquet and said she would be out in a minute. She was learning that people's private business was probably better off kept private. Inside, she grabbed her ivory cable-knit sweater, slipped on her white canvas tennis sneakers and took down the vase from atop the refrigerator, and put the bouquet in it, adding some water. She pressed one of the roses to her nose and inhaled deep and hard. Its sweet smell was intoxicating.

Neal waited for her at the edge of her driveway. They walked up 66th street and then wrapped around 56th drive.

"Have you ever been out on the docks at night?" Tess asked.

"No," Neal said.

"Come on," Tess said dodging across the lawn of the house they stood in front of. Neal watched her. "Come on, Neal," Tess called out. "Come," she motioned with her hand.

"It's okay," she said, making her way through the backyard and up onto the dock. "We're not doing anything wrong," she said in response to Neal's face. "Don't worry. We're just going to look out at the water, right? It's not private property."

Neal nodded.

Tess climbed the stairs of the wooden dock and moved out to the edge that jutted into the water. Once they sat down with their legs dangling over, the water below their feet, Neal sighed.

"The water is beautiful at night," he said.

Tess saw her image bobbing along the water's surface. There was always a moment when she stared into the water's surface that she felt as if the Tess in the water was going to pop up and pull her in. Little sparkling images of her glowed in the faint moonlight.

"Sometimes when I look at the water, I think there's a message for me imbedded in it," Tess said.

"What do you think the message is?" Neal said.

She bit the inside of her top lip. It was sore. Her mother had always told her that she would have bruised lips if she didn't stop biting her top lip.

"I'm not sure," she said. "I used to believe that if I returned to the water every day, the message would seep into me."

"Did you stop believing that?" Neal said.

"No," Tess said. "I don't think so. It's just that life seemed to get in the way of me going to the water each day. Other things became more important, I suppose – work, my son." Tess shook her head. "There are years in my life in which I didn't seem to exist," Tess said.

"I think we all have those years," Neal said. "Life just seems to happen."

Neal looked up towards the sky as if he were basking in the sun. His reflection bobbed in and out of focus on the water's surface. He took out a pen and little pad from his blazer pocket and jotted something down. He folded up the written-on piece of paper and closed his eyes to the sky, breathing in deep, as if he were sealing in a wish.

Tess wanted to ask him what he wrote, but she didn't. He turned to face her now. There was a quality of his face that was always shifting. His moods were unreadable to her.

"What's your passion in life, Tess?"

The water danced under the moonlight. The breeze was getting crisper, and Tess shrugged her shoulders and let them fall. She liked feeling cold right now. A pigeon toed the shoreline and then skirted backwards. Tess was passionate about selling houses, but it wasn't the actual selling she loved so much as the chance to connect with others that it gave her. She was passionate about running her business. Only that exhausted her, too.

"I don't know anymore," she said.

In the distance, past the water's edge, she was able to see the glare of headlights on the Belt Parkway. There was an eeriness to the traffic beyond, as if at some point, she would have to move past the water and travel that road alongside everyone else. She had learned that no matter how much she crawled into her shell, she had to come out at some point. There was an everyday-ness to the heart of life that scared her, made her feel desperate to shake things up. She was afraid that she would spend the rest of her days traveling on roads alone without anyone ever knowing where she was, or wondering for that matter, when she would be returning. She was beginning to know an emptiness that she had never known, and while it would have been easier to run from the emptiness, fill her days and nights with activities, she believed that there was something for her to learn in the silence.

"What are you passionate about?" Tess said.

"Writing, I suppose. Gardening. I like seeing things bloom and playing a role in creation."

The glare of the headlights across the way shone on Neal right now, like a spotlight. Tess shielded her eyes with her hand.

"Do you believe people can change? I mean really change, or do you think we're all pre-programmed?" Tess asked.

"I think we're all always changing," Neal said. "Like it or not."

"Sometimes my life feels like a game of musical chairs, and I just keep getting a chair," she said.

"Maybe what matters is that you keep getting a chair," Neal said.

She nodded. Her fingers and toes had grown stiff in the cool air.

"Should we walk a bit?" Tess said.

They tiptoed their way across the lawn and then walked quickly away from the house so as not to be spotted.

"Do you trespass on your neighbor's lawns and docks often? Neal asked.

"As long as they don't have attack dogs." She winked at him.

The street was silent, as if the breeze had scurried everyone home.

"Isn't it amazing how quiet it is here at night? It makes me wonder what everyone is doing inside their homes," she said.

"In Canada, the nights were so still that you could hear an animal moving across a field. When the owls would come out and cry, their cries would echo so that it sounded like they were screaming into a megaphone."

"Up in Woodstock, the nights were noisy. There would be dharma talks and laughter and chanting. We had satsangs a lot of nights that went on until after midnight."

"What's a satsang?" he asked.

"It's a coming together with other spiritual people. It means associating with people who help you to realize your truth. You sing spiritual songs together and share one another's energy."

In her mind, Tess could see the people sitting around the Woodstock living room, singing and dancing as if waves were flowing through their bodies. She had never realized until this moment what a beautiful thing it was – to be that free.

The church bells began to ring in the hour.

"There they are again," she said. "The church bells. They remind me of the *Sound of Music* tonight," Tess said.

"Is that the movie you mentioned to me a few weeks back?"

"Yes," Tess said. Then, she turned to him. "What are you doing the afternoon of May 1st? It's a Tuesday afternoon."

Neal shook his head. "I don't believe I'm doing anything," he said.

"Would you like to be my guest to go see the *Sound of Music* at the Ziegfeld Theater in Manhattan? I think that you'll love the movie."

Neal squinted, as if he were looking for something in the distance.

"If you can't go, that's fine," Tess said.

He looked at her and smiled his sweet smile that made her smile back at him.

"It would be my pleasure," he said.

Tess was already thinking about how she would arrange her work schedule so that she could get away and go to the movie.

When they arrived in front of her house, they stopped.

"Thank you for walking with me," Tess said. "And for the flowers."

Neal looked at the floor as if he was checking to see if his shoes were still on. There were moments when she felt as if she was torturing him.

"Tuesday," he said.

"Tuesday it is – say around 11am? I can pick you up," she said.

"I'll come here," he said. "If that's okay," and she nodded. She still didn't know where he lived, but it didn't seem to matter to her at that moment. A car passed in the distance and the way that the headlights hit Neal and then vanished made him look like a ghost on her driveway.

She smiled and he began walking away. She caught sight of rose petals on her porch as she opened her front door, and bent down to pick one up, rubbing its velvet against her pointer finger and thumb as she inhaled its sweetness.

CHAPTER 12: EVERY ACTION HAS A REACTION

Tess screeched into her driveway and let the car idle for a moment, catching a glimpse of herself in the rear-view mirror before she turned the ignition off. The pockets below her eyes were puffy. She patted them with her fingertip. She could always have them fixed. But that would be another thing to do. Besides, there was something about looking all tucked, tapered and plastic that didn't appeal to her. She was growing older. Her skin was going to sag. She turned the rearview mirror away and sank back in her seat, allowing her eyes to close for a few moments of precious rest.

She couldn't remember what time she had made it into the office this morning, but she knew that it was dark out when she had left her home. It seemed to her that the more she tried to accomplish, the more she had to do. She wondered what a day would feel like without her to-do list. What would she do? 10:50 am. She never even took a lunch break, and now here she was back at home at 10:50 am waiting for a strange man who she was taking to see *The Sound of Music*. Had she asked him on a date? No. An afternoon movie was hardly a date. She laughed at herself and let out a long, deep sigh.

Neal's knock on her car window startled her. He was on his bicycle, smiling at her through the glass. The front basket of his bike was filled with a large cellophane bag.

Tess got out of the car.

"Good morning, Ms. Tess," Neal said.

"Good morning, Neal," Tess said. "What differentiates a bike day from a walking day?" Tess asked.

"There are days in life when you need to go at your own pace, and there are days when you need to feel the air rushing at you."

"I see," she said.

His dark denim jeans and white polo shirt made him look like he was trying out for the glee club, only his navy and yellow anorak, which he wore tied around his waist, added a sportsman flavor.

"I've come with presents. Ginger cookies, peanut butter cookies, and sugar cookies," he said, holding out the red and blue cellophane bundle to her. "You can share them with your office."

"Thank you. That's very thoughtful of you, Neal," she said. She took the bundle from him and debated putting it inside her house, before she opted against that and put it on the floor behind her seat. She could imagine Michael's inquisition if she were to bring a cookie basket to work.

"Do you mind the windows open?" Tess shouted once on the

highway, her hair blowing helter skelter. She hoped that his bike, which he had put in her backyard, was going to be safe. There was no telling these days who was lurking around the neighborhood. She thought about asking him if he had tucked his bike into the cul de sac, like she had told him to, but didn't. No need to put any more negative energy toward it. If anything should happen, she'd buy him a new bike.

"Not at all," Neal said. "I like the breeze."

She caught more than one whiff of his cologne.

"When I was a little girl, I used to believe that the wind brought us messages," Tess said. "I'd sit on my bedroom balcony and try to decipher them."

"Did the wind tell you anything special?" Neal asked.

Old Spice. He was wearing Old Spice. Each time the wind rushed in, it drifted into her throat. She didn't know they still made the cologne! The sharp musky aroma reminded her of boys she went to high school with who had just started to shave.

"I think that I heard the messages I wanted to hear," Tess said.

"Well then I have a confession," Neal said so that Tess glanced over at him; in the sunlight his eyes were almost translucent blue. "In Canada I used to sit up on the roof at night and have conversations with the wind."

Tess laughed. "I think you're just trying to be like me," she said.

"No, really," he said.

"What did the wind tell you?" Tess said.

"I did most of the talking, I suppose, but it did send me things – leaves, pinecones. It was the wind that told me to return to Mill Basin," he said.

"Really?" she said. "Winds like that would make a fortune in real estate. What did this persuasive wind say?" Tess asked.

"It whispered to me that I had missed something last time I was here. That I had to go back and find what I had missed," he said.

"And have you found it yet?" she said.

Neal paused; he focused out the window now. "I'm always finding things I've missed," he said.

"How's your book coming along?" Tess said.

"Okay, thank you," Neal said. "I'm working out a concept that I've been thinking about for a long time – it's about celebrating yourself."

"As in throwing yourself *I'm happy to be me days*? I think most folks in Brooklyn would have no problem with that."

Neal laughed. "I like that, *Happy to be me days*."

"Hallmark would have a field day – cards, party favors. I can see it now as the next biggest thing. Remember to think of me when you make millions."

"You can be my partner," Neal said and for a moment he and

Tess locked eyes. She wasn't sure how to read him – did he like her the way a man likes a woman or was he just friendly? Tess pursed her lips.

"I was thinking more along the lines of people ordaining themselves what they are in life. So, if you were a grandparent, then you would ordain yourself a grandparent. If you were a mother, you would ordain yourself a mother. A waitress could ordain herself a waitress. The premise is that you should celebrate what you already are in life instead of always trying to achieve something or aspire to be something other than you already are. Not that people shouldn't aspire to be more, but they should also remember to celebrate who and what they are along the way."

"Sounds very empowering," Tess said.

"I see it as a form of acceptance. It gives people a reason to acknowledge themselves and one another for who they are."

"What would you ordain me?" Tess said.

"I ordain you my movie friend," Neal said.

"I ordain you my walking friend," Tess said.

They both jumped when her phone started ringing; she pulled it out of her bag – Michael was calling – and tossed it back into her bag. She didn't feel like dealing with work stuff. The minute it stopped ringing, her blackberry email alert went off.

"How's work?" Neal said.

"People sell homes. People buy homes." When she put it in those terms, she felt ridiculous. Neal's windbreaker, which he had put on, puffed and the hood flapped in the wind.

"Are you cold?" Tess said. "You can bring the windows up a bit."

"I'm fine," Neal said. "What do you like about your work?"

"Making money," Tess said. She had never just come out and said that to anyone. She smiled. There was more to it, but she liked making money. Liked being self-sufficient. "And I like the action," she said. "It makes me feel like I'm a part of life – or other people's lives, I suppose. I get to play a part in people's futures." She paused. That's what she was doing at the heart of it – moving people into their future. "And it enables me to live the lifestyle I want to live."

"And what lifestyle is that?" Neal said.

"I don't know; I can buy whatever I want for one thing, and go on vacation whenever I want," Tess said.

"Do you shop a lot?" Neal said.

"Well, no, I suppose I don't," Tess said.

Neal nodded.

"Do you go on vacation a lot?"

"Well, not recently. Unless of course you count today – I'm on vacation today," Tess said.

"I wonder if the people who earn a lot of money aren't bigger slaves than the folks who earn just enough to get by," Neal said.

"I'd hardly think of myself as a slave, if that's what you're saying. I work because I like to work," Tess said.

"Sure," Neal said.

"Oh, don't think you can throw the slave to work card at me and then get all smug on me," Tess said.

Neal laughed a belly laugh so that Tess laughed too.

"I believe that you love what you do by the fact that you're good at it. You're successful," Neal said.

"What I don't understand is what people who don't work spend their days doing. I certainly don't think sitting around and watching TV or shopping or meditating or whatever it is that people who don't work do is the way to happiness or salvation for that matter. If you want a meaningful life doing nothing, you may as well enter a convent or a monastery."

Neal started to choke, or was he having trouble breathing? Tess moved her eyes from him to the road and back to him.

"You okay, Neal?"

"Sure. Just…"

"Do you want me to pull over?" she asked.

And then Neal sighed and caught his breath. "I'm fine," he said.

"You let me know if you need me to pull over, okay?" Tess said.

The last thing she needed was for this guy to have a heart attack in her car!

"No need," Neal said.

"You looked like you saw a ghost," Tess said.

Neal stared straight ahead.

Tess accelerated and cut across lanes and put out her hand in front of Neal to keep him from falling forward in his seat. "Sorry," she said. "I didn't realize our exit was approaching. Will you do me a favor and get my phone out of my bag to call the movie theater? I didn't know what screening we would make it out here for, so I figured we would just buy tickets when we got there."

Neal reached into Tess's bag and pulled out her phone. He looked at it as if it was a strange animal.

"Just dial 212-777-FILM." Out of the corner of her eye, Tess saw Neal fumbling with the phone.

"How do you turn it on?" he said.

"You've never used a cell phone?"

"No," he said.

"God bless you," Tess said. "You may be the only person that I've ever met that doesn't know how to use a cell phone. Hand it over," Tess said. She veered off the FDR at 42nd street and when the light turned red, she dialed. Neal sat with his face plastered to the window.

"When's the last time you've been in New York City?" Tess asked. She listened to the number prompts and made her choices.

"Not for a very long time," Neal said. "Actually, not for over 23 years."

"23 years!" Tess said. "Wow, you really have been away," Tess said. "Great," Tess said zooming up Third Avenue. "There's a 12:30 show." She tossed her phone back in her bag. "I envy you for not knowing how to use a cell phone. I hate this thing and yet I can't seem to live without it." She made a left on 61st street. "Oh, I think that's a spot," Tess said. They were on 61st street between Third Avenue and Lexington Avenue. "It's a little bit of a walk, but we have time and if you're up for it, I am."

Neal nodded. "Sure thing."

"Just close the door," Tess said. "I'll lock up."

"I'd forgotten how busy New York City was."

They made their way down the street, the tall buildings shielding the sun so that the air was cooler, and a shiver went through Tess.

"What did you do when you were here 23 years ago?" Tess asked.

"My parents took me to St. Patrick's Cathedral, and then to some Italian restaurant in midtown. I left for Canada a few days after our city excursion."

Tess pointed to the Christ Church on the corner of 61st and Park

144

Avenue.

"See that church? It has a quote board in its little alcove. Every few weeks, they put up a new quote." Tess led Neal to the quote board.

I cannot step into the same river twice because I am never the same. –Heraclites

They paused beside one another taking it in. The church clock struck the hour – 12:00 pm.

"We should get going," she said.

I cannot step into the same river twice because I'm never the same. That was true enough – each day existed independent of another; what she may have felt yesterday was by no means what she may feel or think today. She closed her eyes and saw the words. *I cannot step into the same river twice because I am never the same.*

"My treat," Tess said when they came to the ticket counter. "I dragged you here."

"Thank you," Neal said. He put away the money satchel that he had pulled out of his back pocket. It was made of a thick fraying brown cloth. It looked like something a caveman would carry his money in.

Neal turned round and round when he walked into the gala of the movie theater.

"My, oh my," he said.

Tess glanced around – no one was watching them. She wasn't sure if she felt embarrassed or charmed by Neal's reaction. She observed the chandeliers, the ornate gold staircase railings, the burgundy carpets, the men in tuxedos and white gloves tearing tickets. She could have been in a palace.

"It is quite a theater," Tess said.

"I feel like we're going to see an Opera," he said.

"It's probably the last movie theater of its sort," Tess said. "The rest of them have become more like a family basement."

The on-screen movie trivia games before the feature started intrigued Neal. How in the world, he wanted to know, did Tess know all the answers relating to movies? The year *Casablanca* came out, the name of Julia Roberts' character in *Mystic Pizza*. Neal was the first person Tess had ever met that had never seen *When Harry Met Sally*.

When the movie started, the overture of *The Sound of Music* filling the theater, Neal sank into his chair and Tess did the same. It had been a long time since she had gone to the movies mid-day – not since Prakash was a young boy. It made her feel luxurious and free.

No matter how many times Tess saw this movie, she always lost herself in the story of Maria, the postulant, who left the abbey in Salzburg, Austria, to find out what life outside the monastery had to offer her.

"Aren't they adorable?" Tess whispered to Neal when the von Trapp children, who Maria had become a governess for, sang for their father, Captain von Trapp, and his dinner guests. Tess smiled as they sang the goodnight, adieu, song. It was hard for her to restrain herself from singing along.

There were ten or so other folks in the movie theater. None of them seemed to be singing along or even nodding to the music. She felt the tears well up in her with each turning point in the movie: the children falling in love with Maria; Captain von Trapp and Maria, the nun-on-leave-of absence, falling in love; Maria's return to the abbey to confess her love of the captain to the mother abbess; the scene when the abbess encouraged Maria to climb every mountain and find her true love. Tess sat on the edge of her seat during the movie's final scene when the von Trapps hid in the abbey as they tried to escape from the Nazis and make their way up to the mountain. She held her breath as the Nazi soldier that the oldest von Trapp girl had dated debated turning the von Trapp family in. And then the struggle was over, and the family fled into the hills, safe and free, a whole new life ahead of them.

Neal sat silent in his chair when the movie ended, *Climb Every Mountain* softly humming in the background.

"Isn't it gorgeous?" Tess asked, standing up.

Neal remained seated, as if he was waiting for someone to come and claim him.

"Neal, are you okay?"

He nodded. He looked as he had just awoken from sleep – disoriented and hazy.

"Should we leave the theater?"

He looked around. "Sure," he said.

"It's a powerful movie," Tess said.

He nodded again.

"Are you sure you're okay?"

"I just need some air."

Tess motioned him toward the aisle. "Let's go."

Outside, the mid-afternoon air was cool and breezy. It made Tess feel lazy. "Can I get you some water, Neal?"

He shook his head. "I'm fine. Thanks."

"It's so beautiful out. Do you have time for a walk?"

Neal nodded.

The movie had a profound effect on her, too. She walked beside him in silence. He seemed to be moving on autopilot, his eyes focused on the ground, his feet marching. They walked down Seventh Avenue. Men selling beaded necklaces and bracelets and handbags spread out across tables lined the streets. The smell of honey peanuts always made her hungry, but she knew from experience that if she bought them, she would eat two or three and then be done with the bag.

Tess led him into Central Park through the entrance on 59th street and 7th avenue. She loved Central Park. To her, it was the jewel of Manhattan. Side by side, they rounded the park loop, walking toward the

72nd street entrance. The silence began to feel awkward to Tess.

"The movie affected you," she said.

"It wasn't what I expected, I guess. It was very...."

"Intense."

"Yes," he said.

"It usually makes me silent," Tess said. "Although I don't feel as shaken by it today as I normally do – maybe it's because I saw it in public as opposed to in my living room."

Tess led them to the left once they were at the fork in the road just off east 72nd street. As they walked down the steps leading to the fountain at Imagination Point, Tess heard the music and saw the dancers. A woman dressed in a white and red striped skirt and a little red tank top handed her a flyer:

MAY DAY is a festival of happiness, joy, and the coming of summer.

The Anglo-Saxons called it BELANE, or BRIGHT FIRE, which best signifies this joyous day.

MAY DAY is a return to life. It brings with it new hopes for good planting and rich harvests in all aspects of your life.

It is the start of a season of love, attraction, courtship, and mating. Circle the MAY POLE.

It is a skyward symbol of LIFE!

Someone grabbed Tess's hand. She resisted, only to be pulled harder, and then she was part of a larger circle which went clockwise around the May Pole and then counterclockwise. She saw Neal smiling in the distance. The circle kept growing, and they were moving much faster now. In a moment she was able to break free and rejoin Neal.

"That was an adventure," Tess said, fixing her hair into place with her hand. "It never ceases to amaze me how many nuts are in this city," Tess said.

In the distance, crowds of people surrounded the May Pole, new circles forming and breaking up every few minutes as the crowd multiplied. Small children and elderly people alike spun round. Tess turned to face the lake behind them. People in canoes – families and couples – were floating about. They couldn't all be tourists. Did anybody work anymore? One couple lost an oar in the lake and the man stood up, waving for help. Neal waved back at him, and in a moment, the girl was waving at him, too.

"Shall we sit down?" Neal said, motioning with his hand toward the lake.

"On the ground?" Tess said.

Neal took off his anorak and spread it out across the grass.

"So, you won't dirty your clothes," Neal said.

Tess hesitated before she sat down and once she had positioned herself, Neal sat down beside her. His breathing was calmer – he had seemed to let go of whatever anxiety the movie had caused. He sat like a little boy with his legs folded cross-legged, all neat and tidy. He focused on the activity in the lake. She had an urge to trace his cheekbones, to kiss him. She closed her eyes and opened them as if that action would make the thought go away. Up in the sky, there wasn't a cloud. She had feelings for this man. Or maybe it was just that she wanted to touch him. Feel his lips. His breath. She shook her head. No. If they were going to kiss, she would let him initiate; men always made the first move. At least that's how Tess lived her life. And where in the world had all these thoughts of kissing come from? Surely, he was feeling it too – surely this was a vibe between them? Besides, a day kiss meant more than a night kiss. A day kiss was somehow realer than a night kiss because you couldn't hide from it; it would be there, in the wide open. A day kiss was exposure, and yet, what did it really matter? She was almost 56-years old for Christ's sake. What did a kiss matter? His eyes were closed. Now was the time. Before she could give it much more thought, she leaned over and kissed him on the lips, and when his eyes opened, she kissed him again, softly. She brushed her hand across his cheek, so smooth, and smiled into his eyes. Before she knew what had happened, Neal was on his feet, flustered.

"Neal, I'm sorry, Neal –"

But it was too late, because he was shaking his head as he backed away from her and then he was rushing through the crowd, and Tess didn't know what was going on. She stood and bent back down to grab his anorak and then she began to follow in the direction he had gone, but the crowd, it was so thick and there were so many people charging towards her, that she couldn't see him any longer.

"Neal!" she called, only over the sound of the drums and the flutes by the May Pole, it was useless. She hurried back out the way they had come into the park, around the curve, up to 57th street, but Neal was nowhere. She tried to breathe, to stay calm, not to let her pride creep in, which was swelling into a bundle of confusion and humiliation. Surely, Neal would be waiting for her by her car. Perhaps he *was* married? The movie had upset him. She had thought that he would love it, the music, the story. If he was married, then why had he lied? Could he be gay? No. Nowadays it was en vogue. She would have sensed he was gay, unless of course he didn't know it yet?

She passed the church and thought of the quote *I cannot step into the same river twice because I am never the same.* Well, she would never put herself in this situation again, that was for sure. It wasn't like she went around kissing men every day. It had felt like the right moment.

Obviously, it wasn't the right moment to Neal. But to run away? That seemed a bit much to her. When she got to her car, he wasn't there. Was she supposed to leave the city without him? Was she supposed to drive around looking for him? What if he never made it home to Brooklyn? Then she would have been the last person to see him. She waited in her car for over twenty minutes, listening to her soundtrack from *The Sound of Music,* humming along to "Edelweiss." There was a sadness to the song, a foreshadowing, which made it seem appropriate to the turn of events this afternoon. When the church bells rang in 5:00 pm, she started up the engine and pulled out of the spot. She drove down the block slowly at first, pressing the gas pedal lightly, as if Neal might pop up somewhere. He was an adult – he would find his way home. Besides, she couldn't read his mind – she didn't know why he had gotten so upset. She accelerated and suddenly, she was laughing. She had never made a man run away from her with a kiss. The more she thought about it, the more she laughed, until tears began to stream down her face. She began to feel lighter and easier. There was no use trying to concoct reasons on Neal's behalf. The truth always came out sooner or later. When it was time for her to know why Neal had run away, she would find out. That much, she was sure of.

CHAPTER 13: THE CONFESSION

Tess didn't know how long she had closed her eyes when she jumped up, startled. Had the doorbell rung? She rubbed her eye sockets with the heels of her palms, a habit that she had always reprimanded Prakash for. Perhaps she had dreamt that the doorbell rang. Just as she was about to fall back down on her pillow, there it was again – the doorbell. Michael most likely. That was the problem with living in a small neighborhood. If someone was looking for you, they would see your car parked out front and know you were home. She wasn't going to answer it. Michael would have to wait. She saw her answering machine blinking and remembered the messages Michael had left before she dozed off – something or other about a contract, and his thanking her for disappearing that afternoon when they had work to go over. She didn't know if he had worn off on her, or vice versa with his work, work, work mentality.

Slowly, Tess made her way out of her bedroom, down the hall, down the stairs, and pulled open the front door, careful to hold in the alarm button, as she did not need the police showing up at her house right now. She had her share of drama for the day. Perhaps it was Neal coming to claim his bicycle? No one was at the door. She stuck her head out, one hand positioned to keep the screen door open.

"Hello? Anyone? Neal? Michael? If you are hiding, just come out. I'm going to close the door. That's it, I'm closing the door," she said, and that's when she saw the envelope sticking out of her mailbox. Now Michael was writing her letters, she thought, grabbing it from the mailbox. Only she didn't know the handwriting on the envelope. *For Tess.* She looked around for another moment, and closed the front door fast, bolting the double lock. You never knew who was lurking around, watching, waiting to break into your house. Being a realtor, Tess had heard all kinds of stories – burglars following women home from the supermarket and shoving their way into homes as the woman opened their front doors; men posing as delivery men pushing their way in once a person opened the front door. Tess ran up her stairs and looked out her front window before she turned the envelope over to its flap. It was from Neal. He had written his name. She unfolded the sheets of ivory parchment, counting one, two, three, four, five pages, taking in the precise cursive penmanship – had he written it with a fountain pen Tess wondered, noting how the ink bled the paper.

Dearest Tess,

I am sorry that I ran away today. I didn't mean to hurt your feelings. I hope that you will forgive me. The movie that we saw, The Sound of Music, *was very beautiful, but very unsettling to me. I wondered during the movie if somehow you knew my story – if you had figured it out, and that you had taken me to see the movie to show me there was hope, that I may very well live happily ever after as a secular man. I was so preoccupied with trying to figure out if you knew, let alone with the movie itself, that it was too hard for me to even speak. And then when you reached over to me in the park…I will try to explain, but no matter how I say it, it sounds preposterous. I wish I had told you sooner, but there never seemed to be the right moment to say it. And then it somehow became a bigger deal than it would have been if I had told you right away. Your friendship has meant a lot to me, Tess. You have made me feel as if I was a man like any other man.*

I'm a monk, Tess. A Benedictine monk. Or I was a monk. Right now, I am on a six-month leave of absence from my monastery in Canada discerning the vows that I took in the name of St. Benedict some 23 years back. I left the monastery in March; I am expected to return in September, although I can ask for more time if that's what I need – I can ask to be dismissed forever if I so choose.

Most days I am sure that my life as a monk is over. I left the monastery, Tess, not only to satisfy my own desires, but to satisfy God's desires, too. It was God that gave me the strength and the will to go. I believe that my challenge from here on in life is to figure out a way to live in society without compromising my truth.

Coming back to Mill Basin after all these years and moving back in with my mother, into the house that I grew up in, has been a very strange experience for me. It has made me regress in many ways, relive the days, months, years prior to my decision to join the monastery. When I had finished Brooklyn College, I locked myself in my room for three months, reading the Bible and praying. I had started to have conversations with Jesus, and it frightened me. I wanted the voices to go away. My parents, devout Catholics, panicked when I withdraw from everything around me. I thought that they would have been pleased over my passion with religion being the religious people that they were, but instead they treated me as if I was an experiment gone wrong.

They sent me off to stay in the guesthouse of a monastery in Saskatoon, Canada in December of 1979 so that I would have a chance to figure things out – to see if a life devoted to faith and recluse was at heart what I sought. They sent me far away thinking that the distance alone would be enough to make me beg to come home. My parents thought I was going through a phase, and back then, I didn't know what I thought. There had been an afternoon I sat in my bedroom, and I asked to know Christ, who he was, what he was, and I felt something brush my hands and arms and neck and throat soft as a tissue and a voice, hollow and distant, said to me, "I am you."

At the monastery, the monks left me alone at first. In the silence, I was able to think. I watched how they lived – their community was devoted to prayer and study and silence. They helped one another, and although there was an aloneness to being at the monastery, no one there was ever alone in their hearts. We all prayed for one another's well-being as well as for the well-being of others. As I got to know the monks, they talked to me of vocation and how if you heard the voice of Christ, you were to open your heart, listen and not run away.

It was a very long road ahead, Tess. After my three months with the monks, they sent me home so that I could figure out if I wanted to return – this time, for good. Going back home after those magical months was too much for me. I couldn't find focus in Brooklyn. I missed the sound of the wind whispering across the prairie at night, the sound of the coyote's crying, the stillness of the monastery. Every moment of every day was precious there – things were done with purpose. At home, I couldn't hear anything except for noise that sounded like static.

In 1980, I returned to the monastery. It was May 6th, the day I turned 24. I went through a six-month postulate period in which I once again was asked to decide if this life was what I sought. After that, I took on a year novitiate. During that time, I learned about the order I was preparing to join, and I spent my days and nights assessing my call to the religious life. I came to define myself as a monk, and for the first time in a long time my life wasn't a mysterious puzzle. I felt as if I was exactly where I needed to be. I learned the Rules of St. Benedict. After my first year, I took a temporary profession, which lasted for three years. Next, I took a solemn profession. Later, I studied to become a priest, which led to my being ordained.

It's hard to explain how the years passed – but I guess the same is true for everyone – we live and time passing is the consequence. Each day I woke up in the monastery I prayed, dressed, took a walk, ate a simple breakfast. Contrary to what most people believe, St. Benedict's rule requires that a monk work with his hands about six hours a day and earn money to sustain the monastery. At the monastery we earned our living by making cookies and honey. I oversaw making cookies, although it took me over eight years since the day I arrived there as a novitiate to earn that honor.

I stayed in my cell and prayed and wrote and tended to my garden for hours each day. There was always time to contemplate, to write, to think, to read, to speak to the brothers. I had a nice life.

But after many years, there came the nights when I would sit up on the roof of the monastery, looking up into the sky with the abbey's telescope, and I would think about all sorts of things: why certain stars shined brighter than other stars, why I was living there when there was so much more of the world that I had yet to see. I started to question my life; perhaps I was at the monastery because of fear? Perhaps it had to do with a fact that I had repressed: I didn't want to end up like my father who seemed to go through the motions of life; I didn't want to just exist. Over the course of years, decades at the monastery, I had realized that my faith in God was beyond time and place – I knew this because there was no place I needed to be to pray –whether I was in the library, under the night sky, sitting across from my brothers during a meal, or in my garden tending to the land, I was able to speak with God.

I began to think about the choices I had made in my life. The truth was that before my monastic experience, I was a cluttered and preoccupied mess. I knew the Christian truth, but there were so many competing values in my psyche that everything was confused, unfocused, disjointed, and helter-skelter. I had allowed the expectations of others and society's values to influence me, and I had lost my focus. Being at the monastery helped me gain a better sense of who I was and who I was meant to be. But then I began to wonder, what if what I had gone through back then, in my early twenties, was what any young adult experienced? What if I had mistaken a religious calling for the chaos of growing up?

When I turned 40, I began to think about life outside of the monastery grounds. I kept thinking that there was a whole world out there waiting to be explored. The restlessness to look around, explore new surroundings, once born, didn't die. I no longer felt at peace with my brothers. I feared that my restless energy was beginning to filter into the other monks. They looked at me with strange eyes, and I would catch them watching me during meals when they were supposed to focus on their food.

There was more. On the roof each night, the stars above me, I knew that religion had nothing to do with a place or a book. It was about connecting. I started to wonder why I sat in church so many hours a day if I felt purest in my heart and soul when I sat on the roof at night and watched the stars fall, or in my garden during the daylight hours and watched the seeds I'd planted come to life, or even in the kitchen, baking cookies.

I began to skip going into the church and instead prayed aloud, chanting each morning as I walked the five-mile loop that circled the monastery. In the afternoons, I prayed as I sat by the pine trees and meditated. Each time I walked into the church, I felt the prayer go out of me. It was only when I was free, not confined, that I was able to communicate with God. I started writing In Your Own Garden *one afternoon while I tended to the wildflowers that grew out in the fields beyond the potato patches. I began to feel connected to myself in a way that I had never felt before. Finding myself, connecting with God in this new way came at a price: the monastery was no longer my home. I asked my abbot if I could live in the hermitage down the road for a while – to make sense of my heart, be away from the brothers for a bit, and he allowed me to do that. After eight months of utter silence – reading and writing in my journal, long walks, studying the night sky for a sign that never came – I told the abbot that I needed to join the world, see if there wasn't something that I had missed along my way.*

I left the monastery this March feeling like a fugitive. I believed, and I still do, that it was my job to finish my book, to share what I've learned with others – to remind others that going to church or temple each week is not what religion is about. That true devotion is a gift you give yourself, a connection with the universe, with God, who empowers you.

In less than six months now, I need to either return to the monastery or ask the abbot for another three months to discern my vows. I cannot formerly apply for a leave from the church until I am away from the monastery for nine months total. I don't know what is in my future, but I do know that each day since I am away from the monastery, the reasons that I left are changing. Each day I am learning and growing and moving into my life. And seeing that movie today – I took it a sign from God that I was on the right path and that somehow, someway, you are one of my guides.

The cookies I bake each morning are for my mother to take to the nursing home that she volunteers at. It's the nursing home at which my father died. I know that this is a lot to tell you, Tess. Right now, I am in St. Patrick's Cathedral, watching all the people come and go, searching for something outside that they can only find inside. I will light a candle for you, for me, for every soul who struggles, finds, and flees and vows to live this life with heart and soul. I will light a candle and pray that you may see the light always, and that you may be the light, too. I am sorry that I couldn't tell you in person, but I speak to you now as if you were me – for after all is said and done, you are me and I am you. Our struggles and joys and finding and freedom are but one and the same. If you will meet me at dawn by the water tomorrow morning, I will be thankful, as I always am, for your presence.

Yours truly,

Neal

Tess held her knees tight to her chest and sighed, deep and loud. A monk. She laughed out loud and scanned her kitchen – nothing at the window, nothing mysterious on the walls. She almost expected to see a camera set-up zoomed in on her; some new reality TV show about a woman finding out her new love interest is a monk. She laughed again, this time her laugh winding into a moan.

A monk.

Tess got up from the spot she sat in by the window and went downstairs and out onto the backyard deck. The cool May breeze rustled her hair. She looked up into the sky and without fail, the stars sparkled down at her. It made sense to her and yet she felt lost, as if someone had dropped her off in a maze, leaving her to find her way out of it.

She laughed out loud again, and whatever it was scurrying through the tree whose leaves shadowed her, froze. A cat pounced from the tree and landed on the deck with a thud. In the darkness its eyes glowed fire. Little by little, under the starlight, she was able to make out its orange and white stripes. It looked to her like the same mangy cat whose path had crossed hers on her front porch. It danced forward, then back, as if it were walking a tight rope, trying to discern if she were friend or foe. When the wind brushed the trees' branches, the cat darted.

A fugitive. That was what Tess had felt like when she walked away from her marriages. It never mattered who had instigated the breakup. In the end it wasn't about placing blame but about facing up to the fact that sometimes it was best to walk away – to let go of what was and start over. If you never left the old, there would never be room for the new. Neal had told her that.

It came back to Tess now, that old, familiar *I cannot go on living the way I am living one more day* feeling. Not one more day. To jump off a bridge, to stand in front of traffic was always her first impulse. The easy way out. Anything was easier than living through change. The struggle of trying not to compare the here and now of your life with what it had been the day before, then the week before, then the month back. There had always been a glimmer of hope – no, not a glimmer. Hope wasn't a glimmer. It was more like a tiny hand breaking the surface of dark, thrashing waves, pointing her forward, coaxing her toward something that she couldn't quite see, making her feel as if there was a chance she could reach the hand in time, pull it up from the water, rescue what lurked below.

When she had first learned she was pregnant, some 32 years back, Tess had decided that she wasn't going to keep her baby. She loved her husband and wanted her time with him alone. She feared what a baby would do to them – create space, distance. Besides, she didn't want to take a break from her career. Not then, after she had worked so hard to get to where she was. For a few weeks during that first month when she realized that she was pregnant, before she was ready to construct a plan about this thing that was growing inside of her, she had dreamt that a hand was reaching out to her, only she was never able to clasp onto the hand, never able to save it from whatever it was trying to break away from.

The silence she had felt inside those first few weeks of her pregnancy was both deafening and claustrophobic at once. She felt trapped in her own body. Then there was the fear that if she were to fall, get in an accident, she would have an explosion inside. No, she didn't want to have something blooming inside her, crawling and pulling at parts of her she couldn't get to. Feeling this strange creature's every move made her feel as if someone was examining her and she couldn't see what they saw, only feel their frustration, their outbursts. The concept of someone knowing her from the inside out, of her knowing someone from the inside – of this creature sharing her mind and heart and her motions as it grew inside her – overwhelmed her. She imagined the creature listening for her breath, trying to fall in line with it. She imagined herself falling in line with its breath.

It had seemed like so much work. Too much work and pain and examination for any person to endure. She hadn't understood, had not yet taken a moment to consider an abortion as anything other than a physical fix. She saw Neal in her mind, walking out the door of the monastery, not looking back, and she thought of the morning when she had woken up after having clasped the hand in her dream. There was no longer a question of her keeping her baby then, but instead a knowing that was nestled deep inside her. A connection. It was then that she realized that an abortion would go deeper, remove something from her soul. And suddenly, she saw an abortion as a loss of faith.

Even after her mind had made peace, decided to keep the baby, there was a final moment of contemplation a few mornings later when she saw a leaf dangling outside her window and told herself that if the wind let up in the next sixty seconds and the leaf grew still, then it was definite, she would keep the baby. A thought and a non-thought at the same time. A silly promise and then the wind did stop and the leaf grew still and she couldn't remember what number she was up to, and she knew then, the way you know you are going to cross the street even when the yellow is flashing don't go, that she was going to keep the baby, that there had never really been any doubt about her keeping it, that it had been a matter of her accepting her reality and not fighting it.

She knew that morning that she was going to name her baby Prakash, the Hindu word for light. It had been a word her mother taught her years back, although it wasn't until after he was born that her mother reminded her of the context. When she had been a little girl, Tess had asked her mother why Prakash, an Indian man who lived a few houses from them, never came to their home like the others did. Her mother had explained that he was Hindu, not Buddhist, which would be like Tess going to a Catholic church. When Tess had asked why he had an odd name, her mother had explained that it was a beautiful name that meant light. In retrospect, Tess supposed that subconsciously, she had wanted to create a barrier between her son and Buddhism.

Tess had become so much stronger once she had decided to keep her baby, and her new-found strength had scared her first husband, Marc, who hadn't known there had ever been any debate. Tess was able to see now that she hadn't let Marc into her life and yet she had blamed him for staying at a distance. It was baffling the games people played with one another.

Tess rubbed her belly, deflated now. Me, was what she had thought back then, in her twenties, as selfish as it was. My baby. Each time she examined her bloated belly in the mirror, feeling it rise in her like the moon, she had thought *my baby*. But it was more than that, because in the selfishness, there was a sharing, too: she would no longer be on her own. By accepting this baby into her life, she was opening herself up to another human being that she did not yet know or understand – that she may never know or understand.

Her baby, her Prakash. It had been as if she had impregnated herself. It was her gift, her breath, her burden, and she wasn't willing to share. Not back then, at least. As much as she wanted to write this all down here and now, share it with Neal, she sat silent and still and focused on what his first step walking away from the monastery had felt like. That had only been two months back. The newness of his reinvented life. She smiled up at the heavens. Change was an act of bravery. She smiled at Neal behind her closed lids. It seemed unimportant to drag him backwards into her life. Besides, wasn't she an accumulation of all she had been? She remembered what she had felt like inside the moment Prakash pushed out of her – alone, utterly alone in the world, more alone than she had ever felt when she was alone in the dark of the night, listening to her own breathing. She imagined that this was what Neal experienced the moment he walked into the monastery and away from the life he had been living. She imagined that this was what Neal had felt the moment he walked away from the monastery and boarded the plane back to Brooklyn after 23 years.

CHAPTER 14: TRUTH AND CONSEQUENCES

Neal's shadow came into view beside Tess as she toed the water's edge with her sneakered foot. There was something in her that was fighting to keep life simple, to ignore the past and plow ahead. That was the problem with letting someone into your life, with someone letting you into their life – it made you both stop, reassess the directions you each had taken.

"Tess," Neal said. "There you are."

"Here I am," she said, turning to face him.

Standing beside Neal, she was now able to articulate what it was that she had felt the first time that she had met him in the chapel: that he was her comrade. Like herself, she saw him now as a man who had lived a dual life – one that was expected of him and one in which he dared to envision a different life. That was the odd thing about learning about people in a behind the scenes way – once you came to face them, you were never quite sure how to act.

Neal looked at her as if he could walk right through her, keep going.

"Now you know," he said.

"Yes," Tess said. The two of them were quiet and staring ahead, as if their next thoughts might fall out of the sky.

"This morning when I woke up, I stared at the picture on my night table – me standing beside the monastery in my robes. If I lost that picture, there would be nothing to link me to my life. It's bewildering how fast you can wipe out your past."

The water crawled up the shore, staining the oiled sand a deeper gray before it retreated, soft and slow. In the distance, waves bobbed, toppling over themselves. The current can take your life, she thought, but it cannot take the life you've lived. She had contemplated this thought for a long time, and she wanted to share it with Neal, but it was as if she were in a trance. How was it possible that she could think everything and nothing at the same time and yet amidst this static her insides purred as if she were perched on a windowsill, safe from the world, warm in the sun's glow, taking it all in?

"This has been the most peaceful time in my life," she said.

Neal tossed a pebble into the water. Circles opened out where the stone had vanished.

"Yes," Neal said.

"A monk," she said. She smiled. It was easy now to imagine him in a robe – although she didn't know what color robe he had worn – white? Black? She could visualize him dragging along in his puppy gate, a prayer book in his hands.

"I'm not a monk anymore, Tess. When I see myself in the picture with my brothers, I think *oh look, there's Neal.*"

He stared off into the water, and again, she had an urge to touch him, bring his face to hers and kiss his lips, as if with one kiss she could silence him, convert him to her lover. But that wasn't going to happen. They were friends. She was going to be his friend and, in a few months, if he left, she would say goodbye and go on with her life. She laughed so that Neal looked up at her. It tickled her the way that she was wired. So typical, she supposed. The moment she knew he was off limits, she wanted him more than she had wanted him the day before.

"How does one go from being a monk for 23 years to not being one?" she asked.

"Monks are human, Tess. Regardless of what you do in life, your heart comes with you. Your internal battles don't fade. The only difference from me living in the monastery versus living outside of the monastery is that there, contemplation was part of my job. Here, outside of the monastery, it's up to me to find time to be with myself each day."

Tess thought of her marriages. Just because she had taken vows, it didn't mean that her life had changed. The truth was that she had kept on being herself – sometimes confused, sometimes content, always questioning.

"What about women? Did you miss them?" She wanted to know if that was part of his equation for leaving the monks behind.

Neal nodded as if she were asking him if he'd like more mashed potatoes. It was a non-committal, indifferent nod.

"I didn't want to get married. It wasn't in my cards," he said.

"Why? How did you know it wasn't in your cards?" He was gay.

169

Wasn't that what he was saying? "Did you like women, Neal? Before you entered the monastery, did you like women?"

Neal paused. "Yes," he said.

"Did you ever have a relationship with a woman?" She knew that she was crossing lines, that she shouldn't be asking, that he didn't have to answer her, and yet she couldn't hold herself back.

"I had kissed some – in high school, college."

"Didn't you want to be with a woman?" Tess said.

"You mean did I want to have sex?" Neal asked.

She looked down at her feet before she met his eyes. She didn't know why she was suddenly shy to talk about sex. She was an adult. He was an adult.

"Yes," Tess said.

"I was a devout Catholic. I played by the rules. I dated nice Catholic girls who shared my beliefs – sex wasn't an option."

"I see," Tess said. A virgin. Tess had never known a grown man who was a virgin. She looked away from him. Thinking of him as a man who had never lain with a woman made her want to keep him pure.

"To become a monk must not have been an easy decision," Tess said.

Neal took her in and then closed his eyes and opened them, as if there was something he dreaded to say but had to say regardless.

"I hated the monotony of my parent's life. Marriage seemed miserable to me. I wanted something more. I didn't want to graduate college and get a job and get married and have kids. The whole concept of it depressed me. I didn't want the life my parents had. I didn't want to be my father. He went to work and then toiled in his garden and woke up and did it all over again each day."

He paused and Tess didn't take her eyes from him. He seemed to be talking from somewhere deep within, a place where she didn't exist.

"Maybe he was happy. A lot of people like to live simple lives."

"He seemed miserable," Neal said.

"Did you ever ask him if he was miserable?" Tess said.

"No. We all lived within our lanes, I suppose. My father was a quiet man – he wasn't one to sit down and tell me about his life."

"Maybe there was more to your father. More to your parent's lives," Tess said.

"I can entertain that now. At 23 I couldn't."

"He could have been content," Tess said.

"Yes," Neal said. "I never got to ask him. Once I joined the monastery, I never got the chance."

"Do you regret that?" Tess asked.

"I've made it a rule not to worry about regret."

Her mother always said that a life lived from one's truth did not accommodate feelings such as regret. Tess had always wanted to say, *yes, but in real life, people feel real things and regret can be a very real thing.*

"You ran away from a life that was monotonous and yet you chose a life –"

"That was monotonous, regimented, judgmental." He laughed. "I ran into what I was running away from."

"What about the letter you wrote me. About hearing God's voice," she said.

"It's all true. I did have a calling. I felt sure that it was the right path for me; the only path."

"What does your mother say about your being back?" Tess said.

"She's doing the best that she can, I guess," Neal said. "She doesn't say much. She's been alone all of these years since my father passed and now here I am."

"Does she think you belong at the monastery?" Tess asked.

Neal laughed and stared straight into Tess's eyes, revealing an edginess that she hadn't noted until that moment.

"Do I think she's happy to see me? To have the company? Yes. She lives an isolated life. And yet, I think if it were up to her, she'd have me on the first plane back to the monastery."

"Doesn't she want you to do what's right for you at this point in your life?"

"She's a religious woman. Keeping me in her house is the same thing to her as a mother hiding out her criminal son. She doesn't want to mess with God; she doesn't want to be my accomplice."

He had nowhere else to go but back home to his mother. She studied her sneakered feet and moved one foot in front of the other. It wasn't a choice.

"I like you, Tess," he said.

One of her shoelaces needed retying. She nodded as if in slow motion.

"I like you, too," she said. She would be friends with Neal, nothing more. A healthy, friendly relationship. He was a middle-aged monk who lived with his mother.

"Do you think that this is just going to be a vacation from the monastery?" Tess said.

He squatted down and picked up a wood strip scattered on the mud sand. He began to sketch what looked to her like a circle.

"I left the monastery because I couldn't live up to my vows anymore. My life was, is, leading me elsewhere. I took my time thinking things through. And then I asked to leave."

"You were freed, just like that?"

"You make it sound as if I escaped from jail," he said.

"You go back in a few months."

Neal traced the circle again. "In September I can ask for three more months to discern my vows. After that, I must ask the abbot to put my dispensation though. The Vatican has to grant me a pardon and sign papers that dispense me."

If Neal took the route he carved in the sand, he would go back to the monastery. The trees sounded like rain, and Tess looked up to the sky.

"I won't be going back, Tess."

Tess thought of her splits with her husbands. Until she had signed the divorce papers, she had always felt as if she was waiting for a sign from above that would tell her to either go back to her marriage or let it be over. She had always believed that anything was possible after the worst had already happened.

"You don't know that," she said.

"I can live as simply here as I did at the monastery. I can pray anywhere I am. I believe that God hears and sees and knows us regardless of our zip codes."

"The night I met you – you were at the church."

"Yes," he said. "That night I had found the scapula my mother gave before I went to the monastery. It brought back a lot of memories. I put it on and then I road my bike to the church. I suppose I wanted to see if I could get the feeling back."

"Could you get it back?" Tess asked.

"When I was in your presence, I was reminded of why I left the monastery. There was a freedom to you, a lightness. I forgot about the scapula when I met you until you asked me about it when we looked at the paintings. After that night, I put it away."

Tess squatted, placing her hand on the sand, making an imprint and pulling it away. What came to her was a vague, but haunting memory of putting her wedding bands away in her jewelry box. The dismal pain of divorce, the loss of hope, of faith, of love, that divorce was. And yet each time she had realized that she was no longer in love with her ex-husbands, she had felt herself floating, suspended between a state of lost and found. Each loss had allowed her to find her way one step closer to the voice in her that said yes, that said no. There were a lot of no's: Tess had prepared herself, warned herself, *no you are not going to do this again, you are not going to let yourself fall in love again,* but the yeses abounded, because again and again, there she was, a woman in love, a bride, a wife, and then as quickly as the love came, like déjà vu, she was a woman out of love, a woman living alone, rebuilding her life, trying to move away from guilt and loss. If Tess had given up on relationships because they no longer fulfilled her dreams, hadn't Neal done the same with his relationship? Hadn't they both shed skins?

"You don't think that I'm done with that life," Neal said.

"It doesn't matter what I think, Neal," Tess said. What was going through her mind was the fact that if this man could walk away from God, how easy it would be for him to walk away from another human being.

A pack of pigeons in the sky scattered in random directions so that Tess didn't know which one to follow. She was trying to pinpoint the differences between standing next to someone you were falling for and the silent, yet-to-be-spoken goodbye you felt inside when were in the presence of someone whom you knew would not be in your life for much longer.

She felt Neal's eyes on her but didn't feel the least bit self-conscious. She couldn't remember the last thing he had said. It didn't feel fair – that she could ask any question of him when she was not sharing her heart in words with him.

"Tess, I had gone to the church that night to ask God what to do. And there you were. You silenced my questions with your presence. I was in darkness, confused, searching for something, only I didn't know what it was that I sought."

He shook his head as if he was having a conversation with himself.

"In the light, I saw a rainbow in your earring, and I couldn't focus on you, but just stand there like a fool and marvel at the colors – at how bright and true they were. And I thought about what my mother had said about rainbows when I was a young boy: that when you saw them, the other half was beneath the surface."

The waves tumbled and retreated, soft, slight. If she closed her eyes, it sounded to her as if whispering children were tip toeing towards them then away. *The rainbow she had seen on Neal.* Neal had no way of knowing that she had seen it, and a strange *how can this be, but it is* feeling overcame Tess. His presence in the chapel had silenced something inside of her.

"I'm a human being, Neal. I'm not a sign from God. I'm just Tess."

Neal watched her, his eyes cutting her so that her thoughts fell away from her, like soldiers jumping from a moving plane.

Neal reached for Tess's hand and clasped it in his own, and everything inside of Tess fought to hold on to him while at the same time she contemplated letting go. NO. Tess was through with these love-me-tender games, through with these illusory moments of grandeur in her life. People fell in love, found their true loves as often as people got hit by lightning. She didn't want to be anyone's damsel in distress. She didn't seek a knight in shining armor. No. She wanted to wake up each day, drink a cup of tea, go to work, come home, relax. Simple pleasures with simple rewards. No, no, no.

"You were a monk," she said, looking at their joined hands. What came to her were the moments she had first held Prakash, her baby, in her arms. Otherworldly, yet in the flesh.

"Yes," Neal nodded. "I was."

Random runners ran by flicking mud with each imprint of their heels on the mud sand, and as they pounded the earth, Tess thought about movement and the forward motion of life. Tess had allowed herself to believe that she was destined for so many things in life, only now, after all those years of working at marriages, of searching for a way to live her life, of trying to shed her past experiences as if they were skins she could step out of and leave behind, after four husbands all of whom had been good men, but not one of them her one true love – her knowing this because she had always been able to be with these men and also be a ghost looking at herself being with men while she inhabited her own life apart from them – after all of this, Tess didn't know what lay ahead of her. What she did know was that when she was beside this man, this former monk, she felt happy. If darker, more difficult times were to come, she would get through them hoping for more of this lightness.

Neal clasped her hand tighter and brought their clasped hands to his face, kissing the back of her hand. His lips were faint and cold, like a snowflake on her skin. The waves swam gently to the shore, retreating the moment they made their way towards them, and what came to her was that regardless of her adventures and her fast-paced life, she too had led a careful life, not so unlike Neal's she supposed, if you dug under the surface. She had thought out her marriages, deliberated her moves from one of her little lives to another. She had weighed what she would give up with each transition of her life, what she would gain. She had always been cautious in real estate, too. She had made a career of moving people in, making sure they were settled. She had not taken chances, but had calculated risks and moved accordingly, always trying to see into the future, to predict what lay ahead so as not to be unprepared.

The marriages – one after the other – and her workaholic ways had helped pass the hours, the weeks, the years, but in the darkness of her bedroom each night, she saw herself for who she really was: a lonely woman who had started off her career by reading the obituaries to see what homes were becoming available. A woman who liked to drive with the windows open, taking in the trees and the sky, asking herself who and what it was all for, as if one day she expected to hear a voice from beyond answer: *it's all for you, Tess*. It dawned on her now, though, that she had given up on hearing that voice over time, as if she didn't deserve an answer, as if she had missed her turn somewhere along the way and nothing would ever be for her again.

The wind blowing, Tess imagined herself lifting, propelling far and away from the earth, looking down on herself as a piece of a whole, and repositioning so that she aligned the world outside with her internal universe. She imagined herself coming in for a landing, her position sure and steady, and the moment she clicked intact, there was a strange sense of her being able to see everything and nothing all at once. It was as if she were looking into a crystal ball whose images flashed like road signs directing *come this way.*

Her hand in his, Tess imagined Neal leading her into the distance. She was ready to take to the road; whether it was the high road, or the low road didn't seem to matter.

"I'm glad to have met you, Tess Rose."

A tornado of faith and foolishness and knowing and fear escaped when she sighed. Neal. His hand was smooth, soft, and she wished that she could protect it, keep it flawless, keep him safe – from her – while at the same time she wanted to dig in, to bite him, to squeeze him so that she could feel him melding with her. For the first time in a long time, she felt the way she had felt when she was pregnant – two selves in one.

"I'm glad to have met you, Neal Clay," Tess said.

He turned to face her now and staring into her eyes, he kissed her quickly and daintily, so that Tess felt as if an ice cube had dabbed her lips.

In the distance, the sun was beginning to peak out from the grayness, the damp morning fog clearing, as if the sky was a mirror being wiped clean. Tess squeezed his hand tight and hard, and for the first time in a long time, a prayer ran through Tess as she held onto him – a wish that he may find freedom and peace, that he may be safe, always. The sun was taking over the sky now, rapidly, as if it had been there all along, hiding until they focused on it. A shower of birds up above parted, flying in random, scattered directions, and when Neal squeezed her hand back, the birds congregated again, and flew off beyond them. In a moment, Tess and Neal were walking away from the water, their hands at their sides, moving in the direction that the birds had gone. Tess looked back, once, and locked eyes with the gold tabby cat. Her instinct was to tap Neal, to make him turn around to see this cat that had begun appearing in her life, only she didn't. The tabby watched her, held Tess's eyes, not moving, until Neal turned to look, and the tabby fled as fast as it appeared.

CHAPTER 15: ROSE GARDENS

The phone call came from old Jim Creet, her mother's neighbor, at 4:30 am, startling Tess from sleep. Something about her mother taking a fall in the past hour when she got up to go to the bathroom, her hip being out of whack, her calling him in pain, his calling the ambulance and going with her to the hospital, them x-raying her and finding it was just a bad bruise. "She insisted on returning home and shooed me out, but I don't think she can get around too well right now," old Jim had said, and Tess had thanked him and told him she would head up there in the next thirty minutes.

Tess had called her mother only to get her answering machine. She was probably resting, she guessed. But her mind raced: what if something else had happened? Should she call Joe back? More ringing and the answering machine again. She left her mom a message that she was heading up to see her. She wasn't going to panic. Her mother was fine. She would keep her faith and see her soon. Only something in Tess had shifted, so that nothing felt fine.

There was a call to Michael downplaying her concern, a call to her assistant, checking her blackberry to see about which meetings to cancel, and then she was packing up some things and on her way. She knew that all these things had taken place, just as surely as she knew that her foot was now on the gas pedal of her car and that she was moving past the exits on the New York State Throughway, only she felt as if she were moving in a fog. Life was fragile and spontaneous: in an instant, something could happen to her mother and Tess was powerless to do anything but react.

There were times in her life that she had loved this ride, had looked forward to it with its winding roads and its picturesque mountain peaks rich with foliage, the never-ending rows of evergreen trees, stacked like people in a stadium. She had blasted the car radio – Crosby, Stills, Nash and Young followed by the Rolling Stones – and climbed into the mountains rushing full speed ahead. While she had enjoyed the journey in the past, though, the thought of reaching her destination had caused her unease. It wasn't that she didn't love her mother and being in her company, it was that being there, in Woodstock, in the house she grew up in, brought her back to complicated emotions of trying to be a good daughter, trying to act the part of a Buddhist, while trying to figure out who she was as a person. She was more than just her mother's daughter, yet there never seemed to be the time or space to be her true self, so that when she was in Woodstock, under her mother's roof, she had felt like a fraud.

Tess wasn't sure what she felt now as her car climbed the mountain, her hands firm on the steering wheel as she switched from the left lane to the right lane and vice versa to bypass the eighteen and thirty-six-wheeler trucks that made her car buckle. Something like nostalgia tinged with dread. Each time her mind lost thought, a feeling, a premonition of sorts, rushed through her, insinuating that this was the last time she would make this ride up to Woodstock to see her mother.

She tried to brush off the feeling and opened her car window, as if to blow it away. This was how life worked, she reasoned. People got older; no one could outwit old age.

The tollbooth exit towards Route 17 seemed to come up too soon in the journey for Tess. In less than an hour she'd be in the quaint little town of Woodstock where people still made and wore bright colored tie-dyed shirts and canvas-textured ponchos and carved crystals to wear around their necks for healing properties. Now that meditation, Buddhism, and yoga had become mainstream, it made the hippie environment in Woodstock seem a bit more cliché. Time had passed and yet the town had kept its same old-world – Tess searched for a word – charm, she supposed. Whenever someone heard that she was from Woodstock, they would always ask her if she had been there in 1969 and seemed to be disappointed when she filled them in that she wasn't. She had been in her junior year at Brooklyn College then, caught up in an internship. Her mother had invited Tess to bring whomever she wished from Brooklyn back home with her for the concert, which would have caused utter joy amongst her classmates, but the thought of bringing her city life up to Woodstock made her uncomfortable. It seemed funny to her now – most college coeds in the late 1960's would have dreamed of having a bodhisattva for a mother and yet, she had been embarrassed of it. The last thing she had wanted to do with her newly acquired city ways was to take part in a glorified hippie fest.

Tess pulled into the freshly paved driveway of 56 Echo Lane as the sun was beginning to break through the sky, and let the car idle a few moments. She had insisted and paid for the driveway to be repaved in the last few years, reminding her mother that one of her visitors could get hurt on the pebbled driveway and finally, her mother had agreed. She admired the English Tudor design, the picturesque cottage-style architecture of the house. It had been built in 1924. The house was cozy and bright and spacious with its wood, brick, and stucco details. Tess had the glass doors all around the first floor of the house insulated just the past spring to make the home warmer in the winter for her mother and to cut down on heating costs.

Hearing the car, old Jim Creet came out on his porch to greet Tess, while her mother stood at her own screen door, touching the glass so that it looked to Tess as if she were trying to reach her through a fishbowl. Tess waved to Jim and motioned that she would call him later as she made her way out of the car.

"Contesta," her mother said, hobbling out onto the porch and then Tess was hugging her frail frame, holding her and kissing her eyes so that her mother pulled her head away at some point and held her daughter's face in her hands and whispered, "Contesta; Metok Ladron." Contesta had been her American name, while Metok Ladron had been her Tibetan Buddhist name, meaning *Blooming Light*.

Brushing off Tess's concern, "I'm fine, just a little bruise," her mother, overjoyed to see Tess on this random day, insisted that they sit out on the front lawn and watch the sunrise. She reminded Tess how they used to do that when Tess was a child, before she left for school some days, and reluctantly, Tess helped her mother out onto the grass. "Be careful, please Mom, I don't want you to make your hip worse," before she pulled blankets from her trunk. She draped one over her mother, smaller now than Tess ever remembered her being, her thick wavy mane a shiny, silver gray, and placed another blanket on the grass. Her mother held her hand tight, and lying down on the blanket, closing her eyes to the sky as if she was not yet ready to watch the new day dawn, she began to sing in her sweet voice, *I never promised you a rose garden*. Tess caressed her mother's grooved face with her fingertips, smoothing her hair back. It was the first time she had ever touched her mother tenderly, and it surprised Tess how it resonated in her soul. Her mother was under her control at that moment, and it made Tess feel as she did when she carried her baby son in her hands for the first time – the fragility of life, the complete surrender of one human being to another.

Along with the sunshine there's gotta be a little rain sometime

I beg your pardon I never promised you a rose garden.

Tess had forgotten how her mother loved to sing that song, how whenever life was not what a young Tess had wished it to be, her mother had sat on the porch swing beside Tess and sang it to her as she rocked the swing to and fro. Tess wondered when it was that her mother had first heard that song. She would ask her about it at some point. Caroline. Sweet Caroline, Tess thought as she smoothed her hair. That was the American name she had taken when she came over to the United States, although to her congregation, she had remained White Tara, the one who saves, associated with long life and wisdom.

To her mother, Tess was always *Contesta*, the answer; literally, *he/she/you answers* she had pointed out to her mother once she learned to conjugate the verb *contester* in Spanish class. To Tess the literal translation had made the world of difference. She was always listening to a person wondering if they were the he, she, or you who was to supply her with the answer. Her name somehow was a cruel joke to her, a title that would always leave her searching, although she was grateful that her mother had given her what she had viewed as a normal name and that she didn't make her go to school with the name Metok Ladron.

Across the road, neighbors came outside one by one to fetch the newspaper in their robes and pajamas and take in the new day. In Woodstock no one slept past the break of day. Tess wondered where, if anywhere, the townies went for their morning meditation session in the past few months since her mother had become more reclusive; they had still come over each morning through her Leukemia and Tess believed it had kept her mother going in between chemotherapy sessions. Tess had spent many a long weekend sleeping at her mother's home during the chemotherapy months, although she couldn't remember those much. Contrary to all the doctor's warnings about what chemotherapy would be like, her mother had been fine, laughing and cooking dinners as soon as each session was over.

An old man across the way waved to Tess and then there was a man and woman standing beside him in track pants and sweatshirts – their names were on the tip of Tess's tongue – and as they began to make their way towards Tess, she held up her hand to keep them off and put her pointer finger to her lips. She wanted this time alone with her mother. She bent down and kissed her smooth cheek. Her mother was so beautiful with her silken, gleaming skin. It was funny that it wasn't until she was a grown up herself that Tess began to realize how beautiful her mother was, and then came the realization that all those men who had hung around their home as she had been growing up, trying to win Tess over, buying her trinkets – books and miniature statues of Green Tara, the savior, and Kuan Yin, the bodhisattva of compassion – had loved her mother. It made Tess feel silly now thinking about all those men loving her mother, trying to win Tess's affection as a way of getting to her mother. Her mother had never married after Tess's father walked out of her life; it wasn't until Tess divorced Michael that her mother had explained to Tess that the reason she had never remarried was because her life was not about marrying any one person, but about being married to herself first and then to the people that she shared her life with. She had reminded Tess of the second of the Four Noble Truths: "The origin of suffering is attachment." *Nirodha*, her mother had said to Tess, as if it was the first time she was sharing the word with Tess, while in fact her mother had instructed her in the Four Noble Truths and the Eightfold Path of Buddhism again and again. *Nirodha*: the unmaking of sensual craving and conceptual attachment. No clinging and attachment. It had made Tess feel foolish that she had submitted to the various men that had loved her, that she had clung to others, formed so many attachments and brought suffering upon herself.

Her mother continued to sing, and Tess watched her lips form the words, the sound coming out of her mother too beautiful for Tess to interfere with. *Contesta* – that was who she was to her mother: an answer, a voice in the night, a house for her to move into. But as her belly grew, her mother had told her, she had realized that the blooming within her provided her with more than shelter. The life within her was an answer to the questions her heart and soul tossed her way each day: the why's and when and how's of her life could be stilled by her hand caressing the expanse of her belly. Her mother had told her that throughout her pregnancy, she had loved becoming familiar all over again each day with the boundaries of her flesh.

Tess massaged her mother's sturdy, slender fingers. Although the rest of her hands were covered in wrinkled flesh, her fingers hadn't aged.

"I'm sorry," Tess said, and at that moment she was. It wasn't regret or nostalgia, but sorrow, for not adoring her mother, for failing to know her earlier in her life.

"Never apologize for your life," her mother said as if she were speaking from a dream.

"I never understood that you were my ally," Tess said.

Her mother brushed Tess's cheek with her hand.

"You always knew that I was your ally – that's what gave you the strength to lead your own life," her mother said, putting the pad of her pointer finger to Tess's lips so that Tess kissed it.

"Listen," she said, moving Tess's hand to her heart, and Tess heard life pumping through her mother amidst the distant sound of the birds' chattering songs.

What came to Tess was the reality that all those years living alongside her mother, and later, her husbands, she had never known what the beat of their hearts sounded like. The realization overcame her, so that waves of nausea bubbled up in her. Tess had lived her life at a comfortable distance from the people closest to her, and if they knew that she was always apart while she was with them, none of them had ever let on to it. Now, she wondered if there had ever been any truth to her relationships. So much distance between people. So many routes leading into a person, so many routes leading away. Tess believed that there were choices in life that one couldn't go back on. After so many years of keeping a person far away, pulling them in seemed cruel and selfish. A person pulled in would discover that they had been kept away and then the wonder and unrest in them would unsettle them. Endless questions whose answers were irrelevant. You could visit the past, pick up a souvenir or two, but you couldn't undo it. Her mother squeezed her hand, shifting Tess up from her reverie, and Tess held onto her mother, wondering how with this woman whom she both knew and didn't know, she felt so connected.

"*I never promised you a rose garden,*" her mother sang, and Tess rubbed the fingers of her free hand against the grass, feeling the ground beneath her. Under the lingering moon, and persisting sun, Tess began to sing along, letting go of trying to make sense of the feelings washing through her. The rising sun glowed vibrant as it began to dominate in the sky. Tess felt her heart wrenching open, as if it too was making room for warmth and light. She didn't want her mother to die – that's what filtered through her, and yet she knew that her mother viewed the concepts of birth and death as an ongoing process in the chain of living. That was what it was to be a Buddhist: to believe that when one form of life ended, another began.

They went inside when the bugs began to be a nuisance, her mother wanting to rest for a bit, so that Tess helped her up the stairs, then her mother insisting that Tess must be tired, that rest would do her some good after the long drive, telling her to close her eyes, if only for 15 minutes, that work would wait. She patted the bed beside her, setting down a pillow for Tess, so that Tess lied down on the bed beside her mother, like sisters, for the first time in she couldn't remember how many decades. She assured her mother that she would rest for a few minutes and the next thing she knew, she must have fallen asleep.

The second fall came hours later. Tess heard it and in the who, what, why, when of waking, and then she was up and out of bed before she realized that she was in her mother's bedroom. She rushed down the stairs, into the kitchen, where her mother lay in quiet agony on the tiled floor. She had been reaching for a bowl to make Tess pancakes. Silver dollars, Tess's favorite. The emergency surgery – her mother had fractured her hip and dislocated her pelvis – took hours, and even with pain killers, the doctor told Tess that her mother would be uncomfortable for weeks, if not months to come, not to mention that she would need blood transfusions as a precaution for her Leukemia, although she was in remission.

He believed that her mother needed round-the-clock care to get her through the fracture and suggested that they transfer her to an assisted living facility affiliated with the hospital the next morning. Tess proposed bringing a nurse into her home to stay with her mother, or even taking her back to Brooklyn to stay with Tess, but the doctor felt that she would be better off in a facility. "Just to be sure she's monitored and that she heals properly; we can't risk any complications," he had said, assuring Tess that it was temporary, just until her mother could walk on her own again.

With Tess's ultimate consent, they were able to get her a room in the home. When Tess returned to her mother's empty home that night, after packing up a suitcase of what she supposed her mother would need for the move in the morning, she wept. She felt as if she had committed her mother to an institution. Tess wiped at her swollen eyes at the kitchen table and blew her nose – life was not fair. It was not fair to love someone so much only to watch them suffer. It was not fair that such a good woman, a woman who had devoted her life to others, was now going to be stuck in an assisted living home, for who knew how long? How could a life so well lived, so meaningful, turn into this? She wept off and on until her head throbbed, and jaw ached from clenching her teeth, and she moved into her mother's bedroom as if in a trance, falling asleep in her clothes.

Her mother carried on in her most positive manner when she was checked into her temporary home the next day. "How lovely the view is and what a wonderful bathtub," she said when Tess wheeled her around. Tess decided to stay on in Woodstock so that she could visit with her mother each day until, she supposed, either she grew accustomed to this new situation, or her mother did. In those first few days of her mother's confinement, Tess sprouted black and blues all over her body – first a knee, then an elbow, and later, her thighs and calves. Her mother's doctor diagnosed it as a mixture of stress and an eating deficiency. Who, Tess had wondered in her weakest moments, would provide her with round-the-clock care when she needed it? Selfish and small as the thought made her feel, Tess hated the aloneness she felt once her mother was in the home. Nirodha. She read over and over the *Four Noble Truths,* which her mother had engraved into a wooden plaque that hung over the fireplace in the large meditation room of her home.

Life means suffering.

The origin of suffering is attachment.

The cessation of suffering is attainable.

The path to the cessation of suffering.

"Mom," Tess said, as her mother's eyes began to gradually open.

Her mother had tossed and turned in and out of sleep in the narrow bed, for an hour. The sour smell of urine coming from her mother's bedpan had nauseated her, but she had held off on calling in the nurse to let her mother rest. She didn't know how anyone could heal in a room with walls the color of phlegm, and cold, industrial-tiled floors – a mishmash of white and grey flecks.

"It's nice to see you," her mother said.

Her mother was not as sharp the first few days, but the doctor assured Tess it was a result of the painkillers from her fall. To Tess, it was as if in a matter of a few days, her mother had submerged underwater.

"How are you feeling, Mom?"

Her mother sat up in bed and glanced around.

"There's sunlight," she said, her eyes on the window.

"Yes," Tess said. It's a lovely spring day," she said.

Her mother's eyes moved from the window to Tess, sitting in a chair beside the bed.

"Come here," her mother said, and Tess was out of her chair and leaning close to her mother. Her mother patted her hand on the bed. "Sit," she said.

She took Tess in for a few moments before she reached out and touched her hair, her face. Tess felt the tears in her eyes begin to fall. Her mother's touch had always been so healing to her. Tess closed her eyes, letting her mother's fingertips trace her face.

"Contesta," she said, wiping the tears from Tess's cheeks.

Her mother believed that crying was healthy, a way to cleanse the soul.

"I'm here, Mom. I'm here," she said. It had always been the two of them. Regardless of how many people had been involved in their lives, it had always been Tess and her mom.

Her mother reached her arm around Tess, pulling her upper body down so that Tess was resting beside her from her waist down.

"Don't waste your days on this earth, Contesta. Make all the days count, even the ones that may be difficult for you. Make them all count. And make peace with time. It's not an obstacle. It's the keeper for all that you have done and all that you have yet to do."

Tess sat up to face her mother. Her mother's hand traveled down her shoulder until it landed on Tess's hand.

"What is it that you want in your life?" her mother asked.

She shook her head. "I don't know," Tess said.

Her mother smiled her beautiful, gentle smile at Tess. It was the expression Tess wanted to have with her always.

"When I used to ask you that as a teenager, you used to say that you wanted to move away from Woodstock, that you wanted to be a businesswoman. Was that what you wanted?" her mother said.

Tess shrugged. "Back then, yes. I suppose."

"What you think you want is not always what you want," her mother said.

"I want you to be okay," she said.

Her mother laughed. "I'm exactly as the universe believes I need to be."

"Do you think I've made mistakes?" Tess said.

"My dear child. Mistakes? What does any of that matter? There are no mistakes in living. Just living."

Her mother's eyes were on the window again. A sense of urgency rushed through Tess.

"What did you mean when you said that what you think you want is not always what you want?" Tess asked.

Her mother closed her eyes. Tess wasn't sure if the painkillers were making her drift back into her fog or if the conversation had worn her out.

"Mother," Tess said.

"To be open to possibilities," her mother said. "To not always take the route you think is the one you should be traveling on. Your life can be so many things, Tess," she said. "If you are open, it can be so many things," and with that, she was resting.

It was then, sleeping in her mother's bed at night in the house in Woodstock, that Tess began to examine the crevices of herself that she tended to stay away from when her life was in autopilot. Tess began to realize that she had never let her mother inside, had never shared her fears or her dreams with her mother, and maybe that was because Tess had not yet connected with what her fears or her dreams were. It made Tess still and quiet and desperate that there was a chance that her mother was never going to get to know her. Tess began to realize that if you didn't speak up, if you didn't find a way to communicate first with yourself and then with the people you loved, there may not always be the chance to speak up. But what frightened Tess most of all wasn't about anyone else getting to know her – it was the possibility of her never getting to know herself. Each night in her mother's bed, feeling smaller than she ever remembered feeling, she cradled herself in a ball and prayed with an intensity that she had never experienced. She felt her prayers in every ounce of her being before she released them into the void surrounding her, depleting her as much as the new-found space made her feel strangely whole and complete.

The call that her mother had passed came at dawn on her fourth day at the home. The ringing phone had startled Tess. Snakes, she had dreamt of being suspended in a muddy river and snakes trying to get at her, poised to bite her, lurking in every direction as she tried to escape from them. "She passed in her sleep. Sometime in the last hour," the nurse had said. "It seems to be from natural causes. Please come right away." Tess got out of bed and when she hung up the phone, she squatted, closing her eyes, as if seeking shelter from a brutal wind. The gravity of it all pulled her to the earth. Shocks of nausea vibrated her being so that she felt as if she were on the verge of vomiting and stifled back deep belly coughs. Here it was. The day she had dreaded more than any day of her life without her realizing it. Her mother was gone. She felt anchored to the ground while at the same time she felt as if she were weightless, incapable of keeping herself upright.

At the assisted living home, there was a thick, static quality to the air that made Tess gasp when she walked into her mother's room. It looked to her as if her mother was sleeping soundly and yet to the touch, her hand was already beginning to grow cold. She looked peaceful enough – her face calm, serene, her body neat and compact as she lay there, the sheets tucked nicely up by her chest. Tess clasped her cold, lifeless hand in her own and it hit her. She brushed her mother's hand against her face and kissed it once and again, before she knelt beside the bed and with her eyes closed, her mother's hand on her face, she prayed. For her mother to have a safe journey, for her mother to have a joyful ever after, for her to know peace, to love, and to know that she was loved.

She wished she could bring her back, that she could have her mother for only another moment, or hour or week. The tears were free flowing, and Tess felt herself growing weaker, tired, suddenly so tired, exhaustion overcoming her. She rested her upper body on the bed, close to her mother. It was so peaceful there, being close to her. "I'm sorry for your loss," the nurse who walked into the room said, and Tess pulled herself up. "I'll give you some time," and Tess nodded as she walked out. The white board on the wall across from her bed read May 6th. An early May Day. A spring day full of so much hope. The last day of her mother's life. *Sorry for your loss*. The words resonated deep within her.

There wasn't anger or sorrow so much as a feeling of incredible emptiness and then came a feeling of coldness at being so alone in the world, of being separated from her mother in such a complete, permanent way. Tess didn't want to leave her. Her logical mind told her that what she was clinging to was just her mother's shell. That her mother's soul had already moved on to some new realm. Her mother's soul may be right there with her as she swooned beside her. She smiled; she could hear her mother saying, "Why do you weep and cry? I'm right here with you."

A different nurse popped her head into the room: "A few more minutes and then we need to move her."

Tess nodded. The life had gone out of her mother, passed through her and away. Her mother was no longer with her in the flesh. It didn't seem possible to Tess. It was time for her to go. They needed to move her mother. She bent to kiss her forehead and then her hand and her cheek and then she nodded to the nurse who had walked back into the room and said, "thank you," in a meek voice and she was moving down the hallway, out of the building, into the parking lot and she was looking for her car, where did she park that car of hers, and she thought of Michael's comment that it was a funeral car and suddenly she hated the car, hated death and everything associated with it, and then she spotted the car and plopped into the driver's seat and sat there, with her head pressed to the steering wheel, locked in, trying to remember where she lived, how to get there, what was next.

The days following passed with Tess in a daze. She felt as if her heart had shut off, like a valve on a summer home in the winter. There were the funeral arrangements to make, friends and family to call. There were the conversations with Prakash, calls to Michael, telling him that she was fine, that he needn't make the trip up there. As selfish as it may have been, the thought of being around others just then made her feel rushed. She wanted to be alone in the house if only for a bit longer. It was the first time in her life that she had been alone in the house without the prospect of her mother coming home.

The silence and spaciousness of the empty house made her feel eerie and free at the same time. She felt connected to her mother being there in the silence. She walked the upstairs halls, her bare feet grazing the cool hardwood floors, and studied the mahogany wood-framed pictures which adorned the walls – pictures of her mother with her friends, various spiritual leaders whose names escaped Tess. Tess as a teenager, and then a young woman and then a mother, Tess and Prakash. She tried to imagine what it was her mother had felt or thought as she walked through those halls, living alone in the house all those years. There was a level of compassion and acceptance and love, true love, that Tess felt for her mother in those days of solitude.

Resting on her mother's bed, she read the pamphlets on *Four Noble Truths* and *The Noble Eightfold Path* that her mother had formulated and stacked in a wooden trunk in the larger of the two meditation rooms, near the stacks of sitting cushions. The pamphlets had been for the people who used to come to the morning meditations to see what they were all about prior to their becoming regulars at the house –

practicing Buddhists. Tess remembered when her mother had typed up the pages, reading them aloud as she did, and then brought them into town and run off copies of them at the library, stapling each one and how a week or so later one of her followers had volunteered to have them bound with a cover into pamphlets. Tess remembered keeping both pamphlets by her bedside table for a time, tracing the glossy photo of Prajnaparamita, the Mother of all Buddha's, and Yeshe Tsogyal, the Mother of Tibetan Buddhism, alternating reading them before she went to bed, believing that some of the concepts may seep in and make sense to her by the morning, but they never did.

1) *Life means suffering.* Tess agreed with the first of the *Four Noble Truths.* She had suffered over the years, although she was the first to admit that much of her suffering had been self-induced.

2) *The origin of suffering is attachment.* Craving and clinging. It was this concept that had frightened her first as a young child and then angered her as a teenager. She had felt scared not to be attached to her mother – who then would she be attached to? She had wanted her mother to cling to her as the other mothers clung to their daughters – to worry where she was going, what she was doing and with whom, what she ate. She hated the freedom her mother imposed on her. The constant discussions in which her mother would tell her that nothing was permanent. It had made Tess paranoid: each night she would go outside to make sure the sky was still there and the stars and each day on her way home from school she would pray that her house would still be there, that her mother would still be there. Her father had proven his impermanence. Tess had been guilty of craving and clinging for as long as she could remember, whether it had been another person, her independence,

herself. She had clung to the version of reality that she believed was the right one. In retrospect, it had always been attachment that had caused Tess to suffer.

3) *The cessation of suffering is attainable.* It was through nirodha, or the unmaking of sensual craving and conceptual attachment, that one could end one's suffering. One needed to use a fire extinguisher on clinging and attachment. That's how her mother had explained this noble truth. Tess hadn't wanted to cut out her attachments.

4) *The path to the cessation of suffering.* This path could extend over many lifetimes, through many rebirths. It was only as one made progress on the path that delusions and ignorance and cravings would disappear. Tess used to imagine herself suffering for years on end and then dying and coming back to life and suffering some more. What she wondered, was the point of life if it was full of so much suffering?

She closed her eyes and fell back onto the pillow propped up behind her. Right now, she was clinging to her mother's memory, this house, her solitude, and craving her mother's company.

She moved on to *The Noble Eightfold Path*, which was a "practical guide," per the introductory paragraph, on how to end suffering in relation to one's ethical and mental development. The goal of putting The Noble Eightfold Path into practice was to become free from attachments and delusions. It was to "lead one to understanding the truth about all things." Tess skimmed the list:

Right View

Right Intention

Right Speech

Right Action

Right Livelihood

Right Effort

Right Mindfulness

Right Concentration

If it were a true or false test, Tess would fail. Although she would give herself a true for Right Livelihood – she did earn her money in a legal and peaceful way. She was losing her concentration with the pamphlet, which would count as unwholesome thoughts or wrong concentration. She moved onto the books she had found in a wicker basket under her mother's bed. *Open Heart, Clear Mind* by Thubten Chodron, *Be Here Now* by Ram Das, *Food for the Heart: The Collected Writings of Ajahn Chah*, *The Art of Happiness: A Handbook for Living* by Dalai Lama. A typed note fell out of her mother's well-highlighted copy of Jack Kornfeld's *A Path With Heart.*

A guru's job is to help you to know yourself. Nothing more or less. No other human being is going to be able to change your life, but a guru can help you to change your life just by being in your life. And there's never just one guru, but a chain of gurus who keep imparting their wisdom until it reaches you. So be respectful of the lineage of gurus. Your teacher is by no means the end all, be all of gurus. Rather, he or she is part of a lineage of gurus.

The thing about gurus is that the turn up in life when you least expect them. When you seek them actively, when you force that bond, it won't work. Whenever you seek a person thinking that he or she is going to have the answers to your life, it leads to disappointment. However, when your life is on track and you're feeling good and finding your way as best you can, that's when you tend to encounter a guru. And gurus come to us in the least expected ways – a guru can be a friend you meet who has gone through a life experience that you're first embarking on; a guru can be your mailman or your yoga teacher, or your neighbor or High School English teacher. Gurus don't have any special uniforms. It's the knowledge that they can impart to us, and their own life experiences. Gurus are humble and patient, but they're tough on us, too. They may not always tell us what we want to hear, but if they didn't challenge us, chances are that we wouldn't grow.

The word guru *means from darkness to light – if you take away anything from our talk today, I hope you will remember that you are the only person who can bring yourself from darkness to light. External forces can help you to find your way, but in the end, you are the only one who take to your path and make it your own. In* Dante's Inferno, *it's Beatrice who leads the way, but it's Virgil who makes his way from the darkness of the nine circles of hell into the light. Chances are that you've all met gurus in your life, and possibly that you've been a guru; chances are that you will keep coming upon gurus as is necessary in your life. The best gurus are the ones who refrain from preaching and live their lives in a quiet way that enables others to learn from them by watching them live. Of course, there's the famous guru-student relationship in* The Bhagavad-Gita *in which Arjuna learns from Krishna; remember though that it takes Arjuna time to learn and accept the lessons that Krishna teaches him. Often what our guru advises is not what we want to hear, but that's because when we first ask for help, we are not ready to listen.*

That's where it ended. Tess remembered her mother giving lectures. She had always thought that her mother just spoke. She never would have known that her mother scripted anything. Tess wondered if she had been at this lecture or if it had been one that she skipped out on by hiding in her closet. She felt cheated that she had missed out on so much that her mother had to offer because of her own obstinacy. But she had been too young, and she had repelled her mother and her ways because she had been trying to find her own way, learn who she was, she supposed. She hadn't wanted to be the different kid on the block, the weirdo as the other children called her. When her mother sensed Tess's anger and rejection to Buddhism, she would tell Tess that it was okay, that it would make sense to her one day and that had made Tess even angrier. She didn't care about Buddhism, didn't care about dharma and karma and being a bodhisattva. Awakening and spirituality and enlightenment was silliness to Tess. She didn't want to hear about *The Four Noble Truths* and the *Eightfold Path*. To her it was just words about giving up everything she cared about and trying to be perfect by thinking, saying, doing the right things. She wanted to be Tess, whoever that was. She didn't want to be part of the cult – she ran away from it all at any chance she could, opposed it, and her mother's friends had treated her with compassion, meditating for her that she would find her way, awaken. All the talk of awakening made her want to sleep, escape from her life. She had wanted a father like the other children. She didn't care about her mother's need to be free; she had felt like a prisoner. She didn't want to wake up each day to people meditating in her living room and practicing yoga. She had wanted to eat hamburgers and French fries; wheat grass and grains made her want to vomit. She didn't understand why she had to be a vegetarian.

"Mom? Please come to me, Mom. Please let me know you are with me," Tess said as she moved through the empty house. She had always imagined that when her mother passed, she would feel her presence. The absence of her mother's presence made her feel desperate. Would her mother ever come to her? If only she could feel her presence, know that she was okay, safe, then Tess believed she would feel peaceful.

Each day the finality of death, the irrevocable nature of it, hit Tess anew. She was afraid of time passing, as it moved her mother farther away from her. Thoughts of December – cold, dark days – unnerved her. She moved through the house, her footsteps on the wooden floor startling to her in the silence as she made her way into the living room and paused by the large bay windows overlooking the backyard. Outside, the trees swayed in the breeze and Tess plastered her nose against the cool window glass. The endless rows of flowers her mother had planted had already begun to bloom. There were yellow flowers and bright pink flowers, and a patch of what Tess knew to be fresh lavender. She longed to be outside, smelling the fresh, sweet lavender and yet it seemed too far to go. Along the east side of the low wooden fence, there were rows of tulips, some beginning to bloom, others not there. She wished that she had asked her mother the names of all the flowers that she had planted if only so that she could replicate her garden one day. How had she never gotten to that?

Landing in her old bedroom, now a guest room, she tossed herself belly first onto the day bed. The mattress was hard and stiff. She remembered spring evenings nestled on her pillow-top mattress, which had been on the floor back then, candles scattered about her. Long after everyone had left for the night, she had heard the weeping willow trees outside her window shooing back and forth to the gentle night breeze. She saw the beaded curtains that she had strung that separated her walk-in closet from the rest of the room. She had spent so many afternoons camped out in her closet, in this room, candles lit all around her, illuminating the darkness, casting shadows against the wall that transformed into her secret friends, glowing and growing and dancing so that watching them, she would feel what she imagined to be her soul – a wild, lithe creature within her, confined by her flesh – merge with their movements and then she would be up, moving with them, dancing in the darkness like a girl in a trance.

Here and now, it seemed such a simple thing: to have silence in her life, and yet experience had taught Tess that it was one of the most difficult things to achieve. When she had given birth to Prakash, she had given up hours of sleep-in order to have time alone. In those spaces void of sound, she had scripted possible routes for her life. Later, when she grew bored with her own self-imposed dramas, she began speaking to God. Not a God of religion, but a higher force that dwelled within her. Growing up Buddhist, she had only known idols. She had never been able to relate to them. She didn't understand the point of praying to things that were plastic and rested on a table in her living room. To her, they were no different than dolls, except for the fact that she was not allowed to play with them. Once, when she was no more than ten-years old, she had knocked over a mahogany-wood Buddha that had been on a table in

205

the living room. She had folded into herself on the floor, covering her head with her hands, closing her eyes, and prayed to be saved in her next life; she had hoped that harming the idol wouldn't send her too far back in her karma. Moments later, she had opened her eyes to see that nothing in the room had changed. She was still there, the idol still on the floor. She could pick herself up while the idol that she was asked to bow down to could not. Day after day, Tess would stop in the living room before she left for school and wait for the Buddha to say something to her, reprimand her, wink, even nod. Nothing. It was wood through and through.

Although Tess's mother had stopped trying to convert her, by the time she reached high school, she had continued to plant seeds in Tess. Through each of Tess's marriages, her mother had reminded Tess that truly letting someone into your life meant that they moved into your mind and heart and vice versa – there was no divorce from such a connection if it was deep rooted. Her mother didn't understand connections of any other nature. Tess believed that she had experienced deep connections with each of the men she married; it was just that people changed, they grew apart, and sometimes it was a good thing. Her mother preached to her that true connections stopped being about what two people thought or felt in their daily earthly life and took on a deeper life in the couples' souls – a selfless connection that made being together an experience and a shared energy.

Tess's eyes began to close, exhaustion overcoming her, until her mother's comment resurfaced: *what you think you want is not always what you want.* What did Tess want? Did she even know what she wanted? She wanted to live simply. Complication free. Whatever that meant. Or maybe that wasn't what she wanted because she thought she wanted that. Maybe it wasn't about knowing what she wanted or didn't want, but about being open. About following her instinct instead of having a plan mapped out. Maybe that was it. To go with the flow a bit more. Her eyes were growing heavier. Her mind was tired. Sleep began to take over, and she began to lose words, thoughts, and to surrender.

CHAPTER 16: COINCIDENCES ARE GOD'S WAY OF REMAINING ANONYMOUS

The morning that Michael and Prakash were to arrive – two days since her mother had died, although to her, it felt like months – Tess remained in her old bedroom, wrapped up in her mother's thick, ivory Afghan throw blanket. She remembered when her mother had made that blanket. It had taken her over a year; Tess couldn't have been more than 13-years old at the time. Now, she sat on the twin day bed, inhaling what was left of her mother's lavender and sandalwood scent. The trees outside danced their yes/no dance and she smiled; that window had been her looking glass as a child, the trees her private consultants. And the chimes that hung on the overhang of the window – replaced with new chimes over the years – to Tess, their song was the hum of magic. It had been so long since she'd been lulled by the music of the chimes.

There had been nights when she was growing up that listening to the chime's melody, she had tried to connect the dots of her mother's family tree, tried to imagine her mother's life when she was a young girl in Thailand. Her mother's parents had passed while her mother was a young girl and in turn, relatives had raised her. Reaching over to the night table beside the day bed, Tess traced the cool, smooth elbow and breasts of the intricate wood Thai statue of the half girl, half creature that her mother had given Tess when she was a young girl. It was one of the few childhood objects that her mother had brought with her from Thailand. Tess's parents had settled in Woodstock due to business opportunities – Tess remembered hearing once that her father had been responsible for building many of the houses in the area, but Tess had never bothered to ask her mother which ones, although she knew that the very house, she was in had been built long before they arrived, in 1924, as there was an inscription plaque built into the bricks by the front door. She supposed that if she did some research at the library, she could find out which homes her father had been involved in building. She was curious to see if they were houses she would have an interest in selling – she wondered if they would have a connection in that way. Her mother had asked her father to leave. In her mother's words, he had tried Buddhism on, and when he didn't find the fit comfortable, he had tried to undo her way of living. Eventually, her father had moved away from Woodstock and gone back to his family in the Midwest. Tess couldn't remember if it was Ohio or Indiana at this point. Whenever she had asked about him during her childhood, her mother had told her that her time was better spent on learning about who Tess was than trying to know a man who was absent. "We fool ourselves into believing we can actually know others, but we're lucky if we even glimpse who and what we are about," her mother had said. Still, Tess had often felt un-rooted and believed that if she knew her father, she would somehow be more grounded in the universe. That, and the fact that she often felt eerie traveling through life and not knowing if she was related to the person who sat beside her. And now it was too late for her to ever know the details of her father. That was how life worked: you went along believing that there would be time down the road until life taught you otherwise.

Suki. That's what her mother had told her was the name of the

statue. Suki, which meant *beloved.* So many nights before Tess had
drifted to sleep, she had studied Suki with her elaborately detailed hat
and scales and her feathered tail. She had closed her eyes and tried to
imagine what it would sound like if Suki played the guitar that she held
in her hands, tried to imagine what it would feel like if Suki feathered
Tess with her tail. Tess had imagined Suki coming to life and sharing
details of her mother's childhood with her – things that her mother would
never have shared with Tess about herself. But night after night, Suki
struck her wavy pose, mute and lifeless.

Tess picked Suki up carefully; her old energy was still there. As
a child, Tess had imagined that there was something or someone living
inside of Suki and that if she cracked her open, the presence, like a genie,
would emerge from Suki and grant Tess wishes. Tess had never cracked
her open, though. No matter how many times she had wanted to
disappear, vanish from her life, she had decided not to waste her wishes
and instead wait for a time when nothing less than a genie's help would
suffice. Now, 50 years later, Tess wondered if she would ever meet her
genie face to face.

The sun was beginning to make its way through the darkness.
Her time alone in the house was running out. Tess couldn't say why she
felt rushed, but she did, as if there was some secret the house had yet to
tell her that she wouldn't be able to hear once visitors arrived. Tea. She
needed to go out and buy tea and milk and she supposed some food for
her guests. Tess inched open the window. The air, cool and damp,
filtered in and she shivered. There was a hint of summer in the air, a
lightness that the birds embellished with their inquisitive melodies.

Outside, the air lashed so that Tess wrapped her mother's orange gauze scarf tighter around her neck. It felt nice to be moving after being cooped up in the house for the past few days. In the distance the mountains rose as if they were breaking through the sky. The foliage was almost in full spring bloom and the fragrant honeysuckled air made Tess feel lighter. Although she had been in Woodstock for well over a week now, this was the first day that she was able to notice her surroundings, take them in. It was so easy for days to pass unnoticed when you were caught up in the drama of your life. A peace was coming over Tess as she moved outside of herself. She inhaled again, grateful to feel herself transcending the fog she had resided in and becoming a part of life again.

Tess had envisioned herself a city girl through her adolescence, although she had no significant experiences with the city until she went off to college in New York. It was just that in her mind, the city with its diversity and fast-pace and money-oriented mentality, seemed to contradict Woodstock, and Tess had believed that her views and thoughts were contrary to everything that Woodstock exemplified. Only now, she wasn't sure that the breeziness of Woodstock, the quietness, the innate beauty of its peaks and valleys and open fields weren't what she had always sought in the rush of her life in New York. There was a serenity to Woodstock, a rhythm that enabled her to breathe and be.

Tess had felt someone pass her by, but she didn't look up until she heard him coming back toward her. "Excuse me," the man said.

He registered the moment she glimpsed his deep-set black eyes and dark, wavy hair that he brushed off his face with a flick of his hand. His hair was shorter now, more manageable than the locks that had grown down his back when they were teenagers. Tess brushed the tendrils that hung by her face behind her ear, made sure her low ponytail was still in place. She hadn't thought of her own long hair for ages; all through growing up, she had let it grow long and free until it nearly touched her butt. Her unruly red curls had been her safety net, something to hind behind. The first time she cut her hair to her shoulders, during her MBA program, she had felt as if she had been stripped naked. Somehow, along the way of becoming a businessperson, she had been duped into believing that long hair wasn't professional, and if she wanted to succeed in the business world, she needed to play by the rules.

"Tess Rose."

"Luke," she said, and had to stop herself from saying Skywalker; that's what she and the other children had called him.

"It's been a long time," he said. He reached out to embrace her, but she met him halfway a minute too late, so that they offered one another more of a pat on the shoulder.

"I heard about your mother. I'm sorry," he said. "Really sorry."

"Yes," she said.

They stood nodding, silent for a moment.

"It's good to see you back up here, Tess."

"Have you ever left?" she said.

Luke laughed. "Yes, I found life outside of Woodstock," he said.

"I didn't mean –." Tess paused.

"I've moved around a bit, east coast, west, but somehow I

always end up back here. I've yet to find a community quite like this one," he said.

"It's nice to be here; of course, I wish the circumstances were different."

"Your mother would say 'It's all exactly as it should be.'"

Tess smiled, her eyes falling. Her mother would not say anything anymore. That was still more of an idea to her than a reality.

"You look wonderful," Luke said.

She observed her outfit: black track pants and a black zip up sweat jacket with her mother's bright orange scarf; she imagined that she looked like a Halloween cat. She couldn't remember how many days in a row she'd been wearing this outfit and it wasn't until she took inventory of it that she realized she didn't even have on a bra underneath her white t-shirt; things like showers and bras hadn't seemed to matter over the last few days.

"I'm afraid I'm a bit of a mess," Tess said.

"No. The years have been good to you."

She smiled. "The years have been long and hectic."

Luke laughed a soft, muted laugh that sound more like a grunt. There was something sexy about him with his dark eyes: they made him look mysterious and then there were the angles of his cheekbones and chin. Everything about him was masculine, from his throaty voice to his penetrating eyes. Tess couldn't remember how many years younger than her he was – two or three she supposed. He'd been one of her mother's groupies along with the rest of Woodstock, so while she liked him well enough as a child and teenager, she hadn't ever shared any of her thoughts or aspirations with him. Nevertheless, most folks in Woodstock felt that they knew Tess by association with her mother. Of course, there were those who had considered her rebellious and difficult.

Tess didn't know how long they had been locked in a mutual stare, but she didn't feel any awkwardness.

"I should get going. I was on my way to pick up some supplies – my son and friend are coming today to help me put my mother to rest."

"Will there be a funeral? Luke asked.

"She wanted to be cremated so I suppose we'll have a quiet ceremony beforehand. I haven't made preparations just yet," she said, wondering what she had been doing since her mother passed other than lying around the house. She didn't recognize herself as the sort of person to get lost in grief.

"Well, keep us posted. There are a lot of folks in town who will want to pay their last respects to your mother."

"Sure." Tess couldn't imagine having to entertain anyone, although she understood that she'd have to offer some way for the town to say their farewells to her mother. She'd let Michael and Prakash help her to figure that out and have it posted in the local paper.

"It was great seeing you, Tess," Luke said, and this time he was leaning in to embrace her without her fumbling.

She was trying to remember if she had ever kissed him romantically. It was vaguely coming back to her that she had; only she couldn't place the details.

"Nice seeing you, Luke," she said, and then he released her and was on his way.

As he walked away, she realized that she hadn't asked him about his family – how his mother or father were doing. They had been good friends with her mother, as far as she remembered. She didn't even know if he was married and had a family of his own. The church bells rang in the hour. Tess realized that she had heard those same church bells all through growing up and thought of St. Bernard's in Mill Basin. Neal vaguely passed through her mind and then drifted away, like a wish flower. The bells rang over and over. Was it 8:00 am? 9:00 am? She didn't even know where her watch was and then it dawned on her that she hadn't even taken her cell phone with her when she set out for the grocery store. How easy it was for your life to transform once you checked out for a bit.

Just as she climbed the wooden porch and was about to enter Moe's Country Market, the flyer came undone from the bulletin board by the entrance and flew onto her leg so that she had to bend to pick it up unless she was going to wear it.

If you've dreamed of leaving your hectic fast-paced desk job behind, discover the joys of being a yoga teacher. Our 500-hour yoga teacher-training program will teach you all you need to know to be a first-class yoga teacher. Over the course of 8

months, you'll explore <u>Sanskrit, Anatomy, Asana, Pranayama,</u>
<u>Sequencing, Meditation and Spotting Techniques.</u>

The time to become a yoga teacher is now!

Spaces are limited!

Please call today for an application for our exclusive teacher-
training program starting on May 15th in our spacious New York
City studio.

Yoga Zone, NYC @ 1-800-IDO-YOGA

How odd. What in the world would a flyer advertising the yoga teacher-
training program at the studio she went to in New York City be doing on
a bulletin board over two and a half hours away from New York? Tess
thought of Dale – the night the two of them had laughed about the
prospect of joining the yoga teacher-training program at the studio. That
seemed like years ago, but it couldn't have been longer than two weeks
back.

She wished that she could call Dale, share the coincidence with
her, only she didn't know how to reach her, which made her think of
Kyle. She wondered what had happened with the brownstone – if he had
given up on it since Tess had disappeared or if he had followed up with
her agents who were covering for her. *What you think you want is not
always what you want.* Her mother's words were there with her, in the
forefront of her mind. Maybe there was more to her life. *The time to
become a yoga teacher is now!* She folded the flyer in two. She didn't
know at this moment what she wanted, what she didn't want. Her life in

Brooklyn seemed so far away while she was here in Woodstock and thinking of returning, of all the responsibilities that awaited her, a sense of dread filtered through her so that she swallowed hard, nausea overcoming her. She sat down on the bench beside her. Maybe she had it all wrong. Her life. The way she was living. Where had any of it gotten her? And now her mother was gone. In a flash, it was all over. A yoga teacher. The concept of it seemed ridiculous to Tess. She was too old. It was the opposite of all that she had aspired to. And yet, here, now, the idea of delving into something like a yoga-training program appealed to Tess – serenity, peace, a group, a place to go, something to dive into that helped her, calmed her. Something that perhaps would lead her to know her mother more. A link between them. A yoga teacher.

She did the math: her mother had died on May 6th, which was two days ago, which meant that it was May 8th; there was still a week to join the program, assuming there was room. She vaguely remembered something about the program being sold out. Clearly, she was losing it. She exhaled and stood up. She had family on their way to think about, a memorial service to plan, her mother's house to clean out and close up, a job to get back to. A young girl in a tie-dyed poncho making her way out of Moe's Country Market held the door for Tess. She folded the flyer neatly into squares and stuffed it into her sweatshirt pocket. She muttered thank you and passed through the open door.

CHAPTER 17: A DIFFERENT CLIMATE

Tess was unpacking the items purchased on her shopping expedition – organic apples, organic bananas, morning-glory breakfast muffins – when there was a knock on the kitchen window, and she jumped so that the oranges she was holding fell to the floor. Michael peered in at her and motioned for her to open the front door.

"Don't look so glad to see me," he said standing across from Tess in the doorway.

"Actually, I am glad to see you."

"Perhaps you should invite me in? I was knocking for a good five minutes before I ambushed you in the kitchen."

"Sorry, when you're in the back of the house you can't hear anything out front," she said, stepping aside and brushing her tendrils behind her ear. She had planned to shower, but somehow time had gotten away from her again. She felt her face; her eyelids were puffy from crying.

"Gosh, do you know it's been years since I've seen you outside of the city. You look like a bumpkin out here."

"We're still in New York if I remember correctly, so *bumpkin* would hardly be the right terminology."

"Oh, sorry. Upstate New York folks can't be considered bumpkins. I'll have to refer to my almanac next time to see what towns I can associate bumpkins with."

"Do you practice being sweet, or does it just come naturally to you?"

"My girl hasn't lost her edge," he said pulling her to him and squeezing her.

"Ohhh."

"Was that a sigh or a moan?"

"I'm tired. Am I allowed to be tired?" she said, pulling away.

"Slumping around for days and tired? What's becoming of you, Tessy? By 10 am you're usually on fire."

"It's 10:00? Kash will be here soon. I didn't even have time to straighten up yet and I still haven't showered."

"Somehow I don't think that your son will be judging you for how clean you kept the house. Do you need me to pick him up at the airport – wait, is there an airport near here?"

"He's flying into Poughkeepsie and renting a car – it's about a 45-minute drive."

In a moment, Tess was moving around the kitchen, putting away dishes and cleaning off the counters.

"How are you holding up?" Michael said.

"That sounds so dramatic. *Holding up.*"

"Are you ever able to have a conversation without going into attack mode?"

"I'm *holding up* just fine, thank you. Everything is rosy as a matter of fact."

"Sit down. Tell me what I can do to help."

"I have a lot to do, Michael. I appreciate the charity, but the best thing you can do is keep out of my way."

"Didn't you just tell me a few minutes ago that you were glad to see me? I know you're stressed, Tess. Your mother just passed. Let me help you. "

"Can you just shut up?" she said. "Please just shut up."

Tess braced her hands on the kitchen counter and stretched her arms out, leaning her forehead on the granite top. She closed her eyes; the coolness on her forehead soothed her. She wasn't ready to deal with anyone in her space.

"Kitchen yoga?" he asked, beside her now.

Tess straightened and punched him in the chest. "Asshole," she screamed. "You're an asshole."

"Owe," he said, gasping as he bent over to catch his breath. "Slugger, calm down."

"You can never just stop. I asked you to shut up. I just need some quiet," she said and then she was crying, loud sobs coming out of her. "Please, I just want some quiet," she said. The feel of her mother's cold hands filtered through her. *I'm sorry for your loss.*

Gently, he pulled her away from the counter, and took her in his arms.

"You're such a jerk," she said, letting go, allowing him to hold her. "Do you know that?"

"You always remind me," he said.

"I'm so tired," she said in his ear. "I am just so tired. I can't believe she's not coming back."

"A lot has happened."

"I'm sad, Michael."

"I know," he said.

"It happened so fast. She was doing fine and then just like that, she's gone." She sighed, her breath wavering as she wiped her eyes. "I feel unanchored. Like I'm drifting out at sea," and in that moment, she thought of Neal and the walks by the water and the slippery image of herself in the ripples of Jamaica Bay. That had only been a few days ago. It was strange how much could transpire in so short a time; one day you were walking around Mill Basin with a monk on a leave of absence, fighting your desire to kiss him, and the next day you were wandering the halls of your deceased mother's house, and fearing the time when you'd have to dismantle the serenity and silence of that house, pack it all up and leave. Tess laughed so that Michael let up on his grip.

"You're scaring me with your mood swings. What's so funny?"

"What's so funny is that I'm clearly a mess and I haven't showered in a few days, and I don't even care, and I was just thinking about how much I like this house. It's such a beautiful house. I feel safe here the last few days."

"Don't tell me you're moving to Woodstock now?"

"Oh, who knows what's going to happen," Tess said. She pulled away from him. "I guess I should get in the shower. You'll put everything away for me?"

Michael bowed. "At your service."

This was the strange thing about having a grown child: when Tess sat across from Prakash, sharing a cup of tea with him, staring into his chocolate eyes, she couldn't believe that at one time he had been a baby, then a toddler, then a teenager. He seemed so grown up, so much of his own person that Tess couldn't imagine him anyone other than who he was here, now, today. He was more self-assured than she had been at his age but then again, she knew that the heart and soul you bared to the world wasn't always a reflection of who or what you were on the inside during the hours you were all alone.

"Mom."

"What's that, Kash?"

"You realize that you keep drifting off," Prakash said.

"Do I?"

Prakash nodded.

"Are you tired? You must be tired with flying and then driving here," she said.

"I'm fine, but you seem like you may need a nap."

"I've slept more in the past few days than I've probably slept in the past few months," Tess said.

"I forgot how nice it is to be out of the city," Prakash said.

"It is nice," Tess said.

"You seem good Mom. Better than I expected you to be. You're calm. I don't remember the last time I saw you sit still for more than a few minutes."

"I miss her, Kash," she said, reaching across the table to take his hands in her own.

"I miss her, too."

"I only had a few hours with her and then it was all over. I'm afraid that when I leave this house nothing will ever be the same," Tess said.

"It won't ever be the same," he said.

"Being up here has been really peaceful for me. This house, this town. Suddenly it doesn't seem like the worst place in the world to me," Tess said.

"I always loved it up here," he said.

"You did. I couldn't wait to leave when I was a teenager and now, I'm having separation anxiety when I consider packing this place up and selling it."

Prakash pulled his hands away from her. "You can't sell this house," he said.

Tess raised her eyebrows. "Do you want to live in it?"

"I live and work in San Francisco so no, I can't live in it, but I don't want you to sell it. Our heritage is here in this house. You can't just let any old family live in this house," he said.

"I love to see your righteous side."

"This conversation isn't over, Mom."

"I'm getting us more tea," Tess said.

"Tell me you're not going to sell it."

"Prakash, who is going to take care of this house? Do you know how much upkeep it'll need? Someone would have to check in on it every two weeks or so year-round," Tess said.

"You have contacts, you can find someone to do that," he said.

"Well, I don't have to worry about that today, right? There's plenty to deal with the next few days; then I'll figure out the house,"

Tess said.

Tess scanned the audience from the podium that the park officials had placed on the makeshift stage. Each one of the hundred or so fold down chairs spread across the park grounds were occupied, and what she imagined to be at least a hundred more people were standing behind the chairs with dozens sitting on blankets in the grass in front of the chairs. She took a deep breath, smoothing the flowing white dress she had taken from her mother's closet; she had seen her mother wear this very dress to funerals she had presided over. She touched the microphone with her forefinger and the static prickled out all around her.

"Hello," she said, almost stumbling when she heard her voice resonate. She looked for the volume switch and turned it down a few notches. "Is this okay?" she said, her voice shaky, and people in the audience nodded and some called out that they could hear her. She took a deep breath and swallowed a sip of water. Another deep breath. This was her mother's funeral. Her *mother's* funeral. The gravity of it weighted her down. Her palms were sweaty and for a moment she felt as if she would faint.

"Thank you all for being here. My mother, as many of you know, was a special woman. It wasn't until I was an adult living on my own that I began to understand and appreciate my mother and all that she was about. My mother was never too busy to help anyone in need. She was a gentle, sensitive, and compassionate soul who made you feel as if you were never alone. Whether you were suffering or joyful, you always felt like she was right there with you. She didn't judge, and when her immense brown eyes set on you, you felt that she knew you, accepted you, and loved you, and that what you were sharing with her was the most important thing in her life at that moment. She listened. She cared.

"My mother believed that we were all in it together – the universal chain of being is what she called it. Shared energy. 'Smile so that I can smile,' she used to say to me as a child when I was sad, and I would smile because I loved to see her smile. She was joyful and she was not stingy with her joy – she liked when people laughed with her and was known to tell people that the key to a longer life was to let the joy in. She was always clear of her mission and regardless of what she faced in her own life, she never lost track of her mission – to help people find their way. She spoke of dharmas and the importance of finding one's path, but the future never preoccupied her. She lived in the moment and whenever I would wander into the future, asking her to help me to make decisions and to see ahead, she would bring me back. Remind me of right now. She told me that my life's work was to find today, the moment I was in, and that if I was living the moment, then the decisions I made would be inevitable. 'Reality is not the problem,' she often said. Reality, with its ups and downs, twists and turns, my mother believed, was perfect; our distorted minds were the problem, trying to tamper with reality.

"She believed that clinging and craving – attachment – led to ruin, both in ourselves and in the world at large. I suppose that if she were here now, she would scold me for clinging to her, for missing her, for being attached to what she would call her human form. She was not afraid of death – she believed in the great connectivity of life and often said that although flesh may disintegrate, the soul lived forever, passing from one form to another. She taught me to honor the ants and the crickets and the birds of the air just the same as any other human being. 'They too are passing through,' she would say. She taught me to laugh at myself when all I wanted to do was cry and when the next phase of my life loomed hazy, she instructed me to let go – of my fears, my dreams – to just have faith. She believed that the solution was always to breath, and that the only way to get through the tough times was to live each moment to the fullest.

"My mother was a friend, a trusted advisor, and as a result, she was always surrounded with love and friendship. She didn't preach, but rather lived her life in an honest and straightforward way that inspired those around her. She faced health hurdles the last few years of her life, but she never became a victim. She continued each day, always grateful for the gift of waking up, having a new day in front of her. 'There are endless possibilities when one is awake in their life,' she often said.

"In the days leading up to her death, in a lucid moment, she told me 'What you think you want is not always what you want.' A reminder to me to be open in my life – to accept what comes in my path instead of always searching and pushing ahead. I wanted her to live forever in the flesh. I knew that wasn't possible, but I wanted it, nonetheless. I can hear her gentle voice telling me not to cling, to let go, to accept, adapt. She often said, 'when someone impacts our lives, they become a part of our heart and soul, a part of our guiding force.' I pray that my mother lives on in all of us, guiding us always."

After the ceremony Tess didn't remember getting undressed, didn't remember washing her face or getting into her mother's bed, although when she woke up from her deep, intoxicating slumber, she was clear that the ceremony had passed, that some of her mother's cremated remains were scattered across the fields beyond the backyard of the house where she had often seen her mother from her bedroom window, walking, her white tunic and matching wide legged pants flowing in the breeze as if she were a ghost about to take flight. The rest of the remains were in an urn that Tess had placed on her night table. She wasn't sure yet if she was going to leave them here, in this house, or if she was going to take them with her back to Brooklyn so that she could have her mother close to her. Her mind couldn't get that far yet.

Tess remembered the speech she had given more as a dream: she was able to see herself in front of the group, feel her lips moving, hear her voice coming out of her, although she didn't know where the words came from or much of what she said. She remembered that when she was done speaking people had bowed their heads towards her, pressed their hands into prayer, and then Prakash was grasping her elbow, walking her to a seat on the field before he got up on the mock stage and spoke of his grandmother to the crowd.

Waking up to the new day, the cool, crisp air seeping in through the slightly opened window, Tess sat up in bed slowly, inching her way up, as if she were nursing a hangover. She felt utterly disconnected, as if she were in a bubble, unable to communicate or connect with any other living thing, and with this feeling of desperation, came pangs of loneliness, like waves, which washed over her. This was what the feeling taught her: that all the other times in her life that she had felt alone were merely trial runs that fell short of preparing her for this overwhelming moment of her life. Her instinct was to wail and moan, only when she opened her mouth, no sound would come. Hollow. She was hollow. She fluttered back down onto the pillow, only the thought of sleeping more filled her with a sense of dread – she didn't want to be anymore removed from the world than she already felt and as she was making her way up again, bracing her back against her mother's teak bed board to keep herself upright, what came to her was that this was grief. Feelings of helplessness and anger and fear and frustration rushed her, landing in her throat and chest, constricting her breathing so that for a moment she thought she would throw up then and there, until she focused on her breath and quieted her racing mind down, consoled herself by pulling her knees to her chest and hugging her arms around them until she was in a ball, her lips pressing into her knee cap. Her mother had died. Her life was over. This was how it worked: everyone was going to die. It amazed Tess that she had never fully believed this. But now her mother would no longer be there for Tess to call or visit or share any details of her life with. Tess began to rock herself back and forth, the finality of it overcoming her: her mother had died. Caroline Rose was dead. White Tara was no longer of this earth. Her mother was dead.

Tess opened her eyes, squinting as they registered the light. Just like that, not knowing how long she had slept, she felt free again, alive, connected. Her t-shirt was drenched, as if she had sweated out a fever. Prakash was by her bed, his hand on her shoulder, waking her gently.

"Good afternoon," he said.

"What time is it?" Tess said.

"You slept most of the day."

She sat up carefully; she still felt weak, fragile.

"Did I?" she said.

He sat down on the edge of the bed. "Rest," he said, stroking her forehead. Tess was paralyzed by the way he was looking at her and loving her. She couldn't remember ever before being in this situation with her son.

"What's that face?" Prakash said.

"I didn't want to sleep the day away," she said.

"It's okay to rest," he said. "There's nowhere you need to be."

"You're leaving today." Tess pushed herself back up. "I wanted to spend the day with you. Why didn't you wake me sooner?"

"There will be plenty more days for us to spend together, Mom. You needed to sleep."

Tess pulled his wrist to her. "It's 5:00 pm?" she said. "Oh my gosh. Where's Michael?"

"We spent the day carousing Woodstock."

Tess fell back onto the bed. "I'm sorry."

"For what? Needing to rest?"

"Do you need to leave now? Can you stay up here with me for a few more days?" Tess asked.

"I need to get back."

"I suppose I need to get back to my job one of these days, too, if I don't want to get fired," Tess said.

Prakash smiled, and Tess shifted, her mind coming into sharper focus. She leaned up against the bed board.

"Can I ask you something?" Tess said.

He nodded. He was such a handsome boy. Such a good boy. Her only child, her son.

"Have I failed you, Kash?"

"Mom, what are talking about?"

"If I die tomorrow, what do you wish you could have asked me? What do you wish you could have changed about me?"

"You are not going to die tomorrow, Mom."

"It happens so fast, Kash. Life is so fast. Tell me. Have I deserved your love?"

"You have my love. We will always be bound as mother and son."

"But was I good to you?"

He nodded. "Yes."

"But if you could change something?" she asked.

"Mom."

"Tell me, Kash. I can't read your mind."

"Mom, not now."

"Kash, please? Tell me. You're thinking something. Tell me."

"I guess…you did what you wanted," he said.

She took a deep breath and let it out shakily. "Is that bad?"

"No. Not bad. It made me be…responsible."

"I did what I wanted, and it made you responsible?" she asked. "I wanted you to follow your path."

"And I did," he said. "But sometimes I felt like I was on my own."

"Kash, we are all on our own, but that doesn't mean we aren't there for each other. That doesn't mean I wouldn't have dropped anything for you at any time."

He was silent, his eyes on the floor now as he moved his toes back and forth on the wood, as if he were polishing it.

"Do you think I was selfish?" she said.

"I don't think that you meant to be," he said.

Tess shook her head. Her mind was spinning.

"If I kept you from your father, it was because he wasn't good to us, Kash."

"It's not about my father, Mom."

"He wanted another life, Kash. One without us."

"I know this, Mom. I know. I had Brad, and he was great. For me, Brad will always be my dad. It's just all the other relationships. I don't know. I don't want to get into this now."

"Do you think my marriages were selfish?" she asked, but she knew the answer. They were selfish. She had done what she wanted, but she hadn't loved Kash any less because of it, she hadn't meant to leave him out. She hadn't meant to make him feel alone.

"I think we all do what we can and have to in life to survive," he said.

Tess was silent, her eyes on the movement of his toes.

"I can't change what was," she said. The hollow in her stomach was growing. "I can't undo my actions."

"No," he said. "I met some good men because of you." He laughed. "Brad, Michael."

"I'm sorry. I never meant to fail you."

"Mom, you started this conversation. You did not fail me. I wouldn't change any of it – all that we've gone through has made us who we are."

"Kash, marriage is not a trivial thing."

"I don't think it is."

"If my actions have made it seem that way, it's not. What I didn't know then that I know now is that I needed to get married to myself first, fall in love with me, first."

"And have you done that now?" he asked.

"I don't know." She shook her head. "No. I haven't done that yet."

They smiled at each other.

"No one could ever call you a simpleton," he said.

She laughed, deep and throaty. "Crazy, yes," she said.

"I have to go," he said. "Unfortunately, my plane will not wait for me."

She reached for his hand and squeezed it tight in her own.

"We are all always evolving and growing," Tess said.

"Amen," he said.

"I miss you already. Promise you'll call me when you land?" Tess asked.

"Promise," he said.

She hugged him sitting up on her knees in the bed and then in a moment, he was heading out the door, closing it behind him. Tess thought: the hardest thing about loving a person was the knowledge that one day they would leave you.

CHAPTER 18: RETURNING ALWAYS TAKES TOO LONG

Alone again, Tess had started to pack up her mother's things. She had always thought of her mother as someone who didn't have many possessions, but box after box, she realized otherwise. Statues and meditation books and relics from her devotees – stones and crystals and charms. The more she found in her mother's drawers, the more relieved she was that she had convinced Michael to leave soon after Prakash's departure. The thought of him being around to supervise made her cringe, as she was sure he would have had something to say about each item she packed away to the effect of I *can't believe you're not throwing that rock away*. She still wasn't certain what she was going to do with the boxes she was packing away. If she donated them to the folks around town, she had a hunch that they'd go up for sale at a town flea market or in one of the shops on Main Street. The idea of anything belonging to her mother being made available to the public for a price made her feel as if she were violating her mother.

She would send some of her mother's things to Prakash. Kash. She had replayed their parting conversation over dozens of times. Had she been a terrible mother? She couldn't change what was, so all that she could aspire to was to be better moving forward. A new and improved and more aware version of Tess.

There were many things she would take with her: crystals her mother wore around her neck on a thin red string and her very own angel statue. She smiled when she thought about placing that on her night table beside her bed in Brooklyn. Her bed. Home seemed far away. She could see the front of her house, the large rectangular windows looking out onto 66th street, the trees shadowing the sides of her garage, the cherry blossom alongside her kitchen window, the mist of Jamaica Bay rising across the way. Neal. Standing beside him at the water's edge. She couldn't imagine where he thought she had gone. His confession letter. She hoped he didn't think he had scared her away!

Perhaps, though, he didn't imagine at all. Perhaps he was just going about his daily life and hadn't noticed she was missing and one day in the future if they crossed paths again, he'd say, "Oh, hello, Tess," as if not even a day had passed since he had last seen her. But maybe he missed her just a little bit. She shook her head the moment she thought it. Hadn't she just been through this with Prakash? All her relationships. The last thing she needed was another man. She and Neal were friends. Besides, passion didn't seem possible for Tess. Right now, sleeping and waking and busy work was all she could muster.

Tucked away was what Michael had said –" How long do you plan to stay tucked away in Woodstock?" Her mother would have told her that life didn't stop, that it kept going, and while Tess knew that it felt good if only to pretend that life had in fact stopped for a bit. So much rushing about, for what? That's what Tess wondered now. For the first time in a long time, Tess wasn't sure where she was heading – what it was she sought. If she didn't know where she wanted to go, where was there to rush to? Her life felt uncomplicated now, which made her wonder what all the complications had been about in the first place. Had she ever known anything but self-imposed hurdles?

There was a freedom to wondering the halls of her mother's home that made Tess feel luxurious. Like she was a little girl who had control of the house for a few hours until her parents returned home. It still hadn't completely sunk in with her that no one was coming home. That was perhaps the most isolating factor of death: it was irreversible. Tess moved out onto her mother's bedroom balcony. The stars shone in the night sky, like little eyes twinkling down on Tess. She felt as if she were looking up into a stadium packed with faces she couldn't see. The night sky was so bright, so full of hope. She traced the arc of the quarter crescent moon, which hung like a comma. What came before, what came after, Tess didn't know. She laughed. For so much of her life, she had thought she knew the answers, thought she had it all figured out, until little by little all that she thought she knew came unraveled. She smiled. It was okay not to have the answers. For the first time in her life, it felt okay not to know what was next. She gripped the railing and lost her way in the great expanse overhead. There was something to being here, in this house, with that sky overhead. Life was a gift. Tess had always heard people murmur similar sentiments, but she had never felt truly grateful for life as she did right now. A chill rushed through Tess, and for a moment, she felt a presence pass by her, like a faint, gentle breeze, so that she turned all around. Nothing. She waved her hand in front of her, half expecting her mother's fingers to grasp hers from somewhere beyond. Tess wondered what it was she would want to say to her mother if she had a few more minutes with her. Words seemed trite. She supposed what would matter more to her mother was to see Tess live her truth, to witness the actions of her life rather than to hear her speak.

Tess nestled her hands into her zip-up sweatshirt and shrugged her shoulders up to her ears before she sighed, letting go, her shoulders sinking into her body. She pulled out a piece of paper in her pocket and unfolded it. The yoga teacher training flyer. The wind picked up so that Tess had to grip the flyer in both hands to keep it from flying away. Yoga teacher training. She had done crazier things in her life. The prospect of becoming a yoga teacher didn't compare to her decision to open her own business some thirty years back. It didn't compare to the insanity involved with her decision to marry Michael, let alone her crush on Neal, the monk. For one thing, joining a yoga teacher-training program would give her a reason to return home. It would certainly mark a new phase of her life. An experience she imagined that her mother would be proud of her for undertaking. It was an experience that perhaps would lead her to helping people find peace, serenity. She thought back to the crowds at her mother's memorial service. She had touched so many lives. Was it selfish of Tess to want to do the same? Was it wrong of Tess at this stage in her life to want to be like her mother? A voice in her said it was too late – she had already carved her path, while another voice said that it was never too late. She didn't want to go back to the way her life had been. Hectic. Chaotic. Tired. Stressed. Change was the way of the living. Why not become a yoga teacher? Why not try to help people, to make a difference, to venture out of her safe routine?

She looked up at the sky one last time and smiled up into it – she imagined herself moving from star to star, as if she were finding her way through a connect-the-dots puzzle. There were so many choices, so many directions to explore in a lifetime – Tess wasn't sure how you knew if you were moving in the right direction. That was the thing about life: there was no right or wrong, just living. It was easy to forget that, easy to fool herself into thinking that she had made wrong moves along the way. She had grown up being reminded daily by her mother that whatever she was doing was exactly what she needed to be doing at that moment in her life. She had grown up being told each day that everything was always perfect, including herself. Tess had nodded in compliance, silently rejecting those thoughts, all the while choosing to complicate her life by always wishing to be something or somewhere other than where she was. She had convinced herself that life was better wherever Tess wasn't. She had wished away so much of her early years by not living in the moment. For the first time ever, Tess felt that she was exactly where she needed to be – it was a delicious, freeing feeling. Tess sighed, deep and loud, as if something inside of her was escaping. Between that sky and the earth, she felt that there was nowhere else in the world she would rather be but in her own skin. A yoga teacher…why not?

She made her way back into the house, closing the balcony door behind her, and placed the reels of packing tape and labeling markers inside one of the boxes before she began pushing the half-packed boxes into her mother's bedroom closet. She pulled her suitcase out from her closet, and moved from her bedroom to her mother's bedroom, picking up some of her mother's books and the Four Noble Truths and Eightfold Path pamphlets to toss into her suitcase, then downstairs to the kitchen, gathering up more things. She couldn't remember at this point what she had brought with her – it didn't seem to matter to her if she left things behind. What mattered was that it was time for her to move on, to find her way back into her life via a new route. She folded the flyer up again and put it in her pocketbook, beside her cell phone, which was still turned off. She feared turning it on and having to face the countless messages waiting for her. Although she had been in her the-world-will-wait mentality, she knew that the world had been functioning at full speed. Normally, that thought would have induced stress, but here, now, Tess didn't care. She'd take care of all that needed to be taken care of in her own time. Right now, she needed to get herself back to Brooklyn and sign up for the teacher-training program and if the program was sold out, she'd find a way to convince them to let her in. She made one last trip to her bedroom and retrieved the urn of her mother's ashes from her night table, bringing it into her mother's bedroom so that she could sleep beside her.

A yoga teacher. Not exactly a path she had planned to take, but once she determined to do it, it seemed like the right path for her. The path of the daughter of Caroline Rose. She washed her face, brushed her teeth, shut the lights off all around her, and climbed into her mother's bed for one last sweet night's sleep in this phase of her life. She picked it up and held it to her heart. It was hard for Tess to imagine that her mother was stuffed in there, like a genie. "Mother," she said, the sound of her voice startling to her in the silence of the room. "Do you hear me?" she said. "I hope you can hear me." Tears formed in her eyes and began to fall down her face. "I'm going to try something new," she said. "You always encouraged me to try new things. To nurture my soul." She held the urn to her cheek, wiping away her tears, and then to her forehead, the coolness soothing to her. "I miss you, Mother," she said, and it was at that moment that she knew she was going to take what was left of her mother with her to Brooklyn. "A new adventure for us both," she said, placing the urn down carefully on the night table. The thought of having her mother with her filled her with a sense of relief. She wrapped herself in the ivory Afghan blanket, knowing she was going to take that with her, too, and lie down in bed smiling. There were some things that she wasn't ready to leave behind.

CHAPTER 19: CLOSE TO HOME

In the distance, Neal sauntered, pausing in front of a blooming batch of yellow tulips. Tess moved steadily as she caught up to him. Her heart was racing. When she was less than a few feet away, he turned his head, spotting her, and smiled shyly, his eyes downcast, as if he were shielding them from the sun.

"Tess," he said.

"Neal."

"A beautiful morning for a walk."

"It certainly is," Tess said. She fell in line beside him and together they moved on. Standing beside Neal made Tess feel as if time had stood still. She had forgotten the simplicity of Neal, how sharing space with him was uncomplicated and relaxing. Tess focused on her sneakered feet, moving one foot in front of the other as she inhaled the sweet honey suckled air.

"My mother passed away." Although weeks had passed, each time Tess said it out loud, it didn't seem possible; she felt as if she were talking about someone else's mother.

Neal stopped for a moment, facing her, his hands a prayer in front of his heart. His face was steady, even.

"I suppose it was her time," she said, meeting his eyes. She glanced at the ground and started walking again.

"I'm sorry, Tess. The loss of a parent is never easy."

"Yes. Thank you. I'm sorry, too." She sighed. "She believed in reincarnation. Maybe it was time for her to change form?" she said. "But you don't believe in that, do you?"

"Anything is possible, Tess. None of us know what happens when we die. That's one of the great mysteries of living."

Neal smiled his all-encompassing lips-pressed-together Charlie Brown smile.

"I missed your birthday," Tess said. "May 6th, right?"

"Yes," Neal said. "My mother took me out to dinner in New York City."

Tess thought of her last episode with him in the city and wondered if he had thought about it, too, when he was there with his mother. She wondered if his mother had taken him to the same Italian restaurant his parents had taken him to the night before he left for the monastery. May 6th. The day her mother had passed.

Together they looped around 56 Drive onto Whitman Drive North. The houses were more spacious here, the lawns wider – daisies and tulips and blooming rose patches abounded. They had been built later than the houses on 66th street and the houses leading up to 56th drive. It was as if the developers, having figured out that Mill Basin was a desirable place for people to settle down, had decided to create homes on the Jamaica Bay inlet that were bigger than the existing homes. That was the great thing about the real estate market: at the beginning, you never knew what the end result would be. It was a bit of guesswork, a bit of intuition, a bit of market analysis, and a bit of sharp marketing to develop homes in an area that would have longevity and whose market values would soar. In the case of Mill Basin, it had been a matter of creating top-quality homes and what followed were top-notch schools and elaborate synagogues and churches. Over the years, the schools had started to bus in students from various neighborhoods, which helped to boost diversity and create a true Brooklyn melting-pot atmosphere.

Neal moved precisely, each step of his foot following the one preceding it as if he were walking a tight rope, his hands clasped neatly at nape of his belly. It was hard for Tess to imagine that he was the same Neal who had come undone when she kissed him on the lips a few weeks back, the same Neal who had fled from a monastery.

Neal led them around the bend of National Drive. The houses on the water here were more elaborate, ornate, their multi-levels shooting high up into the sky. The corner-most house was encrusted by a large iron gate with sharp, pointy tips, like knives. They paused in front of it. In the driveway there was a Rolls Royce and a baby blue Bentley convertible.

"That house has ten floors," Tess said. "It's equipped with two elevators – one for the help and one for the inhabitants."

"Sounds like a hotel," Neal said.

"The real estate in this neighborhood never ceases to amaze me. People build mansions, but they don't realize that they are not going to make a lot on their investments in the long run. This area is changing. It's not what it was. You drive a few miles out of this area and there are lower income houses now."

"Is Mill Basin still full of mafia folks? When I was growing up my mother used to fear that I'd get involved with the wrong crowd," Neal said.

"The mafia folks are still here. I don't think they'll ever leave Mill Basin. But they're not the only ones investing in this neighborhood – Israelis and Syrians are also building mansions. Our own little United Nations," Tess said.

They turned down Arkansas Drive creating a zigzag and Neal pointed at the sunflowers growing wild in one of the gardens. They looked like crazy children smiling up at the sun.

"*That* house has always interested me," Neal said when they reached the corner and were back at National Drive and the intersection of 56th Drive.

The house was situated on the water. It was a two-tone brick – tan and brown. Tess had always loved this house, too, with its breeziness and its majestic air. It was old and dignified. When it had gone up for sale a few years back, just when she and Michael were getting ready to go their separate ways, she had asked him if he was interested in buying it. She was ready to let go of Michael but having him nearby had appealed to her.

"The view on the dock must be beautiful," Neal said.

"I sold that house to my last ex-husband, Michael, a few years back," Tess said.

"Should I presume that meant you liked the house or didn't like it?"

Tess smiled. "I love that house. When we were splitting up, I wanted him in that house. Now, I may not have been so generous, but back then, I wanted him to have it."

"Do you regret having him close by now?" Neal asked.

"Michael is part of my life. Even before we got together, we worked together – he was the lawyer for my company – still is. I like having him around. I shouldn't have married him, but I don't always do the right thing. Especially when it comes to marriage," Tess said.

A wish flower floated by Tess, and she grabbed it in her hand. She couldn't feel it, but she knew that if she opened her hand to check if it was there, it would fly away. That was the thing with wish flowers – if you didn't act fast and make a wish, they flew out of your reach.

The sun was beginning to beam down now so that half of the sidewalk was in the shade while the other half was in the sunlight. Tess stayed in the shade while Neal was in the sunlight. They were by Gaylord drive. Out of all the blocks in Mill Basin, this was the one Tess was least familiar with. So many of the houses had recently been redone. She imagined that's why so few of these houses had been for sale – the owners had invested in them.

"Do you think you lose part of yourself by marrying another person?" Neal asked.

"I think you get to see another side of yourself when you're married. I think it helps you to grow," Tess said.

"Why shouldn't you have married Michael?" Neal asked.

"He made me restless. But I guess I made myself restless with Michael. I was never able to let things just be. I didn't understand what he loved about me – it made me suspicious. I never felt as if he got me – what I was all about."

"Did you want him to *get* you?" Neal asked.

"I don't know what I wanted, but when I was with him, often, I wanted to be alone. I guess that I didn't want to share my life. I wanted to live on my own terms," Tess said.

"Well, it seems to have worked out fine – you're friends again."

"Yes. We were able to figure it out," Tess said.

They were in front of Tess's house now. She liked looking into her living room from the outside, making out tidbits of her Asian breakfronts; there was so much to a house that you couldn't know from the outside. The cleaning lady neighbor was on her porch, cleaning her screen door with a rag, wearing her rubber gloves and her rubber boots. She was wearing her pink sweatshirt and sweatpants today, which clashed with her apple-red hair. How was it that her son didn't tell her how odd her hair color was?

"How is it that you got stuck listening to me going on and on today?" Tess asked.

"I like listening to you," Neal said.

"How's your book coming along?"

"Fine," Neal said.

"Fine has a scale of 1-10 attached to it."

Neal laughed. "I'll be sure to be more descriptive when I speak to you."

"It's good to see you, Neal," Tess said.

"It's been good to see you, too, Tess."

"And whatever happened between us…" Tess started and stopped as Neal looked down at the floor. Tess reached over and touched his arm.

"I respect you, Neal." Saying it, she wasn't sure if it had come out the right way. She wanted Neal to know that she didn't expect anything from him.

"I understand who you are," she went on, again unsure if she was comforting him or making him uncomfortable.

"Tess, you're my friend."

"I am your friend," she said.

"Will I see you out walking tomorrow morning?" Neal asked.

"Actually, I need to go to some meetings tomorrow morning for yoga. I enrolled in a yoga teacher training program," Tess said.

"I didn't know that you wanted to become a yoga teacher," Neal said.

"Me neither," Tess said. "It just kind of happened – a series of coincidences, I suppose."

CHAPTER 20: SECOND THOUGHTS

Tess held the staircase door open for Dale, handing her a bag of cookies. To Tess's surprise, Dale had also signed up for the yoga teacher training program at the last minute – they laughed together after the introductory lecture two weeks back, remembering how they had both pooh-poohed ever taking the yoga teacher training program at the studio. Dale's thought process had been that since her life was a total mess in her estimation, perhaps studying yoga for eight months would help her get her life in order.

"Bribes?" Dale asked, opening the bag.

The last two-weekend lock-ins at the studio, Tess had accompanied Dale prior to the Friday night session when she stopped at The Bakery around the corner from the studio and bought a few oversized cookies.

Dale bit into an oatmeal raison cookie. "Mmm," she said. "I didn't know you could bake."

"I can't," Tess said. "I happen to know a master cookie maker."

"Are you re-gifting?" Dale asked.

"I won't tell if you won't," Tess said.

Tess pushed the door open into the night. Fresh air. There was something magical to feeling the warm night air after taking an evening yoga class. The carefreeness of it made Tess feel as if she was on vacation.

"These cookies are surreal. Tess, you've struck gold."

"I'll keep them coming," Tess said.

Two weeks into the program and already Tess was becoming disillusioned as to how she was going to juggle running her company and daily yoga classes not to mention weekend lock- ins at the studio. When was she supposed to do things like food shop or clean her house? Still, she did love the yoga classes, and she had made a commitment to the program, not to mention that she spent $8,000 on it. Having earned every penny she had, she wasn't one to throw money away. There was also the fact that she hadn't seen Neal in almost two weeks, not that it should have mattered to her, but somehow it did. When he left her not one, but two bags of cookies on her porch, it made her long for a free hour to go walking with him, but with her having to leave her office every day now by 4:30 in the afternoon to shoot into NYC, she needed to get to work by 7:00 in the morning if she were to get her work done, which didn't leave her time for early morning leisurely strolls.

"Last chance," Dale said. Tess looked at the chocolate chip cookie chunk Dale held out to her and shook her head.

"They're for you."

"You okay?" Dale said.

"Just in a fog from class."

"The more I take these classes, the more confident I become that I'll never be able to teach a yoga class – between spotting all the students and the instructions and keeping it all moving along and then getting us all to conk out at the end. Way too much to deal with," Dale said.

"If you want to teach, you will; you'll figure it out," Tess said.

"You're a bore tonight," Dale said.

"When I first met you, I had you sized up as an affected snob."

"That's sweet," Dale said. She had chocolate on her nose that Tess wiped away.

"I couldn't imagine why Kyle would put up with you aside from the fact that you're beautiful. But the past few weeks of getting to know you, I look forward to your company," Tess said.

"Great. Then you'll be happy to join me for tea. I need something to wash down the cookies," she said. "And I need to hear more of your assessment of me." She linked her arm in Tess's and led her down to Barnes and Nobles on 17th street and Union Square.

From up on the fourth floor Starbuck's Cafe, Tess had a clear view of the kids on skateboards who tried to jump the ramps that that they had set up on the 17th street side of Union Square. One after another, the boys – most likely 13-17 years old – picked up speed, jumped the ramps, and hit the pavement smoothly before skating off. Ultimate precision and skill.

"I put in a touch of milk for you" Dale said, sitting down across from Tess, placing the two steaming teas down on the table and producing a lemon square from a paper bag.

"You're the skinniest carbohydrate junkie that I know," Tess said.

"I've been known to eat four lemon squares in one sitting," Dale said.

One of the skateboarders fell, hard, on his arm and Tess jumped in her seat, but he was up in a minute, shaking it off, retrieving his board and making his way back to do the jump over again. It must have been 8:30 p.m. by now. Tess wondered if the kids had homework. If their parents knew where they were.

"How's it going with Kyle?"

"He wants us, or me, to pick a date for the wedding, a place, the works."

"What do you want?" Tess asked.

One of the smaller skateboarders did a flip off a ramp and hit the ground, standing.

"I guess we should start planning," Dale said.

"Do you have good friends, Dale?"

"I guess, sure. I think they're sick of hearing my indecision about Kyle, my job, my life. I'm on hiatus from them right now. I don't feel like hearing everyone's opinions," Dale said. "Do you have good friends?"

Tess laughed. "I didn't mean it as a competition," she said. She blew on her tea and took a sip. "Or a proposal to be your best friend. I was curious what they were saying to you about Kyle," Tess said.

"And I asked you – do you have good friends?"

"I'm married to my job and my company, Dale. I don't have time for friends and lunches and all that stuff that goes along with friends. I have 50 + employees to manage daily."

"Did you ever have close friends?" Dale asked.

"Oh, don't you go and psychoanalyze me. Yes, I've had tons of friends in my lifetime, but when you get married and divorced four times you tend to lose a lot of people along the way," Tess said. "Satisfied?"

"I'm glad that you have time for tea and conversation with me," Dale said.

"We were talking about whether it's the right time to move on with plans for the wedding," Tess said.

"Well, how I see it is that it's already May, and if we're going to get married by the end of the year like we decided we would, then now is as good a time as any to move ahead, right?"

"Dale, it's only a good time to move ahead with the plans if you feel good about your relationship. Forget the plans. Focus on the two of you. What matters is if he's the person you want to spend your life with. That's what you need to know before you do anything."

"But how does anyone know that? There are so many days to life. So many hours in every day. I tend to change my mind a few times every hour."

Tess took the lid off her of her tea and steam flushed her face. "Did you want to spend today with him?"

"Sure, I guess, but we had to work –"

"I'm not talking about his working or your being busy. If you were the only survivor on earth and were granted the wish to keep one person with you, would it be Kyle?" Tess asked.

"I think I need another lemon square," Dale said.

"Dale, I wish I would have asked myself those questions before each of my marriages. It might have saved me a lot of time and grief in my life," Tess said.

"My heart goes in a different direction depending on the hour of the day."

"We make ourselves scattered, Dale. I do it to myself every day. When I was up in Woodstock earlier this month it may have been the first time in a long time that I didn't feel all over the place every day. I was calm. And when you're calm inside, everything shifts," Tess said.

"So, you're saying I need to be calmer?"

"I don't know what I'm saying, Dale. Trust me, I'm trying to figure it out for myself, but I do know that when you debate something as if it's a chess game – especially your love life – you're going to drive yourself crazy. You need to tune into what you feel, and you'll find all the answers that you need."

"I feel happy being on my own," Dale said.

"If Kyle was to vanish from your life tomorrow, no big deal?"

Dale shrugged. "This is how I see it," she said. "There's you, who I think has it pretty together, and you've gone through four divorces. There's Kim from the teacher training who's going through emotional breaking point about her marriage after nine years – suddenly she's starting to wonder if she did the right thing marrying someone twenty years older than her. There's Sara from the program that's bitter about marriage and is in the midst of a battlefield of a divorce. It all makes me wonder if I shouldn't stay on my own. I don't even know what marriage means. I don't get what exchanging vows is going to do for me. Part of me thinks marriage is archaic and bizarre, and the other part of me thinks it's the most precious thing. Some of my relatives are already asking me if we plan to start a family right away or if we're going to wait. Can you imagine? I think that I would be fine doing yoga and hanging out with friends the rest of my life."

Tess looked away from the window. Against the night sky, Dale's green eyes reminded Tess of the water in Jamaica Bay. Muddy, yet translucent in certain spots, as if a needle had passed through them, pricking holes for the light to seep in.

"I left my job today," Dale said. "Actually, I took a three-month leave. You're the first person I'm telling."

"What? Why? And you haven't told Kyle?" Tess asked.

"I never said I wasn't crazy," Dale said.

"What happened with your job?" Tess asked.

"I don't know if I'm cut out to be a social worker. Or at least a social worker for runaway teens. I felt useless, you know. One of the girls I was working with for months ran away from her home again the other day. Now she's missing. And the other ones...I'm supposed to coax them to go back to their real homes, promise them that their parents and guardians will be monitored from here on out, but if you heard the stories they told me about their homes – I can't tell them to go back. When I bring it up to my supervisor, he tells me it's my job to send them back. I'm sorry, but I can't send these kids back to hell. It's even worse when I have to find them foster homes. I start thinking about myself at 14, 15. I would have rather lived on the street than go to live in some stranger's house and have to abide by their rules. And every time I make progress with one of the teens – find them a decent family, get them set up in school, find them part time work, they go and pull something else that I have to bail them out of: getting caught buying drugs, drinking. I'm a wreck all the time. I never know when I'm going to get a phone call telling me something terrible has happened to one of the kids I'm dealing with. It makes me feel like I'm failing everyone. I asked for a leave so that I can get my life together a bit and besides, I want to focus on yoga teacher training."

"And I thought I was the only one that had stressful days. What's Kyle going to say?"

"Kyle will probably be relieved. He thinks my job is what's

keeping me from everything else in my life. As in making the wedding arrangements and moving."

"Is it?" Tess asked.

"I don't know," Dale said. She was folding the napkin in front of her into neat little triangles, one folding into the other.

"Is counseling teens your passion or is it something you just do?" Tess asked.

"I want to help them, but I don't see how moving them around is helping them. I would love to teach yoga to those teens – help them to build their self-confidence. I want to give them something that they can always utilize, long after my time with them is up. To answer your question, yes, I'm passionate about what I do, or I was." She paused and let out a sigh. "Have you ever just needed a break from your career?"

"I certainly have my melt downs. But there's also something about real estate that keeps me going – the matchmaking aspect of it, the sell, I guess," Tess said.

"Maybe my true calling is to be a yoga teacher," Dale said.

"Or a wedding planner," Tess said.

They both laughed.

"Here's the good news. If you were able to walk away from your career without second guessing yourself, don't you think you would walk away from your relationship if it wasn't right for you, or at least put off moving ahead with wedding plans?"

Dale studied her for a few moments. "I guess?"

"Dale, everyone fears marriage. Or at least some people are. Or should be. Only when you break down the fear, what is it really? Just not knowing what to expect, right? If you knew what to expect, though, it would be a boring life. I used to dread going with the flow. I thought that I could plan everything – still do to some extent, I suppose – but the truth is that I can't. No one can. Expect the unexpected is probably the best advice anyone can ever give you," Tess said.

Dale continued to stare at her before her face softened.

"I do love Kyle. Marriage is just the next step in our relationship. I'm not selling my soul, just sharing my heart with someone. When I listen to myself speak, none of it seems like a big deal. It's when I listen to other people that I get all fucked up – *when are you moving in together, when's the wedding, where are you getting married yada.* The more I have to deal with people, the more I wish I could lock myself away and live in my own little world. Maybe I'll go to an ashram for a break or become a nun."

"Apparently people who lock themselves away in their own little worlds are not the most carefree folks, either," Tess said.

Dale's brow creased. "Have you interviewed any nuns lately?"

If Tess had a daughter, she hoped that she'd be like Dale. There was something about her that was quirky and offbeat – a mess and a charmer in one. There seemed to be no rhyme or reason to her actions, and yet something about her was calculated, as if she knew exactly what she was doing.

Tess smiled at Dale and winked. "Let's just say I have my sources."

"Okay, I'll cross the ashram and convent off my places to escape to list. Remember, coming from a girl who can't leave New York City for Brooklyn, it's highly unlikely that I'm going anywhere," Dale said.

Outside, the skateboarder kids were jumping off their mock mountain again and again. For moments at a time, they were airborne.

"Tell me something about you," Dale said.

Tess wobbled her head back and forth. "My friend the cookie man, who I was starting to like, was a Roman Catholic monk," Tess said.

"What? You're dating a monk?"

The skateboarders were all sitting on the floor now, smoking cigarettes. The show was over.

"And here I thought I was the only one with drama," Dale said.

"He lived in a monastery in Canada for 23 years," Tess said.

"Wow," Dale said.

"I took him to see the *Sound of Music* a few weeks back, before my mother passed away – you know that it's about a nun leaving a convent and falling in love with a man that she marries, right?"

"I know the story. He must have thought you were trying to convert him!"

"I tried to kiss him after the movie, and he ran away."

Dale laughed, slipping back on her chair, the front two legs lifting off the floor so that for a moment, it seemed as if she was going to topple over backwards, until she recovered herself, crashing back down.

"Is he going back to the monastery at some point?" she said.

"He says he left for good, that the monastery wasn't for him anymore. Talk about leaving careers."

"I had a professor in college who was a Roman Catholic priest for over ten years, and he fell in love with a nun and the two of them ended up getting married. When he told my class, we thought it was the coolest thing."

"Well, I'm no nun," Tess said.

Dale laughed. She was picking at the lemon square crust again, breaking pieces off before she contemplated taking a bite.

"Maybe you guys will just be friends," Dale said.

"We are just friends."

"But you like him," Dale said.

"Like I said, we're friends," Tess said.

"But you did say you were starting to like him," Dale said.

Tess shrugged.

"Do you want to kiss him passionately, Tess?"

"When I think of kissing a monk, I feel like a criminal," Tess said.

"Don't worry, I won't turn you in," Dale said.

Tess smiled, all lips, no teeth. "Thanks," she said. "Can we not bring this up for topics of discussion when we lunch with Kim and Sara on Saturday? Not that there's anything to tell, it's just that I don't feel like making it our daily amusement, you know? I think I just needed to hear myself say it aloud," Tess said.

"Scout's honor," Dale said. "They don't need to know about my taking a leave from my job right now, either. I don't want to make a big deal of it and who knows – chances are I'll go back in a bit."

"Deal," Tess said.

As they walked out into the night, Dale wove her arm in Tess's arm.

"Sometimes I wish I could see a year into the future and know how everything will work out," Dale said.

"The answers always come at the right time and place," Tess said.

"Amen," Dale said.

CHAPTER 21: A SEPARATE PEACE

The blackened sky departed gradually at first, like a curtain lifting, until all at once the sky was a shade of bluish gray: the color of morning. The transition from darkness to light was seamless, fluid, so that Tess could never pinpoint the moment when a new day dawned. She wondered if that's what it was like when you reached Samadhi – the blissful state in yoga – or if there were signs all along the way saying, *you're almost there*. If there were, she hadn't hit one of those signs yet.

The steam from her tea drifted upwards, warming her face. Her mother had been gone for weeks now, and still, no sign. She hadn't come to Tess in a dream, hadn't spoken to her. Nothing. Void and silence.

Outside the kitchen window, two birds teetered on a high branch in the cherry blossom tree. In a matter of weeks, the tree had bloomed into a captivating landscape of pink-white flowers and petals that sprinkled the grass like velvet tear drops. The blossoms were flourishing, the branches brushing against the window glass so that it sounded like waves rushing the shore. Late May. It was only a matter of weeks before the tree would be in full bloom. After these 30-plus years, the branches were sturdy and thick. The tree reminded her of a highway with its various routes to follow. The routes that intertwined and overlapped all led upwards. That was a comfort to Tess. No matter which route she traced, she landed beside the others. As a young boy, Prakash had loved to lodge himself in the tree and do a forward bend gripping the branches. She recalled how she used to spy on him through the kitchen window and wish that they were close. Prakash never seemed to tire of his little flip. To know what he had been thinking, if only for a moment, to see what he saw when he turned the world upside down – that was what she had wanted. Seeing him be his own little person, it had amazed her that there had been a time when Prakash was a part of her. It had confounded her that she was unable to enter his mind or heart; that she could no longer hear life beating through him after had shared that rhythm with him for nine months. Prakash was hers to love and not hers, too, and when she was younger and foolish in ways different than she was now, she had felt hurt and stunned by her inability to possess Prakash – by the fact that he could walk and talk and think on his own.

The first divorce, from Prakash's father, had been a rough one. Prakash's father had fallen in love with another woman and packed his bags. When Tess read the note he left her, saying that he would be in touch, she had felt strangely relieved, as if someone had rescued her from a cliff she was about to spring from. There was no hate or anger, just questions that she wished answers to, so that the not knowing transformed into a waiting period. Yet, she had encouraged Prakash to love his father – she had wanted him to have his father, to see him if there came a chance, talk to him if he should reappear in Prakash's life.

Prakash had clung closer to her than he ever had during the abandonment. Not needing her to speak or hold him, so much as to reassure him that she was where she was supposed to be, and he was where he was supposed to be. He would come home from school and call her at work to report that he was home. Courteous, dependable Prakash. And somehow, she had resented that about him, because there were times when she had felt like she was the child, and he was her mother. While she made dinner, Prakash remained alone on the side of the house, sitting on his perch while the other children on the block played stickball in the vacant street by the Yacht Club.

Years later, as a teenager, he called her after school each day before heading to Strickland Park to play handball and let her know what time he planned to return home. If Prakash had not been the conscientious child that he was, she didn't know how it would have all worked out.

When she had told him of one divorce after another, shared the details with him, Prakash listened in his calm and patient way. Husband number two, then number three. Then, with her fourth marriage, it was as if Prakash had sprung a leak. He was done with college by that time, living out in San Francisco, already establishing himself as an architect. He had asked Tess when she was going to be through with this husband phase. *A husband phase.* The words had stuck in Tess's mind like a splinter. What was true was that Prakash remained in her life when all else was gone. She often wondered what her relationship with her son was at heart: what did they talk about these days beyond trivial things? *Are you okay? How's work? What's new?* It was such hard work to form a bridge into someone else's life.

Tess sipped her tea. Silence and time and space to think was underrated. And yet there were moments when she envisioned herself sitting at this kitchen table each morning for the rest of her life and it made her feel hollow, as if something had been sucked out of her. She had struggled with the paradox of wanting to be alone and the fear of being alone for most of her life. When she had been a child, there were days when she had hidden in her closet safe from the crowd in the living room that chanted and told herself stories about how her life would be when she was older. She would live far away in a quiet house by the water and how she'd go out in the early mornings to look at the world and how she would never let strangers in. It would be her own home and to get inside others would need to know the special password that let her know that they were safe, the password that the universe had granted, offering them access to her world.

She remembered evenings when the crowd in her living room was silent, and all that Tess heard were her own thoughts. She often grew fearful that everyone had left the house and forgotten her. Once, when the silence set in when she was home with a cold, worried that her mother wasn't around to take care of her, she rushed down the stairs and into the living room to find her mother and her followers all sitting cross legged with their eyes closed, their chins down, bobbing as they made subtle noises that sounded like voices underwater. She had had the urge to wake them all up. It frightened her to see people look dead while they were living, and yet watching them intrigued her. There was something beautiful about seeing people in their stillness – there was a peace that they exuded, as if they were clouds. In her room, Tess had closed her eyes and sat cross-legged on the floor, imitating the way the people in her living room had sat. She made the breathy sound with her throat and within a few minutes, she grew sleepy. So sleepy that she crawled into her bed and fell right asleep. The more she practiced sitting that way – in her closet for fear that her mother would discover her – the less sleepy she became and the more alert it made her. After a few weeks of the sitting, she began to feel as if she were weightless when she sat, no longer noticing her body, and instead tuned into her mind, which seemed content to think about nothing. The first time the free-floating feeling overcame her, she panicked, wished to come back down, to sink into herself, but once she was moving, there was no turning back. She never knew where she went, but the feeling of drifting was enough to make her keep doing it. She meditated in secret, never once sharing her experiences with her mother. It intrigued Tess that the things that could have connected her to her mother were things that she had chosen to keep them apart.

Tess wondered if she had played that game with her ex-husbands – keeping from them the things that could have connected her to them. Had she ever asked them if they were afraid of anything? Had she ever truly known them? Other than what they liked to eat and the hours they worked, and the trivial things that would make them happy or annoy them, there wasn't much else that she knew about them. It perplexed her that you could live alongside a person and not really know them, that you could be related to someone, that you could give birth to them, and not be able to read their minds and hearts. She knew nothing after all her son's daily life other than the things they told one another during their phone calls. Unless you were to become another person, and that, in this lifetime at least, was impossible, it seemed unlikely that you would ever get to know another person. The truth was that no matter how many people you surrounded yourself with, you were always alone. Tess wondered if a monk ever felt as if he was alone or if he always felt as if he was with God. She breathed in deep and let it go: the fear, the worry, the wishes that lived in her that she was not yet ready to articulate, as if no words could communicate this new song of her soul which had been forming in her during the last few weeks of her life. She felt empty as of late, as if someone robbed her and left her a note: *nothing left to take.* And yet the emptiness left her feeling free and renewed somehow, as if she had to empty out, had to let go of all that was to begin again. That was the thing with changing your route in life – it seemed that once you got on a new road, there was no end to all the directions you would travel.

Tess wondered if Neal had felt the same way since he left the monastery. Perhaps his life away from the monastery felt small. To walk a day in his life. Tess wished that she could see out of his eyes, if only for a moment. Tess imagined the halls of the monasteries: dark and cool, mysterious and eerie, safe from the world. She had a desire to walk in a monastery – to smell it, hear the sounds, eat the food, look at the monks. Neal had done the unthinkable by leaving the world behind and finding his own separate peace.

She yawned deep and wide, her hands reaching toward the sky. Outside, the crickets' throaty hum filled the air. This spring was certainly different from the other springs of her life. For the first time in as long as she could remember, she felt as if she was living each of her days instead of passing through them. At random moments, such as this one, it seemed bizarre to her to spend her days walking in and out of houses, opening and locking them up, balancing check books, holding staff meetings.

The cloud looming outside brought a flash of winter to her mind: deep and dark and cold. She tried to imagine entering life on that late December day so many years ago, over half a century back. Arriving in the world one day late for Christmas – December 26th. Her birthday seemed an afterthought. Winter. The coldness that seeped into her bones. She always felt as if she was on the verge of cracking during December and January, but by the time February set in, she would feel herself melting. She thought of those mornings in December and January over thirty years back when she had been pregnant with Prakash. The loneliness of those days, knowing that her whole life would be different the moment the creature in her decided to show his face. Those February days prior to Prakash's birth, and the few weeks after his birth were probably the only times in her life that she had ever lived as she was living now – apart, and yet connected to the world around her, aware of its movement, aware of the metronome within her beating to the metronome without her.

The doorbell's ring sent Tess from her reverie. Her heart raced. Who would be calling for her at 6:00 a.m.? She peaked out the living room window and saw Michael.

"Yes, it's me, your favorite intruder," he said when she opened the door.

She hugged him close; there was something about the way her and Michael's bodies melded together that always caused her a moment of doubt whenever she was that near to him. Maybe it was just that she hadn't had sex in a while.

"What a treat," she said.

He raised his eyebrows at her and in a moment, he was past her and climbing the stairs up to her kitchen.

"The crazy Israeli neighbor lady is out there screaming at her son while he runs down the block, full speed," Michael said.

"She's not Israeli. Her husband, who's never around, is Israeli."

Michael was filling the teapot and turning on the stove when Tess reached the top of the stairs.

"Would you like some tea?" Tess asked.

"Thank you, I would," Michael said, taking out his favorite oversized ivory mug.

"What do I owe this honor to?" Tess said.

"I knew that if I called, I would be stuck talking to your answering machine, so I decided to pay you a visit."

The teakettle, still warm, whistled quickly, and after he filled his mug, he joined her at the table.

"Did you come to tell me something?" she asked.

"I've been thinking of joining you on your morning walks, but I don't know how your boyfriend would react to me tagging along."

"My boyfriend?"

"The weird guy."

"For your information, dearest, I haven't been out walking with him for weeks, as I've been spending my mornings reading for the yoga program and then getting into the office by 7:00."

"Don't start with me, Tess."

"You come to my house at 6:00 a.m., and tell me not to start with *you*?"

Michael sipped his tea, his eyes lowered, before he picked them up and glanced at Tess.

"Don't look at me with those puppy eyes, Michael. Jealousy doesn't become you. Neal is just a friend."

"We were just friends for a long time. I saw him walking away from your porch a few mornings in the past weeks. Is your 'just friend' spending the night now?"

"I wasn't here those mornings you saw him walking away because I was already at the office."

"I suppose he was just hanging out on your porch?

"He was leaving me cookies if you must know."

"Cookies?" he said.

"He bakes," she said. "Did you come here to interrogate me?"

"I came to talk to you about this yoga teacher training nonsense that you've gotten involved with."

Tess laughed.

"It's funny to you. Your mother dies and now you intend to become a yoga teacher and decide to start hanging out with a guy who is clearly a freak," he said.

"I'm not *hanging out* with a freak, as you call him, and I don't intend to be a yoga teacher."

"Now you don't want to be a yoga teacher?" he asked.

"Will you give me a break – I'm trying something new, that's all. What's this really about?"

"You think I like this – that I want to be here saying these things to you?" he said.

Tess held up her palm to Michael as if she was directing traffic to stop.

"Right now, I don't want to hear what you want."

"What are you going to do with your mother's house?" Michael asked.

"I don't know yet," Tess said.

"Four acres, up in Woodstock, about 3200 square feet house with balconies on each of the bedrooms, all French doors. You would know better than me, but my guess is that you can get over a million for it – maybe close to two. Someone could convert it into two properties – a house and a store of some sort."

"We'll see," Tess said.

"Maybe I'll buy it," Michael said.

"I don't think so."

"Are you sleeping with the weirdo?"

"No, I'm not sleeping with him. Neal and I are just friends. Couldn't this conversation wait until we were in the office?"

"I just have a funny feeling about him, Tess. I saw him with his mother yesterday; at least I supposed it was his mother. They were in the supermarket. Just the way they interacted. His mother seems like a nutcase. And he seems as if he's sleepwalking or something. He functions in slow motion," he said.

"We're all weird, Michael."

"You don't get it, Tess. Trust me. If he's hanging out with you, he's falling in love with you. I predict he's a goner, waiting for the right moment to move in for his kill."

"Michael, not everyone is in love with me."

"No, but most men that know you are," he said.

"I'm sure that he's planning to ambush me during one of our morning strolls," Tess said.

"Perfect crime scene," he said.

Tess laughed. "Michael." She stopped.

"What Tess?"

"The weird guy as you call him, is – was – a Roman Catholic monk."

Michael laughed a deep belly laugh. "A monk?"

"He lived in a monastery for 23 years. He left the monastery in

March. He's only been back in town for two months."

"Wow," Michael said. "You've outdone yourself this time, Tess. But I still say he wants you."

"Michael, I barely know him. He's an acquaintance, someone who I've run into a few times," she said.

Outside, the sun shone bright. Tess stretched her neck left, right.

"And we don't ask one another too many questions – the best type of friend to have," she said.

"What are you trying to say?"

"I need to get ready for work," she said.

"Tess – I miss you."

She watched a pigeon outside walk across the telephone wire. It moved deliberately, gracefully, before it dove into flight.

"You don't care," he said.

"Michael. Don't do this."

"What am I doing, Tess? Is it so wrong of me if I miss you, miss us?"

"No."

"You just don't want to hear it," he said.

"We're friends, Michael. Please. You're feeling nostalgic today, that's all."

"We changed our lives for one another, Tess. You forget that sometimes. I left my wife; you left your husband."

"We did that for ourselves, not for one another. That's just where we were at back then. Now we're at a new point in our lives," she said.

"Now I'm slaving away at your company while you're busy becoming a yoga teacher and seducing a monk," he said.

Tess laughed. "I promise that tomorrow you'll feel differently. You're just lonely today." Tess stood up and stretched tall, and while her arms were in midair, Michael hugged her tight around her waist. She hugged him back.

"I'll leave you to get ready for work," he said. "I hope you're right about today." He kissed her forehead and let her go.

He moved down the steps slowly, as if he had weights on his legs. She lingered at the door for a moment as he got into his car and drove away. Sometimes it was so hard to make sense of life. She couldn't remember why she wasn't with Michael, but when she thought of waking up beside him each day, of going to sleep in his embrace each night, it was enough to make her desperate to wash it all away. Michael had asked for things that Tess could never give another person – permanence, security, herself. When she was with him, she had always felt as if she was playing a game of tug of war, trying to hold onto the parts of her that Michael tugged at. There was no doubt for Tess – she was done with relationships. To think that you could form a union with anyone other than yourself was a myth.

CHAPTER 22: OUT TO SEA

"Neal!" She must have been sitting at the foot of the cherry-blossom tree and reading the *Yoga Sutras* for over an hour, unless Neal was early for their date.

"I didn't mean to startle you," Neal said.

"I lost track of time," she said. "I only meant to come out here for 15 minutes at most."

He pointed to the cat by his feet. "I've brought a visitor," he said.

Tess's eyes met the cats and in that moment of recognition, she understood that it was the cat that had been crossing her path these months. The cat didn't take its eyes off Tess, so that she felt as if she couldn't break the stare, either.

"He's been waiting by the bushes surrounding my house each morning. When I start walking, he follows me – at least for the first block or two. Today, he followed me the whole way here."

"We know each other," Tess said. She held out her hand to the cat, and still, not taking its eyes off her, the cat began to sniff at her finger and then sat down beside her, purring as he rolled onto his back, his belly to the sky.

"Hello, kitty," she said. "You always run away from me, don't you? But now you want to play. It's as if there's a whole world in those eyes of yours, isn't there?" she asked.

The cat nuzzled Tess to pet him and hesitatingly, she reached out and touched his fur.

"You're not such a bad cat," Tess said. "Even if you look big and mean."

He was beat up – cuts by both ears, crusted blood by his nose. She wondered if he had any diseases. "I haven't had a cat since I was a little girl. My mother always had cats running around our house."

She scratched his head with her fingers so that he closed his eyes, his purr growing louder. She hoped he didn't have fleas.

"He likes you," Neal said.

"Do you want some milk, kitty?" she said, and the moment she began to make her way to her feet, the cat darted full speed into the backyard.

"Oh," she said. "I didn't mean to scare him away."

"He'll be back," Neal said. "Cats remember kindness."

"Maybe," Tess said, smiling at Neal, sad now that the cat had gone.

"I'm glad we're doing this," Tess said, pulling out of her

driveway, glancing for a moment at Neal in the passenger seat. The way he strapped in and leaned back in the seat made her smile; he looked as if he were preparing for takeoff.

"Me, too," Neal said.

She had run into Neal out on the shore of Jamaica Bay a few mornings back. Watching the boats pass by in the early morning, Neal had said *In More In Caelo*, going on to translate it: *In the sea in heaven.* He had told Tess it was the motto of the Intrepid upon setting sail. His father had always said it whenever they saw a boat go by and then Tess was saying that she'd never been to the Intrepid and neither had Neal, and so they made plans to spend the following Saturday of Memorial Day weekend, one of her rare Saturdays off from yoga teacher training, at the Intrepid Museum in New York City.

"My friend from yoga has been talking about your cookies to everyone in Teacher Training and giving them a taste. You've got a following. If you ever want to open a cookie shop, it would be a hit."

Neal laughed. "Monk Cakes."

"Or the Cookie Monk."

"The Cookie Monk," Neal said.

"We're laughing, but I'm being serious. I could search for some reasonable real estate for you, and we could make it happen."

"Somehow, I don't think that God intended for me to leave the monastery to become a bakery owner."

Tess was silent as she stopped at the light. She didn't know what to do when he brought up the monastery. Was she supposed to ask about it? Ignore it?

Tess merged into the right lane of the Belt Parkway and eased into the middle lane. Surprisingly, there was no traffic. That was the great thing about holiday weekends – everyone that lived in the city left so that there seemed to be more room, more air to breathe.

"How was your lecture on Thursday night?"

"Fine," Tess said. "It was on the *Bhagavad Gita*. Have you ever read it?"

"No," Neal said. "But I've heard of it."

"It's about Arjuna and his journey through life. He loses his way, and meets up with Krishna, who helps him to find his way or his *dharma*."

Tess merged into the left lane and opened the back windows so that her shirt ballooned in the breeze. On days like this, she wished that she could keep on driving forever.

"How's your book going?" she asked.

"I write a lot each day and then I typically throw away all that I write once I re-read it. It all makes so much sense in my mind, but when I put it down on paper it seems trite."

Neal stared out the window and hummed "My Favorite Things" from *The Sound of Music*.

"What are your favorite things?" she asked.

He lifted his chin up to the sky and Tess had an urge to kiss his neck. He seemed so vulnerable at that moment. She passed through the tollbooth and then they were in the mines of the midtown tunnel.

"I like to see new things. While I was at the monastery, everything was so familiar. That was okay for a long while for me. But now that I'm seeing new scenery, I want to keep exploring. There's so much that I haven't gotten to yet in my life."

"It's never too late," Tess said. She let go of her breath when she exited the tunnel and moved back into the light of day. The sun shining, the sky clear blue, no schedule to adhere to – already she was anxious that this day would come to an end.

Tess and Neal stood before the labyrinth that spanned the black top of the 44th street pier. It was perfectly outlined in white paint.

"On my thirteenth birthday my mother created a labyrinth out of stones for me to pass through. I had to find my way to the center and then find my way out of the maze while everyone in our community watched me."

"Every year thereafter, a week or so before my birthday, she started laying down the rocks, making sure that each of them was in their own lanes, and if it snowed and the stones got covered over, she carved the labyrinth out of the snow. I walked the labyrinth until my 18th birthday."

"The myth is that if you walk to the center of the labyrinth and rest there for a few moments, you'll be inspired, and when you journey out and re-enter the world, you'll have a new sense of purpose."

Neal entered the labyrinth and searched for the route to the center. He beckoned Tess to follow him and at first, she smiled and didn't move; she was hot. But then without thinking, she made her way in and around the circle to the center and out.

"Am I supposed to feel different now?" Neal asked.

"Do you?"

"No."

"Then you're not supposed to."

"What's the cruise to nowhere?" Neal asked, pointing to the metal stand-up sign.

Tess shrugged. "I think you go around the city and back." Tess squinted to make out the small print. "Maybe it's a dinner cruise," she said. "It leaves at 3:00 p.m. and returns at 9:00 p.m."

"Want to go?" Neal asked.

"And not go to the Intrepid?"

"It's such a beautiful day," Neal said. "I wouldn't mind being out on the water."

It was 2:45. They could make it. The weather was glorious. The thought of being out on the ship appealed to her.

"Last call for the cruise to nowhere," a ship hand called into a megaphone.

"Let's do it," Tess said, and she was on line to buy their tickets. "It's my treat," Tess said when Neal took out his money purse.

They boarded the boat laughing, as if they had gotten away with something. From the deck, the waves flowed and retreated. When the motor started up, loud and choppy, she took out two pennies and handed one to Neal.

"Make a wish as we leave the shore," she said, and as they pulled away, Tess closed her eyes and tossed her penny in the water.

"Where is everyone going?" Neal asked a ship hand, as people paraded past them.

"To the casino," the man said. "It's a gambling ship."

Tess started to laugh, and Neal began to laugh, too, so that the ship hand looked from one of them to the other and then walked away towards the crowd.

"I'm fine out here, unless of course you want to go to the casino," Tess said.

Neal pursed his lips. "I'm not much of a gambler," he said, so that Tess laughed.

"I never got gambling," Tess said. "If you ask me, life is a gamble – the thought of standing around a table and betting money on numbers or throwing coins into a machine is beyond me, unless of course it's a parking meter."

"We didn't gamble much at the monastery," Neal said.

"Champagne?" a deck hand asked, holding out a tray.

"Sure," Tess said, watching Neal take a glass, too.

"To our very own memory on Memorial Day Weekend," Neal said.

"What shall we remember about today?" Tess asked.

"That the past is past."

"I'll drink to that," she said.

The boat sliced the water, dividing it dead center. Tess imagined the boat on a tight rope as it plunged on. She and Neal had pulled plastic deck chairs close to the side rail, which they used as a footrest, stretching their legs out. The hum of the motor was in her now, so that she felt the motion in her although she was sitting still. The rush of the boat charging the water mesmerized her; she liked the feel of moving ahead without exerting any energy. Neal peered out beside her. She felt her eyes grow heavier, shutting intermittently, so that each time they opened, she went through the who, what, why, when, where of consciousness.

"You folks still out here?" the deck hand asked as he passed with a full tray of champagne. "It's getting a bit chilly," he said. "Sure, you don't want to join the other folks inside? There's some food in there."

Tess jumped in her seat and turned to Neal. One of her legs had fallen asleep so that she felt the pins and needles prick her when she tried to move it. She didn't know how long she had dozed off.

"I think we're fine out here," Neal said. He smiled at Tess. "Unless you want to go inside."

Tess cleared her throat. She felt cold, stiff. "I'm great out here," she said.

"It tends to get crowded in there," the deck hand said. "If I could stay out here, I would. Let me clear some of those champagne glasses away," he said, offering Tess a fresh glass off his tray.

Tess took a new glass and handed it to Neal, before she took another for herself. She loved the long days that came with the approach of summer.

The deck hand and Neal were discussing something – the buildings in the distance, the speed of the boat?

Her nose to the rim of the glass, the champagne smelt syrupy; the bubbles fizzed to the top and she felt a belch coming, which she stifled by putting her hand over her mouth. With each plunge forward of the boat, they left a stream of foaming waves behind. Tess felt the motion within her, which seemed to be magnified by the sweet smell of the champagne. She bit her top lip, hoping that it would make her mind work: should she drink this? Champagne had a way of making her feel light and happy with her eyes open, and tired and shaky with her eyes closed. She imagined herself riding the waves, going under. She caught her breath and put the glass down. "Maybe I'll save this for a bit," she

said.

The deck hand smiled. "We head back any minute now." The moment he said it, they watched the boat cut the water and turn, waves billowing and crisscrossing as the boat began to retrace its route.

"How much does it cost to ride on this forever?" Neal asked.

"We have a while yet before we dock," the deck hand said. "Enjoy the rest of the ride. I'll be back to check on you."

The sun began to set. Neal was out of his seat now, clinging to the rail. Tess wished that she wasn't tipsy. In contrast to his black t-shirt and black chinos, from where she sat, Neal's bald head dazzled in the fading light, as if it were oiled. In the shadow of the sun's rays, he looked otherworldly. It made Tess want to touch him to see if he was real at the same time that it made her afraid to touch him, as if she would tarnish him. She wondered what it would be like to kiss him romantically out on the water. She wondered what his skin was like under his shirt, how it would feel to have his hands caress her shoulders and suddenly, a strange heaviness, like she had swallowed a bowling ball, came over her. I am not just old, Tess thought, but pathetic. 55 years behind me and I still fantasize about men that are all wrong for me.

In a moment, she was up close to him. His breath was hot and thick, and it made Tess nervous. She wished that she could sober up.

"Isn't it so strange how the day disappears?" Neal said. "Where does it go?" Neal watched her eyes as if he was trying to infuse her with his vision.

"Off to sea," Tess said. She wondered what it would be like to have sex with him. It could go either way—sloppy and horrible, or sweet and passionate. It could be spicy and seductive, too, but Tess couldn't really envision that. There was something too simple about Neal for him to emerge as a seducer. In fact, imagining him seducing her made her laugh. Tess shook her head as if trying to realign her mind, which was all over the place. She imagined that a man who had been celibate wouldn't be the best of bed partners the first time around. Tess would have to be the teacher, and as much as that idea appealed to her, it scared her, too.

The engine roared louder now, so that talking was futile; the pools of green-gray water mesmerized Tess. The water whirled and spun and foamed against the boat. She couldn't see anything in the haze of the whirlpool and yet if she focused on a streak of water, she could see it being paved dead center, mending as it was left behind. In the distance, streams of water bobbed to their own rhythm. She imagined the water ahead calling out to her, its beckoning soft and airy, like the sway of a hula dancer.

She could feel Neal's eyes on her and if she concentrated, she could see his eyes, the way his pupils spread into his irises, little creatures unto themselves. Sometimes, looking at him, she imagined his eyes slithering into her, looking around inside, watching, learning about Tess.

The Statue of Liberty was coming into sight, its green hue making it appear extraterrestrial in the half-darkness. It was the first time since 9/11 that she was seeing the statue up close and what came over her was a higher love for New York, for her life, for freedom. She looked in the direction of where the World Trade Center had stood – empty space.

In the days following 9/11, her mother had asked Tess to come up to Woodstock, and she and Michael did. Everyone functioned at a gentler frequency in the days and weeks that had followed. There was a need to be surrounded by the people one loved. In Woodstock her mother had led meditations that lasted hours, and in the evenings, satsangs in which everyone shared thoughts and memories and feelings about the tragedy. Tess remembered listening to her mother's followers without participating. It wasn't that she didn't have feelings to share, it was just that once she was in that setting, with her mother as a guru, she never knew who to be, how to be. The water thrashed the boat harder now. Above, stars began to fall in the semi-darkened sky. She was about to tell Neal that it was the New Moon, a chance to start again, reinvent, journey toward fullness, but when she opened her mouth to speak, no words came. Neal's breathing was shallower now, and Tess closed her eyes, peaceful and dreamy.

She didn't want this day to end, and yet already, it was, the minutes passing, the night falling. It seemed impossible to her that people found one another in this great big world. The truth, Tess believed, was that people clicked with those who were going in the same direction. My-way-or–the-highway type of people. It was the equivalent of meeting someone at a bus stop and sharing the ride. Neal was going her way – whichever direction that may be – but it was more than that. Where he had been, where he was heading, intrigued her; she could see herself searching for his path, wanting to stay on his route.

The boat shifted so that she fell slightly forward, closer to Neal. They were on a cruise to nowhere and back – back, not necessarily the direction Tess sought, but nonetheless, a destination. So what if he had been a monk? When the Viennese Waltz played over the intercom, Neal reached out his hand for Tess and she looked around for a moment to see if it wasn't somehow a joke, only the other people who had gathered on the deck to see the night sky were a distance away. She took his hand, and embracing Neal, she breathed in the cool night air, following his lead. She stumbled for a moment, and Neal righted her. The water tugged at the boat and Tess fell firm against Neal. They were still standing. At that moment, that's what had mattered most to Tess – that she had found someone that she couldn't knock over.

Neal touched her face, his fingertips gentle as a feather, before he cupped her chin in his hand and tilted her face up toward him. Her body reverberated with anticipation; she felt everything inside of her coming awake.

"Tess," he said, looking into her eyes. In the pull and tug of the boat, their movements were clumsy.

She felt her heart racing.

"I'm afraid," Neal said. His expression was fixed on the floor now, as if he was no longer seeing or hearing.

Tess brought his face back to hers, his cheek smooth to her touch.

"I'm afraid, too," she said, looking into his eyes. In the coming darkness, his pupils grew dark and wide, so that she could see her own eyes in them.

"I'm not sure what I'm supposed to do," Neal said.

"What do you want to do?" she said.

"I would like to kiss you," he said, and in a moment, Tess brought her lips to meet his – gently, faintly, as if she were kissing the air. She pulled away and then Neal was cradling her face in both hands, bringing his lips to hers, planting little kisses so that she felt as if an animal was nibbling on her lips. She giggled and held Neal around the waist as she pulled him to her and began to kiss him passionately, seductively, on his neck, his lips.

When they separated, Neal stared into her eyes and Tess tried to slow down her breathing. Everything inside of her pulsed. She smoothed his chest with her hand and felt the indentation of his ribs. His body was thin and well defined and something in her began to hollow as if all of her was making room for him. He moved her in front of him so that they both faced the water and draped his hands around her waist so that she felt his breath by her ear and his body pressing against hers. A voice in her head said: oh no, not this, please, but the boat kept moving, rushing the water, slapping the waves as it made its way toward the New York City skyline, and for the first time in a long time Tess felt gratitude for all the possibilities that life held.

"It's such big city," Neal said, and Tess nodded, her head brushing against him.

The lights of the buildings reflected in the water so that it glowed.

He whispered in her ear: "I ordain you, Tess Rose, a woman that I like."

The waves gushed all around them, streaming into pools of whiteness that were smooth and calm. There was a silence to the water that one could only see as one moved through it. Standing still, you would never know its power, its peace. As the boat charged the water,

Tess saw herself plowing forward into this next phase of her life – the journey would lead her through rough waters, but there would be calmer waters, too. It was all mixed in – that was what everyone forgot when they searched for their happy-ever-afters.

Tess turned to face him. His eyes swam over her like the sea: restless and wild. No matter how scared she was of him – of herself – in his presence, she felt something that she couldn't ignore: her fierce waters were growing calm.

"I ordain, you, Neal Clay, a man that I like."

In a moment, Frank Sinatra was booming out over the loudspeaker, *Start spreading the word, I'm longing to stay,* and Neal held Tess close, dancing across the deck with her, tripping over her feet.

"I should have warned you that I don't know how to dance."

"You're doing fine," she said, moving her foot before Neal could step on it again.

As they moved across the floor, more people began to gather outside to watch as the boat approached the New York City shoreline. A deck hand walked around offering passengers little cups. When people started to toss confetti from the cups, Tess laughed. Some began to toss confetti at Tess and Neal as they danced. He dipped her slightly before he pulled her up and more people threw confetti at them.

When they docked, *New York, New York* was still booming out over the loudspeaker: *These little town blues, are melting away, I'm gonna make a brand-new start of it in old New York, and if I can make it there, I'm gonna make it anywhere...* Tess and Neal stumbled against one another. The night was silent, still, the sky full of stars. Tess and Neal held one another's hands as if one of them would fall if they were to let the other one go. When it was their turn to disembark, Tess took a deep breath. Her life felt foreign to her, as if she was witnessing someone else's story. She wanted to pause before she moved on to the next chapter, provide time and space for all that had happened to sink in, only the thing about life, about living, was that it kept going, moving you from one episode to the next. When she stepped from the plank onto the dock, Neal caught her, steadying her first step onto land.

CHAPTER 23: HOLDING ON FOR THE RIDE

"Kissing passionately?" Dale asked.

Tess smiled, and in that slight, involuntary movement, pressure from behind her eyes spread to her temples. She imagined a herd of midget hammer men scrambling around up there, taking turns whacking one another with their mini hammers. Bam, bam, bam: a pulse pounding her forehead. She didn't know what had possessed her to get out of bed that morning and meet Dale at yoga. Perhaps because Dale had woke her up at the crack of dawn, and the fact that she had to talk to someone to help figure out what had gone on the night before.

"It's not such a big deal," Tess said. "People get sentimental every day."

"I highly doubt that ex-monks go around kissing women."

"Maybe he's just feeling horny," Tess said.

"No doubt about that," Dale said. "Poor guy hasn't had sex – ever!"

"Can we move into the shade?" Tess asked.

They were in Union Square Park eating corn muffins and drinking coffee. The benches all around them were vacant and Tess breathed in, glad to have space. A squirrel eyed Tess's muffin until she flecked off a piece of it and tossed it his way.

"You shouldn't have done that," Dale said. "Now we're going to be ambushed. And, might I add, if you're going to give your muffin to the squirrels, I wish you'd offer it to me." Tess smiled and placed her muffin bag beside Dale on the bench.

"Tell me more," Dale said.

"An ex-monk likes me, what can I say?" Tess said.

"Do you want to rip his clothes off?"

"If I say I do, does that make me a pervert?" Tess asked.

Dale nodded and Tess leaned back in an overly dramatic motion so that her neck was exposed to the heavens.

Dale pulled Tess forward by her shoulder. "I'm just kidding!"

"When I took him home last night, he told me that he was going to tell his mother about me," Tess said. "What do you think he's going to tell her?"

"He's going to tell her that he plans to have wild, passionate sex with you," Dale said.

"Why am I even talking to you about this?"

"I bet he's going to tell her that he likes a woman – something like that," Dale said.

Tess shook her head. "His mother called me this morning at 7:00

a.m. Who calls at 7:00 a.m. on a Sunday morning?"

"She beat me by a half hour. What'd she say?" Dale said.

"That she wanted to come over to talk to me," Tess said.

"No!"

The swaying of the waves still barged from one end of Tess's head to the other. "Can you be seasick from a cruise to nowhere?" Tess said.

"When are you meeting her?" Dale said.

"Just so happens I'm not going into the office until later tomorrow as I have some houses to show down the street. She's coming over at 10:00 a.m. sharp."

"Do you think she's going to welcome you to the family or threaten you?" Dale said.

"She wanted to come over and meet me this morning. When I told her I had plans, she acted as if she had caught me two-timing her son."

"Are you going to make breakfast for her?"

"Perhaps you'd like to come over and make it. Or maybe I should invite Michael over to make breakfast." Tess laughed. "What have I gotten myself into?"

"It's going to be fine. What's she going to do?" Dale asked. "Threaten you?"

"I feel as if I'm back in grade school."

The sun was sharp and strong on Tess's back. She wiped her brow and pulled her hair up off her neck. The pounding in her head came and went at intervals, as if her brain was in snooze mode.

"In a few weeks' time, we'll be laughing about this: Tess, the ex-monk, and his mother. Great material for a sit-com," Dale said.

"Come on," Tess said. "Let's walk. I need to get out of the sun."

"How about going for a drink?" Dale asked.

"Very funny," Tess said.

"Really. There's nothing like a Bloody Mary to make a hangover go away."

Tess clasped her elbow in Dale's. "What the hell, right? I'm already a doomed woman. Lead the way, my dear."

Out of the Midtown tunnel and onto the Gowanus highway, "Sex World" was the first billboard Tess saw. It advertised live girls and adult fun. How did one seduce a virgin? Sex with Neal didn't seem right. How did love and sex become synonymous in her life? She didn't understand why she couldn't love someone of the opposite sex without thinking about having sex with them. Perhaps that's why she had succumbed to an affair with Michael: her loving him had led her to make love with him, and after making love with him, she felt as if her love for him was something tangible, in the flesh. She wouldn't have sex with Neal.

Thinking that filled her with a sense of relief. She belched and tasted the Bloody Mary at the back of her throat. Perhaps not having sex with Neal would work the same way – be more fulfilling, easier. Anyway, didn't one reach an age when they could decide once and for all they were over sex and romantic love? Oh, who was to say? She imagined that even if she decided that she was through with sex and love she'd fall victim to it at some point down the road. At least that's what her track record predicted. Though, with Neal it would be different.

She turned on the radio and scanned the channels looking for something soothing to divert her attention from sex and Neal – not only was she old and foolish, but now she was becoming a pervert, too. Commercials, weather reports, and more commercials. She turned the radio off and switching into the right line to veer towards the Belt Parkway, she maneuvered her cell phone from her bag and turned it on. Three new voicemail messages. She pressed speakerphone: one from Michael: *Hey, call me back.* One from Prakash: *Hi Mom – it's your own and only son – give me a ring when you have a minute.* A second from Michael: W*ill Tess, the CEO of Best Realty call back Michael, when she has a yoga break?* Tess wondered if Tess the CEO of Best Realty was different from the Tess who was the mother of Prakash, or the Tess who was the wife of four husbands at one time or another. She liked thinking of herself in multiples, like she was a deck of cards, and could deal people a different hand depending upon – depending upon what? Was it about how much people could offer her, or was it the luck of the draw?

She squinted in the glare of the sun, and there it was again – her head flaring up reminding her: *if you drink, you will pay.* Was this the price for becoming a yogi, Tess wondered? One could no longer enjoy a drink without suffering consequences? Or perhaps it was a mini-Neal inside of her trying to get her attention: now that I like you, I will not let you forget, bam. Tess turned off the Belt Parkway at 11N and suddenly all that had been familiar – the roads, the Kings Plaza Shopping Mall looming in the distance – seemed changed to her. She was back at the previous night, driving down 66th street in the dark, making a right on Mayfair Drive, and pulling up in front of Neal's house. The curtains had been drawn, and the moment that Tess stopped the car, the figure that had been looking out the window fled. His mother was at the front door instantaneously, fiddling with the lock, Tess supposed, because then she inched open the screen door. The way his mother stood there like that, in her robe, not moving, reminded Tess of a greedy trick-or-treater waiting to collect.

Neal had turned to Tess. "So, I guess I should tell mother about you," he had said.

She hadn't known what to say – did Neal expect her to say anything? "Sure," she had said, unable to take her eyes off the open door and his mother.

"Until we meet again," he said.

"Goodbye," Tess had said. When Neal walked up the porch, his mother opened the door wider, as if she was a Venus flytrap getting ready to strike. When he was inside, the wooden door closed, then the screen door slammed shut, blocking Tess out. Tess felt a momentary loneliness and it was unlike other spurts of loneliness because she could articulate it: on the water, she and Neal had been a unit. They had been dreamers on that boat, adventurers amidst those seas. On land they were separate.

It was hard to imagine that episode had been less than 24 hours ago.

The moment Tess walked up her porch steps, the cat sprang at her from inside the tree shading her porch, so that she jumped back, almost losing her balance. The cat watched her, as if Tess was a strange creature that he was inspecting. His lips were lined in black, so that it looked as if he had just been lapping chocolate ice cream. In the sunlight, she could tell that he was old. He glared at her like an angry old man and suddenly she wanted to shoo him away, only the way he meowed – long and slow, with an upward arc at the end, as if he was deranged – made her feel sorry for him.

"Hello kitty," she whispered and once again, the cat fled, looking back at her before it vanished past her neighbor's house and then out of sight.

When she walked into her house, her cell phone rang.

"I just wanted to check that you got home okay," Dale said.

"I did," Tess said. "Home sweet home."

"Just sleep it all off," Dale said.

"My encounter with the crazy cat, the Bloody Mary's or the Neal story?"

Dale was silent for a moment: "Everything," she said.

"Sounds like a plan," Tess said. Then, "The house phone is

ringing. Michael. I should get that. Farewell, my dear," Tess said.

She picked up her home phone on the fourth ring. "Hello?"

"This is Neal's mother."

Tess cleared her throat. "Mrs. Clay."

"You said that you had plans today."

"Yes. I just returned home."

"I see. Well, I'm confirming our talk tomorrow morning, Monday."

"I'll be here."

"Fine, I will bring my egg salad to eat." Was Tess supposed to say what she would eat? What she would have available?

"10:00 a.m. sharp," his mother said.

The way his mother annunciated *sharp* made Tess have to place her hand over the receiver to catch her breath. Tess was beginning to understand the extent of her crime against the Clay family.

"10:00 a.m. sharp is fine," Tess said, and a wave of nausea, like she was on the boat again, drifted through her. Then his mother hung up, so that Tess was left bracing the counter, the phone in her hand. It was a few minutes before she turned the portable phone off and placed it down.

She imagined Neal's mom snooping around her house the next morning with evaluating eyes. The countertops would have to be waxed; the crumbs under the dishwasher would have to be mopped up. Tess was about to pick up a sponge, and then she stopped. If his mother saw the crumbs, passed judgment on Tess and her home because of them, so what? Were dropped crumbs proof that your life was untidy and out of control? Tess gripped the counter, trying to steady herself. Suddenly, what she needed was to be out of her house again. She moved to the table slowly, picked up her bag and her car keys and in a few moments, she was backing out of the driveway.

The Religion section in the 17th street Barnes and Nobles was filled with books on Christianity: *The Idiots Guide to Being Christian, The Christian Encyclopedia, All You Ever Wanted to Know about Christianity.* There were three people looking at the books in the section: two old ladies and one young girl. She wished that there was somewhere that she could go right now where she could sit down with someone who would explain all she needed to know about Benedictine monks.

Tess pulled one book off the shelf called *Benedictine*, another book about religious callings, and one by Thomas Merton – *The Seven Story Mountain* – that one of the employees recommended. She sat down with them in the café section and glanced out at the lawn of Union Square Park where just a few hours earlier she and Dale had sat talking. Each day was so many things. Her mind was restless; she read sections from one book and then another, as if she was trying to put together a puzzle.

In the first few sentences to *The Seven Story Mountain* Tess learned that Merton had been a college teacher. So, there it was – the decision to become a monk was one that could come to any man. What Tess didn't understand was how a man could truly seclude himself from the hurdles and challenges of society. Wasn't the true test to be able to keep your faith when you lived amid chaos? Tess moved to the next book laid out before her:

As Benedictines, monks lead a strict contemplative life that separates them from what modern culture proclaims to be essential elements of human happiness: parties, TV, sports, restaurants, fashionable clothes, homes, cars, vacations, even families....

Perhaps the hardest challenge was to be alone with yourself in silence rather than to keep your faith amidst the chaos of society. She thought of herself in yoga class and how when she was forced to be silent, to focus on her breath, she would begin to panic and want to run away, and yet when she stuck it out, there was a benefit to it, a freedom that she earned; a peace that surpassed understanding.

Cistercians are a kind of Benedictine; Benedictines are a kind of monk. It is a question of different ways of ways of being monks, of seeking silence, solitude, and discipline for the sake of living the gospel well, for the sake of growing in love...

It didn't seem so strange to her – to seek silence and solitude, to be disciplined. When she had silence and solitude in her life, didn't it make the most sense? And discipline, wasn't that the cornerstone of any successful person? If she hadn't been disciplined, then Best would have never grown to be what it presently was. Her own mother was the most disciplined person that Tess had ever known, with her waking up at the crack of dawn each day and meditating and praying. Tess believed that to pursue a career, to be successful, it required a certain amount of discipline. She hadn't had that discipline in terms of her love life, and maybe that's why her four marriages had failed.

The search for God is the goal of monastic life. A day composed of the opus Dei, lectio divina and manual work. Cistercian life is basically simple and austere. Cistercians carry out their search for God under a rule and an abbot in a community of love where all are responsible. It is through stability that we commit ourselves to this community. It lives in an atmosphere of silence and separation from the world, and fosters and expresses its openness to God in contemplation, treasuring, as Mary did, all these things, pondering them in her heart...

Tess grew still. It made her think of teacher training, and how when she was with that group, it was nice to be separate from the rest of her life, the rest of the world for that matter. She was able to hear herself think when she was in the yoga studio, able to make sense of things that she couldn't seem to get to when she was rushing around the office or out showing a house.

The fundamental discipline is surrendering our will to God and submitting ourselves to the guidance of another. This does not at all exclude a personal search for the will of God, but it does mean we bring more important decisions to the superior for discernment.

Tess paused over this; was she operating as if she was the one and only power in her life? Did she even look or listen for a higher power in her day-to-day life, or had she believed all this time that she was the higher power in her life? There was something to letting go, surrendering, as her yoga teachers said, hearing someone else in her life besides herself.

Celibacy was a permanent choice made by those taking vows.

Of course, she liked sex. Although she'd had certain partners who she wouldn't have minded being celibate with. She hadn't had sex for a year now, and truth was, she felt fine. Tess remembered something her mother had said to her when she went off to college: that we are sexual beings, but that we are also so much more than that. She had told her not to make a big deal out of sex, which of course was easier said than done for an eighteen-year-old.

Friendship and affection are encouraged. Community amounts to a network of friendships. Yet these must be balanced with the need for solitude and with our radical commitment to Christ...

Neal must have had many close friends. Tess wondered what his leaving had done to the others, if they were able to get on with their lives, if they had debated leaving, too, because of his departure, or if they saw his leaving as a weakness. She wondered what he had said to his friends, if he had said anything, or if his leaving was a shock to them all, a scandal of sorts.

The pattern and regularity of the daily schedule can be a searching discipline. When it is time for the office or other community exercise, the monk goes ...

Vigils, lauds, terce, sext, none, vespers and compline are the seven "hours" of the liturgy or the hours or opus Dei (work of God) as St. Benedict called it in his rule. They are common prayer service: the prayer of the Church as well as the prayer of our community. None of these "hours" lasts an hour. All seven add up to two and a half hours. The purpose of these seven times of prayer is to praise, thank, and petition God as a community and to foster prayer throughout the day. The monks and others who pray the liturgy of the hours do so on behalf of the Church and of all humankind.

Vigils takes place before the sun rises, when the monk is enveloped in darkness; Lauds takes place at daybreak and asks for new beginnings; Terce is said at midmorning and it asks for strength; Sext is said at noon and asks for perseverance; Nones is said at mid-afternoon and it asks for more perseverance; Vespers is said at the day's end; it is a time when one sees beyond the struggles of the day; it is the hour of wisdom and rest in thanksgiving. Compline is the last prayer of the night. It foreshadows life's end and leads back to the darkness of night and the darkness of God's mystery. This prayer is a gentle daily exercise in the art of dying.

A daily exercise in the art of dying. It seemed an awful thing and a wonderful thing, too – to practice dying. To surrender and go to sleep acknowledging that you may or may not wake. If Tess were to go to sleep with that thought in her mind, how differently she would live each day and enter sleep, she imagined.

The monk is a man like other men, and his problems are basically those of other Christians. He is present to the world insofar as he is able truly to experience and share the anguish of his fellow man in the face of suffering, time, evil, and death. What he does more than others is simply that he tries to face this anguish, not with more subtle rationalizations, but with the greater humility and deeper awareness of his own poverty, not in a climate of inner beauty (whatever that might be) but with more intransigent and lucid honesty, not with more stoicism or resignation, but with a conscience more determined because more firmly rooted in the sense of God and in abandonment to him.

Tess sat very still, trying to keep all she read intact in her mind. She remembered her mother saying that Buddhism was the religion of the awakened one. It stressed discipline and morality, meditation, wisdom, insight. You could not become a Buddha until you realized your own nature. Perhaps Tess was never awake and that was why she had not accepted Buddhism. Or perhaps it had nothing to do with being awake for her – perhaps it was a child's rejection of something her mother practiced.

Tess opened the calling book to a random page and came upon the description of grace: *the gift of God's life in our souls, which guides us toward right choices. The gift of God's faithfulness to us.* She tried to imagine what Neal had heard, felt, known, when he walked away from the monastery.

A gentleman approached her table and with his eyes asked her if she was leaving and she shook her head. Sometime in the past few moments, she had closed the books on the table. Tess didn't know if she was headed in the right direction. So far what she knew of life was that each road turned into a highway. She feared that later she would want to turn off this road and what would she do then? And yet projecting into the unknown was what had always led to Tess's not being able to focus on the here and now of her life, to be restless, seek change when it wasn't always called for. Her job was to find the strength and discipline to keep herself in the present, come what may. What came to her was a quote from Ram Das that her mother often shared: *Be there when it happens.* She had committed to many things in her life – her career, her happiness – more often than not. But she had never committed to seeing things through. Something broke and she replaced it, whether it was a relationship, or an object. She had taken the easy way out. Here and now, Tess was done with running away. She wanted to be there when her life happened. *The gift of God's life in our souls, which guides us toward right choices. The gift of God's faithfulness to us.*

CHAPTER 24: THE ENCOUNTER

A sock in her hand midair, Tess paused, focusing on her laundry sprawled out on the kitchen table. There it was again. Was someone knocking at the front door? They could ring the doorbell. 9:15 am. His mother wouldn't arrive 45 minutes early, would she? Then the dreaded thought came to her: Michael. But no, he was at the office. She had just spoken to him. She peaked out her front window and strained to see the porch. When Prakash was a child, she had taught him to look out the window when she left him alone to see who was there when the doorbell rang, only Prakash never got it. He would look out the window and then go and open the front door regardless of who was there. No one on the porch. Strange. She heard the scraping at the screen door again – it sounded as if someone was trying to get in.

When she pulled open the wooden door, there, hedged inside the screen door, was the cat, rangy looking and more beat up than ever with fresh cuts all over its face. There was a news flyer stuffed in the door, and she imagined that the cat had pushed his way in through that opening. Their eyes met for a moment and then he was inside the house, running up the stairs. Tess darted up the stairs after the cat, tripping on the top step, falling forward into the kitchen's entrance, so that she cut her top lip with her tooth. "Shit!" She felt the bump on her lip and when she took her hand away, there was blood.

"Here kitty," she said, looking under the kitchen table and then moving to her bedroom. "Here kitty; where are you?"

She heard it sharpening its claws on her living room couch and by the time she darted there to confront it, the cat had run past her and up onto the kitchen table walking through the laundry. Just as Tess was about to grab it, the cat struck out at her with its claws and then whizzed away. "Damn!" Tess cried. She blew on the scratch; it was already puffy and bloody.

"Okay, kitty, do whatever you want. I don't have time to look for you. Come out when you're ready."

Tess poured some milk into a bowl and put it by the bathroom door. That way, she figured if the cat stopped to drink it, she could trap him in the bathroom. She washed her hands put some bacitracin on her scratch, and then rinsed her mouth to clean off her lip. It stung each time it touched her teeth. Tess stuck a sliver of toilet paper over the cut to keep it dry. She finished folding the laundry, put it away, and still no cat. She imagined it peeing under her bed, or better yet, shitting somewhere that she wouldn't be able to find the shit for days, so that her whole house would smell.

9:30. She hadn't showered yet and Neal's mother would be over in 30 minutes. She glanced at herself in the bathroom mirror. She wet her hair and moved her curls around a bit; damn, the scratch on her hand hurt! There wasn't time to shower and prepare something to eat. She splashed some water on her face and then rubbed in some tinted moisturizer. She slipped into a black linen A-line skirt and a black linen button down which she tucked in and then pulled out. Neutral, unsexy, leisurely clothes. Neal's mom wouldn't be able to judge her by what she wore.

What to make to eat? Tess took out some orange juice and poured it into a pitcher; then she took her fruit basket out from the refrigerator: apples, oranges, pears, and an avocado. She put up a pot of hot water and took out her collection of herbal teas, some sugar, filled a creamer with milk. What Tess really wanted was some cereal. She took down the box, poured herself a bowl of Kashi, cut up a banana and set it down at her seat. If Neal's mother wanted cereal, she could have a bowl, too.

Tess had forgotten about the cat when she heard a car horn beeping. The car backed up in front of her house and beeped again. Tess could make out a woman in the driver's seat. She parked the car so distant from the curb so that it looked like she had abandoned it in the middle of the street.

Tess straightened her shirt and then held the door open for Mrs. Clay. She walked in carrying an oversized brown leather pocketbook without glancing at Tess. She had on a burgundy pants suit. It looked as though it were polyester, with a white and burgundy striped shirt. She could have been wearing an airline uniform.

"Good morning Mrs. Clay," Tess said, motioning her up the stairs.

"I don't take off my shoes," Mrs. Clay said.

"Excuse me?"

"You heard me correctly. Your yogi ways won't work with me.

My shoes stay on," she said.

"Sure. You don't have to take off your shoes," Tess said, and Mrs. Clay was already traipsing up the stairs, standing in the doorway to the kitchen. She peered in both directions as if she were about to cross a street.

Mrs. Clay moved to the sink, looked out the window, then made her way to the refrigerator, opened it and examined the contents. It was packed with condiments: salad dressings, mustard, jellies and jams, some peanut butter, but not much more.

"Can I get you something?" Tess said, and Mrs. Clay closed the refrigerator door firmly.

There was a geometry to her person, with her angular bobbed gray hair, bracket-like graying eyebrows, sharp yet small nose. The arcs of her lips formed isosceles triangles. Mrs. Clay sat down where the cereal was, so that Tess didn't know if she should move it away or if Mrs. Clay thought it was for her. Mrs. Clay pushed the cereal away from her.

"Your house is cold," she said. Her skinniness was exhausting to Tess, she looked like she was about to collapse on the floor.

"I could shut the window," Tess said, and Mrs. Clay watched her now as if Tess were some strange specimen. When Tess turned around from closing the window, Mrs. Clay took a toothpick and a Tupperware container from her pocket book. She opened the container, and with the toothpick, she began to eat her egg salad, picking out the egg white chunks and examining each one before she put it in her mouth. From what Tess could see, it was not mixed with mayonnaise, just cut up eggs with carrots, celery, and scallions. Goose flesh sprouted up Tess's arms and legs; this woman was creepy. Perhaps if she ate, too, it would be less awkward. The cereal no longer appealed to her, and Tess remembered the tuna fish cans in the cabinet. She would make herself an English muffin with tuna fish.

"Excuse me while I prepare something for myself," she said, and Neal's mother looked up from her egg bits.

Tess used a can opener to open the can and then mixed the tuna with mayonnaise while she toasted an English muffin.

"The smell of tuna fish makes me nauseas," Mrs. Clay said, so that Tess stopped and turned around. Mrs. Clay peered at Tess, her toothpick tapping the table.

"Mrs. Clay," Tess said, moving toward her. "What is it that you want from me?"

"Hah," she said.

"Excuse me?" Tess said.

"I know you," Mrs. Clay said, quietly, as if she didn't want other people to hear.

Tess shook her head. "You know me?"

"You're a fancy lady."

"I beg your pardon?"

His mother looked up towards the ceiling and made the sign of the cross.

"You have a lot of other pardons to beg, lady."

"Mrs. Clay, people who insult me are not guests in my home."

"What do you want with my Neal?"

"I don't want anything with him – we're friends."

"You think I'm stupid."

"Neal and I are grownups. I refuse to be treated as a criminal."

Mrs. Clay laughed a thick, throaty, laugh that made the cat peer into the kitchen as if it was aroused by an animal call. Tess kept her eye on the cat: *go away, kitty. Stay away.*

"You've led a big life," Mrs. Clay said. "Neal has not. He is not part of the world that you live in."

"You make it sound as if he's an alien."

"If you were a religious woman you would understand," Mrs. Clay said. "You're poison for him."

"You know nothing about me."

"Hah," his mother laughed again.

"Neal and I care about one another," Tess said.

"Neal is horny," Mrs. Clay said and at that moment the cat jumped onto the table so that the bowl of cereal splattered. Mrs. Clay let out a scream when she saw the cat. For an instant, she and the cat stared up at one another until the cat hissed, growling at Neal's mother before it fled.

"What a disgusting creature," Mrs. Clay said. She wiped the sides of her mouth with a tissue she pulled from her bag.

"I'm sorry," Tess said, looking down the hallway to see where the cat had fled. "He wandered in today." There was cereal all over the table. "Can I clean this up for you?"

Mrs. Clay was studying her.

"Would you like some napkins, Mrs. Clay? I'm so sorry."

"After all of those years cooped up without sex, then he meets you," Mrs. Clay said.

"You're wrong," was all that Tess could say. She stood, as if paralyzed, the cut on her lip stinging; she touched it and felt the toilet paper there, still intact.

"You don't know Neal," his mother said.

She felt powerless with his mother watching her like that, accusing.

"Neal is a monk," she continued.

"He left the monastery," Tess said.

"He took vows."

"Your son left that life behind. He's here now," Tess said.

"A person can never leave the monastery behind. It's everything he is," Mrs. Clay said.

"Neal and I are friends. I'm not keeping him from anything."

"You must be delusional."

Neal's mother watched her so intensely that Tess felt as if she was looking inside her mind, the mess of it. Then, suddenly, his mother lost interest in her and resumed to picking the egg white chunks out of her salad.

"Neal is devout Catholic," his mother said, studying the tip of her toothpick. "There is no place for someone like you in his life."

Tess opened her mouth to speak, but no words came. If she stared at the tiles long enough, the white gave off a blue gleam so that the floor looked surreal, as if it might part at any minute and provide an escape route for Tess to vanish. Mrs. Clay's face was blank now, like a cloud, and Tess tried to imagine how she would react to this situation if it were about Prakash. She had an urge to reach out to her, mother to mother. Mrs. Clay's life was falling apart. Her son had set her spinning years back when he joined the monastery and he had set it spinning again upon his return, only now Mrs. Clay had found a scapegoat in Tess. Tess wanted to tell her that she was sorry, but the truth was that she was not going to be able to put Mrs. Clay's life together again.

"Neal is confused and trying to find his way and then you showed up, willing and able, to manipulate him with your flirtations."

"Mrs. Clay, I am not manipulating your son."

Mrs. Clay picked at her front teeth with her toothpick for a moment, and then sealed her Tupperware container. She dabbed at the sides of her mouth with her tissue and cleared her throat before she stood up and stared beyond Tess's eyes, as if at a spot on the wall.

"I don't see you," she said.

"Excuse me. Mrs. Clay," Tess said, grabbing her arm as she walked past Tess. Swallowing was becoming unreliable.

Mrs. Clay pulled her arm away.

"Let go of me," she said, and Tess moved back. "You haven't seen the last of me," she said. "You go on and have your fun, but you remember what I told you. Don't play with a man of God. You'll regret it," and with that, she hustled down the steps and out the door.

CHAPTER 25: SILENCE AND SERENITY

There were times when Tess thought that she needed to leave this house, this world that she had built around herself, or that had built itself around her. It was hard to tell if one was the gatekeeper or the prisoner of one's domain. In this house, where she was sitting now at the top of the steps, she had watched one husband leave after the other. She had raised Prakash in this house, and then watched him walk down these steps and leave, too. And yet she persisted here.

The cat strolled up to her now and lay down across from her. She hadn't checked yet if he had used the litter box that she had bought for him on her way home from her appointments. He studied her for a moment before he closed his eyes and spread out, his paws moving towards her. She reached out to pet him and at first, he flinched and was about to strike her with his claws, but then looking into her eyes, he softened and lay back. Tess sighed. "See, I'm not so bad." The cat looked up at her again before it fell back. "His mother is bad," Tess said. "Evil."

Tess moved through the kitchen and wandered her halls, passing in and out of the bedrooms. It suddenly struck her as silly – Neal a few blocks away, at his mother's house. The cat followed her into Prakash's bedroom, and jumped onto the windowsill, looking out before it turned to look at her. She was sure that there was something being spoken from this creature's eyes. She felt a gratitude passing between them, and yet she couldn't distinguish who felt gratitude for whom. The cat's glowing green-yellow eyes made her feel as if she was on fire, and it began to cry – helpless little yelps. Tess no longer saw the cat but felt the vibration of its plea and then, she didn't know if she blinked, or if the cat was spooked, but it fled from the room suddenly, darting past her. She lay down on Prakash's old bed, her mother's Afghan wrapped around her like a shawl, and closed her eyes.

It was almost midnight when she woke up and she was reminded of the times in her childhood, when after a tantrum she would lock herself in her bedroom and snuggle in her bed, falling asleep. Outside, the sky was total darkness. Her dreams came back to her in flashes. Something about her in a car that Prakash was driving. She grabbed the cordless phone and went out onto the porch. The air was fresh, cool, the street desolate.

She remembered days when she would sit on the porch waiting for Prakash to come home from a friend's house. She would be thinking of the houses she had to show, scouting her brain for possible matches, and then she would see Prakash's big head and those black eyes staring at her and it would make her very still. His eyes had the power to make her focus on him and lose everything else. They were the eyes of a wise old man. When he was a toddler and she was vacuuming or cleaning, she often felt something penetrating her, and she told herself that she was being silly, that Prakash was in his room, napping, until she turned around and there he was, on the floor, his thumb in his mouth, watching her. She always froze, half expecting him to start speaking to her in a deep old man's voice, and in those moments, she felt as if he knew things about her that she had yet to learn. When Prakash had smiled at her, she had felt safe and good – as if he validated her existence.

"How are you, Mom?"

"I'm sitting on the porch thinking of you," she said.

"What are you thinking?"

"How I used to be afraid of you and in awe of you when you were a baby," she said.

"I thought that you still felt that way about me," Prakash said.

"If I tell you something, promise me that you won't react," she said.

"Don't tell me you're getting married again," Prakash said.

Tess hadn't realized she had plucked some foliage from the evergreen tree beside her until she feathered her ankle with it.

"Mom? You still there?"

"I met someone. I'm not in love and we are not getting married. He reminds me of your grandmother," Tess said.

"Oh, no," Prakash said.

"I met him a few months back, before we were all in Woodstock."

"I'm listening."

"He's an ex Roman Catholic monk who lived in a monastery for the last 23 years. He's from Mill Basin and his mother is a witch who thinks she has to protect him from me."

Prakash laughed into the phone – a small laugh and then an all-out cackle.

"Just when I think you're insane, you go and convince me that you are," Prakash said.

Tess laughed. "I never said I wasn't nuts."

"What are your plans for this guy?" he asked.

"Am I supposed to have plans for him?"

"No. But you're telling me about him, so there must me some motive."

"I just wanted you to know," she said.

"Don't fall in love with him, Mom; you know where that route leads."

"Kash, I am not falling in love with him."

"Is that a cat meowing?" he asked.

The cat was at the door now, trying to nuzzle it open. For a moment, she imagined the cat living in the house and that she was the outsider. She waved to the cat and the cat stood watching her. She pulled the door open, and he dashed out, past her and down the driveway.

"I've taken in a stray cat. Or rather, he seems to have decided that I'm his keeper," Tess said.

"Let me guess – his name is Buddha."

"He doesn't have a name yet, but I think you just gave him one. Buddha," she said.

"How about Buddhi, after my stuffed monkey that I was obsessed with?"

"Buddhi," Tess said. "You carried around that stuffed monkey until it lost all of its fur. Buddhi it is," she said, and the moment she spoke it aloud, the cat paused in the driveway, looking back at her, before he darted across the street.

"A monk," Prakash said. "In Mill Basin of all places." Then, "can someone leave a monastery and be done with it?"

"It's like going through a divorce, I suppose," Tess said. "Feelings change, and you find a new way to live your life." The cherry blossom shadowing the porch swayed in the breeze so that pink-white pedals sprinkled Tess's shoulder. Against her fingers, they felt like velvet.

"You there?" Prakash asked.

"Do you think that life is random, Kash, or that we meet certain people for a reason?"

"I don't think anything is random, but I don't think we can always make sense of why things happen. Sometimes it doesn't all fit together until years later."

"I don't want to be the woman who keeps making mistakes, Kash. I want my life to make sense."

"Only you know what makes sense for your life," he said.

"But I don't always know," she said.

"Does anyone, Mom? Aren't we all trying to figure it out?"

She bit her top lip. "I guess. I wish sometimes that there was someone to tell me what I was supposed to do, what comes next."

He laughed. "If I or anyone tried to tell you what you were supposed to do, you would insist on figuring it out for yourself."

"Yes. I guess you're right."

"It's bedtime for you," Kash said.

"I wish you were here," Tess said.

"Like you've said to me many times: tomorrow is a new day, and you are going to feel differently."

"Tomorrow is a new day."

"Good night, Mom."

"Good night, Kash."

Tess sat holding the phone in her hand. Looking up into the falling sky, she wished that she could propel herself upwards, beyond, see what lay ahead. She wished that she could pick up the phone and call her mother, hear her voice. She thought of going inside to get the urn, to try to sync with her mother in that way, but no, she wasn't ready for that. She wasn't ready to revisit the urn, which she had hidden away in a top shelf in her closet, alongside her cashmere cardigans. The urn was full of death. Tess focused, trying to visualize her mother – her long wavy black hair, her deep brown eyes, her olive skin. Tess lay back on her porch so that the sky was her ceiling.

People were born to change, adapt – that's what Tess believed. She thought of her husbands, each one of them falling away from her life like a leaf in the wind. "Let go," was what her mother had advised Tess when she told her of each divorce. Tess had let go, jumping from the ledge of her life again and again, free falling. Wherever she had landed, she had picked herself up and began anew – it hadn't been a choice, but a necessity. Life kept going whether you were in the game or not.

Tess didn't know how long she had been staring into space. She sat up, scanning her driveway, the yacht club across the street, the sycamore trees lining the sidewalks, their shadows mirroring 66th street. The crickets chirped. "My life," she said. "This is my life." She closed her eyes; sometimes this is what her life felt like – total darkness. She couldn't have imagined that her life would lead her in the directions that it had – each path had led to another path, sometimes Tess kicking and screaming en route, other times an eager traveler. She liked thinking of each person on his or her own path. There had been times in her life that thought had made her feel lonely. Now, it felt empowering. She looked up into the great big sky and made a wish upon a star – *may I continue to find my way and live my truth, whatever it may be* – before she went inside, leaving the world behind.

CHAPTER 26: CLOSE QUARTERS OF ANOTHER KIND

When the car door slammed shut in her driveway, Tess looked up from the page she was reading in *A Path With Heart*. That was funny. 6:30 am. She glanced at the cat sitting at her feet before she made her way into the living room, crouching by the window. Neal waved a little wave to his mother, picked up his brown oversized rucksack from the sidewalk – it looked to Tess like a body bag – and walked up the three steps of Tess's porch. He rang the doorbell. What in the world? She tightened her bathrobe and made her way to the door.

"Tess," Neal said. The way he said her name, as if he had been looking for her in a crowded carnival, made her smile.

"Good morning," Tess said. The cleaning neighbor lady was out by the curb organizing her bags of garbage in the pails. For a moment, Tess had a sinking feeling that Neal had come to say good-bye – that he was leaving Mill Basin, heading back to the monastery.

She motioned him inside and the screen door slammed closed behind him.

"You're packed," Tess said. The cat stood at the top of the stairs.

Neal nodded. "I am," he said. "I mean, I did – pack."

"Are you going somewhere?" she said.

Neal looked at her as if he didn't understand.

"My mother told me…." he turned to look behind him now, as if his mother would be waiting for him in the background, but she had pulled away the moment Tess opened the door.

"She told you what?"

"She told me," Neal said, looking down at the floor, "that you asked her to bring me here."

"Bring you here for what?" Tess asked.

"To stay with you," Neal said, and suddenly Tess understood. This was the game his mother would play. Send him off to her and see what she would do. Fury rose in her throat, so that she had to take a few deep breaths before she spoke again. She gripped the railing with one hand, creating a barrier from where they stood to upstairs.

"Neal, why did your mother send you here?"

Neal took a deep breath and looked deeply into Tess's eyes.

"Do you know why she sent you here?"

"I guess –" he paused. "She doesn't want me to sin under her roof."

Tess used the railing to lower herself down and perched on the steps, shaking her head. No, no, no.

"Neal, you should go. For your mother's sake, for your sake, you should go back home. I'm not –"

"I'd like to stay," he said. "For my sake."

Tess shook her head. "It doesn't work this way, Neal. You don't just show up at a person's house, this isn't – I don't want this. We kissed, Neal. That's all, a kiss."

"I'm sorry. I'll go," he said, picking up his sack. "You're right, I'll go."

"If two people want to live together, Neal, they talk about it, it's a joint decision, they don't just show up – no one shows up at someone's house," Tess said. "You're a grown man."

"Tess, I understand. This was stupid. I should have spoken up to my mother. I should have come to talk to you first. I'm sorry."

"It's none of my business, Neal, but your mother. She needs to let you make your decisions. You're not a child."

He nodded. "I was wrong in thinking that coming back home was the next move for me. At the monastery I was ascribing to their ways and here it's my mother's ways."

"Well, I'm sure you'll figure it all out," Tess said, and the moment she said it, she cringed and closed her eyes as if to erase this scene. Her comment was harsh, yet that was how it worked. She wasn't his keeper. No one was. People figured things out.

He studied her with those blue eyes. His hair was beginning to grow in; Tess supposed that he hadn't shaved it for weeks. Harmless. He was harmless. Childlike. Vulnerable. And attractive. Annoyed as she might be, she was attracted to him.

"I hope we can still be friends," Neal said.

His last residence was a monastery. She shook her head. He might as well have been living on Mars. She thought of his breath on her neck, the tenderness of his lips and something like excitement, anticipation filtered through her.

"I don't see why not, Neal."

She heard the beep of her blackberry telling her she had an email. Work. She had to get ready for work. She had promised Michael she'd get there early this morning to go over some paperwork.

"I can drop you back home on my way to work," she said.

"I'm fine to walk. Thank you," he said.

She nodded her head and stood up on the stairs.

"I'm sorry, Tess. This is awkward."

She nodded again. The guy had nowhere to go – if he went back home right now, it was likely he'd have to listen to his mother's insanity.

"Look," she said. "If you just need a place to stay for a day, I can put you up downstairs. Later today, you head home, talk to your mother, and go from there."

"I wouldn't want to put you out, Tess." His chin tucked into his chest, he peered up at her.

No, she was not going to plead. She'd made her offer. A man who showed up at her house was not going to get away with giving her shy and awkward.

"As you choose," she said.

"I mean I don't want to inconvenience you," he said.

Monk or not, all men were alike – they needed to feel wanted. She studied him for a few moments before she realized she was biting her bottom lip.

"It's just for a day, Neal," she said. Surely Neal's mom would come to claim him before the day was over.

"Thank you," he said, his eyes meeting hers. "I won't be in your way."

"I'll be at work and then yoga. I need to get ready to go to my office, but let me show you downstairs, and I need to get you a key and show you how to work the alarm."

Spare keys were in her bedroom night table – she had learned to put them there after a string of local robberies in which house workmen stole spare keys from kitchen cabinets or countertops. She dashed into her bedroom and scrutinized the bright fuchsia walls. Years back, she had the walls painted the bright, vibrant hot pink on a whim, the way she'd try on a nail polish color and then take it off and paint her nails the same old whitish-pink nude. The ecru walls of the rest of her home were professional, clean, a perfect setting for the mahogany-framed black and white photos that lined them. Photos of 1920's jazz culture – pixie girls, flappers, musicians. Sometime over the years she had stopped seeing the photos, but whenever one caught her eye, she would smile at the familiarity of the image, like an old friend there before her.

She hadn't known she would keep the fuchsia color until one day had passed and then another, and her painter, calling her a week later, asking her when she wanted him to re-paint her bedroom, had seemed shocked when she instructed him to add a second coat of the fuchsia versus painting her bedroom walls the same bland ecru. Nothing seemed to look right on her fuchsia walls except for the mirror on the wall facing her. She liked having bare walls in the room in which she slept – it made her feel expansive. All the accents in the room – the comforter, pillows, the frames lining the dark chocolate brown French antique furniture – were a rich creamy off-white that soothed Tess. The contrast of the shocking fuchsia and the deep brown furniture worked for her – it was an adventurous combination. Michael had found it sexy, said that the room showed the hot and seductive side of Tess, which made her cringe now, as did most thoughts of intimacy with Michael. When she was done, she was done. Neal. Keys.

Tess showed Neal how to open and lock the front door without setting off the alarm, and how to shut off the alarm if it should go off. Should she be doing this? She hesitated more than once – what if he made a backup set of her keys – but he seemed so harmless. She couldn't imagine him bringing any malice to her, although she would be sure to lock her closet, where she kept her jewelry, and now her mother's urn, and take that key with her. He complied when she asked him to demonstrate that he could handle the door locks and alarm on his own.

She led him downstairs to the basement and showed him the study and the den. It had been weeks since she'd stepped foot in the study. Each time she opened that door, she imagined, just for a minute, that she was going to see Prakash sitting there at the desk. It had been his study up until the time that he left for college. Her ex-husbands had never used that room, and Tess was never sure why. She guessed it was the same reason that she never used that room. Whenever she was in there, she felt shut off from the rest of the world, as if she was in a fallout shelter. The room was scattered with bookcases full of Prakash's college textbooks, some architect books, and stacks of old realtor magazines. There were a few mahogany wood filing cabinets that were full of old Best Realty papers. There was a matching wraparound desk, a thick burgundy leather couch surrounded by two windows. When Prakash was in high school, he had sat on the couch talking on the phone.

Neal looked around the room as if he had struck gold. He felt the cold, hard leather of the couch, peered out the window, examined the books in the cases.

"This is perfect," he said. "I can write in here."

Tess's forehead creased. "For today, sure," she said, nodding.

Just as he sat down on the couch, the cat crashed into the room and jumped up onto an arm of the couch, panting, and lied down. Neal smiled and petted him.

"You like it here, huh? The couch must feel cool on your back," Neal said. The cat wiggled under his touch and snuggled up to Neal.

"You've got a companion," Tess said. "Poor kitty – so cut up," she said squeezing one of his paws gently.

"Have you named him yet?"

"My son suggested Buddhi."

The cat squinted up at them. His eyes seemed to say *I know everything.*

"You like being called Buddhi, fellow?" Neal asked him. It was funny to Tess how everyone's voice changed when they spoke to an animal, as if they expected the animal to talk back to them if they hit just the right chord.

"Well, you should be all set then," Tess said. "I need to hurry up."

"I'm all set," he said.

"I'll leave you to do what it is that you do," Tess said. It was hard for her to imagine the passion she had felt for him on the boat just days back. "And the locks and alarm –"

"Yes, I'll be sure to be diligent and lock up if I go out."

"The police will be here in a minute if anything happens," Tess said, once she said it, regretting it. "What I mean was if the alarm –"

Neal nodded. "I understand," he said. "Everything will be fine."

CHAPTER 27: CHALLENGE INCLUDES CHANGE

"What do you mean he showed up at your house?" Dale asked. They were doing karma yoga, which consisted of an hour or two a week of volunteer service at the yoga studio. Today their job was to clean out the yoga mat storage shelves.

Tess looked up from her perch by the bottom shelf, where she was pulling out yoga mats that smelled like un-bathed feet.

"It's so gross that people don't throw their mats away and buy new ones," Dale said. She unrolled one mat that was worn out at the back, presumably where the owner's feet would land in down dog. "Look at that – it's almost worn down to shreds. Grab me a post it and pen from my bag, will you, Tess?"

Dale wrote *time for a new mat* on a post it and stuck it on the worn-out part before she rolled the mat back up.

"Dale!" Tess said.

"What? They need a new mat." She reached for another mat from her shelf. "Of course, his mother put him up to this," Dale said.

"I'm sure that Michael or my son would tell me it's some type of a hoax – that Neal is out to rob me of all my stuff."

"I didn't think of that," Dale said.

"Dale, he's lived in a monastery for 23 years. I highly doubt that he's a criminal. Although it did cross my mind this morning that it could be a scheme."

"Do you want to know my opinion?" Dale said.

"Your opinion about what?" Stephanie, the downtown yoga studio manager, asked.

"Nothing," Dale said.

"About how the mats should be arranged?" Stephanie said.

Dale looked at her like she smelled rotten milk. Tess loved this bitchy, no-nonsense side of Dale.

"We're not talking about the mats," Dale said. "Believe it or not, there are other things to talk about. Tess just lost her mother –"

"And the studio was kind enough to let her join the program late because of it. I'm aware of what took place. When you're all done with that little project, I have a few others for you to do," Stephanie said, smiling. "Karma hours – need to get them all in!"

"This is the only project we have time for today," Dale said. "Some of us have a life outside of the studio."

Stephanie walked away, tossing her long, black straight hair in their direction.

"Such a bitch," Dale said.

"Behave," Tess said.

"Look who's telling who to behave," she said. "So, what are you going to do with your new roommate?"

"I am only letting him stay for the day," Tess said. "When I stopped to check in this afternoon before coming here, he was sitting at the kitchen table reading. Do you think I'm nuts for leaving him in my house?" Tess asked.

"If you did it, you must have felt it was okay."

Tess sighed and shook her head.

"I guess," she said. "What's going on with Kyle?"

Dale pulled mats from the next shelf down onto the floor. She unfolded them one by one before she folded them back up, neat and tight, and fastened them with a wide rubber band.

"Things are fine. Sometimes I think I'm just crazy."

"Join the club, Dale."

"I've come to terms this week with the fact that I'm commitment phobic. You would think someone is asking me to wear a strait jacket by getting married to Kyle."

"Marriage isn't an easy thing," Tess said. "But if you're with the right person, you're not giving up anything – in fact, you're gaining."

"What am I gaining? More responsibility? More accountability?"

"Yes, there's some responsibility and yes, you can't always come and go when you please, but when I was happy and married, I didn't think about that."

"Were you happy and married?" Dale asked.

Tess paused and met Dale's eyes. She was so young; Tess couldn't remember being that young.

"I was. I had a lot of fun with my husbands. And right or wrong, when I stopped feeling happy, then I said goodbye. I don't know if I did the right thing walking away, but I never regretted my choices. My mother called it the flow of life."

"The flow of life," Dale said. She studied a mat before she unrolled it and rerolled it tighter. "I'm beginning to think that marriage is a bizarre concept, and that people shouldn't be wed to one another in any formal way," Dale said.

"Questioning your feelings for Kyle is okay. It's better to do it now than when you're married and pregnant. Everyone thinks it's the jitters, that it will pass, but maybe it's your intuition guiding you."

"Now you're really confusing me. What are you saying?" Dale asked.

"I'm saying that maybe you're not crazy. Maybe your fears are grounded. Just because you're dating Kyle for over five years doesn't mean that you have to marry him," Tess said. "Maybe he's your best friend or maybe he's your lover, or maybe he's someone who makes you laugh. Perhaps he's all of the above. Or maybe he's the most amazing person in this world for you to spend your life with. The important thing for you to do right now is to take the time to figure out who Kyle is to you and let him be who and what he needs to be. There is no right or wrong answer, but you do need to work at it a little – make sense of it all to yourself."

Dale sat staring at Tess as if Tess had just filled her in that there was a choice D after she completed an ABC multiple-choice exam.

"I don't mean to preach, Dale. God knows I'm not one to preach about marriage with all my divorces," Tess said.

"I wish that someone would tell me *this is what you need to do*," Dale said. "But I probably wouldn't believe that person anyway."

Tess reached over for Dale's hand and squeezed it.

"I know it sounds lame and cliché, but you'll figure it all out, Dale. You will. You probably have all the answers already, but with all the noise in your head, you can't hear them."

"Maybe," Dale said. "I'm getting tired of driving myself crazy, which means that change is brewing. I keep wondering if I'd be commitment phobic with everyone that came into my life, or if it's just with Kyle."

"The good news is that you don't have to worry about everyone that comes into your life today. Right now, you just have to concentrate on Kyle," Tess said.

"Conversations like this make me wish that I was working and had all my work nonsense to focus on," Dale said.

Tess laughed. "It's healthy to detox from your professional life now and then. It helps you reassess your life."

"You don't detox from work," Dale said.

"I did for a few weeks when my mother passed away, and it got me here in teacher training."

"And the jury is still out on whether that's a good thing or not," Dale said.

"Good or bad, it's reality," Tess said.

"Yup," Dale said. "A few weeks ago, Neal was just some guy you knew and now he's in your house. No dull moments, huh?"

A few weeks ago, her mother had been alive, and she had just started doing yoga. It was fascinating the way life unfolded, ready or not.

"No dull moments," Tess said. She stopped folding mats. "I hope my house is okay," she said. "I'm going to take him home tonight," Tess said.

"That sounds like a plan. And you never know. You may end up falling madly in love with Neal and the two of you will live happily ever after," Dale said.

The image of him in his monk robes came to her clearly.

She smiled. "Unlikely," she said.

CHAPTER 28: WHAT YOU SEEK; WHAT YOU FIND

Tess held her breath as she pulled into her driveway. 7:00 pm and the sun was still bright. As much as she wished Neal would be gone, there was something in her that hoped he was still there. She didn't realize that she was holding her breath until she saw his bike by the side of the porch and the air seeped out of her. She nodded hello to the wild Israeli boy and his mother, who was pleading with him to get in the car while he shook his head no. It was a matter of moments, Tess imagined, before the mother would be chasing him around the driveway.

"Hello?" Tess called climbing the stairs into her kitchen. The house was quiet so that her heart began to race – maybe he was up to no good, hiding out – until the aroma of fresh baked cookies filtered through her and everything in her slowed down again. She opened the oven and there was a batch of cookies on a tray. They were cool.

Tess picked up the pages propped sideways on the table, held up by the silver Tiffany salt and peppershakers, thinking it was a note for her.

It was in a garden that I tended to that I began to unravel the mysteries of my heart and soul. For a long time – over 20 years – I had thought that I was living my life from my heart and soul. But as the seasons came and went, and I watched seeds bloom into flowers of different colors and sizes, I would wonder what would happen if I planted the seed of my soul: would I bloom in vibrant colors or would I be black and white? Would I grow tall and wild, or would my stalk be stumped? And so, I began to sprinkle seeds of my soul here and there and what bloomed startled me. There were parts of me that I had never seen – parts that I never even knew existed. How could it be that there was so much more to my life that I had yet to uncover?

For a while, I believed that it was a miracle that I had left my hometown of Brooklyn, New York and migrated to the northern countryside of Canada, where there was endless space for my garden. Slowly, though, I began to realize that a garden is not about the space or climate outside; rather, it is about the space and climate within oneself. We can keep searching for a better situation, but it's not until we stop looking outside and venture inside that we begin to find what we are looking for.

In writing this, I hope to share with you what I have learned from spending time in my own garden. My hope is that it helps you find your way back to the land in which you bloom.

The Beginning

Although you may have strayed from the path of your life, it's never too late to change your direction and find your way back to your home. My goal is to help you to navigate through the weeds of your life to your very own garden, where new seeds are always being planted and flowers are always blooming.

Once you enter your garden, though, be prepared – that's where your work begins. It's no small task to plant seeds, cultivate them, let the sunshine in, weather the storms, and become inch by inch. It takes patience and persistence to be a gardener, just as it takes patience and persistence to grow.

Regardless of your commitment, there will come times that your garden will be barren. If you have faith, however, the barrenness will lead to rebirth. For in life, before we plunge into the future, we need to live today. Remember always that it is out of the barrenness that you will bloom again.

You must actively commit to take time for you each day if you are to find yourself in your own garden. You must also accept the fact that you are exactly where you need to be at this very moment of your life. To keep wandering in search of some better plot of land is to keep traveling away from yourself – the farther you journey, the longer the trip back home. It is in the silence and stillness that you will see that you already are in the garden of your life. Always, your garden is blooming, dying, and regenerating.

Committing to be yourself

It's up to us to own up to our jobs in life. We need to acknowledge who we are when we arrive in each phase of our lives. We need to celebrate our evolving identities: one moment we are a child, the next a son/daughter, a parent, a grandparent, an accountant, a teacher. The list is unique for each of us, bearing the stamp of ourselves.

Why shouldn't we be ordained who and what we are for each occasion? Aren't we always all wearing different hats for the different things we do in life? Too often who we are and how we identify ourselves is disconnected – people ask us what we do, and we say: "I'm a lawyer." Yet to answer with such a statement is to ignore all the other things you do in life – it's to ignore the fact that you are also a father and a son and *a husband. To ordain yourself what you are in life – each and everything thing you are in life – is to free yourself, to say to the world "I am a multitude of things," and allow yourself to devote yourself to each of the things you are, instead of hiding behind your job or the title that your friends and family and neighbors have given to you. It allows you to celebrate all of yourself: to become a more holistic version of you.*

You are your own religion. That is, what you believe in and what you wish and hope and dream is your religion. You are your very own lost and found bin and each time you lose yourself, it's up to you to dig in and find yourself. It is only when everything inside of you meshes with everything outside of you that you achieve grace. To know yourself, to be yourself, to practice and celebrate your own religion, to appreciate yourself for all you are, all you strive to be, is to travel the road of freedom. You are only bound if you let yourself be. To fly free, you must commit to be who you are and celebrate the many selves that live and breathe within you.

"Neal," she said. The cat was beside him, watching her.

"I didn't mean to startle you," he said.

Tess placed the pages down on the table as if she were caught reading someone's journal.

"I wanted you to read them," Neal said. "To see if they made sense. I've accumulated a lot of different openings by now."

He looked like a professor in his narrow oval-shaped reading glasses and his charcoal grey wool cardigan. Tess smiled at him.

His preaching was a bit corny by her standards; something a new age freak would write.

"I'm looking forward to reading more," she said.

"And so, you will," Neal said.

"Tea?" she said, and with that, she was taking off her blazer and filling up the teakettle with water and opening the cupboard to take down teacups. She stared incredulously when she opened the cabinet: teacups all lined up and shiny, their stems facing the same direction. Coffee mugs in one corner, espresso cups dead center, neatly stacked on top of each other, resting on their saucers. In all her years in this house, she had never recalled such order in her cabinets.

"I hope that you don't mind," Neal said.

His hands were clasped on the table, his eyebrows arched. "I reorganized a little."

"It's so…efficient," she said.

In the cupboard adjacent, cans of beans and soups were neatly lined up, stacked in neat rows one on top of the other. It looked to her like a mini army had congregated inside her cabinets. Next, she pulled open her silverware drawer – spoons, forks, knifes, all polished and stacked on top of each other with precision.

"I suppose I should have asked you first," Neal said.

"No. It's fine. It's just…unexpected." She cleared her throat to get the lump that had lodged there down. "It's great. Thank you, Neal."

Tess's mother had been super organized – mindfulness was what she had called it. Attention to all things. Tess had spent her entire life trying not to be as orderly as her mother – to mess things up a bit. And yet as Michael and the others had pointed out, she was all about order, structure. Michael had joked with her that he was going to buy her a to do list with the slots filled in for each day: wake up at 5 am, drink tea, get to work, work through lunch, leave work late. Her home was the only place where she had managed not to be so stringent, or so she liked to think, and now here was Neal, imposing order. Did she mind? She supposed not. At least she wasn't willing to mess it all up now that he had put everything in place.

Just then a car horn sounded outside her window. It beeped again and again, so that Tess went to the living room window.

"It looks like your mother, Neal," she said.

Neal was on his feet, rushing down the stairs to open the front door.

"The alarm," Tess said. "Be sure to hold in the alarm button."

"Yes, I've been in and out all day," Neal said.

Here it was: his mother coming to get him. All that worry about what to do with him was for nothing. Tess took out tea bags and placed them in the mugs. When a few minutes passed, she peaked out the living room window. Neal was sitting in his mother's car. The hiss of the kettle made Tess jump so that she bit her bottom lip again. She wiped it with her top finger – blood. When he moved from his mother's car, Tess ran out of the living room the back way, through the dining room, and into the main bathroom. Her lip was now full of blood. She dabbed it with toilet paper.

"Tess?" Neal called.

"Be right there," she called back.

"What happened to your lip?" he said.

"Oh," she said. "It was already a scab and I bit it."

Neal put a cup of tea in front of her.

"Everything okay with your mother?"

"Yes," he said.

Tess nodded. His mother hadn't taken him away. He was still here. He was staying. She could still ask him to leave; it was her house. Asking him to leave would be reasonable.

"It's such a beautiful night," Neal said. "Should we take our tea out to the backyard?" he asked.

Tea in her backyard. She couldn't remember the last time, if ever, she had sat outside in her backyard at night.

"Sure," she said. They could have their tea and she could still get him home by 8:00 or 9:00 pm.

Neal led the way downstairs and had already been out in the backyard, as he had the drapes parted and the back door unlocked; she supposed he had figured out how to shut off the alarm on that door.

He held the sliding door open for her and as she made her way outside, she gasped. Tall candlesticks were scattered about her wood deck railing, and the backyard table was covered with an off-white lace table cloth on which there were four candlesticks and an array of flowers – all sorts and colors of flowers: red, pink, yellow, peach, white daisies and tulips and roses – situated dead center. Dishes covered with saran wrap scattered the table. There was a large wooden salad bowl filled with greens and tomatoes, plates with all sorts of grilled vegetables: zucchini, carrots, eggplant, corn on the cob, and two bottles of red wine. Off to the side there was a bowl of fruit and a platter of cookies. Everything was arranged with what she imagined was painstaking care and order, down to the ivory cloth napkins and silverware. She couldn't recognize if these were her settings – it had been so long since she had put out any sort of formal spread.

"Neal," she said. "I don't know what to say."

"Say you're hungry," he said, lighting the candles on the table. He pulled back a chair for her at the table and Tess sat down, Neal taking a seat beside her, so that they were nestled close. He reached for the wine and poured her a glass before he poured one for himself and then handed her a glass.

"To relaxing after a long day," he said, raising his glass to hers.

"To relaxing," she said, clinking glasses, following him in taking a sip.

"So, what were we talking about?" he said.

She shook her head. "You're surprising," she said.

"I hope that surprising is good," he said, facing her. The way his eyes lingered on her, she wasn't sure if he were about to lean in and kiss her. Instead, he brushed a wisp of hair away from her eyes and then his attention was diverted to serving her food, but she was hungry for his kiss. She sipped the wine slowly: getting drunk would not help her feelings at this moment.

"Good?" he said as he watched her taste one vegetable after another.

"Delicious," she said. "You're quite the chef."

"I'm glad you're enjoying the food," he said.

"So, what else don't I know about you?" Tess said.

"Lots of things," he said. The way he watched her now, his chin pointing toward her, head cocked, his eyes taking her in, as if he was appraising her, made her pause, put down her silverware. She sipped her wine slowly, meeting his gaze.

"I don't let strangers into my house," Tess said.

Neal laughed. "I didn't think you did."

"I thought about asking you to leave all day."

"You didn't ask me to leave yet," he said.

"The night is still young," Tess said.

He leaned in towards her so that their lips were close, their eyes intent on one another.

"I'll leave whenever you want me to," he whispered.

Tess's heart began to beat faster, and her breath grew heavy. She nodded her head. She was inches away from his lips. And then he was focused on the food again, reaching for the plates and serving Tess and himself more.

When they were finished eating – Tess pushed her plate away and shook her head, "No more," she said – the day was at its moody moment, the sun lingering, night ready to take over. The heat of the day had lifted. A faint breeze rustled the trees. In the next half hour, twilight would dawn.

"Shall we move to the deck?" Neal asked.

"You have it all planned out," Tess said.

"Unless you have other things to take care of now?" he said.

Tess smiled. He was sincere; the night could end right now if she said so.

"I'd love to sit on the deck," she said.

Neal was up and pulling out her chair. He grabbed the unopened bottle of wine, motioning for Tess to take their glasses, and with the lighter in his free hand, he was on the deck lighting the candles.

"This is nice," Tess said, reclining a lounge chair. She circled the rim of her wine glass, taking in the sky. Neal pulled his chair beside hers so that if she wanted, she could reach over and touch him. She couldn't remember ever being out on her deck at night, relaxing. It felt good to leave all the dishes where they were, to truly not care about anything other than the moments at hand.

"In Saskatoon, this was my favorite time of day during the summer. I liked how the whole world softened, the temperature fell, the prairie grew silent."

"It must be hard to leave a place after you've spent so much of your life there," she said.

"You adapt."

"Your mother doesn't think you did the right thing by leaving."

"My mother doesn't like change. She had me all tucked away in her mind as being safe at the monastery. And now here I am."

Tess put her glass down and turned on her side to face him.

"Thank you for making me dinner," she said.

Neal scooted down in his chair and turned to face her. "It was my pleasure," he said.

They sat staring at one another for a few moments: his eyes were the color of the sky at that moment, his eye lashes perfectly curled. Tess felt like a little girl, safe and loved. She curled her knees up closer to her chest and smiled at him.

"What shall we do?" he said.

She shrugged her shoulders. She didn't feel the need to move right then.

"What would you like to do?" she said.

"How about giving me my first yoga lesson?" Neal said.

"I don't know that much," she said.

"You know more than me," he said.

Tess set up the mats so that she and Neal faced one another on the deck. Tess laughed each time she looked at Neal on his mat.

"You'll have to take off your socks," she said. She was tipsy. She didn't know how long she'd be able to stay on her feet without falling over. She laughed at herself.

"Oh." He sat down and pulled off one sock at a time.

"Okay, let's start by setting an intention. Stand at the front of your mat," Tess said. She brought her hands to a prayer at her chest and nodded for Neal to do the same. "Close your eyes," she said. "We're going to repeat a mantra three times – *Lokaha samasta sukhino bhavantu*. It means *may all beings everywhere be happy and free.* Let's say it together now." Neal whispered the words along with her. She cleared her throat.

"First pose is mountain pose, or in Sanskrit, *Tadasana*," she said. "It's the basis of all yoga poses. Stand firm, engage your abdomen – it should feel like you're doing a sit up or pulling in your stomach, only you're breathing – and try to feel all four points of your feet pressed firmly into your mat. I like to think of it as the east, west, north, and south of my feet all grounded. It helps to lift up your toes and feel each part of your foot planted down."

Neal lifted his toes and rooted them firmly into the mat.

"Nice," Tess said. "Do you feel strong?"

"I suppose so," he said.

"A few things to remember," she said. "Keep engaging your abdomen; keep your shoulder blades down and on your back; your chin should be parallel with the floor; oh, and your legs are engaged – your thighs strong and your knees lifting up."

"Are you studying to be a drill sergeant or a yoga teacher?"

"I know. It's a lot. It's one of those seemingly simple poses – you look like you're doing nothing and yet you're working hard."

Neal looked like he was about to step into a strait jacket, and she laughed.

"You can relax a bit," she said. "Let yourself ease into the pose."

"Sure, now you tell me," Neal said.

"Imagine yourself a mountain, standing strong and tall; a wind might blow, but you remain firm, rooted. You should feel strong and light. It comes with time, of course – yoga is as much a mental practice as it is a physical practice."

Neal relaxed and he seemed firmer now, more grounded in the pose.

"Good," Tess said. "You got it. You're a natural! Let's do a sun breath in honor of the fading sun."

"What about a night breath?"

"No night breaths, but there's a pose called half-moon or ardha chandrasana, but that one is a bit difficult for a first timer," Tess said.

"Forget I suggested it. Let's go for a sun breath."

"Watch me first," Tess said. "Inhale your arms down, around, and up to the sky. Look up at your thumbs, and exhale as you dive down toward the floor. Your hands come to your shins; or, if you can, they touch the floor and then on an inhale, reach your arms down, around, and up and look past your thumbs again. Exhale, your arms float by your sides and come into prayer position, or namaste. It's like swimming," Tess said. "Ready to try?"

"We're done with Tadasana?" Neal said.

"Ah," Tess said. "We're never done with Tadasana; in fact, it should be a part of every pose. You're always in Tadasana when you practice yoga. A simple translation is that every part of your body is engaged and that your hips are in one line with one another."

"Got it," Neal said, feeling his hipbones and adjusting his torso. "I think I liked you a lot better when we were relaxing on the lounge chairs."

Tess felt light and free on her mat. She laughed, so that her whole body moved.

"You asked for yoga, you got it!" she said. "I was happy doing nothing."

"I didn't realize you were going to really turn into a yoga teacher, or I wouldn't have gotten myself into this," he said.

"Try a sun breath. Come on. I'll do it with you," Tess said.

Tess led them through one sun breath, and then another. When they landed back in Tadasana, Neal asked, "Why are you breathing like you swallowed hot coals?"

"It's called Ujjayi breathing. In yoga, you inhale through your nose and filter your breath through the back of your throat. It should sound like you're saying hah as you breathe. It's to build heat, steady your heart rate, and to keep you from hyperventilating. Here, listen. Tess breathed in and exhaled three breaths, accentuating the *hah* sound in the back of her throat for Neal to hear. "Now you try," she said.

Neal focused on Tess and breathed in through his nose and imitated the sound she made, although he sounded like he was gurgling something in his throat.

"Perfect," she said.

"Why do I sense your laughing at me?" he said.

"Well, you shouldn't quite sound like you're using mouth wash," Tess said. "It will become more natural over time, less strained," she said. "Ujjayi breathing slows down your brain waves. It helps you to stay focused and steady. The breathing is what differentiates yoga from aerobics or calisthenics. And, if you pay attention to your breath, and keep coming back to your breath each time your mind wanders, you can learn a lot about yourself. If you're breathing fast, for instance, it might mean that you're anxious. If your breath is steady, it tells you that you're calm. Your breath is the link between your body and your mind."

She supposed she sounded like an advertisement, but the teacher trainers went over it so much that the phrasing was stuck in her head.

Neal sat down on his mat. "I feel like I should be taking notes," Neal said.

"I'll be quiet."

"No, please, don't. I like listening to you."

Tess sat down on her mat now, too, facing him.

"This one you'll be able to handle no problem. Lie down on your back and let go of everything," she said.

Neal settled back.

"You don't have to worry about your breath when you're doing shavasana," Tess said. "It translates to a little death or corpse pose."

He closed his eyes and Tess could see his abdomen rising and falling.

"Shake out one leg," Tess said. "Then shake out your other leg. Lift one arm and then let it drop to the mat. Lift your other arm and let that drop. Move your neck from side to side, and then tuck your chin towards your chest. Now you can let it fall wherever it feels comfortable."

With her hands, she pressed his shoulders down. They were strong, muscular. She hovered over him, watching him with his eyes closed, before she moved behind him, and cradled his neck in her hands, massaging it gently before she placed it back on the mat. How easy it would be to lean over his face, kiss his lips.

"I like shavasana," Neal said, and Tess watched his lips move. He was so vulnerable at that moment.

"Rest," Tess said.

She traced his eyebrows with her thumbs and with her index finger she pressed lightly on his third eye. His face was calm and clear.

"I ordain you my favorite yoga teacher," Neal said.

Tess laughed. "And I ordain you my first yoga student," she said as she made her way to her own mat and lied down, inching her way up, so that the top of her head touched the top of his head. For a moment, she wondered if her curls were coarse against his scalp, but let it go. He could move away if he wanted. Her eyes open to the falling night sky, the world seemed large to Tess right now.

"It's such a big world," Neal whispered.

"Yes," Tess said.

"At the monastery I used to look up at the night sky and imagine myself living far away on another planet, without the other monks."

The crickets were chirping in full force now.

"Do you know what I used to say to myself each night when I looked up at the sky?" she said.

"What?"

"That my star would shine bright yet. I don't know when I stopped saying that. Maybe I just got tired of looking for my star and not finding it."

"Do you know which star in the sky is yours?" Neal asked.

Tess shook her head. She liked the way their heads were touching as they lied on their backs facing opposite directions. It was as if their minds were connected.

"No," she said.

"If you don't know your star, how would you know if it was shining bright or not?"

Tess closed her eyes and opened them, and the first star that came into view she designated as her star. She liked that there was a chance that at that very moment Neal had chosen the same star. She shivered.

"You're cold," Neal said.

"No," Tess said. "I'm fine."

Neal started to say something and stopped.

"What?" Tess said. "Say what you were about to say."

"For a long time, I wished that I could get closer to the stars, but at some point, I came to like the distance. In that distance – from earth to the stars – I imagined that anything could happen. Over time I've come to believe that it takes a comfortable distance to be objective. When you see something from a distance, you see it for what it is, free of fear and desire. The closer you get to something, the less you see," Neal said.

The stars seemed to dazzle brighter as Neal spoke.

"Do you think there are uncomfortable distances?" Tess said.

Neal paused so that for a moment Tess wandered if he had drifted off.

"I think that an uncomfortable distance is the result of running away from something. There's a difference between running away from something versus letting go of something. You need to be careful about running away. When you run away, it's fear that guides you. When you let go of your need to own something or control a situation, a comfortable distance blooms," Neal said.

Tess tried to remember the situations of her life that she had run away from – her ex-husbands, she supposed. But what about now – was she running away from anything or letting go of things? It was too much to consider here and now. She stifled a yawn.

"You're tired," Neal said.

"Yes," she said. Slowly, Tess sat up and made her way up to her feet. She looked down at Neal on the mat and he smiled up at her.

Neal made his way to his feet so that he stood before her; she felt the tension between them, and nervous tingles filtered through her, making her feel lightheaded. He moved a curl off her face, and she caught his wrist and kissed his hand, their eyes lingering on one another. It was Tess who broke away first. She began to gather up the extra plates and the utensils and salad dressing. Neal rolled up the yoga mats, and then moved over to the table to help her, gathering the garbage and making sure the grill was shut off. She caught him looking up at the sky one last time as they walked in, and once inside, she locked up the door, switched off the backyard lights, and asked Neal to pull the blinds together.

They passed by the basement study on the way up, where his stuff was, and Buddhi darted from the room, running up the steps in front of her.

"I can't believe it's 10:00," Tess said when she put the plates and utensils down on the kitchen counter. She didn't remember an evening that had flown by this fast in a long time. "You can leave the yoga mats by the stairs," she said.

"It's been a long day," Neal said.

Tess thought about Neal's mother dropping him off that morning. That seemed like a week ago. "Yes," she said.

"Can I help you?" Neal asked. "I'm glad to do the dishes."

"No, thank you," Tess said. "I'll run the dishwasher."

Neal stood by the table, the cat sitting at his feet, the two of them waiting while Tess put things away here and there.

"I guess this is goodnight," he said, and she nodded. "Thank you, Tess. I had a wonderful evening."

"Me too," she said. "Thank you for dinner."

"I'll get my stuff from downstairs, if you'll wait a minute to let me out," Neal said.

Buddhi sat still, watching with Tess as Neal walked down the stairs. When he reappeared, satchel in hand, she smiled at him. It had been one of the most romantic nights of her life. One of the most unexpected nights of her life.

He moved toward her and kissed her once on the lips – a quick, firm kiss – before he bowed his head, and was out the door into the cool night air.

CHAPTER 29: ALL IN A DAY'S WORK

"What do you mean he quit?" Tess said.

"Well, usually that means a person won't be working here anymore," Michael said.

"That's ridiculous – he's closing houses left and right. He's my top performer right now," Tess said.

"Exactly. He thinks he doesn't need Best anymore."

"So, he's going out on his own?" Tess said.

"Tess, I'm just the bearer of news, not his biographer."

"When did he call you?" Tess said.

"Five minutes before I walked into your office to tell you."

"Why would he call you and not me?" Tess asked.

"When's the last time you had a conversation with him?" Michael asked.

"That's not fair. I talk to all of my agents daily," Tess said.

"Yeah, to tell them to close deals and instruct them on how to make it happen. When's the last time you asked any of them what's going on in their lives?"

"Michael, I'm running a business, not group therapy."

The intercom system beeped on: "Ms. Rose?"

"What is it, Lynn?"

"I have a Kyle Dunfried on the phone for you."

"Put him through," Tess said.

Michael backed his way out of the room and Tess held up her finger to him motioning hold on.

"Hi Kyle – could you hold a moment?" Tess asked.

"I'm going to call Max when I get off the line, so if he calls you back, let him know he'll be hearing from me," Tess said.

"Aye captain," Michael said.

"Anything else?" Tess said.

"Jana didn't close that house in Bergen Beach," Michael said.

"What do you mean she didn't close it? The couple made an offer and I told her to accept."

"Yes, but she felt she could get more money," Michael said.

"Kyle, one more moment," Tess said into the phone before she put him back on hold.

"Is she kidding? It was a hefty offer they made. I wanted her to accept," Tess said.

"When I asked her this morning if I needed to get started on the closing paperwork, she told me it wasn't a close because they didn't meet her terms," Michael said.

"Great, now I have kids with real estate licenses thinking they can do what they want. A couple offers $750,000 for a house and she tries for more money. These agents I've got are brilliant. Absolutely brilliant," Tess said.

"Sorry, Kyle. How can I help you?"

"Just checking in to see if you have any apartments for me," Kyle said.

"Haven't had a minute to check in the last few days, but I will."

"Did the sale for the brownstone in Brooklyn Heights go through?" Kyle asked.

"It did."

"Right," Kyle said.

"There'll be others. And you know that wouldn't have worked – Dale didn't want to be there," Tess said.

"I wonder if she's going to want to be anywhere. I don't know what I'm supposed to do at this point: keep searching or give up?"

"Look Kyle, not that I'm in the advice-giving business, but if I were, I'd probably tell you to just live today, not worry so much about where you're going to move to in the future."

"Did Dale tell you to ask me to lay off?" Kyle asked.

"Dale told me no such thing. I'm saying that to you to help you keep your sanity," Tess said.

"So, you don't think I should worry about buying an apartment right now?"

"I think you should focus on enjoying your time with Dale. Let all the details fall into place as they will. I'll still keep my eyes open for you, let you know what's out there," Tess said.

"I appreciate that, Tess."

"So, we're all set?"

"Tess, do you think Dale and I will make it?"

"Kyle, that's a question I can't answer."

"I know, but you've been spending a lot of time with her; do you think she wants to marry me?"

The intercom beeped: "Jana is on the phone for you, Ms. Rose."

Tess hit mute; "tell her to hold," she said to her assistant.

"Kyle look, I have another call, but here's what I want to leave you with: just keep getting to know Dale. Of course, you know her, but take time to listen to her – not only to the things she says, but the things she doesn't say, too. Can you do that Kyle?"

"I can try," he said.

"Okay then. I need to sign off, but we'll talk soon. And I'll keep you posted on apartment developments."

Tess clicked into the line that was holding.

"Are you nuts, Jana?"

"They have the money, Tess. I don't see any reason to come down $25,000 for them."

"You don't need to see the reason. They offered $750,000 and I instructed you to accept. It's lovely that you want to go for your maximum commission, but last I checked I'm in the business to sell houses, not to lose deals over twenty-five grand. So, here's what you're going to do: call them back and tell them you'll close the deal today for $760,000."

Jana laughed. "You're too much."

"Thank you. And if they won't hear of $760K, you tell them you need to consult with your boss and call them back in an hour and say okay to $750K. You got it?"

"Yes, Tess."

"Wonderful. Call me later with the good news."

Tess looked up at the ceiling, stretching her neck, and breathed deep and slow before she brought her neck back level. She scanned her to do list in her Outlook calendar and picked up the phone.

"Mr. Genovese," she said when he picked up on the third ring. She put her legs up on the desk and flexed her feet and released them. Since she started her yoga marathon, parts of her body ached that she never knew existed. "Good morning."

"What do I owe the pleasure to Tess Rose?"

"I've got a house for you."

"Tell me about it."

"On the water, 56th drive, four bedrooms/bathrooms, built in pool, marble floors, twelve-foot ceilings, circular driveway. Just on the market, as of yesterday, and it's an exclusive with Best."

"How much?" he asked.

"Why don't you meet me to see it and then we can talk details."

"Have you seen it?"

"Assessed it yesterday – let's just say I can guarantee that it's worth your while," Tess said.

"Why does the family want out?"

"Divorce," she said.

"Got it."

"I can meet you there by 4:00 – I'll have my assistant get back to you with the address and send you the specs," Tess said.

"See you at 4:00 and look forward to hearing from your assistant."

"Sounds good, Mr. Genovese."

Tess sank back in her chair. What she loved about being a realtor was the moments when she knew, without any shadow of a doubt, that a house was the right match for one of her clients – that the match would result in a sale. It was a knowing that she reveled in, a knowing that she had never experienced in any other facet of her life except for her career. She had often laughed at herself over it – she couldn't find the right match in love, but when it came to matching people with houses, she was dead on 98% of the time. She was good at real estate because of her intuition, so why, she wondered, couldn't she tap into her intuition for other segments of her life?

"Lynn, get Max on the line, please," Tess said.

"Yes, Ms. Rose."

Tess tapped her pen against her desk.

"Ms. Rose, I've got Max on the line, but a call from a Mrs. Clay just came in. Do you wish to call her back and get on with Max?"

"Tell Max I'll get back to him; put Mrs. Clay through."

"Good morning, Mrs. Clay," Tess said.

"Neal will be dining at my house tonight."

Tess cleared her throat. "I see," she said.

Ms. Clay laughed.

"You have a sense of humor," Tess said.

"I laughed over your comment that *you see*; that's quite a statement from someone as blind as you are," Mrs. Clay said.

Tess picked up her pen again and began to tap.

"Quite a statement indeed from someone who does anything but see," Mrs. Clay said.

Tess leaned in and held the phone close by her lips, as if she were talking to a bookie. "Mrs. Clay, what is it that you want from me?" Tess said.

"It's one thing if you choose to live recklessly and ruin your life, but I won't have you destroying Neal's life."

"This is between you and Neal. You're going to have to work this out with your son. This is not about me," Tess said.

"After you've got him under your spell?" Mrs. Clay asked.

Tess lounged back in her chair. She had to do something about the fluorescent lights – they felt intrusive, obnoxious. She scurried her chair over and flipped the light switch off. That was better.

"I assure you that I don't have him under any spells, Mrs. Clay."

Tess pulled open the blinds, sunlight piercing the room. It cast a glare on her computer screen so that she titled the screen downwards.

"You obviously underestimate your sexual ways," Mrs. Clay said.

There was a knock at her door and then Michael peeped in: "You got a minute?"

Tess held up her hand and cupped the receiver: "Give me ten minutes."

"Apparently you entertain men at all hours of the day," Mrs. Clay said.

"Mrs. Clay, I don't have time for your preposterous accusations – I'm at my office."

"The truth needn't hurt if you live a moral life," Mrs. Clay said.

"This conversation is over," Tess said.

"You haven't heard the last from me," Ms. Clay said.

"Enjoy your evening with Neal; I'm sure that you two will have *tons* to catch up on," Tess said and slammed the phone down.

Scrawled across the brick wall of the building across the street was RIP in white spray paint, the letters bubbled with red tears dripping from them down towards the name *Ice Man* painted in the same bubbly white letters. *Not to be forgotten* was written below in red square blocked letters – the words loomed like a threat. Tess wondered how many days she had looked out at the wall while she was on the phone without ever really seeing what it said.

There was a knock on the door and then Michael burst in.

"Hey, I need you to…" he trailed off peering at Tess out of narrowed, skeptical eyes. "What's wrong with you?" he said.

"Nothing's wrong," Tess said.

"You suddenly look exhausted," Michael said.

"Not at all. Just thinking for a moment," Tess said.

"If you ask me, that yoga stuff is taking its toll on you; I thought it was supposed to rejuvenate and make you feel younger."

"Michael, the yoga stuff is just fine. What is it?" Tess asked

He handed her a file. "Need you to take a look at the final file for the house on Whitman Drive."

"That deal is done?" Tess said.

"Going to closing today. Max's work. You speak to him yet?" Michael said.

"I need to call him back now," Tess said.

"You sure you're okay, Tess? You look about ten shades lighter than you did an hour ago."

"I'm fine," she said.

He appraised her and nodded hesitantly before he made his exit. Tess lay her head down on her hands on her desk. A long, deep, muffled moan escaped from her. It was unfathomable to her how much had happened in her life in a matter of days: the fiasco with Neal's psycho mother, his showing up at her doorstep. The daily work issues came and went – that's what it was to run a business. She thought of the note Neal had left her on her screen door this morning: *The day is yours for the making. Enjoy all the moments.* He had signed it, *Yours, Neal.* It had made her smile. *Yours.* She wasn't sure how that would feel to her if he were hers.

Hours later, Tess sat cross legged in the corner of her bedroom, squinting up at the ceiling each time she read another of the yamas, as if its description was etched above. The yamas were one of the eight limbs of yoga according to Patanjali, the author of the *Yoga Sutras*. She couldn't imagine ever getting it all straight. Yamas were the things one was supposed to abstain from. That seemed easy enough. You weren't supposed to cause harm, steal, have sex, be greedy, or lie. Not causing harm meant not eating meat, because killing animals to get meat was a harmful act. She had been raised on that philosophy, although back in those days she had thought her mother cruel for not taking her to McDonalds. Now, she didn't particularly care for meat, so no issues there. She wasn't too worried about stealing. Although she was sure that Neal's mother would accuse her of stealing Neal from God. Or stealing him from his mother. Her laugh came out as a grunt.

The fan clocked round. Its seamless motion soothed her. Michael had always turned the fan off when they went to sleep at night. The stillness had made her feel suffocated. There were nights when Michael fell asleep that she had walked into the living room and peered out the window. She didn't know who or what she was hoping to see. But that was in a different lifetime. Or so it seemed. She thought of her mom, her gentle smile. She wondered where she was now. Why she hadn't come to her yet. With all her mother's spirituality, she had counted on feeling her mother's presence when she passed. She closed her eyes. "Mom, I'm here. I'm waiting for you." She could picture her mother's face perfectly. Her expressions, her hair. She thought of her hand, that icy hand. *I'm sorry for your loss.* Tess shook her head. No one could ever be as sorry for her loss as she was.

She couldn't remember ever sitting in this corner of her bedroom before. If someone were to walk in on her, she supposed they would think she was trying to hide. Here, though, in her house, there was nothing to hide from – not while she was alone at least. Her mind could lead her on a merry-go-round. That was for sure. She searched for what it was that unhinged her before she left the office. Ah yes, Max. Convincing him to stay on working for Best by giving him a 10% raise. Did her employees think that she was a bank? A 10% raise for no reason. When she had proposed 5%, he had laughed. He was already earning more than the other realtors. Sure, he was closing deals, but wasn't that his job? One day she wouldn't be in the real estate business. This phase of her life wouldn't last forever. That she was sure of. Like all the other phases of her life, this business-owner phase would end. The book that was in her lap fell shut. She opened back up to the page where her highlighter marked her place. The yamas.

Continence was a yama. No issues there – she hadn't had any sexual relations for at least a year and considering Neal's situation, that didn't seem to be on her top-ten list of things to worry about. Greed – she didn't think she was greedy. She'd never been accused of being greedy either in her personal life or in business. Sure, she was out to make money, but why else was one in business? Some women would see her as greedy regarding having had so many husbands. She saw it as more insecure than anything else. She was a different person now, or so she believed. Hoped. She understood that another person could not complete her. In fact, she had learned that another person could make her feel fragmented and lonely. Experience had brought her that knowledge. Besides, with each divorce, she hadn't asked for a penny or a possession – she never liked to owe anyone anything. The next yama was about lying. She wasn't supposed to lie. Hmm. That one shouldn't have been too difficult, but just then the phone began to ring. She was at home, so was not answering the phone a lie?

"I know you're there, Tess," Michael said into the answering machine. "Please pick up. Tess?"

If she unplugged her answering machine and turned off her phone when she didn't feel like speaking, then she wouldn't be lying. That was easy enough to change. The phone, again. Two rings. Three, and then the answering machine to the rescue.

"Tess? Call me later? Can you do that? I have a simple question for you."

For a moment Tess thought about calling him back – it may be something important about work. Then she let it go. It annoyed her that he was so sure she was home. What if she were out? People were out at 9:00 pm on weeknights. Or what if she were busy doing something with Neal? But of course, he didn't know that Neal being there with her could be a possibility. She would have to remember to turn off the volume on her answering machine when Neal was there, if he were ever there with her again. She didn't know what the future held, but she knew that if it held Neal, she didn't want to have to explain about not taking calls and for Neal to get involved in the whole Michael insanity.

So much for her quiet night. Her mind was on overdrive. She could try to meditate, but it was no use – her mind was picking up random thoughts and spinning them here and there like a spider's web. She was confused about Neal. She sighed. How did her life become so full of drama again? She pulled an oversized pillow off her bed – Michael had never understood why she had half a dozen pillows on her bed – and nestled her head and neck onto it as she held the book in front of her. She couldn't remember the last time she had camped out on her floor. She felt cozy, small, safe.

The niyamas, or the observances, were easier for Tess to digest. Purity, contentment, accepting pain and not causing pain, the study of spiritual books, and self-study. She was tired. Reclining, she closed her eyes and tried to hear her mother's voice. It came to her in waves: she'd catch it and then it would fade away. It scared her – how someone could vanish from your life, bit by bit. It was hard to imagine that she would never see her mother again. Loneliness overcame her, so that she felt as if she was drifting far away from the shore. That's what it was to lose her mother: isolation, disconnection, only Tess couldn't pinpoint what she felt disconnected from – her past? Her heart? She regretted that she hadn't gone to visit her mother more. That she hadn't been more available to her. She supposed that she had thought that her mother would always be around, that there would be opportunities in her life to spend time with her mother, to get to know her, understand her better, and thinking that, she longed for Prakash. When he had been a baby, she had held him wrapped up in her arms, safe from all that was to come, rocking him as she walked through the house, this very same house. There had been times she wished she was the baby, and he was the parent. She glanced at the clock. She could call Prakash. He would still be at work. Only no, she wanted the quiet. Talking right now would require too much work.

Tess reached with her foot and maneuvered her mother's Afghan blanket at the edge of the bed to the floor. She clasped it with her feet and brought it to her hands. She covered herself and nestled onto the ground fully now, her head resting sideways on the pillow as she moved her legs about, getting comfy. From where she lay, the bed looked comfortable, but too far to go. She couldn't remember having slept on the floor in this house ever, although she could recall nights in her home growing up in Woodstock when in her adolescence she'd hidden in her closet and camped out on the floor at night on one of her mother's thick, woolen Tibetan blankets. She had felt hidden and safe those nights. In her closet, she was able to hear herself think. Feel what she was feeling. Her secret corner of the world. That was what spurred her love for real estate: the search for her own corner of the world. She wasn't sure though if she'd know her special spot when she found it. She had thought for a while this home she was living in was her sacred spot, only now, with Prakash gone, with one man after another moving in and then departing this house, it had become more of a shelter for Tess than anything else, a place to distance herself from the world.

With her eyes closed, she tried to imagine Neal at his house. She wondered if he were sleeping, if he were up reading. She wondered what his bedroom looked like, if it had changed in the 23 years since he had left home. She wondered if he thought of her while he was at his home.

She felt close to him. She barely knew him and yet she felt closer to him than she had felt to most others in her life. It was nice to lay thinking of him, Neal, her friend; nice that he had captured her imagination. That's what it came down to: one after the other, the men in her life had captured her imagination. Something about them, or perhaps it was something about her when she was in their presence, had fulfilled one of her fantasies and off she went to explore it. Live out the fantasy until…she didn't know what. Until the fantasy shattered, she supposed. The ceiling fan spun round and round, its movement mesmerizing Tess as she faded off, giving in to the heaviness of her eyes, her mind, sleep encompassing her.

CHAPTER 30: HEART OF YOGA

The ornamental engravings on the ceiling of the ten-foot-high yoga room seemed to uncoil and crawl around each time Tess was in an inverted posture. All around her pairs of helpless feet dangled in the air: shoulder stand, *sarvangasana*. There was something invigorating to being upside down – it was hard to take the world serious from that point of view. The teacher counted the final breathes and then they were in plow, *palasana*, legs reaching beyond their heads, torsos on the ground. One more breath and they would unwind their legs to the floor in front of them and tilt their heads off the floor, chins reaching up towards the ceiling – fish, *malasana*. Finally, they were moving into a deep forward bend, hands reaching towards toes. Tess inhaled deep and with an exhale she inched her way closer to her toes, careful to keep her abdomen on her thighs. The pulling forward motion made the aches in her shoulders and upper back tingle. That's what she got for sleeping on the floor.

The teacher shut off the light fixtures above. Sunlight beamed in through the sunroofs, shadows cutting the glazed bamboo floor at random intervals, so that sections of it looked slick as an ice-skating rink. In this room, Tess felt safe, sheltered from everything that she had to do or be. Here, tucked away, the world would wait.

"Last sun salute," the teacher said. "Inhale, face looks up, arms reaching toward the ceiling. Exhale, forward bend. Inhale face looks up, palms pressed into the earth, jump back, exhale, chataranga. Inhale upward facing dog, exhale, downward facing dog. Five breaths."

"Finish up with an inhale, and when you are ready, exhale and jump through. Lie on your backs and let everything go. Corpse pose, shavasana. Rest."

Tess spread her arms beside her, palm up. Everything in her let go so that she felt as if she was free falling. Freedom, peace, calmness. It wasn't so much that Tess loved practicing yoga, although she forgot that each time she was on her way to the studio, but that she loved how her mind and body felt after she had practiced yoga. Cleansed, focused, unafraid. After a lengthy shavasana, the group of forty teacher trainers sat in a circle on the floor. Tess felt like she was at a college sorority event, not that she had ever been in a sorority. There were things she had done as a teenager as acts of rebellion against her mother, but joining a sorority hadn't appealed to her, not even as an act of rebellion. She was her own girl. Even back then, when it was easy to be one of the group, she had opted to find her own way.

The yoga lock-in weekends went something like this: Friday night yoga classes, meditation, lecture. Saturdays consisted of 9:00 am yoga class, group powwow, and afternoons spent discussing their readings and lectures on a host of topics. Tess loved Saturdays. Sundays were when they practice taught and spotted one another. Tess didn't love Sundays. She never felt as if she knew what she was doing, although the mentors of the program were gentle with her, providing pointers and assisting her until she would get a spot right. It was hard to get people to move their bodies how you wanted them to move and to adjust them at the same time, while you tried to advise them how to move into the pose utilizing all the parts of their body. Sometimes while practice teaching, Tess wanted to run out of the room. In all her years of selling real estate, she had never once felt afraid or insecure enough to want to run away.

When they all came out of their rest, the mentors led a chant to get the group into the right mental space. Today it was "Lokaha samasta sukhino bhavantu," which meant, "May all beings everywhere be happy and free." Next was a ten-minute meditation in which they were instructed to focus on their inhales and exhales, elongating each inhale and exhale up to eight counts. Tess couldn't make her inhales longer than six counts. Then it was time for "re-entry," during which they went around the circle and each of them had to talk for a few minutes, sharing where they were in their yogic journeys now regarding where they were last week. Tess liked hearing everyone's confession. There was an intimacy in this room that Tess had never experienced in a group.

Dale nodded at Ganesha on the stage and gave Tess a thumbs up. Her plan had been to go to the Ganesha temple in downtown Brooklyn on Friday night since they had been given the night off from teacher training. Ganesha, a Hindu God who was known as the remover of obstacles, had become a favorite God of all the teacher trainees. Dale had decided that it was Ganesha who she'd call on to get past her fear of marriage. She told Tess that she had hung little Ganesha stickers and ornaments over all the doorways in her apartment and carried some with her at all times. She had gone so far as to put a Ganesha sticker on her compact mirror and looked at it whenever she opened her bag.

Dale was speaking to the group. She was saying how she was beginning to feel herself open and how she was a lot more emotional these days. Sara shared how she noticed that she was a little less anxious, that she was being gentler with herself. She said that she was petrified of becoming a yoga teacher – that she couldn't believe how much work it was and that she didn't know if she would be able to do it, and everyone laughed – it seemed to be a collective fear. Then it was Tess's turn to talk. Tess looked around at everyone and smiled. She never knew what to say – a two-sentence snippet made life seem trivial.

"I feel a little more open to new possibilities," Tess said, and Dale stifled a laugh.

"To The Bakery?" Kim asked when they were set free for their 45-minute lunch break. She led the way down the block and around the corner.

"I think Dale would have a coronary if we didn't go," Sara said.

"Don't blame it on me. Tess is obsessed with the tortilla soup," Dale said.

Dale had three cookies stacked on a plate – chocolate chip, peanut butter, and oatmeal raisin – that she broke up into morsels. She was in the midst of picking out the chocolate chips and putting them in her mouth.

"What are you going to do with three cookies?" Sara said. "Have a bake sale?"

"It was three cookies for $5 today. I couldn't pass up a bargain."

"It's always three cookies for $5," Kim said.

Tess blew on her tortilla soup before she swallowed a spoonful down. Each Saturday she couldn't wait to get her fix.

Sara dipped her bread flat into Tess's soup and winked at her as she took a bite. "I say we all open up our own yoga studio."

Sara was a well-off retired investment broker that had just turned 40. She was in the middle of a divorce, and on certain days, she was bitter, while on other days she was optimistic and so alive that you felt her energy – manic, but hopeful and exciting – the moment you were in her presence.

"I'm all for that," Kim said. At 30, she was married to a man twenty years her senior and had a five-year old son. She was secure, calm, beautiful at a glance, although more than once, Tess had noticed tears in her eyes during a yoga class.

"If we own a yoga studio, we may become monsters like our mentors," Dale said. "Sorry, but I opt not to become an asshole."

"They're good people," Sara said. "They just don't have a clue about how to run a business."

Kim's eyebrows peaked.

"Good people? We're their yoga slaves, and what's more, we're paying them thousands of dollars to listen to them get into cat fights during training and to work for them for free."

Tess laughed. "Wow, I'm glad I'm off working all day, although they did just ask me to help them look for new spaces for studios."

"Why shouldn't they be looking for new studio space – with all the money they make off us, why not invest in another studio? Think about it: there are 40 of us in the program, paying over $8,000 each," Sara said.

"Just make sure to clock those real estate hours as part of your Karma yoga," Dale said.

"I say that you use that time to look for a yoga studio space for us," Sara said. "I'm being serious. I think that may be my next career move. Not a bad way to spend the extra cash I get from my divorce settlement. Yoga without politics will be my logo."

"I'll work for you," Dale said.

"Do you want to teach yoga, Tess?" Kim said.

"I have a business to run," Tess said. "I think I'd get fired if I left to teach yoga."

Sara hmm-ed and moved on to Dale. "What's the wedding story?"

"I've decided to forget about it for the next two weeks," Dale said.

Kim laughed. "Did you tell that to Kyle?"

"I told him that I need to air out," Dale said.

"So, you're not going to talk to him for two weeks?" Kim said.

Dale shrugged. "I'm taking a little break. If we're meant to be, then two weeks apart shouldn't be an issue."

"Trust me," Sara said. "Marriage is no fun. I would use these two weeks to plan your permanent exit strategy."

"You make it sound like she's escaping from jail. Don't listen to her," Kim said. "It can be fun. Sometimes."

"Ask Tess," Sara said. "She's the marriage expert."

"If I were the marriage expert, I suppose I'd still be married," Tess said.

"Would you marry again, Tess?" Kim said.

"Oh, who knows? If you would have told me a few months back that I'd be in a yoga teacher training program I would have said you were delusional, so I suppose anything is possible."

"Well, I won't be marrying again anytime soon," Sara said.

"I think it's that time," Kim said tidying up everyone's plates and garbage onto her tray and standing up. "We need to head back."

Tess rolled down her car window at the streetlight and breathed in the muggy June air. Others hated summers in the city. She didn't mind them, although if she closed her eyes for a moment and thought of the cool, airy breezes of Woodstock, she longed for those days and nights when she walked around barefoot amidst the trees, the cool grass tickling her feet, waking each morning to the song of the wind chimes that hung outside her window. "Mom?" she said. "Are you there?" Perhaps her mother was busy making rounds with others before she docked with Tess. This much Tess had learned of life: you had your time with a person and then it was over.

She was on the West Side Highway passing by Battery Park, waiting to make the sharp left turn, which would lead her into the midtown tunnel. Each time she passed by the pit where the World Trade Center had stood, a part of her sunk. It was almost two years since and yet when she thought back to closing Best, sending everyone home to their families, staring at her television screen, watching the same scenes over and over on CNN – the planes crashing into the towers, the flames, people jumping from windows like birds with broken wings, the phone calls with her mother, Prakash, it could have been yesterday. The grief that had overtaken the city had been suffocating, as if everyone was caught under a tarp. She had driven up to her mother's house, her car searched at each toll bridge, and camped out in Woodstock for a few days with Michael, while her mother and her followers had meditated and prayed for peace.

Tess turned into the tunnel lanes. Sometimes she would have horrible thoughts – the walls of the tunnel closing in on her, a brick in the wall coming loose and water overcoming her. There was a no-man's land quality to the tunnel, a hollow, no-way-out feeling. Riding through it she held her breath. And then she was out of the tunnel, the pool-blue sky broad and expansive, and she was thinking about the yoga girls and how it was a job to let people into your life, to try and explain in words what was in your mind and heart. People got frustrated when they couldn't understand you, but the truth was that they couldn't even understand themselves, so why would they think that understanding someone else was a possibility?

There were random moments when she was driving, like now, that Tess wished that she could keep going, no destination in mind. She wondered where she would end up if she followed her intuition, turning here and there. Would she know when she reached her destination, or would she be unsure, always? Cars merged onto the Belt Parkway while cars slowed down, switched lanes, and made their way toward the exit. 11N, her exit, was approaching, and all her wishes to keep going faded away. She was anxious to get home, to settle in and relax.

She passed Toys R Us, then Nick's Lobster House, and when she approached King's Plaza Mall, she glided into the right lane, maneuvering her way around buses and gypsy vans. She shook her head in her rear-view mirror at a man in an orange Cadillac beeping at her and giving her the finger, trying to cut her off. Brooklyn's finest. Often, this place was enough to give her a heart attack, and yet she couldn't really imagine herself living anywhere else. That was how things went in life – you got comfortable and then you stayed. When she got to the 24-hour one-stop on the corner of Mill Avenue, she made a right. Maybe, though, staying in one place meant missing out on what other places had to offer. If Neal had stayed where he was, they would have never met – he would never have known this other, away-from-the-monastery life. It was a strange phenomenon, this knowing-where-you-were-supposed-to-be aspect of life. How did anyone ever know? Tess wondered what her life would have been like if she had never left Woodstock.

What the heck? When she recovered from jutting forward, she held onto the wheel and in her rearview mirror there was Michael waving at her. He motioned for her to pull alongside him.

"Are you crazy?" she said, their cars parallel.

"I was just going to ask you the same question," he said. He held up his hand: "Wait. I'm coming with you." Now he was pulling his car over to the curb and then he was getting out of his car and walking over to the passenger side of Tess's car.

"You could have beeped, you know," Tess said. "You didn't have to rear end me and scare the daylights out of me."

"I was calling your name out the window and waving at you – you were in a trance."

"So, you crash into me?" Tess said.

"You want to tell me what's going on?" Michael said.

"If you have something that you want to talk to me about, you're going to have to ask me about it," Tess said.

"What's the story with your new boyfriend?" Michael said.

"He's not my boyfriend," Tess said.

Michael laughed. "You kill me, Tess."

Tess looked in the rear-view mirror and began to drive. One stop sign, two, three, and then through the intersection of 66th street. She followed the arc of Whitman Drive. Michael leaned back in his seat, his head firmly against the headrest, so that it looked as if he was strapped in and ready for takeoff.

"Neal and I are friends, Michael."

"He's living with you now?" Michael said.

"No, he is not living with me," Tess said. She ended up at the Dakota place and 66th street intersection: her house stared back at her from here from across the street. Buddhi sat on the ledge of the living room bay window. Both crazy neighbors were nowhere in sight. That struck Tess as unusual: perhaps the cleaning lady neighbor was in the midst of a big indoor clean session. She made a left turn and drove past the house and up 66th street.

"You got a cat?" Michael asked.

"Buddhi. He was a stray; I've taken him in," Tess said.

"You take in all types now, don't you?" Michael said.

Tess stopped short. "Get out of my car," she said.

"Not until you tell me what the story is with this Neal character."

She was moving again; she made a right at the corner of 66th and National Drive.

"What do you want to know, Michael?"

"You tell me," Michael said.

"I told you that he was a monk for over twenty years," Tess said.

"You're having an affair with a man that was a Roman Catholic monk and you think you're normal?" Michael said.

"I'm friends with him," Tess said.

"Hah," Michael said, slamming the dashboard. She was riding down 65th street now. "Tess Rose, you are a piece of work."

Tess stopped the car short again, put it into park, and turned to Michael.

"What are you doing?" Michael asked.

"What am I doing?"

"Are you on a mission to erase all sanity from your life?"

"Here it comes – Michael's drama," Tess said.

"First you decide to become a yoga teacher in your free time, and now you're caught up in a relationship with some priest or monk or whatever he is," Michael said. "And you call me dramatic?"

"Can't I just live my life without having to answer to anyone? No one has to *get* my life except for me. And as for Neal, if he happens to be an ex-monk, so much the better. At least he doesn't try to change me or meddle in my life. I don't have to be something that I'm not when I'm with him."

"What are you trying to say, Tess?"

"Exactly what I said," Tess said.

Michael shook his head and stared straight ahead – his exacerbated look.

"No one ever knows what life will bring," Tess said.

Michael smoothed the dashboard back and forth now, as if he was trying to erase it.

"You know you'll always be my friend, Michael."

He nodded. "We used to be so much alike," he said.

"Maybe," Tess said. "Maybe not. What people are on the surface and what they're all about inside are two different things."

"What's that mean?" Michael said.

"It means that knowing someone is a complicated thing," Tess said.

"Are you trying to say that he knows you and that I never really did?" Michael said.

"Why is it that each time I talk to you about life you bring up *you and me*? This isn't about *us*," Tess said.

"I told you he was in love with you when you first started spending time with him," Michael said.

"There's a lot of different types of love, Michael." Tess fell back so that her head hit the seat rest. "You would like Neal."

Michael shook his head. "I wish you could see this all objectively."

"I wish you could, too!" Tess said.

Tess was driving again, heading back to Michael's car. When she pulled up alongside it, she stopped and stared straight ahead. Above, the clouds were forming a mass. It looked as though it would start storming at any moment.

"The few times I passed your house in the last week, there was a woman in a navy-blue Honda watching your house with binoculars.

"His mother," Tess said. "She had binoculars?"

He nodded.

She smiled at him. "Next thing I know you'll be out there joining her with your own binoculars."

"I'm going to buy myself a pair right now," Michael said.

"I'm fine, Michael. Everything is fine," she said.

She turned to him and smiled before she gave him a kiss on the cheek and then he was out of her car, situating himself in his car and starting it up before he looked over at her. She waved. The moment she drove away, the cloud broke, rain plummeting down, steam coming off her windshield. She opened her window and stuck her hand out and washed her face with the wetness.

CHAPTER 31: COMING UNDONE

"Good morning," Tess said. She had been walking the perimeter of Lindower Park on Strickland Avenue and saw a man by the swings. On her second time around, she was sure that it was Neal.

"We meet again," Neal said in his calm and collected way, as if seeing her in the park at 6:00 am were the most natural thing.

"Okay if I join you?" she asked.

He nodded, his eyes not leaving hers. He had a way of looking at her, his eyes intent, his lips not quite smiling but showing amusement, which made her heart race. She was excited in his presence.

Tess moved to the swing beside him, and sat down on it, its metal chain pulling tight.

"I haven't been on these swings in ages," Tess said. "Not since Prakash was a little boy." She pushed off with her feet and glided through the air, swinging her feet in front of her to gain momentum. She laughed. "I forgot how fun this was." Neal remained still beside her until she paused.

"I hope I'm not disturbing you," she said.

"Nothing could be further from the truth," he said. "It's nice to see you."

They sat beside one another, swaying on the swings silently as first light began to illuminate the sky.

"It's going to be a beautiful day," Tess said. She loved the month of June: warm air, sunshine, the promise of summer ahead.

"Do you still like living here?" Neal asked.

"For the most part," she said. "I'm used to it, I guess."

"Would you ever leave?"

She shrugged. "I suppose anything is possible. Since my mom passed, I've thought once or twice about going back to Woodstock."

"I thought coming back to Brooklyn would be a big change for me," Neal said.

"And – is it?"

"Sometimes it feels as if I've never left, and other times it feels as if I've arrived on Mars."

"There's no place like Mill Basin," she said.

"It certainly has its charm," he said.

"I wouldn't exactly call it charm," Tess said. "Insanity is more like it. Where else could you get away with parking in the middle of the road to run into a store? Or putting up spiked gates around your house?"

"I've thought about you," Neal said. "A lot."

Her initial reaction was to say *what did you think?* But she didn't.

"Our lives, Neal. They're different. You and I are different."

"If you mean because I was in a monastery all these years, sure, yes, they're different. I believe that at the core, though, people are the same. We both have to get through Mondays and Wednesdays and all the other days."

"You have different obligations."

"We all have our obligations in life. You own a business –"

"Neal, I haven't been a nun all of these years."

"But if you were, you could change your vocation just the way you could shut down your business and open up another one."

"Professions and vocations are two different things. Best Realty wasn't my calling. It's something that I fell into and enjoy. Being a monk is a calling. I assume it wasn't something you chose lightly."

"People change, Tess. What I chose at 23-years old is not what I would choose at 45. I left the monastery for a reason."

"Neal, married 40-something men have mid-life crises every day of the year and buy sports cars or dye their hair or get a girlfriend."

Neal laughed. "You're equating my leaving the monastery to a mid-life crisis?"

"It's normal to get bored in one's life. God knows how many times I have," she said.

"I may have been a monk, but my brain is still intact. I know the difference between being bored and choosing a new path in my life."

"What is it that you want from me, Neal?" Her eyes were fixed on him.

He laughed so that she turned her body to face him on her swing seat, her knee stabilizing her sideways. He stared down at the ground and shook his head.

"What do I want," he said. He shook his head. "I like you," he said. "And I think that you like me."

"Neal —"

"And if you don't, that's okay. If I've misread you, that's okay."

"It's not that I don't like you, it's that we're different."

"You've already told me that."

"Your mother doesn't want me near you," she said.

Neal focused on the floor.

"I'm sorry," she said. "I don't mean to be disrespectful about your mother. I'm just not used to being berated by a man's mom at my age."

"Tess, my mother is delusional. She's acting unreasonable. It has nothing to do with you. She just wants me to go back to the monastery," he said. "Anything other than that is problematic to her."

"Well, right now, I'm the problem to her," Tess said.

"My mother will not bother you again –I'll talk to her."

"You can't control her, Neal. Plus, you're dependent on her right now. She knows that; she's going to use that against you."

"Then I'll get a job and move out. This is about me –not my mom. I am not going to let her dictate my life."

Tess bit her bottom lip and exhaled.

"You think I'm ridiculous," he said.

"It's not that I think you're ridiculous, Neal. I barely know you. Showing up at my house with your bag, and your mother on your tail. Most people would think you're nuts, or I'm nuts for having anything to do with you."

She swayed back and forth on the swing.

"Can I ask you a question?" he said.

Tess stared up into the sky at the birds congregated on a telephone wire.

"Yes," Tess said.

"Did you come out walking today hoping to run into me?"

Tess turned to him, her face pensive, and then back up to the birds that skittered to the right then left, as if they were doing a little tight rope dance. She put her feet firmly on the ground to stop the swaying of her swing. In the distance, the sun was beginning to glare, cutting through the clouds.

"It's nice to see you," she said.

"That wasn't what I asked," he said.

"I walked down by the water first. When you weren't there, I ended up here," she said. "And there you were."

"I came out walking this morning and came to this specific spot hoping to see you," Neal said.

"What are you saying? God willed us to meet here?"

"I'm saying that sometimes things are exactly as they're supposed to be even if it doesn't make complete sense to us."

"Neal –" she was going to tell him that they could only be friends, nothing more. She didn't want anything more. It was too complicated.

"Sometimes you just have to trust and have faith," he said.

What am I to trust and have faith in?" she asked.

"Life. The universe," he said.

She couldn't read his expression – it was somewhere between smug and smiling. She smiled back.

"That's what I like to see," he said. "Tess smiling."

She rolled her eyes and he laughed good-naturedly.

"You like to come off all business and tough, but I've seen the softy in you."

"When? The time you arrived with your bags, and I caved and let you stay? Frankly, I felt bad for you and gave you a break."

"I think you enjoyed your dinner with me," he said.

"Didn't you ever learn not to have serious talks before 7:00 am?

"Is that a Tess rule?

"There's a reason businesses generally don't open until 9:00 am – nothing makes sense before then."

"Really?" he said, moving off his swing and standing in front her now.

He took her face in his hands and leaned over and kissed her on the lips. Gently at first and then with more force. "Nothing makes sense this early?" he asked, and she nodded before he kissed her again, holding her knees steady in his own as she sat on the swing.

"I should go," she said, her lips inches from his. "I should get ready for work."

He kissed her again, his lips pressing against hers, his hands massaging her neck, so that she felt herself softening. He pulled away and took her in so that she had an urge to pull him back to her.

"I don't want to keep you," he said.

"No," she said, unsure of what she was saying no to.

"Shall we walk?" he said. "I should be going, too."

"Yes," she said. He held out his hand to help her off the swing. As they moved forward, she wiped the corners of her lips with her pointer finger and thumb and traced her lips with her finger, dropping her hand when Neal turned to her and gave her one of the mischievous little smiles that she was beginning to enjoy. It was a smile that made her feel as if they were in something together and she smiled back at him, her eyes on the road ahead.

CHAPTER 32: AN OUNCE OF FAITH

Tess pulled the door open slowly, trying to avoid the creaks, but it was no use. The room full of teacher trainers turned to see who was walking in. She held up her hand and mouthed "sorry." Dale, seated up front, motioned to her, pointing to an empty back jack and cushion beside her. She knew that the mentors seated at the back of the room, adjacent to the stacked yoga mats and blankets, were watching her moves. In the past few weeks, she and Dale had been getting called out during yoga classes and lectures for talking and laughing. As she liked to tell herself, she was a paying customer. She was allowed to have some fun – wasn't that the point of the program?

The speaker paused while Tess made her way to the front of the room, where Dale was sitting. She had forgotten that they had changed around the schedule for the weekend – the lecture was to take up all of Saturday with no yoga class and Sunday they would do a two-hour asana practice followed by practice teaching. She smiled at the lecturer in apology, and held his gaze for a moment before the recognition set in. Luke? Was that Luke from Woodstock? He nodded and smiled back at her. It was Luke, only with his head shaved and a slight goatee. He continued, pacing the platform. He was wearing jeans and a white t-shirt that outlined broad shoulders and a well-defined chest. Like the rest of the teacher trainers, he didn't have on any shoes or socks and Tess smiled – a slight memory surfaced of her and Luke and the others running around barefoot in Woodstock late into their teenage years. What in the world was Luke doing here, in New York City, lecturing to her teacher-training group?

"You made it," Dale said, taking her bag from the back jack that was beside her. Before teacher training Tess had never heard of a back jack. Now they were a necessity. She loved that she could sit upright on the floor and have her legs out in front of her while her back rested firmly against the canvas.

"Overslept," Tess whispered. She imagined that it had been well after 3:00 a.m. when she had fallen asleep. At first, she had tucked herself in a corner of the living room, trying to meditate, thinking that would make her ready to sleep. When that hadn't worked, she had sat up in the kitchen reading *A Path With Heart* before she had made her way back to her bedroom and took down her mother's remains from the high up perch where she had rested them. She had taken the urn carefully out of its velvet case and held it close to her chest before she put it down on the wooden closet floor across from her as if it was the most normal thing in the world to sit across from her mother in this manner.

"I miss you every day, mom. I think that the yoga is helping me. I can't say exactly how, but I feel better. Happier." Tess had smiled. "I met someone I like. I'm sure you know that. I don't know what it will lead to. You told me to follow my joy, though, and that's what I'm doing. I know you'd tell me that you're always here with me, so I'm going to try to remember that and listen for you more. You once told me that I have two options in life – to think my whole life away or to live it. I'd forgotten that until just now. I want to live my life. Sometimes it's hard for me to get out of the way of myself, but I'm going to try."

Tess had held the urn close to her heart again before she had packed it up and placed it back on the top shelf. She remained leaning into her clothes for a few moments longer before drowsy eyed and exhausted, she had made her way into her bed and tucked herself in.

When she had woken up again, it was 8:30 am. Her lecture started in Manhattan at 9:00. Even with skipping a shower, no way she'd make it to the studio earlier than 9:30.

"If you're going to evolve," Luke was saying, "you need to learn to let go of your personal desires. Dissect your ego – the root of your personal desires – from your true consciousness. It's not an easy job. If it was about detaching from the distractions that come into your life in the here and now, that's not so bad. Now that you're becoming conscious, that's doable. But what about the desires that you've been living with for 10 or 20 years? The desires that you've been programmed for – success, whatever that means, right? Maybe earning a lot of money, living in a nice house? That's where the struggle comes in – the reprogramming of your brain. You need to let go of the desires that you've been living with for however many years if you want to liberate yourself. Those desires, or impressions – *samskaras*, as they're called – are deep-rooted. They are what come up while you meditate or do asana – samskaras are what make your hips tight, or your knees ache."

"I thought that was the onset of middle age," Dale whispered.

"It's up to you to grant yourself freedom. Samskaras are what keep you from true freedom. It's not until you let those go that you can truly find peace and joy, and really get to know what you're all about.

You're going to reside in no man's land for a while before you clear all that up. And trust me, when it comes to letting go, there's a big difference between detachment and running away, or as I like to think of it, denial."

"What's the difference?" Kim asked. She was seated on the other side of the room, as close to the platform as possible, her notebook and pen poised, ready to take notes – the perpetual good student.

"When you run away," Luke said to Kim, and then addressing the group, "you'll always end up back where you left, because you didn't resolve anything. We're not talking about indifference when we talk about detachment. We're talking about an active choice to move past something, but only after you've fully dealt with it, examined it, accepted it. And remember that you need to be attached to something before you can detach from it. For example, when someone that you love starts blaming you for doing something or other to them, then you need to find that strength within or that switching point that says to you: *What you're saying is not about me. I didn't do this to you. I'm not responsible for your actions, your feelings.* You need to find the strength to know that the person is choosing to feel that way and that by blaming you, they are not getting to what is really the problem. Detachment is the tool that enables you to let that person reflect – it's a ricochet in that respect. By refusing to be the scapegoat, you in turn are empowering the person to take a closer look – figure out what is really going on. Detachment is like saying: *No, your issues are not about me, they are about you.* It's giving people ownership for what's going on in their lives while at the same time giving yourself the freedom not to become burdened with issues that are not your own. In that same vein, detachment requires you not to displace your issues or desires onto other people or events or life outcomes. It requires you to own your issues and desires – to in a sense accept that you're your own priest. Detachment isn't about putting up walls, it's about ownership, acceptance, and examination. It's about moving on, flowing. The more you keep projecting your stuff on other people, blaming this one and that one for things that only you can control, the further away you travel from your core."

"How are you supposed to detach from your desires?" Kim asked.

"Good question. By staying awake. Aware. By getting to know your true self. In your truest state of self, there are no desires. There's just being. Desires are delusions. You tell yourself if I get this, then that – if I had a million dollars, then I would be happy. Think about that. Can a million dollars touch your soul? Can it make you feel complete inside? Sure, it may make it easier to pay the bills and allow you to be worry free for a while, but it's not the actual money that is making you worry. You see a dollar bill and it doesn't make you anxious, right? It's the way we think about money, the relationship that we have with it that creates anxiety. We have the power in our minds to choose how we react to money."

"Detaching from our desires is really about getting rid of all that limits you, and your desires do limit you. There's an inherent expectation imbedded in our desires. Once we start expecting things, then we are no longer acting with pure intentions. It becomes all about us. For instance, if you are so caught up in getting a better job, chances are that you are letting other things in your life suffer. If you can let that desire go, focus on what is, take note of everything and everyone in your life in the present moment, focus on what you're grateful for, live your life with that knowledge, that acceptance, fueling you, then chances are the better job will come to you because of the fact that you are a better person – but when it's your only focus, you are putting obstacles in your path and most likely you're keeping yourself from getting the better job. It's all about balance, right? Yoga is about merging sun energy and moon energy. The three Gunas. Satvic is a balanced state. That's what we're always aspiring to. You're a little tamasic one day, all tired and lazy, and then the next day you're a little rajastic, or manic. And while each state is helpful in some respect, the goal is to attain balance, to be satvic. It's when you let go of the expectations that society ingrains in you, then the expectations you place on yourself, that you're on your way to attaining balance."

"Make sense?" he asked looking at Kim.

She nodded.

"We can go on with these discussions forever, but what I would like you to remember from today, if nothing else, is that enjoying happiness from external things is short lived. Your attachment to your desires and subsequent attempts to fulfill them will always keep you in a needy state. Once you detach from your desires and connect with your true self – the you that's free from expectations – you'll begin to enjoy a steady happiness. And trust me, once you experience that selfless joy, you're going to keep going there. The question is how do you get started? There's meditation. A little each day really helps you to begin to connect. Then there's asana practice. Paying attention to what goes on when you're on your yoga mat is a great way to start taking ownership of your life. When do you start to struggle? What do you do when you struggle? Do you stick with yourself, or do you run away from yourself and start thinking about what you need to do later that day, what your plans are for next week? Do you start planning what you're going to eat for lunch, dinner? The eight limbs, what you've been studying all along – yama, niyama, asana, pranayama, pratyahara, dharana, dhyana, samadhi– that's the route."

There had been so many attachments in Tess's life – to her husbands, to her child, to her business, to her evolving needs and desires. She had told her mom so many times that she was wrong about attachments, that it was healthy and good to need people. Only now, she didn't know. There was a way to look at anything and see it in the right light. She didn't want to be needy. She didn't know what it was she was attached to now, what she clung to – power, she supposed. Looking to the past, she was able to view her attachments objectively, to see how the objects of her desire confined her. The more she had tried to control things, they more they had controlled her.

"One last idea I want to leave you with. I grew up practicing Buddhism," Luke said. "When I delved into yoga, I would get asked a lot what the correlation between Buddhism and yoga was." His eyes were on Tess's as he spoke now. "For me, the connection was palpable. The yogic endeavor as I see it is about dealing with duhka, or suffering, and transcending it. Yoga helps us to move past the small stuff that we tend to obsess and identify with. Both yoga and Buddhism, when it comes down to it, are about moksha, or liberation."

"What were you two talking about after class?" Kim asked. Tess had just met up with them at The Bakery. "Should we grab this table?" Kim asked, pausing at a table for four that was about to be available, as they made their way toward the salad counter in the back.

Dale tossed her sweater and bag onto the chair, and the rest of the girls followed her lead.

"His eyes were stuck on you," Dale said. "If you ask me, someone has a crush."

"I know him – he grew up in Woodstock. I ran into him when I was up there taking care of things with my mom."

"Old love?" Dale asked.

"Childhood friend. He was always at my house," Tess said.

Dale winked. "Always at your house and just a friend?"

"I never said he was there to see me – he was one of my mother's clan," Tess said.

"He's pretty cute," Kim said.

"He's bald and slimy," Sara said.

Tess filled her salad bowl with spinach leaves, almonds, and chickpeas.

"No tortilla soup for you today?" Dale asked.

"What's wrong with bald men?" Tess said, and to Dale, "I think the tortilla soup phase is over."

"Nothing is wrong with bald men, if you're into that. In the summer, their heads get pink from the sun. I couldn't get passionate with a guy with a pink head," Sara said.

"I think we should try to practice what Luke talked about today. *Non-judgment,* and detaching from simple gratification," Dale said. "I reject your statement. I won't be swayed to think Luke is unattractive by what you call his summertime pink head."

"I think bald men can be attractive," Tess said, and a balding man behind her began to touch his hair line so that she bit her lip and Dale clutched her arm, smirking.

They paid and made their way to the table one by one.

"Remind me not to come eat with you guys anymore," Sara said at the table.

"Any divorce updates?" Tess asked.

"Listening to Luke I concluded that I'm attached to the drama of it all. How did you make it through four divorces, Tess?" Sara asked.

"I suppose that while I was going through each one it was consuming and rough, but looking back, I'd be lying if I told you I really remembered the details," Tess said.

"Well, you must be made of stronger stuff than me. I guess I should feel lucky that we don't have any children to get caught up in this mess," Sara said.

"Relationships are headaches, if you ask me," Dale said. "No matter what stage they're at, there are always issues."

"Hello ladies." It was Luke. The way their table was squeezed into a corner, they hadn't seen him coming.

"Sorry, I didn't mean to interrupt anything," he said.

"Just our normal Saturday conversation," Sara said. "Same stuff, different day."

"Join us," Kim said. "We'll find a chair."

"Oh, no, I'm fine. I wanted to take a walk around the block before I head back. Get some tea. It's wonderful outside," he said.

"It's raining," Dale said.

"The rain is a glorious thing," Luke said. "It washes away our worries. I didn't get to ask you if you'd be back up in Woodstock any time soon," Luke added, his eyes on Tess.

"I suppose so," Tess said. "It's been pretty hectic."

"I can imagine, with teacher training and all," Luke said. "Well, I'll be keeping my eye on your mother's home until you can make it back up there."

She tried to imagine herself in her car, driving up on route 17, past Monticello, past Kingston. It was such a long drive. So many miles to cover. And then she thought of the landscape in the fall, her car climbing into the mountains, the evergreens a collage of burnt red and forest green and mustard. The air cool, clear.

"I'll be going back to visit before the New Year," she said.

"I look forward to seeing you up there. A few folks were talking about what a shame it is that the house is closed. That house was an important sanctuary and refuge for a lot of folks in the area. Perhaps you'll be kind enough to have us all over for a morning meditation when you're there."

Tess smiled. "Possibly," she said. She couldn't imagine sharing the house with anyone when she was up there.

"Do you think you'll sell it?" Luke asked.

"No, I don't think I'll sell it. Not now, at least." She looked around at the girls and cleared her throat. The question made her feel unhinged.

"I'm sure that if you keep meditating, your mother will transfuse the answer to you on whether to pass it on or keep it," Luke said.

Tess smiled. At other times in her life, she would have nearly vomited from such a comment, but now, it brought her comfort, as she believed her mother would give her the answer when it was time.

"I suppose so," Tess said.

"Well," Luke said, "I'll see you all back at the yoga shala in a bit."

"The *yoga shala*," Sara said the moment he walked away. "Where does he think we are, India? And your mother transfusing the answer to you? Is it just me or is he a bit out there?"

"I actually do think my mother will tell me what to do," Tess said.

"I think all the meditation has gotten to your brain," Sara said.

"Isn't the whole point of yoga to unite with ourselves, become one with our soul, be open minded?" Dale said.

"You belong at the shala with him," Sara said.

"Guys, Luke *likes* Tess. Did you see the way he was looking at her? I think he's a hot number," Kim said.

Dale laughed. "I think you're sex deprived."

"Have a kid and then get back to me about that one."

"I'll be right back," Dale said.

"Is she going after him?" Sara said.

"She's going to get her cookie fix," Kim said.

"Do you *like* the yoga baldy?" Sara said to Tess.

"No, I don't like him!" Tess said. "I know him. For decades."

"No need to get so defensive. You've been single for a while now, right? Why not have a fling?"

"We went from divorce to relationships suck, to flings in less than 45 minutes," Kim said.

Dale put down a tray in the middle of the table filled with three oversized cookies: chocolate chip, chocolate-chocolate chip, and ginger snap. She had a bag in her hand that she shook: "Dig in," she said. "I've got more for later."

The girls all took pieces of the cookies, and while they were swallowing them down Tess asked, "What's the strangest relationship you've ever been in?"

"I married a guy twenty years older than me. That's as strange as I get," Kim said.

"I dated a dead head once," Sara said. "He and I broke up when he opted to go follow the Dead for a summer. Spill the beans, Tess. Who's the strange guy in your life?"

"No one's in my life," Tess said. "I was just curious."

"Oh, come on. Conservative you asking us about strange relationships? I smell a story there. Someone has a secret," said Sara.

"I'm not that conservative," Tess said.

"You're a realtor who rebelled from your Woodstock roots," Sara said.

"Who's now in a yoga teacher training program," Dale said. "I highly doubt any of us would be labeled too conservative. If you ask Kyle, he will say we're all new-age freaks."

Tess's bravery was short lived – she was not going to let them know she had a crush on an ex-monk. She couldn't imagine having to deal with that discussion for the next few months. No, her private life was just that: private, and better off so.

Sara continued to scrutinize Tess, her lips a straight line until a strange smile came over her face that made Tess know that this was not the last time Sara would press her about strange relationships.

"Okay, you can have your secret, Tess. That's fine. Just because you spend most of your free time with us, you don't need to tell us details. No problem."

Dale tapped on her watch and picked up the last piece of the chocolate, chocolate chip cookie. "It's time for us to go back." She winked at Tess. "Luke awaits," she added, stuffing her mouth with cookie.

CHAPTER 33: FIREWORKS

"Thank you for inviting me to spend 4th of July with you," Neal said. He stood on her porch beside her, while Tess locked up her front door.

"Oh, don't be silly," Tess said. "We're just going to the Yacht Club, Neal – everyone in the neighborhood is welcome."

His hair was growing in a sandy blonde so that there was a bit of a surfer look to him with his blue eyes and his tan chinos and white shirt. A surfer or a golfer, but not an ex-monk.

"I wouldn't have known about it if it wasn't for you," Neal said.

She smiled at him. She was excited that Neal was joining her; she'd been excited about it since she had crossed his path on her way to work a week back and asked him to join her. In fact, she had been hoping to run into him to ask but had been rushing off to work with no time for a walk.

"Was your friend upset that you aren't going to her party in the Hamptons?"

"Dale understands," Tess said. "July 4th traffic can be horrible – I didn't think it was worth it to drive all the way out to the Hamptons for tonight."

Neal nodded.

Her second ex-husband, Brad, had owned a house out there, and for years Tess had spent every summer weekend out in East Hampton. Aside from endearing memories of the twilights when she and a young Prakash would take long walks along the beach and skit the waves as they crawled up the shore, the Hamptons reminded her of her relationship with Brad – all show, lots of wine, and too many social obligations.

"Well, do we have all we need?" Neal asked, picking up the basket.

Tess had packed red wine, cheddar and Jarlsberg cheese chunks, crackers, grapes, strawberries, plastic cups, and napkins. In the canvas beach bag she carried, she had packed sheets for them to sit on.

"I think so. We'll only be across the street. We can always run back and get whatever we've forgotten."

The Yacht Club was crowded. There were senior citizens who summered in Brooklyn and spent the winters in Boca Raton, Florida; there were life-long born and raised Brooklynites who were likely to die in their forty-year-old houses with vinyl upholstery – Tess was usually the one called in to appraise their homes by their children once they passed. There was a new wave of younger couples, too. Some recently married, Brooklyn style, meaning they had graduated high school and gone to work for their fathers. She thought of those wives as the young-and-restless-clan, as they tended to dress provocatively, always had freshly made-up faces, and loved to flirt with anyone from the gardener to the UPS deliveryman. Then there were the couples in their early thirties who were either pregnant or had young children. Tess liked to think of the thirty-something women as the marmee bunch: many of them had grown lazy with their looks, gaining weight, forgetting about make-up, and always rushing to either drop off or pick up their kids from somewhere. Tess usually saw the marmee husbands in the early mornings as they waited at the bus stop in front of the Yacht Club for the Manhattan Express. It was the women of the marmee group that discovered the powers of plastic surgery once they hit the forty-year-old mark.

Diversity was one of the things that Tess had always loved about Mill Basin: the mix of young and old, the divide between frumpy and slutty, the melting pot of Jewish folks living alongside Italian and Russian mafia wise guys. Just when realtors began pegging the neighborhood as mafia haven or Israel in Brooklyn or Asian delight, a tribe of new families of all sizes, shapes, and ethnicities would move in, shaking things up. It had been that way for the last twenty years or so. The common denominator for Mill Basin newbies was cash, as even a shabby two bedroom went for $250,000 inland and if it was on the water, $300,000 minimum. When Tess had first moved in, some three decades ago, every couple that bought a house in the neighborhood was young and either had children or was about to have children. Tess couldn't remember celebrating a Fourth of July at the Yacht Club since back in those days when all the young families gathered, letting their children run free, although Tess remembered that there was always at least one parent who kept their eyes on every child and brought the child back to a parent if the child got too close to the water's edge. Prakash had never gone too near the water – he had been afraid of being pulled out to sea and getting eaten by sharks. It had made Tess feel guilty that she used to wish that he were bolder and braver. Something in his quiet, simple ways had reminded Tess of her mother, and back then, she wanted to shake him up, make him more adventurous.

People were carrying handfuls of shopping bags out to their boats, while others had already lined up blankets on the beach. When they had first moved into the neighborhood, no one had boats. Tess couldn't remember if the docks were even up at that time. There was certainly no paved parking lot for cars as there was now.

Tess scanned the area. In the last few years, she had moved in at least three-dozen families, but at a glance, she didn't see many folks that she knew. Not that them seeing her with Neal fazed her too much; they didn't know her life story the way she knew theirs. That was one of her golden rules when working with clients – listen well to their details, but don't share anything about your life that could allow them to pass judgment. Most of the old timers of the neighborhood, that is, the busy bodies who would have just loved to see Tess with a new man, were likely to be at their Hamptons houses or at their bungalow colony homes upstate. Once everyone's children had grown up and left the neighborhood, the old timers had slowly drifted away from one another, their ties to the neighborhood's events disappearing as well.

"Where shall we sit?" Neal asked.

"You choose," Tess said.

Neal picked a spot adjacent to a family that had already broken out bottles of soda and bags of potato chips. Tess and Neal settled down, laying their blanket down first, and then sorting through the picnic basket and taking out the wine and strawberries.

Neal pulled the cork from the bottle that Tess had already opened and poured Tess a glass before he poured himself one.

"What was your mother doing tonight?" Tess asked.

"My mother doesn't like Fourth of July. She thinks it's too noisy. She stays home."

"Did your father like it?" Tess asked.

Neal stared straight ahead as if he was watching a movie screen. "I don't remember," he said. "But my father was very compliant. He generally agreed with my mother."

Tess still couldn't read him when it came to his father. What she did gather, though, was that if Neal was anything like his father, and his mother and father had a relationship like the one that Neal had with his mother, his father had to have been a saint – or insane – to stay with her.

The wine was dense and fruity. She took a few sips and then a few more before she reached for the grapes and ate a few, putting one in Neal's mouth. "Mmm," he said. "So sweet." She steadied her glass beside the picnic basket and lied down on the blanket. She liked that her head felt tingly. Above, the sky was opening: white gave way to pool blue, to a deeper, nautical blue. A flock of seagulls flew into view and trailed off, forming a single file as if they were in a cha-cha line. Neal rested his head beside her. Slowly, nightfall was overcoming them, as if a dimmer switch was being turned. The sky turned a deeper shade of navy blue. A lone firework launched, sending out a snap, crackle, pop as it exploded into a shower of color and light in the sky.

Tess waved her fingers in the air. "Like magic," she said.

Another lone missile shot up into the sky and Tess watched it explode: a shower of hot pink and royal blue light scattered.

The crowd launched into "Oohs and aahs." One after another now the fireworks took over the evening sky, their colors streaking it and mesmerizing Tess as she squinted in the glare of the falling light.

Neal sat up, sipping wine and eating a strawberry before he dangled one in front of Tess's mouth. She took a bite, and then another, the fireworks falling steadily, and when she reached his finger, she gave it a playful bite. In a moment Tess sat up beside him and he filled her glass with more wine.

"Remember what happened last time we drank together," Tess said.

"Remind me," Neal said.

"Well," she said. "We got ourselves into a little trouble," she said, scrunching up her face as she said the word *little*, so that he laughed.

"Trouble with whom?"

"Hmm. Your mother," Tess said, so that he laughed again.

Nightfall was quickly taking over the sky, so that the fireworks illuminated it and the people and shapes around them began to fade out.

"I'm happy to be here with you," he said.

"How come?"

"I like your wine. And your strawberries."

She laughed.

He traced her eyelashes to her cheekbones to her lips with his pointer finger, moving around the perimeter in slow, swooping movements, following each indent and peak.

"Can I ask you something?" she said, and he nodded.

"What do you want from me, Neal?" she said.

"That question again," he said. "I don't want anything."

"I don't believe that," she said.

He began to brush her cheekbones with his knuckles.

"I like your company," he said.

"I can't read you," she said, and he laughed a deep belly laugh.

"That's funny to you," she said.

"People are not books. We're not meant to be read. We're just living. Sometimes there's nothing we need to know other than just being here together."

She studied him and for a moment he stopped brushing her face with his knuckles as he took her in.

"What I should have said is that I don't understand you," she said and before the laughter came out of him, she placed her palm over his lips so that he kissed her palm.

"I don't understand what you're doing here, why I'm sitting next to you –"

"You like me," he said.

"You're so sure of that," she said, and he nodded.

"I'm a chapter in your book," he said and this time she laughed.

"Why is that funny to you?"

The whites of his eyes shone in the darkness, and she smoothed his face with the back of her palm. The light show above sent colors cascading all around them so that they were in darkness and then in light. There was something so innocent to him, so gentle and she took it all in through those searching blue eyes of his.

"You still there?" Neal asked, taking her in and she nodded.

"Don't go away," he said, and she smiled.

"I'm here," she said.

Chapters had beginnings and endings. She knew that all too well.

"But you're thinking about something that's not here," he said.

"No," she said. "What's it like for you to be here with me now?"

"Natural," he said.

He had never been romantic with a woman like this ever before. Why her? Why now?

"Say what you're thinking," he said.

"I'm not thinking anything," she said.

Their lips were inches from one another. From the continued noise from the crowd, she knew that everyone's eyes were still on the fireworks.

She kissed his lips intently, her heart racing as she felt the smoothness of his lips against her own, felt them taking over her lips and then his inching his body closer to her so that they pressed against one another. She was not one for a public display of affection so close to home, but the warm air, the fireworks, the blanket, she didn't care about anyone else around her as he kissed her. And then the people around them were standing up, packing up their things – the firework show was over, and she and Neal separated, Tess smoothing her shirt and wiping the corners of her lips before she stood up and Neal was on his feet gathering their things and putting them in the basket. Together they folded up the blanket and put it back in Tess's tote bag. They paused on her porch.

"I've had a wonderful night," he said.

"Me too," she said. It couldn't have been later than 8:30.

"Thank you again for inviting me," he said. He made his little salute with his hand, as in so long, goodbye.

"You could come in for a bit," Tess said.

"That would be nice," he said, and Tess opened the front door.

What was she doing? She would tell him it was a mistake, and that he should leave, only he was beside her then as she attempted to unpack the items from the basket, and he was touching her face again, and then he was kissing her, pulling her body to his.

"Neal, you should probably go," she said.

"Is that what you want?" he said.

"This isn't right for you, Neal," she said.

"I like you," he said.

"Neal," she said, stepping back from him.

"What couldn't be right for me about liking you, Tess?" he said.

"If we–," she said.

"Say it," he said. He traced her collarbone with his pointer finger so that chills ran up Tess's spine. She let him pull her closer, so that his hands braced her hips.

"If we go any further, you may regret it," she said.

He shook his head. "What I would regret is not being here with you."

"There are certain things that you can't undo once you do them," she said.

"Do you like me?" Neal said. His breath was warm; his lips were moving closer to her own.

"I want to do what's right," she said. The blueness of his eyes seemed impossible to her – Caribbean Ocean blue. She traced his lush and dark eyelashes with her fingertip and then moved on to his eyebrows. She loved the way his features formed his face; there was a delicacy to him and yet the way he held her; he was a man.

He kissed her tenderly at first and then full force so that it was easy to lose herself in the passion and yet there was something in her that kept bubbling to the surface – fear? Reality? She didn't want to have an affair with a man who was only on a temporary leave; a man who didn't have affairs; a man who was married to God; a man who was going back to the monastery in a few months.

"You should go," she said, pulling away.

"Okay," he said. "I'll go."

Tess sighed and straightened her shirt. She nodded. She moved to the counter to get a glass.

"Water?" she said, and Neal nodded. She poured them each a glass and gulped hers down, Neal taking a sip.

"I didn't mean to make you uncomfortable," Neal said.

"You didn't," Tess said.

"I should get going then," he said, but neither of them made a move.

She didn't know when she had become so moral. It was rare that she wanted to be with a man. She was 55-years old for goodness' sake. Why shouldn't she have some fun now and then?

"What's so funny?" he said.

She shook her head. "Nothing," she said.

"Can I see you again?" he said.

"As long as you behave."

"As long as I behave?" he said, their eyes meeting one another's.

And then they were kissing again, Tess kissing him hard now, and Neal pulling her closer to him so that she felt all his body against hers.

"I want you," he whispered into her ear.

She was trying to forget that he was a virgin. That he had never been with a woman.

"I want you, too," she said. "I just don't want you to regret this."

"No," he whispered, kissing her neck from top to bottom so that all the flesh on her back and arms turned to goose flesh. She let out a slight moan and pulled his face to hers so that she was kissing him again. How in the world he was so sexy, she had no idea. *Please forgive me God. Please forgive Neal.*

In her bedroom, he pulled Tess's shirt off and began to kiss each inch of her flesh, so that her body was a mixture of chills and heat. When her bra came off, she unbuttoned his shirt and massaged his hairless chest until he pulled her against him, his hands kneading her back so that their flesh melted into one another's. Sweat began to pool down her cleavage and her back and she felt him massaging it into her. She didn't remember ever feeling this turned on, this hot for a man. She began to kiss his neck and then moved up to his ear and in a moment, he was kissing her ear lobe and then biting it ever so gently, so that she heard herself moan again. He moved backwards to the bed and made his way onto it, pulling her down with him so that she was on top of him until he climbed on top of her, and his lips found hers again, their tongues meeting like waves. "Neal," she whispered in his ear. He shivered and grew harder in between his legs as he pressed against her and again, he began to kiss her neck delicately, so that all of her wanted him, here, now.

"Tess," he whispered, his breath sending a chill through her so that her whole body shuddered. She looked into his eyes, kissing his lips, and seeing him that way, his eyes so close to her own, their bodies against one another, creatures of desire, she didn't care if he was a monk. He was a man, and she was a woman.

Neal pushed her to the side and began to unzip her pants before she took over, pulling them off, her panties still on, while she fumbled with the button on his pants, which he opened and then unzipped and pulled down. They lay on their sides facing one another while Neal smoothed his hand up and down Tess's torso, his palm passing over one nipple and then the other before he lingered there, raising his other hand, so that his palms caressed her nipples. Tess was alert, her insides tingling with anticipation from his touch. She traced his belly button before she moved down and lightly stroked his underwear. In a moment his hand was in her panties.

His breath hot in her ear, he was saying her name and she reached into her bedside drawer – please, she thought, let me still have condoms.

"What's wrong?" Neal said, and she shook her head as she pulled out a single condom and opened it. Neal was still as she pulled off his underwear and peeled the condom over him, bracing her hands on his chest as she sat upright on him, helping him to move into her before she began to circle forward and backward, slowly at first, their bodies merging, and then harder, so that in a matter of seconds, their bodies created a delightful friction and then he maneuvered his way on top, situating her below him.

"You feel so good," she said, and now she was squeezing her legs around him, shifting her body so that she could feel all of him moving into her. It didn't seem possible to her that he could be this good, this sexy.

"You feel incredible," he said, as he continued to thrust, and then she knew he had hit his magic moment and she tried to join him.

"Oh," he said, and she closed her eyes and felt him moving with her. Her legs were tingling, then he was panting and there was another "Oh, Tess," and she felt everything inside of her flaming, rushing, tingling. "Neal," she said. And then he collapsed on her chest, their flesh soaked with sweat, so that they both laughed and then he was kissing her lips, giddy, so that she could feel him smiling as he kissed her.

He smoothed her curls from her forehead and kissed her there.

"I don't believe you're a virgin," she said, and he laughed.

"You're the sexiest woman alive," he said. He cupped her chin in his hands and kissed her lips hard, moving his lips back and forth against them.

"I'm glad that I waited for you," he said.

"Shhh, don't say that."

"I am."

"No, it makes me feel as if I did something wrong."

"Are you still worrying about that?" he said, his hands exploring her body as he pulled her tight against him and she snuggled in the envelope of his arms.

She remembered nights when she had gone to sleep next to Michael with her back to him. It was nice to want to be close to someone, to feel safe like this. She kissed the crook of his neck and glanced at him one last time. His breath hummed, and the drowsy way he moved his head, she felt him drifting off. She closed her eyes and rested her face on his smooth, firm chest, trying to fall in line with his breaths. In a few moments, the crickets serenading her, she lost the earth.

CHAPTER 34: THE NEW MOON

Tess had gone through a range of emotions, it not yet being 7:00 am. She had woken up in the middle of the night in the nude, disoriented and disheveled, her neck slightly stiff, before she remembered that she had gone to sleep beside Neal, who was no longer there beside her. She had seen his note on the kitchen table that he would meet her in the morning by the water and that she should sleep tight. She had checked the front door and saw that he had locked it, which confused her as her keys were on the kitchen counter, until she realized he must have taken the spare key?

She had put on a night gown, and gotten back into bed feeling anxious, restless, turning up the air conditioner to cool her down. The next day's to-do list surfaced as it always did when she knew she should sleep, but couldn't, and she sat up to catch her breath. 3:00 am. She still had some hours to rest before she had to tackle it all.

When she resurfaced some hours later, the thought of going into work struck her as impossible. No, her mind was too busy to add any new information outside of her and Neal. She called into the office and left a message on her assistant's voicemail that she couldn't make it in, something had come up and that she would be in later this morning.

At Jamaica Bay, Neal stared off into the direction of the water, the sun, not yet risen, floated in the background, as if it were mustering all its strength to rise and spread across the sky. Seagulls congregated and scattered. Her heart raced at seeing him, and she forced herself to take a few deep breaths. He turned to her as she approached him, and she felt something in the pit of her stomach sinking. He smiled and all the passion of last night came back to her; she couldn't help but smile back. Relief, that's what she felt at seeing him. Relief tinged with desire and neediness to be near him, to know that he was in it with her.

"Where do you think they're all going?" Neal said.

The seagulls spread into flocks now, all heading in the same direction, at different altitudes, different speeds.

"Off to their next destination, I suppose," she said.

She wanted to touch him, to hug him, but she remained still. Watching the seagulls leave, she thought of his leaving in the middle of the night, of his leaving to go back to the monastery. She wondered if having an affair was part of his agenda all along.

"Can I ask you something?" she said.

His expression was pensive, his eyes warm. He nodded.

"When did you think about having sex with me?" she asked.

Neal laughed and then, his eyes on Tess, whose expression remained steady, he cleared his throat.

"Last night was one of the most special nights of my life. I didn't take it lightly, Tess. I've been thinking about you nonstop."

"Answer my question, Neal."

"I thought about sex that first day that I saw you in your car."

Tess shook her head; she felt a hurricane rising in her. No, this isn't what she wanted to hear although she had asked it.

"You were a woman. A very attractive woman. It was probably the first time in decades I felt –"

"What? You felt what?"

"The feelings that a man feels for a woman. I liked you the minute I saw you."

"Was your plan to have sex with me before you went back to the monastery just to see what it would be like?"

He shook his head. "Tess, no. I didn't have a plan. I like you. I feel as if you've helped me."

"Helped you?" she said.

"It didn't come out right, Tess." He moved to put his arm on her shoulder, but she backed away from his reach. "What I meant was – when I saw you that first time, I was busy thinking about God and my vows, and meditating if I was doing the right thing and when I saw you, I stopped thinking about that."

"Because I made you think about sex," she said. She laughed; it sounded preposterous to her.

"I wanted you in my life that first time I saw you. I didn't have it all figured out and didn't intend to seduce you or anything of the sort, but I wanted you in my life."

She laughed again. The seductive monk.

"Well, you got what you wanted, right?" she said. She felt herself on the verge of tears and cleared her throat. What was going on with her?

"Tess, it's not like that. There is no conquest for me. I wanted to be in your presence. When I'm with you the monastery and that whole life seems impossible to me."

"So, I keep you from the monastery – that's my role?"

"What I'm trying to say is that when I'm with you, I feel like a man who likes a woman and that type of man has no place in a monastery."

The tears began to build up in her throat again. She stifled them with a cough and then another cough. What had she done? Who in the world would have sex with a 45-year-old virgin? A man of God? And now he was saying because of her, he knew he didn't belong in the monastery? She needed space. She began to walk towards the dock.

"Tess!" Neal called, walking toward her. "Wait, please."

She sat down by the edge of the dock, studying the muddied water lapping the dock's poles. She saw an outline of herself in the water, but no details. In a moment Neal sat down beside her so that she glanced over at him. Here it was: she had feelings for this man and already felt him leaving her. Going back to where he came from. She didn't have the energy to like someone.

"What we did last night shouldn't have happened."

"I'm glad it did."

She shook her head. Something like disgust rose in her – her mind was in conflict between the enjoyment she had experienced last night and the uneasy feeling that she had done something wrong. Something that she couldn't undo. How was it he didn't feel the same conflict?

"Don't you worry if you did something wrong?" she asked.

"I did everything with the Lord in my heart," he said.

This was too much for her to process – now God was involved in their sex.

She wanted to shake some sense into him. "Aren't you going back to the monastery in September?"

"I wrote and asked for another three months."

Tess didn't realize that she had been holding her breath until he spoke the words. He was going to stay. For now. She was searching for a folder in her brain to store this information. He was going to stay for a bit longer. And then he would leave. This was temporary. All of it was temporary. A sigh from deep inside of her escaped and Neal reached for her hand and clasped it in his own. But wait, what if they didn't grant him another three months? That was possible, wasn't it?

The sea gulls were moving back towards them, and for a moment Tess thought they were going to land right by their feet, as if to be witnesses.

"Do you think they'll approve it?" Tess asked. This was the problem for her with falling for someone: her mind skipped ahead, began worrying about all the possible outcomes that might or might not happen. Falling for someone meant trying to control the future.

"Yes," he said. "They already did."

Three months was 90 days. Anything was possible in 90 days – she could fall madly in love with him, fall out of love with him. She loosened up. A sense of calm came back over her.

"What did your mother say?" Tess said. She wasn't sure if she meant about his going home in the middle of the night last night or about his extension. He tossed a pebble into the water and then picked up another and began to sketch in the sand.

"She's struggling," Neal said.

"About me or you not going back yet?" Tess said.

"About my not going back yet, I'm sure; and most likely about you to some extent."

The water tip toed up to the shore and then darted away.

"I somehow imagined that she'd be happy about my being back," Neal said.

Tess thought of something that Prakash had said to her about her break up with David – he had been in his twenties by then – that after a certain age you didn't want things to be so haphazard. You wanted to believe that you knew what to expect.

"She was used to her life, Neal. You changed her reality."

"She was so sad when I first left for the monastery – she said that she was losing her only son and I wanted to comfort her, but what was there to say? It wasn't about her – it wasn't about me, either," Neal said.

Neal tossed the stone in his hand into the water, and it made a splash, sending nearby pigeons into flight.

"It was about life. I had to go. There was nothing else for me to do but follow the voice that was leading me," Neal said.

"You need to give your mother time," Tess said.

"I don't know if that's the case for her, Tess."

"What does she think of me?" Tess asked.

"She doesn't understand. You can't be hurt by what she thinks – she doesn't know you," Neal said.

Tess stared straight ahead. "I don't want to be an obstacle for you," Tess said.

"You're not an obstacle," he said.

"Maybe not now, but in the future –"

"Right now, we're living our lives, Tess. That's all we can do."

The water dragged up the shore, slow, lazy. It reminded Tess of the school children she saw walking into the elementary school each morning.

Tess tried to imagine what it was like for Neal to walk up to his porch his first day back, ring the doorbell. How his mother felt when she saw him standing there with his duffel bag. How it felt for him to walk into his house after being gone for twenty-three years, to cross that threshold. How it felt for him to sleep in his bed that night.

"Do you miss the monastery, Neal?"

He stared off into the distance: the waves a muddy green as they trickled up the shore. Beyond, she was able to see the cars on the Mill Basin draw bridge.

"When I think of my time there, of walking through those fields, of working in my garden, of eating meals, morning, noon, and night with the brothers, it seems like it was all in some other lifetime. It's as if that reality couldn't possibly exist amidst this reality," he said.

He chucked a shell into the water. The ripples mesmerized Tess.

"If I didn't leave, I would have never known that all of this was waiting for me," he said.

Tess thought of her relationships. How each time she moved past one there had been a whole new reality that she embarked on. The sun cut the clouds, its initial rays a deep russet as it streaked the sky, and she had a fleeting sense that there was something more – something ahead that she was yet to do in her life, something that would make this chapter fade.

Neal touched her shoulder and Tess jumped. "You okay?" he asked.

She took all of him in: the layer of sea mist on his forehead, his translucent eyes, his peach fuzz head of hair, his long and sturdy fingers.

She nodded. "I'm fine. I'm just trying to figure this out. It's new for me, too."

Neal nodded. Tess fingered the sand and drew two stick people at a distance from one another.

"What do you miss most about the monastery?" she asked.

"My mentor, Father Demetrius," Neal said. "He was – is – the assistant abbot," Neal said. "That's like being the vice president."

"He sat with me during the afternoons that first summer I spent out on the prairie and told me about his life – about how he was an undertaker for over 20 years before he found his home at the monastery. He'd been married at one time, too, but he had decided early on that marriage wasn't right for him. The way he put it was that he had spent too much time trying to please his wife and not enough time trying to please God when he was married. For a long time, he had loved being an undertaker, loved being there for people in their time of need, but after a while, he felt that each time he sold someone a coffin, helped them to plan a funeral, a part of him was being locked away in a box and buried."

A stray pigeon inched its way closer to Tess right now. She locked eyes with it, telling herself that if it stayed, Neal would stay. If it flew away, Neal would flee, too.

"He went through chemotherapy three times in the past few years – the cancer just wouldn't go away, kept spreading from his lymph nodes to his breast. We saw him go through some hard times, but he never once complained, never once stopped being there for us. He's in remission now. I worry sometimes that if he passes, I won't be there to say goodbye to him," Neal said.

"Have you been in touch with him since you've been home?" Tess twisted her torso around, looking for the pigeon. There he was, behind her, bopping around.

"A monk on leave isn't encouraged to reach out to his brothers while he's discerning vows. I think they fear it would cause an epidemic. I've spoken to my abbot, and he's assured me that Father Demetrius is alive and well," Neal said.

"What did Father Demetrius think of your leaving the monastery?" Tess asked.

"He assured me that we all had our moments of doubt. He believed that strength and renewed conviction was what waited for us once we got past our doubts. He told me that if he'd given in to his doubts, he would never have survived cancer three times. The Benedictines view doubt as a sickness. Our belief is a faith that surpasses understanding. To doubt is to –"

"To show that you're human," Tess said.

The pigeon hopped away from Tess but didn't yet take flight.

"Everyone talks about having faith in things outside of you – religion, your friends, your spouse, the universe – but no one ever stresses how important it is to have faith in yourself," Tess said. When she finished talking, she realized that she had been watching the pigeon as it took flight.

"Oh," she said.

"What is it?" Neal said.

The pigeon skimmed the surface of the water. It strained its head in her direction before it flapped its wings and soared higher.

She shook her head.

In a moment, Neal was on his feet. "We should go back. You have to get ready for work," he said.

Tess nodded in what felt to her like slow motion, and he clasped her hands, pulling her to her feet.

He looked into her eyes, searching, and Tess saw the little boy in him. It made her feel helpless, incredibly helpless and what she wanted more than anything at that moment was to move inside his mind, his heart, his body. To know him from the inside out. To hold him beyond the physical realm, to reach him. She didn't believe she had ever felt that way before with a man, with anyone.

She draped her arms around his neck, gently nudging his head into the safety of her shoulder. She felt his breaths against her and fell in line with them, rubbing her ear and chin into his flesh, like a mother tending her cub. She felt him loosen, melt into her. He was so fragile, so vulnerable, and silently she promised to be good to him, to care for him, her sweet boy, her Neal.

When he lifted his head from her shoulder, she took all of him in, a smile overcoming her. He lingered, his eyes intent on her, and then they were moving, making their way back.

CHAPTER 35: CONFRONTATIONS

"Look who showed up for work this afternoon," Michael said from his office as Tess passed by. He was drinking iced coffee and jiggling the ice around in the plastic container.

"And how are you, today, Michael?"

"Rough morning with the monk?" he asked.

"Thanks, I'm great."

"Is the affair at the hot and heavy stage?" he said.

Tess backtracked and walked into his office, putting her briefcase down on his chair. She bit her bottom lip.

"Ah, Tess is nervous. Have I struck a chord?"

"What's that supposed to mean?" she said.

"You only bite your bottom lip when you're nervous," he said.

"It's funny, in all the years I've known you, I never knew how jealous you were. It doesn't become you," she said.

"Jealous? I don't think so." Michael slurped down the rest of his ice coffee. "Look, I know you only come in late if it has to do with sex."

"Oh really?"

"Are you forgetting our adulterous mornings?" he asked.

"Now you're comparing our relationship to mine and Neal's?"

"See, I knew you were involved with him. Platonic my arse, my dear. I know you, Tess Rose. Don't forget that. Just answer me this one question: are you sleeping with him on the bed we shared?" he asked.

Tess shook her head and forced out a grunt-laugh. "You are too much." She picked up her briefcase. "If you remember, this is still an office, and while we're here, we work," she said. She nodded at the folders piled up in his inbox. "No time for coffee breaks, buddy. Looks like you got a lot to do."

"That's my girl. Always the boss lady. If you're back to business so quickly, the sex couldn't have been that fulfilling," he said.

"Fuck you," she said.

"Ah, I touched a nerve," he said.

"I don't have time for your interrogations. Excuse me while someone here gets to work."

"I think all of the yoga has made you lose your mind," he said.

"Have a great day, Michael," Tess said on her way out.

Tess plopped down in her office chair, took a deep breath, and let it go. She felt as if she were a balloon losing air. There were folders scattered all over her desk with post its on them – *please review* –

pending sale. Can we talk about this ASAP? Sometimes she felt as if her agents were her children: all needy, all the time. When she glanced at the list of messages in her phone log, she realized that she had left her reading glasses in her car. Michael waved to her with his Ronald McDonald smirk as she walked past his office on her way out.

She searched the passenger seat, and then under her seat: no glasses. There was a car idling next to her – she held up her hand – she would be out of the way for the person to pull into the adjacent spot in a moment. The car beeped. She held up her hand again. Damn, can't a person wait a second? Another beep. Asshole! Tess stood up, saw the blue Toyota, and thought immediately, *her*, Neal's mom. Mrs. Clay stared at Tess, her hands gripping the steering wheel and Tess stared back at her. Was she supposed to wave? Was she supposed to walk over to the car?

Mrs. Clay leaned over and opened the passenger door.

"Get in," she said.

Tess looked around.

"Get in the car," Neal's mother repeated. Neal's mother beeped her horn. "I won't stop beeping until you get in."

Tess looked up at her office window and then at Michael's. The coast was clear. Her heart was racing. The last thing she wanted to do was get in the car with the raving lunatic, but if she didn't, there was the possibility Mrs. Clay would keep beeping; the possibility that Michael would come to the window to investigate the commotion. Mortified by the possibility of a scene in front of her office – the embarrassment! – she made her way over to the car and got in.

Mrs. Clay drove off, her eyes straight ahead.

"Would you like to tell me what it is you think you're doing?" Mrs. Clay asked, her voice calm and weighted, so that it made Tess feel as if she were sinking.

Tess cleared her throat. "Excuse me?" Sweat began to pool on her upper lip. She flipped the air conditioner vent up and down. No air.

"Aren't you ashamed of yourself? You seduce my son and then you go off to play at work with your ex-husband."

"Stop the car," Tess said.

Mrs. Clay kept driving.

Tess braced her hands on the dashboard. "This is kidnapping. Stop the car."

Mrs. Clay glanced at her and then back on the road. Her glare – insistent, deranged – made Tess sprout gooseflesh.

"You realize that you've destroyed Neal," Mrs. Clay said. She spoke matter-of-factly now, clinical.

How in the world was she so stupid as to get in her car? Tess opened the car door while the car was in motion and Mrs. Clay stopped short.

"Are you crazy?" Mrs. Clay asked.

Tess caught her breath, her insides pulsing. "Are you?" Tess asked.

"Close that door," she snapped. "You'll get us hit," she said, reaching over Tess to close the door, so that Tess pushed her away.

"Keep your hands on the steering wheel!" Tess screamed and closed the door. "Are you trying to get us killed?" A car swerved around them, beeping.

Mrs. Clay was in her zombie-driving trance again.

"Look, I have a son, too," Tess said. "I'm sure that this is a lot for you – your son coming home and meeting me. I'm sorry if you think that I'm this evil woman who's corrupted your son's life. That's not the case. I was doing fine on my own. I didn't want to be bothered with anyone, quite frankly. You were the one who pushed him on me that first time you brought him over to my house."

"Not on your life, missy. Neal told me that he wanted to go to your house," Mrs. Clay said.

"I never invited him over," Tess said.

"Hah! You think I was born yesterday? You seduced him and then you better believe he did whatever you told him to do. Neal follows orders well."

"You should know," Tess said.

Mrs. Clay pressed her foot to the gas, her neck disappearing into her shoulders so that she looked like a hunched-back witch.

"Stop this car!" Tess said, her body damp now, her adrenaline flowing so that she had to fight to take slow, steady breaths. She was not going to have a heart attack over this woman. *Slow and steady* she told herself.

"Mrs. Clay, I did not seduce him, and I did not tell Neal what to do and if you don't slow down, you're going to cause a wreck."

"So now you're pleading innocent?" Mrs. Clay said.

"I'm not guilty of anything," Tess said. Mrs. Clay had driven around in a circle. They were making their way back towards her office.

"Things would not have *just happened* had you let him be," Mrs. Clay said.

"Trust me, the last thing I need is to chase a man. I'm a successful, independent woman."

"Who happened to have multiple husbands. I'm sure according to your calendar, it was about time for your next husband."

Tess kept her eyes on the road; ahead, there was a four-way stop.

"For the grace of God, how could you have let things progress between the two of you once you knew he was discerning his vows? Twenty-three years in a monastery and some slut who has had God knows how many relationships, decides to seduce him. Haven't you done enough harm in your lifetime? Do you realize how confused Neal is?"

"Stop," Tess screamed, her hands pointing to the stop sign before she braced the dashboard and Mrs. Clay slammed the brakes, looking left then right before she moved forward.

"If anyone is confused, it's you. Neal, for your information, is happy," Tess said. "Or are you too blind to see that in his face?"

"You're having sex with a man who is married to God," she said.

They were four blocks from Best Realty. Tess opened the car door again. "Pull over," she said. "Now! I'll call the cops on you for God's sake."

Mrs. Clay made her way to the curb.

"You're corrupting Neal," she said, her voice faint.

Tess swallowed and smoothed the creases in her blazer jacket, biting her bottom lip before she turned to Mrs. Clay, whose eyes faced straight ahead. Tess moved closer to her, lowering her voice.

"You're obviously a miserable old hag who's desperate to control everything and everyone in your life. But you know what, Mrs. Clay? You can't control me. I won't play your games."

"You'll be sorry. You wait and see how sorry you'll be," Mrs. Clay said.

"No," Tess said, bracing herself to get out of the car, feeling her face flushed. "I won't be. You'll be. A mother should always support her son, no matter what he chooses. If you can't accept Neal and stop trying to control him, you're the one who'll be sorry."

Tess slammed the car door shut and walked away without looking back. She was wearing sling-back stilettos: *perfect* walking shoes. For a moment, she froze, imagining Mrs. Clay following her back to work and then coming inside her office and causing all sorts of havoc in front of her employees. This was ridiculous. Tess would not run scared from this crazy woman. How idiotic could she have been to get into her car! Tess waited for the light to turn green and crossed the street. She practiced her ujjayi breaths: one slow inhale followed by a slow exhale. She imagined that she looked as if she was preparing to give birth. Composure. Calm. She sighed. Mrs. Clay was nowhere in sight. Tess sighed and moved faster now. He was a grown man, monk or not. A grown man with a mind of his own. She made her way back towards her office, where she saw her car in the parking lot, the driver side door swung open. There, on the floor, under the door, were her glasses.

CHAPTER 36: THE RHYTHM OF LIFE

Tess sat up and stretched tall in her bed. 5:56. She had set her alarm for 4:30. Her plan was to get up early and meditate, read a bit before the morning work rush. She supposed she needed the sleep, although tinges of regret gripped her. Lost time was simply that: lost. In the early morning sunlight that pierced her room in two, dust particles danced about. When she was a young girl, she had thought of the particles as secrets floating all about. She certainly had her share of secrets these days. She fell back into bed and smiled, last night coming back to her. In the week since she and Neal had first made love, he had come to visit her three times. That had become their unofficial code word, "If you're around tonight, I'd like to visit," he would say during their morning walks. Yesterday she had asked him if he wanted to visit her in the evening. She glanced over at the pillow a few feet from her own and could still make out the indent of his head. As they had cuddled in bed well past 10:00 pm, she had pleaded with him to stay the night, playful at first – she understood that he would have to deal with his mother if he didn't show up at her house – but she surprised herself when she felt the longing in her voice when she asked him again. That was silly night talk though. At least now it seemed as such. It suited her just fine that he went home and that she settled in and got a good night's sleep and woke up alone in her bed, in her house, the way she liked it.

She reached for his pillow and pulled it tight against her so that her insides rushed for a moment; she could smell his clean soapy scent on it if she held it close. It was a masculine smell. He made her feel sexy, alive, and desirable. "Mmm," she said aloud, her body tingling thinking about his body.

It was time to get up. Tess put on her gray zip up sweatshirt that was on the floor beside her bed and searched for her panties on the floor. She peeked down the stairs to check if Neal had locked up the front door as he said he would and peering back at her at the bottom of the stairs was a glistening pair of eyes that sprang up the stairs when they met her gaze. In a moment, Buddhi was there beside her in the kitchen, rubbing up against her, doing a long downward facing dog while she scratched his back. He was becoming more of a housecat in these weeks. When she opened the door for him, giving him the option to leave, he would sniff the outdoor air, and then run away from the door and up the stairs. His favorite spot was sitting on the living room windowsill. He would move from side to side as if he was clocking how long it took people outside to walk from one end of Tess's house to the next.

She microwaved some hot water – it was faster that way – and then sipped her tea at the kitchen table, opening Charlotte Joko Beck's *Everyday Zen*. For the past few days, she had taken to opening it up to a random page, fixing her eyes on a sentence, and letting that be her mantra of the day. It had been a game she had played when she was growing up – she would pick a book from mother's collection, close her eyes, open it up to a random page, and whatever sentence her eyes would focus on she would let be the theme of her day.

We refuse to see the truth that's all around us. We don't really see life at all. Our attention is elsewhere. We are engaged in an unending battle with our fear about ourselves and our existence.

Tess thought for a moment about this here and now of her life and wondered if she was in fact refusing to see the truth that was all around her. Was she somehow deceiving herself by becoming a yoga teacher while working her hectic pace at Best, and having some fun with Neal? She imagined that in some way she was, but for the first time in a long time, she was enjoying living and not worrying about what was right or wrong, not worrying about the consequences – if there were any at all. Was her attention elsewhere? She believed that her attention was where it needed to be – in each moment of her life as she lived it. She was beginning to let go of her fears and letting someone get to know her without putting on a show, which didn't mean that new fears wouldn't spring up. She closed the book and yawned deep and loud, her hands reaching for the ceiling.

Buddhi made his way up on the table and plopped himself down on *Everyday Zen*. He sniffed at the steam rising from her tea, then feeling the wetness, wrinkled his nose and shook his head, resting it back down on the table.

When the phone rang, both she and Buddhi jumped. 6:15 a.m. Her heart sank – it was too early to deal with Neal's mother. She took a deep breath and cleared her throat.

"Hello?"

"Hello Mother."

"Prakash," Tess said. "What are you doing awake? Didn't you just get home from your Mexican retreat?"

"Yes. I couldn't sleep."

"Are you okay?" Tess said.

"Is there something you need to tell me, Mother?"

"I appreciate your calling me Mother."

"Michael told me you're in a relationship with the monk," Prakash said.

"Michael has a big mouth," Tess said.

"Please tell me he's wrong. After our talk in Woodstock, I thought you were done with all of that."

"Prakash, I am done with the marriages."

"You told me that you had to fall in love with yourself first."

"Kash, nothing has changed. Why are you so upset? What's going on?"

"Michael seems like a mess, Mom. He still loves you."

"Please don't listen to Michael. He feels sorry for himself. It will pass."

"I just don't want you to go through this again."

"I am not going through anything again, Kash. I promise that I am not getting married."

"Michael said he's a weirdo."

"He reminds me of your grandmother. He's unique."

"No one is going to be able to take the place of grandma."

"No one," Tess said. "So, did you meet the woman of your dreams in Mexico?"

"I did yoga and meditated and hiked," he said. "Perfect getaway."

"You'll meet her yet," Tess said.

"Mom, marriage is not on my mind."

"No, but some amazing girl is going to love you and you are not going to be able to resist her."

"What I love about you, Mom, is that you're an eternal romantic. No matter that marriage was not all fun and games for you. You still believe in it."

"Marriage is a beautiful thing when there's honesty in it," Tess said. "Oh – know who I saw last weekend at yoga teacher training?" Tess asked.

"Who?"

"Luke from Woodstock," Tess said.

"What was he doing in New York City?"

"Giving a lecture on Patajanali's *Yoga Sutras*. He knows one of the mentors of the teacher-training program. He took some classes somewhere with one of them."

"Mom?"

"Yes, Kash?"

"Don't go and get married again."

"Your wedding is the only one I'll be attending any time soon," Tess said. "Get some sleep. And do not listen to Michael's ranting. Just because he thinks he knows it all, he does not."

Tess surveyed her bedroom from the doorway: she moved toward Neal's side of the bed and picked up the photograph that he had brought to show her last night and left behind. There was Neal, in his faded black robe, dead center. All the monks were smiling. The skies were a vibrant blue, the fields beyond them a lush green. Tess traced Neal in the picture. His robe reminded her of a dyed potato sack. A monk. There was a blankness in his eyes – as if he was looking beyond the picture. Yet there was an earnestness in his expression that Tess had never witnessed. She studied it for a few moments longer before she moved to her bureau and picked up a picture of herself with hands spread, motioning *ta da* in front of the Best Realty office. There were grand opening banners in the window. So many years ago. So many Tess's ago. People changed. Tess changed. If she did, it was possible Neal did, too. She placed Neal's picture beside her own. *That was then,* she supposed the title for the pictures could be. She wasn't sure what photos would go under the caption: *this is now.*

She made up the bed, letting the flat sheet air out before she fastened it onto the mattress, tucking the corners in first and then the sides. She folded the blanket down just right, smoothing it before she fluffed up the pillows and set them up against the bed board. She liked that sometimes order was easy to attain.

As the shower's hot spray slithered all over her body, she sighed. There were mornings that starting over again appealed to Tess. There were other days, however, such as this one, in which the thought of putting on makeup, doing her hair, and picking out clothes to wear seemed like impossible tasks to accomplish. How nice it would be to lounge around and relax in bed, read. She laughed. Is that what feeling content did to her? She wondered what her days would consist of if she took a leave of absence, like Dale. But no, it wouldn't suit her not to work. She liked to work. Just sometimes she longed for a break. Heck, even Neal was taking a break. Sure, he was busy baking his cookies and writing and discerning his vows, but he was on an extended vacation. Michael had once told her that she was the only person he knew that didn't need a vacation and her response had been, "if you love what you do, your whole life is like a vacation," only now she wasn't so sure of that. Was her life like a vacation? Or was it so heavily cloaked in work that she was disconnected from what she really felt or believed? The skin on her fingers began to prune – Tess turned off the water.

Drying off she started to run over the things she had to do that day at work – she knew that there were some closings she had to review. She moved to the kitchen in her robe and pulled out her blackberry. Thirty-two things spanned her to-do list. Michael had emailed her over a dozen times already from what she could tell as she scrolled down her inbox. There was Max who was making noise about the commission on the deal he was in the middle of closing and the house on Strickland Avenue to show and the house over on Indiana Drive that she needed to check out. So much movement all the time. She felt the tumult rising in her. It was too much for her sometimes – too much to think about, to do. She pulled out her orange post it pad and began to write herself notes – call Mr. Distifano and confirm time for showing house on Strickland. In parentheses she put down Mr. Nelson – she could see him as being interested if the price was right. Couldn't hurt to call him about it.

She was in the bathroom blow drying her hair and then blending moisturizer and concealer – the best way to even out her face and cover her freckles – when she heard her cell phone ringing. Michael. Where was she? He was waiting for her. They needed to go over some contracts. Story of her life. She paced her bedroom, listening to Michael reading from the contracts, giving his input. Her eyes were stuck on Neal's monk picture. It seemed ridiculous, all of it – what Michael was saying, Neal being a monk, having to put on mascara and pick out an outfit. Absolutely ridiculous, and yet it was her life.

"Are you listening to me?" Michael said.

"No," she said. "I'm not."

"Well, that's nice. I'm glad that you're otherwise occupied."

"I wish you didn't feel you had the right to share my business with my family," she said.

"That's what your attitude is about," Michael said.
She could hear the smugness in his voice.

"Yes, Prakash called. I like how you assume you know what's going on between me and Neal."

"Whatever you do with your freak boyfriend is your business."
She laughed and breathed out deeply into the phone.

"I'm glad that you have a sense of humor about it."

"I never knew that jealousy could make you pathetic," she said.

"That's a lovely comment," Michael said. "Now I'm jealous and pathetic. Anything else?"

"You assume you know what is going on with Neal, but you're wrong," Tess said.

"I know when you're having sex," he said.

She laughed again. "Do you realize how absurd you sound sometimes? You know when I'm having sex. Uh oh, can't get one by you, Michael. What are you, the sex psychic or something?"

"I can tell by your mood. You're spunkier when you're having sex," he said.

"Okay, conversation over. I'm getting ready, and I'll be there in a bit and then we can discuss whatever work stuff you need to discuss with me," she said. "I am not discussing my personal life with you. Bye now."

She picked out a navy suit – simple, appropriate – and a crisp white button down. Michael would tell her that she looked like a flight attendant. She didn't care. Right then she was craving simplicity.

Dressed, she dabbed on some mascara and fixed up her lashes with a Q-tip. She adjusted her hair with her fingers, pulling a curl this way and that. The wind would do its thing with her hair. She wished she had more patience, or discipline, to blow dry it straight, only it seemed like too much work for too little reward, especially with the humidity that was sure to attack her when she set foot outside. She grabbed her orange post it, stuck it on her blackberry. Why she didn't use her blackberry as her phone was beyond him, Michael liked to say, but Tess wasn't big on having everything in one place due to the dependency factor. Yoga breaths. That's what she told herself, but she didn't feel like yoga breaths. Her mood was all over the place, a mixture of everything and nothing. Life sometimes. As she drove down 66th street, doing a good 15-miles per hour faster than the 35-mph limit, she slammed her brakes when the yellow light turned red at the Avenue U intersection. There, at the bus stop shelter, her smiling face stared back at her, wrinkles and all. Best Realty. Who, she wondered, was Tess Rose minus Best Realty, minus her fancy suits and Mercedes and blackberry and cell phones? Stripped of everything that she defined herself by, who was she?

CHAPTER 37: WHERE YOU'VE BEEN

Dale nibbled on the pieces of the oversized chocolate chip cookie that she had spread out on the napkin in front of her. She sat across from Tess at a table nestled up by the front window of The Bakery. Tess looked from Dale to the scene of passersby outside. She couldn't decide if she felt as if she were on display or if the people passing by were on display. She could tell that Dale was processing what to do with the information that Kyle had called Tess that morning. Their two-week break was a day or two from being up.

"What did he want?" Dale asked.

"He was asking about apartments – if anything new had come up."

Tess sipped her tea. She took the cover off her tea to cool it and the steam rose out of it. For a moment, she felt as if she was getting lighter, clearer, watching the steam vanish. Friday – finally, the end of what had been a long and tiresome week in her life.

"So, he's still looking for a place to live," Dale said.

"Want my opinion? And I don't think one has to be too much of a detective to figure this one out," Tess said. "Kyle was searching for information on you. The apartment stuff was his way of easing into a conversation with me."

"What'd you tell him?"

"I told him about some apartments that were on the market, sent him the email links to take a look at them and told him to call me if he's interested," Tess said.

Dale was playing with her cookie, breaking it up into more pieces, searching for chocolate chips.

"Has he called you?" Tess asked.

"He's into sending me emails and text messages now," Dale said.

"And?" Tess said.

"And I don't know. I read what he writes me but then I'm powerless to respond to him. I have this lethargy when I think about writing back to him. Of course, I don't know what to say because I'm not sure what I feel. My life is fine without him. Sometimes I can't even imagine that I was with him," Dale said.

"I can relate to that feeling. It's how I felt about all my ex-husbands after each divorce. Out of sight, out of mind – that's what Michael used to say to me. Of course, since I always got to see him, he felt that I was still thinking about him."

Dale looked over at Tess's watch.

"We've got about fifteen minutes," Tess said.

"What do you think I should do?" Dale asked. Her eyes were intent on Tess.

"If I was in your situation, I would keep on going and trust my feelings. Sooner or later, you'll know what to do. I don't think that you have to rush anything. And you certainly don't have to put pressure on yourself."

"I'm sure you're right," Dale said. "I hope. It's just so hard to keep on going with so much unknown and unsolved in my life."

Tess smiled. "My dear, we all have tons of unknowns and unsolved issues in our life. Thinking we know the answers is the real joke. But the answers do come. All you have to do is live and they happen."

"How's the monk?" Dale asked.

Tess glanced on either side of her to take inventory of who was sitting alongside them: all strangers. She took a deep breath and filled Dale in on the kidnapping by Mrs. Clay, the sex on the 4th of July, the not-quite sleepovers.

"You've kept this from me for all of these days?" Dale asked.

"You were in the Hamptons!"

Tess glanced at her watch and stood up. "We have to go. Yoga time."

Once outside, "Do you think he's going to stay?" Dale asked.

Tess shrugged her shoulders, the cool evening air invigorating. She linked her hand in Dale's elbow. "It's a big mystery. Right now, he's here until December. After that, his abbot has to write to Rome to get him an official pardon from the Pope."

"The Pope? What? This is the stuff soap operas are made of. But if he has fallen for you, Tess, and I am sure he has, he's staying."

"Remember, I'm up against his mother, the wicked witch of Mill Basin, and the Pope."

Dale paused, bringing Tess to a stop. "Like you told me, Tess. The answers will come."

"I know. And I also know that nothing lasts forever."

Tess started walking again and Dale fell in line beside her. There was a hint of fall in the air. The season of transition and change.

Swarms of people were walking down the city streets. Work people done with their day, moms with their children, groups of teenagers in uniforms on their way home from some extracurricular school activity, she supposed. Everyone had somewhere to go.

Dale paused by the tables of earrings, necklaces, and belts that were being sold on the street in front of the yoga studio. She picked up a chunky gold medallion necklace and exaggerated its weight before she put it back down. She held up a spiked red leather belt and Tess shook her head.

"It looks like a collar for an evil dog," Tess said.

Before pulling open the door to the studio, Dale turned to her. "He probably won't go back, Tess."

"How does everything get so complicated, Dale? One moment I'm enjoying life, the next moment psycho mother is stalking me, and I have to worry if a monk is going to go back to his monastery."

"Que sera, sera," Dale said.

"Amen," Tess said.

Church bells began to ring in the distance and as Dale held the door open for her, Tess paused a moment – their tinny chimes sounded to her as if they were from another era; there was a beckoning element to them. She thought of *The Sound of Music*, the ominous sound of the church bells toward the end, as the family made their escape, but at that instant Dale released the door and Tess moved inside before it slammed on her.

CHAPTER 38: NEW LINES OF COMMUNICATION

My Dearest Tess,

I have reached a point in which preaching to others no longer fulfills me. I ask that you read my pages, as I leave them for you, one section at a time. Perhaps the only way to really know one another with any truth and honesty is in a behind- the-scenes way. I hope that my writings will help you to know me and understand me. The truth is, Tess, that I don't have any answers. In my own garden, there are just daily questions. What I can offer you is my story. What going to the monastery was all about for me and what I discovered there. I believe that if no one knows your story in life, you will never be known.

Fondly,

Neal

In Your Own Garden

Finding Your Way

It took me a long time to realize that life is all about accepting the unknown and learning not to expect. It's when we expect that we lose our focus and become fixated on goals that are figments of our imagination. The beauty of each act is in the doing of it. Of course, this is an easy concept to preach, and a much harder one to practice.

As a young monk, I prayed each day, my goal being very clear to me: I wanted to know God, to be at one with him. Each time I prayed, I waited, believing that THIS would be the day that God would come to me – speak to me, through me, guide me. I sought my own goals in praying to God and lost sight of everything else. After a few years of waiting and wishing, my faith began to dissolve and as a result, I began to doubt God and my calling to serve him.

It was at that time, when I had hit a low, that a transformation occurred. I stopped looking outward for a sign and began looking inward. I asked myself what it was that I sought in life and realized that I already had everything that I wanted: my health, a supportive community, and hours each day to read and come to know myself. The less attached and concerned I became with results, a funny thing happened – the more immersed in my prayers I became. In time, my prayers were heart, soul, and action all in one. It was in that focus and honesty that God did come to me – not as a voice or a face, but a presence as gentle and as subtle as a breeze.

And yet, once I found God, the soft guiding God of my life, there was no major shift in me, just a silence that I hadn't been able to hear before. Each day, I prayed and toiled in the fields and tended to my garden. Looking back, I guess that I had deceived myself into believing that when God came to me my life would change as it had done many years back, when his voice led me to join the monastery. When I reconnected with God at this later date, nothing much changed – my life was still full of the same hurdles as it had always been. The only difference was that I was no longer searching but living.

On the days when I struggled, I wondered if my being at the monastery was a selfish act or if in fact it was my calling in life and if

God still wished for me to be there in his house. I worked in my garden,
tending to the weeds and making sure that the soil around the tulip bulbs
was moist and firm, and waited for God to come and console me and tell
me, YES, you belong here. God never told me that.

One May night, two years ago, on my 42nd birthday, after I had
been at the monastery two decades, I had a revelation. It was after
nightfall, when we said our last prayers of the day and were supposed to
be in our rooms, reading and contemplating. I stared out my window at
the towering evergreen trees waving in the wind like shaky old men and
closed my eyes as the coyote's song infiltrated the fields. I prayed for the
safety of all the smaller animals that might find themselves in the
coyote's path. It was in one of those moments of pure love and concern
for others, that I realized that no matter how much we may want
someone else to experience our lives for us, feel our pain and fear,
console us, they cannot. In truth, we are all alone. It was that night that I
came to understand that God is not a force who can provide us with
answers or take away our loneliness. God is the strength within us that
helps us to surpass our fears, helps us to be strong not only for ourselves,
but for others, too. It was that night, after all those years of living within
the walls of the monastery, that I came to know – not just accept, but
know – that each of us is an image of God and our job is not to wish for
others to remove our pain or to add to our joy, or confirm our actions,
but to live our lives without any expectations and to always tend to our
garden first, for it is only after we weed ourselves and nourish our soil
that we may bloom, and in turn help others to do so.

In the coyote's song that night I came to understand that God is
our mirror: if our faith in Him is strong, His faith in us flourishes; if our
faith in Him begins to falter, then His faith in us falters, too. Our

connection to God is reciprocal and everlasting. To wait around for God to give us a green light is to forget that we are already on the same journey. When we go, God travels with us. When we stop, God stops, too.

If I had begun to suspect that perhaps I was not destined to live the remainder of my life at the monastery, it was on that night – the day of my birth some 42 years back, May 6th – that I realized that life was not always about a straight path, but that sometimes there was a crooked progress to our lives, and it was not something to be ashamed of, but rather something that we needed to accept. People would and did get lost along their ways, and it was only in getting lost that there was a hope of getting back on one's path. I prayed that night as I got into bed and the owls began to cry, reminding me that there was a time each day for everyone to be heard, that I would be able to accept not only my crooked progress, but the crooked progress of others and to appreciate that crooked progress as much as I appreciated my straight- path progress. For a moment, as I fell asleep, my mind deflating after so much thought, I remembered the tulip stems in my garden whose weakness I had tried to undo by placing sticks up against their stalks, trying to change their direction and make them straighter, stronger. There was always in this great big world the chance that some force, some presence, without asking any questions, would try to help you find your straight path.

CHAPTER 39: ALL THE THINGS ABOUT YOU

"Are we almost done with standing poses?" Neal asked.

Tess paused mid sun salute to wink at him and then kept going, her body flowing into plank, then chataranga, into upward facing dog before she spoke. "If you want to be, sure." And then she was in downward facing dog and jumping through into a seated position.

Neal made his way to a seated position on his mat. "How you do that fancy jump through thing is beyond me," he said.

"It's a repetition thing. One day it just happens," she said.

Tess smiled at him in his white undershirt and navy Adidas track pants. She wiped the thin layer of sweat from her brow. It was a brisk September evening and she had turned the heat on to warm up her home. Now she was hot. She couldn't tell if it was menopause or the heat or the yoga, but her body was damp all over and she liked it. After so many years of no physical activity, she liked feeling as if she was getting in a workout, liked feeling a relationship with her body again, the aches and stiffness in her joints from activity.

"Practice is the key," Tess said.

She wondered if Neal was thinking what she was thinking; thoughts that belonged in the bedroom and not on a yoga mat. That's what he did to her – turned her on in some foreign way.

"After about the twentieth sun salute, my middle-aged body says no more," Neal said.

Tess laughed. "We did not do twenty sun salutes," she said. She was leaning forward now, inching her hands toward her toes in a deep forward bend. Pachimotinasina. "Anyway, you have ten years on me. I'm the one with the middle-aged body," she said.

Neal was doing as she did and leaning forward, his hands barely making it to his knees. "Ouch," he said. "This is what I get for going for a jog today."

"You're tighter than usual. And since when do you jog?"

He fell on his back, bending his knees, and reached and pulled her so that she fell back beside him. They looked at one another on their sides, Neal smiling so that Tess smiled.

"I jog as of today," Neal said. "I always used to jog, but then I guess I stopped for a few years. Or maybe a few decades," he said so that they both laughed. "But today I decided to start again."

"Why today?" she asked. Her voice was light and gentle. It felt nice to be resting on her back. She had to get rid of the stucco ceiling downstairs one of these days. Jeesh. She didn't know how she had let it go for so long. Who had stucco ceilings anymore? No houses she sold. She'd put it on her to do list.

"Why not today?" Neal said. "It was brisk and cool, and I felt the inspiration to go do it. Thirty minutes. I'd like to say thirty minutes of bliss but today it felt like –"

"Hell," Tess said. She leaned on her side so that she sat facing him. "I said it, not you."

"I was panting like a big sweaty dog during and after, but I felt great," he said. "I'm going to give it a try again tomorrow. Thirty-three minutes."

"Why thirty-three?" she asked.

"Just because," he said.

"I see," she said.

"I'm putting you to sleep."

"Nope," she said. "I'm relaxing."

He adjusted himself to his side so that he faced her directly. He moved a stray tendril from her face to behind her ear. "You have the prettiest hair color," he said. "It's ginger. Or cinnamon. But more ginger," he said. He twirled the tendril around his finger now.

"I started to read what you left for me," she said.

He nodded. She reached to touch his face with her hand, tracing his eye socket down to his cheekbone and then moving her finger over his lips. It was hard sometimes to remember that he was a person, that he was more than just the feelings and thoughts she had of him. He was a person sitting across from her who she liked and with whom she had been intimate. A human being with his own active mind and complexities. He kissed her fingertip with his lips. A soft, slight kiss.

"You have a lot of good things to say," she said. "I liked what you said about the crooked progress of life. My life has been pretty crooked." Tess laughed and Neal kissed her finger again and then he was sitting up and rolling over to her yoga mat so that she laughed some more.

"One mat per customer," she said.

"I want to share your mat," he said, and she scooted over, making room for him so that their bodies were close together, their faces inches apart. All Tess could take in were his blue eyes that reminded her of the Caribbean right now, of diving into a foamy white ocean.

"I love spending time with you," he said. "I love talking to you."

Tess didn't move her eyes from his. "Why?" she asked. His pupils spread so that they were almost taking over the blueness.

"I get to be myself with you," he said.

"Who were you at the monastery?"

"A man following rules."

"Who are you in your mother's house?"

He laughed. "A man following rules."

Tess brushed his cheek with the back of her palm.

"Sounds like a lot of rules everywhere," she said.

"No rules with you," Neal said.

Tess laughed. "Yet," she said.

He wrestled her onto her back playfully, his face looming over her.

"What does that mean?"

"It means that you never know what you're getting yourself into."

"What do you think I'm getting myself into?"

"Hmm." She could have told him that he was getting himself into a steamy relationship in which she could see herself becoming insatiable. She laughed deep in her throat. For a moment she was silent as she debated, *what am I getting myself into?*

He waved his fingers in front of her eyes. "Tess to earth," he said.

"Do you believe in points of no return?" she asked.

He studied her, his eyes taking all of her in, first her face and then traveling down her body in her tight black yoga top and tight black yoga pants. She blushed, suddenly conscious of her body. He steadied her chin with his hand and then smoothed her hair off her forehead and kissed her there.

She didn't believe in points of no return. She had learned that no matter how deep you were in, it was always possible to back out – that had been true for her in love and in business matters.

"Do you?" she asked.

"Do I what?" he said. His fingertips were massaging her ear lobes and then moving down to her neck. Slow rhythmical movements.

"Believe in points of no return?" she asked.

"I think I know what you're asking me," he said. He kissed one cheek lightly, then the other cheek, a symmetry to his movements.

"What am I asking you?" She whispered now, letting herself be pulled into his seduction, letting him have his way with her, her pulse rising with anticipation. She had been asking him if there was any way back for him. Back to his old life, back to the monastery.

"I don't have the answer yet, Tess."

She nodded, his lips hovering over her own and then moving up to her eyelids, kissing each one, so that she felt herself easing up even more behind closed lids. She smiled and felt his fingertip tracing her lips, which made her smile broader. He was her lover. For now, that's what they were, lovers.

He leaned down over her and covered her lips in his own, kissing her lightly at first and then harder, so that she felt her insides come to life, and rolled closer to him, their bodies pressed together. She loved this about them: how they seemed to fit, how their joining wasn't awkward, but comfortable. She pulled him closer to her and then his hand was up her under her shirt and he was caressing her bare back. Gooseflesh spread and she eased into his touch, craving it all over so that she began to caress his back, his skin soft and smooth, and then she wanted his shirt off so that she could feel his flesh against hers and in a moment, she was pulling off his shirt and then he was pulling hers off.

"I could kiss you for hours," he whispered. "Hours and hours." He moved his lips from hers for a moment so that she craned her neck from the floor to reach his lips, only he pulled further away, so that she couldn't reach him.

"What?" she said. "What is it?"

"I bet that I'm not the only man who's said that to you."

She laughed and let her head fall back down to the floor.

"Neal," she said, and then his lips, his person was closer to her again and he rested his head on her chest, so that she felt the racing of her heart against his cheek.

"That's funny to you," he said.

"No, not funny." She stroked his growing-back, silky straight hair with her hand, her fingers arranging strands this way and that by his ear. "I wish I met you a long time ago. And yet, I think I met you at just the right time. I wasn't always who I am now; you may not have liked me if we met any other time."

"Have other men said that to you – about wanting to kiss you?"

"I don't know. Maybe. What does it matter, Neal?"

She leaned up, her head bent, and kissed him on the cheek. "Right now, I want you to kiss me," she said. "No one else."

Neal faced her again and began to kiss her slowly, passionately, so that she couldn't contain the excitement, the pure desire that rushed through her body. As if he could sense the shift in her, the neediness, he began to undress her right there, pulling off her yoga pants and then pulling down his own sweatpants, his hands exploring her body, right there on her yoga mat.

Afterwards, their bodies relaxed, he rested his head on her belly, so that they pulsed, ever so slightly, with each of her inhales and exhales.

"It matters," Neal said. "It matters because I wish you were in it with me – I wish this was our first experience together."

"It is, though, Neal. No one has ever been like you."

His hand traced the inside of her thigh so that she quivered.

"You're cold?" he said, and she shook her head although he couldn't see her.

"No," she said. She glanced down at him on her naked body and had the urge to cover herself but then feeling his hand move along her lower back and then her mid-back, the feeling passed. She liked this – being exposed with him.

"I like you, Tess," he said.

She was silent for a few minutes, thinking and not thinking. Taking in the moment, the two of them exposed in the fading light of day. She smiled. How could she ever practice on this mat again without reliving this scene?

"I like you, Neal," she said, but a darker thought was passing through her just then. So, what that she liked him? What would come of it? She had liked men before; what had ever come of any of those feelings, those relationships?

He stirred, and moved up to her now, so that they rested side by side and she felt her body stiffen. She wondered if he had sensed the shift in her. He began to smooth over the profile of her body, his hand swooping at the indent of her waist as he made his way from her hip to her breast and she felt herself soften, lose herself against his touch which both nurtured her and made her feel safe, secure, desirable.

"What are you thinking?" he asked.

"I like being here with you," she said, at which he pulled her close to him, his arms cradling her.

"Are you comfortable? Should we go into my bedroom?" she asked.

They lay silent for a few moments, until she peeked up to see if he were sleeping.

"Neal?" she whispered.

"Uh huh," he said.

"Do you want to go to bed?" she asked.

"I need to go soon," he said.

"Home?" she said, and he nodded.

"You can stay," she said, suddenly feeling desperate for him not to leave her. "For a little bit?"

"For a little bit," he said.

They got up from the floor slowly, Tess gathering their clothes as Neal rolled up the yoga mats and placed them in the corner, and then Neal was following her up the stairs and Tess felt self-conscious again – she couldn't remember a man ever following her naked from her downstairs to her upstairs, and she was grateful that the lights upstairs were off. They stumbled into her bedroom, laughing, Neal bumping into her more than once, and fell onto her bed, undoing the covers and sheets as they got inside and held one another close. It didn't take long for Neal to be excited again, which got Tess excited, and then they were kissing passionately and making love – a dreamy, desirous love in which Tess let go, gave into him, gave into her desire and moaned once and then again, in harmony with Neal's moans. There was a recklessness to their actions; she couldn't define exactly why or how, but she felt it in her being. Reckless abandon was the phrase that came to her; a phrase she had never identified with any of her actions.

"Stay the night," she whispered as they drifted off to sleep. "I want to wake up next to you." She felt vulnerable once she said it, but beyond caring if she sounded needy. She was needy of him right then.

"The cookies," he said. "I have to make the cookies," he whispered, so that they both laughed.

"What if the folks at the nursing home don't have any cookies tomorrow?" Tess asked.

"They have to have their cookies, love," he said and hearing that word, *love*, she felt a rush of tenderness pass through her. *Love*. No one had ever called her that.

"Okay," she said, her mind too tired to think, to make sense anymore.

"Neal?" she called out, sitting up in bed. She couldn't tell if she had awoken due to him stirring or if he had left hours before. 3:15 am. She got up, grabbed her white cotton nightgown from the drawer beside her bed, slipped it on, and moved to check the front door – it was locked. He was gone. On her kitchen table he had left her a note on a post it: "Sleep tight, Tess. Until we meet again." He had made a smiley face on the bottom, and the thought of him drawing the smiley face made her smile.

She sat down at the kitchen table, and rested her head on it, the cool glass soothing against her sleep-warmed flesh. She laughed. It struck her as funny that her lover – her lover Neal, because that is who and what he was in her life – had to go home so that his mother wouldn't get angry with him. Or maybe it was more than that; maybe he had to go home because there was a fear in him that spending the night with a woman would solidify his downfall. Did she think that his waking up next to her would be a sign that he was going to stay away from the monastery? The complexities of the mind. She often couldn't figure out herself, so the possibility of her figuring out Neal was slim. She could fight him, petition him to stay the night, but was that what she really wanted? At this point in her life, did it matter? No. She liked waking up alone, liked making her tea, sitting with her yoga books. She could remember times in her life when having to chit chat with her partner in the morning exacerbated her, how she had felt desperate for some time to herself, some peace and quiet. This is what age and experience had done to her: made her set in her ways.

She yawned. Who knew what came next? Perhaps he was only hers to borrow; this time she had with him was limited. Maybe it was for the best that way. Tess had no way of knowing if he would wear on her emotions, her heart, as the others had done. Not that she had wanted it to be so, but she knew that time could transform things in mysterious ways – that it could lead her to love what she had once despised and to despise what she had loved. Or maybe it wasn't time, maybe it was Tess who transformed things; maybe she blocked others out when a relationship started to keep them from getting close to her. She controlled the on/off switch in her mind and heart and maybe it wasn't any more mysterious than her trying to protect herself. From what, though? Life? She couldn't protect herself any more than she could will Neal not to return to the monastery. She simply didn't have the control to master her universe. It was all larger than Tess, larger than her thoughts and feelings. Her mother had always tried to instill that in her to no effect and yet here, now, the night sounds thick outside her window, she felt herself moving through some understanding, some membrane of thought, of logic, and she felt herself closer to reaching a truth. Only she was tired. Her eyes began to close, her eyelashes brushing against the glass table. She wanted to stay excited about Neal, open to the possibility that he was the one. The one what though? She knew that no one could change her life or make her life better. That was all her work, her role in life – she had to be her own savior and inspiration. She had to take ownership of her life.

She knew all of this, and yet in the darkness of this night, she wanted Neal to stay – she wanted him not to return to the monastery. She knew that people didn't belong to one another, that everyone was on loan to one another. *I know Mom*, she spoke aloud. *I know that*. She felt honored to have Neal in her life during this time of change and tumult for him. For her. She knew that what she had with Neal may only be temporary, but she still wanted it. All of it.

She moved into her bedroom, into her closet, got up on the step stool and took down the urn, removing it from its velvet case and placing it on the closet floor, pushing her black patent leather pumps out of the way so that she could sit down beside it.

"I know you are trying to rest, Mom," she said. "But I needed to be near you. I needed to be in your presence. I never realized how much I disliked ambiguity." Tess laughed. "Isn't this what I'm struggling with? Ambiguity. I am not calling the shots and I don't like it." She laughed again; a defeated, tired laugh. "I don't like not being in control," she said. "Not one bit," she whispered.

Tess yawned loud and stretched her arms broad, before she nestled her way onto her closet floor, curling up in a ball on her side, the wooden floor cool and smooth against her body, pushing a shoe here and there out of the way with her feet.

"I miss you, Mom," she said. "I miss you." She wished for a moment that a voice from above would say, *I'm right here with you.* "Silly, silly me," she whispered. "Good night, Mom. May we both only know peace," she said with a faint apprehension that life wouldn't be peaceful for her, that she had entered into a realm that included unrest. "Shhhh," she said to herself, "shhh," quieting her mind, and closing her eyes.

CHAPTER 40: A CHANGE IN TEMPERATURE

In the distance, Tess saw Mrs. Clay walking towards her. With each step forward, their intersection became evident. Tess was on 56th drive, blocks from Neal's home. What in the world was his mother doing out walking? The last thing Tess needed was an encounter with Mrs. Clay to rile her up. Besides, Tess had to get home and get ready for work. She shook her head – no, not going to deal with her today – and the slight jolt aggravated the ache she had awoken with in her lower back. Served her right for sleeping on her closet's wooden floor.

There was no one on the other side of the street – she could still cross over to avoid a direct intersection, only she was sure that Mrs. Clay had already seen her. Anyway, if Mrs. Clay wanted to avoid her, she could just as easily cross to the other side. Tess was holding her ground – she wasn't going to let Mrs. Clay change her course. She had been walking by herself for the past few days, or whenever it was that Neal had taken up running, and she had never seen Mrs. Clay. This was Tess's turf. His mother had no business being out on her streets.

Tess bit her bottom lip and hastened her pace, breezing past towering oaks and gardens filled with blood red and vibrant pink and yellow **chrysanthemums**. When she whizzed by a sweet-smelling honeysuckle bush, she breathed in deep and long, letting its sweetness fill her. In a moment, Mrs. Clay would be beside her. She breathed out one, two, three, four.

"Mrs. Clay," Tess said.

Mrs. Clay didn't move.

"Beautiful day, isn't it?" Tess said.

Her eyes were not raging today and with her hair growing out of its angular bob, she seemed duller, harmless. Tess took a deep breath, as if she were bracing to blow up a balloon.

"Why is it that you despise me so?"

Mrs. Clay stared straight into Tess's eyes so that Tess felt as if she were invisible.

"I'm not an evil woman, Mrs. Clay. Your ill feelings for me are ungrounded. You don't even know me."

"I know your type," Mrs. Clay said.

"And what type is that?" Tess said.

"You're out to have a good time. You don't realize or care that other people can get hurt from your actions. You don't realize that it's not always about you, that the world isn't out to please you," Mrs. Clay said.

"You've got me pegged as someone that I'm not," Tess said.

"You've been married four times. This is a game for you – conquering a monk, making him fall in love with you," Mrs. Clay said.

"I respect your son and whether or not he was, is, a monk, is not what this is about," Tess said.

"There are so many single men out there. I'm sure that you meet men all day while you're out showing houses. Why can't you victimize one of them?" Mrs. Clay said.

Mrs. Clay began to walk, and Tess moved with her, trying to keep up with her.

"I am not looking to meet any man. I'm fine on my own," Tess said.

"Then let Neal go," Mrs. Clay said.

"You make it sound as if I'm holding him hostage," Tess said.

"You are. His heart is with the monastery, not with you," Mrs. Clay said.

"He can do as he pleases. I've never asked him for any commitment."

"Neal talks to me about the monastery each day. It's in his heart, always. If you think anything else, you're kidding yourself. And he's not free to go while he's with you. Neal is loyal. He won't walk away from anyone that he believes needs him. He'll come to you until you tell him that it's okay for him to go," Mrs. Clay said.

Tess didn't know if there was any truth in this. Perhaps Neal did want to go back? Perhaps his mother was right, and he was with her now because he thought that she needed him.

"Neal is free to do as he pleases," Tess said.

Mrs. Clay turned down 64th street and began to head up towards 56th drive. Tess didn't care for this block, with its two-family homes that reminded her of row houses. So out of place in Mill Basin, so dated, and yet they sold quickly – grown and married children who wanted to have their parents live downstairs seemed to swoop them up and were willing to pay for them.

"How don't you understand?" Mrs. Clay asked. "This isn't about what I want or what you want. This is about Neal following his path in life. This is about what God wants, not what we want. It's about divine destiny, not selfish motivations." She stopped abruptly, as they neared the end of the block and were at the intersection of 56th drive, so that Tess almost stumbled into her, the ache in her back jolting down her legs so that she grimaced. The home they stood in front of had Halloween decorations – scaredy-cats and pumpkins – on the windows and Tess wondered if they were still up from last year.

"Are you even listening to me?" Mrs. Clay asked. Her eyes were clouded with tears and for a moment, the way she moved her hands, almost reaching out to Tess, Tess thought she was going to start shaking her, so that she backed away an inch. "It's not about what we want," Mrs. Clay said again, and Tess nodded. Mrs. Clay could have been saying the lawn is green at this point and Tess would have been nodding – Tess had brought her to tears.

"Open your eyes," Mrs. Clay said; her face had grown softer. It was the face of a mother pleading for her child. "He's my son, for Christ's sake. I've lost him for so many years and believe me when I say that I wish he would stay here with me, but that's not up to me. When a person has a vocation, it's not about what you want, or I want – it's about life and one's duties to oneself and to powers that are larger than oneself. When God asks you to live in his house, you can't decide that you want to move out – there's no such thing as moving out. God chooses few, but those that he chooses are not randomly chosen. There is a higher power to the world. Whether or not you choose to acknowledge that, it's true. Do you understand me?" Mrs. Clay asked, and Tess nodded.

She understood, but somehow couldn't believe that she was involved in this drama. She glanced up at the scaredy-cat arching his back with his bugged-out eyes. Why was she involved with Neal, with this drama? What was she doing?

"Because I'll keep talking until you hear me," Mrs. Clay said.

"I hear you," Tess said. Tears dripped down Mrs. Clay's face. Tess felt as if she was a statue, solid, still, like she would fall over in one motion if the breeze were to blow a bit harder.

Tears seeped from Mrs. Clay's chin onto her chest and Tess wanted to hug her, to comfort her. They were both mothers. Tess could offer her that solace, that understanding. Instead, Tess pulled a tissue from her sweatshirt pocket and handed it to Mrs. Clay, who used it to dab at the corner pockets of her eyes before she cleared her throat.

Mrs. Clay began to walk now, faster, and like a dog clinging to its owner, Tess followed, close beside her.

"Mrs. Clay," Tess started. She didn't know what she was going to say, what there was to say.

"Lyla," Mrs. Clay said. "My name is Lyla." She cleared her throat again, wiping away the last of her tears.

"Lyla," Tess said. "I never meant to cause any problems. I never meant to confuse Neal or to hurt you. The day you called me into your car – I didn't deserve that," Tess said. "You've made me into a monster, but I'm not. I'm just trying to live like you or anyone else. My goal in life is not to go around hurting people."

The sun had disappeared behind the clouds, the sky a faint white. The trees were beginning to change to hues of deeper forest green and brown. Tess had never noticed how quickly fall set in, how in a matter of days, the rich, bright green leaves became crunchier. She wasn't ready for the summer to end. Fall always made her feel lonely, as if everyone and everything was going to drift away.

"If it weren't for you, Neal would have returned to the monastery long before his six-month discernment was up. But he likes you. He likes being with you," Lyla said.

Everything inside of Tess was shifting – she was a mix of indignation, anger, and desperation. She wanted to make things okay. As a mother herself, she wanted to set things right.

"You don't know if he would have returned. Maybe I'm just a distraction, and if it weren't for me, there would have been another distraction. You don't know."

"Look," Lyla said, "If you can be his friend and not be sexual, then I almost don't mind your friendship. I actually think you could help him find his way back to the monastery."

Tess was still trying to digest the sex comment. Did Neal tell his mother that they were having sex, or was this Lyla looking for confirmation? They were crossing the street now. She surveyed Lyla, her worn out Ked sneakers, her navy polyester pants, her white short-sleeved polo shirt, her black – no doubt freshly dyed – hair. Like Tess, she was the mother of a grown man. A mother who feared losing her son, or had already lost him, without knowing where or why.

Lyla paused and put out her arm, like a toll, so that there was no way around her unless Tess broke through and pushed her arm away.

"I need you to stop the sex," Lyla said, her eyes intent on Tess, as if she were picking her out of a line up. "Do you understand?"

Tess shook her head. "I, I –" she said.

"You will," Lyla said, and then she was moving again, and in a moment or so, Tess began to move again, too. They walked on alongside one another in silence, up 56th drive, past Tess's house, her cleaning lady neighbor pausing in her task of raking leaves from the driveway when Tess and Lyla approached, following Tess with her eyes and nodding as they walked by. Tess and Lyla looped around National Drive, and headed back down 66th street, until they turned onto Barlow Drive and stopped in front of number 56.

"There's a reason he's running now," Lyla said.

"He told me that he always used to run," Tess said.

"People run when they're trying to get away from something," Lyla said.

You is what Tess thought. He's trying to get away from *you*.

"What is it that you think he's trying to get away from?" Tess asked.

Lyla's eyes didn't leave Tess's. "I'll be walking tomorrow morning at 6:00 a.m.," Lyla said. "And I trust you'll consider what we've discussed."

Tess stared at her, and Lyla moved up her driveway, onto her porch, opened her front door, and then she was gone, letting the door slam shut gently behind her.

CHAPTER 41:AWAY FROM HOME

The cars were lined up all along the turn onto Whitman Drive and parked bumper to bumper on Michael's semi-circle driveway. Tess imagined that the neighbors across the street would be calling the police due to the commotion. Regardless of her nudging, Michael hadn't grasped the concept of inviting all his in-view-of-his-home neighbors so as not to have them "tell" on him to the police. Michael claimed that his neighbors had nothing to do with Best Realty and therefore he was under no obligation to include them in his second annual Best Realty Labor Day/Birthday Celebration Bash.

Tess paused for a moment and hid behind an evergreen two doors away from Michael's house to adjust her ivory pants suit. Michael would appreciate her navy Gucci loafers. She took a deep breath. Parties made Tess feel small, like a tiny fish swimming in an ocean. All those people but no real connections, talk for the sake of talking. She couldn't picture Neal there with her – walking in with him and introducing him around seemed like too much work, especially having to elude Michael's comments, not to mention causing a stir with her staff. It was for the best that she hadn't mentioned the party. Besides, it's not as if they were truly a couple; they were just people who spent time together.

Michael stood at the backyard door greeting everyone that

walked in with his sheepish grin and his sparkling blue eyes. She envied this of Michael – his freedom at gatherings, his ability to socialize and not feel as if he had to run away to get back to himself. When he winked at her, though, holding up his glass in a mock toast, she remembered how the non-stop show of Michael had tired her. How she had felt lonely trying to get to the real Michael, as if he was covered with a web, and no matter how hard she tried to break through to the real Michael, she couldn't. It had only been after they split that she had glimpsed the real Michael, and, in those glimpses, he had been desperate to get her back, as if she were something to be won.

She was sure that Michael would say the same about her – that he hadn't been able to know Tess while they were a couple, and most likely he was right. It wasn't that she didn't want people to know her, but she understood that letting a person know her meant that rejection was a possibility. It was hard work to be yourself. Thinking about this made her feel like a kid in grade school. Foolish and insecure. Which reminded her of how she felt towards the end of her marriage to Michael – that he was more like a child to her than a husband. He was always expecting something or other of her. Tess didn't like to be counted on for things. It wasn't that she was stingy or greedy. It was that the expectations of others made her nervous. What if she couldn't live up to them? What if she failed to satisfy others? She believed that she could give a person topical things – money, conversation, companionship – but she could never give herself. People couldn't give themselves, and it was probably a good thing, too, she supposed, because no one really wanted you anyway. It was parts of you that people wanted to fill in the gaps within themselves.

Michael embraced her and feeling it go on a bit too long, Tess pulled away.

"Come on, it's my birthday," Michael said. "Give me a break."

In the distance, out by the dock, she saw some of her agents. It was hard for her to imagine them having a life outside of her office, or maybe it was hard for her to imagine them in her social circle. It wasn't that she didn't like them; it was just that seeing them made her think of all the things she had to get done at the office. Aside from Michael, she had been careful throughout her career not to mix business with pleasure. Michael leaned to kiss her on what looked like it was going to be her lips and she turned her cheek to him so that his kiss fell dead center on her cheek.

"You've had a bit too much to drink, my dear," she said.

"Wow, tonight I'm a dear."

"You're a dear when I don't want you to make an arse of yourself."

"My girl." He pushed her an arm's distance away from him to take her in. "You look very nautical tonight," he said. "The navy Gucci loafers, great touch. I'm ready to get on board."

"Did anyone ever tell you that you're too much, Michael?"

"Where's the weirdo? Oh, let me guess, he's at Mass?"

"Now I know you've had enough to drink. Perhaps it's not too late for me to cancel the case of wine I got you for your birthday," she

said.

"It's a legitimate question for a religious man."

"For your information, I chose to come alone tonight," Tess said.

"Which means to me you're not staying, just here to make your appearance."

"I'm glad you have it all figured out," Tess said.

Just then a few guests, a couple that had bought a starter house, and Michael's research assistant, were gathering behind her, waiting to greet Michael and make their way into the party.

"I don't want to hold up progress," Tess said, nodding towards the line that had formed behind her.

Michael made a sweeping gesture with his hand for her to enter. "Enjoy yourself, dearest," he said.

Tess whispered in his ear, "Last drink for you for the night."

He saluted. "Aye-aye, captain."

Tess made her way to her team. There were three of her agents, her assistant Lynn, and two more of her agents were walking over to the group as she made her way from the opposite end of the backyard. No one had brought his or her spouse, but then again, she couldn't remember if everyone was still married or even married at all. Over the years she had been invited to some of their weddings, but in general, there was always so much drama going on in the office between this house and that house, agents in and out of the office on their way to show houses, and buyers and closes and contracts, that there'd never been much time for her to catch up on their personal lives. Her mind paused: did she regret that? Did she wish she were more connected to her team, that she did group dinners and such more? Heaven's no. She didn't have time for that. She was running a business. And then she remembered her small and informal wedding to Michael at her favorite, since closed, Italian restaurant in New York City to which he had insisted on inviting the office. Tess cringed thinking about that. She imagined that the office had a field day gossiping about her and her fourth marriage, not to mention seeing her in a romantic sense. At least she had worn a tan cocktail dress versus a virgin white gown.

"Anyone know where to find a good deal on a house?" Tess said.

"I have a few to show you," Max said. Laughter erupted amongst the group.

"And I'm sure you'd give me a good deal, too," Tess said.

"I learned everything I know about good deals from you, Tess," Max said.

"Remember when Tess used to drag each of us with her when she was showing houses so that we'd see how it was done?" Max said.

"I tape recorded Tess once so that I could study her selling techniques until I realized that she changed her dialogue for every sell. *No two buyers are alike*. I heard that so much my first few months I thought I was going to lose my mind," Jana said.

"What'd you used to call it, our pledging semester? Remember our weekly drills? Tess would give us case scenarios and make us create dialogue around them. It was like taking acting classes," Max said.

Tess laughed. "I'd forgotten about that. I used to be a rough boss, huh?"

"Used to be?" Lynn said, so that the group laughed again.

"Oh, come on, Tess has softened up a lot in the past few months," Max said.

"Do you mean that?" Tess asked.

"You seem less bothered by it all," he said, "and I should know with all the stuff I pull." Laughter again.

"What would I do without you all?" Tess asked.

"Probably close 50 deals a month on your own," Max said.

She smiled at the group, and winked at Max. "If you'll excuse me for a moment, I need a drink."

Tess made her way up to the refreshment table and poured herself a glass of Perrier. Her agents were laughing hysterically about something now. She didn't know if they liked her, if they thought she was a jerk, but this much she knew: she had helped them all to become successful and long after they had progressed in their lives, whether they moved past Best Realty or not, Tess would be able to reflect that she had helped their careers. She made her way past the perimeters of the backyard party space, and making sure no one had detected her wandering, she walked down the steps leading to the dock and made her way onto the beach. Her loafers made an impression in the moist sand. As she moved closer to the water's edge, sand got into her shoes, but she didn't mind it. She made her way onto the dock and moved across it further out into Jamaica Bay. The water glistened under the lazy, late afternoon sun and she looked up to the sky under the cool breeze, feeling it rustle her hair. The faint promise of fall was in the air, and she remembered the spring night, not more than a few months back, when she had brought Neal to this spot. His first time out on the docks. So much changed so fast. The nature of life. She believed in change, had imposed it on her life again and again, via the comings and goings of her relationships, but had she ever changed at her core? Maybe it was that people never really changed so much as they evolved into different versions of themselves at different points in their lives, their core remaining the same. But if at her core she had remained the same, then who was she really? Her mother's daughter, the independent businesswoman she had whipped herself into, a wife, a mother, a flop? The comings and goings of the waves mesmerized her. Always in motion. When and for what would Tess stop?

For a moment, she imagined Neal beside her and turned to look: flocks of birds surrounded her on the dock, and she closed her eyes in the lazy breeze. Life made more sense with her eyes closed. The feeling-Tess was so different than the seeing-Tess, who was programmed in ways that were sometimes counter to her feelings. She thought of Neal at home with his mom. She couldn't imagine if they were formal and awkward when they were alone together or if there was camaraderie between them – if they laughed and reminisced.

The screech of the pigeons resounded in Tess's ears. When she opened her eyes, they seemed to be surrounding her on all sides. Her instinct was to ask *what do you want from me*? But instead, her eyes locked with one pigeon and the inability to know this creature – what it was thinking or feeling – overwhelmed her. There were so many walls in life, too many for any one person to break through. Above, the flames of the candle torches blew in Michael's backyard to keep the mosquitoes away and people mingled and laughed amidst the reggae music that was blasting. She imagined Michael making his way through the crowd swaying his hips – he loved reggae music. The pigeons had opened their circle around her, scattering, and she began to make her way from the dock and onto the beach. She liked the sinking sensation under her feet, as if she were moving into the earth with each step. She walked slowly on the sand back towards the yacht club and her home and for a moment, she paused. It was only right to let Michael know she was leaving and then she thought the better of it – she didn't want to go through the fuss of saying goodbye, the possibility of Michael berating her for leaving after only a few minutes at his party. She kept going, her eyes on the coasting waves, skirting them as they rode the shore, as if she were dancing with them.

The breeze made her shudder so that she picked up her pace; suddenly she felt eerily alone in the great big world and wanted to be at home, in her room with the door closed, under her blanket, small, safe. But where had her desire to be alone, to have her space, gotten her? She wondered for a moment if it wasn't herself that she was trying to get away from. The thought seemed cliché. But there was some truth to it. Hadn't all the distances she had created been unsuccessful in making her feel complete? She wished that she could call up her mother, only she didn't know what it was that she wanted, what she needed to talk to her about. The breeze came at her fiercer now and she stopped in her tracks for a moment, pinched by the idea that her mother was there with her. The sky was a fading electric blue, the clouds moving in from the distance. It struck Tess as preposterous that she had spent so many years wishing to be away from her mother when now, often, she sought her company. How one's feelings could change. Perhaps, she thought, that's all this was, change settling over her, shaping her world anew. She couldn't imagine what her mother would say to her, how she would direct Tess, but she believed she would start by asking her if she was happy. On the good days, yes. Today, Tess didn't know. "Happiness is your birthright," her mother always said. "It's yours to have."

She was moving again, one foot in front of the other, the sand in her shoes irritating her toes, so that she bent down and pulled her shoes off, slapping them together so that the sand trickled out of them as her bare, smooth feet trekked the sand, moist and cool to the touch. In a few minutes, she would exit the Yacht Club and cross the street to her home. She anticipated Buddhi waiting for her in the living room window, watching the world go by from his perch. Her mother, Prakash, Neal, Michael, Dale. The characters in her life. How she wished she could cradle them all into her at this moment – if only to feel as if her life was in one place. Regardless of what she had told herself in the past, she needed people – people who she loved – which made her wonder if anyone needed her. She slipped on her shoes to run across 66th street to her home. She fumbled with the lock on the door. Did anyone need Tess? When she swung the door open, Buddhi dashed to meet her, his purr reassuring to her as she scooted him out of the way and pushed the door shut, blocking out the world beyond.

CHAPTER 42: SHOW AND TELL

"How was Labor Day?" Dale asked.

Tess plopped down next to Dale, who was sitting at a table for two by the window in The Bakery. Dale pushed one of the large teas in front of Tess.

"I don't remember when these holidays started to bring me down. I vaguely remember that I used to look forward to non-imposing holidays like Memorial Day, July 4th, Labor Day. Now, they feel like work," Tess said.

"Non-imposing?"

"Any holiday that doesn't involve gifts or family is non-imposing. Thanksgiving, Christmas, Easter – those are the imposing holidays," Tess said.

"So, I take it Labor Day was a bit labor-some?" Dale said.

"Michael had a birthday party that included all of my staff," Tess said.

"Michael is the infamous ex that was at yoga with you that first night I saw you here?" Dale asked.

"That's him. Ex, business partner, friend. The party was fine, nothing out of the norm for his parties, although I couldn't get out of there fast enough, which makes me feel like something is wrong with me."

"Did you take Neal?"

"Heavens no," Tess said. "I didn't want to complicate anything with my office folks and all."

"Are you still chumming it up with his mom?"

"We walked together a few more mornings," Tess said.

"What do you talk about with her?" Dale asked. Tess shifted in her seat to shield off the sunlight piercing her eyes.

"She talks to me about Neal – how he was growing up."

"Sounds exciting," Dale said, and she and Tess laughed.

"It makes me wonder if she's ever had anyone to talk to. With her husband having passed away and all. She seems lonely to me. I had thought she was this hostile monster and I'm still not sure she won't snap on me again, but I see her differently now. Her life was devoted to her son and her husband and her volunteer work at the nursing home. Normally I would think what a boring life, and yet I find myself thinking that she's altruistic," Tess said.

"The witch has won you over," Dale said.

"I've been talking to her about Prakash and that's new to me." Tess pulled her blackberry out of her bag. They still had 30 minutes until the yoga class time. "We're okay for time."

"You don't mention your son much," Dale said.

"When it comes to him, I never know what to say. He's one of the great mysteries in my life."

"I can't believe you have a son who's older than me," Dale said. "You seem so young."

"I'm an old lady all right," Tess said.

"To me, you're one of the sweetest, most caring people I've ever met. I'm sure that you're a great mother," Dale said.

Tess leaned in closer to the table, as if she was about to share a secret.

"Really? You think of me as sweet and caring?" Tess said.

"Yes," Dale said. "You're the first person I've opened up to in a long time."

"I don't think anyone has ever described me as sweet and caring, let alone a good mother," Tess said.

Outside people moved up and down the street, all on their way somewhere. When she had moved to Brooklyn, she had often sat out on the college campus quad watching the students and professors coming and going and wondered what each of their homes looked like, how their bedrooms were decorated.

"Did you want to be a mother?" Dale asked.

Tess studied Dale. She was still so young and free from any real mistakes. Her routes were all still wide open. Would Tess have done anything differently if she were Dale's age? She didn't know if that was up to her or up to higher powers.

"I was petrified of being a mother. I wasn't sure I was going to go through with it; it took me a few weeks to commit."

"You would have gotten an abortion?"

"I thought about it a lot," Tess said. "An abortion was a lot more complicated back then than it is now. But I thought about it. Of course, I'm so grateful I had Prakash."

"What's he like?" Dale said.

"Prakash is like Kyle in some ways. I thought that the first time I met Kyle, before he brought you into the picture. They look alike. Same penetrating eyes and curly hair and thoughtfulness," Tess said.

"That explains why you chose Kyle over me when you met us," Dale said. She winked.

"You were a brat," Tess said. "How I saw it was that you had a guy who wanted to buy a gorgeous million-dollar brownstone and you didn't want to leave New York City. You were ridiculous as far as I was concerned," Tess said.

Dale raised her eyebrows and opened her mouth wide before she shook her head.

"Tess Rose, you judged me without even knowing me.

Very un-yogic!"

They laughed. "When I saw you at yoga, I thought if that girl likes it, I certainly won't," Tess said.

"I take back what I said about you being sweet and caring. You're a monster," Dale said.

"Time changes everything, right?" Tess asked.

"What does Prakash do?"

"He's an architect. Designs office buildings and condominium complexes. He tries to convince me to move out to San Francisco. Promises to get me a good deal in one of his apartment buildings. Like mother like son, I suppose."

"Sounds like you two can go into business one of these days," Dale said.

"Oh, and he's a yogi, no less. He took a teacher trainer program one summer while he was in graduate school. Of course, I panicked that he was aspiring to be a guru like my mother."

"Seems like he turned out just fine," Dale said.

"I worry about him getting married. He's 32. He still has time, I know, but I think that a mother always wants to see her child married. As if then they'll be safe or something." Tess laughed. "Of course, I couldn't stay married myself, but maybe that's just me. Not to change the subject, but anything new with Kyle?"

"We spent the weekend together," Dale said.

"You waited all this time to tell me groundbreaking news? That's great! Right?" Tess asked.

"Yes. Only I still don't know what I want to do – if I should marry him or be on my own."

"Dale, you know by now that you can't make life decisions based on a weekend. You need to just keep going. The answer will come to you. Sooner or later, you're going to be sure of what you want. It's going to be evident," Tess said.

"What if it's not?"

"Then the decision may be made for you," Tess said.

"I'm beginning to wonder if that's what I want – for him to make the decision," Dale said.

"How's he doing?" Tess asked.

"Fine. He seems happy. He's joined this basketball league and plays with the guys a few nights a week and then goes out with them afterwards. He told me he's busy," Dale said.

"And you are, too," Tess said.

"Now that I don't have my work stuff to talk to him about, I feel like a little bit of a loser for not working. He didn't make any comments, it was just that he kept talking about his daily work stuff and I had nothing to offer from my work stuff, obviously, and I didn't think he'd care to hear about our yoga stuff," Dale said.

"It's not about what you talk about. If this is the person you want to be with, it's about how you feel when you're with him. Do you feel like you can't wait to get away from him or that you want to keep spending time with him?" Tess said.

The knock on the window glass startled them both: Sara and Kim smiled and waved and then they were making their way in.

"To be continued," Tess said, and Dale nodded.

"It's divorce week!" Sara said standing in front of the table. "We reached an agreement!"

"You seem festive about it," Dale said.

"She was practically skipping down the street," Kim said.

"I'm getting a lot of money. Taking him down," Sara said.

"How yogic of you," Tess said.

Dale choked on the sip of tea she had just taken so that Kim patted her on the back. Sara pulled up a chair from an empty neighboring table while Dale made room on her seat for Kim to sit down.

"I think I'm dropping out of teacher training," Kim said.

"What?" Sara said. "You didn't mention that on our walk over here."

"You were too busy going on about your divorce; I didn't have a chance to get a word in," Kim said.

"Why would you drop out now? We're more than halfway done," Tess said.

"Tess, you work all day – you don't have to deal with the yoga maniac-women like I do."

"They are nuts," Dale said. "But I'm not in the studio with them all day – I'm out at the high schools in the afternoons teaching kids yoga – karma hours."

"They're just running a business, Kim. The training is for you," Tess said.

"Yes, but they're making my life hell," Kim said. "I'm doing menial work for them – folding yoga mats, cleaning up the studio, answering phones. I have a nanny that takes care of my housework so that I can go to the studio and do their busywork."

"Send them your nanny in your place," Sara said.

"Very funny," Kim said.

"Sounds like a good idea," Tess said.

"I think we're all tired of their rules and regulations," Dale said. "But Tess is right. This is for you. At the end of the program, it's not them you'll have to deal with, but yourself."

"Spoken like a true therapist," Sara said.

"They certainly remind me of why I went into business for myself – so I didn't have to deal with someone else barking orders at me," Tess said.

"You're not really dropping out, are you, Kim?" Dale asked.

"I almost did twice this week," Kim said.

"And?" said Sara.

"Well, I was all set not to show up for whatever task they asked me to do, and then I ran into one of the mentors on the street and next thing you knew I was walking up to the studio with her."

"Just tell them you're busy during the day. You don't see Tess or me here. Do what's right for you," Sara said.

"I think I'm going through a pre-midlife crisis. I guess I don't know where I need to be, so it's easy to blame them for ruining my life," Kim said.

"You and I both," Dale said.

"We need to get going," Tess said.

"Anyone know what's on the agenda for today?" Sara asked.

"I think that the Sanskrit teacher is coming," Kim said.

"Hours of fun ahead," Sara said. "Why they bring in all these teachers at 9 am on Saturday mornings is beyond me."

The cool September air was invigorating. Tess searched her mind – she wasn't sure what she was happy about. There were certainly things she could feel bad about right now – work issues, what she was doing with Neal – and yet at this moment of this day, she was outside, walking, the sun beginning to shine, the air crisper and cooler than it had been in some time, and she felt light, free, and hopeful. Hopeful of all that was: the day ahead, the time she was allowing herself to spend in the yoga studio, giving herself the opportunity to grow, to evolve, to experience different pastures of her life. The girls chatted on. She felt peaceful in not having to join in. They all had their share of drama to discuss and analyze. That was in part what living was about. The other part was about being and feeling. When she climbed up the stairs to the yoga studio, for the first time in decades she thought of something her mother used to tell her when she was restless: that just maybe, this was going to be the very best day of her life.

CHAPTER 43: WHEN WE MEET

"Picture meeting you here," Neal said when Tess opened the door. She had been in her bedroom, her backside nestled up to the wall, which held her legs upright, lying on her back as she read Iyengar's *Light on Yoga.*

She had opened the door expecting it to be Michael – hadn't he left her a message saying he was dropping by, something about bringing her some paperwork to review prior to Monday morning and grabbing dinner up at the Italian place on Avenue U? She hadn't called him back on purpose as after the endless activity and chatter of one of her final three yoga lock-in weekends, she craved a quiet night. The thought of making small talk seemed miserable. She had planned to catch up on her reading and get a good night's sleep before the Monday morning work insanity.

"Neal," she said, fixing her hair, which she realized was doing all sorts of uncooperative things from static electricity with the carpet. She was still in her black yoga tank and black leggings, which she and the girls had come to refer to as their uniforms. She had planned on showering, but somehow didn't get to it just yet.

"If you're busy, I'll go."

"No," she said, holding the screen door open. "I was reading." She rubbed her eyes, massaging her cheeks a bit to bring some color into them. "I'm glad to see you."

"It's a nice night," he said and making no move to walk into her home, Tess stepped out onto the porch. The coolness of the bricks against her feet sent a chill through her.

"Out for a walk?" Tess asked.

"I came out to see you," Neal said. "It's been a while."

"It's nice to see you," Tess said.

"I knew you were tied up all weekend," he said.

"Yes. Teacher training. We're almost done."

"Would you like to join me? We could go out to the docks," he said. He took a flashlight out of his anorak jacket. "I'm prepared," he said.

Tess moved beside him slowly, the sand cold and damp against her bare feet, a burgundy pashmina shawl draped around her upper body smooth against her skin. She carried her loafers in her hand, the glow of Neal's flashlight illuminating the way so that they steered clear of any shells or other sharp remnants scattered amidst the sand. The stars up above shone brightly in the darkened sky; the chilled air refreshed her after being in her warm bedroom. Neal glanced sideways at her more than once and she smiled back at him, closing her eyes after each glance to capture his expression. There was something about his person that drew her in – a blend of sexy and commanding, so that at any moment, he could have stopped to kiss her passionately and she would have responded with all her being. He had the power to mesmerize her, with his clear and stoic eyes. The insanity of it all. After all her failed relationships, no less. She laughed a quiet, slight laugh.

"What's so funny?" he asked.

"Nothing," she said. The moment he spoke, she missed the silence. There was safety in silence at times, a sense of being in something together. Words were sometimes an intrusion. And yet, once he spoke, she felt the need to talk, too – to keep things friendly, light.

"Did you have a nice weekend?" Tess asked.

"I ran some. Got lots of writing done. Baked some cookies," he said.

"Sounds productive."

"I thought about you," Neal said.

In the near distance there was a dock; in the dark Tess couldn't make out right away who the dock belonged to. Her eyes moved to the shoreline to attach the dock to a house, but then Neal was moving towards it, and she followed, realizing that it didn't matter who it belonged to, that they were going to park themselves on it for a bit and hope the owner didn't think they were vandals.

"I thought about you, too," she said. What she wanted to tell him was that she always thought about him, but she paused. She didn't know if he felt the same. He could have changed over the past week. People did that. Neal was in the midst of making a decision that would affect his whole life. He was kind. She didn't want to obligate him.

Their shoulders touched as they sat on the dock, Tess swinging her feet, so that every now and then she brushed his leg with the motion. What she wanted to ask him was if he had reached any new conclusions, but she didn't have the energy, or maybe it was the courage, to ask. The limbo that was somehow always between them transformed her into an insecure, needy Tess – a person she didn't care for much. And then she paused, turning to face him. Perhaps it was her limbo. Perhaps he wasn't as concerned about it all as she was. Perhaps it was the controlling Tess that needed to know something, as if knowing would solidify what was between them. But Tess knew another truth: knowing didn't always shape things. Sometimes knowing only lasted until someone changed their mind.

"Kiss me," she said, and the moment she said it a shrill delight ran through her. She couldn't remember ever asking a man to kiss her, ever letting herself be that vulnerable. She would have repeated it – I want you to kiss me, but by then his lips were gently grazing hers and she felt them moving into one another, their lips enlarging as they encompassed one another and then they were fully entangled. She let him take control of her, let her passion seep through her and into him, infusing them. It was a mingling of two minds and hearts, a meshing of lust and desire, a surrender of sorts, although she couldn't have said just then what she was surrendering to him – couldn't differentiate what was hers and what was his. And then he was pulling her closer, his hands on her shoulders, pulling all of her being closer to him and what she felt between them, what was there was unlike anything else she had ever felt. It was more than lust, more than desire. It was a tenderness, but there was also a strength as the intensity between them grew more powerful. She was a stronger person when she was intertwined with him like this. It wasn't a physical aspect, but a strength of mind, of character. With this kindness, this honor she felt for him, she was a more powerful person. A better version of Tess. She thought all of this, and yet wondered if she weren't somehow more selfish when she seduced him, or maybe he was seducing her; it was hard to say where one ended and the other began.

Neal pulled away just then, so that their eyes took in one another with an intensity that Tess couldn't read.

"What?" she asked.

He shook his head. "Nothing."

She traced the contours of his cheekbones with her fingertips before they made their way to his lips, which she outlined and then leaned in close to him, kissing him deliberately there once and then again. Neal's pupils enlarged, his eyes intent on hers.

"I like you," she said, so that he laughed, a deep, unexpected, boyish laugh. She backed away from him, but he positioned her chin in the wishbone that his thumb and forefinger created and pulled her face closer to his, their lips almost touching.

"I like you," he said before he kissed her gently and then hard, their lips enveloping one another's, so that this time she began to giggle.

"You're such a beautiful woman," he said. "Sometimes I want to devour you."

She laughed and shook her head to his quizzical look. "I'm not laughing at you," she said. She was laughing at the insanity of them, the unlikeliness of their passion.

He reached for her hand and cradled it in his lap, tracing each of her fingers, and then his eyes intently on hers, he brought each of her fingertips to his lips, planting a soft kiss on each one.

"I miss you when I don't see you," Tess said, a moment of tenderness overcoming her.

"I miss you, too, Tess."

For an instant, her mind drifted to the possibility of his leaving, of missing him terminally. But then her mind told her another story – she had missed herself in many relationships she had been in – missed the independent Tess who always adapted her life for a short while so as not to make another person feel second rate, as if she was always trying to get away from them. She could not be that person again. No, she would need to be herself if she was going to be happy in any relationship. And herself meant that she might make someone else feel bad. The redeeming quality of Neal was that he too had his own agenda, his own to do list each day. She felt relieved and then sad that she might never be his priority.

"What are you thinking?" Neal asked.

The stars were out in full bloom. Off in the distance, the headlights of the cars traveling the Belt Parkway glistened and twinkled, like stars moving across the road. She was thinking nothing and everything. That she was content sitting here with Neal; that she may have to give him up; that she had so much work to do before tomorrow morning; that she wanted to take him home and make love to him; that she was so tired of drama in her life; that he was worth whatever obstacles that came up; that she was willing to go the distance for him.

Tess shook her head, her eyes finding his again. "I'm not thinking," she said.

He massaged her temples with a soothing, kneading motion. "I see that mind of yours working," Neal said.

"If it's working, it's not consulting with me."

"What are you thinking?" Tess asked.

"Oh, the old switcheroo," Neal said, and she laughed.

She shook her head. "No switcheroo. I can never tell what you're thinking."

"If you could, you would be physic," he said. "But remember I came to see you tonight."

She smiled. "Should I assume you wanted me?" she said.

His forefinger raised her chin so that their faces were parallel. It was a small gesture, but something in his sureness, in the masculinity of it, made her insides throb.

He kissed her deliberately, with abandon, and then he was pulling her up and they were making their way back, stopping every few moments to take one another in, to share a kiss. There was a giddiness to their interaction, a knowledge that they were in it together, that the passion between them was real. If all else faded, this much Tess would know: the passion between them was real.

They put their shoes on and jogged across the street, her hand in Neal's as they moved up her driveway and then up her porch stairs. She knew that she should leave well enough alone, that she should savor these moments, these feelings, but as she unlocked her door to let them in, she couldn't hold herself back.

"Stay the night. Just this once, wake up with me," she said, twisting the key in the Segal lock round, pushing the door open as she removed the key. Her eyes glanced up at him and he paused before bringing his eyes to hers.

"I know," she said. "The cookies."

"The cookies," he said, backing her into the doorway as he kissed her.

"I can make the cookies with you," she said. "We can do it together at the crack of dawn," she said, so that he laughed his deep belly laugh.

"My dear, I wouldn't think of depriving you of a minute of beauty sleep," he said.

She moved her hand under his shirt, feeling his flesh, the outline of his belly as she made her way up to his muscular chest. How she loved his skin, his body. She inhaled the nape of his neck and kissed him there, making her way up his neck to his chin, which she tilted down, kissing his lips.

"I just may give you a reason to stay the night," she said, and they both laughed.

Tess locked the door behind them. He took her hand and led her up the stairs, stopping to kiss her at the landing, then backing her through the kitchen, down the hallway, and into her bedroom, so that she giggled. She couldn't remember the last time she had walked backwards this way and it reminded her of how Prakash used to practice moon walking on the kitchen tile.

"What's so funny?" Neal said, peeling off her sweater, caressing her neck before he kissed her there.

"Nothing," she whispered.

He was lifting off her shirt and then she was taking off his. All of her wanted him and then they were on the bed, her side of the bed, and she was wrapped around him, and he was taking her in, and their kissing was an energy between them, electric and tender all at once. The passion she felt for him, with him, was unknown to her; how could she have lived for so long without knowing this passion, and then she was free, no longer thinking but feeling, moving with him, because of him. And it didn't matter who or what Tess was, all that mattered was that moment, their union, their love, for what other than love could this feeling of oneness be called?

Cold. She was cold and her throat dry and raw. She sat up, her eyelids sticking together as she peeled the mascara off, allowing them to open a bit. She pulled the blankets around her naked body, which was sideways on her bed, before she plopped back down. She couldn't tell if his leaving, the front door closing, was what had woken her up or if he had been gone for hours. She sat back up and squinted at the clock. 3:30 am. He had been long gone. Or maybe he had overslept and just left. She sighed and with her hands, she righted herself on the bed so that her head rested on her pillow. She traced the contours of her body, moving from her stomach, and up to her breasts. She wondered how she felt to Neal. If he liked touching her. She could feel his presence all over her.

There was a faint feeling of panic in her for a moment: she would not let him destroy his life. No, she wouldn't allow that. She sat back up and took a few deep breaths. But that was not happening. No one was destroying anyone's life. No. She laid her head on her pillow, turning one way and then the other, trying to get comfortable. It would all work out as it was meant to work out. It would all work out, she told herself, before sleep overcame her.

CHAPTER 44: SEEKING SERENITY

Buddhi purred and nuzzled up to her, his wet nose rubbing her forearm. She was in down dog on her yoga mat but paused to stroke his fur and glanced out the living room window before she positioned herself back into the pose. She had never practiced in this spot before, beside Buddhi's windowsill perch. She had drawn the blinds semi-shut for privacy, which was fine with Buddhi, as he chose to watch her today rather than look out at the street. His cuts and scratches were beginning to heal, his hair growing in over his wounds in patches that looked like hair transplants. The way he looked at her with his yellow tiger-eyes made her feel as if there was a person inside of him that was trying to communicate with her.

"Scoot," she said gently pushing him away from the mat and he meowed, lingering.

She did a few sun salutes to wake her up before she made her way down onto the mat for some forward bends. Clouds lingered above with light blue peeking out here and there. She could tell that when the sun broke through the haze it would be a warm day. Tess was ready for the summer to officially end – for the clocks to fall behind, the foliage to make its appearance, the cooler air to settle in. There never seemed to be any downtime during the summer. The more hours of daylight, the more she felt that she had to accomplish each day. She was ready for fall, only a few weeks away now, and yet the approaching season induced a sense of melancholy. Fall: back to school time, crunchy used-up leaves tumbling to the ground, cool nights. The thought of Halloween and then Thanksgiving unsettled her. She imagined costumed children ringing the doorbell for candy and big family dinners and the possibility of having to tackle those events alone, induced a heaviness in her chest. She breathed into the forward bend, moving her fingers from grasping her big toes to the sides of her feet to stretch deeper. It wasn't that she wouldn't be okay if Neal returned to the monastery, it was just that it was hard for her to know that decisions that would affect her life were being made behind the scenes and that she wasn't the one making them. She wondered what he had been thinking, doing, in the week since they had last seen each other. Had he thought of her? She imagined he did. She thought of him. She could go by his house, ring his doorbell. Only no, she wouldn't do that. He would come around when he was ready. Or maybe he had – who would know with her schedule the way it was, between work and yoga.

Tess squatted and then sat down and lay back on the mat for a moment, taking in the shifting sky. What did she seek in this great big universe? Some moments, she wanted to fast forward life, to see what was around the bend for her, while other moments, she was grateful that she didn't know what would happen next. She sighed. She felt impatient with life, impatient with herself. She felt defeated that she couldn't make sense of what was brewing in her mind and heart, or maybe it was that she didn't know what was brewing in Neal's mind and heart. It would be so easy for her to ask him, and yet she couldn't, or didn't.

Tess closed her eyes and focused on her breath. Small, shallow breaths. Her insides were racing. She wanted more than anything to want what she had in life. *Yoga chitta vritta nirodaha: yoga stills the fluctuations of the mind.* Only her mind didn't feel like being still just then. Tess wondered if she wanted to be a yoga teacher – if that had ever been an option for her and yet if she didn't want to teach yoga, why was she devoting so much time and energy to the training? She could always continue to focus on Best, although her passion for her business was shifting. Sitting in an office doing paperwork, answering calls, and then running around to show houses seemed silly to her. She sat up. Silly? No. She didn't want to think that all those hours and days and months and years she had devoted to her career were silly. And yet, here, now, what did any of that matter? Where had it gotten Tess? Sure, it gave her nice possessions, but beyond that? Buddhi meowed and rubbed up against her arm. It was ridiculous to think that moving people in and out of houses was anything more than silly.

On her back, she exhaled, and tried to focus on her breath. No one knew what was to come – that was the mantra that she repeated over in her mind. That's what living was: filling in the blanks.

Ow! Buddhi's claw penetrated her skin as he attempted to climb up on her chest, and Tess jolted up only to catch a glimpse of Neal running by, right in front of her house. Was he looking up at her window? Did they exchange a glance at that moment? She certainly saw him, but did he see her and keep going? No, she was imagining things. If he saw her, wouldn't he wave, stop? It was Neal. Sweet, kind Neal, who would surely stop for Tess even though she hadn't seen him in a week. Six days to be exact. And yet she could have sworn that their eyes met at that instant. He moved efficiently down the block, a lithe figure in his black running pants and his deep purple windbreaker. She wondered what he thought of when he ran, what his internal dialogue was, where the running took him emotionally. She wondered what he would ordain her now, what she would ordain him.

She lay back down on the floor, pulling her knees into her chest. If he wanted to run, that was fine. So, what if they no longer walked together. He was his person, and she was hers and it was a free country, and he was allowed to do as he chose. Soon, after she settled down from yoga, she would go out to walk. It was fine. He was doing his thing and she was doing hers and sometimes that's how life was, and it wasn't good or bad, it just was. Her job in life was to take care of Tess. *Lokaha samasta sukhino bhavantu: may all beings everywhere be happy and free.* Buddhi crawled onto Tess's chest now, kneading her with his paws and she gasped from the weight of him. His purring grew louder, and she tried to breath in line with it. *Ishvarapranidam*: surrender to a higher power. Her mind was noncommittal, passing by topics, thoughts, like a train en route. It was hard work to live in the moment, not to seek the future, not coast to the past. If she let go of all she had to do and what she had done, what was left in her mind and heart? This moment.

Neal's mother was waiting for her on the corner of 66th street and Indiana Drive in her new black Nike warm-up suit. It tickled Tess that their morning walks had been reason for Lyla to invest in new gear. When their eyes met, Lyla stared straight at Tess. Tess understood now that there was a harmlessness to her, an eccentricity that governed her actions. When they stood together, Lyla didn't offer any salutation, just started walking with Tess alongside her, their feet falling in line. Lyla knew Neal's morning route (she had trailed him in her car on multiple mornings to make sure she had it memorized) and led them down blocks so that they wouldn't intercept Neal. It was understood that Neal didn't need to know about their daily tête-à-têtes.

"So, when will you be a yoga teacher?" Lyla asked. She said *yoga* as if it was a dirty word.

"There's two months left in the program. We have to take some tests in November."

"You have to take yoga tests?" She kept looking straight ahead, so that it was hard to tell if she was talking to her or having a conversation with herself.

"There's a comprehensive exam and also a practical exam – we have to teach a class in front of the mentors," Tess said.

Lyla glanced at Tess as if she were trying to figure out if Tess were making fun of her.

"That's ridiculous. Tests to become a yoga teacher."

"It's like becoming any other type of teacher, I suppose. You need to be qualified to teach. We're working on people's bodies." The moment Tess said *bodies*, she wished she hadn't. She imagined Lyla immediately thinking of Tess working on Neal's body and cringed.

Lyla was crossing the street now, moving in the direction of Mill Avenue. Tess followed closely at her side, looking both ways more than once as they crossed. Lyla seemed oblivious to traffic. Lyla's failure, or maybe it was her resistance, to realize that the rest of the world existed at times, fascinated Tess.

"Where will you teach this yoga?" Lyla said. Tess couldn't tell if she was genuinely interested or if there was a motive behind her questions.

"I don't know yet if I'll actually teach. It's all kind of random that I signed up for the program," Tess said. It was too long a story to share with Lyla. "I took it to learn more, deepen my practice," she said. The mentors loved to throw around the concept of deepening one's practice. Tess smiled to herself. Dale would have laughed if she heard Tess say it.

"Humph," Lyla said. She was leading them through Strickland Park now. They passed by the gated aboveground pool and then the monkey bars enclosure, empty now that the children had gone back to school. How Prakash used to love to swing on those monkey bars. They moved past the sea saw and Tess remembered the days when she and Kash had played together on the sea saw, since replaced, her keeping him suspended in the air until he pleaded with her to let him down, giggling and screaming all the while in his excited five-year old way. It seemed impossible to her that those moments had existed in the same lifetime as the one she was in now.

"What did you want to be when you grew up?" Tess asked. Lyla didn't slow down, but the way she looked at Tess, sideways and fast and then back at her again, made Tess wonder if anyone had ever asked her anything personal.

"I wanted to be a businesswoman," Tess offered.

Each time they got to a corner intersection, Lyla held out her arm, as if Tess was about to rush out before her.

"No one in the community I grew up in was a businessperson," Tess said. "Except for my father, and he bolted from the community when I was two and went back to his home in the Midwest. I suppose I was just looking for a way out, too, and being a businessperson was the way out."

"What did your mother think?" Lyla said.

"My mother kept all the doors open for me. I didn't realize that until much later in life, though. Maybe even just this year. I had always thought that she wanted me to be like her, but that wasn't the case. In fact, that was counter to all she believed in," Tess said.

"I wanted to be a nun," Lyla said.

Tess stared straight ahead, trying not to show any emotion. Of course, she had wanted to be a nun. It made perfect sense to Tess.

"Were you ever?" Tess said.

"No," Lyla said. "No. My mother wouldn't hear of it. Once, when I was a teenager and I tried to tell her that I wanted to be a nun, how I liked being with the Sisters, she went on and on about how the sisters were a big facade. How they sat around praying all day and trying to convert people and win them over while she had to cook and clean and take in work as a seamstress and do other people's laundry to help support her family. She was intent on me marrying someone with money so that I wouldn't get stuck like her."

"Was she a single mother?"

"My father died when I was young, and she never remarried. Said she didn't have time to date with me being around to care for."

Tess nodded. "So, you abandoned your dream and got married."

"He was a local boy – we grew up together in Bensonhurst. His family owned a few hardware stores that became a chain. We got along well, Neal's father and me. He did his thing for the most part and I did mine, with raising Neal and being active in the church and volunteering and whatever else it was that I did to pass the time," Lyla said.

"Did your husband have any idea you had wanted to be a nun?" Tess said.

"No. I never told anyone. Except for one of the Sisters and she's long gone now. She wanted to help me run away – send me off to a convent outside of Brooklyn."

"You wouldn't go?" Tess said.

"I was never much of an adventurous spirit. I suppose you would have run off," Lyla said.

"I did run off – to college in Brooklyn," Tess said. "It's never too late to be a nun, is it?" Tess asked.

"Surely you're kidding," Lyla said.

"I've never been more serious," Tess said.

"Dreams change," Lyla said. "Just because I wanted that then doesn't mean it's what I want now."

"And yet you don't want Neal to walk away from what he once wanted," Tess said.

"We weren't talking about Neal," Lyla said. She stiffened up, clearing her throat, her lips forming a straight, stern line. "Besides, it's different with Neal. In my heart, my mother's instinct, I believe that the monastery is the place for him."

"You've made that clear," Tess said.

"The way Neal talks about the monastery makes it clear to me that he belongs there," Lyla said.

"That's all he's ever known, Mrs. Clay. He spent 23 years there. That's half of his past; the other half he lived with you and his father," Tess said.

Lyla sped up so that Tess had to move faster to keep up with her.

"Do you ever wonder if you've somehow infused your desire to be part of the religious order onto Neal?" Tess said.

"That's ridiculous," Lyla said. She was moving quickly across the streets now. In a few moments, she would be back at her house.

"What I wanted and what I want for Neal are two different things," Lyla said.

"What do you want for Neal, Mrs. Clay?" Tess said.

"I want him to live the life he was meant to live, free of

complications," she said.

"You're insinuating that I'm a complication?" Tess said.

Lyla paused when she reached her home, turning to face Tess. The ivy bordering the windows made the house look ominous, as if a giant winged creature would perch on the sill at any moment and torment Tess.

Lyla looked down at the ground before her eyes met Tess's. She looked tired, worn out, and Tess wondered what was going on in that brain of hers. Could her whole life revolve around Neal right now, his staying or going, or did she have other issues that pulled at her?

"I don't think it's unrealistic to believe that if Neal wouldn't have met you, he might have gone back to the monastery by now," Lyla said.

"Which wouldn't mean it's the right thing for him. For all you and I know, Neal was never meant to be a monk. Who knows? Whatever Neal chooses, that will be what's right for him because now, today, this time in his life is still unscripted," Tess said.

Lyla shook her head. "He doesn't want to let you down, Tess."

"Maybe it's you he doesn't want to let down. Maybe he thinks he needs to be at the monastery because of you."

"I think we both want the same thing," Lyla said.

"And what do you think that is?" Tess said.

"To get through the days," Lyla said.

"No complications, right?" Tess said.

"Precisely," Lyla said. "Go on, now. You have to get to work, I have to get ready to get to the nursing home and Neal will be coming home any minute."

"Mrs. Clay?" Tess said.

"Lyla."

"Lyla," Tess said. "I still think it's never too late."

"Are you talking to me, or to yourself, Tess?"

She held Lyla's eyes. She didn't recognize her as the same woman she had met weeks back at her home. That woman had struck her as impossible, asleep. This new Lyla that was emerging was assured, awake.

"Maybe both of us. What I do know is that every time I thought I was done with whatever I thought I was done with, I wasn't," Tess said.

"My life has turned out exactly as it was meant to turn out," Lyla said.

"Are you happy?" Tess asked.

"Life is about hard work, faith, duty, right and wrong." Lyla held her screen door ajar.

With just a little push, Tess could make her way in, look inside.

"But if you're not happy, the hard work and faith and duty are meaningless," Tess said.

"To you with your hedonistic ways, that would be the case."

"You seek the security of knowing you're living a morally righteous life, but where will that get you?" Tess asked.

"It will get me to heaven!"

"That's what you hope, but you don't know. None of us do," Tess said.

"We can discuss your theories during our walk tomorrow morning. 7:00 am sharp," Lyla said, and Tess thought she sensed a smirk on her face. With that, Lyla pushed open her wooden door and walked inside, shutting Tess out.

CHAPTER 45: WAY LEADS TO WAY

Tess screeched into the Best Realty lot, maneuvering her way into her parking spot and stopping short so that the folders on the seat beside her slid to the floor. She tossed her keys in her bag, checked her lipstick in the rearview mirror, and leaned down for her fallen folders before she opened her car door and stumbled out. Either she was getting old, or her high heels were getting to be ridiculous.

"Sounds like it's time to bring your car in for brakes," Michael said. He was waiting by the building's side door.

"A welcoming committee. How thoughtful of you," Tess said.

"I was actually getting some air," Michael said. "Couldn't resist – such a gorgeous morning. Unlike you, I don't take an hour stroll around the neighborhood each morning – someone has to get into the office first thing to take care of business," Michael said.

Tess rolled her eyes and shook her head before she took in the sky: pale blue with not a cloud in sight. The brisk air made her feel excited, awake. September had set in with its boundless energy and optimism.

"It certainly is a beautiful day."

"We could play hooky, go into the city," Michael said. "Hang around Central Park. What do you say?"

He had on his European charcoal grey slacks and a navy button down with his black Sergio Ferragamo loafers and matching belt – his casual, yet collected look, as he liked to put it. It was funny to her that she knew his wardrobe, knew his actions, his expressions as well as she did. Sometimes, like now, when she was near him, she couldn't believe that she'd slept next to him for a few years of her life. Once she had been passionate with him and now, he was just a friend, a work partner, a buddy.

"Earth to Tess?" he said, slicing the air between them with his hand.

His graying hair was longer than usual, the bangs straying onto his face – she knew it was only a matter of days before he cut it short again, but she liked it. He looked freer, sexier. He was a good-looking man. A sweet man when he chose to be. She smiled and he smiled back at her. She couldn't imagine picking up the pants he had on from the cleaners, getting dressed beside him. She couldn't imagine any of it, and yet it had all occurred in the not so distant past. Going home with him from work, sitting beside him at the kitchen table. So many chapters to a life. So many routes to take. Who was she to say what was the wrong route, the right route?

"You're thinking about playing hooky with me," Michael said. "I can see it in those mysterious eyes of yours. You're considering a day in the city with your favorite guy."

"Some of us have to work for a living, Michael," Tess said.

"That's a no," Michael said.

"Not today," Tess said.

"You're no fun," Michael said.

"Who said life was supposed to be fun?" Tess said.

Michael followed her in.

"I suppose you want me to make you coffee?" he said as they made their way to her office.

"I wouldn't think of it," Tess said.

"You know it's already brewing," Michael said.

"That's one of the reasons you get paid the big bucks," Tess said.

Michael stood in her office doorway as she took her suit blazer off. One minute she was cold, the next minute she was hot. Welcome to middle age, she thought.

"Anything else?" she said, pulling out her plush swivel chair.

"How's yoga training?"

Tess sat down in her chair and stretched her arms and hands tall. "It's moving along I suppose."

"You know you never thanked me for getting you to a yoga class in the first place," Michael said.

"You got me there, my friend, but certainly were not the inspiration for me to keep going. Remind me, how many classes did you attend after that first one?" Tess said.

"Got your point. But, if you should ever teach, you can bet on me being in attendance."

"I won't hold my breath," Tess said.

"That would be against yogic principles – holding your breath," Michael said.

"Is there something you need?" Tess asked.

"I heard from your son," Michael said.

"Great," Tess said. "When he reaches out to you it usually means trouble."

Michael moved into her office and sat down across from her. "He thinks that you've lost it with this monk affair. He wanted to hear from me that you're not totally insane."

Tess slammed her hand on the folder in front of her. "If he thinks I lost it, it's no doubt because of the ridiculousness you tell him."

"I tell him the truth – that I don't know a lot about the guy. Other than that, his mother seems nuts."

"She's actually a nice woman," Tess said. "I've been walking with her in the mornings now."

"Just when I think you've shocked me as much as possible, you manage to outdo yourself," Michael said.

"Thank you," Tess said.

"Let me get this straight. While the monk runs, you've taken up walking with his mother?" Michael said.

"Did you ever hear of going with the flow?" Tess said.

"You've given that expression a whole new meaning," Michael said. "Perhaps I'll come out and join the two of you tomorrow morning."

"Don't you even think about that Michael," Tess said.

"Look at you, getting all bent out of shape," Michael said.

"She knows who you are. She already thinks of me as a man-izer. The last thing she needs is to hear how we interact," Tess said.

"How is it that we interact, Tess?"

"Michael, what else did you tell Prakash, so that I know how to mitigate the damage?"

"He wishes that you'd leave Brooklyn and head out west. He thinks it would do you good," Michael said.

"Of course, he forgets I run a business," Tess said.

"That's true," Michael said. He was playing her desk with his fingers, his eyes intent on hers.

"So," Tess said. "Anything I should know in terms of business?"

Michael shook his head. "Everything is moving along. We're busy."

"Very good," Tess said. She had logged on to her computer and was opening email.

"Is that your way of dismissing me?" Michael said.

"We are at work," Tess said. "Things need to get done."

Michael stood up.

"Tess?"

"Yes?"

Do you plan on seeing this guy much longer?" Michael asked.

"Michael, last I checked, I don't own a crystal ball," Tess said.

"So, you're going to keep romancing him," Michael said.

She turned away from her computer to face him. There were times, like now, when she didn't know how much she could trust him with, when it was better to stay quiet.

"I think he'll be going back to the monastery," Tess said.

"Wow. That one caught me off guard," Michael said.

"It's just a hunch I have. I don't know if that's what's going to happen. God knows it's what his mother wants to happen," Tess said.

"I can't imagine anyone wanting to leave you," Michael said.

"It's about Neal and his life. He has his own responsibilities and commitments. It's not about me."

He nodded. Phones were ringing down the hall and Tess heard

the agents talking in the kitchen. Best Realty was coming to life for the day.

"I know, I know," he said. "You have to get to work." He winked at her and was out of her office.

The roof to the low-rise medical building adjacent to Tess's office seemed like a great escape route. Only what was she looking to escape? Sometimes all of it seemed so ridiculous to her. Life. Taking herself so seriously. She wasn't sure how she arrived at this here and now. Part of her was relieved that she got to start over again each day, but there was also a part of her that wondered what the point was to starting over if the same issues kept coming up. Work, relationships: it all was one big circle. A stray cat sauntered along on the street below, stopping to sniff the grass and then moving into a downward facing dog, before it rolled onto its back. Tess reclined her head back in her chair and closed her eyes. Relationships overall exhausted her. All the wondering, the not knowing, the detective work that the mind employed.

And yet, no matter how much the same issues did come up in her life, it intrigued her that each of the days was so different. Days were reminiscent of one another – she recognized feelings of loneliness, fatigue, doubt, joy, and love – but the ingredients of each day were so unique. She had the power to change the direction a day was taking, to take a different approach, try something new. She wished she remembered that more. *Joy was a choice*. Her mother used to say that to her. Joy was a choice. And if that thought failed to inspire, she reminded herself that whatever she was thinking, or feeling was only right now.

She gathered the folders on her desk in front of her and the folder with the study sheets Kim had made for the comprehensive yoga teacher-training exam fell out of the bunch. She fingered through the sheets and smiled. Anatomy, asanas, Sanskrit, philosophy. It seemed like too much for any person to know amid all else there was to know in life. She couldn't imagine ever having to go back and relearn all she knew about real estate, or life, relationships. And now she was trying to master the whole yoga thing. For whom and for what? That's the question that came to her. Wasn't it enough to just do yoga? Did she really need to know all this stuff? She tried to imagine what her mother would say and now her phone was ringing, and she was sure it was something or other about work and she wished that she could float away from it all. Work, this life, the tasks she busied herself with all day. She wished it would be her mother calling, only she didn't know what it was she wanted to say. That was the strangest thing about someone you loved being gone – there was no way to reach them. She was sure her mother would smile at Tess in her incredulous way, insinuating that Tess was missing the obvious: that of course she could talk to her, and that communication had nothing to do with a phone. But at importune times, Tess was a realist – there was only so much she could sit around talking to herself.

Her admin Lynn was asking her to pick up line one and then she was doing just that, mechanically, not hearing who it was. It took her a few minutes to register the voice on the other end.

"Luke," she said.

"I hope that it's okay I called you here," he said.

"Sure," she said.

"You gave me your card when we crossed paths at the yoga studio."

"Right, I must have," she said. "Actually, I had wanted to ask you something," Tess said. "The flyer for the teacher trainer program that was in Moe's Country Market – did you put that up?"

"I did. In fact, someone took it down and I had to put a second one up," Luke said.

Tess stopped tapping the pen she held in her hand. Her face was caught somewhere between a vacant stare and a smile. Luke had led her to teacher training. How her mother would have enjoyed that karmic crossing, as she would have called it. Way leads to way is what she would have said.

"The reason I'm calling has to do with your mother's house," Luke said. "Your house."

"Is it okay? Did something happen? Jim Creet didn't call me," Tess said.

"Everything's fine. You know that the house is a landmark up here," Luke said.

She wondered what her mother would say to hear her home called a landmark. Probably that the house was only as special as the people who spent time there or something to that effect. She saw the sprawling front lawn, the rounding drive leading to the front door, the cherry blossoms by the kitchen, like at her own home, and the massive evergreens shadowing the grounds.

"The foliage must be starting," Tess said.

"The colors are spectacular," Luke said.

There was silence on the line for a few moments.

"If I wasn't so tied up with teacher training on the weekends, I'd make a road trip," Tess said. "But that won't be possible until December, when my weekends free up again."

"I'm calling you with a question," Luke said.

"Ask me," Tess said. She was sitting up straight now. What could Luke need to ask her that was so important that he was hemming and hawing to get it out?

"Any decisions yet about if you plan to move back?" Luke asked.

"Move back to Woodstock?" A pigeon on her windowsill was intent on watching her. Tess knocked on the glass to shoo it. It pecked its beak against the window once, and then again. "I don't think I'm moving back," Tess said.

She moved to open her window – she didn't want it to fly away, but then it was too late. The pigeon had leapt to flight. It glided through the air, free.

"I know I've already asked but thought it couldn't hurt for me to check in again about your plans. Do you intend to sell it?" Luke said.

"I don't know. I guess not much has changed about that since I saw you last. I haven't thought all of the details through just yet," Tess said.

"I'm sorry, Tess. I know it's none of my business and that it's only a few months since your mother passed. I probably shouldn't be making this call to you. The truth is that folks here would like to buy the house and they put me up to reaching out to you after I said I'd run into you recently."

"You're the messenger," Tess said.

"Yes, I suppose I am. I'm sure it's no surprise that the people here have a long-term relationship with your home. They would like to convert it into a temple," Luke said.

"I see," she said. She heard his words and waited for them to register. Sell her home. Give up the place where she had spent her youth, where her mother had acclimated to America and spread her ways. She couldn't imagine parting with it, and yet if she wasn't going to live there, she believed that her mother would want the town people to keep it alive.

"Perhaps it's something for you to think about? A seed that I'm planting?" Luke said.

It seemed to Tess that she had a lot to think about: the prospect of Neal leaving, becoming a yoga teacher, whether she wanted to spend the rest of her days as a realtor, and now, did she want to sell her childhood home? She wished for a moment that someone could tell her what she was supposed to do regarding everything.

"Sure," Tess said. "Something to think about."

"I haven't upset you, have I, Tess?" Luke asked.

"No, not at all. I'll think about it."

"That's all I can ask for," Luke said. "You take care, Tess. Namaste."

"Namaste," she said.

The moment she hung up there was a knock at her door and then the door opened, and Michael was in her doorway.

"You look like you saw a ghost," he said.

"Usually people wait for a 'come in' before they open a door," she said.

"Yeah, well I'm not 'people.'"

Tess swiveled her chair around to face the window and then back to face her desk again. Michael made himself comfortable in the plush leather reclining chair off to the side of her desk, nestling his head in the headrest. Tess thought of it as her counseling chair – no clients ever sat in it – it was reserved for agents having a rough day or for Tess when she wanted to get away from herself. She couldn't remember Michael ever sitting there. He generally sat in the chair across from her and put his feet up on her desk, which tended to remind her of the way he used to put his feet up on her living room coffee table and how he didn't see anything gross about it. Once he had told her that his feet, which she now found offensive, were the same feet that were in bed with her each night beside her own feet.

"Isn't life supposed to get dull at some point?" Tess said.

"The mother threatening you again?" Michael asked.

"An old friend from Woodstock. He wanted to know if I plan to sell my mother's home."

"What'd you tell him?" Michael said.

"That I hadn't thought it through yet," Tess said.

"You know what I think?" Michael said.

"What?" Tess said.

"I was expecting you to say you didn't care what I thought," Michael said.

"What do you think, Michael?" Tess said.

"You sell it. Those people are attached to that house in a way that's a bit nutty if you ask me, but you and I know that in this business, it takes all kinds. People love houses. People hate houses. But that house, those folks up there *love* that house. That was pretty clear to me when we were up there for the funeral."

"What if I want to keep it?" Tess said.

"As a souvenir of your life?" Michael said.

"To live in," Tess said.

"Tess, you living in Woodstock is like…it's like me joining the Peace Corps."

Tess laughed and bowed her head down to her chest so that her curls sprung forward. Michael's idea of charity was writing a check.

"Exactly. Laughable," Michael said.

"People change their lives all the time, Michael. You never know. I could become a yoga teacher; invite people into the house to meditate in the mornings. Teach some yoga classes."

"You're scaring me, Tess."

She laughed again. "I'm going to hold onto it for now. My mother's crew is not going anywhere, and I don't need the money," she said.

"They could be in there using it, keeping the spirit of your mother alive," Michael said.

"The spirit of my mother is alive of its own free will for your information and your desire for me to sell that house is enough reason for me to keep it for now," she said. "And I know what you're thinking – that I'm a piece of work – but don't you dare say it," she said.

"I was actually coming in to tell you that I'm planning to go out to San Francisco to visit my step-son," Michael said.

"Really?" she said, massaging her temple. "Let me guess, you're joining him out there to devise a plot to separate the monk and me?" Tess said.

"You're a real sleuth, Tessy. Tell you a way to foil our plan."

"I'm on the edge of my seat," Tess said.

"Join me, us," Michael said.

"Michael, I think I have a bit too much going on for a holiday at the moment."

"He's your son. It's a plane ride away," he said.

Tess bit her bottom lip and took him in. She was too tired to play his games.

"You've gone to see Prakash, mmm.... never in the past few years. What's this all about?" Tess said.

Lynn buzzed in over the intercom just then: "Prakash called, wants you to call him back."

"Shall I ring him back so that he can fill me in?" Tess asked.

"Prakash wants us to partner with him on a new property he's designing. Part residential, some office buildings. He'd like Best to take on the sales and rental aspect of it – get an agent onsite in San Fran. I told him I'd take a look. Of course, we'd like you to be there, too."

"One big, happy family," Tess said. She smiled. "You go and tell me all about it. Send pictures. As my trusted adviser, I'll take your word for it."

"We could go over the weekend, take in some sights, have some fun," Michael said.

"I'm busy with teacher training. Only a few weeks to go," Tess said.

"Right. How could I forget?" Michael asked.

"Be sure to let him know I'm still planning on visiting him around Christmas time," Tess said.

"I take it I'm dismissed," Michael said.

Tess's eyes followed him to the door. He about faced once he reached it. "Tess," he said.

"Michael?"

"Please don't move to Woodstock. Really. I like having you here."

"I'm certainly not going anywhere today," she said, her eyes holding Michael's for a moment longer than was comfortable. She knew that he was waiting for her to say something more definite to him. Nothing was definite, though. He nodded and closed the door behind him.

Tess swiveled to face the window again. Outside, the birds continued to coast – they made it look so easy to be free, to float, to move on, away. They certainly didn't seem worried about where to live, what to do next. There were moments, like now, when the not knowing was torturous to Tess. Only no, that wasn't true, it wasn't torturous. She smiled at her melodramatic mind. She just wished she knew what the future held although she knew that the wish was in vain. For that's what living was, the not knowing, the not being sure what was next. She wondered what her life would be like if she could once and for all let go, live, coast with the birds in the sky. Her intercom was buzzing but she didn't have the strength to turn around.

She wondered if her life was an act of free will, or if her course was already predetermined and someone up above was laughing at her struggling, trying in vain to figure it all out. Her mother had often spoken of "getting into the flow of one's life" as if it was a lane on the highway that one could move into. Her mother believed that if you were living, there was no need to worry or wonder about what would come next as life was unfolding one moment at a time. It wasn't that Tess wanted to preoccupy herself with what to do next in her life; it was that she didn't know how to let go. After a lifetime of clinging, of trying to create her outcomes, control them, she didn't know how to go with the flow. She believed that with a few words, her mother would help Tess to make sense of everything right now. Loss, regardless of what the spiritual said, was tangible. But just maybe, she didn't need anyone to guide her. Maybe it was about listening to herself. Maybe she had all the answers to the questions she faced and to all that lie ahead, if she tapped into Tess.

In Your Own Garden

From Here to There: May 1980 – Getting There

     The flight from JFK Airport to Minneapolis that May was uneventful. I was still caught up in college graduation and the fact that I wouldn't be going back in the fall, that classes were over, exams all past. I wasn't sure what I had learned those four years as a math major. How to solve equations and manipulate numbers, I suppose. So, while I wasn't sure about my past at that point, I did feel strongly that my vocation was to devote my life to God. That last year of college the feeling, the knowing, as I believed it, was intensified, until I knew that I would act on it. I wasn't afraid to be on my way. After landing in Minnesota, there was the flight to Saskatoon, Canada. I remember becoming a bit uneasy boarding that flight as mostly fathers and sons were in line. They all carried packed up rifles and fishing gear. I began to feel dispirited – why wasn't my father with me? How was it that we never did father and son things? I thought about calling him then and there and asking him if we could spend more time together but then I realized that didn't fit in to the life I was discerning. Amongst all those fathers and sons, I wondered if my father viewed me as a failure if I didn't take a wife, didn't have children – if he would think me unmanly. My stern, distant father who believed in hard work, in discipline. I wondered if I were an embarrassment to him, and if he would ever embrace those terms, admit that truth to himself, or go on resenting me, disapproving of me, silently.

     It was a small plane, a jet, with no more than 90 or so seats. I sat in a window seat and during the flight, I didn't think. I focused on the world outside the window: fields, dry and parched; acres and acres of fields that spanned in every direction. I remember that I didn't want the plane to land, and then it did just that, and there I was, in Canada, walking off the plane, the men and boys around me laughing and carrying on. There was the urge to call my father again, tell him that I'd changed my mind – that I wasn't going to devote my life to religion after all. I was desperate for him to love me, accept me, only if I did make that call, I'd be lying to myself, and I believed back then that living a lie was a harsher fate than feeling unloved. Besides, I believed that God was calling me, and, in the end, I feared disappointing him more than I feared disappointing my father, my own flesh and blood.

I claimed my luggage and made my way to customs, feeling isolated and afraid – it was my first time in a foreign country. The customs officer detained me. He didn't buy my story about going to the monastery, said he'd never heard of some monastery out in Muenster. Asked me why I was there and then when he opened my bag and saw all my books and journals, my Bible all marked up with my notes, I could see he was starting to wonder if I wasn't telling the truth. It was then that another customs officer gave him a look, pushed him aside, stamped my passport and waved me on. I guess I had been holding my breath, because when I walked, I felt dizzy and weak. I suppose that a part of me had wanted them to hold me back, to ask me to return to Minnesota where I'd get a flight back to New York.

None of the taxi drivers at the airport knew where Muenster was, let alone the monastery. There was a woman taxi driver – I guess she sensed that I was near tears because she approached me and asked me where I was going and when I told her St. Peter's Abbey in Muenster, she nodded and told me to get in her car. It wasn't until we were driving away from the airport that she told me she didn't know where the monastery was, but that Muenster was about two hours away. She asked me why I was going to the monastery, and I told her that I was discerning taking monastic vows and she nodded at me, and then when we reached a stop sign, she turned to look back at me and said, "You are becoming a priest," with a slight smile on her face. Her accent was thick and deep, so that her words slurred a bit. I didn't bother to tell her that I was considering becoming a brother, which was different than a priest, far less learned, and that becoming a priest was something that I would consider later. She, Dora, seemed content to think of me as a priest and I was content to watch her wispy chestnut-brown shoulder length hair blow in the wind and the way she focused on the road, her eyes squinting as if it was all too much to take in. When we reached a traffic light, she studied me in the rearview mirror with her black eyes and asked if it was okay if she stopped to pick up her husband – he was home as it was his day off – so that he could drive with us as she wasn't a hundred percent sure of the way. That made me feel a bit uncomfortable – my imagination was already on overdrive, and I envisioned the two of them kidnapping me or something of the sort. Things like that happened in foreign countries.

Dora was in her house for about five minutes when she emerged with a stocky, short, balding man, who made his way into the driver's seat. He, Alex, didn't say much at first although he smiled at me solemnly in the rear-view mirror at times, so that I couldn't tell if he felt sorry for me going off to a monastery or if he felt sorry for himself that he had to drive so far on his day off. During the ride across barren, deserted roads, the dry, penetrating heat rushing in through the open windows, Dora told me about her life in Romania and her two children. Alex warmed up to me during the ride and told me about how they had come *to Canada and how they had managed to make a life for themselves. Endless miles of sun-parched land loomed out the window. It seemed absurd to me that people in Brooklyn lived so close together, on top of one another, while all these miles of desolate land existed. There came a point in the journey as I listened quietly to Alex and Dora going on about their families – both in Romania and the one they had in Canada – that I felt a change of heart. I wanted to ask Alex and Dora to take me back home with them, let me stay with them for a few days, meet their children, give secular life another try. I craved space and time away from God, from my family, from myself. I wanted to be amidst these people, who I believed were sent to save me from a mistake I was about to make.*

When we pulled off a deserted road into the monastery grounds, Dora turned to me, smiling. We were there, St. Peter's Abbey. The road leading in was about half a mile long and the grounds were covered with burnt grass and weeds that were four-feet high. It seemed deserted and I began to question if we were headed in the right direction. We crossed over railroad tracks and then there was the entrance – a gravel drive with a solid oak tree that had a tinny St. Peter's Abbey plaque nailed to it. It felt as if we were riding horseback as the car maneuvered its way on the gravel, following the signs to the main chapel. Dora was searching in her bag, facing me still, and then handed me a card with her phone number and Alex's work phone number in case I needed to reach them and taking it from her, I felt calmer. There was a way out if I needed it.

Alex was taking my bag from the trunk and then I was out of the car, my body damp and sticky beneath my khakis and button down, so that my pants stuck to the back of my knees. The ride had taken a little less than two hours. The sun was still burning strong. The sky was a vibrant periwinkle blue and then a peaceful breeze swept by so that I felt some relief. I heard the birds chirping and the hum of the crickets – Dora had told me it was crickets – and all around, there were tall, thick Evergreens. The prairie, the first I had ever been on, was flat and seemed to go on forever. It was in those moments of taking it all in that I knew it was going to be fine. I saw the Abbey's college in the distance, and that made me feel better, too, as my parents thought that teaching at the college on the grounds would at least make my four years of college studies worthwhile. There was also a press building and a farm and a sign for a gym with an arrow pointing in the distance. After only a few moments standing on the grounds, I began to imagine starting a life there.

Father Demitrius, the guest master, thanked Dora and Alex for driving me, asked them if they wouldn't come in for something to drink or eat, but they assured Father Demitrius that they had a long ride back and should leave before it grew dark. Together, we waved them off. Following Father Demetrius into the building in his flowing brown robe, I wondered if he was hot and if it was difficult for him to move around in his garb. He was tall, over six feet, slightly overweight and mostly bald and I smiled when I saw that he was wearing sandals. There was something sad to his movements, slow, methodical, and yet his presence was warm and inviting – I felt safe with him immediately. Father Demetrius showed me around the grounds a bit before he left me at my room. I was to stay in the guest quarters while I was discerning my interest. My room was a white-walled square with white and black speckled linoleum tiles that were reminiscent of a dentist's office. There was a window with white tinny blinds through which the sun beamed, casting a shadow on the floor and walls, and above the window was a cross. The cot was dead center of the room, and beside it was a small desk with a lamp on it and a Bible off to the left. There was a closet with hangers and a spare blanket folded up on the top shelf – he told me that it grew surprisingly cool at night. Then he opened another door, which exposed a bathroom with a shower – I hadn't expected that and was pleased. My quarters reminded me of a hospital room with its disinfectant smell and its cold, bare feel. Down the hall was a kitchen and a common area where he told me guests often sat to read and talk amongst themselves. I asked him if there were many guests and learned that there were a few nuns on retreat from other parts of Canada and a few like me, discerning their monastic interest and some lay folks who were there taking a break from life. He left it at that and then excused himself. He promised that he would give me a tour of the preserves in the basement and the apiary and potato farm in the next few days, and that I should make myself at home in my surroundings for the time being, and that he would see me in the chapel when the church bells rang.

That first night, after supper with the other guests, during which we all sat quietly as we ate the salad and soup that was given to us – I had learned that the heartiest meal of the day was eaten at lunch time – I went for a walk with the guests around the five-mile trail that bordered the monastery grounds. It was my first real experience of the prairie, in which objects appeared much closer than they were. There were a few times during the walk when I was sure the massive church bells adorning the chapel were just a few feet away, only to realize that they were miles beyond. None of us said much. For me, there didn't seem to be anything to say once I was there. When we returned to the grounds, the church bells began to ring, and we made our way in to Vespers.

In the pews, I looked from brother to brother, each of them in their tweed brown cloaks and tried to imagine myself sitting beside them. There were 31 of them per my count, and they crossed all age groups, from 20's to what I imagined 60's and they seemed to be in good humor, gentle. I couldn't tell who the priests were versus the brothers, although I knew that there were about six among them. One of the brothers stood out with his wild, curly, long-black hair. Later, I would learn that he, Brother Kurt, was a painter, guitarist, and psychology professor. As the weeks went on, I studied his paintings scattered throughout the guesthouse and the university library and lounge. In the late afternoons, I would listen to him play folk songs on his guitar outside by the picnic benches near the dining hall while I sat in my room, journaling, with the window cracked open slightly. He would be the one to tell me about Father Demetrius's cancer – how he was battling it for the third time around, and that the chemotherapy had begun to take a severe toll on him.

Later that first night, I wandered outside of the guest quarters into a little garden that was wedged in between the guest common room and the chapel. The daylight slowly began to fade, the moon taking over the twilight sky. The air grew cooler in a matter of moments. I had my journal in my hands and was trying to sketch the scene although I wasn't much of an artist. When the clock struck 9:00 pm, the sky was still verging on darkness. It was then that I saw a rainbow arcing the sky and it seemed to me to be one of the oddest scenes, as I hadn't ever remembered seeing a rainbow streak the sky when it wasn't raining. I began to think of all that had transpired in the past 12 hours, between the plane rides and the car ride and moving into my room, and the shared meal and the chapel and the tins of cookies that were left for the guests in the kitchen – ginger and chocolate-chocolate chip cookies that I couldn't seem to eat enough of – and the bird garden and the fields, and the garage where they kept the 20 or so cars and trucks that the monks shared to run errands and deliver goods which they made – cookies and honey and jellies. It seemed impossible that it was still light out and that it was still the same day. I was exhausted. It was time for me to sleep. I went to my room, opened the window, and then pulled down the blinds so that they rattled ever so slightly in the breeze. I decided to move my cot by the window so that I could feel the fresh air. I wasn't thinking about religion that night or the world outside of the monastery or about my family or what was right for my life. When I got into bed, there was nothing that I wanted or needed or wished or hoped for. I just was. For the first time in a long time, I felt that I was exactly where I needed to be. Through the chinks in the blinds the night sky shone black, and the crickets hummed, and the owls tooted their who who's. *I closed my eyes. I was home.*

CHAPTER 46: THE LONG AND WINDING ROAD

Tess thought she heard footsteps in the hall of Best Realty and froze. Who would be coming into the office at 7:15 am on a Saturday morning? Since Yoga Teacher Training had kicked in, she hadn't been to the office on a weekend. Would it be Michael? Not this early. She waited, holding her breath. Maybe it was just the cleaning service. Silence. She moved back into the hall and saw the cleaning lady putting away her cart in the hall closet. She let out her breath, closed her office door, and sat back down, opening her email.

In the email she had sent to the guest master of the Benedictine Monastery in Morristown, New Jersey, she had inquired if she could come in to talk as she was writing a novel about a monk. When he had told her that there was no one who could sit down with her, that they were all very busy working and carrying out their responsibilities, he offered that she email him her questions and that he'd do his best to provide her with some information.

She scrolled down her email inbox. There it was – she clicked it open.

Ms. Rose:

In our experience, once a monk takes leave, he usually

536

does not return to a monastic setting. Most who take leave eventually ask their Abbot to put through a dispensation request. Once officially dispensed, it is not easy to return. One would need to start over as a novitiate before professing vows.

Perhaps what may be most beneficial for you is to visit the monastery, look around and attend some of our services. We welcome day visitors and offer weekend retreat stays, which must of course be booked well in advance as our guest quarters are limited and seem to be in high demand throughout the year. You may find our address and hours of visitation on our web site and if you wish to schedule a weekend retreat stay, please get back to me with some dates and we will see about a reservation.

Kindly,

Brother Nick

Tess read the letter again and then a third time. She didn't know if she was horrified or charmed that the brother functioned as a travel agent. She clicked on the monastery website link and looked at their address. She supposed it was about an hour and a half drive from Brooklyn, give or take. Weekday morning prayers were at 6:30 am. She would be able to drive out there and back before work. Why not go? Wasn't this what she wanted – a chance to see what Neal's life was all about?

Sunlight penetrated the yoga studio so that the floor glistened like wet pavement. Dale was lying on her back towards the stage beside

Kim, each with a roll pillow under their knees. Tess grabbed a pillow and a blanket from the bin and joined them.

"Déjà vu," Tess said.

"They should let us sleep here," Dale said. "I feel like I live here. Or maybe that's just me and my boring life."

"If they let us sleep here, they would probably charge us a fortune. Nothing comes cheap with yoga," Kim said.

"It's nice to talk without them telling us to quiet down," Tess said.

"The benefits of being early," Dale said.

"Ahhh," Tess said, as she lay back. "Who knew the floor could be so relaxing?"

"Can you believe we have less than two more months of this?" Dale said.

"I can't remember my life before this program. What did I do? "Kim asked.

"Come on, you love it and are having the time of your life," Dale said. "Where else would you rather be at 8:30 am on a Saturday morning after spending 6-10 pm here Friday night?"

"To be young," Tess said.

"And what does that mean?" Kim said.

"I actually like being here, so I'm attributing that to my old age.

Where else would I be? I don't have children to tend to and surely no one needs a realtor on a Friday night or first thing on a Saturday morning."

"Oh, well I have tons going on," Dale said. "I have to pull myself away from all the activity to get here."

"What's the Kyle update?" Tess asked. She held her legs up over her head, alternating flexing her feet and pointing them. Watching them move, they didn't seem to be a part of her body.

"I told him that I needed to focus on the yoga exams for the next few weeks," Dale said. "I know, I'm being a jerk. I need to either let him go or try to make it work. It's just that I seem to change my mind every day. If you don't feel like listening to me talk about him, no problem, just tell me to shut up. I know I must sound like a nut."

"Time is okay," Tess said.

"He told me he's resurrected his house search," Dale said.

"Greetings girls," Sara said. She plopped down next to Tess. "What a gorgeous day it is."

"I think I liked you better when you were a grouchy and going through a divorce," Kim said. "Your peppiness depresses me."

"Well, the grouch is gone, and the good times are ahead! Four days of being single and I'm loving it," Sara said. "I'm ready to become an anatomy expert today," she added.

"Are we having another anatomy lecture?" Dale asked. She sat up.

"That's what they said last night," Tess said.

"I must have been dozing off when they said that," Dale said.

"By the way, we need to get started on our study group in the next week or so," Kim said. "Did you look at how much we need to know for the comprehensive exam? I heard from the mentors this week that it's going to take between three to four hours. I haven't taken a test in over ten years."

"Three to four hours for an exam?" Dale said. "Are we in graduate school?"

"I'm more worried about the practical exam," Kim said. "We have to teach a class for 30 minutes and we won't know until it's our turn whether we're going to be asked to teach a beginner class or an advanced class."

"Remind me why I signed up for this?" Dale said.

"We have two months to get ready girls. We'll be fine," Tess said.

"She's right. Two months is a long time. And, if we fail? Who cares?" Sara said. "It's not the destination, it's the journey that counts. Right?"

"I don't want to fail the yoga test," Kim said. "Not after all these months. I think I'd have a nervous breakdown."

"Not like you're on the verge of one anyway," Dale said. She laughed. "Of course, I'm right there beside you. Wasn't this program supposed to enhance our lives? Is it my imagination or are we all falling apart?"

The mentors walked into the room – Tess heard them laughing amongst themselves and sat up. The room had begun to fill up. She smiled at some of the girls across the room as they sipped their coffee, and then at the older couple, each of whom had lost over twenty pounds since the program began. She liked being part of this group. Liked this new family where nothing else in her life seemed to matter except for yoga and simple gossip. She would miss seeing these people each weekend; she would miss this camaraderie, this journey. She tried to absorb the sentiment, as she was sure to forget her joy at being here by the time it turned 6:00 pm that evening and they were still learning about flexion and quadriceps releases and contraindications of doing poses.

In the glare of the streetlights, Tess spotted Lyla's car parked across from her house. The car lights were off, and she paused as she made a wide turn onto her driveway, trying to see who was in the car. She believed that she saw Lyla and Neal beside her in the passenger seat. 10:00 pm. She was too tired to entertain anyone, too tired to try to make sense of Lyla and Neal's evening powwow in front of her home. Her dinner out with the group after the morning lecture and afternoon yoga class and practice spotting session had exhausted her. She tried to remain calm, to keep her shoulders from tensing. Sometimes, like now, it was hard for her to remember why she was putting up with this all. If she wanted a relationship, weren't there plenty of single middle-aged men to choose from who were not discerning monastic vows and living with controlling mothers.

Please don't let them want to come in and talk, she thought as she gathered her sweater and shawl from the front seat and left her yoga mat and bag in the car – she'd be heading back to the studio at 8:00 am the next day.

The moment she slammed her car door shut, Neal emerged from Lyla's car. Lyla made a sharp U-turn and disappeared down Dakota Place. Neal caught up with Tess and walked beside her up the driveway to the porch.

"Hello, Neal," she said. He had on his navy anorak, white polo, and tan chinos. It had become his uniform as the fall weather set in.

"Hello, Tess," Neal said.

"Out for a ride with your mom?" Tess asked. She stifled a yawn. She vaguely recalled being in her office that morning at the crack of dawn and reading the note from the guest-keeper monk. Was that today? Sleep. She needed sleep, not complications, right now.

"Yes," Neal said. "Actually, we were waiting for you to get home."

"Shall we sit on the porch?" Tess said. "I've been cooped indoors all day."

Tess draped her shawl on the bricks and Neal sat down beside her on the top step. Above there was a multitude of stars. Tess leaned back a bit and rubbed shoulders with Neal. She felt his body stiffen, and she sat up taller, careful so that her body was clear of his.

"Get any writing done today?" she said, and once she said it, she wasn't sure what compartment of her brain it had come from. What she really wanted to ask was how much longer are you going to keep everyone in limbo?

His eyes were on the sky, so that she looked up. She searched for her star. It was no use, though. Right now, they all looked alike.

"Some," Neal said.

There was a noise in the street, a louder than necessary uh hum, as if someone was trying to get her attention and sure enough, there was Michael, in black running shorts and a matching top running by her house. He was in the street versus on the sidewalk.

He waved his hand and called out "beautiful night," as he passed by.

Tess wasn't sure if Neal recognized Michael in the dark, but she didn't point out to him who it was. Was this Michael's idea of competition? To outshine Neal as a runner? He had looked fit coasting by. Which is what she was sure he wanted her to notice. Her life had become ridiculous. Utterly ridiculous. She sighed so that Neal glanced over at her.

"Fall is approaching," Neal said. "This time of year, it's already getting cold and crisp in Muenster. We work hard to get all the farming done before the frost sets in."

We. Neal and his brothers.

"The college students must be settling into their classes, too. There was generally a lot of excitement around the campus in

September."

He was smiling so that the creases on his face softened, and she felt it – that urge to protect him. To forgive him for anything and everything that he did, to remember that it wasn't about her. Things Neal said and did were not about her. He was trying to find his way just like anyone else.

"You would like Muenster in the fall," he said. "The way the stars take over the night sky. All the constellations right there up above."

"I'm afraid I wouldn't know any of them even if I saw them," Tess said.

"I'd teach you," Neal said.

She felt his body beside her loosen, his shoulders close to hers, relax. She wished that she could see through his eyes at that moment to know what he was feeling – what thoughts he wasn't saying out loud. If he had made up his mind to go back, she wanted him to feel comfortable telling her. Or maybe his mind didn't work that way. Maybe he only lived in the moment he was in and wasn't worried about what was to be tomorrow or the next day. Maybe he would just know his next move when he knew it and then act on it. And yet, it had taken him months of discerning his initial choice to leave the monastery before he acted on it. A sense of unease gripped her and as quickly as it did, she let it go. She was not going to live in fear. Whatever was supposed to be, would be.

"My mother used to host new moon ceremonies in our backyard during the fall and winter. Everyone would gather and set up blankets and sleeping bags in our yard and when the sky grew dark, my mother asked everyone to write whatever it is that they wished to free themselves of on a slip of paper. One by one they'd walk up to the fire and toss the slip of paper into it. I always wrote *Woodstock* on my slip of paper and watched the fire eat it up, but year after year, I was still in Woodstock, so I suppose that I didn't believe in the ceremony."

Neal was staring straight ahead, and she followed his gaze. The sky over Jamaica Bay gleamed black, so that it seemed as though she was looking into the water.

"I spent so many years of my life wishing I was somewhere else. I had so much to be grateful for in Woodstock," Tess said. "Of course, I had to leave there to figure that out. A person can waste a whole lifetime searching for things without seeing what is."

"Maybe the time spent searching isn't wasted time," Neal said. "Maybe that's just part of the process of finding one's way," Neal said.

Neal was a nice person who she happened to intercept in her life; it was no one's fault if they had fallen for one another. It was no one's fault if they had entangled one another in a mess of emotion.

"Maybe," she said, their eyes focused on one another. This, she thought, was the distance between two people: she couldn't read his thoughts.

"You look tired," he said.

She nodded. "Yes."

"I should leave, let you get some rest."

She nodded again, but he made no move to leave, nor did she make any move to get up.

"What made you come here tonight, Neal?"

"I wanted to see you. My mother and I went out to dinner, and I wanted to see you and I told her, so we stopped by on the way home."

It was a simple answer for a simple question and yet it unnerved her. He got to do what he wanted, but if she had wanted to see him, she couldn't just show up at his house. It wasn't that anyone had told her she couldn't, but it was understood. His mother was the gatekeeper. This was the inequality between them.

"What's wrong?" Neal said. He moved a curl from her eye.

"Nothing," she said. "I've had a long day."

She wished it didn't have to be so complicated with him. That they could just be a man and a woman and not worry about each move so much. She could invite him in. He wouldn't stay the night anyway. She liked making love with him. It would be a nice end to the day. And yet, she wanted to be alone. She paused for another moment, focusing on her loafers. She wanted to be alone. To walk into her house and put on her pajamas and just be. It was the first time in her knowing him that the neediness was not there. The first time in her life that she liked a man but was choosing to be alone. She wanted to do what she wanted to do this night. She let her mind explore this feeling to make sure that she was clear, and then she was up on her feet, feeling stronger than she had when she pulled into the driveway. She was choosing to be alone. It meant nothing and everything to her at that moment.

She smiled down at him. "Time for me to go to sleep," she said. "It was nice to see you tonight, Neal," she said.

He nodded and paused for a moment, but after she leaned down and kissed him on the cheek and said goodnight, he stood up and said, "good night," and remained standing in place while she opened her front door, went inside, and waved goodbye.

CHAPTER 47: FOLLOWING THE PATH

Buddhi dashed ahead of Tess and began to scratch at the front door. He too wanted to get the day off to an early start. She pulled open the front door slowly, scooting Buddhi out before she pulled the door closed behind them. The fall air was chilly, the dew making it thick, heavy. The Israeli husband, who she never saw, was on his porch, locking his front door before he made his way into his car in his driveway. She remembered the wife telling her that he owned some sort of wholesale business in Manhattan, but she couldn't remember what. She hadn't sold them the house – it had been a direct sale, owner to owner. She let her car run for a few minutes on her driveway before she backed out and was on her way, the Israeli husband close behind her as she made her way down 66th street.

4:45 am. She'd be in Morristown, New Jersey in time for 6:30 prayers and would make it back to her office no later than 9:30 am. Not ideal for a Monday morning, but it would have to do. She pulled out the directions she'd copied down from the website and spread them out on the seat next to her. At the traffic light on the corner of Avenue U and 66th street, she unbuttoned her blazer. She'd opted to wear a conservative navy pants suit with a crisp white button down and simple navy heals – what she considered slight pumps. Her outfit made her feel middle aged and uptight. It was something she had purchased during a phase when she was still trying to prove her professionalism. She felt that it was perfect for her monastery visit – the type of outfit that blended in.

It was close to 6:00 am when the sky began to break, the darkness receding, exposing clouds that threatened rain. Tess was a few minutes away from the monastery per the signs on the road, and then she saw the entrance up in the distance and made a right turn into the grounds.

The buildings scattered about were red bricked – Tess couldn't make out what the signs in front of each of them said. And then there was the cathedral off to the side with its substantial steeple and bell tower. Tess pulled into the gravel parking lot and turned her car off in a spot close to the road. In the rearview mirror she fixed her hair, scattering it a bit about her face and pushing it off to its side part and then she was applying her lipstick before she thought better of it and wiped it off with a tissue from her bag. Best not to look too made up she supposed. She opened her car door. The air was cooler than she anticipated, and she reached into her back seat for her ivory pashmina, which she draped around her neck.

She tried a side entrance, but it was locked. 6:21 per her watch. Her heart began to race. The last thing she wanted to do was enter late and make any sort of scene. She moved to another entrance that was part of a long hall and it was open. The air inside reeked of eucalyptus-spice smelling incense and she immediately thought of St. Bernard's Church, which she had been in with Neal months back. It was cool, air conditioned, and the lighting was dim and faint. Along the ivory walls there were bronze antiqued sconces, with thick, tall white candles burning in each one. Tess wondered whose job it was to light the candles each morning – it seemed like so much work to go through when there were such things as track lighting. Tess's shoes echoed on the white hospital-like linoleum tiles as she moved slowly through the hall, with its low, dropped ceiling with removable white panels. She never liked those panels – cheap and eerie. Always made her feel as if someone hiding out up above could remove them and jump down to the ground. The atmosphere was a blend of business and antiseptic, in no specific order.

At the end of the hall, she came to the mini birdbath which she knew contained holy water, although she wasn't sure what made that water any holier than say the water that gathered in puddles on her deck after a rain storm. Beyond the holy water pool loomed two mahogany wood doors with dulled brass handles, which she intuited was the entrance to the chapel. Why weren't the doors open? They were sturdy, severe. Of course, given the rest of the décor, they could be hollow.

If she were a Catholic, she would dip her finger in the holy water, make the sign of the cross – she'd seen people do that at weddings and funerals. She considered dipping her finger in it to see what it would be like, but then one of the monks in his coffee-colored robe was rushing towards her, or perhaps he was moving towards the chapel. She looked behind her at the still-closed doors. He stopped by her and bowed slightly, or maybe he was bowing at the water, and then he was dipping his fingers in the water, making the sign of the cross, and then moving into the chapel. One after the other now the monks appeared in procession, as if they were part of a wedding party following a cue to proceed into the chapel. Tess moved by the doors to get a glance inside.

There were people in the pews facing the monks – that's where she was to go, she supposed – and at least ten monks already in place in the front of the room in their pew. Tess wasn't sure if she should cut in front of one of the monks and make her way in or if it was best to wait for them to all file in. She decided to make a move and darted in when she saw the next one still a way off. She found a spot next to an older man dressed in chinos and a white anorak still zipped up, and she thought of Neal in his uniform. She kept some space in between her and the man and he smiled at her slightly and she smiled back. There were two nuns in the row in front of her.

A few more men and women entered the chapel. Everyone seemed to arrive alone. Maybe that was how it was with religion – people tended to it independently. She imagined many of them must have been locals. She wondered if it was part of their daily ritual or if there was anyone, like her, who was there for the first time.

Then the organ music began – one of the monks was playing and everyone stood up in their pews and began to sing along. Tess could make out the words *The Lord* but didn't know where to find the words to follow along and then the organ stopped, and it was time to sit and the monk who was positioned at the podium opened his prayer book and began to speak. He wore glasses and was bald, with a fresh face and Tess found it hard to concentrate on his words as she was caught up in taking in each of the monks. Some had facial hair that was cropped close, while there was another monk in the back row with unruly facial hair. There was a monk who looked Indian to her, and a few younger men – she imagined one of them was in his twenties – and an African American monk. In total, she counted 32, each one so unique that she couldn't come up with a word to summarize the group other than that they were men. She tried to imagine Neal as one of them, which seemed simple enough to her. He *was* one of them. If she were to see him in that context, in a row beside the other monks, she would have accepted that he was unavailable to her. She would not have let herself feel for him. He would have simply been a monk, not a man who she was involved with.

The organ player was at it again and the monks were standing and so were the people in the rows surrounding Tess. She felt herself go red and stood up. She wanted to hear what they were saying, but was caught up in the tone, a melancholy tone that reminded her of the incense smell – somehow the two were connected in her brain. There was a sense of loss and longing in the music and then her eyes caught the surreal glow of the stained-glass window across the church's glossed marble floor, and she felt that she was going to cry and swallowed once and then again, trying to smooth down the ache in her throat. She was relieved when it was time to sit down again. She practiced her deep inhales and exhales, closing her eyes while she tried to calm herself down. There was a creepiness to the music, the shadows, the incense and the smoke that rose from them – a profound sadness and suddenly she couldn't imagine Neal as a part of it. She didn't want him to be a part of that despair. She found that with her eyes closed, she was able to hear the monk speaking better, although his words still escaped her. He spoke in a sing-songy way and with her breath calmer, things made more sense to her. He was praying, leading the others in prayer. He was speaking to the Lord. A peace began to envelope her so that she was able to open her eyes and see the monks now anew. This was their life. This praying and pleading with the Lord was what they were about. It was their calling, just as Best Realty had been her calling and being a mother had been her calling, just as yoga was her calling right now. These men were living their lives in the best way they knew how.

These men had made a separate peace. They had done the unthinkable by renouncing sex and marriage and material goods and devoting their lives to God. Neal had been one of them for most of his life. Until he had decided to flee the monastery and return to Brooklyn. For all she knew, if it weren't for her, he may have only stayed in Brooklyn a week or two until his mother sent him back. Or he would have wanted to return on his own free will. People did that. Left. Returned. People were always changing their minds. But then he met her. Neal met Tess and it was like his mother said. He was horny. Maybe she had flirted with him. Who was she to say how the story went from his point of view? Maybe he felt that Tess needed him, and he didn't want to desert her. The aroma of the incense was stronger now, as if it had been turned up a few notches and Tess felt nauseous, terribly nauseous, and queasy.

The man next to her was waiting for her to move out into the aisle. She didn't understand – was it over? Then she realized that the congregation was lining up to receive communion and she saw the smoke from the incense rising and felt it settling in her throat so that swallowing was becoming unreliable. She made her way out of the aisle, letting the man next to her pass and then she began to make her way to back of the room, toward the tall, thick wooden doors, cognizant of the echo of her shoes on the marble floor. She turned back once and locked eyes with the youngest monk who had not yet lined up for communion – his row seemed to be waiting for the congregation to take communion first. His eyes were full of joy, or perhaps it was tears. Tess couldn't tell from the distance, but then she caught his smile and couldn't help but to smile back. She imagined she was making a spectacle of herself escaping from the service or perhaps it was that he wished he were leaving with her. She held his eyes for a moment longer, smiling back, and then he nodded, as if to let her know that it was fine, it was okay, everyone felt the need to get away sometimes and he was moving down his pew now, making his way to receive communion and then she rushed to the end of the hall and pushed the door open to the semi-lit hallway, pressing it closed behind her. Leaning against the door, she let out a deep breath.

She heard the organ from inside the chapel and from here it sounded softer, less dramatic. There was something about the atmosphere both in and outside of the chapel that had a shadowy effect to her, as if objects could be seen, but were too far away to touch. She made her way down the hallway slowly now, but surer of herself than earlier. There were some intricately designed metal crosses up on the walls – crisscrossed patterns of thin metal strips woven together – and some busts of old, austere looking men on podiums with plaques noting who they were. At the end of the hall, she came upon a showcase.

Monastic Horarium

Vigils   6:30 am

Lauds   9:00 am

Holy Mass   11:00 am (Mon-Sat.) 10:30 am (Sun.)

Vespers   5:00 pm

Compline   8:00 pm

Tess wondered why this church didn't follow the seven daily prayers that she had read about in the religion books. Nevertheless, praying five times a day was a lot of time spent praying. She supposed that it wasn't so different from all the time she spent working. There were brochures set out about weekday and weekend retreats at the monastery. She could spend a few days living there. Praying with the monks. Eating with them. She fingered the brochure and then put it back down. Something about staying at the monastery made her feel uneasy, as if she were peeping into Neal's life. She heard people in the hall now and supposed the services were over. She didn't want to see anyone, not after she had rushed out of the chapel. She moved quickly to the end of the hall and followed the red exit sign that led her to a glass door leading out.

The breeze was brisk, refreshing. She looked left and right to get her bearings. The parking lot. She'd have to find the parking lot, which shouldn't be too difficult as she had only walked down a few hallways. She made her way back, in the opposite direction, and sure enough, there was the lot with her car close to the road that would lead her out of the complex.

She turned off the air in her car and opened her window, the cool air rushing in at her. The spicy incense aroma was thick in her throat, but she couldn't tell if its memory was lodged in her nose or if she had acquired the smell on her person. She imagined Michael making his what-smells-horrible face when he walked into her office. She'd leave her blazer in the car, not take any chances. In the daylight, the buildings loomed less intimidating to her, like schoolhouses. She passed one after the other, wondering what went on inside each of them, and didn't hit her brakes until she saw the red-bricked cloister up ahead. Out front a sign read: "Guests are not permitted beyond this point." It looked like a dorm with its three stories and rows of windows with the same white shades. Or an institution. She thought of the monks, each one of them going off to their rooms at night. She wondered what each kept in their rooms – books, pictures, a lamp, she supposed. She wondered what Neal's room had looked like, if he had switched rooms in his 23 years in the monastery, or if he had slept in one room all those years. She wondered if it was warm or cold, if he had a rug on the floor or tile and what came to Tess first was the faces of the monks she had glanced earlier in the morning, the one young monk with whom she had shared a smile, and then she realized that there were rooms in this world that she would never see. She thought of the corners in which people retreated and how far inside some went and how they often never came out. It was easy in this world to be invisible, to hide away so that no one could find you and more than that, sometimes it didn't even require hiding away. You could live amongst others without letting them know your thoughts, your heart, your dreams.

There was a car behind her now, waiting for her to move along, and she hit the gas, needing to go fast, needing to get away, far away, to be out of this place and then she was on the road, amongst traffic, moving, and she felt herself coming back to Tess, to the world. All around her there were cars moving fast and traffic lights and road signs. The silence made her uneasy – in it she heard the hum of the monks. She rolled down all the windows, letting air gush in from all sides as she merged onto the highway, moving into the middle lane and then the left lane, and now she felt safe, passing things by. She reached for the radio and turned it on, pressing the stations until an orchestra version of *Climb Every Mountain* came on and suddenly there was nothing else but this music and she was gliding down the road, coasting on the song's waves of hopefulness, on all that song had meant to her over the years and her mind narrowed in on the months leading up to now, early May, when her mother had still been alive, when all that was between her and Neal was still light and easy. Before Neal had written the note to her detailing his past, before she had gone up to Woodstock and her mother had passed on.

She sang along, her voice unsteady at first and then growing stronger:

> Climb every mountain, search high and low
>
> Follow every by way, every path you know
>
> Climb every mountain, ford every stream
>
> Follow every rainbow, till you find your dream

And then she saw the sign that said New York City and merged onto the Belt Parkway, making her way back to Brooklyn. She didn't know how long the tears continued to fall down her face, how long ago it was that the music had ended as she continued to sing.

CHAPTER 48: DIFFICULTIES AND DIFFERENCES

"I waited for you the other morning. You didn't show and your car wasn't in your driveway," Lyla said.

"I had an obligation," Tess said.

They walked along beside one another in silence for a few moments, Lyla leading the way down Ohio walk. Tess thought back to the morning, month's back, that Neal had led her down this same path. The trees had been in full bloom then.

"Do you believe in God?" Lyla asked.

Tess turned to Lyla, but Lyla's eyes were on the ground in front of her, no expression on her face.

"Yes, I believe in God," Tess said.

"I've wondered that. With you being raised a Buddhist, I assumed you prayed to many Gods. Isn't that the way with most Buddhists?" Lyla said.

"I suppose many Buddhists pray to multiple Gods, but I always believed that there was one higher power. Something about praying to the statues on my mother's mantel didn't really appeal to me. I like to think of the God I pray to as someone up there," Tess said, her chin jutting to the sky.

Lyla was leading them across a street now, maneuvering them into another walk.

"Do you have a place that you go to when you want to pray?" Lyla asked.

"If you're asking me if I go to a temple, the answer is no."

"Hmm," Lyla said.

"If it matters to you at all, Lyla, I pray in my home, in my office, in my car. I can pray from wherever I am. I don't need to go somewhere to pray," Tess said.

"Neal is trying to convince himself and the world of as much in that book he's writing," said Lyla.

"Have you read any of it?" Tess said.

"Heavens no," Lyla said.

Tess couldn't place her tone – if Lyla was mocking Neal's project or if she was indifferent to it.

"The Lord created churches and temples for a reason," Lyla said. "In fact, they've been around for quite some time from what I know."

Tess wanted to say that she thought it was man who created churches, temples, and man who invited people to come and worship in them, but she didn't.

"All through growing up, my home was the neighborhood's place of worship," Tess said. "Everyone – Buddhist or not – was always coming there to meditate and pray." As soon as she said it, she felt silly – it made her home seem freakish.

"I see," Lyla said.

They walked on in silence, with Lyla zipping her hooded gray sweatshirt up higher and lodging her hands in the pocket. She continued to move faster, so that Tess was practically jogging to keep up with her.

"Sometimes I think about moving back to Woodstock," Tess said. She wasn't sure where she was going with this. She wanted to change Lyla's impression of her home – make it more desirable in Lyla's eyes.

"Really?" Lyla said.

"My mother left me the house up there – it's beautiful," Tess said.

"You're hardly the country-living type," Lyla said.

"People change," Tess said.

"Not very much from what I've seen," Lyla said.

Tess stopped in her tracks for a moment, but seeing that Lyla was going to leave her behind, she got moving again. How was it that this woman continuously had a way of making her come undone and why in the world did she subject herself to it?

"Have you told Neal you're thinking about moving back to

Woodstock?"

Tess smiled. Ah, there it was. Lyla was thinking of Lyla. Tess leaving meant Tess and Neal would be over. Or maybe Lyla was worried it meant Neal would go away with Tess.

"It's just a thought. There's nothing to discuss," Tess said.

"I see," said Lyla. She had slowed down considerably. "I think I'll be heading home now. I've had enough of a walk this morning."

Tess didn't say anything; she kept moving along side of Lyla, taking in the trees that lined the sidewalk. They were un-leaving more on this block, Indiana Drive, than on other blocks, and the shrubs were already a deeper green. She supposed that this block was a bit more shielded from sunlight than the rest. That was something that she'd keep in mind for future reference, if she were to be in a position to sell any of the houses on this street. Older folks tended to like living on less sunny streets as then they wouldn't have to worry about getting into their cars in the warmer months and dealing with hot leather seats or the sunlight penetrating through their living room windows and discoloring their couches.

Tess wondered about the shrubs surrounding the porches – who had decided that each of the houses on this block would have them bordering the three to four step porches? She imagined that whenever the next inhabitants would take over and move in, they would tear down those porches, create their own design and the folks that would take over each of the other houses would follow the new design. That was how it worked – no one wanted to be behind the times when it came to the newest fad on the block. Tess had seen trends catch on in a matter of weeks, houses transforming one after the other, until a block, sometimes a whole neighborhood, became unified anew. The lawns she passed were scattered with mulberry and orange-colored leaves, some deep russet-colored leaves here and there. Soon it would be October and pumpkins would line the porches of houses in which children lived. Tess wondered what she'd be for Halloween if she were to dress up. When she'd been younger, much younger, and had taken Prakash trick or treating, she had always put on a black dress and a witch's hat. With her red curly hair, which had been longer then, curlicues tumbling down her back, it seemed appropriate for her to be a witch.

"What would you do for a living if you were to live in this Woodstock house?" Lyla asked.

Tess had gotten into her groove so that she had almost forgotten Lyla was moving alongside her.

"Going to Woodstock is something that I'm toying with in my mind. An idea, really. But if I went anywhere, Best Realty would remain open."

"Is your home still a Buddhist temple? Do people go there each day?" Lyla asked.

"No. It's closed up now. I don't think that I'd carry on in that tradition, though."

"No, I can't see you doing that," Lyla said. She was walking in the opposite direction of her home now. Apparently, she had decided that she wasn't ready for their conversation to be over.

"Lyla, I'm not going anywhere just yet, so if you're worried about my taking Neal away, you have no need to worry."

"Neal wouldn't go with you anyway," Lyla said.

Tess stifled a laugh. Her instinct was to take the defensive, but she breathed instead. Let the moment pass.

"Why?" she said. "Why wouldn't Neal want to go?"

"His home is at a monastery in Canada."

Tess moved alongside of her, silent. This line of reasoning again. Lyla was moving quicker now.

"Did you ever visit Neal in the monastery in Canada?" Tess asked.

Lyla crossed 66th street, moving into the walk entrance on the other side of the street, scooting in front of Tess as she did so. The lane wasn't wide enough for them to walk side by side. Tess wondered what would happen if she were to suddenly stop, leave Lyla to rush away on her own.

"No," Lyla said.

"Why?" Tess asked.

"He told us not to bother whenever the family days would come up. Said it was too long a trip for us to travel."

"Weren't you curious to see how he lived?" Tess said.

"He sent us pictures," Lyla said. "He told us he was at peace. What more did I need to know?"

"I went to visit a Benedictine Monastery in New Jersey the other day," Tess said.

Tess waited for Lyla to comment, but she kept moving without looking back.

"I don't know what I was expecting. I just wanted to see what it was like."

"And now do you suppose yourself an expert on monastic life?" said Lyla.

"I wouldn't say that," Tess said.

Lyla was making her way down 65th street. Tess imagined that she was leading them back to her block, back to her house, where she would excuse herself.

"What were your impressions of the monastery?" Lyla asked.

"Quite frankly, I was a nervous wreck," Tess said. "I felt like someone there was going to find out I wasn't a Catholic and ask me to leave. And once I got past that, I was overwhelmed – by their singing, the smells. I tried to envision Neal up there with the other monks," Tess said.

"And could you?"

"I don't know. I suppose. I practically ran out of the chapel," Tess said. "I felt stifled. Or something close to that," Tess said.

"I've been to that monastery," Lyla said.

"Why?" Tess said. "When?"

"For the same reason you went. To see what it was all about. It was years ago. Close to twenty. I stayed there for a few days, did a retreat. I wanted to understand what Neal was doing each day. I didn't tell my husband that I went. I believe that I told him I was going to visit a relative. Might have been the only lie I kept throughout our marriage."

"Did being there help you?"

"If you're asking, did it help me to understand Neal's choice, no. I don't think so. There was nothing in the lifestyle that was reminiscent of Neal to me. Sure, he was a quiet boy, and sure he was studious, but I couldn't see him living by that order, that rigidity. But it helped me to accept his choice. Seeing the monks go about their daily lives, their sense of conviction, I came to realize that I had no control over his calling. That his path in life had nothing to do with my wants or desires for him. He was following his own path in life. I came to know that at the monastery," Lyla said.

"Yet now, you try to steer him," Tess said.

"I try to remind him. I try to keep him grounded," Lyla said.

They were moments away from Lyla's house and sensing their conversation would reach an abrupt end when they reached their destination, Tess began to move slower, so that Lyla had no choice to slow down if she didn't want to end up talking to herself.

"I went back to that monastery many times. Once or twice a week, for years. They all came to know me well there. Neal and my husband didn't know. Being with the brothers, I felt that I was getting to know Neal better," Lyla said.

"Do any of them know that he's come home from the monastery?" Tess said.

"Oh no. I haven't been there or in touch with any of them in years now. I didn't seem to need to go any longer. I suppose my questions were answered."

"Why didn't Neal go to that monastery? Canada is so far away," Tess said.

"He seemed to know that his place was in Canada. Perhaps it would have been too easy for him to return home if he were in New Jersey."

"Didn't you ever ask him?"

"No," Lyla said.

Lyla had stopped in front of her house. Her car was pulled up close to the garage door, as if she had debated driving through it. She glared at Tess long and hard. Lyla had the ability to transform into so many different Lyla's in a matter of minutes: hard, sweet, caring, dismissive.

"I believe that people tell us what they want us to know – what they need us to know," Lyla said.

"We can't read each other's minds, Lyla. If we don't ask, we may never get to know the answers," Tess said.

"What are you saying? That I don't know my son because I

didn't ask certain questions?"

"I've regretted keeping quiet, assuming. When my mother passed, so did my chance to ask the questions I had," Tess said.

"I'll be going now," Lyla said.

"Yes," Tess said. "You're home."

"Have you been asking him questions?" Lyla said.

"No," Tess said. "I haven't."

Tess held her gaze for a few moments longer before Lyla broke away and made her way up her driveway to her porch. Tess didn't turn to watch her enter her house; she heard the creaking of the door as it was pulled open, and the familiar slam shut.

In Your Own Garden

At the Monastery – En Media Ras 1985

There were three white houses and one red-bricked house out on the hermitage grounds. There were no bathrooms in any of the houses, but there were refrigerators and a stove and a freezer, too. In each there was a middle room with a couch and in the bedroom, there was a bed and a dresser. The furniture looked as if it had come from a garage sale – slightly beat up and aged. It was a ten-minute walk from the hermitage to the main chapel. One used the shower in the guest wing when staying out in the hermitage. The hermitage was near an apple orchard, which wasn't far from the apiary and the honey house, where Father Demetrius purified the honey before it was ready to be eaten. You passed the farm equipment on the way out to the hermitage as well as the roosters and chickens – there were dozens of them.

I had always wanted to live out in the hermitage, to see what it would be like to experience that solitariness, but a brother wasn't able to just go out to live in the hermitage for a few days. One had to commit to being out there for a long period of time. I was never ready to make that commitment. I suppose that I craved the company of the brothers too much.

In the church, the pews faced each other, one closer to the east wall, the other closer to the west. When I first saw the set up, it reminded me of the television show Family Feud, with the holy table and pulpit in the middle ground, just like where the Family Feud host was situated. I was positioned across from Brother Kirk. He was the eccentric amongst us, with his long, unruly black curly hair and his pronounced nose and his tall, lanky frame. He was a painter and a musician. Many of the paintings that adorned the walls of the university, and the chapel were by Brother Kirk. Some were religious, but many were of nature – trees and mountains. He liked to play folk songs on his guitar and sometimes, sitting out by the picnic tables, he sang James Taylor songs. The students at the college loved him and his psychology classes were always full as a result. He used to teach me about art and sometimes we got into discussions about Freud and Jung. He was one of the few people at the monastery that I shared my ideas about religion and the church with. I don't know if he agreed with me or not, but he always listened. He seemed to have found his separate peace in the monastic setting and if he was able to paint and play music and teach in the university, he was happy to stay put. I often wondered if the brothers I lived alongside wanted to stay in the monastery because they felt passionate about the life they were leading or if they felt it was the only option for them in life.

In the same vein that Brother Gerard was considered the organist, Brother Kirk the painter, and Brother William was the stained-glass maker of the bunch, I suppose that I was considered the writer. I contributed to the newsletter we produced – The Prairie Messenger *– and oversaw editing it quarterly, before we sent it off to press. I also was responsible for taking the people visiting the monastery on tours of the grounds. Father Demetrius believed that I was better suited to escort the visitors around than he was. He believed that I was gentler and friendlier than him. I liked to take the visitors out to see my gardens and to see the endless jars of preserves we prepared in the basement, as well as the vast farmlands that were rich with potatoes sprouting at certain times of the year.*

As the years went by, I came to spend more and more time in my garden, carefully labeling each of the flowers I was growing and caring for them as if they were my friends. So, in that respect I believe I became the gardener of the bunch, too. There was a small statue of Jesus Christ in my garden. A gift from Father Demetrius. I surrounded it with stones, some white, some black, and a few larger, red stones. In the winter, when the winds blew fierce, I would move the statue and the stones into my room, to protect it from the elements. Each day during the brisk winter I smiled at Jesus, and he smiled back at me at me as if we were sharing a joke. I don't remember specifically what I was smiling about – life, the universe, my love for everything around me. Looking at him, I envisioned the spring and the flowers that would blossom and how I loved that coming to life of the earth.

There was a bench facing the chapel in my garden and circular flowerbeds with gnomes scattered in each of them. There were also butterflies made from wire in the center of the flowerbeds and some small wire bees and a wooden yellow jack and a Canadian flag. These decorations had all been in the garden long before it fell into my care. Sometimes I sat on the bench and studied the stained-glass murals that blocked out the church interior. I imagined myself sitting on the pew in my spot and I wondered if I looked at home in the chapel or if I looked like an imposter. I'm not sure the first time I had that self-conscious thought and what inspired it, but it was there in me. There was a constant, slight breeze in my garden that lulled me. At odd hours of the day, even in the winter, the sun visited the garden, but it never made me feel too hot in there. There was a tranquility to my garden that possessed me. There, I didn't have to think about what was next in my life. Each moment unfolded independently of any other moment in my life. There was a timelessness to the hours I spent there, a feeling that the world would wait – that it was my insecurities and neediness that imposed time on anything. I began to wonder why my days were structured around the sound of church bells beckoning. I began to question following the rules. For whom was I following them and why? To what benefit? In the garden there was nothing to do but be and question and explore my mind and heart. It was there, in my garden, that I began to ask questions and seek answers.

Tess waited in her car at the corner, until she saw his mother make a right turn onto 66th street, en route to the nursing home. She pulled up in front of Neal's house, put the letter on his porch, then inched a bit away from his house, beeped twice, then again, until she saw him open the front door and walk outside, and then she drove away.

Dear Neal,

The other night when I didn't invite you in – it was not about you, Neal. Not that you assumed I was trying to shut you out. That's just my insecurity in thinking so. It was about my need to be alone that night. I share this, as often in my life, I didn't explain things. I took it for granted that the other person would understand and sometimes the other person did and sometimes not. What you may not know about me, what I've recently come to discover myself, is that I am struggling to keep my life simple. To keep it uncomplicated. My mother used to say that certain people always chose to complicate their lives even when simple solutions were available. I wonder if I am one of those people – I know the simple solution is to leave you alone. To send you off, to tell you to work through what you must work through on your own, without my being a part of the equation. I know that logically. But selfishly, when I am with you, I don't care about what's simple or hard, what's right or wrong; I just want to be with you.

I hope that as you read this letter, you know that it wasn't easy for me to write to you. I have been a coward often in my life by avoiding sharing what is in my heart, in my mind. I've lived my life keeping many of my feelings and dreams and desires inside. I don't know why – maybe I was afraid that someone would say my dreams were impossible or that I would get laughed at or hurt. Or maybe it was that I wasn't always in touch with my dreams. I don't always know why I do the things I do. That is what happens sometimes when one chooses to live a fast life. It's more action and less thought. But lately, I am trying to make space, to take time to think things through. I don't want my life to be random.

You must figure out what is right for you. My feelings are my own. Only you know what your next move will be and regardless of what you choose, of what chooses you, it will be the right decision. That's what I have come to believe. When you do what's right for you, there is no guilt, no fear, no shame.

I am sure the transition back to secular life has been a lot for you. I am sure it's not what you expected when you chose to come back. Which makes me realize that I have never asked you what it is that you really want?

You have been so many different things to me, Neal. You are a gentle spirit. You have helped me to become in some respects, a better version of me, and because of that, a part of me wants to own and possess you. Perhaps take you up to Woodstock and live happily ever after with you. I worry and wonder, though: would we grow tired of one another? Would our friendship grow old? Would we get bored, day after day, being together, loving one another, taking pleasure in simple things – walks and cooking and nights spent talking and making love? Could that ever be me? Could I ever live a simple life and be satisfied with it? Or would I need to bring in complications? Would we grow tired of one another and would your heart start longing and wishing for the monastery? Would you miss the brothers and the prairie grounds, and would I miss Best Realty? In short, can we ever lose ourselves and create a new life in which we find new ways to live and love and grow?

My mother would say people don't give one another anything, but a listening face. But your presence in my life has impacted me in the most positive way, which has also led to my feeling a little lost and afraid. Because now that I have found you, I have grown attached and I am fearful of losing you. I am fearful that losing you will cause me to unravel in a way that I have not yet experienced.

Or maybe I am confusing things. Maybe it's the loss of my mother that is overshadowing all that I feel. Losing my mother this year was the most profound experience in my adult life. I miss her in a way that surpasses all that I have ever felt and experienced before. In her loss are the loss of parts of myself that were only known to mother and daughter. Our bond was complicated but there was so much love there. I feel uprooted in my life – homeless in a sense and yet my mother would tell me that she and I were bound for life and our home is always within one another, free of time and place. She would remind me that it was no simple act of fate that she was my mother. That it was chosen, that we belong to one another. She believed that there were no random acts in life. While she would insist she is with me, I miss her in my tangible world. I miss her voice, her face, her guidance.

There is a desperate plea in me that says, don't leave me, Neal, don't go. But if I search within, there is a voice that says, follow your heart, your path. It's a loving voice, a gentle voice, one that is deep-rooted in my heart, in my soul. I want you to live your life as it's best for you. I don't want you to do anything other than what is right for you. I want you to be happy, Neal. As trite as that may sound, it's what I want for you. It's what I want for me. I pray that you find peace, find your way, and that you move towards whatever light calls you. We will never lose what we have shared. In some way, I believe that we will always be bound.

Fondly,

Tess

CHAPTER 49: AFTER SILENCE

Tess stared at the phone beside her on the kitchen table before she picked it up. Without realizing what she was doing, she had dialed her mother's number. When her mind began to register what she'd done, she held the phone away from her ear as if she was holding it out to some invisible person. It was the rising beep beep tone followed by the recorded message saying that the number was no longer in service that accounted for her hanging it up, slowly. She didn't know what it was that she had to tell her mother, what she had to ask her. It was more an instinct, an inherent need to hear her mother's voice, to listen to her.

The clock above the kitchen sink ticked away. One second followed another. The refrigerator hummed. She thought of the nights when Prakash had first gone off to college on the West Coast, and she would sit in the kitchen after midnight, as she was doing now, missing him, wishing that he would call, knowing all the while that she could call him, but not wanting to be a nagging mother. She had wanted him to live, to enjoy his life, and not feel burdened by her. It was only during that phase that she had glimpsed what her own mother may have experienced when Tess had gone off to Brooklyn College.

12:30 am. A whole night ahead of her. She didn't understand where this loneliness, this desperation was coming from. She couldn't tell if she was regressing or perhaps moving closer to some unknown point in her life, some new understanding. She could study *The Four Noble Truths* right now. Re-implant non-attachment and non-suffering concepts into her mind. Only no, she didn't feel like it. She was tired of trying to live up to words written by other people.

This very moment. Each second. Awareness started with a fraction of a second. That's what her mother had said, only she had never examined the statement, had just nodded her head, yes. A fraction of a second. If she could stay present in the fraction, then it would lead to a second, then a minute, but there she was, already moving on, beyond that fraction. It was so hard to be present. Her mind was like an airplane on a runway, picking up speed; now she was thinking about work, to the calls she had to make come morning, to all the things that she had yet to cross off her to do list. She thought of yoga training and how in less than two-months' time she would stand up in front of a class and have to teach them yoga. That seemed an impossibility to her – the concept of telling people how to move their bodies, the attempt to make them feel good, centered, by way of her directions. But no, she wasn't going to get stuck on that now. She had two months to prepare. Her hand was still on the phone. She thought about calling Michael. That would make for a good distraction, perhaps some amusement, but that might lead her to have to talk about work and she didn't want to go there. Not now. She had a fleeting wish to call the young brother at the monastery in New Jersey, and tell him her Neal story, only what was it that she wanted anyone to say about it? And besides, what would another's opinion matter?

She closed her eyes and focused on her breathing. The present moment. It was amazing to her all the things she could think about to leave the moment. She focused on her inhales and exhales. With her eyes closed, it was easier to lose everything else, go inside. Until her insides began to panic, and her to do list – food shopping, laundry, yoga reading, practice teaching, work calls to make, the fact that she would feel tired tomorrow from being up so late – began to wreak havoc, darting from her mind to her gut, where it gripped at her, so that she grasped her knees into her chest, hugging them to calm her insides. No, she whispered to herself. No, no, no, go away. She began again, focusing on her inhales and exhales. Within a few minutes the chaos within her began to dissipate. Inhale, exhale. Steady, slow. All she had to do was breathe.

When the phone rang, she froze – its sound pierced the silence – before she picked it up on the third ring.

"Mom. I thought that I was going to get the machine. You usually turn off the ringer at night."

"I'm so relieved you called," Tess said.

"Please don't tell me you've been worrying about me. I'm fine," Prakash said.

"I was practicing being present and it was giving me palpitations," Tess said.

Prakash laughed. "You're my favorite yogi," he said.

"Everything okay?" Tess said. "Work? Life? Are you eating healthy?"

"Everything is fine. I was just checking in. I think about you sometimes, you know," Prakash said.

"Well, that's nice to hear," Tess said. She put her legs up on the chair adjacent to her and slumped back in her chair.

"Remember when we used to make cookies – oatmeal raisin were your favorites."

"We used to eat them up before they even cooled."

Tess laughed. "It's funny, the things you remember from a lifetime," she said. Then, "What made you want to be an architect?"

"There are a lot of reasons," he said.

"Like what?" Tess said.

"You were so interested in real estate – every house we passed that was for sale or being built, you commented on. I guess it made me pay attention to houses and buildings – how they were made. I often looked at a house and thought about the ways I could make it better. "

"I'm glad to hear that I played a role in your career," she said.

"Yeah, well, I was either going to be an architect or a spiritual guru, but I knew that wouldn't be a hit with you," he said, and they both laughed.

"You're a good architect," Tess said. "I'm proud of you, Kash. Really proud."

"What made you want to go into real estate?"

"I liked houses. Something about getting to go inside all of them, and matching the right person with the right house, appealed to me.

Sometimes, though, I wonder, Kash. If I'm on the right path. Or if I missed my exit somewhere along the way," Tess said.

"Mom, more than anyone I know, you've never been afraid to make a change in your life," Prakash said.

"Sure, I got divorces and got remarried and all that. But what if I was meant to follow in my mother's footsteps? What if I was so caught up in what I thought I wanted that I missed out on what was supposed to be?" Tess said.

"Grandma always used to say that we're exactly where we need to be in life, down to the second," Prakash said.

"Yes," Tess said. "You never wonder, though, what else you may have been?"

There was silence for a few moments. "Right now, I'm focused on what I'm doing now, and I suppose when or if the time comes that I lose that focus, I'll start wondering," he said.

"Spoken like your grandmother."

"I've never heard you doubt anything," Prakash said.

"Maybe I'm losing my focus, Kash. Maybe it's time to make changes." The clock ticked on.

"Well, if you want to teach yoga, San Francisco is the place to be," he said. "I'll get you a good deal on a condominium."

"When you get married and have grandchildren, I'll consider moving to San Francisco."

Kash laughed. "It's too late at night for you to bring up relationship talk."

"I just want the best for you, Kash. I want you to be happy and have more in your life than work."

"I know, I know. When it's time for me to settle down, I promise you will be the first to know."

She heard a sound at the front door, and it was a moment before she realized that it was most likely Buddhi. She hadn't remembered letting him in earlier that night. She moved to the front door and pulled it open and then unlatched the screen door. Buddhi scrambled into the house and up the steps before her like a mad man. When she made her way back up to the kitchen, he was already busy at his food bowl.

"Someone there?" Kash asked.

"Just the cat," she said.

"So aside from saying hello, I was calling to let you know I'm thinking about coming east for a visit," Kash said.

"Wonderful. It must be my lucky year to see you twice in a few months' time."

Buddhi had finished drinking his water and splashed it about with his paws before he made his way under the kitchen table and began to groom himself.

"Well, if I wait for you to come here, who knows when I'll see you again," Prakash said.

"I meant what I said about visiting you for New Years," Tess said.

"Maybe we could meet up in Woodstock and spend some time up there. What do you think?" he asked.

"I think it sounds great. Is it a vacation or do you have a hidden agenda?"

Prakash laughed. "I have some ideas for the house. I was thinking about fixing it up a bit. Restoring some of the rooms. Assuming you're not going to sell it that is."

"I'm not selling it, Kash. Michael doesn't see any point in holding onto it, but he doesn't understand the history of that house. I told him that I might consider moving up there to live one of these days," Tess said.

"You wouldn't," Prakash said.

"Maybe I would," Tess said. "Create a little yoga studio at the house where I can teach. I'll leave that to you to figure out, if you're interested in the job."

"You may have to fight me for the house," Prakash said. "How about we meet there around your birthday, stay there through New Year's and come up with some building plans?"

"You're on," Tess said.

"And Mom, it's never too late to change anything – if you're not on the right path, you'll figure that out. Just live your life and let the answers come to you," Prakash said.

"Don't power my way through it," Tess said. "Let life unfold as it will."

"Exactly," he said. "Grandmother Caroline taught us well."

"You turned out okay," Tess said.

"You're not so bad yourself," he said. "Crazy, but okay. Get some sleep, Mom."

It wasn't until Buddhi nudged her hand that Tess realized she was still holding the receiver, a busy signal buzzing. Buddhi darted down the hall. He was ready to settle into his basket at the foot of her bed. When she placed the phone in its cradle, the silence of the house, her house, her life, set in. She felt strangely happy, content. Tomorrow was a new day. A lone meow echoed in the hall. She turned off the kitchen light, glancing to make sure the front door was locked before she made her way into the hallway, where she turned off the hall light en route to her bedroom. Buddhi's eyes sparkled in the darkness. She would be okay no matter what happened in her life. She believed that. She had always been okay. Buddhi kneaded the blanket in his little bed, as Tess got comfortable and pulled the blanket up over her. She stretched her legs to the left, taking over the empty side of the mattress that at various times in her life had belonged to various men. They had come and gone with the years. And still, she was okay. Better than okay. She didn't know if it was her mother's presence, she felt with her or her own, but what she was sure of as her eyes closed and before sleep overcame her, was that tomorrow may be the best day of her life.

In Your Own Garden

Another Time and Place: Brooklyn, fall 2003

The sounds of the prairie are with me always. The echo of the wind as it whipped at my windows at night, the rustle of the tree leaves and branches in the darkness, the foxes traveling stealthily across the campus, frozen in their tracks when the wind brushed past them, or the crickets yelped. In the summertime white cotton wisps floated through the air, dancing, somersaulting about, lodging themselves on my robe so that I'd have to pick them off when I went indoors.

The church at the monastery was designed in a neo-Gothic style and the pipe organ was built by Fr. William Thurmeier, one of us. The stained-glass windows portrayed the River of Life in the New Jerusalem as described in the last book of the Bible, Revelation. Above the altar, the windows portrayed the adoring angels. The bell tower was the focal point of the abbey and the college grounds. It was built in 1994 and before that we had one that was a bit dilapidated. There was an orchard that had many crabapple trees. There were also plots for raspberries and other vegetables, especially near St. Scholastica Residence, which became a guesthouse. For many years it had been home for the Sisters of St. Elizabeth who lived and worked at the abbey from 1913 to 1990.

I often wish that I could tour the monastery grounds with you as we used to tour Mill Basin when we first came upon one another. You would like the grounds, as they are full of history. I've witnessed your love of the history of place without your ever having to tell me. The grounds of the monastery have their own story to tell, and you would be able to narrate it to me, teach me about the different styles of architecture.

There's so much that I want you to know, Tess. Too much for my mind to compress into words. I decided to become a monk because of all that I was. It was my destiny, my path, my home, my calling. I didn't worry if it was the right thing because it was the only thing for me. Benedict's primary attention was to truly seek God. That was my primary intention. I wanted peace of mind and heart. I wanted to work and pray because I was thankful, because I believed. I wanted to live in moderation and balance, stability, mutability. I wanted these things and there was a way to them with the Benedictines. When I met you, I took to you as I would take to anyone – the Rule of Benedict says, "All guests are to be welcomed as Christ." When I first saw you, I was attracted to you. I thought you were a beautiful woman, but I didn't think you would be someone I would fall in love with. I didn't know what it meant to fall in love with a woman, to fall in love with anyone other than Christ. When I saw you, I believed that you would be my friend, my confidante; I wanted you in my life, although I cannot explain why.

To be or not to be a monk? That's the question I'm asking of myself. That's the question that you are asking me with your silence and your acceptance. I ask myself often what a man is. What his job on this earth is. Life as I see it is very complicated and complex. I don't know if one finds the answers to one's life and helps others by being tucked away in a monastery. I similarly don't know if one finds the answers to one's life and helps others by being a part of this larger picture, this larger life. In this world everyone seems too busy, too caught up. I don't even know if finding the answers matters. Perhaps our role in life is to keep finding the questions. But then what – what do we do with the questions?

Use them to further confirm that life is a mystery?

So many years back, after I returned to the monastery to stay, on my third night, May 9th – I remembered the date because it was my parents' anniversary – there was a full moon. When the sun finally set, around 10:30 pm in the evening, I walked outside and wandered a bit down the path to the church. At first there was one star, and then two and then the stars began to multiply beside the moon, white and glowing and magnificent in its fullness, and I thought that between that earth and that sky, if I never got anywhere, it would be fine, because I was exactly where I needed to be. I returned to bed feeling at peace. It was a long while until I felt that feeling again, maybe a few times more at the monastery, and then when I met you.

I watch you Tess and I try to understand what the meaning of your life is. I'm not measuring you in any way but trying to take in your life and learn so that I can better understand my life. For 23 years I've lived by a set of rules. By a to-do list, much like the ones you create on your post-its and on your computers. I'm in earnest to know whatever it is that I need to know. I believe that there's a reason I'm here, a reason for my meeting you, for us. The story is not yet fully formed in my soul, which leads me to believe that there's more to it – more to us – and until we live our story through, until I live my story through, I won't know what it is that God wanted me to know, to learn.

CHAPTER 50: ALL THE DAYS

Tess propped her legs up on her windowsill, slinking back in her office chair. How quickly the fall set in, the leaves a medley of rust, mustard, and forest green. It was still too early for the brown leaves – they came later, closer to Halloween. Her shoulders were tight; she supposed that all the chatarangas were taking their toll. She rolled her neck left, then right, and up. She felt a slight release, her shoulders dropping. It felt good to be in her office before everyone else, to have this time and space to herself. She didn't want to listen to Lyla or Michael or anyone, and here, in the privacy of her office, the day just dawning, she didn't have to. Michael had called this need for *Tess time* the isolationist in her and she had always reminded him that it was her private time that enabled her to deal with him. She believed this was the dichotomy of Tess: she loved being alone as much as she enjoyed her time with people. And it wasn't that she loved one time more than the other, it was just that when she went for more than a day without the Tess time, being with others grew tedious for her.

So many hurdles to overcome en route to enlightenment. She smiled. She could imagine her mother saying that to her with a sympathetic face. Soon Tess would get up and put on the coffee machine. For now, it was nice to be quiet. She scanned her mind – nothing was bothering her at this instant. She hadn't seen Neal in the last week or so, and that was okay. She liked being pen pals; besides, she was busy, and he was doing whatever he had to do to figure out his next move. She had learned to give people their space when and if they needed it. She reached for her hard covered, encyclopedia-sized volume of *The Realtor's Guide to Success* which was situated on the shelf adjacent to her window, beside photographs of Tess and her Best Realty team over the years – mostly pictures taken for Christmas cards and congratulations cards Best sent out after closing deals. She couldn't remember the last time she had picked up the book and brushed dust off the top of it. She believed that Marc, her first husband, had bought it for her when she had acquired her realtor's license. Leafing through the chapters on getting to know your clients and getting to know the neighborhood, and how to close the deal, she came upon a handwritten note embedded within the pages.

Marc

Pros: supportive at times, strong (mentally and emotionally), fun

Cons: womanizer, liar, irritable, self-centered, fighter

Brad

Pros: stable, kind, intelligent, creative, easy to talk to

Cons: competitive, irresponsible in terms of money

David

Pros: attractive, independent, interesting – knowledgeable on opera, wine, etc.

Cons: boring, self-centered, moody, depressed

Michael

Pros: understands what I do for a living; good to work with; good conversationalist; hard working; attractive

Cons: tends to be annoying/insecure, loves to be out on the town all the time, hard to read at times (who is the real Michael?)

She studied the list, remembering the day she had crafted it – it had been a cold wintery day, a few days after she had split with Michael. She had gotten off the phone with her mother after breaking the news of her upcoming divorce and afterwards, she had wondered what her life was all about, or rather, what the men in her life had been about – if there was a link between them all. After reviewing the list on that day, she had concluded that aside from being male, seducing her in their respective ways, making her laugh, they had all just been men whose path she had intersected at the right time and place. Only she didn't know what it was the right time and place for. Companionship? Growth? After each of her relationships, she had felt exhausted for weeks, months, before the freedom, the exhilaration of being on her own again overcame her. It was on that day, after she hung up the phone with her mother and constructed this list that she had promised herself that her man phase was over. She was going to be Tess, on her own, for better or worse, in sickness and in health, to the end.

She added Neal to the list

Neal

Pros: sweet, considerate, gentle, quiet, kind, introspective

Cons: Roman Catholic Monk

She crossed that out. Being a monk wasn't a con. It was what he did, in the way that she was a realtor. Only no, it was more than that. It was how he lived his life. A pro? No. Not a pro. It just was. She crumpled the paper into a ball and tossed it into her garbage pail. She didn't know if there would be any more men in her life. It didn't seem to matter anymore. No more promises to herself or others, only living. If she stayed true to Tess, then whatever happened next was exactly on course. No wrong or right paths, only paths.

Michael knocked on her door and walked into her office.

"I was busy you know," she said, closing the book and resting it on her desk.

"*The Realtor's Guide to Success*? That's what you're busy with? You could probably write that book," Michael said. "Did you have your coffee yet?"

"Good morning to you too, Michael. I've only had my tea back at the ranch," she said.

"Why is it that you only drink tea in your home but at the office you only drink coffee?" Michael said.

"Tea soothes me, and, in my home, I want to be soothed. Coffee stirs me up, breaths fire into me, and in my office, I want to be fired up," Tess said.

"You have an answer for everything, don't you?" Michael said.

Michael moved closer to her desk and scrutinized Tess so that she lifted her eyebrows in return.

"Can I help you with something?" she said.

"I'm worried about you, Tess."

"Here we go again. It's true-life confession time at Best Realty," Tess said.

"I mean it, Tess. You don't seem right. I'm worried," Michael said.

"Whenever someone says that to me, you know what instantly goes through my mind?" Tess said.

"Something tells me I'm going to be sorry I told you how I feel," Michael said.

"I think that you're worried about something with you but are displacing it with telling yourself that you're worried about me," Tess said.

"Have you been studying psychology now too?" Michael said.

"Michael, I'm fine. I don't know if I've ever felt clearer headed," she said, leaning forward in her seat so that the tightness in her shoulders pinched her neck and she winced.

"You look like you're in pain," Michael said.

"My shoulders," she said. "Tight from all the yoga."

"Glad I didn't join that bandwagon. Last thing I need is more pain in my life," Michael said.

"The drama doesn't suit you, Michael," Tess said.

"If you want to know why I'm worried –" Michael said.

"I don't want to know why," Tess said.

"Between his mother and her freakish ways and your traipsing off to yoga morning, noon and night and now you're going to spend the holidays up in Woodstock with your son," Michael said.

"You must be awfully bored to concoct lists that pertain to my well-being. I have better things to do, like run a business and live my life, rather than to console you about my worrisome existence. And I'm really looking forward to the holidays up in Woodstock. I think it's going to be wonderful for Kash and me," Tess said.

Michael nodded. He moved toward the door and turned back to Tess.

"The famous walk to the door and turn around move. If I gave you a dollar for every time you did it, you'd be a wealthy man."

"I'm going to put up the coffee," he said.

"Wonderful. Thanks for making yourself useful," Tess said.

He nodded again but didn't move to go.

"Can I ask you something, Michael?" Tess said.

He remained still, his eyes meeting Tess's, insinuating a yes.

"Do you ever miss your first wife?" she asked.

"Why would you ask me that?"

"Curiosity, I suppose. When I think of my ex-husbands, they all sort of mush together; it's more of a slide show that passes by. You were the shortest of my marriages and probably the most far-fetched, but I remember our times together vividly," Tess said.

"Far-fetched?" Michael said.

"Michael. Don't take everything to heart. You know that I cared about you. I loved you. We were far-fetched in that we didn't need to get married. We had a great relationship. We had fun. We could have just been together and worked together. I think that you and I got married so that there was a legitimate reason to get divorced from our spouses at the time. Otherwise, they would have had the hope things could have been worked out. I think we both had a need to terminate those relationships," Tess said.

"You've got it all figured out," Michael said.

"Michael," Tess said.

"Sure, I think about my ex-wife. For most of my adult life, she was all I ever knew. I wish her well. Just because I wasn't in love with her doesn't mean she wasn't a good person. I'm glad that you loved me."

"I think that we helped each other. I don't think that our getting together was random. I think it was part of our paths," Tess said.

He rested his head against the back of the door and smiled at her

– it was a tired, defeated smile.

"Do you regret me, Tess? Us?"

"No. I don't. I just know that nothing is forever."

"Sometimes it is forever. I think that's a choice people make," he said.

"People change. They grow apart just as easily as they grow together."

"What about people who survive 50 year or more marriages?" he asked.

"Just because they're together doesn't mean they're happy."

He nodded. "Maybe happiness is overrated."

"Maybe," she said.

He nodded and then shut her office door gently. There were emails that had accumulated, and she was sure that if she scanned her to do list there were over half a dozen clients that she had to call back. She rested her head down in the triangle of her arms and gave herself permission not to think for a few minutes before the workday began.

CHAPTER 51: THE POWER OF LOVE

Tess paused at her kitchen table – sometimes her mind played tricks on her, but listening closer, the knock came clearer. If it was Michael, no, she was off limits tonight. She had to get herself ready for the yoga test tomorrow. Tonight, she had to focus. She wouldn't answer the door. Only now someone was knocking on it.

Out of her living room blinds, she saw Neal. The moment he saw the blinds move, he looked up so that their eyes met. He had the power to still her with his glance, so that she smiled regardless of what was going through her mind – yoga test, fear, rush, no time to hang out. *Neal,* she said out loud, making her way to the front door.

She smiled at him, and he was smiling back.

"It's been a while," he said. "I hope it's okay I'm here."

"Come in," she said, smoothing her white tank top and white lounge pants that she had changed into when she got home from work. Study clothes loose enough to practice yoga poses in. She closed the door behind him.

"I'm glad to see you, Neal."

"I'm glad to see you, Tess," he said.

"Come upstairs, join me," she said, so that he slipped off his sneakers and followed her up the stairs, his feet so light on the steps she could barely hear him behind her.

When they stood in the kitchen doorway, he hugged her, tight and hard, so that her nose and lips nestled into the crevice of his neck, inhaling his clean, soapy smell; there was a masculinity to him that unnerved her. It wasn't deodorant or cologne; it was simply his smell and she liked it. In a moment, she was kissing his neck, making her way up to his ear before she realized what she was doing and pulled away, their faces in line.

"I'm sorry," Tess said, "I didn't mean –"

"Why would you be sorry?" Neal said, his arms still around her.

"I don't want to confuse you – I write you one thing and then do the other. I'm terrible," Tess said.

"I care about you, Tess. I don't have the answers either, but I care about you. I came to see you tonight because I can't stop thinking about you. Do you ever think about me?" he said.

She nodded. "I think about you. I think about me. I think about my life and your life, and how we are impossible. And then I think about how I want you. And then I keep myself busy so that I don't have to think about you and wanting you."

He laughed. "I'm glad to hear that you want me sometimes. Even if you try not to think about me." His hands were on her bare back now, smoothing her gently there.

"Studying?" he said, surveying her kitchen table, where her books and note cards were scattered.

Tess nodded. "Tomorrow is the big yoga test," she said.

"You're going to do great," Neal said. "From the nights you taught me, I can attest to you being a natural."

"You're probably the only person in my life who would say I'm a natural at teaching yoga. Most people think of me as a neurotic workaholic."

"Remember, you're doing the yoga training for fun. No one is going to knock down your door for you to teach them yoga – it's a choice. If it happens, wonderful, and if not, you are still wonderful."

"Thank you," Tess said.

"I should go," Neal said. "Let you get your last-minute studying in."

She stared into his eyes, his beautiful blue eyes, and smoothed back his sandy-colored hair, which was shaggy now that it was growing in. She nodded. He should go, she knew this in her brain, but she didn't want him to go. She wanted him to stay.

"You could study with me," Tess said.

His hands were making their way up her back, his fingers exploring her shoulder blades and kneading her skin.

"Mmm," she said. "Feels good."

"I could give you a mini massage and then go," Neal said. "I could even do it while you study."

She remained in his arms and nodded. She was sure she needed to study more, only the way he was touching her. She wasn't going to do this; she was going to send him off and away. She was going to be on her own and let him go and yet…his hands were gently inching into the waist band of her pants right now, careful not to be intrusive, just loosening up her lower spine before they moved up her back again.

"You've been at it for months now. You're going to do great, Tess."

"And if I don't?"

"If you don't, the world won't come to an end. Everything will be fine. You will go on being Tess, running Best Realty."

She smiled. "Yes, I suppose that's how it will be," she said.

"You're going to do wonderfully, Tess. That's who and what you are."

She lifted herself up from her slumped stupor against his body.

"Thank you, Neal," she said, looking into his eyes. "Whoever said pep talks are overrated hasn't had one in a while."

She wanted to ask him to tuck her in, to lay with her before he had to go. She wanted to kiss him. Instead, she let herself be held by him without making a move.

"What are you thinking?" she said.

"That I want to kiss you. That I want to hold you. I don't want you to think though that I came here because…"

"You wanted to have sex?" she said.

"It's not like that for me."

"I don't believe it is, Neal."

"I keep my distance. I know that you're busy and I know that I must try to figure out what is right for me. And yet, sometimes, like tonight, I cave in."

Tess traced his lips with her fingertips and moved her lips onto his, before he started to kiss her back, taking over.

"I've missed you, Tess," he said.

"I've missed you, Neal," she said. And then he was kissing her passionately, as only he, Neal, kissed her, walking her backwards into the bedroom, so that she giggled.

"If you want me to go – if you want to keep studying – I'll go," he said, and she kissed him in response.

"I want you to make love to me," she said as they paused in her bedroom doorway.

Neal planted gentle kisses on her neck, and then he was pulling her shirt up over her head and she was taking off his shirt, so that their bare chests collided, his long fingers smoothing her shoulders, so that goose flesh spread across her arms, and then he pulled her close, shadowing her face with those same long fingers, her insides melting into him, wanting him at those moments, needing him. Tess had wanted men in the past, but it was different with Neal; she was immersed in the moment, there was nothing else, no to do list, no yoga test tomorrow. She was willing to toss it all away for him, for this moment, this collision of flesh, breath, and bodies. She kissed his lips gently and then they were immersed in something more – a finding of one another, a digging, a longing to get closer, to have more of each other and then he moved her onto the bed, asking her gently if she had set the alarm – even amidst the passion he was responsible. He didn't want her to oversleep for her test. "I'll wake up," she whispered, and then their lips were on one another's again, their tongues intertwined.

She woke up to the cat peering at her, his eyes glowing a fluorescent yellow in the darkness. It took her a few minutes to remember what had happened – she didn't have any clothes on; she patted the bed beside her. Neal was gone. She sighed a long and lazy sigh, tracing the flesh of her stomach and moving down to her legs. This is what he did to her – left her feeling luxurious and desirable, peaceful and happy. She reached for her grey zip-up sweatshirt on the floor by her bed and put it on, sitting up to zipper it, before she reached her legs up to the ceiling and plopped them back down on the bed. The sudden movement made the cat dart from beside her and begin to cry once he reached the kitchen. She couldn't remember if she had left him food and water and got up from the bed to check.

On the kitchen table, propped up against her teacup, Neal had left her a note. She smiled before she even read his words.

You are made up of so much more than you will ever know. I wish you a peaceful and joyful morning, and lots of success and fun on your yoga adventures. Remember that your star is always shining bright – all you need to do is to look up in the sky.

Your admirer and devoted friend,

Neal

Buddhi's meows startled her, and she put down the letter and went back to seeing about his food bowl and filling up his water bowl, which was empty. When he was taken care of and eating, she made her way to the living room window, and peering out and up into the sky, she searched the stars, until she focused on one that was shining brightest; it was her star, there in the sky, waiting for her to take notice. She took in its brightness for a few moments, before she closed her eyes, as if to seal it into place. Sleep. She needed to get back to sleep. She moved down the stairs to lock the double lock, and then made her way back towards her bedroom, Buddhi following her after a momentary pause.

CHAPTER 52: JUDGEMENT DAY

The yoga studio was packed when Tess arrived, which was the norm for Saturdays, she supposed, only she was used to arriving there by 8:00 am at which time she didn't have to deal with the 9:00 am class crowd that was signing in at the front desk and then making their way into the smaller studio. The teacher-training group swarmed the larger studio, spilling out onto the wooden benches in the hall with some waiting on line for the bathroom. Dale smiled and waved when she saw Tess in the doorway, which made Kim and Sara, who were busy in conversation, halt and turn and wave, too. The three were situated in a circle of sorts with an extra back jack and meditation pillow beside Dale set up for Tess. The thought of taking a three-hour long comprehensive exam on the floor with props to support her back didn't particularly appeal to Tess, but she supposed that there weren't too many choices at this point. Besides, she figured that the setting would make it feel as if they were at one of their Saturday lectures and there was comfort in that. They had from 9:00 am through 1:00pm to complete the written part of the exam. The practical exams would start up at 2:00 pm and go through the following day. Tess had been assured her practical would take place today and she was relieved – she didn't know if she would be able to make it until tomorrow. Her nerves made her giggle as she tiptoed her way through the crowd towards the girls. She couldn't remember the last time that a test had caused her such anxiety.

Sara nodded to the clock when Tess sat down. "It's show time in two minutes," she said. She had two pens and a pencil set up before her with a steaming cup of coffee to the side.

Tess put down a large tea, and out of her bag took a liter bottle of water, and a sliced-up orange in a Ziploc bag. "Feel free to help yourselves," she said.

"I didn't think to bring food," Dale said. "Do you think I'm going to be hungry?"

"You're going to be taking a million-question test," Sara said. "I don't think your brain will have time to consider hunger."

"To think we struggled through the last few months and now we have to deal with these tests doesn't make sense to me," Kim said. "And we paid for this no less."

"We struggled?" Dale said. "I thought we had some fun."

"While all of you were busy working and figuring out your relationships and debating your careers and such, little old me was at this studio being a yoga slave each afternoon and then going home to take care of my darling little boy," Kim said.

"Sounds awful, Kim. If I had known you were having such a hard time, I would have invited you to run my business for a few weeks for a break," Tess said.

Dale laughed and Kim shook her head and rolled her eyes at

Tess.

"Hey, I'm sort of a yoga slave, too, Kim. Not to mention, I'm the most indecisive fiancé ever, and I'm on leave of absence from my job. So basically, I'm a total loser."

"I'm proud to call you girls my friends," Sara said.

"Remember that you were miserable for the first four months of teacher training until your divorce was finalized," Kim said.

"Shhh." "They're waiting for us," Dale said, her eyes on the mentor at the front of the room who was talking now, greeting the group and letting them know what to expect.

Two other mentors were walking around the room, distributing the exams and making certain everyone was set up with pens and all that was needed for the test. The group was instructed to take their time, and to get up and stretch and use the bathroom when they needed to.

"Good luck," Tess mouthed, and Dale gave her a thumbs-up.

"There will be no talking during the test," the mentor was saying and then Tess no longer heard what was being said as she was focused on the twenty-page exam in her hands.

Tess didn't particularly remember finishing the comprehensive exam, didn't remember running to grab lunch with the girls other than her tasting a few spoonfuls of her tortilla soup and hearing the girls say this or that about the exam – the anatomy section was difficult, the

English to Sanskrit pose translation section was okay, the pranayama questions were too complicated. The group's giddiness during lunch was appreciated – the hours of focus had worn them out and made any meaningful conversations impossible. When she arrived back at the yoga studio with the girls, she couldn't decide if she was nauseous or had the beginnings of a migraine, but her tension was high.

She heard someone calling her name and then one of the mentors was in front of her with what Tess considered her sugary sweet full-of-shit smile, informing Tess that she was first up for the practical and that she had a few minutes before it was time to get started.

Get a grip, she thought, looking at herself in the bathroom mirror. The water she had splashed on her face was trickling down onto her tank top. You're not making a presidential speech, just teaching a yoga class in front of your yoga friends. She knew that deep breaths would help, only each time she tried to breathe she felt as if she was about to hyperventilate. There was a reason for this anxiety, she was sure of that, only she couldn't imagine what the reason was. This was yoga. She loved yoga. She had given endless presentations in her organization, spoken to thousands of clients and lawyers over the years. She had dealt with Lyla for Christ's sake.

First up. She wondered if it was because she was the oldest. Were they discriminating because of her age? Were they trying to kick her out of their little yoga club because she wasn't gung-ho to help them with their real estate pursuits? She didn't specialize in commercial reality. She had let them know that. Did they pick her to go first so that she, the elderly one, could be the example to the others as to what they should avoid? Did they hope that she would mess up so that they could let loose on her and then…and then what? She was going to be fine. She was fine. This would be fine. And then she walked out of the bathroom into the yoga room, and she was standing up in front of the group and the mentors were calling for a dozen or so of her peers to participate in the beginner yoga class that Tess was to teach while the rest of the group got to watch. The mentors had lined up three rows of four mats each for the mock class to use. Dale was up on her feet, as was Kim and a host of others so quickly that like an outcast from musical chairs, Sara had to sit down.

Beginner yoga class. That meant that she had to focus on the breath, spend time explaining each of the poses, and keep it simple. She could do that – after all, hadn't she taught Neal how to do yoga? Start on the floor seated, teach them ujjayi breath, cat/cow, down dog, some standing poses and then back on the floor, hip openers, backbends, shavasana. She had the sequence down pat. Now all she had to do was to speak gently, slowly.

Tess's eyes circled the room, and she smiled warmly at the fellow teacher trainers staring back at her. There was something to this for her, being in front of the room, having a captive audience, and she felt herself relax; she felt almost overjoyed.

"Welcome and congratulations to all of you for finding your way to beginner yoga. Let's all find a comfortable cross-legged seat and if your knees are high up off the ground, please feel free to use blocks to rest them on. I'm glad to bring you blocks if you need them." Tess scanned the room, but everyone seemed to be situated comfortably.

"Let's start focusing on our breath. Notice your inhales, notice your exhales. If your breath is choppy, your focus is going to be to make it even. Focus on your inhales and your exhales. Slow and gentle. In yoga, we use what's called ujjayi breathing, which sounds like Darth Vader breath." Tess demonstrated and went on. "You keep your lips closed and inhale through your nose, nice and slow, and exhale at the back of your throat, all the while, your lips are closed. We're all going to try it together. Inhale through your nose and hold and then exhale at the back of your throat."

Tess took in her fellow yogis and smiled; they were all calm and serene as they focused on their breath. The sound reminded her of a gentle breeze by the ocean.

"Wonderful," Tess said. "You're all natural yogis. Now we're going to try to link the breath with the movement. That's what yoga, or union, is – linking our breath with our movement. It's our ujjayi breathing which differentiates yoga from calisthenics or gymnastics. If we can steady our breathing, we can steady our mind, our hearts, our souls."

"Inhale through your nose and raise your arms overhead. Exhale and your arms twist to the right, brushing your left knee." Tess moved onto her mat at the head of the room to demonstrate. "Inhale through your nose and your arms raise and fall to the left. Wonderful. Inhale arms up, exhale your arms and twist. Again, inhale arms raise, exhale arms fall."

"Let's all come onto our hands and knees now. You want to position your knees in line with your hips and your hands in line with your shoulders." She moved around the room and made some minor adjustments, directing the yogis to move their knees or hands in. "With an inhale, look up to the sky and let your chest open and tilt your pelvis, and with an exhale, round your back and look towards your belly. Again, inhale, open your heart, exhale round your back. Beautiful. Keep going at your own rhythm, focus on your breathing."

"We call it yoga practice as there's no destination to arrive at. No perfect poses. Just movement linked with breath."

"On your next exhale, I want you all to straighten your legs and come into our first downward facing dog. Your feet want to be reaching towards the ground, your arms extended, palms firmly planted on the ground with your fingers spread; your eyes should be focused again on your belly. That's your dristi, or one point focus. Move into the pose slowly. Find the strength in your arms and legs, engage your core. This pose will eventually become your resting pose. Now it may feel like work, but trust me, once you practice more, this will be your rest. Inhale and exhale. With each breath, try to move deeper into your pose – if you need to bend your knees, that's fine. When you feel yourself reaching your edge, when your mind interferes – *no, I can't do this, I don't like this, I don't want to do it* – let go. Surrender. It's only a passing moment of your life. Don't cling to it. Let the moment happen. Watch it come, watch it go. Don't be attached to it. Focus on your breathing. Surrender into it. Inhales and exhales."

"Wonderful. You all look great. Gently, please walk your feet forward so that they're in line with your hands, or as close to that as you can get. Forward bend. Let yourself hang here for a bit; keep focusing on your inhales and exhales. Again, you can bend your knees if you need to. You want to think about your belly resting on your thighs. So, it's not about how straight you can get your legs, but about how much you can engage your core and lessen any strain on your lower back. Your breathing is what will help you to go deeper."

"Slowly, I want you all to roll up, feeling each vertebra of your spine as you do. Inhale your arms and sweep up. Exhale, dive down, inhale face looks up, exhale, I want you to all walk back into downward facing dog again. Stay here for two full inhales and exhales." Tess breathed in line with them.

"And then exhale, walk your feet forward."

She guided them through triangle, right angle pose, and then a gentle lunge and twist before she glanced at the clock and realized it was time for her to wrap it all up. That had been part of their training – to make sure that they finished up class on time. People in New York City were on tight schedules and a yoga class running over was not good – it could stop students with busy schedules from coming to your class. She had her students make their way to the floor, do one gentle forward bend, a seated twist to strengthen and open their backs, one hip opener – a gentle bhaddakonasana – a beginner bridge pose followed by an inversion – shoulder stand – and then she had them move onto their backs with 5 minutes to spare.

"I want you all to let go, rest, shavasana. Corpse pose. Fall into the floor; make yourself comfortable. This is a time for you to just be. What you have to do next, where you need to be, let it go. Give yourself permission to let all the rush and doing go. Now it's time to just be."

She weaved in and out of the people, adjusting their necks left and right with her hands, making a delicate imprint on their forehead, where their third eye was. Normally, she would feel odd to touch people, but right now, after what she had been through with them, after witnessing their transformation into calmer, restful beings, she felt loving, confident, and calm. It was possible to help people, to lead them in a gentle and loving way towards peace. It was the first time in her life that she had felt such compassion so quickly and for no reason. She was gushing with love and there was nothing she expected in return. The experience had been that complete for her, that satisfying.

"For me, yoga is about trusting and opening my heart, my life; when you do that, anything and everything is possible. It all starts with showing up and focusing on your breath."

She brought them out of shavasana after she had placed her loving hands on each one.

"Let's all come into a seated pose for some final breathing," she said. "Roll onto your side, take one more minute in this solitude, in this place of rest and gratitude, and when you're ready, find your way to the front of your mat in a cross-legged pose as we began. Once again, listen to your inhales, your exhales. And together, we will chant the sound of Om; this is not a religious sound, just the sound of the universe coming together, our oneness as people who do life together. You may repeat after me, or just take in the vibration."

"Om," Tess hummed. "Om." She let the sound drift from her throat to her lips, feeling its vibration in her whole being. "Om," she hummed for a final time before she bowed her head to the earth and raised herself up.

"Thank you for allowing me to share this journey with you all," she said. "The light in me bows down to the light in each one of you. Namaste." The yogis chanted back in unison, "Namaste."

In the moments of silence which followed, Tess understood what her mother had felt – how it must have been so satisfying for her – outright joyful – to guide others as she did.

And then the silence broke and everyone in the room, mentors included, applauded her, Tess, the first teacher trainer to complete her practical exam. It had been fun, natural. She had let go, trusted herself and plunged into it and now she felt dizzy and light headed from the experience, unable to remember any specifics of what she had said or done during the time that she was the teacher. She moved to find a place on the floor beside Dale and the others who had seated themselves after her class, and then the mentors were speaking, thanking Tess before they started their critique of her class, which had caught her off guard – she hadn't expected them to discuss her class in front of the room of forty students.

There was a consensus that she had slowed down, and that there was a new graciousness to her, a joy that radiated from her. One of the mentors commented that she saw a more open-minded and accepting Tess than she had seen that first night that Tess came to take a class at the yoga studio. Tess could remember that night, which seemed very long ago, the closed mindedness she had felt towards taking a yoga class, the bickering with Michael en route to the studio. So long ago, but it was only eight months back. So much had happened since then, between meeting Neal, her mother dying, the new friends she had made, yoga. Was she more joyful? She didn't know. Her life certainly had taken on new dimensions. The mentors went on to say that they had witnessed

Tess's evolution into a more compassionate person, into someone they would want to take a yoga class from. "A tough act to follow" was one of the comments a mentor said regarding her class. The mentors bowed to Tess and said Namaste, the rest of the room following, and Tess did the same to them and then it was time for the next teacher trainer to perform.

It was over. All that prep and worry and fear, and just like that, it was over. That was what Tess thought as she made her way through the Midtown Tunnel and towards the Belt Parkway. Relief, that's what she felt. She yawned. Relief and exhaustion. Revisiting the day's events, she believed that she had done fine on the comprehensive and she already knew that the mentors felt strongly about her practical exam. The question that came to her was the one she had asked herself again and again over her lifetime each time that she had completed a deal or relationship or endeavor: now what? *Now what?* Tess didn't know. Her mother used to tell her followers, "Before enlightenment you have to take out the garbage each night and after enlightenment you have to take out the garbage each night."

Not that she was enlightened, but it was the sentiment that she associated with. Things may change on the inside, even if they appeared the same on the outside. That fascinated her about life – how just looking at another person she couldn't know much of anything.

The yoga tests were over. It was hard to believe all that time and energy and now she was free. She sighed. She felt as if she had accomplished something. Exactly what, she wasn't sure of, but she was sure that a few months back, the thought of standing up in front of the room and teaching a yoga class and enjoying herself was unfathomable in her life. That was enough to make her insides rush, as if she were plunging down a waterfall. Who knew what was to come next in life? She would give it a go being a yoga teacher. Sitting in the city traffic, the thought of living in Woodstock appealed to Tess. Wide open spaces, not all the rushing around. She could try it. See if she liked it. But she'd feel ridiculous teaching yoga, wouldn't she? It was a nutty thought, but so were most of the ideas she had acted on in her life. She didn't have anything left to prove – she had been a successful entrepreneur for three decades now. Moving up to Woodstock, teaching yoga in the old house was a real possibility for her. Prakash would be supportive of that. Michael, well, he would get over it. Neal would want her to follow her path. He would support her regardless of what she chose to do. Oh, but she was being ridiculous. So, she had fun teaching her yoga class. So what? She enjoyed lots of things at first, but over time she got sick of them. The 11N exit for Mill Basin was there in the distance. Tess maneuvered her way into the right lane. She followed the curve of the exit onto Flatbush Avenue. There was certainly something to the familiar, but she knew that with time, everything new became familiar.

In Your Own Garden

The Return: April 2003

     Most days I woke up and read and when the bells rang, I made my way to my pew in the chapel. I liked to get there early. Sometimes I had my own words with God. Sometimes I sat and had no thoughts. I took in the stained glass and felt warm in its glow. I nodded to the other monks when they walked in. I was always uneasy seeing others first thing in the morning. I would think, here we all are again and while it was a glorious thing for me to see my brothers alive another day, I was never quite sure what to do with us all being there again. We came together every day, throughout the day, both in the chapel and for meals and to work, so that after time I began to feel that there was no mystery in the everydayness of my life. I began to wonder what would happen if I stayed out in the fields gardening when the church bells rang or if I walked down the road, away from the monastery on my own pilgrimage. I wondered what it would feel like for me – would I feel guilty? Free?

     So much of the Benedictine rule is based on fear of the Lord. Eventually you cast out fear and love God and that becomes your reason for doing everything. Sometimes I felt that I was out of the shadow of fear for the Lord and in the sunshine of his love, but then I would be praying, and it was fear that was there with me, not love. At those moments, I felt away from God's grace.

     "What do you seek?" the abbot asked, and I responded, "The mercy of God."

     But at some point, in the months before I left, I had stopped seeking the mercy of God and sought to be with God on my own terms.

To construct a tunnel between us and not keep building a rope bridge that God could cut lose at any moment. I didn't seek his mercy so much as I sought a mutual relationship with Him. I sought a union that wasn't based on subordination. I wanted oneness. After all my years in the monastery, I didn't see how being there was leading me any closer to God.

"What do you seek?" the abbot asked, and I thought freedom, a chance to find God on my own terms. To let him know me not for my actions, but for who I was at my core. I wanted God to observe me being me as I struggled in the world and took chances. Who would I be outside of the monastery? After twenty-three years in the monastery, I had ceased to think it terribly important what label I wore when it came to my relationship with God. Monk or man, religious or secular.

Something in me shattered when I told myself that I was going to leave the monastery, as if my body were made of glass. Moments later, when the words I had spoken to myself sunk in, I felt light, weightless. I was going to leave. As quickly as a part of me died, a part of me came to life. I felt giddy.

The journey home was long. Father Demetrius drove me with my suitcase to the Muenster Family Restaurant, where the bus stopped that would take me to Saskatoon. He didn't look at me during the drive. When it was time for me to open the car door and get out, he nodded, and I nodded back at him. There was an end-of-the-world tone to our parting, and while a part of me longed to stay, to override the feelings within me and go back to the monastery and carry on, whatever it was that had awakened in me gave me the strength to keep going. I waved goodbye to Father Demetrius as he made a U-turn and headed back to the monastery, but he didn't wave back.

The world seemed flat and endless en route to Saskatoon. So many miles of barren, burnt-out land. Nothing had changed, or so it seemed, in all those years that I was tucked away. I passed cows and graveled roads and trucks. I had worn my heavy black robe for so long, that sitting there in my old black pants and black sweater felt odd to me, like I had shed my skin.

The Saskatoon bus station was dingy and cold. From there I took a cab to the airport and when I rolled down the window, I shivered in the breeze. I felt frail and hollow. If the cab driver tried to make conversation with me, I didn't notice, as I was preoccupied with the scenery. It had been so long since I had seen anything other than the Muenster prairie. I thought back to the day many years prior when the young Romanian couple, Dora and Alex, had driven me to the monastery.

The abbot and Father Demetrius had spoken to someone in the Canadian passport office to renew my passport so that what I held out to the airport personnel was a copy of an old passport with a letter from the monastery and the passport officials. Once they let me through, I was detained at the security check. They had decided to pull me off the line to go through my luggage and as a security officer was examining the few articles of clothing and toiletries in my suitcase, I wanted to tell him that he was not going to find anything – that I had just left a monastery where I had been a monk for 23 years – but hearing it in my mind, it seemed a ridiculous thing to say.

At the gate waiting for my flight to Minneapolis, I had the urge to call Father Demetrious, to let him know that I had made it to the airport okay. But he wasn't expecting to hear from me. My ties to the monastery were broken. There was no one there who was waiting to hear from me.

I thought about calling my mother, but I feared that she was still in shock and unclear as to what I was doing with my life. For the first time in as long as I could remember, I didn't feel as if I belonged to anyone or anything – I was just Neal on his own and I felt a sense of gratitude and longing for all the years in which I had been part of a brotherhood. And then I remembered that I wasn't alone even though I had left the monastery, that God was still with me, and that made me feel lighter and easier with myself.

My flight from Minneapolis to New York City was delayed for hours. At first, I read into that – it was a sign, a chance for me to change my mind, to return to the monastery. People around me were chatting, complaining, laughing. I thought about how easy it was for me at the monastery, how I never needed to speak or explain my silence. It was acceptable to be quiet at the monastery. Here, amongst people making small talk, I felt uneasy, as if I was a freak. I decided to close my eyes, meditate. Think and not think. I called my mother and told her that she shouldn't head out to the airport, that we were delayed and that I would simply take a cab from the airport. Four hours later I was on a plane heading to JFK airport in New York.

On the plane, I sat next to a woman who was a chaplain at a San Francisco hospital. She was 27-years old with strawberry-blonde hair, a pale complexion with freckles, and pool blue eyes. I told her that I had just come from a monastery, and she didn't ask for any details. She told me that she was scared when she had to talk to people about their impending deaths as what did she really know about death? She mentioned that she had faced and overcome her own illness but with the dying there was even a sense of guilt about that as they hadn't been able to triumph over their illnesses. She wondered how and why God had trusted her to counsel these people. She told me that she thought of running out of the room when she was with the sick because she felt like a phony, an imposter, only somehow just at her breaking moment she would know what to say to them, how to be with them. I mostly nodded listening to her. She was so young to have such a big job was what I thought.

She was going to New York City to meet up with her boyfriend, who lived in Boston. She was taking him to a wedding where she would introduce him to her parents for the first time. She had anxiety over this – it mattered to her that her parents liked him.

I started thinking about my parents. My father having passed away and how strange it would be to see my mother after all the years that had passed. What did we even know about one another? At the monastery, she had written to me regularly and vice versa and we had spoken on the phone now and then. Her letters were mostly about her activities at the nursing home, how the seasons took over the landscape and such. My father's funeral 10 years back had been quick – I had orchestrated much of the ceremony during which time my mother and I had spoken only briefly and then after taking care of some legal issues with her regarding my father's will, I was back at the monastery. We were virtually strangers to one another, and it made me feel apprehensive that I was going to be living alongside her in the next few hours, as I didn't know what I would say to her in this period in which I was trying to figure out if I were a monk or a secular man. I had a fleeting wish that I could go off and live alone for a bit but then I realized that everything ahead of me was exactly as it should be, exactly what God had prescribed for me. I was going to say yes to everything and not get in the way.

When the plane landed, I walked with the girl to the luggage claim and there was her boyfriend, who had waited for her at the airport for hours because of our delayed flight. Saying goodbye to them both, wishing them a good weekend, made me feel lonely – lonelier than I remembered ever feeling and I thought again about the monastery, about turning around, about going back to the life I knew. Being at the airport in New York, it was all too much for me. So much had changed in my life since that day I started out so many years back. And then my duffel bag appeared on the baggage claim carousel – the items within linking to me to the last 23 years of my life: my books and journals and some pictures of the brothers which I had taken with me. If I closed my eyes, I could see my room as I left it back at the monastery: the thin white bed sheets pulled back slightly on my cot-sized bed and my desk lamp positioned just so on the narrow desk that was positioned against the wall adjacent to my bed. There lay my Bibles that were too heavy to travel with and some books and articles I had accumulated over the years by Thomas Merton and C.S. Lewis and the like as well as my gardening books. I could see the door to my small, hollow closet in which I had two robes hanging – both worn and in need of repair. I had left some possessions as an act of faith. I wondered if Father Demetrius would clear out my room now that I was gone or if he'd leave it as is, in the hopes that I'd return. Through my confusion, my doubts, he had never voiced his opinion as to my leaving, although I knew that he didn't approve of it. The unspoken view was that to leave the monastery was a breach of devotion.

In the taxi ride from the airport to my home in Mill Basin, the final leg of my journey, I felt like I was so many different Neal's. I had lived in Brooklyn for my first 23 years, and I had been on the prairie for 23 years. My life split in half. Thinking about what was to come, all the unknowns ahead, I felt a sense of liberation as well as a tinge of fear. It was easier to change one's life than I would have deemed imaginable. One morning I was one place, and later that day, I was in another place. Wherever I wandered on the prairie, whatever time of day, I searched for the church cross way up high to lead me back to the monastery. At that moment, nightfall approaching, I looked up into the night sky. Stars were beginning to appear, the moon still a shadow. Here, in Brooklyn, I didn't know what my guiding star would be, my landmark. Coasting on the Belt Parkway all seemed familiar, yet different, smaller. I remembered sitting in the olive-green Oldsmobile beside my father, en route to Buddies Fairyland Arcade across from the Floridian Diner, where he would take me to go on rides and eat French fries and chocolate éclairs after church some Sundays. I didn't remember much about the rides we went on or our conversations those Sundays, but I remembered how proud and important I felt riding in that big car beside my father. He was never much of a talker, but sitting next to him, I didn't have the need to speak. There was a time in the first grade that I had made a Halloween decoration in class – a black and orange scary cat cut out – with the help of my teacher. I had kept asking my father to hang it up in the window of our house as a decoration and I suppose I had gotten annoying as he had grabbed the decoration from my hands and before I knew it, he was ripping it up in front of me. Startled, I had run out to the porch and cried – one of the most intense cries I ever had in front of anyone. In between my sobs, I went on about how I was going to get in trouble at school because he ripped it up and my mother had come outside to comfort me, promising me that she was going to help me to make a new one and then I was screaming that I didn't want another one, that it was an ugly stupid cat, and I didn't want another one. Later that afternoon, when I sat at the dinner table with my mother and father, we were quiet and polite, as if the incident had never happened. There were times my father could make me feel that his having me for a son was the joy of his life, but there were other times he made me feel like I was an annoyance.

The taxi driver was making his way off the Belt Parkway via exit 11N, and I felt myself stiffening up. This was it. The last few minutes of my journey were coming to an end. I would be face to face with my mother, setting foot in the house I had grown up in, the house I hadn't seen in over two decades. We passed Kings Plaza and there was the familiar Brooklyn traffic at the intersection of Avenue U and Flatbush, cars beeping, some turning, others going straight. And then we were at 66th street and I felt empty inside, as if someone had turned me upside down and shook me out. I was still thinking that I could turn around, that I could go back to the monastery, but the driver was asking me for the exact house address, and I was telling him 56 Barlow Drive and he was making the left turn off 66th street onto Barlow, pulling up in front of the house.

My mother came outside the moment the taxi pulled up – she had been perched at the front door – her "lookout post" was what my father used to say. She walked up to the driver with her wallet as I was gathering my suitcase from the trunk, and I felt awkward to let her pay him, yet I didn't have much money with me – just the remains of the hundred dollars that Father Demetrius had given me for my journey. When the driver pulled away, there we were standing face to face. My mother looked to me like my mother, only her hair was cut shorter than I had remembered it and her face was more drawn so that it gave a frailer appearance. Looking into her eyes, which were neither questioning nor challenging, I knew that I was exactly where I needed to be to sort things out.

Dear Neal,

I survived the yoga test. You told me I would be fine, and I appreciated your comments, but I still couldn't imagine myself standing up in front of the room and teaching yoga. More than completing the test, though, I enjoyed myself during the practical exam. It made me feel happy to guide people through an experience that I believe settled them. I felt peaceful witnessing them become peaceful.

I have thought long and hard about my fear of teaching yoga to a group, and I believe that it has to do with the thought of tapping into a part of myself that is not my comfort zone, and letting people see me as something other than a businesswoman. What happens in life, or what has happened in my case, is that for a long time, I have hidden behind a title. A realtor. That title enabled people to know what I did and allowed me to hide anything else that I was. In everyday life, people never asked me what I cared about, or for, or anything of myself. Everyone that I interacted with was a prospective homebuyer, and so we talked to one another and interacted at a topical level. I think it's only with my son that I ever ventured into other territory – the territory that includes soul searching and what I'm about – the things that matter to me in my life.

Much like you, Neal, I have lived a safe life. I have kept the real me tucked away and gone through the motions in many respects. I've taken chances in real estate and in marrying and divorcing, I suppose, but those chances couldn't really affect my soul. I don't think that I ever truly let anyone in. I mourned the losses in my life like anyone else, but now I am beginning to understand that what I mourned had to do with attachment rather than anything deeper. I suppose what I am trying to say is that nothing or no one has ever affected my soul before, and teaching yoga, being so vulnerable in front of others – it has impacted me in a profound way.

There's so much that you don't know about me. That's the thing about life that often bewilders me. We are all here doing it together, and yet we never truly have a chance to tell one another about ourselves. Or maybe that's just how I've lived my life – rushing from one event to the next. I do believe that my mother knew things about me innately, without my ever telling her, but I wish I had talked to her more – not just the small talk, but that I had gotten into the details with her – told her about my fears, my passions; let her guide me in her way. I understand now that her insight would have been invaluable to me. How foolish we are at times to let things slip away in our lives – because there is not always a second chance.

You have shared so much about yourself with me, but I understand that what you shared are just moments, thoughts, and feelings captured at those moments. What is it that we as humans can truly share with one another, other than experiences, moments of bliss, moments of pain, and if we're lucky, moments of understanding?

There were so many memories that I shared with my mom, but what plays in my mind beyond all the others is that morning that I drove up to Woodstock a few days before she passed. I had no idea that morning that her end was so near; I don't believe that she knew either. That morning, we sat out on her front lawn on blankets, and she sang her song, "I never promised you a rose garden," and I sang along. I never knew why she loved that song as she did, but she had sung it to me for as long as I could remember. She had all her spiritual songs that she always sang to her congregation and hummed around the house, but whenever she would come into my bedroom at night to tuck me in and sing me to sleep, that was the song she sang. Maybe there was more to it than I ever understood. I never promised you a rose garden...it serves as a reminder to me that happiness is something that I, you, all of us, have to work towards, to earn. It's never promised to any one of us.

I wonder in some ways if the song was linked to my father and their relationship. He brought her over to the US. I'm sure they were in love and I'm sure that she had hoped and wished for a certain type of life – a life that she had believed they would share in together. I don't think my mother would have brought me into this world if she hadn't have believed in the bond between she and my father. She was too deeply spiritual – too much a believer in the universe and in the power of transcendence. And when that relationship failed – when the life she chose to pursue was not the right life for my dad, and he left, I suppose it's what stuck with her – that life was not a rose garden. That there would be hard times and that it wouldn't be easy and beautiful all the time. I don't know. I'm filling in the blanks. When I was younger, I hated my mother in some respects, as I believed that her spirituality was what drove my father away. I tried as hard as I could to distance myself from her as I didn't want to be like her. I didn't want to turn into her. I told myself that if she were like the other moms, a regular person, that my father would have loved her, that he would have stayed. Now, I understand that it was my father's loss to leave my mother. That he gave up a life that could have been filled with a love without barriers, a true love, if he had been willing to believe, to trust, to accept. But he had his own path to pursue. And I know that after the hurt, after the pain of his leaving her, my mom was able to wish him well and mean it – she was able to believe in his goodness even if he had hurt her; she was able to get past the hurt and love him in a new way; a way that didn't wish for or want anything of him. A way that enabled her to believe that their paths had crossed as that was what the universe wished for and that their paths had frayed as that too was what the universe wished for. They had done their dance was what she would have said if I asked her. She would have said, what more could anyone in this world ask for than to have their dance with another human being?

Thank you, Neal, for listening to me.

Thank you for knowing me.

Tess

CHAPTER 53: REMOTE PLACES

"Thanks, I'd love to come in for tea," Michael said.

He walked past Tess and up the stairs into the kitchen.

"My housekeeper has taken over my kitchen to clean, so tea is off limits at my place. And I know the freak isn't here because I just saw him, and his freak-o mother get into her car by her house and drive away. Are you going to come upstairs and join me, or are you expecting someone else?" Michael said.

Tess pushed the front door closed and made her way up the stairs.

"Look, Michael –" Tess said.

"I got your resignation letter," Michael said, pulling it out of his jeans pocket and flapping it at her. "You're one surprise after another these days, aren't you?"

He pulled his sweatshirt up and over his head. "It's hot in here," he said. He was wearing a t-shirt that said, *Have more fun in bed*, with the word *Sleepy's* sprawled across the top.

"Your shoes, Michael," Tess said.

He looked down at them and back up at Tess suspiciously. "What about them?"

"Please take them off."

"Are you kidding me?" Michael said.

Tess held out her hand, motioning Michael to hand her the letter and his sweatshirt as he took off his shoes.

"Is this some new yogi thing?" he said.

"Is your t-shirt some new sex ploy?" Tess said.

"You're a funny gal, Tess."

"All through growing up, my mother was insistent that we take off our shoes before we entered the house – for her it was about oneness with the earth and not bringing the dirt from outside into one's sacred space. Don't you remember leaving your shoes on the porch when we went up there? Anyway, being at the yoga studio so much, I've gotten to appreciate the ritual of being barefoot."

Michael shook his head.

"What?" Tess said. "You wanted an explanation and you got one."

"Since when do you write me letters about your life decisions that involve me? At least when you wanted a divorce you told me to my face," Michael said.

"I'm ready to talk. I wrote you a letter so that you could digest it.

I knew you would react just like this."

"How else should I react?"

"You should be on a daytime soap opera," Tess said.

Michael sat down at the kitchen table in his chair. When they were married, he had always sat in that chair. It was funny, Tess thought, but even after time had passed and things had changed, you would catch a glimpse of a person in a certain way and for an instant, it would seem as if a time machine had transported you backwards.

"It's a good thing I didn't put on socks with holes in them today," he said.

"You don't own socks with holes, Michael," Tess said.

He motioned to the teapot on the stove with his chin. "Tea still hot?"

Tess shook her head and turned the stove on. She sat down at the table across from him. "Few minutes," she said.

"Do you want to tell me what the heck your letter is all about?" Michael said. "And if I belong on a daytime soap, you certainly should be the star of one."

She had written it up last night at work and had dropped it in his garage mail slot on the way home from work, where she knew he'd see it in the morning when he went to pull out his car.

"It's about exactly what it says. I'm strongly considering moving back up to Woodstock for the New Year, and in order to make that a reality, I'm turning the business over to you to manage. We'll still coordinate, and I'll still make some decisions I'm sure, come into the office now and then, but you'll be the in-house CEO," Tess said.

"Let me get this straight. You're leaving your company not to mention your home for the last 30 something years, to move up to Woodstock and teach yoga?" Michael said.

"I'm not leaving anything. I'm just making some changes so that I can live a life that's in accord with who I am today," Tess said.

"*Who you are today*? Am I missing something because I still see Tess sitting across from me," Michael said.

"People do change over time, you know, as in priorities shift and so forth. Look at you – you were a high-powered corporate attorney in Manhattan, and now you live in Brooklyn and are a lawyer at Best," Tess said.

"Oh, I get it. People change, as in you were sane of mind and now, you're not. As in you loved running a business and now you want to become some sort of Mother Teresa and teach yoga," Michael said.

"You are so off base, Michael, that I won't even waste my breath on your stupidity," Tess said.

"Let me ask you this. I see you every day. When did you make this decision?" Michael said.

"It was brewing, but last night was when I sealed it. That's when I wrote the letter. You're the first to know," she said.

"Aren't I lucky?" he said. His chin jutted up at the ceiling and he closed his eyes as if he was breathing something in. It reminded Tess of how he looked when he slept – vulnerable in an exhausted way.

"You're a goddess in this industry, Tess." His mouth moved, his face and neck still in the same position. "You make an incredible living. You're willing to toss that all away?"

"What good is the money doing me if I'm always working?" Tess said.

"Always working? You just played semi hooky for months with your yoga stuff."

"I'm glad that you consider 60-hour work week's semi- hooky," Tess said.

"You seem to forget that you love it, too. Don't tell me you've forgotten that. I've been there with you every time you close a house. You glow. This yoga stuff has really brainwashed you," Michael said.

"Michael, nothing has brainwashed me. It's okay for a person to want to change things, to take some chances. Anyway, who are you worried about – you or me? You'll do an amazing job. The agents will be thrilled to work with you. I have total faith that you can run this business as well as I did, if not better," Tess said.

"Tess, I'm a lawyer," Michael said.

"Right. And you've been working with our agents for three years now. You have nothing to worry about," Tess said.

"You've been brainwashed," Michael said.

"Call it what you will. How I see it is that there's only so much living that you can go on doing without stopping to see what's really going on in your life," Tess said.

"I just want you to be aware of what you're doing."

"Trust me, Michael, I am."

The teakettle began to whistle.

"I suppose that's another sign," Michael said.

"Cynicism doesn't suit you well," Tess said.

He stood up, took cups from the dishwasher –" Clean?" he asked, and Tess nodded. He put in the tea bags, poured the steaming water into it and brought the steeping hot cups to the table. The steam rising between them fixated Tess. She imagined for a moment that she and Michael were suspended within it and that when it dissipated, so too would the heaviness of this conversation.

"I'm just trying to understand you, is all," Michael said. He was leaning forward now, his eyes intent on Tess. In the heat of their relationship, it had been this expression he had worn before he pulled her face to his and kissed her. Tess moved her tea bag around in her cup. She could feel that Michael's eyes were downcast now, too.

"You know a person for so many years, you were married to them for Christ's sake, living with them, working with them, and then they start changing their life all over the place, leaving you to pick up the pieces, and you wonder what the heck is going on with them. I think that my concerns are pretty valid," Michael said.

Tess leaned back in her chair, her eyes meeting his. His drama was putting her over the top – she had often felt that she was the husband, and he was the wife in their relationship, and she felt precisely that way right now. She cleared her throat to make herself sound more serious – she knew that if he sensed her lightness of heart for even a moment, he would erupt.

"If you think I should sell Best Realty, fine, I will. But I really think that you can run it, no problem," Tess said. "And you'll certainly be compensated very well, I might add."

"You know, sometimes you truly infuriate me," he said.

Tess couldn't conceal her smile.

"Don't even think about being cute," he said. "The fact that I'm having this conversation with you is pathetic to me," Michael said.

"Pathetic?" Tess said. "The fact that I want to get on with my life and do what's right for me, is far from pathetic, Michael. In fact, what's pathetic is your berating my decisions."

"I'm not berating your decision," Michael said, his face all kinds of sour. "I'm just trying to keep you from ruining your life."

"If you don't think you're the right person to run my business, no problem, Michael. I'm sure that it won't be hard work to find someone who's capable and enthusiastic to run a multi-million-dollar business."

"It's not about me running it. Be reasonable. If you leave, your company will lose its best agent. You're the master house seller," Michael said.

"Somehow I don't think that's what I want on my tombstone – *Master House Seller*," Tess said. "You of all people I would think can understand. You left a Fortune 500 firm because you wanted out of the high-pressured corporate insanity. If I remember correctly, that's what you told me when my ex-husband introduced us. Now it's my turn to wake up. I am not going to let a job and money dictate how I'm going to live the rest of my life. There's a whole world out there, Michael. Life is not about working in an office and running around all day, scrambling to please other people. Life is about –"

"What is it about? Tell, me, Tess. What's it all about?"

"Living," Tess said.

"And helping people to find houses, interacting with people from all walks of life each day isn't living?" Michael said.

"Sure, it is, but I think of living differently now. It's having time to take two-hour walks each morning – watching the sunrise. Living is about connecting," Tess said.

Michael sipped his tea, watching her closely.

"This is about him, isn't it?" Michael said.

"Neal? He has no idea that I'm planning to go to Woodstock."

"So, when were you planning to tell him? The day you leave? Or let me guess, you're going to write him a letter telling him so?" Michael said.

"All I need to know is if you're open to running Best or not," Tess said.

"Just don't get so far away from yourself that it's impossible for you to get back to yourself," Michael said.

When Michael had divorced his first wife, he had told Tess that he felt as if the real him had been held hostage at some far away territory while he was married to her.

"Michael, this is about getting back to me."

Michael picked up the letter and folded it into a paper airplane. He sent it off in Tess's direction.

"I'll give you a week to think this through a bit and then we can revisit," Michael said.

"You'll give *me* a week?" Tess said.

"Just because it seems like a good idea today, doesn't mean it will seem like a good idea tomorrow. Trust me, I learned that the hard way," Michael said.

"What does that mean, *you learned that the hard way*? What are you referring to Michael?"

Michael stood up and laughed. He slipped on his sweatshirt and loafers.

"Michael?"

"Use your imagination, Tess."

"Now you're blaming your present situation on decisions you made with me? Are you saying you regret having married me?"

"No," he said. "You're the one who likes to make it clear that you regretted marrying me. How we could have just stayed friends and not complicated things," Michael said.

"Michael, everything happened how it should have," Tess said.

"Please," he said. "What I was referring to was taking you to the yoga studio – I thought I was doing you and me both a favor that night. If I ever thought yoga would be the cause of these shenanigans –"

"Taking me to that studio was the best thing you ever did for me, Michael."

"Save it," he said as she followed him down the stairs.

"You'll owe me big time if I help you with Best," he said. "As in major."

She smiled at him, and he grabbed her face with both hands and kissed her succulently on the lips before she could pull away.

"Michael!" she said, licking her lips where he had bit them. She tasted blood.

"I'd like to see the monk kiss you like that," he said already beyond her, en route to his car. He shook his head and laughed wildly, before he opened the car door, slid into the driver's seat, and sped away.

CHAPTER 54: FOR MANY REASONS

Tess hadn't been sure she was going to the monastery in New Jersey until she arrived at the compound and pulled into the graveled car path, inching her way to the church parking lot. She had driven in a trance, thinking and not thinking at the same time, following the curves of the road, the drivers in front of her. The car still idling, she searched her brain for what came next. 7:45 am. Did she turn around and go back to Brooklyn? She could still make it in to the office by 9:00 am. Slowly, she turned the ignition off, took the keys out, and grabbed her ivory pashmina from the seat beside her, wrapping it around her neck. Morning services were at 6:30 am. She made her way out of her car and moved toward the chapel, the brisk air hastening her steps – November air always chilled her in a teeth chattering way, whereas by December her body had grown accustomed to the cold, and she braved it better. When she pulled the heavy wooden door open, she let out a sigh of relief: there was no one there, just the crackle of lingering candles. Making her way inside, the sharp scent of incense overcame her – to her it smelled of rubbing alcohol and licorice. She covered her nose until she acclimated to the intensity of the aroma. It seemed to seep into her veins, her very core, so that she felt as if she were immersed in it. She wondered how the smell affected Neal – if it was soothing to him or if it unnerved him as well.

Her footsteps resounded on the marbled floor. She hadn't realized how high the ceiling was – over 12-feet, she estimated. She moved around the perimeter of the room examining the stained-glass windows: on each one there was a dramatic portrait of one of the Apostles. So lifelike, so ordinary they all appeared with their taut, defined frames, chiseled faces, and their expressions of pain and sorrow so that Tess cringed, almost feeling their pain in her body. The hues of the stained glass were earthy, yet somber – deep reds, mahogany, navy, emerald greens. They made Tess feel heavy. She moved to the pews and began to weave through them, row by row. She didn't know what she was looking for, hoping for. She just needed to move. She made her way to the pews the monks sat in. She wondered what it felt like day after day to sit in those pews. The thick, dark mahogany wood of their frames was slick, cool to the touch. There was seriousness to the pews, a stand-at-attention look and feel. Surely God wasn't such a disciplinarian that this type of formality was required, or was he? Or perhaps it was the brothers who needed to create this setting to create order. What lured these men here when there were so many other choices in the world, innumerable choices? Did the brothers desire this life against all others? Did they feel joyful that they had become monks? Did any of them wish for a different life? Did they regret being monks? She knew that she was being ridiculous – searching for answers that she wouldn't find and more than that, searching for things that in the larger sense of the world, didn't matter, that couldn't affect Tess one way or the other – the monks, like her, were just living their lives. This much she was sure of: no one, monk or otherwise, was wondering about Tess's life and why she did what she did.

"Oh!" she said. "I, I –"

The youngest monk was a few feet from her, reaching for his bible, which rested on the pew an arm's reach from Tess.

"Please. Sit. You don't have to get up," he said. His voice was low.

She hadn't heard him come in any more than she had realized that she had sat down in the pew.

"I'm sorry," she said, standing up and hurrying out of the row, in the opposite direction so that she didn't have to pass him. "I was just going." She had made her way from the monks' pews so that she stood before the table that held the candles and the Bible and a looming metal cross. The young monk moved to the table, standing across from her. His robe looked too big for him, but those eyes, she remembered those deep-set chestnut eyes from the first time she had visited the monastery. They seemed to take in everything in one glance.

"Really, you don't have to go," he said. He set his Bible down and from a drawer below the table, he took out fresh candles, incense cones, a rag, and a cloth. He began to clean out the incense holder with the weathered rag.

"You're free to stay – the chapel is open to all, always." He worked as he spoke, focusing on his task at hand. His voice was like a song to her. Low but full of melody.

"Your accent," Tess said. "Where are you from?"

"Canada. Ontario."

"I have a friend from Canada," she said.

He began to polish the cross with the cloth. He moved vertically across it and then made his way horizontally.

"It's nice there," he said.

"But you came here. Why didn't you go to a monastery in Canada?"

He smiled.

"I'm sorry," Tess said. "My manners are terrible. You don't have to answer me."

"It's fine," he said. "My family relocated here, to New Jersey, a few years back. One day, perhaps, I'll go to a monastery in Canada."

"Have you been a monk for long?" she said.

"I've been with the brothers for four years now – I'm still in my temporary profession phase. It's a long process to brotherhood."

"But a worthwhile one," Tess said. It was a question as much as a statement.

"Yes," he said. "A necessary one."

She nodded. "Necessary because it was your calling?" Tess asked.

He stifled a laugh in the cup of his hand. There was a boyishness to him that in other contexts Tess would have considered charming. Here, in the church, it made Tess feel sad. He seemed so young to have renounced so much.

"I'm sorry. Really. I'll be going," she said.

"Please," he said, stopping his work on the cross to focus on her. "Stay."

His hair was closely cropped, and his skin was smooth and pale. He had a masculinity to his person, a solidness. For a moment, she was able to envision him as a husband to some young, beautiful woman. A father.

"A man becomes a monk for many reasons," he said, his eyes intent on hers.

She nodded again. She wanted to ask him if he ever thought about changing his mind, about leaving, starting a new life.

He smiled and worked on replacing the incense in the canister.

"You're not a Catholic," he said.

"No," she said.

"You don't seem comfortable in here."

"It's just that – it's new to me. I was raised a Buddhist, but I'm not that either. I'm not sure what I am. I believe in God," Tess said. Then, "Did you always want to be a monk?"

"I wanted to be many things," the boy said.

"I wanted to be many things, too," Tess said. "I used to think that once you made a choice, it was forever, but now I feel differently."

"Why's that?" he asked.

"I've realized that I can change my mind and take a different route. I didn't discover that until this year. It's all very empowering," she said.

"I believe that my path is to be a monk," he said.

"I know a monk," she said.

"Is he your friend from Canada?"

Tess nodded. "He's actually here now. Not here, but in New York. Brooklyn. Where I'm from. He's a very nice person," Tess said.

She didn't know where she was going with this but felt a thread between them. Her desire to speak was mingled with what she believed was his need to know. Maybe he was just being a man of God? Tess wasn't sure. She studied the marble floor, a medley of tan and white and wondered how many people had moved across this floor over the years.

"He's been a monk for 23 years," she said, imagining how many hours in 23 years Neal had been in the church in Canada. "So much time."

"Time is relative," the young monk said, gently.

"Do you remember me from a few months back?" Tess said. "I was here one morning, and I saw you. We locked eyes and then I left."

"There was something in your eyes that made me feel unsettled," the young monk said.

"I was sorry that you were here, that this was your life," Tess said. She caught her breath; she knew she should stop talking but couldn't. "I felt sorry that one day you may not want this life anymore and how complicated it may be to undo your vows."

The monk moved closer to her now, so that he stood before her. He was tall, over six feet, she imagined, so that he looked down upon her. If she reached out her hand, it would touch his chest. The intensity of his eyes on hers made her feel light-headed. She could feel the breath seeping from her half-opened mouth, the back of her throat becoming dry.

"Neither you nor I have foresight into the future. All I can do is live each day as it arrives," he said.

"Have you ever regretted your decision?" Tess asked.

"I'm human," the monk said. "I still think and feel and imagine at times."

His eyes were down cast now, his chin sagging toward his chest as if he were caught in a lie. Before she knew what she was doing, Tess reached for his hand and clasped it in her own. She felt him resist for a moment before his hand grew limp.

"Forgive me," she said. "I have no right to question you."

The monk didn't pull his hand back nor did he look up at Tess. He took a deep breath and Tess heard the quiver in it as he exhaled.

"Your friend of 23 years," he said. "Is he in town for a family emergency?"

Tess felt her heart racing inside her chest. The candles on the table flickered and with a final cackle, one of them was out, smoke seeping away from it in a thin, shadowy line.

Tess released his hand, their eyes searching one another now with an eagerness, as if they had misplaced something between them. He seemed so young, younger than Tess had imagined, and she had an urge to take his face in her hands, to pull him to her breast, to nurture him, protect him.

"Has he left the monastery?" the boy asked, a sense of quiet urgency in his voice, and Tess nodded.

"He's discerning his vows," she said.

The boy nodded.

"Do you think he'll go back?"

"I don't know," Tess said, although at that instant her heart was telling her that he would. That entangled in his desire to live a secular life were roots deeper than she could imagine, entwined in ways that were incomprehensible to her. Heaviness came over her heart so that breathing was laborious, and she held her hand to her chest.

"Are you in love with him?"

"I want him to do what's right for him," Tess said.

"Do you love him?" the boy asked. There was a pleading in his eyes.

"Yes," she said.

"Does he love you?"

"I don't know," Tess said.

The boy nodded. "The Lord will lead him in the right direction. Even if he loses the Lord, the Lord won't lose him."

Tess felt that he had checked out of the intimacy of their conversation and was on autopilot. She wrapped her pashmina tighter around her neck.

The young monk replaced the candles now, lighting them, and Tess bowed her head to him. She moved towards the wooden doors, her footsteps resounding on the marble floor. When she reached the exit, she looked back at the boy one last time. He looked up at her and they held a glance a few moments.

"Life is a mystery," he said, his voice echoing through the chapel, like an organ's chords. "There is no formula for living."

Tess nodded. There was no formula for living. Life was in fact, a mystery. The young monk nodded to her before she pushed open the heavy door, making her way into the sunlight.

CHAPTER 55: THANKS AND GIVING

Tess finished whipping the sweet potatoes, folded them into the evaporated milk, and whipped the mixture some more before she poured it all into a cinnamon and nutmeg sprinkled pie tin. She'd bake that for 40 minutes and then later, when her guests arrived, she would add the freshly diced pineapple on top and sprinkle some more cinnamon. She inhaled the sweet nutty flavors of the sweet potatoes and cinnamon and smiled. Mmm. Tess loved Thanksgiving. Loved the smells of holiday goodies baking and the variety of flavors and colors on the table – brown gravies and pumpkin pudding and cranberry sauce and vegetable bread-crust stuffing, her signature dish, along with her baked tofu stew and sides of steamed broccoli and spinach. It was a shame she didn't get to cook more – she seemed to forget how much she enjoyed cooking until each year she put together a feast. In the past, she had done so for each of her husband's and their families. Some years Prakash and a friend or two of his had joined, although more often over the years she and Prakash had met up at her mother's home a weekend or two prior to Thanksgiving for their own private pre-holiday family event, during which time she and her mother had shared in the cooking responsibilities. Her mother used to make a spicy and sweet pumpkin porridge that Tess craved for months after the holiday. Tess never was able to duplicate it just right when she made it herself. She remembered her mother

humming as they worked together in the kitchen steaming and baking –
her mother always seemed full of melody.

Each year on Thanksgiving Day, beginning when Tess was a
little girl, her mother had led her followers on pilgrimages to local towns
to work in soup kitchens, feeding the less fortunate. Through all of her
resisting her mother, Tess had been fond of those Thanksgiving
missionary trips and as an adult, when she was busy preparing her own
Thanksgiving meals on Wednesday night and Thursday morning, Tess
would think of her mother and neighbors on the yellow school buses they
rented, a kirtan in motion as they made their way to various shifts at soup
kitchens in upstate New York.

She inhaled the sweet potatoes and closed her eyes. It was hard
at times for her to see her mother – her eyes, her face. It was easy enough
to call upon memories, but there were moments, like now, when a
desperation came over her, a panic that her mother was fading from her
grasp, that her memories were dissolving into countless other things.
With her eyes closed, she summoned herself to the morning she rested on
the grass with her mom; she could feel the skin of her mother's face, hear
her mother's gentle voice, see the wind rustle her mother's hair. All the
details were so vivid, so clear to her if she just focused; "Mother," she
said. "I miss you." The tears swelled up in her eyes. She could see the
way her mother looked at her – as if Tess was and always would be her
little girl. How simple it was for the two of them to co-exist, to be mother
and daughter. It was hard to imagine that over six months had passed. If
her mother felt this far away in six months, she feared how it would feel
in a year, in two years.

The phone was ringing. Tess opened her eyes and wiped her

hands on the dishrag on the counter and picked up on the third ring.

She cleared her throat. "Good morning, Lyla," she said. It reminded her that her answering machine had gone off twice earlier in the morning while she showered; she would need to check the messages, but assumed they were from Lyla and Michael.

"You and Neal may come over any time you'd like. No, nothing is wrong. I'm fine. Yes, 1:00 pm is perfect. I'll be here all day."

When she had told Lyla that she didn't eat turkey, never had, Lyla had told her there was no such thing as Thanksgiving without turkey. Tess had learned: when it came to topics that were irrelevant to her heart or sanity, it wasn't worth it to argue with Lyla. Her mom would have been proud of Tess. "Never deny people of the simple things that keep them happy," she had told Tess more than once. If Lyla insisted on turkey for Thanksgiving, then Tess was not going to deprive her. Lyla would bring the turkey with her, and Michael would supply his famous spinach pie, made this year with low-fat ricotta, and a low-fat graham cracker crust. He had told Tess that he was on a new health-conscious mission to watch his weight and his cholesterol. "Lower or watch?" Tess had asked him, and he had given her his very cute smirk in response and told her that not everyone could be naturally thin and healthy like her.

Tess drained the red beans and the black beans which had soaked through the night. They were ready to be cooked. Next, she took the tofu chunks she had been baking out of the oven. She placed them into her casserole dish and added in the steamed carrots, peas and corn with a touch of vegetable broth. Later, she would add in the cooked beans and bake her stew.

She opened the window to let some fresh air in – the oven made the kitchen warm, and the warmth made her feel sleepy. The air that rushed in was damp and dewy so that she shivered. Perhaps later, after the guests had left, after the cleanup, she would take a walk. Maybe Neal would join her. It had been some time since they walked together. It would be the first time that she was to be in the presence of Neal and his mother, and the first time Michael would officially meet them. She was past being nervous, past caring. If they clicked great, and if not, what could she do? The phone rang again.

"How can I help you, Michael?" she said. "Oh, Michael, please. Lyla is fine and Neal is a very sweet man. Don't give me that you can't believe you're dining with the freaks. Please behave yourself today. Can you promise me that? You'll behave? What time can I expect you? 3:00 pm is perfect."

She tried to remember the two Thanksgivings with Michael when they were a couple – how could it be that she couldn't remember a few years back? Oh, right. Zihuantanejo, Mexico. That was year one. And then the second year they had gone to Isla Mujeres, Mexico, only there she had contracted a stomach virus on her first day and Michael caught the bug on their second day so that most of that vacation consisted of them tossing and turning in separate beds. She remembered walking along the beach with him in Zihuantanejo, holding hands and looking out at the ocean. She had been happy with him at that time, content, or maybe it was just the scenery, the beautiful white sand beach and aqua water – she remembered it all being fairytale like, miles of beach and the cliffs up above, like giant sculpted look-out towers. That was when they were first getting used to being a married couple versus friends and colleagues who slept together.

He had still been Michael, only she had felt excited to be with him back then, as if he was the one she would work with and enjoy in her down time and grow old with. That was before his neediness and attachment to her had grown tedious. They had gone out to that quaint restaurant on the mountaintop on Thanksgiving night, their close-to-the-floor table scattered with tea candles and a vase of vibrant tropical flowers. Tess remembered that after that trip she had wanted to redecorate her home with chunky wood furniture that sat low to the floor – a mix of Aztec influence and her mother's Tibetan Buddhist influence. But like other things, she had never gotten to it, because life as always had intruded with its pressing responsibilities, she supposed. That was how it all seemed to go along – ideas, passion, romance. Urgent and exciting one moment until other things came along and cancelled out the urgency, dulled the excitement. She spoke in her heart to God, and thanked him for her life, for the joy he had brought her, for the love he had allowed her to experience.

This time Tess picked up on the third ring.

"Dale! No, no you didn't wake me. I was reminiscing and praying in no particular order," Tess said. "Yes, I'm cooking for hours already. His mother is making the turkey and Michael is making a dish. Yes, she knows I don't eat turkey, but it's fine. If she wants turkey, she can have it. I miss you, too. Oh, good! I'm glad that you're spending the holiday with Kyle. Dinner with your family – that sounds safe. Dessert with his, perfect. Yes, I think it's great. No expectations. Dale, whatever you choose to do is the right thing. One day this will all seem silly. Yes, I promise. I'm looking forward to yoga and brunch on Sunday, too. Yes,

yes, I'll check in with Sara and Kim. Have fun today. Big kiss. You enjoy too. Bye."

Tess wondered if women who didn't work all week spent their days cooking and talking on the phone. She checked on the beans – water wasn't boiling yet. She was sure she'd enjoy it for the first week or two, but the thought of being confined to the kitchen and chatting day in and day out made her feel exhausted. She tried to remember how it had been for her when she gave birth to Prakash. She was sure she'd taken off some time, but then remembered that after he was a month old, she was already back at work. Her mother had come down from Woodstock and stayed with her and Marc for a few months to help with the baby. Her mother hadn't questioned her choices, hadn't thought Tess was a bad mother because she wanted to be at work. It was one of the few times that her mother stayed in Tess's home for an extended period. Tess tried to remember what it was like with her mother as a guest, but she couldn't. Whenever her mother had visited in Tess's twenties, it had never been for more than a few days and to see her grandchild. By the time Prakash was in grade school, her mother's visits to Brooklyn had stopped so that Tess instead drove up to Woodstock every other month or so for a long weekend – how Prakash had loved those weekends in the old house.

Her eyes were stuck on the calendar inside the cupboard door she had opened in search of spices for her stew. New Year's was a little more than a month away. She intended to meet Prakash up in Woodstock, as they had planned. She would drive up on the 26th of December, her birthday, weather permitting. That would give her a few days to prepare the house before the New Year. Prakash had mentioned flying in on the eve of the 30th. For the New Year she would honor her mother and fill the house with fresh cooking and light the fireplaces and candles, and she and Prakash would practice yoga and meditate and bring in the New Year with peace, lightness, and love. If some of the neighbors wanted to come over and be with them, she would welcome that, too. The thought of it all made her feel warm inside. And if she chose to stay on up in Woodstock for months, even years, so be it. Michael would be able to handle it all. As for Neal, she hadn't gotten that far yet. Surely, he would be invited. It was too far away to worry about. First, she had to get through today.

Tess nestled herself into the corner of the kitchen floor across from the table, where she had an adjacent view of the stovetop where the beans cooked. She dialed Prakash's number and let her back sink into the crevice of the wall as the line rang.

"I remember when you were just a little boy and we made turkey cutouts by tracing your hand," Tess said.

"Good morning, Mom," Prakash said.

"I wish you were here with us," Tess said.

"We've been through this – you know how crazy the airports are on Thanksgiving. Flying into New York this time of year –"

"I know, darling," she said. "I understand. It's okay for me to miss you, though, isn't it?"

"You're becoming more and more warm and fuzzy the older you get," Prakash said.

"I'm sure that Michael would firmly disagree with that statement," Tess said.

"Are you done cooking?" Prakash said.

"Almost," she said. "I made your favorite sweet potato pie. I'm still not able to visualize my guests in one room, but I'm sure it will all be okay," Tess said.

"If you're asking me if I think Michael will behave, the answer is yes. Remember he can be quite charming," Prakash said.

"Lyla Clay is not quite the to-be-charmed type," Tess said.

"But don't you like her now? Last I heard, the two of you were competing for the best walker in Mill Basin title."

"Very funny," Tess said.

"It's our first Thanksgiving without Grandma," Prakash said.

She pressed her free hand palm down on the cool kitchen tiled floor as if she could lift off from it.

"Yes," Tess said. Her palm had left a faint print on the white kitchen floor. She was an orphan. It was an unsettling feeling. It made her feel as if she was floating, until she heard Prakash's breath on the other end of the phone, which grounded her.

"I'm looking forward to meeting up in Woodstock next month," Prakash said.

"Me too."

Prakash yawned and Tess heard what sounded to be his sitting up.

"We're you sleeping?" she said. "Did I wake you?"

Prakash laughed. "I was planning to wake up at 7 am on my day off Mom, no worries."

"Go back to sleep. I'm sorry, dear. I wasn't thinking for a moment. Call me later if you want," she said. "Wait, Prakash, do you have plans today?

"I was invited over to a girl friend's house."

"A girl friend, as in someone you date?" Tess said.

"Bye, Mom," Kash said.

"Kash –"

"Miss you. Have fun today," and with that, he hung up the phone.

Tess sat cradling the phone to her chest and smiled. She made her way to standing a bit clumsily, leaning on the kitchen cabinets. So much for all the yoga, she thought.

The beans were done for now. She turned off the stovetop, drained the water from them, and poured them into the casserole with the rest of the stew, repositioning the tofu chunks and the carrots and celery to make room for the beans. She sprinkled some homemade breadcrumbs throughout and mixed in a dash of cinnamon and cardamom – a la her mother's recipe – and set it on the middle rack in the oven, alongside the seven-grain bread that she would heat up later. She would bake the casserole about 30 minutes prior to mealtime. She covered all that needed covering with aluminum foil – sweet potato pie, homemade cranberry sauce and cabbage and beet salad, and strategically positioned everything between the refrigerator and the stove top, so that all that needed to cool and all that needed heating up later was in its proper place. She took the carrot cake and apple angel-food cake she had made the night before out of the refrigerator and put those on the counter to warm up to room temperature. There, everything was all set. Now it was Tess time.

Tess made her way downstairs into the playroom area of her basement. She drew the playroom blinds to the backyard door to let the early morning light in. She unrolled her yoga mat and positioned it in the center of the room, facing the doors. She began to focus on her breath and moved into her sun salutes. Shine out, she thought, opening her arms wide at her sides, and as she flew them up towards the ceiling, she felt herself soaring toward all that was above and beyond. Diving forward, she was humbling herself to the world, bowing down in servitude. She was a warrior, firm and solid, and soft too. Her breath was steadying now, uniting the movements with her inhales and exhales.

Tess moved into triangle, right angle, some one-leg balance postures – tree, arda chandrasana, and bow. Then it was time for her to move to the floor for forward bends and back bends. She loved being able to be with herself, in her own mind and space, while the world outside her went on. When it was time for shavasana, final resting pose, she felt herself melting away, her breath falling in line, the November sunlight cutting the floor through the blinds, warming her face and body.

It wasn't until Tess heard bells ringing over and over, that she jumped up. For a few moments her brain searched where or why until she smelt the food upstairs and she realized that she had fallen asleep in resting pose. There was someone at the front door. She hadn't even showered yet!

Tess clumsily picked herself up, still lightheaded from the intensity of the rest, the jarring of the doorbell, and rushed upstairs, to the front door, which she pulled open with her finger on the alarm, disabling it.

"Lyla," she said, unlatching the screen door.

Lyla eyed Tess suspiciously and shook her head when Tess waved her to come inside.

"I've come to drop off the turkey," Lyla said. I've been busy all morning cooking the turkey for your party and then had to cook two more turkeys for the home. I haven't had time to relax," Lyla said, eyeing Tess up and down.

Tess imagined her hair was going every which way from her brief nap. She tried to smooth it down a bit.

"Sounds like you've been plenty busy," Tess said.

At that moment Buddhi hopped out of the orchid tree and landed on the porch, his back hunched, his teeth showing as if he was about to attack. He sniffed at the air a few times regarding the turkey Tess was holding, and then scrambled past Lyla and Tess through the open screen door, darting up the stairs.

"Oh, my goodness!" Lyla shrieked. "That nasty creature does not belong in your house," she said and for a moment, Tess felt dread at the possibility of Buddhi getting at the turkey; she would have to be careful with it.

"We'll be back at 1:00 pm prompt," Lyla said, and with that she about faced and hurried down the stairs. Tess stood for a few moments watching her move away from the porch, and then focused on the car parked by the curb in which Neal sat. He waved at her, and she waved back. See you later, she mouthed, not knowing if he was able to make out what she was saying, but she could have sworn she saw him mouthing it back to her.

"I was ringing the doorbell forever," Michael said, letting the screen door slam shut behind him as he followed Tess up the stairs.

"It seems to be a theme today," Tess said. She paused at the landing. "Excuse me, but do you think you could maybe close the front door?" she said. "And your shoes, please."

"Geez," Michael said. "You'd think the host would be in the holiday spirit. The weirdo here? I'd like to see you ask his mother to take off her shoes."

"Neal is with his mother, and for your information, I was chasing a lunatic cat around my home for the past hour – he ambushed me in the shower and practically tore a hole through my leg with those claws of his and now he's vanished," Tess said.

"And I thought you answered the door in a robe to turn me on.

Ambushed you in the shower, huh?" Michael said.

"Don't start with me," Tess said. "I have Neal and his moody mother arriving soon, I'm not dressed yet, didn't get to do my make-up and I still can't find that cat who for all I know could be waiting to attack the turkey that Neal's mother dropped off, or worse yet, attack her."

"Look at you, all un-yogi-ed out," Michael said. "The yoga gods might expel you from the kingdom today if they came for a visit."

"I can always count on you to cheer me up," Tess said. "Ah! Did you just see him dart by? Downstairs, he went downstairs!"

"Didn't you tell me you loved that cat a few weeks back when I told you he was mangy?"

"That was before he decided to crash my party," Tess said waiting by the stairs, whispering *here kitty*.

"Well at least I know you're consistent in your loving-something-one-day-and-tossing-it-away-the-next pattern," Michael said.

"I'm glad that you can find a way to compare yourself to a stray cat," Tess said.

She sat down at the kitchen table, tightening her robe. "I give up," she said.

"You're surrendering your love to me?" Michael said.

"You don't stop, do you?"

"The holidays make me nostalgic," Michael said.

"Where's your spinach pie?" Tess asked.

Michael pointed to the bag he put down on the counter by the sink. "I wouldn't leave home without it," he said. "It's quite delicious, I might add."

"Isn't someone else supposed to judge that?" Tess said.

"I made two pies and ate a hefty piece of one last night and I went back for seconds. I would have had thirds if I wasn't middle aged and didn't have to watch my waistline."

"Time for me to get ready," Tess said.

"When are Lyla and the weirdo making their appearance?" Michael said.

"You're coming with me to get ready?" Tess said, glancing back at Michael who was following her to her bedroom.

"Should I sit in the kitchen alone?" Michael said.

"Maybe you want to pick out an outfit for me," Tess said.

"My pleasure," he said, sitting down on her bed.

"Can I ask you a favor? Can you please behave today? I don't want to have to babysit you," Tess said.

"For your information, I'm an absolutely charming gentleman and will be nothing less today."

"Thank you," Tess said.

"Have you told him about your moving to Woodstock and trying to stick me with your company yet or is that topic off limits?"

"Michael. Please. Not today."

"You haven't told him. You've already created a contract for me, but you haven't even told the person you're in a relationship with, not to mention your employees."

Tess dabbed on her burnt red lipstick, touched up her hair with some conditioning cream and made her way past Michael into her closet, pulling the door slightly closed behind her.

"Hiding away won't help you my dear," Michael said.

"If you don't want to sign the contract then the sooner you let me know the better," Tess said, going through her suits – no, it wasn't a suit day – before scanning her casual rack and deciding on a charcoal grey cashmere turtleneck and matching charcoal heather slacks, which she'd accessorize with her black patent leather Gucci belt and matching loafers.

"So that you can put Best up for sale?" Michael said.

"So that I can make other arrangements," Tess said. "I'm going up to Woodstock in a few weeks as you know and I'm going to do what's right for me, regardless of my business, which has been my life for the last few decades."

"I'll assume temporary leadership," Michael said. "For a few months. Two or three let's say. And then we go from there."

Tess walked out of the closet, dressed and messing her hair with her fingers to add fullness. "Are we playing let's make a deal?" she said.

"That's my offer. We can revisit in March and make more definitive decisions at that time," Michael said.

Michael leaned against the bed's backboard, paging through the *Bhagavad Gita* he'd picked up from her night table. He closed the book and focused on Tess.

"It's a deal," Tess said. "And we don't tell the employees anything other than that I needed to take care of some out-of-town business and will be back in a few months."

"That sounds like a change of heart," Michael said.

"Strategic planning is how I see it. A trial period for you. Meaning, if you should opt to bail out of our agreement or fail miserably and I need someone else to take over, at least I can save the team from having to deal with too much confusion in the transition. I'll expect you to draw me up an agreement of sorts that we can both sign off on."

"Always business," he said.

"You're the lawyer. I would think that you'd be mandating the contract," Tess said.

"If I told you I wanted to go with you to Woodstock —"

"I'd tell you to focus on your own dreams, Michael. Was that the doorbell?" Tess said.

Michael paused until they both heard the bell ring again.

"Saved by the bell," he said.

"You'll be fine with or without me at Best," Tess said. "And perhaps you'll be able to get on with your life without me around."

"You're saying that you don't think I've moved on with my life?" Michael said.

"Michael, we're divorced for two years and you're sitting on my bed on Thanksgiving while I'm getting ready," Tess said.

"And your point is?" he said.

Lyla stood at attention when Tess opened the door. She'd told Michael to busy himself in the kitchen by taking out drinks – white wine, seltzer, water and glasses. Neal was making his way from the car parked across the street carrying a few red cellophane cookie platters, which protruded from a large white shopping bag. Tess noticed the rainbow streaking the sky and pointed.

"Look."

Lyla about faced and Neal, seeing them looking off in the distance, turned around when he reached the curb. Tess moved out onto the porch. The rainbow seemed to take over the entire sky, like a backdrop.

In a moment Michael was beside them on the porch and Tess noticed that her neighbors on both sides were also on their porches as were the neighbors across the street on Dakota Place. Tess imagined unicorns coming into the picture, scattering across the lawns of Mill Basin. In this surreal moment, anything seemed possible and then she thought: this is how life works, people gathered, looking beyond at something better, without noticing what's right there, within reach. She was guilty of this. They all were, she supposed, even Neal and his mother with their religion. Planning for the next life but what about the joy of right now? Wasn't that what her mother always preached? To prepare for right now versus the future. *The other half of the rainbow is beneath the surface.* That's what Neal had told her. His mother, who stood beside her now, had told him that, and it made sense to Tess – there was no pot of gold, but a depth, a beauty, beneath the surface.

Tess turned to the cleaning lady neighbor, to wish her a happy holiday, but she was already gone, back into her home. The Israeli neighbor had fled, too, her son not putting up any fight that they could hear.

"I think our Hallmark moment is over," Michael said.

Lyla's lips curled up in a smile and Tess sighed. It was going to be okay. "Mrs. Clay, this is Michael O'Shay," Tess said.

"I know who you are," Lyla said, looking Michael up and down so that he glanced over at Tess and smiled. "I see you when I walk past your house – you live in that mansion – and sometimes I see your car in Tess's driveway."

"You're very observant," Michael said, holding the door open for Lyla and Tess to pass through. "It's my pleasure to meet you, Mrs. Clay."

Lyla cleared her throat, glanced at the shoes gathered by the door, glanced at Tess, and walked up the stairs.

"It's nice to meet you," Michael said, holding the door open for Neal, who was now on the porch. Tess paused at the foot of the stairs, waiting to do damage control if necessary. "I'm Michael. I've heard a lot about you, Neal," he said, patting Neal on the back. Neal smiled and nodded.

"Thank you," he said.

"You have been cooking," Lyla said, inspecting each of the dishes that Tess had set about the kitchen and in the oven. "I'll need you to clear out the oven to warm up the turkey and stuffing," she said.

"I'm glad that someone here cooks turkey," Michael said.

"Well, that's one of the Thanksgiving rituals that most normal people follow," Lyla said.

Seated around the dining room table that Tess had taken much care to set and decorate, using the winter-white china she had taken from her mother's house – it was her way of including her mother on this day – and red cloth napkins and candles, Tess watched and waited for Lyla to eat a piece of the turkey that Michael had carved and placed on her plate. She ate all of Tess's food: her spinach salad, tofu casserole, her sweet potato pudding, Michael's spinach pie, and still not a peck at the turkey.

"You haven't touched your turkey," Tess said.

Michael, Lyla and Neal, who had been caught up in a debate over court cases that they had all seen on court television in the past week – was that what Neal did at his mother's house? Watch court TV? – all turned to Tess.

"You went to all the trouble of making a turkey and you haven't touched it," Tess said.

"Maybe she's saving the best for last," Michael said, putting a piece of turkey in mouth.

"I don't care for turkey," Lyla said and continued her conversation with Michael and Neal.

"How about the spinach pie?" Michael said. "I made it."

"It was my favorite dish," Lyla said.

Tess tried to make eye contact with Michael, but his eyes didn't budge from Lyla's. Since they had sat down, he seemed to be caught up in her. She was giggling from Michael's story about whatever the heck he was telling them about law school – law school, what was that 30 years ago? – and Tess tried to remember if in all their walks, Lyla had ever giggled from something she said.

"Tess, you never told me how charming Mrs. Clay was," Michael said.

Tess smiled. "Surely I did, Michael. Must be your selective memory setting in," she said. Michael turned to her and gave her a cutting look, as in behave and play along.

"Neal, Tess has told me that you've turned into quite the runner. We should go out running together sometime," Michael said.

"Since when do you run, Michael?" Tess said.

"Just last week I did," Michael said. "I think you two even saw me when you were outside moon gazing."

"In all the time I've known you, I never remember you being much of a runner," Tess said.

"Well, that's because my boss is a work-hound who doesn't leave me much time for leisure," Michael said, to which Lyla gave Tess a sharp, accusing look.

"I'm not much of a runner, myself," Neal said. "But you're welcome to join me whenever you'd like."

Tess stood up to clear the table. "I'll pack the turkey up for you, Lyla. That way you can take it to the nursing home."

Tess picked up the turkey plate and made her way into the kitchen.

Neal joined her in the kitchen a few moments later, bringing in some of the dishes, moving next to Tess as she rinsed dishes and pans in the sink.

"Your food was delicious," he said.

"Thank you, Neal," Tess said. "Please, go back and sit down, enjoy yourself. I'll take care of cleaning up."

Neal stood close to her, their bodies practically touching. She felt Neal watching her and looked up at him, their eyes meeting.

"Your mother seems to like Michael," she said.

"He's very nice," Neal said, and Tess stifled a laugh so that it sounded like a sigh. Neal and his mother liked Michael. Why wouldn't they? He was fun, charming. She had married him. With all her yoga and all of her trying to stay calm and focused, Tess found it amusing that she could still revert to an angry woman ready to lash out. Standing next to Neal, she felt herself ease up, her shoulders drop, so that she felt lighter. There was something to him, to his aura, that pacified her; she simply enjoyed being next to him. What she wanted to say to Neal then and there was *what am I going to do without you*, and then she remembered that before she met him, she had always done without him.

"Tess," he said, his eyes focused on hers now.

He took her face in his hands, his fingers smoothing her cheeks, tracing her cheekbones until all of her was overcome with a tenderness and then his lips were on hers, warm and plush, so unlike those first few kisses way back when his lips had felt to her like a corpse. He moved from her lips to the crevice behind her ear and then onto her neck and then he was pulling her close to him and she clung to him as if they were in the middle of a slow dance that she didn't want to end. She brought her face back to his and her lips found his, planting small kisses on him, slowly, and then she was grasping his bottom lip in between her own before they were locked in a passionate kiss. Tess felt herself letting go, becoming more involved in him, as he clutched her tighter. Tears that she didn't know had been building in her began to flow down her face and

667

feeling them with his fingertips, Neal eased away from the kiss, holding her close, his hands smoothing her shoulders and then rubbing her back.

She pulled away to look at him, to concrete this moment, as she understood that this exchange would serve as one of the reference points in her life the way certain memories did. She rested her head on his shoulder and he hugged her to him.

It was Michael and Lyla's laughter from the dining room that made them ease away from one another abruptly and then Tess was facing the sink and Neal stood beside her, picking up the dishtowel. At 55-years old, she was afraid of being caught kissing a grown man by his mother and her ex-husband, who were in the next room in her home. Sometimes life was stranger than fiction. She began to rinse off one of the plates and handed it over to Neal, who dried it and then placed it on the counter. Tess imagined that from an outsider's perspective, they looked like any other middle-aged couple. Her old feelings of domestic dread crept up on her, the reminiscence of the walls of her house closing in on her at the prospect of becoming a housewife and yet now, it seemed a calming thought, a peaceful life. From the corner of her eye, she saw Neal smiling and she smiled back. She moved on to the pots and pans.

What did anyone know about anyone else? It was so hard to know one's self – so hard for Tess to know Tess. At points in her life, she had believed that time and proximity were the ingredients of getting to know another person, but now she thought otherwise. She had been with herself for all these years and still didn't know all her selves, so how could time and proximity help her to know anyone else? People just got used to one another. She no longer believed that getting to know another person had anything to do with the ability to listen to another person, which she had always believed was crucial. After a while, what did people really say to one another – what was there to be said? She was sure that there had been more that she had kept inside over the years than she had shared. She had not yet even admitted everything she felt and thought to herself. The depressions, the joys, the sorrow, the excitement – it all passed through in waves so that what dominated one day didn't exist the next. No, talking wasn't the way to know another person. Perhaps getting to know another person was just an illusion. Perhaps one only got to know another if they were sharing a journey, getting off and on at the same stops.

Michael popped his head into the kitchen. "Dessert?" he said.

Tess pointed to the pies and Neal's cookies that she

had gathered on the kitchen table.

"Right there," she said.

"There are still lots of dishes on the table," he said.

"Well, here's a thought: you can stack them all up and bring them here to me, where I'll wash them. Then the table will be clear for you to serve the desserts to Mrs. Clay."

"You won't be joining us?" Michael said.

"You and Mrs. Clay sit and enjoy yourselves. I'm busy with the dishes for now."

Michael lingered. He cleared his throat, but neither Tess nor Neal turned around from their task. As capable as he was in some respects, there was a helplessness to Michael that irritated Tess. He had moved his cleaning lady from two visits a week to three in the past month, which made Tess pause to wonder what there was to clean three days a week for a man living on his own. When he had lived with her, he'd been relatively neat or maybe it was that she was a compulsive cleaner.

"Go on and bring me the dishes," Tess said, and in that instant Lyla walked into the kitchen with stacks of dishes and placed them on the kitchen table.

"That was Michael's job," Tess said. "He was just going to clear the table."

"Then the least I could do was to help him," Lyla said, to which he nodded his head and said, "Thank you."

Tess wiped her hands on a dishtowel, steadied the cakes on her arms, grabbed the cookies, and brought them into the dining room. "Come and get the desserts," she said.

When she returned to the kitchen, Michael and Lyla were still standing by the kitchen table chatting and laughing. Tess stacked up some cake plates and made another trip to the dining room to put them down before she was back at the sink with Neal, cleaning the dishes.

"Can you put up some tea?" Michael said, still in the kitchen with Lyla.

"My pleasure, Michael," Tess said. She caught Michael's eyes and shook her head lightly at him.

"What? Is it too much to ask for tea with my dessert?" he asked, Lyla already in the next room.

"Not at all, Michael dear," Tess said. "It's my pleasure to serve you."

Hours after Michael, Lyla, and Neal had left, Tess lay in her bed and stared up at the ceiling. She felt unstable and yet calm. She was relieved to have peace and quiet. She had believed she had grown over the past few months, but now she felt otherwise. She was smaller, weaker than she had believed. She was still reacting to others, still struggling to keep her peace when confronted with other people's stuff. Her mother had been much more advanced than Tess had ever realized. Her ability not to waver, to love regardless of what she faced. To show Tess patience and kindness even when Tess opposed her mother's ideas and beliefs with a vengeance. She had never lost her cool on Tess. With all her tantrums and all her teenage fear and hatred, her mother had not wavered in her devotion and love for Tess. And yet, these were all Tess's perceptions. What did she know about her mother's feelings, the thoughts that went through her brain? That was the distance between people – she could only assume from outward appearances and what another person told her, but she didn't really know what anyone else thought or felt. All she could know was what Tess thought and felt, and many times Tess wasn't even accessible to herself.

Was that the doorbell? Tess sat up in bed. It rang again, and then she was making her way to look out to see who was there before she opened the door.

"Neal," Tess said. "Are you okay?"

He nodded. "Did I wake you?"

"I was resting but awake."

"I hope it's okay that I came to see you," he said.

"Of course. Come in," she said, and they made their way up the stairs into the kitchen. "Can I get you anything?" she said.

"No," he said, standing beside the table. Tess was unsure if she should sit down or if this was going to be a short visit. He was in sweats and his black Nike windbreaker, and for a moment, she wondered if he had been out running. His hair was a bit disheveled. His face and hands were bright pink with cold.

"Can I give you something warm?" she asked, and he waved his hand no.

"My mother likes you," Neal said.

"Sometimes," Tess said.

"I like you," Neal said.

Tess looked down at her bare feet. She nodded.

Neal moved closer to her and studied her face. She wiped the crook of her lips. Neal took her hand in his and held it.

"You look beautiful," he said. He leaned down to kiss her and his winter cold lips against her warm lips excited her. One kiss led to two and then Tess felt her instincts take over and she was kissing him as if there was nothing else in her life but this moment, this man. He led her to the bedroom, where she pulled him onto the bed and held him close to her and then he was taking off his windbreaker and she was taking off his shirt and he was kissing the nape of her neck, her shoulders and she felt herself melting into his passion so that it became her passion and she was hungry for him – for his body, his love, for his warmth.

"I miss you," he whispered in her ear, kissing her lobe gently and making his way down her body with faint kisses, before he made his way back up to her lips.

"I haven't gone anywhere," she said.

"I care about you, Tess Rose," he said, his hands tracing her figure before he began to move under her clothing and feel her flesh. She moaned softly.

"I care about you, Neal," she said as the back of his palm smoothed her cheek and made its way down her neck before he lifted her clothes off her. He pulled away for a moment, taking her naked body in and then leaned up and over to shut off the light on her night table, darkness enveloping the room as he pulled her onto him.

In Your Own Garden

What I Remember When I Remember: Before the Monastery

    If my father were a season, he would be late fall, days before winter: crisp, cold, more dark than light. He was in many ways a mystery man to me. I had always wanted to find a way into him, to know his heart, his mind, but as a child, then an adolescent, in my awkwardness, I didn't know how to get closer to him. He lived in his world and there I was in mine, and it seemed like our worlds would never collide, and in his lifetime, they never did. When I was about eight or nine, I used to watch him from my bedroom window in his garden out back, on his knees, pulling weeds and pressing the soil so softly with his fingertips in the spots he had planted seeds, making certain that the soil was well packed and moist, I suppose. He had never touched me with that gentleness.

    Sometimes I think he was more afraid of me than I was of him. Each time he was in my direct proximity, I'd panic, worrying about what questions he might ask me and if I would have the right answers for him, and if I would bore him so that he would want to get away from me as quickly as possible. He never seemed to be much of a father man – he was quiet, to himself, and spent hours of his downtime reading and organizing. He was always organizing something – the tool shed, the knick-knacks in the garage, the bathroom cabinets. Perhaps it was his way of controlling things. From an early age, I intuited that I would never be a father; or perhaps it was that I never wanted to be like him.

    When my father knew I was leaving for the monastery, there was a sense of disbelief in his eyes when he spoke to me, and later I understood that look, both stern and inquisitive, to be more of a sense of wonder. He never asked me why I was going away; rather, he focused on the minutia of my decision – did I have my plane tickets and the phone numbers for the monastery in a safe place? Did I pack the right clothes for the brisk Canadian winters? In the days right before I departed for my life at the monastery, he became more restless, moving around the house as if he always had someplace. He started one project and abandoned it for the next, so that my mother cleaned up after whatever he had started. It was then that I began to question if he had ever wanted to be a man of God – I'm not sure what elicited those thoughts but something in my soul brought it into focus, more of an intuition than anything else. Perhaps I was following a route that he had dreamed of. It wasn't completely ungrounded: he went to church a few times a week, read the Bible in the early mornings, worked hard at his hardware stores and lived simply, preferring his time in his garden to playing golf or tennis like folks in the neighborhood did, or watching sports games on television.

The story I composed in my mind went something like this: perhaps my father had wanted to be a man of God but couldn't commit, or his family wouldn't accept it or perhaps as a young man, he had not received a sign from God beckoning him and then there was my mother who he had known since grade school and liked enough and then when everyone else was getting married, he succumbed to the pressure of fitting in and then she was pregnant and then I came along and a life time of wanting and waiting for a signal from God was suddenly thrown off course due to responsibilities that popped up along the way. A wife and child to take care of, a mortgage. The bookends of his life confining him. I could have asked my father if he had lived the life he dreamt of. I could have learned about him while he was still alive, but I never asked.

When there was frost and freeze in his garden during the winter months, he sat a few feet away from it in a lawn chair in the early mornings, steam rising from his mug of hot water and lemon, which he always drank, watching the garden for I don't know what. Perhaps he was looking for life, movement. Warm in my bedroom, still in pajamas, I watched him out my window, positioning myself carefully so that if I sensed him looking up, I could tuck myself away from his line of vision. He was so close by and yet we kept our distances from one another. It's odd how people living in such a close proximity do that – we study one another from afar when it's so easy to move closer. I wonder now if he was praying or meditating with his eyes on the garden, as I often did in my garden in Canada. I had wanted so badly to sit beside him while he watched his garden, but I never went downstairs. I never made the attempt, never even explored his garden when he wasn't home for fear he'd know. In my mind, it was his sacred spot and as much as I wanted to move into his life, I respected what I believed were his boundaries. And yet, where did respecting his boundaries get me? Farther away, I suppose.

The thing about life is that you can't repeat the past – life flows, it goes on. My father was here and now he's gone. I had the chance to know him, and now I don't. I often wished at the monastery that I could freeze time, make the world stop if only long enough for me to think a thought through before the church bells rang and beckoned me away. I wished there was a lever to pull to stop the earth, to allow me to be in a time and place for just a bit longer, to linger. But there's not. In the last few weeks, I have let go of trying to control the unknown or maybe I've accepted that it's bigger than me. Life and the what-will-be's are bigger than all of us. I'm beginning to understand that it's not the unknown that I fear – in fact, none of us can fear the unknown as it's unknown to us. Rather, it's my fear of losing what I know that paralyzes me, keeps me holding on to what is, from moving into the future. Each phase I arrive at grows comfortable and then I don't want to move on, as I am afraid of losing the comfort and having to start again. I am afraid of the prospect, I suppose, of being uncomfortable. And yet, life must flow. Life does flow. I must flow to keep growing, keep experiencing, keep living.

I wanted to tell you everything. I wanted you to know me from the inside out. Only I no longer believe that I – any of us – can tell another person all there is to tell. We are too complex to simplify our lives into words, which are not the things or the feelings, but only symbols – representations of what is. And I believe that our stories have borders. There are points where we enter each other's lives and points where we leave one another's lives so that there is no one, all-encompassing story, but an array of stories – a host of starts and stops in a life. I no longer believe that we live sequentially but rather that our lives are a maze that we spend our lifetimes making our way through, each twist and turn a part of our path. If I could tell you only one story, it would be the story of how I have lived on the opposite side of a glass wall and how I always wanted to shatter the glass, to find a way in, a way through. To my father. My mother. God. You. I've put myself on the opposite side of the glass and I haven't let anyone in. I don't know anymore. Maybe we are meant to break through the walls of others and let them break through our walls, or maybe the beauty of each of us is that we exist independently of one another and it's not our job or our joy to know another but to know ourselves, to break through our own barriers, shatter our own glass and know our hearts and our minds and our souls.

Sometimes I wish that I could live two lives. One here with you and one on my own, exploring all that I was meant to explore. You may see that as selfish. There are choices in life. I'm aware of that. And yet I want it all – I want to experience all the lives worth living. People make promises in life that they sometimes can't live up to. I'm guilty of making promises that I didn't live up to, although I don't feel guilty so much as honest. What if it wasn't that I was walking away from something by leaving the monastery but walking towards something? Every ending is the beginning of something new. *That was inscribed in the first Bible I ever received from my mother, which she had received from her mother.*

CHAPTER 56: THE BOOKENDS OF A LIFE

It was in the silence of early December that Tess started to feel a shift from the inside out – a restlessness that propelled her forward. Sitting out in her backyard on an early Saturday morning with a down comforter draped around her, watching the tree limbs shake and shiver in the pre-January coldness, she felt as if she had been far away and was returning. How odd it was to be yourself, she thought, and yet not know all the things that you were made up of.

Buddhi pounced onto the tree overshadowing the deck and glared at Tess. His orange, tiger-striped fur was mangy again and he had scratches all around his eyes. He stared at Tess as if he were challenging her.

"Hello Buddhi in the tree," Tess murmured. The sound of her voice, cracking in the cool air, startled her. And then Buddhi vanished.

Yesterday, while showing a house to a young, newly married couple, a couple full of hope and possibility for their life together, she had felt very definitely, that she was done. That she could only go on doing this for so long. She had showed them each room of the house, helped them to envision what they could do with each room – colors, lighting – and then locking the house up once they told her they wanted it, they were going to take it, driving them back to their car, she had felt as if she were an actor shooting the last scene of what had taken her years to perfect. There was no big dramatic moment, no lightning bolt. Just a very concrete knowledge: she was done. A few more appointments to finish out the year, and then this phase was over. Curtain closed. People moved on. That was how it worked. A time came when moving on was the only choice, the right choice. *Every ending is the beginning of something new.*

The snow fell all around her, lightly, softly, like whispers, but vanished as it made its way to the ground. To be of the earth, to know that there was a ground that you were searching for, a place to land, but not to hit the earth and leave a mark. The snow had a spiritual aspect to it. The wet flakes kissed her nose, her hands, and she had a sudden urge to be naked in the snow, to know that freedom. But as with all urges, her mind intruded: it was cold, she wasn't much of an exhibitionist, her neighbors were close by. She could hear the cleaning lady doing something or other in her backyard – it sounded like sweeping. Tess craved exactly what she had: silence, the wind blowing, right now.

This much Tess knew: she was done with arbitrary days. She sought a destiny. She was done with reaching a point each day only to misplace the thought until so much later in the day. She was tired of false starts and the way she was always losing and finding herself. Always changing and always the same. Buddhi showed himself again, and suddenly Tess wanted him beside her. "Here, Buddhi," she said. Their eyes locked and then Buddhi darted away, and Tess felt an old familiar hollowness drift through her. She couldn't pinpoint if she were hungry or tired or about to cry. Her mind began to race, searching for a to-do list, for something, anything to latch on to and then she remembered to breathe, to follow her inhales and her exhales and the angst began to dissipate, flowing out of her so that she sunk back onto her chair, tension releasing its grip on her body. People, places, events, came and went. The flow of life. The comings and goings. It was what had troubled her about her career, without her ever having been able to articulate it until this moment: each connection she had formed as a realtor led to a split. Getting to know the couples and helping them to find their dream homes, drawing up the contracts, consulting with them on mortgages. And yet once all the paperwork was signed and she handed the new homeowner the key, the door she had opened for them, with them, closed on her.

It had never been hard for her to say goodbye to people close to her – she had said goodbye to her mother as a teenager and left Woodstock. She had said goodbye to one husband after another and had gotten on just fine without them, so that in the months following her estrangements, her lives with them seemed like someone else's story. She had watched Prakash go. She had watched her mother go. And yet, they were all eternally intertwined, part of one another's stories.

Her mother had often told her about the dances of life, how people had their dances to do with one another and when the dance ended, it was time to move on to the next person, the next song. That had been how her mother explained to a young, pre-adolescent Tess about her father's departure from Woodstock and Tess's life: their dance was over. For her mother, there was no apparent sense of sorrow attached to it, no sentimentality. Her mother had told her that people moved into ones lives and out of it with a sense of purpose, grace, kindness. Her mother had told her that a true companion left everything intact when the dance ended and if they didn't, then steps had been missed along the way. Endings, she had told Tess, were inevitable and necessary for the next dance to begin. It wasn't until Tess was away at college and the other girls' fathers sent them money and flowers and other niceties, that Tess had questioned the dance image regarding her father, for if her father and mother's dance had ended, what did that have to do with the dance between Tess and her father? Perhaps their music had not yet started; perhaps their dance was yet to come. Like many dreams, though, Tess believed that she had tucked that one away somewhere between her own college love affairs, exams, and graduation.

What if, though, it wasn't that people were the dancers but rather that they were being danced? What if it wasn't up to a person to start or stop a dance but if people were puppets in the dance of life? The more she lived life, the more she was beginning to believe that she, people, were not in control so much as they were part of the grand scheme of life.

The wind rushed past her, and she nestled under the blanket, shaking her legs out on the lounge chair. She couldn't remember a time when she had ever sat out in her backyard in the cold and yet it was stimulating – the cold gnawing at her while she camped out under the blanket, the warmth of her house a few feet away. When she was a young girl, she had loved to sit out on the porch swing in Woodstock, rocking herself, the roof of the house a shield as snowflakes trickled to the earth. Her neighbors had walked by and waved to her and once her mother had come out on the porch looking for her and finding her there, she had smiled and told Tess to keep warm, motioning to her to wrap herself in the throw blanket set there for that purpose. Her mother had let her be.

Tess understood now what an accomplishment that was for a mother. How if she would have seen Prakash out in the cold, she would have told him he had to come inside. Her liberal up bringing had been a gift – a chance for her to develop and become whoever she was to become, and she had been too blind to see that all those years. She had treated it as a curse. If only she could have redone it, relived it all, she believed that she would have been different, that her life would have been different, although she didn't know exactly how.

The comings and goings of life. So many comings and goings. She believed there was a reason for all the movement and would have liked to believe it had to do with growth, only she wasn't sure. There was no way to measure growth in a lifetime – people grew older, taller, shorter, fatter, thinner, but there was no gauge to measure internal growth. She wanted to believe that she had grown – yoga had helped her with her life in the past few months – only who was to say if she grew internally or was only standing still, substituting one thing in her life for other things? It was hard to be honest with oneself and harder yet to surround oneself with people who could be objective enough to tell her the truth about herself that she was sometimes blind to.

After making love to Neal on Thanksgiving night, she had become needier of him again. She had warned herself that she would get hurt. That she needed to let him be free and yet she couldn't help wanting him. Non-attachment. *The Four Noble Truths* – suffering due to attachments was the enemy.

Perhaps he would stay. The part of her brain that believed that people were unpredictable told her that. The part of her brain that believed people were predictable told her that he would leave. The thought of him leaving made her feel hollow, alone. She didn't necessarily understand that as she had always been alone, while she was in relationships and out of them, and it wasn't exactly as if she and Neal were a couple in any normal sense of the word. It was just that his presence made her feel protected. Loved in a way that had nothing to do with passionate love or maybe nothing to do with the concept of love that her mind had created. She would have never thought of herself as sentimental, but the thought of Neal's leaving made her cling to the times they had shared – exploring Mill Basin, their first kiss in Central Park, the cruise to nowhere, their yoga practice under the stars.

The church bells were ringing. Outside, people were going about their business; inside Tess felt cold and tired. It was so hard to separate what was in her mind from what was real. And how did a person know what was real, what was an illusion? Why couldn't the world just stop for a few moments so that Tess could find her way and either choose to keep going or take a different route? Tess wondered if from here forward, the church bells would always remind her of Neal or if after some period, she would stop hearing them because she'd be too busy living in the next here and now of her life. A wave of emotion – sorrow, then stillness and then a slight perceptible joy – rushed through her, and she felt a truth coming to her, but she lost it, like how you lose a star when you blink. She wanted so badly to know what was ahead of her but wondered if she were given the chance to know if she would instead choose not to know. Wasn't that how it always was? We wanted what we couldn't have but when by some chance of fate, it was granted to us, we ran from it.

CHAPTER 57: CROSS ENCOUNTERS

"Finally. I've been waiting for you for over fifteen minutes," Lyla said. She was walking in small circles at the corner of Dakota Place and 66th street, directly across the street from Tess's house, well positioned so that she was blocked out of view by a tree.

"It's cold out here," she added.

"I didn't know that we were meeting," Tess said, the wind brisk and harsh on her face, her eyes tearing. She adjusted her scarf so that all the nooks of her neck were covered. Snow loomed from the white-grey sky.

"You could have rung my doorbell and come inside if you were out here," Tess said.

"You've been avoiding me," Lyla said.

"That's not the case," Tess said.

"You've been taking different routes on your walks the last few weeks. Don't think I didn't see you strolling around the neighborhood," Lyla said.

"If you saw me and wanted to walk with me, you could have very easily have joined me or called me to meet you or whatever it is that most people would have done so that we could meet up," Tess said.

"I'm not most people," Lyla said, her feet moving quickly, her arms flapping at her sides as if she were gaining momentum to take off in her black bubble coat and her red ski gloves with matching red ski cap pulled down over her ears.

"When I didn't hear from you, I didn't think that you were interested in walking with me," Tess said. "But I wasn't intentionally taking different routes – I was just living my life."

"You sound like a fifth grader. *I didn't think you were interested in walking with me*," Lyla said, mimicking Tess so that Tess didn't know if she should laugh or wring her neck.

"I came out for a walk. The cold is punishment enough, Lyla. I thought that we were past this. I thought," Tess said, stumbling over her words, "that we had become friends."

"When someone purposely avoids another for weeks, friendship isn't the word that comes to mind," Lyla said.

Tess was about to respond, defend herself again, but Lyla had paused in front of a three-story mansion full of Christmas decorations – flashing white lights on each of the towering evergreen trees and a sleigh on the roof, complete with reindeer and Santa sitting at the reins, and a glass enclosed garage with the title *Santa's Workshop* above it filled with mechanical elves that bent down, and hustled left and right, passing wrapped gift boxes to one another. At some point Tess had stopped, too, and stood a few feet away from Lyla as she took it all in.

"It's hard to imagine Christmas is only a few weeks away," Lyla said. "Time goes so quickly."

They were moving again. Each house outdid the others with its gaudy Christmas decorations. There were ice skating snowmen on faux ice rinks and waving Santas who bowed to passers-by and enough lights draped around some homes to illuminate the Atlantic Ocean at night.

"If you were a Catholic, you would understand what you've done. I remind myself of that sometimes. You can't know as you're not a Catholic."

"If you don't mind, I will be excusing myself from this walk," Tess said. "I came out for some fresh air, not for a lecture on all of my shortcomings according to Lyla Clay."

"You will continue this walk with me," Lyla said.

It was more of a statement than a threat. Tess quickened her pace to build up some heat. She could turn around, leave, head back home, but something in her wanted to hear what Lyla had to say. Her hands and feet tingled so that she had to keep making a fist and releasing it quickly to keep her fingers from freezing up. It was hard to imagine that a few months back everything in Tess's life had been different – she had worked hard, lived a quiet life. She never had to deal with the biting cold gnawing at her on a morning walk, because there hadn't been any morning walks, not to mention older women who berated her.

"You should never have divorced Michael," Lyla said. They were in a groove now, their breath creating tiny clouds before them. "He's fun, easy to be around, interested, interesting."

"I would be thrilled to set you up with him," Tess said.

"He's of the same world you are," Lyla said. "Like belongs with like."

"I'm glad that you have it all figured out but let me help you with a key fact: I didn't love him like that," Tess said.

"Love," Lyla said. "Love has nothing to do with anything. No one even knows what love is. We love the Lord; we don't love other people. We enjoy them, we talk to them. Are you going to tell me that you love Neal?" Lyla said.

"Why don't you ask Neal how he feels? Why are you always making this about me?" Tess asked.

"Neal is as naïve as a young boy. Before you, he was a virgin. He doesn't know how he feels; he's confused right now," Lyla said.

"I enjoy when you accuse me of corrupting Neal," Tess said. "Let me remind you that he left the monastery of his own free will. He didn't even know I existed back then. He debated it for months and then he left and meeting me was a consequence, not the catalyst," Tess said.

"If it weren't for you –" Lyla said.

Tess stopped and faced Lyla.

"What? If it weren't for me, what? Neal would be back at the monastery? Neal is free to do as he pleases," Tess said. "Let go of that nonsense that you've planted in your brain of me keeping him prisoner already. I'm living my life. I don't control Neal. You do that," Tess said.

They walked on in silence, crossing 66th street, which was free of traffic in the early morning hour, and made their way down Basset walk. Tess's stride hastened, as she was sheltered from the wind by the trees on both sides of her. The walk was narrow enough that they had to walk single file and when Tess looked back, Lyla was a few feet behind her. Tess couldn't tell if she was keeping her distance on purpose or if she couldn't keep up.

"You're a mother, too," Lyla said when they were in stride again. "You threw that comment at me once, if you remember. So, while you pretend not to understand my concern, I believe that you do see my point of view and would do the same."

"My son is a grown man," Tess said. "He makes his own decisions and I accept them."

"I don't believe that," Lyla said. "While your son is thousands of miles away, it's easy to preach that grown-man stuff. But if he were here in Mill Basin with you destroying his life, I'd like to see you mind your business."

She was too cold to argue with Lyla any longer. Who was to say what one would do in a situation until one was in it?

"Do you miss your husband?" Tess asked.

Lyla was quiet for a few moments so that Tess wasn't sure if she'd heard her.

"Do you miss –"

"We lived our separate lives," Lyla said, her voice barely a whisper so that Tess had to slow her pace and move closer to Lyla.

"Did he want Neal to go to the monastery?" Tess said.

"We didn't talk about it much," Lyla said. "It happened quickly – Neal started to feel that he should go and then he visited with the monks for a bit and then he left. It wasn't something that we had planned for."

"Did you want Neal to go?" Tess said.

Lyla walked on in silence again. They crossed Mayfair Drive North and moved towards 56th Drive. Tess couldn't tell if her body had acclimated to the cold now or if the temperature had warmed up a bit. The morning dew was lifting, and the sun began to peep through the clouds. In the distance, she saw a runner making his way down 66th Street from 56th Drive. Lyla must have seen the runner too as she came to a halt, Tess stopping beside her.

"I suppose that I was relieved when he decided that the monastery was for him," Lyla said.

They were moving again, in the direction that the runner had just left. Lyla was walking slower now, and Tess supposed it was to give the runner, who they both assumed to be Neal, time to get ahead. They had yet to encounter him while they were out together. Tess dabbed at her sniffling nose with a tissue she pulled from her coat pocket. Her nostrils were raw to the touch.

"Relieved?" Tess asked.

"That my job of raising him was over," Lyla said.

"He was 22. Your job *was* over," Tess said.

"Not with Neal. He was very young for his age, very innocent. He had never had a girlfriend you know," Lyla said. "He had never gone out with his friends as other boys his age did. He was content to read, go to church. He kept to himself."

"Surely if Neal hadn't joined the monastery, he would have found his way," Tess said.

"I think that he always knew he was destined for a religious life although he may not have understood that until he grew older," Lyla said.

"He seems to have adapted well to everything now," Tess said.

"He's had you in his life. A worldly, wealthy woman to teach him."

"I love how you think you can sum me up in a few words without really knowing me. And don't give me your *I know you well*, junk. You don't. My relationship with Neal is something that happened – it's no one's fault," Tess said.

"You let it happen even once you knew he was a monk," Lyla said. "That was your choice."

"No one chooses who they like. You just like certain people."

"You could have stayed away," Lyla said.

"Did you ever ask him what he wanted? Why he came back home?"

In the distance, Tess saw a man running at the intersection of

Mayfair Drive and Mill Avenue.

"He came back home because he needed time to think. Which is what he would have done if you didn't come along."

"If it were up to you, you would have shipped him back to the monastery already," Tess said.

"That's where he belongs," Lyla said.

"Because you say so? Did you confer with God, and did He tell you 'I want Neal back?' Neal belongs wherever he chooses to be. It's his life. His decisions. You can't send him away because it's easier for you to be alone. It has nothing to do with you, Lyla."

Tess started walking again and after a few moments Lyla was beside her.

"I don't hate you, Tess," Lyla said.

"I can't keep up with your mood swings, Lyla. We're enemies, we're friends. I don't know what you want from me," Tess said.

"You're so free and so successful," Lyla said.

"Lyla, my life has been full of ups and downs and lots of my own induced messes. Just like anyone else's life. You can't judge another person's life on what you perceive it to be," Tess said.

"You have all these men chasing you and this business to run," Lyla said.

"None of that defines me."

"If Neal were to spend his life with a woman, I would want it be you. But Neal doesn't belong with a woman," Lyla said.

Tess swallowed hard and deep. This was a compliment. Lyla was paying her a compliment.

"It's not for us to say what Neal should or shouldn't do," Tess said. "When will you understand that?"

"Neal chose to be a man of God. One cannot go back on that," Lyla said.

"But he did, Lyla. He did go back on it. And you know what? God is okay with it because Neal hasn't been struck by lightning and the heavens haven't parted and sent down a rope ladder to take him back," Tess said.

"Oh, what do you know, Tess? What do you know about God and right and wrong? You think you have all the answers, but you don't."

"I don't," Tess said.

The evergreens on Barlow drive were full of icicles, so that the weighted down branches looked tired, heavy. They were a few feet away from Lyla's home. The houses surrounding 56 Barlow Drive were decked with Christmas lights and the house next door to Lyla's had a menorah in the window. Lyla's home had no decorations. Tess paused in front of 56. Lyla took her house keys out from her pocket and dawdled by the edge of the driveway with Tess.

"So much happens in a lifetime," Lyla said. Her eyes were on

Tess now. "Dreams get lost, and you just become whatever you are even if it's not what you planned on being. Your son goes to a monastery, your husband dies, and then your son returns."

"Nothing gets lost. People leave us, but they don't fully go away. Dreams get misplaced and it's up to you to uncover them. And sometimes what were once your dreams, no longer are. So, you assess what you want in life and create new dreams."

"Is that what you tell yourself?" Lyla asked.

"That's what I know," Tess said.

Their eyes lingered on one another's for a few moments before Lyla nodded with an uncharacteristically faraway look in her eyes and made her way up to her porch. Moments later, Lyla made her way inside.

CHAPTER 58: WHATEVER WILL BE, WILL BE

Tess had driven around for thirty minutes – up and around 48th street, 49th street, down Fifth Avenue and up the Avenue of the Americas, taxi cabs cutting her off, city busses veering into her lane, before she had pulled into a parking garage. She was already running a few minutes late to meet Dale and was tired of circling the same blocks with no luck. New York City during Christmas time was not a place to deal with finding a parking spot. As soon as she was out of her car, moving along the bustling city streets in her stilettos amidst men and women bundled up in coats, scarves and gloves, some of the men coatless in just their suits, she felt alive and giddy. When Dale had called her that morning to see if she couldn't convince Tess to join her in the city to go to see the Rockefeller Center Christmas tree, take an afternoon yoga class, she had shocked herself by saying yes, making a U-turn before reaching Best Realty and getting on the Belt Parkway.

"You're doing what?" Michael had said when she rang him in the office. "Taking a personal health day?" She laughed now. The endless rows of office buildings offered a shield against the snapping wind so that Tess loosened her red cashmere scarf.

She spotted the Atlas Shrugged statue across from St. Patrick's Cathedral with mobs of people surrounding it, snapping photographs.

Not yet 9:00 am and Manhattan was a tourist haven. Crossing the street, making her way through the crowds to the heart of Rockefeller Center, she glimpsed the Christmas tree – grand and glamorous with its array of colored lights – shimmying and swaying in the wind, as if it were shivering. There were skaters of all ages scattered around the rink with crowds surrounding the rink on all sides, taking it all in. Joy. That was the atmosphere around her, and she marveled at the thought that she had almost spent her day tucked away in an office, away from all this life, this energy. She made her way through the multitudes of bundled up onlookers and the carts setting up to sell roasted chestnuts and salty supersized pretzels. The aromas filtered through her, warming her and stirring her stomach with their burnt and doughy scents. There, by the third trumpeting snow angel lining the path to the Christmas tree, she spotted Dale waving to her, a pale pink pom-pom hat with ear flaps on her head.

Tess hugged her tight – she couldn't remember ever greeting someone with so much affection, so that when the thought registered with her, she felt slightly embarrassed and pulled away, but Dale kept clinging to her.

"You're here! You came," she said. "I got Tess to play hooky from work! I can't believe it."

"Thank you for reminding me that there's life outside of an office," Tess said.

"We can skate," Dale said and the moment she said it both she and Tess squinted their eyes, shook their heads. It was cold, crowded. "Or we can warm up inside and have some breakfast," Dale said.

"Let's walk a bit," Tess said. "I'd love to go see the Christmas window displays."

They made their way up Fifth Avenue, arms linked, crossing to the east side of the street and pausing by Saks Fifth Avenue's windows to glance at the already crowded Santa's Workshop displays, complete with *Jingle Bells* booming through loudspeakers. They moved further along up towards Bergdorf Goodman, where Tess marveled over the paper props of Christmas trees and cut out snowflakes. She lingered by the window decked with countless time pieces – clocks of all shapes and sizes, some antique, some modern; grandfather clocks, miniature alarm clocks; the backdrop a giant-sized calendar of all twelve months.

"If a window display could sum up my life, this would be the one," Tess said. "Years of rushing from one appointment to the next and setting my alarm clock to get up before dawn so that I had time to do whatever it is that I had to do before I rushed into the office. So much preoccupation with time."

They made their way up Fifth Avenue and entered Central Park at 59th street, moving past a row of artists selling caricatures and portraits. Dale shook her head no to the artists who approached them. They moved past the ramp onto the 6.2-mile loop, looking both ways before they crossed to the inside lane, safe from the darting cyclists and horse-drawn carriages. Runners passed them on either side, some dressed in shorts and t-shirts in the near freezing temperatures, others decked in tight fitting running pants and fleece tops. Tess smiled thinking of Neal in his track pants and sweatshirt as he ran up and down the streets of Mill Basin.

"Any status on Neal's staying or going?" Dale asked.

"No. His mother is convinced that he belongs at the monastery."

"What do you think?" Dale said.

"I'm too caught up in trying to figure out where I belong," Tess said.

"What are your choices?" Dale said.

"Lately I've been thinking about going back to Woodstock and spending some time there."

"As in you're thinking about moving?" Dale asked.

"Maybe. The house up there is beautiful and there's so much land and space. Prakash is going to join me there for a few weeks – we're meeting for New Year's Eve. I could teach yoga up there and take long walks and read and live a little bit."

"Wow," Dale said.

She pulled Dale out of the way of a cyclist who was heading toward them. Walkers passed them and Tess glanced down at her heels. Her feet were holding up. She could always buy a pair of sneakers if they hurt. In the past, she had been able to walk for miles in her heels, but ever since she had gotten involved in yoga, she was a bit more precious with her feet.

"Did I mention yet that Lyla thinks I should have never divorced Michael?"

"Since when did she fall for Michael?" Dale said.

"Since my mess of a Thanksgiving dinner," Tess said. "That was on my check list to share with you. Thanksgiving eve Lyla and Michael became best friends, and I had a night of hot, steamy sex with Neal."

"What?" Dale said, stopping to face Tess. "You are full of surprises today."

"Of course, afterwards I felt needy. Then desperate thinking that he is going to leave, and I will be all alone. Then I was desperate thinking that he might stay, and I would be stuck with him forever and what if I couldn't keep him happy?" Tess laughed. "I don't understand how after all of these years and all of this introspection I can still be so nuts."

"We're all nuts," Dale said. "You're just better at articulating your insanity."

"I'm already tired of talking about me. Tell me something new about you," Tess said.

"I'm going to move in with Kyle," Dale said. "We spent Thanksgiving weekend together and while I'm not ready to get married right now, I want to live with him, give it a try. He's going to call you this week about a brownstone he found in the East Village that he wants to buy. We're going to move in together as soon as we can and not worry about getting married or any of that just yet. One thing at a time."

Tess shook her head. "Wow to you." She hugged Dale's arm tighter and rested her head on her shoulder. "I'm thrilled for you, Dale. You've made a decision and you seem calm and happy about it."

"I am happy," Dale said. "I've decided not to over think things and just do what feels right. This feels right for me. Kyle agrees – he's open to seeing what happens and not worrying so much about the planning and the details. There are no guarantees in life, so why not just move in the direction of what feels right?" Dale said.

"No guarantees for sure," Tess said.

They came around the bend and crossed over the east 72nd street entrance to the park, dodging cyclists and runners at the intersection as they made their way up the little hill, approaching the Central Park Boat House.

There were runners congregating by the bathroom of the Boat House, moving in place in the cold, little puffs of air coming out of their mouths as they waited in line and made small talk. Tess thought of Neal, how he would enjoy running in Central Park in the morning and taking in all the sights and people. If he stayed on, she would take him there as soon as the weather warmed up. Perhaps take a stroll around the loop while he ran.

"Should we have lunch here?" Dale asked. "I haven't eaten here in ages."

Tess led the way into the Boat House. There were people scattered throughout the restaurant eating and sipping from coffee cups. The overhead heaters were on, the ceiling fans attempting to circulate the heat, but the wooden building was cool and damp. They were seated at a table by the window, overlooking the lake. It had been years since Tess had been here to eat – she recalled some business luncheons and a few engagement parties and bridal showers at various points in her life. The lake was still. In the distance Tess could make out a few ducks drifting along, the canoes piled up by the shore, locked together. She remembered the day, month's back, when she and Neal sat by that shore and watched couples and families paddle by on the lake. There were still so many possibilities back then, before she knew he was a monk, before the future had come upon them. She snuggled in her coat and tightened her scarf around her neck to keep out the slight breeze that seeped in through the windowpane.

"Sometimes I wonder if I've done more damage to Neal than good," Tess said.

"You've allowed him to be himself, to lose some of the structures that his mother and the Church most likely built around him," Dale said.

Tess shrugged. "Either that or I've perpetuated his confusion."

"You've helped me to find my way. Just by being in my life and not thinking I'm crazy or telling me what to do. You've made me feel more normal," Dale said.

"Well, that's good news. I don't feel too normal myself and I'm sure that Lyla would tell you I'm nuts, as would Michael. When I told him that I might move up to Woodstock and leave him in charge at my company, you should have heard him. He thinks I've lost it once and for all," Tess said.

"He probably feels left out that you didn't ask him to join you," Dale said.

The waiter took their order: French toast with fresh berries and a bagel with cream cheese for Dale and an egg white omelet with spinach for Tess, fruit instead of hash browns and hold the toast, to which Dale told him to please bring the toast with lots of strawberry jam on the side.

"I'm a growing girl with a carbohydrate fetish," Dale said when the waiter left.

"Power to you," Tess said.

"Have you told Neal about your trip to Woodstock?"

"It hasn't come up yet," Tess said.

"It hasn't come up yet or you haven't brought it up?" Dale asked.

"I don't want him to think it's an invitation or that I'm giving him an ultimatum or any of that type of stuff," Tess said.

"Or maybe you don't want him to join you," Dale said.

"Can you imagine how his mother would react if he wanted to come?" Tess said. "She'd probably bring me up on kidnapping charges."

"I was going to say I'm no therapist so don't listen to me, but the problem is that I am a therapist," Dale said, and they both smiled.

The waiter placed Tess's tea and Dale's orange juice on the table along with a basket of miniature blueberry muffins, which Dale started picking at.

"It seems like what you're saying is that you want to do what's right for Tess regardless of Neal. And right now, going to spend some time in Woodstock with your son is right for you. Or," Dale continued, finishing a sip, "you want to clear out of the way so that it's easier for Neal to leave."

"Tell me about Kyle," Tess said. "Did he take you to see the brownstone? Should we go see it together today?"

"You can't dodge me," Dale said. "Or you can dodge my questions, but you can't dodge yourself and your questions, Tess. I believe that whatever you do is the right thing to do. Know why?"

Tess shook her head. She suddenly felt tired. Tired and older than she had ever remembered feeling.

"Because that's what you told me more than once and it's been dead on. Whatever you do is right and of course whatever you do can always be undone," Dale said. "Nothing is forever."

Tess thought about her mother passing, her son. Some things were forever. Her mother wasn't coming back to Tess in any recognizable form. Prakash would always be her son. She would always be Tess, although the players and places in her life may come and go. Thinking that made her sit up straighter. There were consequences in life. Doors opened; doors closed. It was easy to forget that or deny it when she was feeling optimistic and assured herself that nothing was forever. Dale's eyes were on her, waiting, watching. She was tired of preaching, tired of trying to make sense of herself, of anything. *Whatever will be, will be* was what came to her. It seemed silly to try to figure anything out. She imagined her mother saying that her only job for today was to live today and then tomorrow she would have to live tomorrow. She didn't know what was right for her, for Neal or Dale or Michael or

anyone. And even if she did, what did it matter? Each one of them,
herself included, still had to go through the living to get to the knowing.

It had been over two weeks since Tess had made it to the yoga
studio. She was immersed in her own practice as of late, enjoying her
time to experiment with all she had learned in the early morning hours.
The solitude had been a time of growth for her practice, although the
moment she walked into the studio she felt a sense of relief, a sense of
coming home. Now that all the teacher trainer activities were over,
although she still owed the studio over twenty hours of assisting classes
or teaching her own classes to earn her 500-hour teacher training
certificate, there was a gaiety to being there. After all the hugs and kisses
and carrying on with the mentors and some of her former teacher training
mates –" I miss you's" and "How are you's?" – she and Dale settled
down in the yoga room, their mats close to one another like old times. At
the front podium half a dozen tea candles flickered, casting shadows on
the walls, while earthy music played – a mix of flutes and light drums.
The sweet, spicy scent of nag champa incense filled the air, the aroma
circulated throughout the heated room by the white metal over-sized
ceiling fans, which rocked gently, twelve feet above. Lying with her back
on the mat, the skylight directly above her, she could make out the
chalky sky, snowflakes lingering, like miniature parachutes floating
downwards. She lifted her legs to the ceiling, her feet flexed. Supta
dandasana. Her eyes grew heavy and for a moment she debated taking a
nap, how easy it would be to shut out the world and rest in this
environment, only then the teacher, one of her mentors, was in the room,
asking everyone to come to a cross-legged position, and Tess was

following along, her legs in lotus, her hands at her heart center in Namaste, readying her mind and body for the journey ahead, her inhales and exhales balanced and calming.

When they moved out of shoulder stand, sarvangasana into fish pose, matsyasana, and the teacher eased them slowly onto their backs, one last twist to the right and then left to open up their thoracic and lumbar spines and release any pressure, everything inside of Tess let go so that she felt as if she were floating and for a moment she opened her eyes to look up at the snowflakes, still falling and then with her eyes closed she imagined herself falling with them, lightly, gently, landing right there onto her mat. In the moments before she drifted off, she felt joyful and free. It was as if she were here again, in this classroom, this sanctuary, for the first time. She felt the old familiar faith she experienced each time she lost herself in a yoga class, in life. A faith that all that was would pass, that her thoughts and feelings and the events of her life were all in flow, constantly shifting, no feeling final, no thought a reality until she was living it and even then, it would be replaced by new thoughts, new moments, new realities. It was a play, an ongoing drama that was neither good nor bad, but just was, like the sky, like the snowflakes, like her breath. Inhales followed by exhales. The flow of life. Of peace. Of freedom.

"It's really no problem for me to drop you off," Tess said. She felt lighter, as if she had left the unpleasant parts of herself behind in the yoga class.

"I'm fine. I'm going all the way uptown and you need to go

downtown," Dale said. She was hailing a cab.

When a cab stopped in front of them, they hugged, tight and hard, until the cab driver beeped.

"I'm so glad we were able to spend some time together," Dale said.

"Me too," Tess said. "I needed this – thank you. And I'm very happy for you. I'll wait to hear from Kyle about the brownstone."

"Saturday morning class?" Dale said and Tess nodded.

"Absolutely. Brunch at The Bakery afterwards. Let's invite the girls to join in."

"Love you," Dale said, and in a moment she was off.

Tess tightened her scarf around her neck and made her way across Fifth Avenue to Park, heading uptown. She thought about hailing a cab for the twenty-block haul but thought better of it as she caught one green light after another. There was something to being outside in the cold, taking in the people on the streets all bundled up in their coats like snow people, the Christmas decorations adorning store windows, the giant electrical snowflakes strung along the streetlights, connecting the blocks and avenues. The sidewalk was slick from the snow, which had stopped for the time being. The sky had grown lighter, hints of blue around the white edges and Tess spied a sliver of the sun over by the West Side Highway, lingering in the distance as if debating making an appearance. She passed stands with men selling roasted chestnuts and peanuts, warming their hands over the roasting nuts and stuffing the nuts into little paper bags. It reminded Tess of the days of Prakash's early birthdays, when she would hand out similar pouches as party favors to the little boys and girls who came to Kash's celebrations.

Time passed. People changed. The older she grew, the more relief that sentiment gave her. Tess changed. She hit one green light after another, they rhythm of her feet on the pavement mesmerizing her so that she felt as if she could keep going forever, keep passing it all by, taking in the manic energy that was New York City at Christmas time.

When she hit her first red light, she was already at 48th street. The lights of the Christmas tree glared in the distance, and she wove her way through Rockefeller Center for one last look at the tree. The skating rink was packed now – children, adults, groups, made their way around the ice, some stumbling while others glided by. Endless movement. One little girl in a pink bubble jacket moved to the center of the rink, weaving figure eights, first moving frontwards and then skating backwards. As she gained speed, she seemed to be at one with the ice, her movements so precise that they ceased to become movements and instead became a dance. When she stopped dead center, Tess felt jarred until the little girl began to spin in place, recklessly at first, her arms flailing until she tucked them to her side and grew more and more compact and erect as she twirled round and round, a torpedo spinning, so that Tess could no longer make out her features. Sometimes she had moved so quickly in her life that she'd felt like that little girl spinning, everything a blur, fast, furious and yet somehow there had been grace and ease to it all. As quickly as the girl had gained speed, she slowed, moving away from the spot she had launched from and back into the flow, cutting figure eights in the center of the rink once again. That was how life worked, Tess thought. We take off haphazardly but come in for a gentle landing. A seamless return was possible.

In a few moments Tess was standing beside the trunk of the looming Christmas tree, the boughs above her, like a Grecian crown. She had never been so close, had never realized how enormous the tree was, how small she was in comparison to it all. Your *little me* is speaking is what her mother used to say whenever Tess was obstinate and fought to get her way. "I only hear Tess when she speaks, not *little me*," her mother had said, and it had made Tess furious. She smiled thinking back to the countless times she had protested that it was Tess speaking, not *little me*. She thought back to the postcard of Chagall's "Me and My Village" that her mother had given her after introducing that concept, pointing out the shrunken people in the painting to give Tess a visual of *little me*, to remind Tess that she was just a small part of the bigger picture that was always going on at every moment, in each corner of the earth. Tess had used the postcard as a bookmark for some time. As a young girl, she had thought the painter was some follower of her mother's that had given it to her, until years later, when she had been in a museum and seen other paintings by Chagall, which made her wonder how her mother had obtained the post card and what it meant to her. So many memories tucked away that came and went, like hunger, like love, like life.

A plump middle-aged policeman standing by the tree's branches smiled at her, his red scarf wound around his neck so snuggly that his face took on the same hue.

"Everything okay, Miss?" he asked.

Tess nodded and smiled back, waiting until he turned away before she took off her gloves and touched the limbs closest to her. It was hard to imagine that the tree surrounding her had been alive at some point. She inhaled the rich pine scent and plucked a few needles from a branch before she moved on, inhaling their spiced scent deeply before she let them fall to the ground.

Her toes tingled and ached with cold, so that it was becoming difficult for her to move quickly because of the prickles that she felt with each step. She was eager for the warmth of her car, to sit down, when she noticed the crowds clustered on the steps of St. Patrick's Cathedral, and suddenly she was moving in that direction, away from the parking lot where her car awaited her. She made her way up the steps of the church and maneuvered her way through the crowds. Everyone around her seemed to travel in extended groups of all ages, and she slipped into the church via a door that was being held open. The muted darkness and the thick scent of incense enveloped her – there was a somber aspect to the church. It felt important, heavy. Tourists were clumped together at all corners of the church lobby, some lighting candles, some taking in the elaborate arches of the dais in the distance, while others moved along the perimeter of the church, lingering over the artwork adorning the walls as they made their way around. Tess took in the high ceilings – over 20-feet she imagined, the walls strewn with crypts and artwork. The center aisle, which led up to the altar, was roped off with thick, red velvet ropes, like those in a theater. The arches up by the dais were sharp and commanding with their wrought iron tips, like swords. They reminded her of miniature church steeples, and she imagined that Kash would be able to tell her all the details of the architecture.

Her shoes echoed as she made her way across the marble floor, pausing at the red velvet rope blocking her way. It felt old to her touch, the velvet rough. It was hard to imagine that this setting was authentic, that priests and religious folks passed through here each day and felt any real connection with God. There was a hollow aspect to the church, a damp, cool, vacant aspect, so that she felt as if she was on a movie set. The setting was so unlike the warmth of St. Bernard's church in Mill Basin, so unlike the monastery in New Jersey she had visited, which was mysterious in its way, but more accessible to her.

She walked the perimeter of the church interior along with the others, not taking in the scenery so much as trying to understand what this setting had meant to Neal, trying to imagine what he had thought about, felt, when he was here that day over 23 years back, when he had visited this very place the eve before he left for the monastery for what he had anticipated would be the rest of his life. No one knew at the beginning what the end would be. Her mother had told her that the only way through something, the only way to get to the end, if there was such a thing as an end, was to live through each of the moments. While Tess believed that to be true intellectually, she couldn't grasp it on an emotional level. She had tried to force outcomes based on her agenda and in the end, she had felt betrayed and disappointed when things didn't go according to her plan.

When she came to an open pew, she made her way to the middle of it and sat down. The people in the pew in front of her were kneeling while others sat silently with prayer books on their laps. A teenage girl and boy in front of her held hands and whispered in one another's ears. Tess smoothed the wood of the pew with her hands and knelt for a moment on the wooden bench to see what it felt like before she scooted back up onto the seat. No need to bruise her knees. She closed her eyes with her hands folded on her lap, her pocketbook between her feet. She followed her breath in and out, until everything inside of her slowed down and she felt herself drifting away, the sounds of the church – hushed voices and a few young children crying and carrying on – still vivid in her ears, but somehow distant, as if she were underwater. She felt herself drifting in and out and realized how tired she was. So tired. It would be so easy to sleep here, to let go and rest for a bit, but just then the organ started up so that her mind raced with the deep-pitched dramatic overture. She thought of Neal running to this very church on that day back in May after she had leaned over and kissed him in Central Park in broad daylight. She imagined how different it would have been if he had been wearing his monk robes – she wouldn't have looked at him let alone touched him if that had been the case. She doubted she would have even known him, would have said more than one word to him if he had exposed himself as a monk from the beginning.

And yet he had known who and what he was and put himself into that situation. She wondered where he had sat, where he had constructed his confession letter. A monk. She wasn't sure if she felt the manner of his confession was brave or childish, looking back now. He had to tell her at some point. There was only so long he could have endured his secret if he intended to keep seeing her, keep getting to know her, she supposed. Could he have told her face-to-face? It was a long story. He was a writer. He felt more comfortable communicating on paper. He had done the best he could.

The organ played on, taking over the cathedral, like a giant sweep of thunder full of crescendos and valleys and she thought back to the little girl ice-skating. The rhythm of it all, the great big dance of life and then she was thinking of the dance she shared with Neal on the cruise to nowhere. Holding him close, feeling his cheek beside hers, his breath by her ear. So much changed over time. Or maybe it was that things didn't change so much as they revealed themselves. There was no short cut to the long run. That was for sure. The organ was softer now, the melody almost sorrowful so that Tess felt an overwhelming sadness come over her. She had never meant to do Neal any harm, never meant to cause anyone any pain. She scanned the rows, trying to imagine which row Neal had sat in as he labored with pen and paper and wrote her the story of his life, the story he had wanted and needed her to know, to accept. She wondered how things would have turned out if she hadn't responded to Neal after reading his letter – if she hadn't met him by Jamaica Bay the morning after. Would he be back at the monastery now? But maybe it was all exactly how it was meant to be. Maybe Neal had told her because he knew that she could, would, accept him. Perhaps he had seen her as flawed in some way, like himself, and felt comfortable with her. What if Neal was still around because he felt his job was to help Tess with her life? What was it about Tess that Neal knew? What if his visit had nothing to do with Neal and he had been sent by some higher force to help fix Tess? The thought made her laugh out loud – Neal being sent to her from God. And yet, who knew for sure? The people in the pew in front of her had turned to see where the laughter had come from. She was tired of her mind. Tired of the places it traveled when she lost her way. She stood up and excused herself as she made her way out of the pew, which had filled up in the last twenty minutes or so.

She moved to the candles by the lobby. Brisk air seeped in

through the wrought iron doors, which opened and closed with hordes of tourists entering and exiting the church. She stood in line and picked up a wooden stick and a stack of votive candles. She watched what the people in front of her were doing and lit her stick from glowing candles. She placed the votives in empty candle holders and before she lit each candle, she thought of the person she was sending a prayer of well-being to: Lyla, Neal, Michael, Kash, Dale, her mother, and then Tess. When she was finished with her prayers – simply may he or she be well and safe – she lit one more candle for her father, the father that she had never known, who may or may not have come looking for her at some point of her adulthood. Lighting one more candle – it became addictive to her to light and pray – she prayed to be open to anything and everything that came her way, to accept her fate, regardless of what the universe dished out to her. When she heard the woman behind her remark to her friend about how long she was taking, Tess looked up to see that the line behind her had grown steep. She fished in her wallet for a twenty-dollar bill and stuffed it into the donation box before she moved away.

On her way out of the church, she lingered by the gift shop, looking over the medals of St. Francis and St. John and the various prayer books and rosaries for sale. She wanted to get something for Neal, a token of sorts, only she wasn't sure what he'd like. When she saw the laminated prayer card with an ocean flowing up a sandy shore, adorned with three little gold embossed footprints in the sand, she brought it up to the cash register. It was corny, and yet she believed that in years to come, if she should no longer know Neal as she did today, it would serve for him as a reminder of their time together and she wanted him to remember, not to lose her in his road ahead. As selfish as the thought was, she wanted Neal to love her regardless of the route he took. She wanted to be the woman who had changed his life, she supposed. She laughed at herself. If she had read such lines in a novel, the melodrama would have been off-putting. She couldn't remember ever having wished such a thing – had she even cared what any of her exes thought of her? No. She supposed not. Old and foolish, she smiled to herself. Tess Rose, you are old and foolish.

CHAPTER 59: FULL SPEED AHEAD

"Tick tock, tick tock," Michael said as Tess brushed past him in the office kitchen.

"I assure you that my biological clock stopped ticking years ago," she said. She reached around him for a spoon on the counter to stir her coffee. "Do you prefer to be in the way, or does it just come naturally for you?" she asked.

"The ticking clock was referring to your departure, for your information, and most normal people would say excuse me, at which I would gladly move out of the way," he said.

"It's 7:00 am. I came into the office to get some work done while it's quiet, not to defend my life choices to you again. For that matter I could be out walking with Lyla. Oh, I forgot, I shouldn't be talking bad about your new best friend Lyla."

"First of all, she's *your* new best friend, so don't give me that propaganda," Michael said.

Tess stared him down with her hands on her hips until he looked up at her from his coffee, his chin to his chest, eyes lowered, the lines of his forehead deep and grooved.

"Wipe that look off your face – you're creating wrinkles on your brow first of all, and second of all, people who criticize me and condemn me to hell aren't best friend material," Tess said.

"Say what you will, but I know that you wouldn't be walking in the early morning hours with someone whose company you didn't at least somewhat enjoy," Michael said.

"Amusing people amuse me," Tess said.

"What purpose do I serve to you?" Michael asked, his eyes appraising Tess.

"Right now, you annoy me," Tess said. "If you don't mind getting out of my way, I'd like to finish making my coffee."

"You realize that ever since you gave me your adios-I'm-out-of-here letter you've avoided me," Michael said.

"I see you in the office every day."

"Except on the days you play hooky to hang out with your yoga friends, and on the other days you're busy every minute," Michael said. "Whenever I try to get your attention, you're on the phone or on your way to a meeting and if I try to find you at home, I have to worry if the monk is around."

"What do you need to know?" Tess asked, facing him, a sugar sweet smile on her face.

"For starters, if you're still serious about ditching work and running away to Woodstock and if so, when do you plan to let the team know about the transition?"

"I still intend to go up to Woodstock to spend the holidays with my son and perhaps stay on a bit. As for letting the team here know, I don't see that as necessary. Last I checked with the boss, I'm allowed to take a vacation. I'm sure I'll send out a memo before I head out that in my absence, they can all go to you with questions. And of course, you or they can always reach me when I'm in Woodstock. It's not like I'm going around the globe – I'll be a few hours away."

They made their way down the hall to Tess's office. Michael paused beside her at her office door, waiting for her to lead the way in.

"You're not going in your office?" he said.

"I prefer to finish this conversation out here," Tess said, peering in at her desk, which was covered with stacked-up files and post its arranged according to her color-coded criteria of urgency. "I need to get work done once I walk in there. Someone needs to keep closing deals to keep the business alive," she said.

"So, you're not going to let them know you're leaving," Michael said.

"For goodness sakes, Michael. Are you familiar with the saying *Live and let live*? Let me live my life. Just feel excited to run the business. You may not ever have this chance again," Tess said.

He bowed down to Tess.

"Yes, mighty one. Thank you for this most honored gift," he said, and Tess laughed.

"You think it's funny," he said.

"I think you're funny, Michael. It's like you want me to be someone that I'm not just to keep your life in order."

"You seem to forget the fact that you're running away from your responsibilities and tossing them to me," Michael said.

"Say it, Michael. Say what it is that's really bothering you," Tess said.

"You already know," he said. "I don't want you to go. I feel like your life is still here with me. Working together at Best."

Tess opened her mouth to speak, but no words came out. She could have reminded him that they were over – that they hadn't been a couple in a long time. She could have told him that her life was where she chose it to be, not where Michael believed it was. She could have told him to get a grip, to let go of her, to get on with his life. She could have told him that change was an inevitable part of life, a beautiful part of life. There were so many things that she could have said, but none of it seemed necessary.

She reached out and touched his face, her open palm against his cheek, making its way down to his chin and then dropping down to her side. It felt like more of a motherly gesture than a romantic one.

He nodded and Tess smiled.

"It's all happening exactly as it should," she said, and he nodded again and made his way down the hall to his office.

Tess sorted the folders in front of her, each one labeled with a different address – somehow, she was responsible for each of these deals. Off to the right of her desk in her in-box were folders from her agents, deals they wanted her to look over before they acted. That was part of being the boss – overseeing her agents' transactions. She focused back on her folders and put the Johnson house sale on top. That would close today if the bank guaranteed the mortgage. She knew the young couple buying the house was on pins and needles for everything to be final with the woman being six months pregnant. She began to look through the papers, see what the buyers still needed to review, what would need signing for the transaction to move forward, and then let the folder fall to her desk. What did it any of it matter? That's what went through her mind and yet some distant voice in her brain reassured her that it did matter – it was her job, there were people involved whose life dreams depended on it, whose futures would be shaped by these transactions. One day way back her future had been carved when she moved into her home on East 66th Street in Mill Basin, Brooklyn.

7:20 am. It was too early to call Prakash and yet…. He picked up on the second ring.

"You're awake," she said.

"Mom," he said. "How'd I know it was going to be you?"

"Telepathy," she said. "Why are you awake?"

"The same reason you're in your office right now – working."

"The new complex still?" Tess asked.

"Whatever I come up with, the investors seem to have their own ideas," he said.

"Why don't you ask them what they want and create it?" Tess said.

"That's what I thought I was doing but they seem to keep changing their minds."

She paused. "Do you like your life, Kash?"

"Is this going to be an existential talk?" Prakash said.

She could hear that he had put down his pencil and imagined him leaned over, rubbing his eyes with the heels of his palms as he used to do when she woke him up for school, his piles of thick, curly black hair springing forward.

"The thing is a person can make all this money, be busy, and yet still not know what's missing, what's right, what's next," Tess said.

"A person can also waste time worrying about what's missing, what's right, what's next, and neglect to live in the moment and enjoy all that is," Prakash said. "And if something makes you feel bad, you get to change it. That's the beauty of freedom."

Tess put her legs up on her desk and studied the scuffed points of her heels from the snow and salt on the ground. They needed polishing.

"Freedom is a complicated concept," Tess said. "Our right to exercise our freedom affects others."

She heard Prakash walking around his apartment. Perhaps he

was looking out his window, high up on the 22nd floor. It was 4:30am in San Francisco; she imagined it was dark, cold, and foggy there.

"I got my plane tickets by the way, so we're all set for our New Year's getaway," Prakash said.

"I'm looking forward to that," Tess said.

"Have you invited anyone – Neal? Michael?"

"No," Tess said.

"Are you still planning on staying up there?" Prakash asked.

"Yes," Tess said. "I've let Michael know."

"How did he take it?"

"Obstinately. But he'll live."

"I'm going to stay on through the first week in January, so you'll have some company for a bit," Prakash said.

"That will be nice," Tess said. "Be sure to pack warm clothes. It gets a bit torrential up there this time of year," Tess said.

"Thanks for the tip – I was going to pack shorts and t-shirts."

"Will you get some sleep tonight?" Tess said.

"It's already tomorrow," Prakash said. "And I'm fine. Remember that I learned my work ethic from you."

"That's what frightens me," Tess said. "You know I'm proud of you, Kash. Really proud of you."

"I know. Do yourself a favor, Mom: don't waste another minute today worrying – just live," Prakash said. "Like you used to say to me – *this is it, this is life*."

"Yes," Tess said. She vaguely remembered her little mock top-hat tipping gesture when she would say that to her son.

"Birthdays tend to cause anxiety, Mom. Whatever you're feeling is perfectly normal," he said.

She stopped tapping her pencil against the desk and closed her eyes, smiling.

"I don't know how I got to be 56 years old," she said.

"I don't know how I got to be 33, but somehow, it happened. That's how life works. Another day, another 24 hours older." They were silent for a few moments before Prakash cleared his throat. "Back to work for me. See you soon, Mom," he said to which Tess replied, "See you soon," and then he was gone.

Outside, the birds made their way from the telephone line across the street to the one adjacent to it. One after the other, they seemed to follow, scooting on the thin wire to make room for one another. The trees waved in the wind, their branches brittle under the gray-black snow laden sky, as if they were about to snap off. Tess was grateful to be indoors, warm, the heat booming through the vents. She felt tired, but when she thought about sleep, that wasn't what she wanted. She had slept plenty. No, she was restless, tired in her brain. Uneasy about what was to come. There were moments, days, when she felt strong, confident and open-minded about the future. So how was it that on the opposite end of that spectrum she felt so afraid, so unsure? She had her tools: meditation, pranayama, yoga. Only she didn't feel like any of that now. How quickly all that she had learned went out the door when fear cast its shadow over her. She wondered how her mother had managed it all – how she had remained so steady through adversity, of which she'd had her share. Perhaps her steadiness had been an act. Perhaps underneath it all was the very same desperation that Tess was feeling. People were masters at hiding their truth, wearing masks. Why would her mother be any different? The birds were in flight again, moving beyond her sight. Where would she go if she had the power to fly away? She didn't even know.

The sound of a new email in her inbox jarred her from her thoughts. It was from Michael.

I honorably request your presence to join me for brunch this Saturday, December 20th, in New York City, to celebrate your birthday and the New Year. As I know that you will be heading up to Woodstock on Friday, December 26th, your birthday, I am hoping this will be satisfactory to you. Kindly RSVP no later than 8:00 am.

Tess responded:

Thanks for your most generous invitation. Regrettably, I have early morning yoga and subsequent brunch plans with yoga friends on Saturday.

Michael would live. He was attached to her companionship. Once she was gone, he'd be fine. They had been divorced for a long time now – they were friends. She wondered if he would even care about her whereabouts if Neal hadn't come into the picture.

Work. Organizing her files. That was the task that was in front of her. Focus. She took a deep breath, kicked off her shoes under her desk to stretch her toes, and got back to it. She would go through her own files and then get to her employees' files and get them the answers or approvals they needed. Systematic and orderly. Her goal was to be through it all by 9:30, at which time she would depart for her 10:00 am appointment. It was a new lead – a gentleman who was looking to buy a home in Bergen Beach, something about his having family there, in laws, she believed, and him wanting to find something large and grand that he and his newly pregnant wife could move into ASAP. He was a partner at a law firm in Bay Ridge, and from their initial conversation, it seemed that he had money to spend. She could always tell by the tone of a potential buyer's voice if he was worth her while to take on – a buyer with money, a quick-close type of sale – or if it would be a longer, more drawn-out type of sale, an insecure buyer with less money to spend, which she'd hand off to one of her agents based on their experience level. This gentleman could very well be her last client for some time. Depending on how the meeting went today, she'd determine if she'd be able to close it out in the next few weeks or if she'd have to make a trip back to Brooklyn to finish it out. She knew exactly which house she'd show him if he had the money to spend that he insinuated he did.

When her cell phone rang, she hesitated before picking it up – the area code was Woodstock, only the number wasn't familiar. Perhaps a realtor looking to buy her mother's home?

"Luke," she said. "Hello. Good morning to you…. No, not at all – it's a fine time to reach me. Sure, old Jim gave you my cell phone number. Is everything okay?" Tess paused. "The house okay? That's good to hear…. Yes, it's quite cold down here, too…. I am coming up for New Year's – actually a few days before. My son will be joining me…. A New Year's Eve meditation sounds nice," Tess said, putting him on mute while she shushed Michael, who had just knocked and entered her office, plopping himself down in one of her plush brown leather chairs situated across from her desk. "Luke? Let me check with my son…we hadn't really talked about our plans, but I'll see what he had in mind…. Sure, New Year's morning would be nice, too. Okay, we will consider both and let you know what works best…. I'm sure you'll have no trouble rallying the troops…. I agree – my mother would want it to be…. I'll see you soon, Luke…. Yes, yes, you will hear from me in the next few days…. You take care, too. Have a good day…. Namaste."

"Luke? Isn't that the Woodstock Don Juan? I see you have all your bases covered," Michael said.

"He called me, Michael," Tess said.

"Absolutely. All your courters call you. What's your point?"

"I came in to work. I could be at home doing a dozen other things right now and none of them involve explaining myself to you," Tess said.

"No wonder you haven't told Neal about Woodstock yet. Everything reveals itself over time," Michael said.

"If I had the energy to bend down, I'd throw my shoe at you," Tess said.

"I see how you had the time to marry four husbands. You work quickly. Out with the old and in with the new."

"For your information, Luke called me as he heard from my mother's neighbor, old Jim, who has been keeping an eye on the house for me in my absence, that I was coming up there for New Year's and he wanted to know if I was open to having a midnight meditation at the house on New Year's Eve," Tess said.

"Well now that you have New Year's plans all settled, what about Christmas and your birthday? Are you planning to go to church with Neal?" Michael said.

"Get out of my office," Tess said.

"What? That's a legitimate question when your boyfriend is a monk," Michael said.

"My plans are to do whatever it is I do," Tess said.

"You don't have to tell me, but I'm hoping you share your plans with your boyfriend," he said.

She picked up the folders in front of her and started to go through the paperwork again. Michael sat where he was, his eyes intent on hers.

She spoke into her intercom, calling her assistant, who answered her. "Lynn, please don't let any calls come to me prior to my leaving at

9:30 am – all to voicemail. Thank you," Tess said, clicking the intercom off.

"If you don't mind, I have a lot to accomplish in the next hour and a half," Tess said. Michael stood up and made his way to the door. "Please be sure to close my door on your way out," she said.

Their eyes lingered on one another's for a few moments. There was unrest in his eyes that was familiar to her and yet not something she could articulate.

"Michael," she said, just as he was about to go. He stopped and turned to her, holding the door with his hand. "It's all for the best," she said. "Everything is going to be fine," she said, and with that, he closed the door behind him.

CHAPTER 60: KNOWING

Tess sat at the traffic light on the corner of Avenue U and E. 68th street, her fingers tapping the steering wheel as if the action would speed the light to turn green. Ahead of her on the corner was Temple Shalom and behind it was St. Bernard's Church.

The prospective buyer, Antonio, or Tony as he had asked her to call him, was very promising. He had good taste and seemed to have the funds to back it up. As she had suspected, he had absolutely loved the posh home on Royce Place in Bergan Beach. She had saved the best property for last, a tactic she had learned early on in her career. Tomorrow she would give his wife a grand tour. Not bad at all in terms of progress and momentum, although she hadn't expected to spend so much time with him – nearly three hours. He certainly knew the right questions to ask, which was fine with Tess as she had the answers, and if it led to a quick sale, and she anticipated it would, then it was worth every second of her time right now. Of course, she imagined the paperwork would drag it out for a few weeks, but still, if his wife loved the house as much as he did, then Tess could get the ball rolling in the next few days. Her plan was to head back to her office for another few hours of work, and then she was going to call it a day. It amazed her: she could be done with this house stuff, ready to leave it behind, and then get pulled back in so easily. Perhaps there would never be the perfect time to walk away until she just did it. The light turned, finally, and hearing the church bells, she made the split-second decision to make a left turn and pass by the church.

The school day was over – children were walking out of the school building, and parents were scattered all about the entrance, some talking, some straining their heads, she supposed, to find their kids. On the right side of the street loomed the church with its three church bells reaching over 10 feet into the air, the sound of their ringing resonating as she moved closer. She inched her way to Veteran's Avenue, careful to be mindful of the children crossing the street, the double-parked cars scattered about, and there, out of the corner of her eye, she saw Neal. Was it Neal? He was standing looking at the church, with his back to her. The minivan behind her beeped; yes, she was sure – it was Neal. Why was he looking at the church? Then as if in answer to her question, he made the sign of the cross, turned around, and was moving away from it, parallel to her, so that if he looked to his left with the slow-moving traffic, he would have seen her. He walked as if in a trance, like he had just exited a movie theater into daylight. Had he been in the church, or had he only stood outside of it? He was making his way to the bike rack; yes, he had deliberately gone to the church, rode his bike there. The car behind her was beeping again and she had to move, step on the gas, reach the corner, make a left turn and head back to her office where work awaited her, but something in his trance struck her. Ah, damn that car behind her! She pulled off to the right and motioned the car to go around her, but due to the traffic on the other side of the road, there was no room.

In the ruckus Neal turned slightly, almost seeing her before he faced forward again, and then as if someone had tapped him on the shoulder, he turned fully now, just as he approached the bike rack, so that he and Tess's eyes met. Or was he looking beyond her? She exhaled, not realizing that she had been holding her breath, and her instinct was to keep going, to pretend as if she didn't see him, but she was stuck in traffic as the crossing guard on the corner held the cars still while she beckoned students to cross the street. Neal gazed at Tess, and she gazed back and for those seconds, it was as if the world had stopped, as if there was nothing else to see or know or feel but that moment.

The car behind her beeped again; now there was a steady lingering of beeps from various cars, all desperate to get themselves out of the gridlock, to move on to the corner, to turn left or right, and be on their way. She could pull over to the curb, that much she could maneuver, only then what? What was there to say? *I know*? I understand why you were at the church today. Because she didn't know. This was guesswork, this was what she feared most and so thinking it so was easiest for her. What if he had decided no such thing? What if he had spoken to the priest and told him that he was leaving the church forever? That too was a possibility. Why was she so fatalistic?

They held each other's gaze and she kept driving, kept moving, making her way to the corner and as she passed Neal, she stared back at him in her rearview mirror and he was still, watching her with his gaze, not moving, expressionless. She thought of that very first night they spoke at this same church, how when they had parted, she had watched him on his bike in her rearview mirror. How free and happy and serene he had seemed that night. And now? How did he seem now? Pensive, serious.

At the corner, she was free to pull over – wait for him to come to her or go to him. His eyes still on her in the distance, she hesitated. What was it in his eyes? What was he trying to say to her? And in that instant, she knew. She understood. She glanced left and right before she made her way through the intersection, and as she moved forward, tears formed in her eyes, and the heaviness that had manifested in her heart and throat overwhelmed her, so that she fought herself from pulling over and weeping. He was going back. She had seen it in his eyes – the silent confirmation. He had received his message from God.

Jodi Weiss

In Your Own Garden

A Separate Peace: December 2003

> *"What do you seek?" the Abbot asks.*
>
> *Truth. To know myself and to know God in myself.*
>
> *"What do you seek?" the Abbot asks.*
>
> *The one life.*

> *With each departure, a return is implicit. I understand that now. It is not about coming or going, but about reconnecting. I am trying to come to terms with the fact that back does not mean backwards. Back can be a movement towards the future, the unknown.*
>
> *I had thought that I needed to be away from the monastery to be closer to myself. I had thought that I needed to be away from God and voices telling me what I should believe. I have begun to understand that it's not about where I am. I have begun to understand that the world becomes one place once I tap into the one life.*
>
> *I chose to be a monk because I was chosen to be a monk, not because I was looking to escape anything. Monastic life is human life. I knew that at the monastery, but ideas of the secular world tempted me into believing otherwise. Now, I am sure that we are all the same – monks, lay people. The problems that riddle people outside of the monastery are problems that riddle those of us in the monastery. The*

732

human heart is a region of conflicting desires. Of wanting it both ways: now this, now that. Hearts are not left at the gate of the monastery. One brings oneself wherever one goes.

The biggest struggle of my life as a monk was the everydayness of being a monk. The routine. Waking each morning, praying, reading, scrambled eggs, tea, work. I had wished for diversion, newness, but I had taken a vow of conversion, stability, which had to do with staying in one place, under a rule and an abbot. That vow was taken so that I might put down roots. I had taken a vow in the same way that lay people take marriage vows. If I kept moving from place to place, I would never be grounded. My vow was not to be an obstacle in my life as I let it become, but a guidepost.

I have spent days watching trees – the way their leaves dance in the breeze, the way their branches sway. If a tree wasn't rooted and firm, it wouldn't be able to sustain itself against the wind or the rain or snow – it would collapse. It's only the grounded and rooted trees that endure. I understand that now.

I was afraid of the solitude in the monastery. Although my brothers surrounded me, I often felt secluded. I didn't want to always be so alone. Now, here, with you, I've come to accept my aloneness a bit more. I've begun to understand that aloneness doesn't mean lonely, it means being okay with myself, enjoying my own company.

God spoke to me. That is why I became a monk. It wasn't in a complete sentence and the voice came and went, but it came to me. As much as I want to pretend that it didn't at times, as much as I want to run away, to be free to do and live as other men, God is with me, speaking to me, through me. He asks so little, but still he asks: "Do not harden your heart to my voice."

To love, I believe, is to possess the capacity to receive and to be touched, to be drawn into something more. Something beyond the self, beyond this realm.

I have always lived by my heart, letting its deepest desires drive me. I often wish I could share my heart with you. Show you how it works, but no matter how much I try to share it, I am always left with something of myself that I cannot give to you. That is something that I am coming to accept. I cannot give away my most pure thoughts and feelings, as there is always something that gets lost in translation because I am me and you are you and our interpretations are distinct and unique. I had mistaken that being trapped within myself was a monk thing but now I understand that it's a fate we all share regardless of our paths.

I entered the monastery because I wanted to be near God. The voice influencing me to stay here now – to keep going and living as I am – may never fade, but in the silence of each morning, the silence of each night when the world is still and I can be alone with my thoughts, I believe that my vocation is to be with the Lord. To wake up this Christmas morning and say Mass with my brothers. It doesn't always make sense to me why that is my vocation, but that doesn't make it any less true in my heart. My first love was, is, God. Just because I have walked away from the monastery doesn't mean that I have walked away from my heart, which is where the God I love and know resides.

"What do you seek?" the Abbot asks.

The mercy of God.

Dear Neal,

    I've always felt it's easier to talk to a person face to face, but I understand now that I haven't been able to do that very well, as often, what I think is not what I say. When opportunity arises for me to talk to you, I am only able to make small talk although there are so many questions that I want to ask you. I want to know me through your eyes. Only I don't know if that's possible – as you've said, there are limitations as you are you and I am me and things get lost in translation.

    I used to think that if I had someone around me, I could get away from myself for a bit, and now I've begun to embrace my aloneness and honor it, crave it, because it's the space in which I get to know myself. I sought company all along when it was me that I sought – the chance to know and hear and see and feel and listen to me. I think that's why no man was ever right for me – it had nothing to do with another person. That's why working all those hours for all those years helped me to pass the time, but never filled me up. What I sought had nothing to do with accomplishment. That's why my mother never made me feel the security I felt I deserved, that I craved. All along, it had to do with me wanting me and not knowing how or where to reach me.

    I've been thinking about moving back up to Woodstock. Somehow in my mind, that has seemed to be the logical thing to do. Return. Start over. Try again. I'm not sure if I am trying to redo anything or if I feel that parts of me never left there. I'm beginning to believe that life in many ways is circular and that where we start is where we will end. When you told me that the other half of the rainbow is beneath the surface, I thought I understood it, but today it is a bit clearer to me. All the beauty, along with the sorrow and the joy and the mysteries, are always in motion. Life keeps going, round and round, one big giant circle, so to think there's a place to get to is an illusion. We are always exactly where we need to be.

I don't know if I'll go back to Woodstock for good. I'm not sure that's the answer, as I don't yet know the question. Somehow, we have arrived at the same place, one of comings and goings and the questions or answers to our riddles are irrelevant. Perhaps whatever we each do is fine.

In The Bhagavad Gita, *Krishna tells Arjuna that he must follow his dharma, which is to fight his family and friends in battle, but he reminds him to keep his feet pointed at the lotus heart of the Lord – to remain open to love, to life's wonders. Krishna reminds Arjuna that one must embrace one's duties while remaining mindful of a more timeless reality – that one must sometimes act without consideration of the immediate results. We must each follow our paths, Neal, but we mustn't lose our joy, our love, and we must remember that there is a higher reality than this one.*

I think sometimes about a reality with you other than this one, Neal. A timeless reality when you and I may share our dance for a bit longer, without any choices to be made or places to go; without any other duties than to hear the music and move to it, together. I think so many things at so many different points in the day that I wonder what it would look like if I were to draw a map of my thoughts. Would I have traveled anywhere or remained in place? I've clung to my life as I know it because it's what I know. I've resisted change while the world changed around me. The other day, I drove to New York City, and I didn't know why I was there until I arrived at the church quote board.

A caterpillar who seeks to know himself would never become a butterfly. – Andre Guide

Perhaps all this trying to know oneself, trying to understand oneself, searching one's soul, is what keeps us from the next chapters of our lives, which will come, inevitably, whether we continue to cling to what is or not.

The plane ticket included in this letter is for you to return to Saskatoon on Christmas Eve so that as you desire, you may wake up amongst your brothers on Christmas day. I hope that you will take this gesture as I have intended it: my seeing to your safe return, my honoring your decision, and as a token of my respect for you. I will miss you, Neal, and I'll never forget this path we have traveled together. I am not sure if we ever truly know if we're traveling in the right direction, but perhaps if we listen – to our hearts, our soul – we will always arrive.

Fondly,

Tess

CHAPTER 61: THE WANDERER

The dew was thick and heavy, the air frosty as Tess made her way from her porch, silently, adjusting her scarf so that no skin was exposed. She felt moody knowing that for the months to come, each time she went outside she would need to bundle up, delve into her shell, isolating herself from all that surrounded her. Cold weather made other people seem out of reach.

There was solitariness to Mill Basin in this pre-dawn hour that was both unsettling and appreciated – she turned in her tracks to make certain no one was behind her and then kept going, moving with precision and a sense of purpose as she coasted down 66th street, the rhythm of her feet hitting the pavement her metronome. She had woken up at 3:00 a.m. alert and preoccupied, her mind darting from subject to subject, like a bird in search of prey. She had stared at her ceiling for some time, trying to focus on something, anything, until it registered that tomorrow was Christmas Eve, the day that Neal was set to leave. She wondered if she would see him before then. She was free to visit him at his home – she couldn't imagine what Lyla could object to at this point. He had left her a note in her mailbox that simply said: *Thank you, Tess Rose.* He was leaving. The thought flashed in her mind as though it were a neon sign: *Neal is leaving, Neal is leaving* until the next thought registered: in three days it would be her 56th birthday. Life was so short;

why was she filling it with so much worry, so much anxiety, when in truth, she only got to live such a short time? She would die, as her mother had, and then there would be darkness forever.

She moved past the houses quickly. Not too much was stirring at this 5 a.m. hour; some of the houses were still darkened, some adorned with flickering Christmas lights and yards decorated with lit-up plastic snowmen and sleds pulled by Santa. In some of the homes she could make out Christmas trees in the windows and a sense of warmth filled her thinking of families with young children and grandchildren all gathered around. She wondered if Lyla had put up a tree with Neal, but she didn't make a move to turn down Barlow Drive to investigate. There were some houses with lights on inside and for a moment, she wondered what went on in other people's homes, behind all the closed doors.

As the sky transitioned into its darkest moments before it gave way to dawn, Tess felt a fleeting desperation mingled with a desire to scream, not to be so invisible, and then it passed, as quickly as the twilight did and the first rings of daylight grew visible beyond the houses, where she envisioned Jamaica Bay to be still and silent. She took in a deep breath, coughing as the rush of hard air hit her throat, her lungs. It was a few moments before she reconnected with her mind, her feet moving faster than was her normal pace, and she wasn't sure if they were attempting to carry her away from the cold or if they were working to keep up with her darting mind. In moments she lost the cold, lost the motion of her feet, and was trying to recall what it was she aspired to. People that were insistent on following their dreams had surrounded her at different phases in her life. Her first three ex-husbands had wanted to make enough money so that they could retire in their fifties, but was that a dream or was it greed? Tess believed that those type of trade-off dreams – if I have this, then I will do that – were not dreams at all, but little contracts one made with oneself and voided once other things came up, replacing those wants and desires. She had made her share of trade-off dreams: if I can get distance from Woodstock and my mother, then I will get to figure out who I am. If I can just not be pregnant, then I will focus on my career and be a better wife. If I can just get through this divorce, separate myself from this person, then my life will make more sense. All those dreams had seemed tangible to her, something to strive for, something she had strived for, but each of them had focused on the future, ignored the present.

Perhaps the real dreams of her life weren't to be realized by running off recklessly, but staying put, facing the day, what was. And perhaps the truth was that there was not any one dream, but an evolving, all-encompassing dream to live her life as truly as she could. Perhaps what separated those who lived their dream versus those who dreamed their dream was that they acted on them and understood that it was never any one action that would help them to realize their dreams, but all their actions. Because in life, everything did matter – and if there was one thing that Tess wished she had learned sooner, it was that fact: everything did matter.

In the bus stop ad for Best Realty, a perfected Tess Rose smiled back at her. In her image, she was able to see herself at different stages of her life: as a teenager in Woodstock, walking to school; and in another glance she saw herself in her first marriage, sitting across from Marc, listening to him and wondering how long she would be able to go on listening to him. She imagined that she had seen people like Marc as puzzles to solve, but now she thought differently: a person wasn't something for her to solve. Her job was to learn about herself and through that learning, try to build a stronger bridge to her core, as well as a stronger bridge to the core of people she loved. Puzzles suggested that you could make things fit, that they were solvable, but Tess had been shown again and again that life was about continually figuring out how to resize things to fit the moment at hand. She could see herself as a mother, alone and afraid with her child; and then as a middle-aged woman, grappling with relationships, trying to pass the time as best she could with dinners and wine, and now. Externally, she had changed, all those faces of Tess, and yet she was still Tess: sometimes confident, sometimes afraid, quiet and outspoken, alone. "Hello, Tess," she whispered, her breath forming a smoke cloud before her. She smiled at the picture of herself for a moment longer and felt something peaceful and soft, like love, like acceptance, for the woman in the picture. "It's nice to know you, Tess," she said.

In moments the sky lightened, the first true peak of daylight surfacing as the outline of the clouds became visible. In the distance cars were approaching, the streetlight on the corner of 66th street and Avenue U turning from green to yellow to red in seconds. Stop. Tess thought of what a mess everything had been at various stages of her life, but that it wouldn't always be that way. The light turned green. "Have a good day, Tess," she said, and then she was moving again, making her way up 66th street, back the direction she had come.

The wooden planks of the docks across from her home were covered in spots with thin sheets of ice. Tess treaded carefully, holding

ᅟ

ᅠ

firm to the handrails as she made her way across the dock and down the stairs to the sand. The sky was white and crisp, the sand moist, packed. Seagulls congregated at the shore's edge, darting to and fro as the gentle waves smoothed the shore. She put an ungloved hand into the water and retreated – it was icy. She quickly put her glove back on. In the distance, she was able to make out a runner, see the smoke of his breath, and for a moment, she was sure that it wasn't Neal, he didn't move his hands that way, but as he moved closer, it was Neal – he was waving to her. She didn't know if he would stop, or if he would keep going, and then he was beside her, panting, moving his jaw up and down as if he were trying to loosen it up so that he could speak. Tess felt awkward, as she had felt meeting him here after she had read his confession letter. She kept her eyes on the ground, shifting about in the sand from one leg to another.

The snow began to fall all at once, the flakes hurdling themselves to the ground, and Tess took in the darkening sky, the cold seeping into her face until her nose was numb, her eyes tearing. Beside her Neal too looked up at the sky and then she felt his eyes on her. She knew that they couldn't escape what was coming next in their lives – Neal's returning, her moving forward without him. She would go on as she always had.

Neal took off his clunky sports gloves and reached for her hand. His beautiful, sturdy hand with his long, lean fingers and she kissed his knuckles as they faced the water. She thought back to the first time they had shared a dance on Memorial Day weekend on the cruise to nowhere. They had gone out to sea and come back – it was the rhythm of life, the waves coasting away and then returning.

"You are my special friend, Tess Rose," Neal said.

Tess nodded; there was a finality to his words that pacified her. After all they had gone through, that's what it came down to: he was her friend.

"You are my special friend, Neal," she said.

"Shall we warm up?" she asked after some time, and Neal nodded.

They walked back towards her home, hand in hand, silent, their steps slow, measured. There was a strength in letting go, in opening the door for a person, in being unselfish, in surrendering that which she wanted to keep. She believed this. A chill gripped her as they crossed the street, sending a shiver through her. She couldn't tell if it was induced from the cold inside or out. Neal squeezed her hand tighter, and the action reminded her of the cool autumn mornings she had walked Prakash to school, squeezing his hand when a wind rushed them as if with that one squeeze of the hand, she could instill in him the confidence that she was there to take care of him, protect him. At the edge of her driveway, Tess paused. Responsibility set in – she should check the backyard to make sure that the outside water was turned off so that the hose didn't freeze up from the snow. She would have to make a list of things she had to take care of before she left for Woodstock. Neal offered to go with her, but she insisted on letting him into her house, telling him to go inside, warm up, and promised that she would come inside in a few minutes.

This is the way of the world, she thought to herself, the snow trickling down on her, as she watched Neal move inside and made her way past the now barren cherry orchid shadowing the side of her house and through the backyard gate. People came and went in life. She was trying to keep her logic about her. To pretend there was a future past the moment she was living was to be absent from her life. Tess was trying to grasp this, to buy into it, to be in this moment, but in the almost day-lit sky, the lingering moon's impression pushed her forward. In two more days, it would be full. The end of a phase, the coming of a new phase. She saw herself alone in the days to come, a woman who had returned a man that never truly belonged to her, gazing up at the moon, full and complete for that one night.

She moved the water valve one way and then the other, making sure that it was off. Snow fell across the wooden deck of her back yard, dusting it in whiteness. She pulled the cushions off the deck chairs and stacked them in the little shed that stood before the corner alcove where the stump of the dying Evergreen tree she had removed the year before stood. She moved into the alcove and there, nestled in the corner, was a garden. Had her gardener done this? He hadn't mentioned it. It looked vulnerable in the cold. She inched closer to it, kneeling beside it, as if under her watch it would be sheltered from the impending storm. Each of the sections had little plastic name tags describing what they were and when they would bloom, and it hit Tess that Neal had done this – this was his garden for her. It touched Tess to think of him fiddling with a label maker and then placing the labels just right in the soil, laminating them to keep them safe from the elements. How was it that she had never wandered into the alcove to see this gift? As a child, Prakash had often hidden out in this alcove, and once she remembered Brad building him a mini club house there, which Prakash had to abandon when the neighborhood stray cats moved in, deeming it a cathouse and raising their kittens there, all which Brad had helped Prakash to find homes for.

There were delphinium, coreopsis, purple cone flower, asters, daisies, bachelor's button, foxgloves. Aside from daisies, Tess had never heard of any of them. For all her years in real estate, she had relied on her gardener to go to a house that she was selling and spruce it up with colorful flowers and shrubs indicative of the season. She had also relied on him for her own house and had often felt lighter hearted at seeing the blooming tulips and colorful flowers in her front garden as she backed out of her driveway in the mornings. Is this little garden what her gardener had been referring to when he left her a voicemail asking her about her science project? She supposed it was.

Neal had labeled many sections perennials, and from her mother, she knew that meant they would bloom in the very same spot, year after year. In another corner of the mini-garden Neal had planted yarrows and written in parenthesis "for butterflies," and virgin's bower and in parenthesis "hummingbird plant." She smiled, imagining butterflies and hummingbirds congregating in her backyard. How her mother loved butterflies. And hummingbirds. Her hair was getting wet, falling flat. The snow was coming down harder now, sticking to the ground, so that accumulation was likely. Tess stood up. The flowers that he had planted would sprout some time the following year, when he was no longer around. A twinge of sorrow gripped her so that her heart felt tight, and yet there was something beautiful in knowing his garden would bloom in the future, as if in his own way he was leaving behind bits and pieces of himself.

She made her way into the house, stamping her feet on the mat before she sat down on one of the steps to take off her sneakers and jacket, dust her hair with her hands, air drying it a bit. The moment she pushed the front door shut, double bolted the Segal lock, there it was, that impossible restlessness in Tess, a feeling of needing to scream and cry, of needing to make something happen, only what was there to make happen? What did she want to happen? She had an urge to go back outside and pulled the door back open, only there was nothing out there that she wanted right now. The desperation raging through her began to dissipate. Okay. She was going to be okay. She was okay. She closed the door again. This passing lowness was part of life. It was a wave. *I'm okay*, she whispered, leaning her back against the door for support. She smiled. She was better than okay. It was her life and there was so much yet ahead of her.

"Tess? You okay?" Neal called, his eyes on her now as he stood in her kitchen. "I put on some hot water for tea," he said. "Hope that's okay."

"Sounds great," she said, making her way up the stairs. "Can I lend you some dry clothes?" she asked, and Neal shook his head.

"I'm fine." He stood by the stove. "My clothes are still dry," he said, checking his top with his hand as if to show her all was dry.

Perhaps he was afraid of going back; perhaps he feared how the brothers would react to him, if they would see him as damaged in some way, if he would ever truly be a part of their brotherhood again.

"It seems to be coming down harder," Neal said, his eyes on the window, before he shut off the stove, the teakettle whistling. In a moment, he was opening her cabinet, taking down two cups, filling them with water, taking out some tea bags – he held up the green tea bags and Tess nodded.

"Shall we sit?" Neal said, and then he was making his way to the table, placing the teacups down.

Tess smiled at him. It seemed so normal for him to be here with her. "It's nice, the snow," Tess said. Outside, the thick, sturdy branches of the cherry orchid had begun to shelve the snow.

"It slows everything down a bit," he said, and Tess nodded.

She should be getting into the shower for work – the last day the office was open before she was to close it for a week – but she didn't.

Neal stirred his tea first one way and then the other. She closed her eyes to still herself; her breath was slow and heavy.

"I don't want you to go," she said. "I don't want to lose you." She had been thinking the words but hadn't intended to speak them aloud. And while she meant the words, she also felt a sense of relief in knowing that he was leaving. Waiting for Neal to decide if he was going to return to the monastery had hovered over Tess for months, like an eagle, wings spread, casting a shadow.

He nodded, his eyes on his hands on the teacup, as if he were considering her comment – as if staying was an option.

"I wish it wasn't all so complicated," he said.

"I know that you must go back, or that you want to, or that you will. I understand that," Tess said.

"I'll think of you, Tess."

"I'll think of you, Neal."

He was silent. He looked tired. Tess wondered if he had been sleeping or if like her, he was restless.

"We each have our paths," he said. "Our duties. You've reminded me of that."

Tess nodded, her eyes fixated on his hands. The veins in them had risen to the surface so that they looked like the hands of a man about to break free from his skin.

"Do they know that you're returning?" Tess said.

"Yes," he said.

She nodded. "Your mother must be relieved."

"Yes," he said again. He looked up at Tess and paused before he looked back down at his hands on the teacup. "She's grateful to you, Tess."

The clock ticked and the wind slashed against the window. The snow seemed to be coming down with a vengeance now. The first snowstorm of the season.

"Grateful to me?" Tess said.

"For instigating my return. For understanding," Neal said.

"The day I saw you at the church, I felt sure that you had made up your mind. That you were already checking out."

"It's who I am, Tess. It's part of my make up."

"You have to live your life as you see fit," she said.

Neal nodded.

She wished that she could fast forward from this moment. That Neal was already back at the monastery, that she was already in Woodstock. Somewhere in the house, she heard her blackberry buzzing, and she thought of the paperwork she had to work through with Michael today before she headed out of town. The people in her office now knew that she would be gone for the month of January and already there was unrest and Michael was anxious.

"I should get ready for work," she said. "Today is going to be my last day at the office for a while."

"You have your trip to get ready for, too. When do you leave?"

"Christmas Day," she said.

"You'll be up there for your birthday," he said.

"Yes," she said.

The wind whipped harder against the window, snow flinging against the glass, like pellets. There would be snowdrifts. The drive to Woodstock would be treacherous if the weather continued this way.

"Would you take me to the airport tomorrow, Tess?"

She swallowed deep. "If you'd like me to," she said.

"It would mean everything to me," he said.

"And your mother?"

"We're eating dinner together tonight," he said. "I wanted you to be the last person I saw before I left."

"I'd like to take you, Neal," she said.

He stood up and she rose with him. His beautiful blue eyes; his now lush sandy-colored hair. It didn't make sense to her, but her feelings were real.

He reached out for her face and cupped her chin in his hands, his index finger tracing her lips and in a moment her lips were on his, clinging to them, kissing them gently, and he didn't pull away. They stood, lips locked, inhaling one another before Tess sucked his bottom lip in hers, and kissed him passionately, knowing that it was to be the last kiss with this man. She felt the tears come down her face and with his fingers, Neal wiped them away, his lips still on hers.

CHAPTER 62: THE END OF SOMETHING

Tess awoke on Christmas Eve morning sluggish, irritable. 6:30 a.m. and her bedroom was dark as midnight. She was tired of this winter season before it even set in. She sunk back onto her pillow. Her dreams had pulled her in, resisting her urge to wake up more than once and yet when she tried to decipher them, her mind was blank. Her eyes acclimated to the darkness, so that in a few moments the familiar shapes of her room came into view: her teak bureau, the oversized rectangular mirror above it, the picture frames lining the bureau: photographs of Prakash, her mother, a younger Tess smiling for the camera. The events of her life on display, although she couldn't remember the last time she had really looked at those pictures, thought about what she was feeling in the moments they were snapped. That was the thing about photos – they were placeholders more than anything, a dog-eared page in a chapter of life. Her fuchsia walls became visible now and she smiled.

As predictable as she often was even to herself, here, now, in the silence of her bedroom, there was a joy in the fact that she had strayed at times, that she had allowed a different side of Tess to break through – that her next moves were not always scripted. Just when she had thought her life was slowing down, that all she had to discover was before her, she had met Neal. She had become a yoga teacher. She had decided to take some time away and go up to Woodstock.

The wind outside made itself known, so that she pulled her blanket up closer to her chin. She didn't hear the snow. Soon she would get up and look outside her front window to see if there had been any accumulation through the night. She wondered if Neal was out running. She closed her eyes again and snuggled under her covers. It was nice to rest. Yesterday had been so many things between Michael at the office launching into yet another one of his tirades about her irresponsibility and how it wasn't fair that she was abandoning ship, leaving him to clean up her messes. She smiled. Never in her career had anyone ever accused her of making "messes." In her personal life, yes, but never in her professional life.

Christmas Eve. She tried to remember past Christmas Eves and her mind scattered to an array of parties, mostly with her ex-husbands, to laughter and dinners and drinks. Nothing memorable stood out. Just experiences. People, places. Had she been happy? She couldn't say – but there were no regrets she held onto. Everything, she believed, had unfolded exactly as it was meant to. She had fun. And when the fun ended, when she felt her life becoming a routine, when the tedium of everyday pulled her under, she had found a way to unravel it, to start again.

The wind's gusts picked up ferocity, the trees crashing against her home. Her home. It sounded odd in her mind. One day, it would belong to someone else, just as her mother's home now belonged to Tess. Time passed; things changed. That was the way of the world. One phase of her life ending, the next year of her story beckoning: in two days she would be 56-years old. She smoothed her arm with her palm, her hands still weak from sleep. Her skin was soft. She wondered when she would start to feel like an older woman to herself or if age was something that only other people characterized one by. The idea of embarking on the next chapter of her life in less than 48 hours sent shivers through her body. She didn't know what was next and then caught herself: no one did. That was both the joy of life and the fear – there were no guarantees, no maps to follow.

Neal's departure. He was leaving today. Her life would go on, it always had, and yet it seemed inconceivable that tomorrow, and the next day, he wouldn't be around. Neal would leave and she was still going to be Tess.

It came back to her what he had told her before they parted yesterday: that he couldn't write to her when he returned to the monastery, at least for the first few months. That his superiors would keep a close eye on him, watch for any signs of weakness, any desire to return to a layman's life. It wasn't that they wanted to keep him prisoner. It was that they wanted to help him find his way – to help him know what was right for him. If he were busy writing to her right away, they would assume his heart wasn't committed to God, to being back at the monastery. He had told her that although he couldn't reach out to her, he would speak to her nonetheless. That each morning when he went out for his run, he would talk to her in his mind. The thought made tears come to her eyes. She knew that in the early morning hours, in the depths of her soul, she would be listening for Neal. His words had made his departure more final, more rigid. At least she wouldn't be waiting around for a note from him, letting her mind run haywire if she didn't receive one.

In a few hours from now she would drop him at the airport and say goodbye and then she'd come home and get ready to leave for

Woodstock first thing tomorrow morning. He would wake up in the monastery on Christmas morning. A resurrection of sorts, a rebirth. She followed her breaths. Later today would come, tomorrow would come. Her mind was too restless for her own good. Right now, this moment. That's what she had to focus on.

Unfurling her blanket, she reached for the fleece lined zip-up sweatshirt on her night table and snuggled into it before she made her way out of her bed. The house was cool even with the heat blasting. She moved into her closet and sat down on her floor, pulling the door slightly closed and reaching behind her shoe racks for the white and gold embroidered box that held the vase with her mother's ashes in it. She undid the latch, smoothing the magenta velvet interior, before she took out the vase, shiny black, iridescent in the muted darkness, and held it close to her heart before she put it down in the middle of the diamond shape her legs formed.

"You were right, mother," she whispered. "About everything."

She looked down into the vase's stem as if there was the chance that her mother would still rise out of it. She imagined her mother tapping her on the shoulder and asking why Tess was speaking into a vase of ashes when she was right there with her, all around her. That thought lifted her spirits – maybe she wasn't as alone as she sometimes felt she was.

"I think it's time for us both to move on," she said. "Spread our wings a bit. See something new. That's what you always encouraged me to do. Thank you for teaching me to be independent, for showing me in so many ways that my happiness never relied on anyone else – that my happiness was within me. I searched outside for so long but all that I found, I lost over time. My life, Mother, has been very happy. I am happy, although I may not have known that until now." Tess held the vase close again, as if infusing her heart with her mother's aura one last time before she packed it up and put it back in its box.

To tell Neal her plan or somehow place it in his bag? She hadn't gotten that far yet, although having to tell him seemed exhausting to her today. She moved to her night table, pulled out a TR monogrammed note card and wrote:

Dear Neal:

Please set my mother free where you see fit. My only wish is that her spirit explores new pastures and knows peace. She would have loved you – I feel safe knowing that she's in your charge now.

Warmly,

Tess

She wedged the card into the box, wrapped it in a towel, and ran down to her garage, where she placed it in her trunk. She would be sure to have Neal place his bag in her trunk.

She pushed the inside garage door closed and made her way upstairs at the moment the doorbell rang. She made sure her sweatshirt was zipped up – she was still in her pajamas – and felt her curls to see where they were before pulling down on the ends. She hadn't even brushed her teeth or looked in a mirror.

"Lyla," she said, the cool air rushing in at her so that she shivered and moved from one foot to the other.

"You're up," she said. "I didn't know if you'd be up – you weren't out walking."

Lyla paused and pulled off her snow boots by the front door. Her car was parked practically in the middle of the street, in front of Tess's house. Tess smiled and pushed the door shut against the cold and wind and followed Lyla upstairs.

"Oh!" Lyla said, Buddhi darting past her. He let out a long, whining yelp. "I can't believe that creature is still here!" He stared at Lyla and let out a few more yelps. "What does he want from me?" Lyla said.

"He wants to go outside," Tess said, making her way back down the stairs to open the door and let Buddhi out.

"Really, Tess, do you think you should keep that cat? And what are you going to do with him when you're away?"

"Lyla, like everyone else, he deserves a place to rest his head and food to eat. I'm planning to take him up to Woodstock. I think he'll like it there."

"Well, I'm glad to know he won't be around your house anymore."

"Tea?" Tess asked and Lyla nodded. She moved to take out mugs to place on the table, when the doorbell rang again.

"Are you expecting company?" Lyla said. "It's 7:30 in the

morning."

Tess shook her head and made her way down the stairs.

"Oh, look, it's Santa Claus," she said when she saw Michael at the door carrying a large shopping bag.

"That freak of a cat of yours is running up and down your front lawn, playing in the snow. Either that or he's searching for penguins to eat," he said. Then, taking Tess in, "I'm glad that you got all spiffy for my visit," he said.

"Haven't even brushed my teeth yet," Tess said, backing away and moving around him to close the front door again. "Your shoes, Michael. Take off your shoes before you go upstairs."

"It's nice to see you in drill sergeant mode," Michael said.

"You can walk around your house with your snowy, soppy shoes, but not here," Tess said. He tossed her his wool jacket and made his way up the stairs.

"I was passing by and saw your car, Lyla, and couldn't resist stopping by to wish you a Merry Christmas," Michael said, holding out his hand to take Lyla's, which he kissed, before he pulled a large fruitcake out of his bag and handed it to her.

"Oh, Michael," Lyla said. "Aren't you a thoughtful boy?"

Tess smiled at him curtly. She dreaded him taking anything out of the bag to give to her in front of Lyla. Knowing Michael, if he had gotten her anything, it would be sentimental.

"I have something for both of you," Tess said. It wasn't how she had planned to give out her gifts – she had envisioned doing it privately, leaving her gift for Lyla later today when she picked Neal up, but she felt desperate to take the attention off Michael and what he may have for her. She moved to her bedroom and pulled out the bag of gifts from under her bed. She was never one for gifts, aside from the yearly bonuses she gave her employees, and the random gifts she had bought her ex-husbands, including Michael. Those had been spontaneous gifts – ones that she saw and knew her partner would like.

She had gotten Lyla a cookie cookbook, complete with a basket of cookie ingredients and an apron with an oversized chocolate chip cookie on it. The thought of Lyla in that apron had made her laugh out loud in the store. Lyla smiled shyly when she opened Tess's gift and nodded before she looked up, her eyes meeting Tess's, and thanked her.

"So that you can keep up the cookie deliveries," Tess said.

Lyla had something for Tess, which she pulled out of her bag. It was wrapped in faded red and green wrapping paper with little Santa Clauses and elves on it that looked as if it had been lying around for 20 years. Out of it Tess pulled a hand-knitted rust colored scarf. It was long enough so that Tess could wrap it around her neck a few times. It felt luxurious against her skin. Her mother had always made her scarves – something she had forgotten until this moment. Bright colored ones of hot pinks and electric blues that had made Tess feel giddy to wear in the snow.

"I made it myself," Lyla said. "It's a good color for you."

Michael winked at Tess, nodding in agreement.

"I love it," Tess said. She did. She was touched thinking about Lyla at home, working on her scarf for hours on end.

"Thank you," Tess said.

"I even have something for you, Michael," Tess said. They had certainly given one another gifts for birthdays – she recalled a bracelet, a ring, he had given her, but she couldn't remember what she had given him for either of the two Christmases they spent together.

"An hourglass," he said, setting it down on the table so that the sand instantly began to travel from one side to the other.

Tess had seen the silver and mahogany wood hourglass in the Bergdorf Goodman Christmas window display. When she went back to the store to purchase it for Michael, the clerk had told her that the hourglass was the only timepiece that represented the present as a fluid movement between the past and the future. He had said that it served as a reminder that the present was fleeting.

"It matches your office," Tess said, all their eyes on it now. "It's to serve as a reminder that now is what's always happening, not the past or the future."

"Thank you," he said, their eyes meeting in a way that made her feel unsettled so that she raised her eyebrows, trying to discern what was wrong, only Michael looked away, his eyes on the sand's movement. She couldn't tell if he liked her gift or felt bothered by it.

She left the gift she had made for Prakash in the bag – a photo album full of photos from when he was a little boy, a teenager, and a young adult. Photos of him and Tess, of him with his father, with Brad, with Michael. She wanted him to have it in the hope that there would be days in his life that he would be nostalgic, and the photos would help him to relive all that was. She had found a printing shop in New York to bind copies of The Four Noble Truths and Eightfold Path pamphlets into a hard cover book for Dale. On the cover she had inscribed: *There Are No Wrong or Right Paths, only Paths.*

"I was thinking about maybe going to see the tree at Rockefeller Center tonight," Michael said.

"The city will be crowded today," Lyla said.

Everyone focused on their teacups. Tess took a sip – hers was cool, but it didn't faze her. She wondered what Lyla was going to do this evening, if she would be home alone. She wondered if she felt lonely, or if she enjoyed her solitariness. Maybe she was planning to go to Mass. It suddenly seemed ridiculous to her that people, each of them, should spend a holiday alone. She had been looking forward to the solitary evening ahead, time for her to pack up, to get a good night's sleep before she headed out on her next adventure.

"Perhaps we should all go to see the Christmas tree this evening," Tess said.

Michael's face lit up. Lyla puckered her lips in her no-nonsense way, and Tess predicted she'd decline, that she wasn't interested in being part of the group, so that when she said that she'd like that, Tess felt her eyebrows lift in mild shock.

"Then it's a date," Tess said.

"I'll pick each of you ladies up," Michael said. "Say 6:00 pm?

We could get some dinner, too."

All nodded. Neal would be on his way by then, at his stopover in Minnesota. She wondered what it would be like for him to arrive at the airport in Saskatoon, to see Father Demetrius, who would be there waiting for him. What it would feel like to pull into the monastery grounds – if it would seem like years had passed or if time had stood still.

"I should get going," Lyla said. "I want to say goodbye to Neal and then head to the nursing home." Tess wondered if she should ask Lyla if she wanted to accompany her to the airport, only she didn't. She believed that if Lyla wanted to join them, she would let Tess know she was coming along.

"Goodbye, Tess, Michael," she said. There was a gentleness to her that Tess had not yet witnessed. She looked at Tess with – was it compassion? Acceptance? The acknowledgement that they were in it together.

Tess stood, but Lyla motioned for her to sit again. "I can let myself out," she said, waving to them both before she made her way down the stairs.

Michael remained seated at the kitchen table, his legs stretched out.

"Tonight will be fun," he said.

"Interesting is the word that comes to my mind," Tess said. She was carrying her and Lyla's teacups to the sink. Outside, it had begun to flurry again.

"Lyla is a nice person, Tess," he said. "For all of her insanity, she's a nice person."

Tess nodded. "Yes," she said.

"I suppose I should get going myself," he said as they stood facing one another. "You know, it's never too late for you to change your mind about Woodstock."

"Woodstock is tomorrow. Think of your hourglass. The present moment."

He pulled her to him and hugged her close.

"You're so dramatic, Michael. I'm going to see you later today."

She followed him down the stairs and opened the door for him.

"Your gift is in your mailbox," he said. "I got shy to bring it in with me."

She laughed. "I got bold and gave mine out because I was fearful that you were going to give me something sentimental."

He reached into the mailbox and then moved back into the front door landing, handing her the neat little rectangular Tiffany's package with a big white ribbon. Tess's heart pounded in her chest. It was too big for a ring. Or was it? What had he gotten her? Her heart raced faster.

"Open it," he said.

"Michael –"

"Tess, open it up. I didn't get you a wedding ring, I promise."

It was an hourglass – a solid, sterling silver hourglass and engraved on it were the words, *Time and Time Again*. She laughed.

"I didn't intend it to be funny," he said.

"I'm laughing because we got each other the same thing. We bought each other hourglasses, Michael. It's funny. What are the chances?" she said.

"Cosmic connection," he said, and Tess nodded.

"Cosmic connection," she said.

"Do you like it?" he said.

"I love it," she said. "I absolutely love it. Thank you, Michael."

"Time and time again you make me lose my mind," Michael said.

He smiled, still holding the screen door open. "I want to come up to Woodstock and visit you," he said, with one last lingering glance at her before he made his way down the porch steps and into his car, without looking back. Tess watched him start up the car and drive away. The sun had come out in the last few moments, shining and bright. Hopeful. It made Tess feel hopeful.

The steaming shower was soothing, refreshing; she was trying not to think, to just do and be – her mind was tired of all the activity. In the past few minutes, things had stopped making sense so that she felt as if she were watching a movie version of her life, taking it all in as opposed to driving the action. Neal having come and now leaving. His mother, Michael – the fact that he was still in her life. Dale having asked her to be in her wedding party, when and if she did get married; and that Sara had met a new man and that Kim and her husband were working out their issues. The concept that these characters were all a part of her life fascinated her. A year ago, apart from Michael, she hadn't known that these people existed. A few months ago, her mother had still been alive; she had spoken to her, heard her voice, sat on the front lawn with her at the crack of dawn in Woodstock. So much had changed. She closed her eyes, the water beating down on her like rain, washing away all the residue of what was. If only she could just stay here, be here, but life kept moving, regardless of where Tess hid herself away. The water flowed. It moved past her and beyond her and while it wasn't a race, Tess understood that she too must flow, and for all her growth, at her core she was exactly who she had started out as, just a bit more aware, a bit more awake in her little life. And for all her worrying and planning and her trying to find herself, the question that permeated as she toweled herself off, massaged on her body lotions and face cream, was *what did any of it matter?* She laughed at herself. Her mother used to smile sweetly at her, smoothing her unruly hair, as she told her that it would all pass, whatever drama that Tess had been upset about, her mother had told her it would pass. And it always did. The days were all so unique, so different from one another.

"Aren't the days all so different, Contesta?" her mother used to say, but she hadn't understood what her mother was talking about then. She was just a girl and the days had all seemed exactly alike to her. She had often felt as if she were drowning in the monotony. But they were all so different. Now, she understood.

She pulled on black turtleneck and black wool slacks – her staple. Simple. She wanted to keep things simple. She glanced around at her bedroom. She would return home after dropping Neal at the airport and then pack up so that she could relax for her evening with Michael and Lyla. It would be nice to be with them tonight. She surprised herself with that thought, but it would be nice. They were all in it together in some respect. Tomorrow morning, Christmas day, she would close her house and take the ride up to Woodstock with Buddhi in the carrying case that she had bought for him. She didn't know how that would work out, but it was all part of the adventure. She would wake up in Woodstock on her birthday morning, December 26th, and pick up Prakash, who was taking the redeye, from the airport. Neal would be at the monastery, all settled in by then.

She beeped once in front of his house and he came out, pulling the door closed behind him and locking it, carefully placing the key under the front door mat. He had on chinos, a black sweater, and his black bubble jacket. She popped open the trunk and motioned for him to put his bag back there. When he closed the trunk and got into the front seat beside her, she smiled at him. And then she remembered her plan.

"One minute," she said, and she was out of the car.

She opened his rucksack and placed her mother's remains inside, carefully positioning it under his books and undergarments, his new running clothes and sneakers, and the few pieces of clothing he was taking back with him – two pairs of chinos, two white button downs, two sweaters, and some dress socks. She liked knowing what he would have with him at the monastery. She brushed the sweaters with her hand for a moment and noticed a small plastic bag next to his luggage. It contained the framed picture of Neal at the monastery with his brothers, the one he had brought to her home, months back, to share something of his former life with her. On it was a post it that was addressed to Tess, with the words *Be Merry In All Things*, Deuteronomy 16:17, written in bold capital letters, signed *Your Friend, Neal.* She stared into the picture and with her finger, she touched his image.

"For you," she said, getting back into the car and handing him a small, shiny red bag with ribbons on it. She had bought him a rustic brown leather-bound journal and monogrammed on it were his initials: NC. She had hidden the bookmark she had bought at the church inside, so that one day, he would come upon it and think of Jamaica Bay, of Tess, of his time in Mill Basin, their morning walks.

He opened it up, his hand tracing his monograms on the journal and smiled up at her.

"Thank you, Tess. I love it," he said, his voice tired, small.

Tess kept her eyes focused on the road en route to the airport. She put the heat on high, then lowered it, then put it on high again until she turned it off. She wanted to feel a little cold and cracked her window open an inch. The skies were clear, and, in the distance, the sun was beginning to break through the whiteness. Once she merged onto the Belt Parkway, she turned on the radio. Christmas songs were playing: an instrumental of "Let it Snow." She was glad to be on the highway, glad that it was congested so that she had to focus on the road. She had butterflies in her stomach and her fingertips grew cold, impossibly cold, so that she took turns opening and closing her fists. She glanced over at Neal, but his eyes were glued to the road before them. She tried to think of something to say, something to ease the awkwardness, but she couldn't think of anything. Maybe she was the only one who felt awkward. Maybe Neal was already past all of this. Perhaps he was enjoying the ride, taking in the scenery.

"How's your mother?" she asked.

"Fine," Neal said. "She mentioned seeing you and Michael this evening. She's looking forward to it."

"Yes," Tess said. "It will be nice."

When she saw the signs for JFK airport, she moved into the middle lane, which veered off right, leading to the airport exit. She followed the curve of the road, focusing on her breathing. Shallow inhales followed by exhales. As she pulled into the underpass and parked the car up in front of departures, snowflakes began to tumble from the sky. *O Holy Night* played on the radio, and she was able to make out a small smile forming on Neal's face. Perhaps he was relieved, at peace.

"Here we are," Tess said, her eyes straight ahead.

"Here we are," Neal said.

Tess nodded. She didn't want to cry.

"If anything goes wrong with your flights, you can call me," Tess said.

"Okay," Neal said.

"Sometimes this time of year, there are delays. I'm here if you need me," Tess said.

"Thank you," Neal said, and now she felt his eyes on her, so that she turned to him.

She pressed the trunk button and got out first and, in a moment, Neal did the same, moving to the trunk to gather his rucksack. By the back of the car, they looked into one another's eyes and smiled a slight smile. There didn't seem to be anything to say. Tess reached out to hug him, a slight hug, keeping a distance between them. He patted her back and then she pulled away. They took one long, last look at each other. His eyes had never seemed bluer to her, and she longed to be closer to them so that she could see her reflection in them.

"I'll think of you, Tess," he said, and then he broke their trance and looked down at his feet. He had on his running sneakers. Seeing them broke her sorrow for a moment.

"I'll miss you," she said, and he nodded. "You should go," she said.

"Yes," he said. "Listen for me," he said.

The lump in her throat was growing. "I'll listen for you," she said.

They held one another's eyes for another moment and then he was walking away, moving into the airport, the sliding glass doors parting for him, so that she had a surreal image of him walking into the monastery, the doors closing behind him, keeping all else out. Keeping her out. This was the image, she believed, that would always stay with her: their paths a wishbone broken in two.

She peaked into the trunk and saw again the bag with the picture – he had left it for her. Later, she would study it. Now, she needed to move, to get away. She pulled away from the curb and back onto the road, following the airport exit signs, the snow falling furiously, coating the trees alongside the road and in her mind's eye, she envisioned the snow transforming Neal's layman clothes into his monk robe. She opened her window and stuck her hand out, the flakes damp on her flesh, like kisses, before they vanished.

She felt as she did the moment she had been handed her mother's ashes and realized that she was never going to be able to pick up the phone to call her ever again. "Silly silly girl," she said aloud. "Silly girl." The snow fell steadily, its whiteness covering the earth, erasing all that was, creating a new landscape. She was going to be okay; she was okay. It was all part of the cycle – people came and went. As messy as life was, as complicated as the journey was, Tess believed that it was worth it. Perhaps that was what her mother had infused in her or what she had come to believe on her own. What she sought more than anything at that moment, was the courage to keep going.

When she turned on the radio "I never promised you a rose garden," belted out from the speakers. It couldn't be. She waited a moment, as if her mother was going to appear on the side of the road or in the seat beside Tess. She pressed the buttons, and on all the other stations, Christmas songs were playing. She went back to the first station and there it was:

Jodi Weiss

So smile for a while and let's be jolly:

Love shouldn't be so melancholy.

Come along and share the good times while we can.

She smiled at the impossibility of it all and opened all the car windows as she cruised along the highway, the cool air rushing in, snowflakes randomly landing and dissolving on her arm and the car's interior. She blasted the song and began to sing along, softly at first and then louder, just as she had done that day months back with her mother, on the front lawn of her home in Woodstock.

Along with the sunshine, there's gotta be a little rain sometime

I beg your pardon, I never promised you a rose garden.

And finally, never lose hope. – Rule of Benedict 4:74

ABOUT THE AUTHOR

Jodi Weiss is the author of several academic books and short stories, and is a regular contributor to LinkedIn, *Ultrarunning Magazine,* and a variety of online magazines.

She possesses over a decade of editorial experience in academic publishing at McGraw-Hill, Golden Books, and The Princeton Review. For the last 15 years, Jodi leads a division of the Nonprofit and Higher Education Practice at a global executive search firm.

Jodi has served as an associate and adjunct professor, teaching English and creative writing at New York City and Florida colleges and universities. In her free time, Jodi is a devoted yogi and avid ultra-runner with over thirty races completed at the 100-mile or more distance.

Jodi holds a Bachelor of Arts degree in English from SUNY, and Master of Arts in English and a Master of Fine Arts in Creative Writing from Brooklyn College. *From Comfortable Distances* is her first novel.

www.JodiWeiss.net

Made in United States
North Haven, CT
26 February 2022

16554198R00427